Silvrin Shards

Volume IV in
The Saga of Magiskeep

By
Jean E. Dvorak

**Cover design by
David Melanson**

Printed in the United States of America

First Printing, 2015

ISBN-13: 978-1-942481-00-3
ISBN-10: 1942481004

Jean E. Dvorak
293 Deans-Rhode Hall Road
Jamesburg, NJ 08831
http://jedvorak.wix.com/magiskeep
http://www.magiskeep.blogspot.com

This book is dedicated to David Melanson, a talented and generous friend whose imagination and creative skill have played in important part in creating the *Saga*.

About the Author

Jean E. Dvorak is a retired high school teacher. An avid horsewoman, she has competed and trained two horses to FEI level in dressage. No longer competing, she still trains her horses and those experiences are evident in the novels where horses play a significant role. From the author: "Fantasy writing is very liberating. It allows the writer complete control of the world. Where else can magic exist and anything at all can happen? The writer makes the rules and can take the story anywhere imagination allows." "The Magiskeep Saga" was "born" in 1984 as a response to a challenge from her students when she assigned them a writing assignment: "What would you do if you had a magic power?" Since then, encouragement from a group of gaming fantasy fans on "The Halfwittenberg Door" message board sparked more writing. The result is a total of five full novels and several shorter novelettes in the collection. Ms. Dvorak has also written a number of stage musicals, plays, and vocal musical pieces, all of which have been performed locally in New Jersey, where she lives.

Other books in *The Saga of Magiskeep:*

- *Kingdom Beyond the Rim*

- *Honor's Way*

- *The Wall Between*

Darkwing's Daughter

Chapter 1

Jamus sighed and tossed the scroll on the study tabe. "From Kala," he explained. "Lovental Province. I didn't know she was responsible there too."

Salene picked up the parchment and read the lengthy message, shaking her head towards the end. "Apparently, she was called because of her expertise in the Magic," she said, smiling. "Our visits to Turan granted her a reputation she'd just as soon forget, I suppose. From the tone of this, she'd rather not be there."

"She should have contacted me through the Way," Jamus said, leaning back in his chair with even more resignation than Kala's message suggested. "If I'd talked to her…"

"If you'd talked to her directly the conclusion would have been the same," Salene said. "She needs your help, it's as simple as that. Magiskeep does tend to limit one's perspective." When she saw the gleam in Jamus' eyes, she knew she'd said the right thing. He'd been plagued lately by his old restlessness, caught in the trap of responsibility to her and the Keep even as the Rivers of Magic tugged at his every thought. Sending him to Kala was perhaps the better choice among the many the River offered. She smiled. "I'll be fine here. I can't begrudge your loyalty to an old friend."

His eyes darkened. "I can't just pack up and leave. The Keep…"

"The Keep existed long before you were its Master and it will exist long after. Sarn did well the last time he was in charge and I'll be here to keep his ambition in check. There's been no hint of trouble in Sevenstins. Do you think as soon as you go the towers will start to crumble?"

"I won't be gone long. It sounds like a simple matter. If the girl is Gifted, and her parents agree, I could simply bring her back here."

"If what Kala says is true there'll be more to it than that. The village is up in arms and ready to burn her as a Wayard. By the Hand, you'd think those old superstitions would have died circles ago."

"Eldenlore is part of Turan's life," Jamus replied. "I've read many a tale about Sorcerers who used the Magic for ill in times past. It's just a matter of twisting the River's currents to harm instead of help, as if the good are the enemy instead of the cherished. Rule and Vow are only a matter of honor, you know."

"As we've seen even here more than once. When I was a child, I thought Magic's River had no path but a good one. Then some other Prentice played a nasty prank on me, and I discovered how wrong I was," Salene said sadly. "I only hope this girl has not touched Darker waters and can be reformed."

Jamus shuddered involuntarily at the mention of the Darkness, the old wound from Sagari's Spellfire throbbing as it always did with the memories. He'd never escape that pain, and he knew one day he would have to confront it once and for all. A Black Dragon lurked ever in the shadows, holding sway over forces he had only just begun to understand. If this girl had any connection to them, he wasn't at all sure he was prepared to deal with it. "I hadn't thought of that," he said at last. "I should take Simen with me and perhaps Jessa. She's been studying the old tomes."

Salene nodded. "Sharia needs to go with her mistress, and it might not be a bad idea to have a girl her age along. Sometimes younger ears listen better to younger voices."

"Kala did say this girl was only fourteen. Good idea. So that's it then. Four of us to Lovental Province. We'll cross the Rim in Spheres and lift our way through most of Telma. After that, we'll have to ride cross country since I don't know the roads."

"I'll send a message to Kala through the Way mirror," Salene said. "You should reach her in a Sevenstin or so?"

"That should be about right," Jamus agreed. "I'll tell the others. We should be able to leave by Windchange."

****

Kala busied herself unpacking in her room at the Tallowtail in Loren, the little village nestled in the southeast of Lovental. She'd sent the message to Jamus with a carrier bird more than eight winds before, and since, Jiana had been thrown into the little dungeon below the village lawkeeper's office, shut up in utter darkness where, the villagers hoped, she could do no more mischief.

Now, with her there, they were already preparing for a trial, more than eager to rid themselves of what they considered was a dire threat against their homes. Spoiled crops, sickly animals, and cheese refusing to set had plagued them ever since the slender little girl had passed her thirteenth circle and now, as her fourteenth neared, even her parents had become convinced she was the source of every misery the village suffered.

To Kala, she was a mystery. Even a sifting had revealed nothing unusual about her, except for the vaguest hint she had the ability to touch the River. But even that power seemed elusive to her Sight, a most unnerving situation. Never before had she found herself unable to See the Truth in a person's intent, but Jiana had somehow "felt" an innocent, despite everything. Yet called to trial, there was no proof except for repeated witnesses who claimed to have seen her working spells and curses in the village square.

The testimony was exact and frighteningly consistent. "She waved her hands about, chanting over and over," one woman insisted. "And before ye knew it, my casks of wine had turned to vinegar, all account of that I wouldn't give her a jug for her father. Said if I 'twas to be so selfish 't'would serve me right to drink as sour as my answer to her."

Another woman nodded. "I was there. Girl kept saying over an' over, *'Bitter much is this reply, all her answer I decry . Hand of power, reach to me, spoil the grape for all to see.'* Them's her very words."

"Aye," the first woman agreed. "Her very words, an' I be sworn the casks all begun a creakin' an' a moanin' like they was cryin'. T'weren't but a moment more than the cup in my hand went sour and every drop with it. Lost a season's vintage I did. T'ain't the market for sourbrew, ye know. I hardly gots denerets to rub together for the Chillmonth now. The Hand bless me my husband's crops were clear of her this harvest."

"Mine weren't," a man declared at that point. Dressed in homespun with breeches sagging to his knees, he pointed an accusing finger as his voice trembled another accusation. "She told my son he was a fat riverslug an' she'd fix it good so he'd wear his ribs to the outside next time he tried to tell her what to do. Seems alls he did was ask her to move her wagon a mite so's he could drive past. By the time he did, the whole load o' corn had molded an' three quarters of my field had rotted too. You ask 'im, just ask 'im."

The boy's face reddened, but at his father's urging he added to the tale. "She pointed her hand at me an' said somethin' like, *'Send the power with my hand ta rot the harvest on his land.'* There was more, but just hearin' that near froze me wits. I can't say I even heard a word o' the rest, 'specially after I saw what she done to the wagonload."

These were only a few of the tales racing through the village, and Kala had heard there were dozens more. Confronted with the accusations, Jiana had simply stared, her lips tight, her eyes narrowing as tears trickled from their corners. She didn't even shake her head in denial, but let them bind her hands and feet and carry her down into the dim pit where, at least the village wisewoman said, she could do no one any more harm.

"Can't ply the Wayardcraft when she cain't see," Carila told them.

At least Kala saw some sense in that, for Jamus had told her much the same thing. When they had been trapped in a cave together, even he, the Rivermaster, had been powerless without light to see. But that memory only made things worse, for thinking of Jiana locked away in a black hole in the ground was a horror in itself. No one deserved such torture.

And so she had sent the message. If indeed Jiana was plying the River, who better than its Master to know what to do with her? All she needed to do now was wait for him to arrive.

She pulled her traveling pack onto the bed and pulled out a well-wrapped mirror of silvrin she carried with her on every journey. Peering into it, she saw a simple message awkwardly scrawled in the reflection. "A Sevenstin and two," it read. She smiled. Salene's handwriting, she thought, by the looks of it, even though it had been written backwards.

Hastily, she wiped her hand on the mirror, careful not to let more than her fingertips slip through its enchanted surface lest the power of the Way drag her inside. As soon as Salene's message was erased, she blew on the shining surface to fog it and then traced a reply, forming words and letters backwards so those in Magiskeep could read the reflection easily. "I will be waiting. " Then she set the mirror against the western wall of her room and left it.

Jamus was on his way. All she needed to do was stall the trial until he arrived.

****

"You're leaving me in charge?" Sarn asked, trying to keep his face sober despite the urge to laugh in Jamus' face. "Completely in charge while you're gone?"

Jamus sighed. It seemed Sarn never tired of the game. He knew right well he was the obvious choice, but each time, he pretended surprise."Don't think me a fool, Sarn. Salene is here and I trust Mistresses Joria and Sarena will not let you stray too far from propriety. You know as well as I do you're still the most qualified to sit as Master of Magiskeep should anything ever happen to me. Why do you always feign such surprise whenever I give you authority?"

"Because I know you don't really trust me," Sarn replied evenly.

"You're an arrogant rimsnake without an ounce of compassion for anyone except yourself, it's true," Jamus said readily, "but you've learned the good of Magiskeep is your good as well. If anything, I'm sure I can depend on you to protect its wealth and its Magic from anyone who'd try to destroy it. If I can also depend on you to leave most of its daily affairs in the hands of those who know them best, then I'm content."

Barely recovered from the sting of Jamus' first remarks, Sarn bowed stiffly. "Fair enough. At least I know where I stand." Then he grinned, surprisingly sheepish. "Besides, despite your opinion of me, I have learned a bit since we were children. I do respect you, you know."

Jamus did not smile back. "It's all I ever asked for, Sarn. Guard the Keep. Stay watchful for the Darkness. I've had no hint there will be any trouble here, but the quiet has been more prolonged than usual."

"Tamor's planning something?"

"I don't know, but he and his minions are never far away from my thoughts. Best you keep them in yours. He'll do anything to turn the waters black and though I've set hard dams against him I doubt even my Magic can hold forever."

Sarn sighed heavily. "Your enemies abound, My Lord. Haven't you ever just wanted to run from them and find peace elsewhere?"

"Every day of every season," Jamus answered. "But the Hand named me Rivermaster and until my circle closes, I can't escape. Consider yourself the lucky one, Sur. You can sit in my chair and relish its power, but in the end, none of it rests on your shoulders."

"And to think, once I would have tried to take it all from you."

"Once I might have given it to you. Now, it's too late. Keep watch, Sarn. I shouldn't be gone long, but remember, 'There is no time in the Way.'"

Sarn swallowed hard as the old words touched his memories. Too many times the Way of Mirrors and its secrets had threatened Magiskeep, and though he'd been loath to enter its twisting passages, he knew more than he cared to of dark reflections and shadows lurking behind mirrors seeking a way out into the world of light. "I will be vigilant, My Lord."

"It's all I can ask," Jamus said as he left.

****

"Pack lightly, Sharia," Jessa told her young Apprentice as she folded a simple dark green gown into her own saddlebag. "One gown for anything formal and an extra set of travel garb. Lord Jamus says we're going to a Province village and we'll need to blend in as ordinary travelers. If we need anything else, it's an easy matter to spell."

"Then why don't we just spell all our provisions, Mistress Jessa?" the girl asked, her pale blue eyes wide with curiosity. "What good is the Magic if we have to carry everything we need with us?"

"Magicians are not welcome in Turan proper," Jessa answered. "Now how do you suppose it would look to even the casual observer if we took to the roads with no packs at all, eh? Worse if we should be stopped and searched by someone from the King's Guard."

"I hadn't thought of that. I've never been out of Magiskeep, you see."

"Few of us have. It's been the way of this world since Wizardchase, and a wise way as well. Mortals resent our powers and when some of our kind tried to use them selfishly, all they did was breed more hatred."

"Then why does Lord Jamus keep going out into the world? Wouldn't he be better off just staying here?"

Jessa laughed. "Oh, little one, you ask so many questions with so many answers, I can hardly keep up with you. It would take a lifetime to explain that one. Suffice it to say it is not Lord Jamus who craves the world, but the world who craves him. His Magic does have a place in Turan, even if it's not always wanted there."

"He's a great man, isn't he," Sharia said, her own question its answer.

"Perhaps, one day, the greatest," Jessa answered. "But for now, like us, he'll travel as a most ordinary man."

"Secrets?"

"Secrets," the mistress replied. "Ones we must keep."

****

Jiana curled up in the darkness, letting it wrap itself around her like a thick blanket. She wasn't afraid, for even here she could feel power tickling her fingertips like so many slitherskins coiling about in their shells poised to strike at the first thing passing by. She needed no light as long as whatever she wanted pictured itself in her mind with sharp clarity.

In fact, the blackness was comforting. With nothing to see, there were no distractions to take her mind away from the direction she sent it. Concentration had always been her short suit, and the old Hag of the Mountains had warned her of it more than once.

"Don't be so eager to watch the rain fall, girl, when ye need to find the sun. The River will laugh at ye if you dip thy toes instead of leaping in full ready to get soaked."

"Oh, Zanda, must you always talk in riddles? You sound like a Seer from one of the High Houses."

"The swirlypot speaks to me, lass, but so does the Dragon. If ye'd shut your mouth long enough to listen, ye'd hear it too."

"The Dragon hisses, Milady. I can hear him in the wind. Don't you?"

"Don't mock me. I've lived long enough to be your granddam's granddam, and more. There be Dragons still."

Jiana grew serious at that. "I know that, Mistress. It's just their color I can't see. Someone once told me they were silver in the Eldenlore, but all I've seen are gold and black."

"Black?"

"Like a great hole in the sky. Kind of all empty and dark."

"Not a storm cloud?"

"No. A hole in the blue, going nowhere and everywhere all at once. If you hadn't told me the darkness was evil I would think it a wondrous sight. How marvelous to see so far beyond the world!"

"Hush!" the Hag nearly screamed the command. "A hole is nothing! *Nothing!* Do ye hear me, girl? There's nothing there to see, nothing to hold on to, nothing to give, and nothing to take. Better ye take hold of that golden Dragon's tail and hold on tight than even look at her brother. Mark my words, lass. 'Tis a sad day when the likes of us marks the Dark One's passing over Turan."

"Why, Mistress? How could any Dragon be bad? They're so beautiful and Magic flies with them."

"Aye, Magic flies and wears the color of their scales. All that emptiness is a sorrow to man and Mage alike. It's the blackheart in the thief, the bloodlust in the murderer, and the false words of the liar. Hurt rides with it on the winds, and circle's end meets as sure as the day blows into Norwin. It calls misery to men, child, misery."

But how could such power be bad when using it brought her so much pleasure? Just the feel of the tendrils of power curling about her hands sent shivers of joy through her whole being. Calling the golden Dragon always posed a challenge, demanded hard thought and careful deliberation. But Blackwing came on a whisper and always did her bidding with a laugh of triumph.

Jiana loved the Darkness. She could always depend on it.

****

Whim, delighted to be out beyond the borders of Magiskeep proper, fretted in the bridle, trying to break into a trot. Jamus checked the silver stallion's rein repeatedly, keeping him at a walk the other horses could follow with no trouble.

Windstep.

"Be patient," Jamus said. The horse obeyed reluctantly, too caught up in the anticipation of lifted strides to stay calm.

Jamus felt his own heart skipping as well, surprised at how eager he was to leave the kingdom for a while. He'd thought he'd finally found a sense of contentment there in the quiet solace of Magic's study, but now, he was nearly his horse's match in looking forward to the Rim.

The enchanted mountains loomed to the west, their peaks and canyons riddled with illusions few could sift in order to pass through. Long before, the great Sogol had set the barrier to keep mortals from reaching his kingdom. But since, they had lost much of that power, for Magic had sifted its way between Turan and Magiskeep often enough that a crossing was always a possibility.

Jamus had been the first to manage a passage since the Eldentimes, but even he tried to avoid the land trails whenever speed mattered. He had chanted many of the mountains' illutions away on on a widing trail he alone knew and could even lift strides for much of the crossing along the familiar passage.

Now, in the shadow of the foothills, he stopped the party. "Simen, you take Jessa with you. She's done this kind of thing before, so if there's any trouble, she can support you. I'll take Sharia."

The little girl blushed prettily at the decision, pleased to find herself chosen to keep the handsome Master of Magiskeep company in such an important moment. She pushed Pebble, the little brown mare, up beside the towering silver stallion and smiled. "Thank you, My Lord. I am honored to ride at your side."

Jamus half-smiled back, almost distracted by her charm. But, he caught himself quickly and answered sternly. "You must do exactly as I tell you. Pebble has experience at this and will not start, but if you do, and I have to catch you from falling off her back, I might lose my concentration. We need to follow the path exactly so I have to be careful to keep a sharp lookout. You do know about lifted strides, don't you?"

Sharia's mouth formed a pout. "Second year Prentice Art," she scoffed. "Of course I have. I am Apprenticed now."

"Then you understand the weaving takes great skill to keep the threads of Magic solid enough to hold our weight - and then even more focus to land in all the right places.."

"Yes, My Lord. I'll help if you want me to."

This time, Jamus did smile. He would not tell her he could create and direct riders accurately with just a finger of one hand if he needed to. As Rivermaster, the waters of both Gold and Silver were ever eager to leap to his command, and he had studied the currents so well he could command their power in his sleep. "I think I can manage on my own, Mistress, but I thank you for your offer. I will be sure to ask if I need you." Then he looked over at the others. "Simen, you can manage on your own to follow close behind?"

Simen, the brother Jamus had drawn from the Way of Mirrors and welcomed to flesh and blood, was more than an accomplished Magician in his own right. A part of Jamus' reflection, the blood of the Rivermaster coursed in his veins and the waters answered his hand with ease. "No problem, My Lord. There are only two of us and Jessa is more than able to handle any crisis." He smiled at the dark haired sorceress whom he was growing to love more each day. "We'll be fine."

"Hmpf," Jamus puffed, hiding a grin behind the admonition. "Just be sure you set yourselves down close by and not off in some secluded spot so you and you Lady can have some privacy before we go on again. I don't want to have to wait for you."

"My Lord!" Jessa cried, laughing lightly at the suggestion. "Certainly you don't think Master Simen would dare do such a thing?"

"Master Simen would do as he pleases whenever he pleases, My Lady. The sooner you realize you're courting affection from a rogue the better."

"Condemn a poor Follyman for his song, would you?" Simen sighed with mock sorrow.

"It's not your singing I'd worry about if I were Jessa," Jamus answered. Then, he heard Sharia giggle and started to laugh himself. "I hope we're in as jolly a mood when we get to Lovental. From the tone of Kala's message, we're going to need something to lighten things up."

"A Wayard," Jessa said, shaking her head. "Eldenlore and fools' tales to frighten children at the fireside. Poor little girl's probably twice as terrified of the villagers as they are of her."

Jamus nodded and moved his fingers gently in the air.

An instant later, before Sharia could even take a breath, she, the Lord of Magiskeep, and their two horses were engulfed in the shimmering threads of his chanting and then swept up into the wind to sail high above the Rim.

The sunlight glittered around them, sending light sparking off on all directions.

Chapter 2

Blue and pink clouds scalloped the sky above the Rim, now behind the travelers from Magiskeep. The sunset lingered in the east, Weswin falling slowly in the warm spans of the Warmmonths. Given the chance, Jamus too would linger here in the foothills, enjoying a respite at the Telma Host House, but the call to Lovental commanded him. One night would have to do.

"We'll rest here," he said, reining Whim into the pine shaded clearing in front of the rustic house. "There's no point in riding on now. We can make fine time at Easwin through most of the Province and make it to Kala before Weswin turns again."

"That soon?" Jessa asked.

Jamus smiled. "I know the trails well in and around Tulene. Once we reach the Lovental border, we'll have to move by ground, but according to the maps, Loren's at the most a wind into the Province."

They settled the horses in the stable at the edge of the clearing and carried their packs into the Host House.

Well stocked with provisions for any traveler who happened to need haven on a journey through the provinces, the Host Houses were set throughout the wilderness of Turan. Each visitor was obligated to assure the cupboards were full again within a Sevenstin of leaving and few houses ever found empty shelves for long.

Jamus wasted no time preparing a fire, for Weswin had brought an unexpected chill. Magic lifted the logs onto the hearth and one lift of his hand should have set them to flame. But for an instant, flakes of snow seemed to flutter above the stones, and he frowned, forcing himself to concentrate on calling the River. "I must be more tired than I thought," he muttered, as the flames finally crackled to life in the dry wood.

"Are you all right?" Simen whispered, startling Jamus out of his near trance. "I saw the snow."

"Strange," Jamus answered, sighing. "It was as if what should have been just a mere thought demanded my full attention to a weaving." Then he checked a weary laugh. "I guess I have been spending too much time confined to Magiskeep's luxury. I'm out of practice."

"The Rivermaster needs no practice, Jamus. I did nearly as much as you did today holding our sphere together and lifting strides, and I actually feel invigorated. I've done no more and no less than you in the Keep these last seasons. Are you sure you're not ill?"

"That's why you asked?"

"I've never seen one of your spells go awry, My Lord. It worries me."

This time Jamus laughed aloud. "We must be too close to the Rim's enchantments. Neither one of us is making any sense. Since when do you address me so formally when we're alone?"

"I…" Simen's voice dropped into a sheepish grin. "It seemed right, but by the Hand I have no idea why. Could it really be the mountains?"

"The Rim's weavings are old. Who's to say if the illusions and deceits might not be spilling from loose threads? Even Sagari worried about that. We've always patrolled the borders of Magiskeep. I never thought much about this side of the range."

"No one would notice. Magic's an alien force in this part of the world," Simen replied. "That's why we're here, isn't it?"

"The girl," Jamus said, sinking into a chair by the fire. "I'm a bit worried about all of this. It's not like Kala to need our help. There's something to this beyond what she's told us, I'm sure."

"She is a Seer, Jamus. You can't deny her Vision. If she needs your help, it's a true need."

"I know, but there's something…"

Just then, Sharia ran out of the bedchamber ahead of her Mistress. "I'm hungry," she proclaimed loudly. "Did you cook anything yet?"

Simen shook his head in mock sorrow. "The Lord of the Keep is a failure in the kitchen, I'm afraid. We'll just have to eat cold biscuits and cheese."

Sharia's face fell, her blue eyes drooping to near tears. "I don't like biscuits."

"An adventurer must learn to eat almost everything, my lady. Why, suppose we were stranded in the desert with only bugs and wickergrass around us? We'd have no choice but to gobble them up to survive."

The little blonde sorceress folded her arms defiantly across her chest. "Magicians never starve, Master Simen. Don't you know that? If they get really hungry they just spell up a nice fat cavel roast."

"Oh, it's that simple, is it?" Simen teased. "My goodness, that's something I never would have thought of."

"Then you are just a bad Magician. Everyone knows it's perfectly all right to conjure when you have need, and what could be more necessary than food?"

"Do you think you could spell some for me now?" Simen asked. "I'm hungry too and we haven't even started to think about what to make for Lastmeal."

Sharia's arms locked tighter. "No. That would be wrong."

"Why?"

"Because the cupboard is full here and we have everything we need to make a meal without using Magic." She loosed one arm and wagged a finger at him. "When there's no need, 'Then deeds had best be left undone.' Don't you know the Rule and Vow? Lord Jamus should have taught you better."

Jamus laughed at that. "I must admit, Mistress Sharia, I have been somewhat lax with my brother's training over the circles. He has a stubborn head about some things and I just find myself giving up when I try to teach him."

Simen grinned back. "I have always been the better part of you, Jamus. Reflection of your more determined self, I suppose?"

Jamus paused before answering that, trying to remember if Sharia actually knew Simen's true origin. Once a Shadow from the Way of Mirrors, he had been Jamus' reflection, the image of a happy day when the Lord of Magiskeep had laughed and sung his joy before a mirror and the enchanted world beyond had captured it. Granted true life by the Rivermaster's power, the Follyman had long since become his true friend and brother. The story was well-known in the Keep by the elder masters, and many of their Apprentices, but whether it was common knowledge among the Prentice classes was another question. "Do you know who Simen is, Sharia?"

She nodded now. "You brought him to us through the Way. Mistress Jessa told me all about it. She's been in the Way, you know. Just a little. Simen's taken her to show her what it's like. Mistress Jessa said it's important we all understand about how the mirrors take a little part of us sometimes because we have to be careful that we don't send bad faces there. She says all the back reflections of us hide there, hoping one day we'll set them free the way you did Simen."

Jessa stepped out of the shadows by the hearth and nodded to her young Apprentice. "If Sharia is to learn the history of the Eldenlore and master its arts, she needs to understand the dangers as well. We must never take what we do in the River's Way lightly."

"It's so," Sharia agreed quickly. "Mistress Jessa says every little bit of Magic we do makes a big difference in the world. And that's why when we have plenty of food in the kitchen, we should cook it like mortals do instead of waving our hands around casting spells."

At that, Jamus pushed up from the chair and pulled the fieron cooking pot from the rack by the fire. "Well, then I'd best get busy - that is if the rest of you can stand a pot of my stew. It's the easiest thing to cook in the wilderness."

"If you let me add the seasoning," Jessa replied, "I should think we could all manage to eat a bowl."

"If there's flour, I can make dumplings," Sharia offered.

Soon the travelers were busy in the kitchen, laughing and sharing the preparations.

The flames in the hearth sputtered as flakes of snow sizzled onto the logs, as if challenging the heat. But the fire persisted, wrought by the Rivermaster's hand and his own fieron Will.

****

Kala paced the wooden floor of her room at the Tallowtail Inn with uncommon impatience, her nerves frayed by constant frustration. Vision, her hold on reason when the common world insisted on spinning out of control, had somehow failed her in dealing with the problem of Jiana. Each time she'd tried to sift the girl with her Sight, the bright white light of Seeing had shadowed into smoky darkness, shimmering with the silvrin rays of reflections of truth in place of knowledge. Strange as it seemed, it was as if each searching she sent bounced back into her own consciousness, revealing far more about herself than about the girl.

"I'm getting older," she sighed, pausing in front of the mirror standing by the dresser. Still slim, and dressed in a long dark turquoise tunic over loose-fitting trousers, she looked no more than twenty circles to men's eyes, but to her own, she saw wrinkles and streaks of gray fading into her short auburn curls. She rubbed her green eyes with her fingers, massaging away the tiredness, and looked again, sighing to see her young face staring back at her once more. "Illusions?" she muttered, leaning in. But nearly as quickly, she pulled back, less too much concentration on her image send a new shadow into the Way. "The last thing I need as another Kala stumbling about in the mirrored halls trying to find a way out," she said aloud, as if her words could challenge the Magic behind the silvrin surface. "You won't have any part of me to play with in your reflections!" Then, she shuddered, knowing all too well how easily the Way's enchantments might have already snared one more shadow from her.

She'd packed lightly, bringing only one formal gown of green velvet for any formal functions in the town and her white Seer's robe for the often-necessary dramatic impact of a Seeing. A leather tunic and leggings for travel and the simple outfit she wore now were usually more than enough for a short stay the average Juris' hearing required in a Province town. But already, Loren's demands had held her longer than the Sevenstin she'd allotted and the wait for Jamus was adding days more.

Worse, she was no further along in making a decision regarding the girl than she'd been when she first arrived. Jiana had been accused of being a Wayard, the worst kind of Sorceress in Turan's Way. Simple Sorcery held no malice for others and, though hated by the people of the Provinces, required no more than banishment. But Wayardcraft, the use of Magic with evil intent, demanded imprisonment at the least and death as the ultimate punishment. It was here the Province Juris became an essential member of the judging trial. It was her duty to decide first whether or not the charges were true and then, if so, just how far the accused had fallen into the ways of darkness.

Normally, it was a simple matter of judging after a quick Vision. In all her circles as Prime Juris of Telma Province, Kala had found only one Magician and at least two dozen such accusations. Superstitious Provincers were prone to blame old widowed women and lonely old men for their troubles when crops failed or cavel were barren, rather than admitting to their own failures as farmers and keepers. If the keldherb was bitter, or a well went dry, evil Magic was as easy explanation for poor skill and nature's caprice. Somehow, not knowing why offered far less comfort than finding a scapegoat in a bearded hermit on the hill above town.

But this time, the accused was a young girl, pretty to a fault and sweeter than surlep candy when she proclaimed her innocence. On the face of it, Kala wanted to believe her, even longed to declare her unjustly accused.

But, Vision refused to confirm her sense of it. Jiana "felt" guiltless, true, yet to the Seer, whose very life was founded on the principles of the Sight, Kala could not render a decision without assurance of Truth.

For some reason, Jiana's nature would not let her See it.

Instead, she'd crashed into her own mortality, driven to self-examination every time she confronted the girl. "Jamus will know what to do," she repeated, almost as a comforting mantra.

"Jamus?" Jiana asked, her eyes wide at Kala's evident confusion. "Is he another Juris? You will call on another to judge me?"

Kala sighed. "He is a judge of sorts, lass. At least one who understands the threat of Magic far better than I do."

Jiana shivered. "He's a Seeker then? One from the alabaster halls of Aberdeen, sent by the King himself?"

"Not precisely. Jamus is a friend who has had some experience with Sorcery. Sometimes people who have seen the Magic firsthand can sense it far better than those who haven't."

"But I heard you were in Tulene when the evil Sorcerer tried to take over the city. That's why you became Prime Juris of the eastern Provinces. That's all Master Depner ever talks about when

they bring up your name. He says that's why he insisted Lord
Manison send you to judge me."

So that explained it. Kala checked a curse under her breath.
Loren was outside of her usual jurisdiction, south enough to belong
to Kerth. At least now she understood why she had received the
calling instead. "I did witness the Sorcerer in Tulene, but I never had
a chance to sift or study his power," she said at last, telling truth
tinged with falsehood. While it was true she had never really studied
Sagari, Jamus was another matter. "I had little acquaintance with his
Magic. I suppose, though, of all the Judgers active in the Provinces, I
am indeed the most experienced."

"And this Jamus is better," Jiana asked, twisting a lock of
her dark hair nervously around her finger. "Is he scary?"

"Scary? Why would he be?"

"Well...," The girl's voice faltered. She swallowed hard
before managing to go on, "I heard some Seers aren't as nice as you
are."

Nice was not a word Kala thought to apply to herself in her
profession. Just, efficient...calculating, perhaps...but not nice. "It's
easy to be kind to someone like you, Jiana."

"Then you think I'm innocent?"

"I think you may be innocent, and for now, that's enough.
Master Depner and Keeper Naven will not harm you as long as I
extend my protection to you. To that I am duty bound until I See
otherwise."

Jiana beamed, her face lighting up with obvious relief at the
reassurance.

For the first time in all her meetings with the girl, Kala
wanted to cringe away. Just how many deceptions could hide in a
smile like that?

****

Jamus had not dreamt his childhood nightmare in long
circles, its terror forgotten once he had faced the loss of his parents
in the cave of Cowltop in the Rim. The dream was so distant, that
when it began, he smiled in his sleep and tossed aside the first
fragments.

But the darkness persisted.

The cave floor was littered with bones, remnants of the tark's feasts. It was, after all, the great mountain cat's lair and he an unwelcome intruder, even though the cat was off hunting.

He climbed the sloping ramp up to a narrow opening in the wall above and looked in.

The world began to spin beneath his feet, whirling him into the vision and remembrance.

"Jami, you stay down there," his mother said, laughing lightly as she pushed her husband playfully up the slope. "Your father and I will look for the stone ourselves."

"It's Jami's cave, my Love," his father said. "He found it first."

"Our cave now, Jarel. Go on. Where's your spirit of adventure."

Jamus wanted to follow, to pull them back into the light, for once to save them, but his feet were rooted to the ground. "I can't let you die again," he said aloud. "Maman, Papan, don't go in there! Don't go!"

"Silly boy," his mother returned, her eyes blazing with determination and something new he'd never seen before—greed. "We'll be rich! Rich enough to throw dirt on those Provincelords who spit on Mountmen like us."

Jamus shook his head, trying to remember. She'd never said that before, never shown a bit of resentment for her life. "Maman, please. We don't need the money."

"I never knew you were so ignorant," his father replied gruffly. "Stupid boy. Gold and silver are all that matter in this world. Don't you know that? If there are as many flamegems in there as you say, we'll fill our pockets with denerets and to blazes with the fools who think to mock us!" He laughed harshly. "Dirty ungalens who'd steal a man's home right out from under him if it meant a profit."

"Lords and ladies, too high- nosed to look down far enough to see the likes of us," his mother added bitterly. "All their coins cover their eyes, blinding them to honest folk like us."

He'd never heard them talk like that. His parents would never talk like that. It wasn't the old nightmare. It was a new one. He tried to shake himself awake.

The dream went on.

He flailed out, gasping for breath in the utter blackness.

And mercifully, awoke, sweating and shaking.

It had never been so horrible.

The room hissed.

He knew.

"You have no power over me," Jamus said aloud.

Everendings ever be, in thy sleep I come to thee.

"I've beaten your nightmares before, Blackheart. Do you think I'm not able to do it again?"

Mine the waters drowning thee, thus thy soul belongs to me.

"Never. Your river languishes in boggy pools against the golden currents I command. Go soak in its putrid depths where you belong. Enough! It is enough!"

The hiss rose to a whine as harsh scales slithered across the floor.

The room burst into the brilliance of a maglit torch.

"Jamus? Are you all right? I came as soon as I felt him," Simen said, letting the rays of the torch fall full on Jamus' face.

Jamus stared into the light, his grey eyes confused by the brilliance after the utter darkness of the nightmare. "Simen?"

Simen moved over to the bed, dropping the glare of the torch to the side, his own eyes searching Jamus' face with concern. "You're pale and sweating. Do you feel all right? I can Touch you."

Jamus blinked and shook his head, but dizziness swept over him and he had to sink back into the pillows. "Give me your hand and the River's Healing, at your will. I..I feel...."

"It's all right," Simen answered, letting the torch fall as he reached out his hand and held it gently on Jamus' chest.

The world lurched away from them both and had Simen not been bred of the shadows himself, he might well have been swept away by the rush of waters slamming into them.

Black as pitch, a huge wave engulfed them both, but the Follyman gritted his teeth and held his breath as it swallowed them into its darkness. He'd felt the emptiness before, and knew how quickly it could drain life into reflection. Born of the Way, he'd been the hollow image of life himself and to him, instead of fear, it offered familiarity.

Instead of fighting to stay afloat, he embraced the dark waters, sinking into them with a sigh of homecoming, holding tight to Jamus. "Courage, brother," he whispered. "It's only the night, and Easwin will come. Believe. It is all you need to do. I'll do the rest."

He felt Jamus relax, smiled at the trust, and dropped his own head on Jamus' arm and simply lay, limp and quiet.

Something roared in his ear and a tentacle coiled about his ankle, tugging, as another probed his neck. There was a predatory hiss behind him, and a lick of black flame to his left. But he did not react. The darkness fed on fear, so he simply refused it.

The black waters ebbed, sighing and moaning as they drew back. A moment more, and the golden waters of the True River flowed over them, soothing and warm.

Jamus breathing steadied. The color came back into his cheeks.

And both men started awake, staring wide-eyed at each other at the crimson light of Easwin filtered in through the open window.

Chapter 3

"Don't pander to me, Madame," Lord Manison said. Taller than Kala by a head, the dark-haired man glowered down at the Seer with all the pomp and arrogance a petty Province Lord could muster in the face of Aberdal's authority. Apparently, Kala's youth and fresh face emboldened him, and he obviously felt he had the upper hand. "You are here at my insistence and will render your decision as I demand. You will hold formal judgment before tomorrow's Weswin or you will answer to my authority."

Kala smiled serenely, tilting her head almost coyly up at him. "The Prime Juris does not even answer to the King in the Way of Sight, Sur. I will not answer to you."

Manison tried looming, as if physical intimidation would have better effect. "I am Lord here, Mistress Kala."

"Jur Kala," she corrected quietly, her green eyes meeting his with a piercing glare. "I See you have little future in the King's service if I deem you unworthy of your heritage. I See a man whose pride will surely precede his fall if he continues to travel the path he's choosing. I See regret too late and sorrow to follow."

She watched his throat bob as he swallowed hard, his gaze wavering in a vain attempt to match hers. "I need your voice, My Lady. The people are tired of waiting."

"Then is it not your duty and responsibility to soothe them, Sur? Does not the Lord relieve the worries of his citizens with assurance? Does the word 'patience' not fall easily from your tongue? Better you expend your efforts ordering your people than ordering me."

Manison sagged visibly. Clearly she was more than his match. "They fear her, Madame Juris. And fear is a difficult enemy to pacify."

"Indeed. Tell them their concerns are first and foremost in my mind, but I will not render judgment without a fair hearing. Tell them if the girl is condemned with any less, then how can they expect more for themselves in time to come? If justice does not serve one, it will not serve many. Better to wait for its fullness than harvest the half-grown ear and starve at your own table on the morrow."

The petty lord's brow furrowed. "How can I explain that to the people? Old adages mean little to the farmer whose crops lie molded in the field. Words won't fill his family's belly in the Chillmonths."

"Then make it simple. Tell them the decision is mine and if they have quarrel with it, then let them face my justice themselves. I will treat them with the same courtesy they insist I extend to Mistress Jiana."

"They won't be pleased," Manison replied.

"That's your problem. You have soldiers, don't you?"

"For the defense of the Hold and village."

"If your people defy me, the village will need defense," Kala said firmly. "Of that I can assure you. Perhaps it would be wiser to use your men at arms to keep order, eh?"

Manison was completely deflated now, sagging into the collar of his ornate red velvet tunic, his face pale against the crimson. "I will assign guards to the streets as you suggest, My Lady. You'll have all the time you need to make your decision regarding the girl. You have my word."

Kala smiled. "You're a wise man, Sur Manison. I'll be sure to give you credit when all this is resolved."

She watched as he bowed and slinked from the room, reduced to the man he actually was beneath the pomp of social rank.

It seemed she did not always need her Sight to uncover the truth.

****

"He's coming," Jiana whispered into the darkness. "It's just as you said it would be."

"She of the Eyes of Truth has learned to trust the Sorcerer above all men."

"I shall play him as you wish."

"Be the innocent in his eyes, Daughter of my Darkness. We have already shadowed the White Waters with our reflections. Now it's up to you to dull the Gold's and Silver's wits with your cunning."

"The skin I wear has power to blind the unsuspecting. But he knows the Way."

"More concern is the one he brings along, once kin to our kind. He will have to be dealt with quickly. Our lot, not yours."

"I'm ready," she said softly. "I've even practiced my smile in the mirror."

****

"By the Blood," Jamus cursed aloud, his frustration peaking as the horses grounded after one final lifted stride which should have taken them to the south of Telma's Green Lake. Instead, they'd landed on the north shore, at least a span from the trail he'd intended to take. "How many more miscalculations am I going to make before we're through with this trip?"

"It's been seasons since you've been here, Jamus," Simen replied. "Things change. Perhaps you've forgotten some of the details."

"A fine excuse that would have been if I'd set us down in the middle of the lake instead of on the shore."

"We all know how to swim, My Lord," Jessa said lightly. "I wouldn't worry too much about it. Even Sharia is competent enough to conjure her way to safe passage after a lifting."

"Well, we don't have to concern ourselves with my carelessness the rest of the way," Jamus answered, raking his hand through his dark hair and sighing. "We'll just be riding from now on, though it will take us a bit longer than I'd planned."

"There's plenty of daylight left," Simen said. "One span more won't make any difference, unless Sharia is too tired to trot that pony of hers."

Sharia squared her shoulders and sat up in the saddle. "I ride all the time, Master Simen. Big horses too, not just ponies like Pebble. If she weren't so over matched by Magwin, I'd race you to that tree over there and beat you soundly."

"Oh, you would?" Simen returned. "I'll take you on."

"That's not fair to Pebble," Jessa said quickly. "Her legs are too short to keep up with him. I'll tell you what. Suppose Sharia and I trade mounts? Flax could use a run and I'm not in the mood."

Simen looked over at Jamus. "My Lord?"

Jamus smiled wearily and waved his hand in dismissal. "Go on. A little fun never spoiled a day. I'd let Whim join in, but I didn't sleep very well last night."

Simen shot Jessa a warning look and covered it with a grin a moment later. "Fair enough, ladies. Magwin and Flax are a fair match. I'd say it's up to the riders if one wins over the other."

Jessa slipped to the ground and gave Sharia a leg up on the golden mare and then mounted Pebble herself, holding the reins snugly to keep the little bay from joining in the fun. "On my word, competitors. Ready, set, go!"

Leaning low over their horses' necks the two kicked forward and galloped towards a lean willow near the south shore of the lake.

Whim danced under Jamus, but his master's quiet hands held him in place and he settled into a sedate walk beside the bay mare and her new rider almost at once. "Not this time, my friend," Jamus said, stroking the stallion's silver neck.

"It's not like you to not sleep, My Lord," Jessa said. "Was something wrong?"

Jamus shrugged. "You and Simen are of like minds."

"How many circles have I known you, Jamus? We've shared enough trouble between us for a mortal's lifetime. Can a little more hurt?"

"I was visited by an old dream last night, that's all. One I thought I'd long forgotten."

"The cave."

He nodded. "It wasn't the same, though. This time my parents were strangely different. They were greedy, vindictive, quite the opposite of the people they really were. I think that disturbed me even more than being there again."

"And the darkness?"

"There too. Trying to coil itself about me. I've dealt with enough to command it."

"So you say. But if it catches you unaware, or when you're too sick to hold against it, who's to say what might happen? Do you think the dream is part of a larger plan to wear down your Will?"

"You've been reading too many of the Eldentexts, Jessa." Then he reconsidered. "It's always possible. As long as the Black

Dragon has wings, I'll have to keep watch over his waters. It has been quiet lately."

"As if the army is mustering forces readying an ambush," she said, shivering. "You're right, I have been reading too much of the Eldenlore. When Kala's first message came through the Way, I studied a bit about Wayards. Sorase is the only Elder who seemed to know much about them."

"The Rightful Text," Jamus said. "A theory that they are not of the True Magic."

"The histories don't mention very many proven cases, so there hasn't been much to study over the circles past. It would seem we're dealing with something quite rare here."

"If the girl is a Wayard."

"It bothers me that Kala can't seem to decide one way or the other."

"It bothers me too, Jessa. In the Sorase text, it was a Seer who named the girl the elders examined. They confirmed it later when she tried to kill one of them with some kind of chanting."

Jessa nodded now. "Exactly. And that's when Sorase observed that the weave was alien to the River, *'emptiness where threads should have knotted,'* she said."

" *'A hollow in the hand, and thought without thought,'* she said," Jamus added, quoting the old text with ease. "Strangely unsettling."

"Maybe that's where your dream came from," Jessa said. "You've been closer to the Darkness than any of us. Perhaps your reading stirred old memories?"

"I hadn't thought of that," Jamus replied. "If that's it, then I shouldn't be bothered again. 'Once a man sees the face of his foe, the battle is half won.'"

Jessa pointed towards the tree beyond the lake. "It looks as if the race was a tie. I think Sharia and Simen are arguing it out now. If you're feeling better, perhaps we could move out a little to get over there before they come to blows. I wouldn't mind a good canter."

Jamus grinned and nudged Whim into a trot. The stallion slipped into a long fluid stride, his hoofs skimming the red earth of the trail. Pebble, with little urging from her rider, burst into a gallop to keep up with him, her short legs pounding out two strides to his one, as side by side, they headed for the drooping willow shadowing the lakeshore.

****

Gunder settled himself on the log he'd pulled to the lake's shore two seasons before, his bottom finding the dent in the wood he's always found the most comfortable. He'd brought a haversack of bread, cheese and fruit, but before opening it, he fastened a squiggler on the hook at the end of his fishing line and let the supple cane pole snap the bait out into the crystal surface of the water.

He hardly ever caught anything. Larsel, his best friend and self-proclaimed fishing expert, insisted his log was at the worst possible place along the shore, but Gunder didn't care. The best part of fishing wasn't the catch anyhow, it was the waiting.

The warm sun, a pleasant breeze, and the soothing shade of a nearby willow eased the day along like nothing else, and in the quiet he could think.

He had just about solved the problem of bringing water to Master Tantum's far cornfield when the horses came. Two riders with careless abandon and reckless speed charged down on his tree, their mounts' hoofs thundering into the grassy shore.

Gunder leapt to his feet, waving his arms furiously as they neared, trying to ward them off, but they were intent upon their goal and kept coming. He dropped his pole, snatched up his haversack and darted off to safety an instant before the horses, almost as one, leapt his log and skidded to a stop just short of the water.

"I beat you!" the girl on the golden horse shouted triumphantly.

"No how!" the man on the magnificent black countered. "Magwin's hoof hit before Flax's after the jump."

"That's only 'cause she jumped farther," the girl argued back. "Look, you can see she landed a half span past him."

"And they were neck and neck even then," the man replied. "I tell you, his nose was in front past the tree."

"Yours, maybe," the girl laughed. "You were leaning so far over his neck you had your nose stuck out to sniff at victory before I did, but Magwin wasn't ahead of Flax."

The man dropped the rein on his horse's neck to let the animal walk in a wide circle as he caught his breath. "Hah, losers always make fun of winners' noses. Typical."

" 'T'weren't but a hair between ya, from where I was standing," Gunder said, stepping back to his seat. "But assure I was runnin' fer me life when ya near trampled me so I ain't the best judge. Hard ta see clear when yer runnin'."

"Oh, dear," the girl said, her hand flying to cover her mouth, opening in surprise at the fisherman's sudden appearance. "Oh, Sur, I am so sorry. We didn't see you here. We never would have been so reckless if we had."

The man slid quickly from his saddle, dropped the reins to the ground and hurried over. "Are you all right, Sur? We didn't harm you, did we?"

"Nah, jest a start is all. I'm still pretty quick on me feet."

"Please know we had no intention of causing you distress. I'm afraid the lady and I were a bit too caught up in the competition to pay enough attention to where we were going."

"Cain't see the need of it. Fine lords an' ladies ain't got reason ta worry 'bout whose feet they step on."

"That's not true," the girl countered. "Lord Simen and I are no better than anyone else. Just because we have fine horses and fine clothes it doesn't mean we can't have manners."

Gunder squinted his eyes up at her, trying to make out her features in the sun's glare. "Yer a young'n to be talking so wise, ain't ya?"

"Lady Sharia and I come from a Keep where respect for others is the first rule."

"Strangers, then. Loren ain't quite so hospitable. Folks like me are most forgot by the velvet and shaenis ranks. 'T'ain't much a trial 'cepting when it come ta the law. Take now, fer instance. Them lords got a little girl in the dungeon, locked up tighter than tark's claws on a duskit. Now it may be she's guilty and it may be she ain't, but I kin tell ya fer sure if she was a highborn she'd be in the town inn eatin' cavel roast whilst she waited fer the Judger to name her."

"The girl," Simen asked, "do you know anything about her? We heard she was charged as a Wayard."

"Jest knows she's a lass from farm country up north, by the Jug Hills. Now me neighbor Rill says she done turned his popple trees ta the rot jest 'cause his wife wouldn't give her no pie, but I cain't say I had call ta agree to it. Course, I ain't run acrost her in any dealings meself. Still, I think it's her homespun shift an' tied-on shoes what threw her in the clink, not some rotten popples."

"Has the Judger trialed her yet?"

"Nah. Some kind o' flitter in the ointment I 'spect. I heard there somewhat amiss with that Judger an' she's calling fer back up from some Lord Seer or somewhat."

Sharia giggled. "Lord Seer? That sounds exciting."

"I'm sure the Lord Seer would be pleased to hear it," Simen agreed. "It's not often he gets a chance to participate in such affairs."

"Whatever," Gunder said. "Don't make no difference to me one ways or other, long as the lass gits heard fair. You'd think , though, her ma an' pa'd come already. Lessen they gots trouble at their own farm it sure woulda been kind to give the lass a hug now an' then."

"She has a family then?"

"So's I hear. But ta tell ya, first cut hay's comin' in an' the beans need pickin' 'bout now. 'T'ain't easy leaving the field when there's season work ta be done, even fer yer kin an' blood."

"That's sad," Sharia said.

"The heart an' the hands cain't always go the same way, Missy. Not when yer whole Chillmonth's provisions is waitin' in the rows. If ya ain't lived a hard life, it's easy ta criticize them what do."

Jamus and Jessa rode up, at a far more leisurely pace just then. When Gunder saw them, he bowed instinctively. Jamus leapt from Whim's back and quickly offered his hand in the customary greeting. "No formality, Sur. I haven't a scepter in my hand."

"I...," Gunder was suddenly at a loss for words, as if Jamus' presence had somehow stunned him.

"This gentleman," Simen offered quickly, surprised at Gunder's silence, "was just telling us about the young woman the town's holding prisoner. He seems to think she's a victim of social prejudice."

"I din't say that," Gunder said, finding his voice. "I said if'en she was a Lady like the lass on the golden mare she never woulda been arrested in the first place."

Jamus smiled. "I see. So you think she's innocent."

"Don't think one ways or 'tother. That sure be a fine horse yer ridin' me lord. Man oughta be mighty special ta be straddlin' sech a critter."

"I'm just lucky," Jamus said. "I found Whim when he was a skinny little colt. No one expected him to grow up so magnificently. If I'd listened to half the advice I got about him, I wouldn't even own him now. But, I kept him and fate granted me a marvel to ride."

"When I first seen ya I thought ya was a ghostly, all shimmer silver an' stuff. Kinda stopped me breath fer a bit there."

"I can assure you both he and I are quite alive, Sur."

"Pleased I am, that I kin tell ya," Gunder said, grinning. "Me name's Gunder."

"And I am Jamus and this is Lady Jessa. We've come to Loren to see the Juris."

"Yer the Lord Seer?"

Jamus frowned. "Lord Seer?"

Simen kept a straight face, but he had trouble keeping his voice from quivering with laughter. "Master Gunder has heard that Jur Kala had sent for the Lord Seer to help her make a decision about the girl. I would presume he's referring to you, My Lord."

"Ah," Jamus sighed, weighing his options quickly. Perhaps adopting a false identity could have some benefits. "I'm just not used to being called by that title," he said, checking Simen's gasp with a glare. "It will do as well as any while I'm here, I suppose. I take it the village of Loren is not far from here?"

"Yon," Gunder pointed down a road heading south. "Less a quarter span by horses, I reckon. I walks it in three quarters if I ain't hurrying. A man's got ta take his time when he's goin' fishin', elsewise there just ain't no point."

Jessa looked down at Gunder's discarded pole, snapped in two by the racing horses' hooves. Taking the risk that the man had not noticed, she gestured with her fingers, repairing the damage. Simen caught the movement out of the corner of his eye and let Magwin step into Gunder's line of vision. "Did you catch anything?"

Gunder grinned sheepishly. "I ne'er do. 'T'ain't the point, if ya knows what I mean. Rill says all I do it drown squigglers, but I figger getting' a line wet an' enjoyin' a quiet day in the sunshine's more'n worth a whole basket of fish."

"It would be nice to catch one once in a while, wouldn't it?"

Gunder shrugged. " 'T'would make me look less the fool in the village," he said. "But I been the butt o' the joke so long I kinda got used ta wearin' it." He moved past Magwin and picked up his pole. "If you folks is going ta town, ya best be on yer way. It's near Sowin an' if ya hurry, ya kin jest make midmeal at the Widow's Peek. Aggie's always got somethin' special on the fire."

"We'd be delighted if you'd join us, Master Gunder," Jessa said. "It would be nice to have a friend in town."

Gunder waved her off. "Nah, Mi Lady. It gots me fishin' ta do and you don't need no extra friend in Loren. Onct ya open Aggie's door ye'll have all the friends any stranger could want. Tell Aggie if I catch anythin' I'll bring it by fer Lastmeal. Elsewise I'll be lookin' fer a bowl o' her duskit stew." He strolled over to his log, cast his line back into the water, and began to whistle.

Jamus and Simen remounted and reined their horses down the trail.

"Do you think he'll catch anything this time?" Simen asked, smiling.

"Oh, I think he will," Jamus replied, nodding over to Jessa who winked back at him. "I think he most definitely will."

Chapter 4

Strong fragrances of warm bread beckoned as the travelers approached the main entrance of The Widow's Peek, one of three inns lining the main street of Loren. Four buildings down, they had found a clean, well-appointed stable to board their horses and then, as Gunder had instructed, headed right for Aggie's tables in a cozy gathering room set with ten tables and a short wooden serving counter next to a wide set of double doors.

To the left, in back, a polished wooden banister lined a set of stairs leading to an upper balcony lined with doors. Simply decorated, the lower room seemed most welcoming and as soon as they entered, a neatly tunicked young man led them to a table with four cushioned chairs and a basket of fresh rolls in the center. "Mistress Aggie's baked a sweet ham roast today," he said. "Collie greens, cut corn, and baked tubers come with it. I can say ye won't find better roast in all of Lovental, so ye won't go wrong if that's what ye order."

"We heard from Master Gunder that no one can cook as well as your mistress," Jamus replied. "He recommended her special meal to us. If my companions are agreed, that's what we'll all have." When the others nodded, he placed two gold sovereigns on the table. "I hope this will cover the bill."

The young man slid one of the coins into his hand. "They'll be six denerets back, My Lord."

"Put the rest towards two rooms for us, then, if you will," Jamus said. "We will be spending a few days in town and I think we'd enjoy sharing some fine meals while we're here."

"Ye be in luck, My Lord. Two rooms are all that's left. With the trial and all, travelers have been coming in from all over. With ye, we're full up."

"Trial?" Jamus asked.

"Aye, My Lord. We've a Wayard in the town jail, near set for the fire or rope, so they say. Telma's Prime Juris is to hear her testimony any day now. Been a crop of folk come in from the hills to witness. They won't stay for the execution, of course. People around here have no blood lust like they do in the cities, but they do want to have their say. Seems the Wayard's done a bit of damage most everywhere she's been."

"Have you seen her?" Jessa asked.

"Only for a moment," the young man replied. "They had her all trussed up with rope and carried her into the town in a farmer's wagon. Whisked her right into the Sheriff's hold before anyone had a good look at her. She looked real young."

"So you've never met her, then."

"No, My Lady. Mistress Aggie says she saw her once at her parents' farm up north, but that was circles ago. The Mistress used to buy her grapes and surleps direct from the growers then and drove the wagon herself. 'T'was a mite ago, I'd guess. She doesn't get around much now, at least not since her husband's circle closed and she renamed the inn. It used to be The Peeking Window back then 'cause it had such a nice view of the hills out back."

"Your mistress has a way with names," Simen said, taking a bite of one of the rolls. "And a way with the oven. This is delicious."

"Wait till ye taste the ham," their waiter said, grinning. "I'll go fetch it now."

"So, the town seems to know little of their prisoner," Jamus said.

"Or it seems to say little of her," Jessa replied. "He seemed very nonchalant about it all, didn't he? I would think an accused Wayard, a trial presided over by the Prime Juris, and a possible execution would rouse quite a bit more excitement."

"I agree," Simen added. "As a matter of fact, the whole village was quieter than I expected. There were only two people in the town square and half the shops appeared to be closed. With all the travelers who are supposed to be here business should be booming."

"It is a little strange," Jamus agreed. "As soon as we finish eating, I'm going to find Kala. It seems there's more to this than she's told us."

****

"Don't ye set foot in the street, Warem O'Dell. I'll not have my husband turned into a toad."

"That's just plain nonsense, Ledia," Warem said, turning his jug empty jug of hearthbrew upside down to show her there wasn't a drop left. "Is a man supposed to go thirsty just because his wife hears a fearsome little lass' eye will catch his?"

"'T'ain't her eye I fear. 'Tis her hand. Ye know far well Wayard's have the lust for fine men to chant. She'll waggle her finger and snatch you right under her covers, and if you think I'm going to stand by and let some little bud have her way with ye, then ye'd best think again. Every woman in Loren knows how those women work. Put her in the darkest hole of the Rim and she'll still send her call to every fool man within a wind of her."

"So how come I'm here, then? The Sheriff's is only two doors down."

"Because I put wards on the doors and windows, that's how come," Ledia answered. "Plucked a basket of willyherb and shillow from the ridge as soon as I heard she was coming to town and tied bunches everywhere. Her Magic won't cross in and ye won't cross out so long as I'm here to watch over ye."

"The Ridge is a far piece off, Leddy. Musta took ye a long day just to fetch the flowers. Ye did that for me?"

Ledia reached out and pulled him to her. "Man like ye is worth a hundred winds more even," she said softly. Then she kissed him hard on the lips.

Warem, kissed her back, and pulled slightly away and grinned. "Can't say she's all Wayard if this part is her fault."

****

"You feed the fear," the darkness hissed. *"By it you grow."*

"I cannot see their terror," Jiana said. "The darkness is a wall between us."

"Your friend it be. Mock it not. Trust my word. Your name is dreaded. They quake before your handd. Feast to the body be their apprehension. Rouse their rage and power more be yours."

"And yours. Do you think I don't know how little you truly care about me? I'm just your puppet. Were I not of use to you, I would be nothing but shade in the sunshine."

"He cannot be conquered by might. The Great shall ne'er o'ercome him. The child shall conquer. Be as you appear."

"This skin is weak and immature. I want better."

"No. It suits the need. Wear it as it must be worn. Use it as it must be used. Eyes will trust, ears will listen. It will be well."

"You will give me the light I need?"

"He will give you light. Treasure your own darkness and drink its power. Patience be yours."

****

Gunder was grinning from ear to ear. He'd caught four big fettlefish from the lake, more than enough for a fine meal at Aggie's. For once, when he returned to the inn, he would not be the laughingstock for all the spans he'd wasted along the shore.

He leaned over the still water, studying his reflection with a certain delight. Even the scar under his right eye where the tree branch had hit him last season seemed to fit today. "Gives me character," he said aloud. "Dignity, methinks. Man needs ta look like he's done a thing or two in his life." He reached out with his hand to scoop a drink.

But as his hand neared the water, the crystal surface rippled and the hand's reflection met his fingers above the water.

"Wha…!" he cried, startled by the feel of cold flesh. But before he could leap back, the hand gripped the edges of his vest and yanked.

Gasping and flailing, Gunder was dragged into the mirrored water, disappearing beneath the surface in an instant.

****

As soon as Kala heard strangers had ridden into town, she sent out one of the servants Manison had assigned to her to find out the details.

Mori was scared to go out to the streets, but the command of the Prime Juris outweighed fear, sending her feet flying out into the near deserted streets. It took her less than half a span to find out who the strangers were and exactly where they were.

"Four strangers at the Widow's Peek, Milady. Story goes one's the Lord Seer ye sent for. Would he be riding a great silver horse?"

Kala smiled. Jamus would certainly find his new title amusing. "Yes, Mistress Mori. He'd be so mounted. It sounds as if my friends have indeed arrived. It's earlier than I expected them, but so much the better. I will be going to the Widow's Peek myself. Would you like to come?"

The girl shook her head. "I'd as soon stay here, Milady, but 'tis not my right to disobey thy command. If ye need a handmaid, I am for thee."

"There's nothing to be afraid of, Mori. My friends have keener skill than even I have in dealing with Magic, if that's what we're dealing with. You can stay here if you wish. I have no reason to have a maid at my side."

"You will dress?"

Kala looked down and her tunic and breeches and shook her head. "No need for formalities either. My friends know me as I am, not as the rest of the world expects me to be."

"I'll come with thee, Milady. It's not fitting ye should be unattended, even in the face of thy friends."

Kala smiled in gracious acceptance of Mori's loyalty. Though Jamus might not care whether she had servants to attend her, the citizens of Loren would notice if the Prime Juris were so little regarded. Already her judgment had come to question. The less she did to compromise her reputation the better.

The Widow's Peek was a short walk from the Tallowtail, several blocks over from the main street of town. She had chosen the less central inn for herself to avoid attention. She found it curious that Jamus would head for the most conspicuous spot himself. Usually he was of her mind regarding public notice.

But the delicious odor of well-prepared food provided one answer as she approached the Peek's door. Fragrant spices, and the welcoming scent of fresh baked bread seemed to beckon from within. Her stomach was surprisingly eager considering she had eaten a full Firstmeal at the Tallowtail well past Easwin.

Despite the wonderful smells, the dining room was sparsely attended. Finding Jamus was a simple matter, and as soon as she spotted him, she strolled over to his table. "So, My Lord Seer, I should have known I'd find you where the food was plentiful."

Jamus bounded to his feet as soon as he heard her voice, his arms spread wide to welcome her into his embrace. "By the Hand, My Lady, you'd think a man could finish a meal before such beauty steals his appetite. It's so good to see you!"

Letting herself savor the feel of his body against hers for the moment, Kala leaned into his arms, and sighed. "It has been too long between friends."

"Lives lived in separate worlds, I fear."

"And yet again, I need you here."

He pushed her gently away to hold her at arm's length, his grey eyes searching her face. "Your coming here to find me so soon suggests more concern than I expected. Is there a reason for such haste?"

She shrugged. "To the village, there is. To me, personally, none at all. But the girl has been a disturbing presence ever since she arrived. I've managed to do very little to calm the fear she's brought."

"You haven't been able to See the truth of her?"

Kala's eyes stole a quick glance around the inn to see who might be listening. Somewhat reassured, she still kept her reply guarded. "The Vision is limited, it seems. I would think your skill will serve us much better this time."

He nodded. "Do we need to do anything now? I was enjoying the meal."

Kala laughed. "I could see that plain enough. Your whole party seems quite content."

Simen picked another roll from the breadbasket, and held it out. "I would have offered you something sooner, but you seemed quite satisfied by my brother's arms."

"Well, it seems your sense of humor has not improved since last I saw you, Sur," Kala returned. "I hope, Lady Jessa, he has not tormented you too much with his follies."

"I've laughed enough at Simen's pranks to last a lifetime, My Lady. However, he has minded his manners in my company for the most part."

"Then all's well between you."

Jessa smiled at Simen, gently placing her hand over his. "We've shared a great deal."

"And I hope to share more," Simen added, smiling back at her.

They were interrupted by the waiter, who arrived with Sharia at his side carrying a tray of pastries. "Mistress Aggie showed me how to fold these," she said, placing a pile of flaky turnovers on the table. "She says the next time I can help her make the dough. She says I have a good hand in the kitchen."

Kala stiffened. "Who is this?"

"Sharia," Jessa replied. "My Apprentice. Is something wrong?"

"She looks...," Kala shook her head. "She looks familiar. You've always been in the Keep, child?"

Sharia nodded her head. "My mother and father were of the East Village. This is the first time I've ever been away from there."

"No family anywhere else, then?"

"No, My Lady. My grandfathers were farmers in the South. I have two aunts and an uncle, all in Magiskeep proper. I cannot think of anyone else who might be related."

"Why did you bring her, Jamus?"

Jamus shrugged. "It seemed the natural progression of things. I asked Jessa to come because of all her knowledge of the Eldenlore, full of stories of the Wayards. Sharia is her Apprentice, that's all."

"No more?" When Jamus shook his head, Kala sighed. "I've grown too suspicious. I guess when Vision fails I start imagining things of my own. I am sorry, but Sharia...well, you'll see for yourself. Maybe I'm just overreacting."

"That's not like you, My Lady," Jamus said. "Why don't you sit down and join us for a good meal. Maybe some relaxation will settle your nerves."

Kala let him pull up a chair next to his and sat wearily. "You may be right. Ever since I arrived here I've been strangely uneasy. Nothing has gone as it should have. By all accounts the question of Jiana's guilt is an easy matter for a seasoned Seer. I've spent well over two Sevenstins and managed no better than the lowliest novice in my Art."

"Wayards waken the evil, Milady," Mori said quietly. "I tried to tell her, Milord, but she said it was all hearthtales and nonsense. Naught goes well when the curses have fallen. Until the lass is tended to, none of us is free to dream."

Jamus stiffened. "What do you mean, Mistress?"

"They mock us in the night, Sur. Haven't ye heard the tales? 'Tis the darkness they love and it's when they work their weaves. Come to us in the night, they do, and when we sleep, they comes into our dreams and make 'em as they will. Wayards got the power, they do."

"Jessa?" Jamus asked. "Does any of this make sense to you?"

"The Eldenlore speaks of Dreamkeepers, but you already know of that. The only other references I recall are of the Shadows."

"I've met enough of them too," Jamus said softly. "Both in my dreams and out. If they're involved, you were right in calling me, Kala."

She leaned back in her chair and took a deep breath. "There was no one else to call," she said.

The door of the inn swung open and Gunder swaggered in, his basket full of fat fish. The triumph seemed to have transformed him, for his head was high as he called loudly, "Aggie! Set the griddles to flame! I got me a pile of good fish fer the whole inn!"

Petite and slender, dark-haired Aggie pushed through the swinging doors of the kitchen. "Gundèr of Farmwell, what makes ye think ye can barge into me inn stirring up such a fuss as all that? Where are thy manners?"

"Hush up, woman. When a man's got a passel o'food fer yer larder, ya ain't got call to make him account fer how he comes through yer door." Dramatically, he slung the basket on the counter. "What's ya got ta say fer that, eh?"

"I say a man ought to mind his manners no matter what he brings here."

"Come on, Aggie, ain't ya got at least one word o'praise fer me? How many's the time yer mates mocked me out fer setting by the lake keepin' me line wet, eh? So now's I brung ya the prime catch o' the whole village an' ya cain't even say a word o'thanks?"

"If ye wasn't so much a braggart it'd be a mite easier. T'would be a bit kinder if ye hadn't plopped the fish on my clean counter too. Still, I'll grant ye favor, Gunder, and say ye done a fine bit of fishing this day," Aggie replied, checking the weight of one of the larger fish. "I had no idea the lake bore such fat fellows."

"I been tellin' ya all, but no one's been listening," Gunder answered, giving the little woman a playful punch in the shoulder. Though he rocked her back on her feet against the counter, he didn't seem to notice. "Now get to cleaning and cooking, Mistress. I aim ta see the whole inn feasting on me catch!"

Aggie rubbed her shoulder briskly and frowned, but instead of making an issue of it, she gathered the basket into her arms, hefted it, and lugged it back into her kitchen.

Hands on hips, Gunder stared at the door for a moment, then turned and strolled over to a table near the window. As he passed their table, Jamus smiled at him. "Well, done, Sur. I see you made a fine catch after all."

"What be it to ya?" Gunder asked, scowling a bit. " 'Tis what I do fer me keep, is all. Ya want's ta make somewhat of it?"

"Not at all, Master Gunder. I am just pleased you had a successful day after all the trouble my friends and I cause you."

Gunder's brow furrowed as he considered this. Then he grunted. "Fair words from a stranger, I s'pose, though I cain't say it makes sense ta me. Still, I ain't a man what's so greedy he don't share. Ya be sure yer here fer Lastmeal come Weswin, eh? Mistress Aggie batters up the best fish in the whole Province." Then he walked away to settle himself in a chair where he banged loudly on the table for the waiter to bring him a flagon of ale.

"It seems Master Gunder keeps short acquaintance," Jessa said. "He acted as if he didn't remember who you were."

"I suppose to him everyone who dresses in fine clothes looks alike," Simen replied, laughing a little.

"I'd thought I'd made a better impression than the average lord," Jamus said. "I guess my manners failed me once again." He laughed too, but deeper in his mind uneasiness nudged at his memory.

Kala sensed it. "What's wrong, Jamus?"

He shook his head. "I'm tired. I haven't slept well the last several nights."

"Dreams," Simen told her. "As soon as we'd crossed the Rim."

"The mountains again," Kala said. "Old visions coming back?"

"It's nothing," Jamus said. "Just my imagination at work. We were at the Telma Host House. I guess I was just remembering."

"Are you better now?"

He nodded. "I think so. But I could use some solid sleep."

"Then you don't want to see the girl now?"

He took a sip of water and sighed. "That's why I came, Kala. There's no point in waiting for a new day when we've a wind left. I don't know how helpful I'll be just yet, but it's certainly worth the effort."

"We'll all go," Simen said, pushing up from the table."

"No. Not yet," Jamus answered, waving him to sit back down. "The poor girl's probably terrified as it is, under arrest as she is. We don't need to overwhelm her with interrogators just yet. Let me go with Kala and assess things first. Then I'll decide what to do."

With Mori leading the way, he and Kala left.

Simen took a long drink of ale from his mug and tried to settle back to the meal. But for some reason, he'd lost his appetite.

****

Sweet smiles and light touch. Go to the heart, pretty one. He comes.

"Can I use a charm?"

Be charming, but beware. His eyes are keen. Magic is to his hand as leaves to the wind. If you weave, be light.

"That's not easy, but I can do it. I'll just think backwards."

Chapter 5

Jamus was cautious with the intensity of his maglit torch as he accompanied Kala down to the dungeon cell below the sheriff's office. If the girl did indeed have Magic at her disposal, keeping the area as dark as possible did work to his advantage. It was hard enough for him to work spells in the darkness unless he was certain of his surroundings. A lesser mage would find it nearly impossible, and he simply refused to overestimate Jiana's possible talents.

Soon they reached the end of the tunneled stairs descending into the dungeon. Aside from the faint glow of Jamus' light, it was totally dark. Ahead, he could just make out the frame of a large wooden door, completely solid and girded in fieron bands.

"Is the girl that dangerous?" he asked incredulously.

"The villagers think so," Kala replied. "They've a terrible fear of dark Magic here, any Magic, for that matter. You'll have to take care too."

He shrugged. "I can usually take care just fine, but I appreciate the warning. Errant spells would be a decided problem here. I did make the torch look quite normal."

"I saw that," Kala said, nodding approvingly. "Regardless, don't take any unnecessary chances—either out there or in here."

"Does she frighten you too, Kala?"

"She is not a part of my realm, Jamus. For some reason, her being refuses the quest of my Sight. It's a very disturbing thing and aside from you, it's never happened with anyone else before. I truly think she has Magic, but its nature eludes me."

"Well, let's have a look." He stepped aside to let the Juris unlock the heavy door with a broad fieron key. Then he moved back in front of her and pushed the door open.

The feeble light revealed a small figure huddled in the far corner of an irregular chamber. The body was trembling with whimpered sobs. "I didn't do nothing, I didn't. Why ye keeping me in so dark? I hate it. I hate it. Please, I want to see the sunshine."

"Answer what we ask and perhaps you will," Jamus said calmly. "You are accused of Wayardcraft. Do you know what that means?"

A pale face, almost transparent in the dim silver light, lifted to meet his gaze - two dark, dark eyes, round and frightened, searching for his. "Who be ye? Ye ne'er been here afore."

"I am Jamus--a judger of sorts, like the Lady Kala, but skilled in different arts. She says you haven't cooperated with her."

"I do what she asks. Why not be satisfied with what I be?"

"They say you used evil Magic in the village. Is that true?"

"I do what I do. 'Tis not good for people to be unkind. Sometimes I just think and it happens."

"Think what, Jiana?"

"Bad things."

"And these bad things just happen?"

"Sometimes. Sometimes nothing. Sometimes what I think."

"Your parents, Jiana. What are their names?"

"Lorna and Sandu, from the north hills. They have a farm there."

"Have either of your parents ever talked to you about Magic?"

Jiana sniffed hard and shook her head, her dark hair, oily and dirty, barely moving against her lighter skin. "Not a whit. Me Papa are a maker, though. Rybus of the next farm over says he cain't grow crops like me Pa 'cause he ain't got the Gift of Making, ya know?"

Jamus frowned. The girl's speech was a curious mixture of classes as though she had been raised in more than one simple world. "I'm not sure what you mean, Jiana."

"Rybus says me Pa calls on the waters to feed his fields, that's all. He calls it the Making. Says even if the rains don't come, Papa's gonna have a good crop 'cause it's his Gift."

"Have you ever seen or heard your father call on the waters?"

She chewed her lip thoughtfully, then brightened a little. "Sometimes he sings rhymes. Like, '*Rise to meet this hand of mine, waters as a Greenmonth sign. Flow to field with evercare, freshing all the seedlings there.*' He'd say that and it was like the water just came up from the ground around all the corn."

"Did he say other things?"

"Oh, sometimes. He'd kind of sing to the grapevines and Mama said even she could see them growing taller and stronger on the arbor. Proud he is of his plantings. 'Tis a pity our farm ain't closer to the big cities. He could make a fine profit there, steada just making by. It's why I come here ta earn me own keep. I was ta find work carin' fer some kidlets or keeping a house. Then afore I knew what was happening…," she started to cry in earnest now. "They was all so mean ta me. Said I was just country dirt, not good enow fer their fine houses."

"What did you do about it, Jiana?

Jiana sniffed hard, recovering her composure a little more. "I thought bad things and then said them. Mistress Poly's wine turned sour. She threw a bucket of leavings at me when I asked her for a popple from her tree. I was hungry, but she said I was a dirty little wretch and said if I wanted food I could eat slop like the rest of her pigs. She was mean, so I fixed her."

Jamus clucked his disapproval. "She certainly was mean to you, Jiana. I can understand why you were angry. What about the other people you thought bad things about?"

"Master Parkins laughed at me when I fell in the mud. His son tripped me, ya know. I was all wet and cold and he laughed. I fixed his well good and dried it all up. Man cain't make mudholes for people to fall in if he ain't got no water."

"Indeed not," Jamus agreed. "But it was a very big bad thing to do for such an insult. Could you make his well fill up again if you wanted to?"

Jiana chewed her lip again. "I s'pose. But why should I? Ye don't expect a lass to forgive a man what don't make apology, do ye?"

Jamus frowned, noting the change in her accents again, as if she were putting on airs just to make her point. "If he said he was sorry, would you fix his well?"

"I'd think on it," she answered slowly. "But I'd hafta feel real good to do it. I cain't make things happen lessen I feels real strong about it. That's when I can wish best."

"I see. Well, that's enough for now, I think. Will you promise not to make any wishes unless I say it's all right?"

Jiana shrugged her scruffy shoulders. "Why for?"

"The sheriff will keep you locked up here in the dark for a long time unless I can convince him you won't do any mischief while you are under my care. But, I will not speak on your behalf if you don't promise me this. I will do my best to be sure you keep any promise you make, Jiana, but I will not even try if you are not ready to do as I tell you."

"Ye'll get me out of here?"

"I will do my best."

" 'Kay. I promise," she said softly.

"Lady Kala," Jamus said, "I will stand for this child. She is not a Wayard in the true sense, but an unskilled practitioner of the Art, unschooled and undisciplined in its workings. She is a threat among those who refuse to treat her kindly, but I have teachers who can guide her. Will you speak to the Council on her behalf?"

Sliding easily into the pretense, Kala nodded. "I will speak for thee, Master Seer, for thy wise counsel is highly regarded by the Juris. Mistress Jiana, your fate is in your promise to Lord Jamus. Be true to your word and you will soon see the sun again. Come, My Lord, the sooner we speak to the villagers the better for the child." Then, letting Jamus light the way, she head out the door.

Once more in the corridor, with the lock firmly in place behind them, Kala asked, "Is she a sorceress, then?"

"An Unperceived, not a sorceress. She is the daughter of a Natural, one to whom the River lifts as a gift. Were this the Eldentimes, she would have been tested and called to the Keep for training, or one of the Wise Ones would have sifted her out and at least taught her the common decency of her power. Instead, she's been allowed to run wild, calling to the River with whatever fire burns in her heart. If she is angry, afraid, or sad, her mind reaches out without conscious will in these "wishes" of hers—spells of a sort. She doesn't know how to control them or shape them beyond her immediate desire for revenge or justice, so more often than not, the consequences are bad. Did you hear how uncertain she was when I asked her if she could fix the well?"

"I did."

"Knowing what to do to bring back the water requires logic and an understanding of exactly where the water is, how it flows and how a well fills in the first place. She's never been educated in how to weave spells."

"But she uses Magic."

"In a manner of speaking. Because she has the Gift of Magic, the Silver River answers her intense pleas. It's like Spellfire - Magic Unrestrained, the dangerous branch of that River as filled with illusion and deception as the Rim itself. Apparently, whatever she wants has a strong enough vision painted in her thoughts that her spells aren't completely random. That's a bit of a blessing."

"I don't understand. If she's hurting people, how can that be a blessing?"

"She's only hurting the people she wants to hurt and in the way she wants to hurt them. Can you imagine how terrible it would be if she wanted Mistress Poly's wine to sour and instead soured every barrel in the village? It could happen as easily as Spellfire could burn down every house. Apparently, Jiana's desires are specific enough to pick the right target and the right retribution."

Kala shivered. "That could happen?"

"Why not? The River is Turan's very soul, not some stream of inches. Evoking its power is no small matter."

"Spellfire of another sort, I suppose. Then it's a good thing I called the Rivermaster himself to sort this out. You can control her, can't you?"

He shrugged. "I should be able to. If I put a sphere of protection around her and weave it tightly, it should do the trick. Any spells she casts will be reflected back instead of escaping. She might sting herself a time or two, but it's the first lesson a Novice needs to learn."

"Then you'll take her to Magiskeep?"

"Eventually. That's where she belongs. But I'll need to see her parents first. It's not like the Eldentimes when children were stolen without their parents' permission."

Kala sighed. "It was true of Seers once as well. The Masters of Grandisite would scour the countryside for Worthies and practically kidnap them. Now most parents are proud to offer a child to the Sight."

"Magic doesn't have that luxury this side of the Rim," Jamus replied. "I'll have to be cautious. But if her father is Gifted as well, he may be more willing to let his daughter go. It sounds as if he has some rudimentary understanding of just how complicated Magic can be in the hands of the uneducated."

"But what about him? Isn't he as much a danger as his daughter?"

"He hasn't come to the village. Apparently, all his Magic is confined to his own farm. Let him ply whatever spells he will on his own lands. What harm can that do?"

****

The door had closed again, plunging the chamber back into the inky shadows.

She sighed contentedly, wiped the streams of tears from her cheeks with one small charmed gesture and then conjured a soft down bed to lie on. Her chants worked easily in the no-light, fed by the very darkness into rich solidity.

She could have shattered the door with a word, but that would spoil everything.

He be fool indeed, this Rivermaster.

"I don't underestimate him. Didn't you feel his Power?"

Too light. Too bright. Too much for one hand. The child blinded him.

"There's more to do. He has no fear."

There is a way. Keep your smile and your tears. They will serve us well.

****

Jessa rolled up the scroll and stuffed it into her knapsack. The ancient words had shed little light on the topic of Wayards and she was feeling completely useless in the matter. "I don't know why Jamus insisted I come," she said. "There's nothing I can do to help in any of this."

"Jamus seems to think you can," Simen replied. "You should have more faith in him and in yourself."

"To what end? There's nothing useful in that scroll and the only thing I'm any good at is interpreting the Eldenlore."

He reached out to take her hand. "That's not true, Jessa. Why, ever since you first met Jamus, you've been his one staunch friend and ally in the Way of Magic. He needed someone here he could depend on. Someone who would understand the possible dangers and be ready to help."

"Someone like you, Simen. If anyone is his ally, it's you."

"But I'm no expert in the old knowledge."

"But you understand the nature of Shadows."

He offered a lopsided grin to match the shrug of his shoulders. "I was born in the Way, that's true. I suppose I should understand the Darkness better than most. If this girl is practicing such a craft, I might be able to sort it out. But Jamus is just as capable as I am. After all, we are reflections of the same soul." He winked now, laughing at what he considered a joke.

Jessa shivered as a chill coursed through her at his words. "I hadn't thought of that in circles, Simen. I've gotten so used to the idea the two of you are brothers."

He shrugged again. "What else can a man's reflection brought to flesh and blood ever be but a brother, My Lady? We are close kin in nature."

"There's nothing natural about your kinship to Jamus and you know it. Bless the Hand you are alive and of the flesh and blood you speak of, but you are no ordinary man. Once you existed only as his reflection in a mirror, a mere image trapped in the Way. But now you are a part of him as surely as the River is. You're here because he needs that part of himself."

"That's a harsh condemnation of me, Jessa. I had hoped you saw me as more than just an appendage to the Lord of Magiskeep."

She caught her breath and then sighed heavily. "Of course I do, Simen. It's just that, well, ever since we crossed the Rim I've had this uneasy feeling every time I've even so much as passed a mirror. It's as if my own reflection is staring at me, even if I'm not facing it."

Simen frowned now, his brow furrowed in deepening concern. "I thought I was seeing things myself in the mirror in my room. Now I'm not so sure it was my imagination. Come on," he reached out for her hand. "There has to be a large mirror somewhere in town where we can really study the reflections it offers."

"Do we really want to do that?"

His frown broadened into a wide grin. "My dear mistress, what need ye fear? I was born in the Way. Who could be a better master of its secrets than I?"

Chapter 6

Sharia tossed the wad of dough onto the kneading board and pushed hard with her fist.

"Don't murder it, child," Mistress Aggie reminded her. "Steady rolling works better with hurleydough than violence."

"I'm sorry, Mistress. I was just a little upset about Mistress Jessa. She and Master Simen left the inn just before Sowin's turn and told me I had to stay behind. It's my duty to follow my Mistress."

"Perhaps she and Master Simen had private business together."

"What kind of business they wouldn't want me to know about? I am her student. It's her bound duty to teach me all she knows."

Aggie bit her tongue and her laugh before she answered. "Ye are but a young lass, Sharia. Some lessons need a few more circles under thy belt before it's time ye learn them."

"Like what?" Sharia asked, setting her hands on her hips, the flour puffing down her apron.

Aggie wiped her own hands on a towel and motioned the girl over to sit on a stool across from her. "You're about thirteen, aren't you lass?"

"Just turning," Sharia answered proudly. "Two more Sevenstins."

"Too young and too old all at once. 'Tis a new time coming for thee. Ye'll need to know men and women rarely make the best of friends."

"But Mistress Jessa and Master Simen like each other."

"'Tis so, from what I've seen. But me old eyes oft times see more than young ones like thine. Ye had a mother and father, did ye not, child?"

Sharia nodded. "I still do. They live in the village near near the Keep where I go to school." She took a deep breath, proud to have remembered not let slip any hints of Magic. As kind as Aggie seemed, she was still a mortal, born and bred on the wrong side of the Rim to understand or even tolerate the idea of Magiskeep.

"Are they but friends to each other?"

Sharia considered for a long time, her sweet face curling into
a frown of intense concentration as she thought of her parents
together. Then, she remembered the closed door to their bed
chamber, and the stern warnings to her about disturbing them unless
invited in. Once, just once, she had opened the door a crack and
peered in to see them wrapped around each other sighing and
groaning. It meant little to her then, but the strange sight had led her
to tell her best friend, Mirian about it.

"It's how they make babies, silly," Mirian had said. "The
kissing's what does it. Man puts the command in the woman's
mouth, an' says, 'Make me a son or make me a daughter,' and if the
woman loves him, she does what he says. They tangle up like that
'cause he needs to hug her belly when he says it so she knows where
to put the baby."

Sharia had nodded wisely as if she'd known that all along,
but had just needed confirmation. It was strange, but she was already
well used to Magic and ready to accept most any explanation just so
she wouldn't have to peek into that bedroom again.

"Mama and Papa make babies together, so they are more
than just friends," she said at last.

Aggie's face spread with relief. At least she had avoided the
need to explain the basics to the girl. "There then. Well, it appears to
me that Mistress Jessa and Master Simen feel about each other a lot
like your parents feel. Unless I be wrong, and I don't think I am,
maybe they need some private time too, eh?"

Sharia's face darkened a bit, but, as before, she nodded
wisely. "I hope Master Simen doesn't ask for a baby right yet. I still
have a lot to learn from Mistress Jessa and a baby'd get in the way."

"Poor little snip," Aggie laughed. "Ye think of thy Mistress
as thy own mother, don't ye."

"She does take care of me and love me like my Mama. It
would be hard to share her right now."

"Ye be an honest lass, I'll say that. I have a feeling thy
Mistress is as honest. She'll not make such a decision without telling
ye. Now, go on back to the bread. We've a fair bunch of mouths to
feed for Lastmeal what with Gunder's fish on the menu. Like to
knock me other with a feather seeing him come in with that full

basket. Man's ne'er caught so much as a minnow in all the circles he's been wetting his line in that lake."

"He seemed quite proud of himself," Sharia said.

"Too proud and too loud of it," Aggie agreed. "Gunder's always been the shy type. I didn't think fish'd change him so. I can't say I like it much. Swagger has a way of starting brawls in Loren and I like my furniture in one piece."

"Master Jamus would never let a fight start in your inn," Sharia said. "Why he'd stop it with one…" Her hand flew to her mouth.

"With one what, lass? I didn't see a blade on his belt. How'd he stop a pair of ruffians from coming to blows on me tables, eh?"

Sharia improvised quickly. "Well, Lord Jamus is really smart and strong too. Stronger than he even looks. He'd figure a way, that's all. He's a brave man and the best Lord ever."

Aggie laughed. "Well, that's a fine assurance then. I'll feel right safe with your Lord here then. Right safe."

****

"So, Madam Juris, the only assurance you offer us is the protection of Lord Jamus?" Sheriff Depner asked, leaning back in his chair, his hand tented below his ample chin. "Am I to trust the safety of the whole village to a stranger?"

"Sur, I am bound by oath to the Truth of all things. Even you know the Juris' Vow is as Sacred as the Hand itself. I can tell you Lord Jamus is the best and only Keeper in all Turan qualified and able to keep this child from harming anyone."

"Then she is a Wayard?"

"Not precisely. She has acted as a Wayard might in times of what she felt was danger to herself. But we see no darkness in her heart to brand her further. She has been ill-treated and ill-taught in her young life and needs more understanding than condemnation."

"Poor little wee lass I'm supposed to feel sorry for, then? She's turned the village on its heels, ruined the livelihoods of a half dozen good citizens, and you expect me to offer mercy?"

"I expect you to be reasonable and to obey the King's Law. I am his Juris and this is my decision. Abide by it as you have sworn to do."

Depner sank down into his chair as the wind sagged out. For all his titles and bravado, he was really only a figurehead in the sheriff's office, far more used to arresting drunken brawlers than dealing with matters of State. As many men had tried, he'd made his stand against Kala, and like them withered at last under her authority. "Take her and good riddance, though I'll not say you'll have an easy go of it. It may be the law, but the people of Loren are not as bound as I to its strict interpretation."

"Is it not your duty to protect its governance? Lord Jamus and I expect at least that courtesy."

"I cannot be in all places at all times, Madame Juris, and I haven't the manpower to sit a guard at your table. I will declare your right to take the girl to the citizens and issue the appropriate proclamations. After that it's the will of the people and your own common sense 't'will make the difference."

"And your Council will agree to this.?"

Depner's confidence boosted back in an instant. "The Council'll do whate'er I tell them to, My Lady. I am the voice of Loren in the end ye see. Whilst I can't command the folks 'round here to behave themselves, I sure can make the Council toe the mark."

"Well, I am glad to hear that, Master Depner. It should be a help to us just knowing the governing body of this town stands behind us." *Far behind us*, she thought, *and well out of reach should any of the townspeople decide Jiana should be burned. No guard to sit at the table, and no official to stand at our sides. Bless the Hand, Jamus and I have been through worse together.* She smiled. "Lord Jamus is outside. If you will be so kind as to give me the key, he and I will escort Jiana to his rooms at the inn. We will rest for at least a day and then be on our way."

"Where are ye taking the lass?"

"Where she will learn how to live a worthwhile life, Sur."

****

Loren, it seemed, was short on mirrors. The Widow's Peek had only small ones above the dressers and quick visits to the Tallowtail and Sparret's Call proved no more useful. There was only one house of any substance nearby and it had been boarded up while Lord Manison spent his time in one of the better located villages in the Province.

Simen remained determined, certain that if he just had enough space to see beyond the limits of his own face, he would be able to figure out just what was lurking in the edges of the Way. He was about to suggest he and Jessa conjure their own silvrin mirror when a simpler solution struck. "The lake," he said grinning. "I should have thought of it sooner. The waters were still and clear along that shore. It's the very reason Master Gunder wasn't catching any fish. Will you ride with me, My Lady?"

Jessa curtsied prettily, accepting his teasing formality with some of her own. "But of course, kind sir. How could a lady refuse such a gentlemanly request? Perhaps we should have Mistress Aggie pack us a picnic basket? The trip doesn't have to be all business."

"A picnic means a blanket," Simen replied, grinning slyly. "Two of us, alone, under a tree?"

Jessa tilted her head coyly and smiled back. "Several blankets, I think, and a long day of it, provided we can find a bit of seclusion."

"Did I ever tell you I think I love you?"

"More times than I can count," she answered. "Get the horses ready. I'll take care of the rest."

Sowin's warm breath caressed the grasses as they rode out of town, laughing and talking, caught up in their own adventure in Jamus' cause. "At least I feel like I'm doing something worthwhile," Jessa said.

"Jamus is going to fuss about it when Sharia tells him where we've gone," Simen answered, "but I'll take his scolding over the boredom of sitting around doing nothing any day. I am my own man, despite what he may like to think."

"He trusts you, Simen. There's been nothing here pointing to any real danger anyhow. Even Jamus said the girl is just a little slip of a thing, no more trained in Magic than a puplet to the hunt. Why, she doesn't even know what it means to cast a spell."

"And yet she's done it nonetheless," he replied. "Sometimes Magic comes unbidden to a Gifted hand. It's the same as when the Way reaches out to capture a reflection of a face staring into it. Random power drifting in and out of the real world without logic or intent."

"Is it dangerous?"

He shrugged. "Who's to say? If the Shadows themselves reach out, it is. But just the Magic? Some say each time a reflection is captured a little piece of the person in front of the mirror disappears into the Way. Jamus keeps insisting I am his music, you know."

"You are a masterful bard, Simen."

"At least I can make a tavern laugh, which is more than I can say for the Rivermaster." He frowned then. "But what if, rather than being part of what he is, suppose I am something he one day wished to be as he stood before his mirror?"

"You mean he wanted to be a Follyman and imagined himself one as he looked at his reflection?"

"Exactly. Does the angry child really want his parents dead when they've punished him? If he says he does, it's his rage speaking, not his heart. But the Way does not distinguish reality, it only reflects what it sees, or captures the face before it."

"Then you are just a part of Jamus' imagination?"

"My essence is his invention, yes. His Magic gave me life, flesh and blood as solid as any man's. I am real, but only because he had the power to make me so."

Jessa reached over to touch his arm. "For that I am ever grateful, my love. Jamus blessed me with a great gift when he gave you breath."

He laughed and reined Magwin to a stop at the grove of trees beside the lake. "Flattery from your lips makes a man blush, Jessa. Thank goodness we have some shade and cool water nearby so I won't melt in embarrassment."

Jessa swung down from the saddle, laughing with equal delight. "The day you are embarrassed, Master Follyman, will be a day this world will never see." She pulled a blanket from the back of her pack and spread it out on the ground. "Come on, Sur. Mistress Aggie in the Inn's kitchen prepared us a fine midmeal. It's yours to enjoy if you can get down off your high horse."

"Ouch," Simen replied, dismounting. "You have a sharp wit yourself, My Lady. Are you sure you've no Follymen in your family?"

"I'm a keen observer," she answered, pouring a cup of keldherb for each of them. "I've learned a great deal since we've met."

Simen took a sip of the brew and moved over to the water's edge. "The lake is almost perfectly still today. It should prove a fine mirror. Maybe we should do our investigating first and eat later. I'm not really hungry."

Jessa walked over to stand beside him. "We'll have to get our feet wet to see the reflections. The angle's not quite right from here."

He took her hand and together, they waded in until the water was just at the ankles of their riding boots.

Simen peered down, studying his face in the surface of the waters, letting his eyes search both his own features and beyond. He focused past the reflection, letting his eyes drift lazily into the image.

Something moved behind the vision. He tightened his grip on Jessa's hand even as he felt her fingers tense in his.

She saw it too. Something more, sliding behind their images.

The water roiled and spumed as clawlike hands and muscled arms snaked out from the depths, clutching at the couple.

Jessa barely had time to scream a single word of protest before both she and Simen were yanked into the water and pulled, flailing helplessly, beneath the surface.

****

Jamus frowned as he tied the last loop in the weaving of his sphere around Jiana. Curiously tired from what should have been a simple construction of reflective Magic, he puzzled again for a moment before dropping his hand. His mind reeled with images of threads twisted upon themselves, reflecting castings in the wrong direction, completely out of his control. Yet, as he studied the essence of the shield around the girl, he could perceive no flaw. It had been harder than he'd ever expected to curve the silvrin surface inward to send back to her own hand any Wayard spells she might cast, but in the end, the barrier appeared perfectly set.

He sighed wearily. "I'm going to disguise who you are, Jiana. When people look at you, we don't want them to recognize you. That way, no one will bother us."

"I ken no fear of bother, Me Lord, but if that be the way ye see it best, so it be for Jiana."

"For now, it's best, My Lady. The people here don't understand the powers you have and it frightens them."

"Fear be a power of itself. So my Papa oft says. Scares make folks do wrong when right be just at the edge of their eyes. 'T'ain't no greater danger to a man's heart than what's inside, my Papa says."

Jamus' gray eyes studied her face intently, his own heart thundering in his ears responding to her words. Her voice had a hollow quality, probably because of the sphere, and something in the tone nudged at his own eldest memories. The worst fears did indeed come from inside. "Your father is a wise man. I hope I can meet him one day."

"He will be honored, me lord, an' more'n pleased."

Again the echo of her words rang in his ears. Jamus shook his head to rid himself of the odd sensation. "Well, then, let's get ourselves a good meal in the village and talk about getting you home to see your Papa again, shall we?"

In short order, they had settled themselves in the dining room of the Widow's Peek, ready to enjoy a good midmeal and take in any gossip that might pass their way.

Gunder swaggered across the common room of the inn, his chest puffed out. He stopped at each table, making sure the diners knew the succulent fish bedded in piles of fresh vegetables had been caught by his hands and he related the tale of his angling prowess more than a half dozen times before he reached the table where Jamus, Kala, and Jiana were sitting. "Fine welcome fer strangers, I say," he said, looking down from his lofty demeanor. "Feast o' sech greatness ain't the common thing, ya know. Takes a catch of a special fisherman ta set a platter like that."

"I should say so, Master Gunder," Jamus agreed.

"How ya know me name, eh?" Gunder asked, peering down.

Jamus smiled slightly. "I suppose you've forgotten, or else," he laughed, "I made far less of an impression on you than your scaly friends here. You were rather busy when we met."

Gunder frowned. "T'ain't shy on names most times, but I fergit yers."

"Jamus. But it's no matter. You have far more important things to consider than my name. Why, it looks as if you've supplied enough fish to feed the whole town."

"T'were fair leapin' inta me baskets," Gunder replied proudly. "I tole everyone that nook o' the lake were rich, but no one believed me. I showed 'em now, I did. Only trouble is they'll be flockin' there theyselves I'm gonna haft a find me a new spot, I reckon."

"My Papa always says the fish like the shadows by the rocks in the warm seasons," Jiana offered quietly. "Too much sun sends them to the darker waters."

Gunder stiffened slightly, before letting his face break into a lopsided grin at the girl. "Yer Pap's a wise man, lass. 'T'ain't many what knows the secrets of the shady spots. I done caught me two prime whoppers not too long past."

"Only two?"

"'T'ain't but fished there fer a wind so far. Figger I'll be spendin' more time in the days ta come. Onct word gits out about me catch I won't have much a choice but ta go off somewheres like that, now, will I?"

"I guess not," Jiana replied, smiling up at him. "Most likely the whole village will be trying their luck at your spot on the shore. I do hope they're careful. As I recall, the banks can be pretty slippery along there."

Kala shifted uneasily in her seat, Sight nagging unbidden in her mind. It was all she could do to hold back her Vision. She took a sip of wine, holding it on her tongue to let the acid taste focus her attention. She glanced over at Jamus, whose expression seemed strangely impassive. Somehow, she too felt detached, as if Jiana's and Gunder's conversation had nothing to do with either her or Jamus.

And yet, she was sure it did.

"You say the lake's dangerous?" Jamus asked absently, his voice too casual for the question.

"Not at all, My Lord," Jiana replied.

"Lovely banks all about," Gunder said. "Sandy slopes go gentle into the water."

"Children play there all the time."

"T'weren't for ta scare the fishes, I'd go fer a swim meself." Gunder deliberately turned his back and made his way to the next table.

Jamus merely nodded and took another bite of the moist fish. "It was a good catch Gunder made. He proved to be a good fisherman after all."

Kala nodded sharply, her head not at all clearing from the movement. "Surprised almost everyone. They all said there was nothing in that lake to fish for."

"Every lake has something in it," Jiana said quietly. "That's what my Papa says, and Papa's never wrong."

Chapter 7

Simen gripped Jessa's hand so hard she gasped. Breath came easily, surprising her as they seemed to sink through, rather than into, the water. Though she struggled to find the surface, whatever had grabbed them pulled with incredible strength.

Despite every effort, they were forced first to the bottom of the lake and then plunged swiftly sideways into a tangle of vines and roots nearer the shore. Then, as was the nature of the Way of Mirrors, reflection burst forth, blinding them with the brilliant light of day somewhere in Turan. From the other side, a stiff wind took over from the lake's currents, sucking them into the sunlight where, within its gusts, they tumbled to the sandy ground beside an outcropping of rocks edging a strangely purple mountain range.

"More fish for the stew," a voice laughed.

Simen squeezed his eyes shut to rid them of the last of the water, then opened them again to peer cautiously into the light, his gaze shaded by a tall silhouetted figure just a span in front of him. Gradually, his pupils adjusted and he could make out details of a flowing lavender robe framing what appeared to be a shapely woman, taller than he by at least a half foot. He sighed heavily. "Shaidra, Mistress of Shadow. Ill met even when it was my own choice."

"Dear, dear, Simen, I have always cherished you. Since we first met in the Way, I wanted you for my own. To think, I took one of your Reflections when could not take you and now, you are here. How my heart aches to hear you speak so harshly of me."

"That can't be. You have no heart."

"I see your Folllyman's garb still wears well, the barbs sharp as ever. Though I do say you've hit the mark there. I do not have a heart, but I am by no means immune to your insults. I should have thought you would have been more pleased to see someone you know after your hard journey."

"It wasn't bad enough to outweigh seeing you again."

"Another wound! Perhaps I should dull your tongue." Shaidra raised her hand, her fingers flexing, but then, she let it drop loosely at her side, the soft folds of her shaenis sleeves hiding her

intent. "No. A man does not suffer unless he is full of his senses."
Her dark gaze turned now to Jessa. "You are a pretty thing. When
your Shadow took form, I had thought it mistaken to shape itself so
prettily. I can see now I was wrong."

Jessa frowned, her own fingers gripped harder onto Simen's
hands before she finally replied, "You speak in riddles, My Lady. I
find it hard to answer when I don't know the subject of the game."

"Ah, you've chosen a wise one, Simen. Not too quick to leap
into the fray, I see." Shaidra swept her arm towards the hills beyond.
"This is my kingdom, for now. Not much to look at, but plenty of
space. Your world is peopled with many of the flesh whose lives can
give sustenance to my kind. But, as your Riverlord has proven time
and time again, it is not easy for us to exist among you without risk.
So it is our lot to take from one world and give to another or, to take
from one world and take again." She laughed at that, if she'd made a
joke far better than Simen could ever understand. "You, see, my
Simen, even now Shadows take your place in the world you know to
ply the wishes of Darkwing."

"Shadows? Reflections, you mean, freed from the Way."

"Your name for his minions, I suppose. However named,
their purpose is the same. Fear will rise from their hands to feed their
power. Then the drinking of the blood will fill our bellies and give us
power over the rest."

Simen shook his head. "It's not going to happen. Jamus
knows about your ambitions. He's already bound your Dragon
once."

"The Black River has many tributaries, Follyman. And
Darkwing has many reflections. Even the great Rivermaster himself
cannot always see clearly in the dark. He too will be shadowed in
Shadows and fall with the rest."

"Never."

"How I have always admired your optimism. Such
confidence." Shaidra turned her gaze on Jessa. "And I have also
admired your taste. This lovely lady on your arm. Jessa, as I recall?"

Jessa stiffened defiantly, then smiled. "I am Jessa, Madam. If
it matters to you, as it seems Lord Simen is far more interesting to
you than I am."

Shaidra's thin lips curled up in evident satisfaction. "Jealousy becomes you, Mistress. One must conclude you are more than a mere friend to the Follyman, eh?" Her hand snapped out, clutching at Jessa's wrist. Simen lunged at them, missing completely as Shaidra's smiled opened into a mocking laugh. His eye caught an almost imperceptible flicker of the Shadowmistress' free fingers and then she and Jessa vanished in a swirl of dark fog.

"No!" he cried, pawing helplessly through the dark mist.

His voice echoed in the emptiness of the sandy plain.

****

Jamus shuddered as the last sip of keldherb hit is tongue. He nearly dropped the cup, steadying it at the last instant with his other hand to set it clattering down on the table.

Kala caught his movement and frowned. "Are you all right, My Lord?"

"Something...," he muttered. Then, he too frowned. "I don't know. By the Hand if you were not the Seer between us, I would think I had the Gift for a moment there. It was as if a terrible danger had dropped its weight on me."

"What kind of danger?"

"Someone...something I love. I don't know. It was as if a heart had been ripped in two."

"I thought ye be the High Seer, me Lord," Jiana said quietly. "Sure, if that be so ye kin tell the truth of a Sight. Me Papa always told me the Seer's eyes are clearer than the crystal waters of Stillwater Lake."

"To Vision bidden," Kala answered hastily. "But even the greatest Seer can be caught unawares by a glimpse of truth and not recognize it."

" 'T'would be a bother, I should reckon," Jiana said, a trace of a smile passing her lips at the first word and vanishing at the second. "Ye must be a strong man to keep from breaking."

"Power does have its drawbacks," Jamus agreed, rubbing his brow with his hand. "I'm more tired than I thought, Jur Kala. I think I'll make a short night of it and get some sleep."

"A good idea," Kala replied. "I'll see if I can drag Sharia out
of the kitchen and take both young ladies to our rooms. You have
warded, have you not?" She left the question hanging without further
explanation, still wary of Jiana's knowledge of Magic.

"I've taken care of every circumstance I could imagine,"
Jamus answered. "And a few more," he added, smiling tiredly. "It
should be a quiet Norwin for us all."

Left alone with Jamus at the table, Jiana lowered her gaze
demurely, toying with her napkin. "'Tis a wide world ye've traveled,
I suppose, me Lord. Ye look young to be a high Judger."

"I'm old enough," Jamus replied. "Circles do not make a
difference to the River."

"Ah, yes, me Papa always said there is no time in the Way."

Half-hearing them, Jamus started at her words. "What did
you say?"

"I said the food was very good here, My Lord, and I thank ye
for bringing me here to the table."

"I thought...," Jamus voice trailed off. "You are most
welcome, Mistress Jiana. I'm sorry the village did not welcome you
better when you first came here."

"People be wary of strangers, I suppose. An me bein' from
the uphills, 't'were concerning. I tried ta get work and earn me keep,
but none'd give me a care. This be the first good meal I had since I
come."

"Poor child."

"Hunger 'tisn't the worst of it, me Lord. It's all the hate I
been suffering. How could people be so cruel to a lass like me?"

Jamus rubbed his eyes tiredly, finding the words difficult.
"It's not you, Jiana. It's the Magic they fear. I'm afraid this world of
men does not accept our Power very well. The story's too long to
relate, but someday, when you are safe in the Keep, you will hear it,
and then, perhaps you'll understand."

"Magic," the girl said, as if she needed to chew the word
carefully before she understood it. "That's what I do?"

"It would seem so," he answered. "But you must keep still
about it as long as we're here. It won't be safe to speak it to anyone."

"No one? Not even those what come here with you?"

"They already know," Jamus replied. "They'll be careful for you."

Jiana nodded. "I'll do as ye say, Me Lord. Exactly as ye say." Then, she covered a sly smile with a mouthful of bread. Lying was becoming easier and easier.

****

Completely disoriented by the sameness of the terrain and a curious dizziness, Simen trudged along the winding path through Shaidra's wasteland. He had trouble following the twists and turns between the rock, finding himself more than once scraping his shins when he tottered against one.

Finally, nearly exhausted, he stopped, hoping to clear his mind. "Ouch! By the Blood," he cursed, rubbing his right calf where he'd banged into another sharp edge. He looked down at the boulder to his left, his thoughts drifting an instant before touching vivid clarity.

He'd hit the boulder with his right leg.

He reached down with his right hand, ignoring the clear vision of the rock to his left and hit the stone sharply with his fingers. He took one step forward, until he was level with the boulder, and as he did, it suddenly slid into the edge of his eyes to the right, where he'd actually found it. A careful step back, and it slipped back to the left as he'd first seen it.

"Reflection," he muttered. He bent down and picked up a pebble, tossing it deliberately to the left. He traced it in the air as it arced defiantly right to land with a clatter. "The whole landscape before me is reflection," he said aloud, assuring himself with the sound of his own voice. "Well, then, Mistress Shaidra, it seems you've left me a maze to follow. But this time, you've chosen the wrong man to torment. I am of the Way." He raised his hand, then swept it down over his own body, surrendering to his lineage.

Ever so subtly, to anyone who might have watched, his appearance shifted. The dagger at his belt shifted to his right hip, the lock of hair teasing his left forehead slid over to the right and his eyes, the same clear gray as Jamus', blinked to clear away the illusions of Shaidra's world with simple ease.

Reflection now, walking in reflection, Simen peered towards the horizon, saw a wisp of smoke, and, for the first time since he'd emerged from the lake, he set a certain course to the east. He could hold the chantment over himself indefinitely as long as he did not need to physically exert himself too much.

Reflections and shadows had little strength against the muscle of reality.

Simen breathed a sigh of edgy relief to see how quickly he closed in on a chimney up ahead. A few more measured paces along the deceptive trail brought him close enough to see three little cabins clustered together under the shelter of a lipped cliff with a foaming waterfall and a grove of green trees.

He checked himself from running headlong towards the houses, all too aware of the dangers of recklessness amidst all the illusions surrounding him and instead, called out, using his best Follyman's voice. "Hello! Hello! Anyone there who can hear me?"

A door opened, and a pale face peered out into the fading sunlight. "Come on if you can! 'T'tain't safe to come for ye, so's it's yer problem to make it here. Be welcome if ye can, and Blessing of the Hand on ye if ye can't." With that, the door slammed shut.

Grinning despite his own fatigue, Simen hurried as best he could, cursing once or twice as his ankle hit a stone he misjudged. In short order, he managed to reach the center cabin where he knocked on the door.

It opened a crack, with two wide eyes meeting his in obvious surprise. "Ye be fast of foot through the lies. Who ye be?"

"Simen, a Follyman," he replied. "Too foolish, I suppose, to really see what's underfoot."

An arm snaked out, grabbed him by the elbow and propelled him inside the cabin.

Simen's head reeled, not from the yank, but rather from the sudden settling of the world back into normal perspective with reflections swirling away to the hard reality of everything's being exactly where it appeared to be.

"Here, sit," a woman's voice commanded. "Takes a while ta git yer bearings back onct ya come in. We keeps it dark thinking mayhaps the sun's the culprit outside making everythin' all backwards and whatnot."

"I still says the Lady built the cabins so's we won't go all mad whilst we be here," another voice said.

"Like she cares a whit," a third person scoffed.

"I knows ya," a fourth voice said. "We met by the lake. Ya musta fallen in too!"

Simen blinked at the fourth voice. "Master Gunder? The fisherman?"

"I be. Leastwise I was. Ain't nobody here."

Simen frowned as his vision cleared. "You, Sur, are not nobody. Don't ever speak of yourself that way. If a man thinks little of himself, then little he will be. You are as good a man as any I've ever met."

"See, Gunder! I tole ye so!" the women cried. "If'en it takes a Follyman to convince ye 'stead of Molly, so be it. Ye listen to him, eh?"

Gunder's face fell. "'T'would be a sad day now ta find me worth. Place like this, a man ain't got need o' pride." His eyes lifted hopefully to Simen's face. "Ya come ta take us back? I figger they might miss even the likes o' me by now."

Simen checked himself before answering. There was no point in telling the poor man he would never be missed. There was already a Gunder in the village. And, Simen suspected, there was probably already another Simen and Jessa there as well. Seeing Gunder had solved part of the riddle already. They had all been trapped in Shaidra's world while shadows of them all had gone into Jamus' world in their place. Reflections escaping from a world of mirrors now stood in their stead, ready to…ready to what? "How many people are here, Gunder?"

"Two dozen, more or less. Seven in this cabin, five and six in the others. I come last. They all bin here more'n two Sevenstins far as they can figger. Hard ta tell, what with the sun an' all. Go out there," he gestured towards the door, "and ya lose track o' most everything 'cept how ta put one foot a front o' t'other so's ya don't fall on yer face or bark yer shin. Found Dimend lyin' stark cold at

the bottom o' a ravine t'other night where's he shoulda took a left
step steada a right. Near killed 'im."

"It wouldn't have done for him to die," Simen said, almost
to himself. "Hard to keep a Shadow's substance when the true flesh
dies. It'd be different if the Shadow took the life itself, but she's not
doing that yet."

"Whatcha muttering 'bout? Ya gots a tech of the sun, I
reckon. Mebbe a cool drink'll clear yer head, eh?"

Simen smiled wearily. "I wish a cool drink were all I needed,
Sur. Anything to blot out what is becoming all too painfully clear."
He took the offered cup, sipped a little and sighed. "This lady you
speak of. Do you know where she lives?"

"Aye," Molly answered. "T'ain't but a span's walk from
here ta one what knows every footfall. I done a bit o' cleanin' fer her
when I first come. Not like she really needed me. One wave o' that
spider hand o' hers an' the whole place'd be swept cleaner than
silvrin. But, since I was the first one here, I figgered she were a bit
lonesome and wanted me ta think I was here 'cause she needed me.
Onct she got herself a few bandies ta keep her company she sent me
off like an' ol' dishrag."

"You can lead me there, then?"

"What fer? I ain't got no stomach ta see that place agin, I'll
tell ya. Why'd ya want to go?"

"Someone I love is there," Simen replied quietly. "There is
no way I will ever leave her with your lady a moment more than I
have to. If you won't take me, then just tell me which direction I
have to go and I'll find my own way."

"Ya'd be riskin' more than yer life, lad," Molly answered.
"Ya'd be risking yer brain, ya know. Sech a trip kin make a man
mad."

"I doesn't matter," he said. "If I lose Jessa, I'll be just as
mad. I might as well lose my sanity in a worthy cause."

Molly grinned. "Man talks like that must be in love. I always
been a soft heart fer sweethearts. If'en ya kin wait til the sun goes
down a bit, I'll take ya. 'Tis far easier ta ignore yer eyes in the dark
ya know. We find the dim light makes any journey quicker
hereabouts."

Simen nodded reluctantly and took the plate of food one of the other women offered him. He was not hungry, but tried to eat anyhow. Filling his stomach might offer at least a little comfort to the deadly pain filling his heart.

****

"Jamus, wake up," Kala insisted, shaking his arm roughly. It was already well past Sowin and he had not stirred since she had first tried to rouse him a span earlier. She'd gone down to midmeal, fully expecting him to be right behind her. But, after finishing a second mug of keldherb, the Seer had returned to his room to find him in an even deeper sleep. "This isn't like you. Get up."

"H-m-m-m-m?" he mumbled incoherently. The world was a haze of fog to his half-opened eyes. He rolled over, threw his arm over his face and tried to drift off again.

"Jamus!" Kala shouted now, her frustration edging towards fear. "What's wrong with you? Are you sick?"

"Sick," he muttered. "Sick." Something sparked him then and he pulled his arm away to squint up at her. "Not sick. No. Tired. Why's so bright?"

"The sun's been up for spans," she replied. "I thought you wanted to make an early start. Simen and Jessa are back from wherever they wandered off to, so we can leave the girls behind here at the village when we go."

He rubbed his eyes sleepily. "Might be best. Sharia wouldn't have left her home if she didn't have to. Going back's hard." He was having trouble making sense. He shook himself, pushing his body to wakefulness. "I've never been this tired before."

"Is it Magic, or nature wearing you out?"

"Huh?"

"The sphere you wove for the girl. Is it harder than you expected?"

Jamus swung from the bed, letting his feet hit the floor hard enough to jolt his body. "No. I locked the threads of that weave so I didn't have to worry about it." He rubbed his side, stretching a little to work out an unexpected kink. "Kind of sore here. Maybe I wasn't as fit for a long ride as I thought. I've been doing a lot of studying

lately. Could be I'm just out of shape." He grinned. "Pitiful idea.
Old age creeping up on me, maybe?"

"By the Hand, Sur, the day you get old without intending to,
the River itself will dry up! Maybe you're catching something.
Simen has a Healing Hand. Do you want me to call him?"

Jamus shrugged. "Might be worth the bother. If he can't cure
me, he can spare a little energy at least."

Magiskeep's Master sank back against the bedpost, his head
in his hands as Kala left. He had not told her the whole truth, trusting
her not to look beyond the surface of his words. Though she was a
Seer, she was bound by tradition and oath not to use her Art without
his permission, and now, he relied upon those promises to protect her
from the fear creeping into his own thoughts.

Magic had twisted upon itself.

In the early darkness before Easwin, he'd risen and tried a
simple spell to kindle the fire in his hearth to ward off the night's
chill. Instead of flames, a shower of snow had fallen from the
chimney, sizzling to steam and water on the sooty stones. He
remembered shaking his head with an initial laugh, tossing off the
mistake as Prentice foolishness born of his own half-sleep. But then,
fully awake, he'd tried again, only to see shimmering icicles rise in
the shapes of fire from the sodden logs.

He'd shivered then, less from cold and more from dread. His
Master's hand barely faltered. Once, perhaps, but not twice. The next
two spans before the sun's first rays hit his window brought even
more concern and with it, an inexplicable exhaustion as he struggled
again and again to reach the River's purer waters.

But over and over, his fingers groped through murky waters,
tainted by black currents turning each chanting upon itself. Hot
became cold. Wet became dry. Light dimmed to darkness, and even
a simple lifting dropped a water pitcher to the floor in shattered
splinters of pottery. When he'd tried to mend it, the shards repelled
each other.

Only after total frustration, did he manage, by completely
reversing every complexity of his spell was he able to restore the
pitcher and then, with even more wobbly success, command his
Magic to replace it beside the bowl on his nightstand.

Complete reversal. Every thought, every concept, every understanding completely the opposite of what it should have been. The effort had been so exhausting and draining it had collapsed him on his bed where Kala found him spans later.

Now, in the light of day, the disturbing realization of what had been happening washed over him in a cold chill.

If Magic had reversed itself here, what else was reflection of itself?

And if, indeed, it were reflection, could Shadows be far behind?

Simen's arrival was a welcome relief. "Well, Jamus," he said with his usual lightness, "Lady Kala tells me you aren't feeling well. Blessed be if I can do much to help you, but I'm certainly willing to try."

Jamus shrugged. "It's more mind than body, but I would think an ounce of your strength wouldn't hurt."

"Mind?" Simen asked. "Do you mean you've lost a part of it?" He laughed a bit too brightly. "By the Blood, brother, I could have told you that circles ago! The day you turned your heart away from this lovely Seer, I knew you were half-crazy. Could it be that being here with her now has cost you the other half?"

Kala blushed despite herself. "I'd be honored to think it, Simen, but this time I doubt I'm any part of the problem. Otherwise he would have gotten out of bed to spend some time with me."

"Out of bed?" Simen laughed. "I would think quite the opposite, Mistress. Any man I know would want you in bed with him."

"Lord Jamus is not 'any man,' Sur," Kala replied quickly, reacting sharply to his suggestion.

"And you are not 'any woman,' my dear," Simen answered. "A countryweight more luscious than most and already his bed partner more than once. Come, come, don't you think you deserve a bit more credit in this? Look at him. If ever I've seen lovesickness…."

"Damn you, Simen," Jamus cut in, "it's not Kala that's bothering me. If you'd stop your Follyman ramblings for a moment and sense the air you'd know better. It's Magic that's awry, not my manhood."

Simen grinned broadly. "And aren't they one in the same, My Lord Rivermaster?"

Jamus' jaw dropped.

"Come now, Jamus. You can't deny your own allure, can you? How many times has a Sorceress seduced you for your Power? Why shouldn't it betray you now when your lust for a woman overpowers your own reason? Look at her. You know as well as I do how much she loves you. Can you deny how easy it would be to return the favor? How much more natural could it be?"

The silence in the room was a thick as Magic's Hand weighting the air.

Chapter 8

Simen followed Molly easily along the trail, his mirrored perception anticipating each footstep before his eyes registered the opposite of what he sensed as truth. When Molly veered left to pass a boulder, his body shifted right, staying two paces behind her.

"Ye have a keen eye," Molly noted, not even turning to check on him. Instead, she held a small sliver of reflective silvrin in front of her and peered into it. She paused for a moment, as if confused. "Ye walk easily, Follyman. It took me more than three Sevenstins to figure the way of this world."

"That long?" Simen asked, quickly adding, "You have been here so long?"

"Hard to say, truly," Molly answered, polishing the silvrin with her apron. "Time twists with the roadway here, but I be counting the suns and 'tis five Sevenstins passed since I fell into the pond."

"A pond? Not the lake?"

"Aye. Along with my little boy. The lady took him right off. She keeps him in her palace like a puplet. 'T'ain't cruel to him or naught, and she lets me visit near ever I want to. But a lad ought ta be with his true mother, not with a pretender."

Curious, Simen thought. A child? Not what he would expect from Shaidra. At least not the apparent kindness. Letting the mother visit? Keeping the boy well? What was she up to? "And she's been taking good care of him?"

"'Pears so," Molly answered. "Boddy seems happy there mostwise. Misses his m'am, but be it so, he's well fed and cared for. The lady shows a kind hand and talks gentle to him."

Stranger still, Simen thought. "And you've let him stay?"

Molly laughed derisively. "Ye may be keen of sight, but ye be dull of understanding's far as that lady's concerned. None has say 'bout what she wants 'cept the lady herself. If'en thy eyes can't see it right off, thy heart will know it short. Look yon," she pointed to a tall palace that seemed to be receding as they neared it.

Simen blinked to clear both of his visions, confused by this latest anomaly. Even in a mirror places drew closer as you neared

them. Apparently Shaidra had laid one reflection upon another as far
as her home was concerned. He made quick note of the image,
forced himself to see through the deception, and realized they were
already on the path leading to the broad brass bound door.

****

    With Simen's words ringing in his ears, for once, Jamus had
nothing to say. The thought that his own power had at last found a
way to become his enemy was not at all surprising. But to hear
Simen suggest it was another matter. This man he had learned to call
his brother had keener insight than anyone he had ever met.

    "No answer, My Lord?" Simen asked, still grinning.

    "It's not a joke," Kala said quietly.

    "Hah!" Simen spat, edging his voice with mockery. "And
I'm not allowed to laugh at the pitiful lust of my brother? Come,
come. Isn't he the one who's spent a lifetime lecturing and pursuing
virtue? How easily he falls before your charms, Mistress. Even the
River fails him in your presence."

    Kala's jaw tightened. "Since when have you become so
cruel, Simen? You sound like a man scorned by his own love,
jealousy dripping from your tongue."

    "I? Jealous? I have a lady, thank you very much. One to a
customer, so they say. Better may you look to the surplus of ladies
in my brother's life—just as there always has been. You're only one
of many, you know. Every head in the Keep turns his way when he
passes. He's not in command of his own power that way."

    "I've warded…," Jamus replied hesitantly. But Simen's
accusation hit hard. He had never really mastered his feelings
towards Kala. Perhaps all his efforts to keep other women from
being attracted to him should have reflected back into his own heart
as well. He'd never really thought to ward himself. Had his Magic
finally rebelled? He flexed his fingers experimentally, sending a
simple spell back at the fireplace. As before, instead of sparks, flakes
of icy snow fell on the logs. He snapped his hand back, wiping his
palm brusquely on his tunic as if to wipe away the errant spell.

    Simen smiled. "Twist and turns along a dark path you've
learned to follow. Perhaps you need to be alone until you sort it out."

"No," Kala said sharply. "If you're right he needs someone with him who understands."

"I have to go to the Northern farms anyhow to find the girl's family. If I go by myself, I'll have time to think this through."

"Not alone," Kala repeated. "Master of Magiskeep or not, the Provinces do not welcome Sorcerers. By the Blood, Simen, you should know that."

"It's only a bunch of farmers," Simen replied. "No kings or princes with suspicious eyes."

"He's right, Kala."

Kala shook her head. "I don't need Sight to see trouble ahead. I've already seen it here in this village. The people here aren't princes either and yet they were ready to burn a girl just because they suspected she was a Sorceress. One spell caught by a rustic's eye would be enough to condemn a man in those hills. I've been there, or at least in places like that a dozen times myself. The ancient lessons of Wizardchase have keener meaning there than they ever had in the city."

"So you'll go with him?" Simen asked, grinning. "His safety a fine excuse to share a blanket in the wilderness?"

Kala jaw clenched, but she kept her temper. "A traveling Follyman is always welcome in country inns. I should think you could even earn a deneret or two if you could manage to replace that poison on your tongue with some sweeter syrup."

"It's not a bad idea," Jamus said. "If Simen is right, he has far more understanding of my Magic than anyone else. I thought the Prime Juris and a wise Seer would be an asset if I needed to judge the hearts of men, but who better than my own reflection to judge my own heart?"

"So, just the two of us, then," Simen replied. This time, he hid the corners of his last grin behind a façade of quiet acceptance. The first hurdle had been easily overcome. Without the Seer's keen Vision, Jamus would never see him for what he was. All he needed to do now was lead the Rivermaster in the right direction.

****

"I hate her," Sharia said, her hands balled up on her hips where the kitchen apron still hung, covered in flour. "She ruined my hurlycake."

"I didn't mean to," Jiana answered. "Honest, Mistress Aggie. All's I did was give it a punch to see if it was done."

"That's not all you did!" Sharia replied. "And you know it. It's as flat as a plate cause of you. I heard you." Her voice trailed off, as she realized the dangerous track her accusation was taking. "I'm gonna tell Lady Jessa."

"Now, now, child," Mistress Aggie said. "There's no need to bother the fine lady with a kitchen argument. "I don't think the lass meant any harm. 'T'ain't easy even for the best cook ta know when the hurly's ripe to hold and when it's fresh to fall. Better to test it with a broom straw than a fist, but mistakes'll happen."

Sharia glared at the other girl. "She did it on purpose."

"Didn't," Jiana countered.

"Did too!"

"Ladies!" Aggie cried, struggling to keep herself from laughing at the two little combatants. "What do it matter when it's so easy a fix?"

"The hurly's ruined, and I was makin' it special for Lord Jamus and Master Simen 'cause they're leaving come Easwin next."

"Says who?" Jiana asked, her voice quieting.

"Lady Jessa tole me. Lady Kala was gonna go with him to see if they could find your Mam and Pap. Now it's gonna be the two lords instead. I wanted to make something for them to take from me. Now I got nothing."

"Now, child, the hurly's never lost." Aggie pulled a curious contraption out of a cabinet and began to bolt it to the edge of her counter. "Now this here is a grinder. See, you put the flat hurly in here and then you wind this handle. See? The hurly'll come out all fine like flour."

"Good for sparret feed," Sharia muttered.

"Good to make the dark nut bread," Aggie corrected. "Hurly makes the best dark bread ever. We'll mix in some nice chopped dates, some nuts, a good egg, and some sweet strap. Bake it up, and

we gots us a loaf any man'd be happy to have in his trail pack. Good
enow fer a Lord's table too, should he sit at one."

Sharia wiped her eyes with her little hand. "That true?"

"True a word as I kin say," Aggie assured her. "Now go on,
grind it up. Jiana, you come over here and help me chop the dates
and nuts. Better way to use that fist of yours on a chopper than into
the hurly, eh?"

Jiana nodded meekly, and slid over beside the older woman.
"Me Mam used ta let me help her in the kitchen."

"Good Mam's do," Aggie said. "Me Mam taught me all I
know and look at me now, mistress of me own inn with a fair pocket
of silver ta keep me well enow."

"What about yer husband?"

"Ain't got one, lass. Had a beau, but he up and left a season
gone, looking for stags in the hills. Don't seem he's never gonna
come back, so I make me time by meself."

"There be a few men what comes into the common room
that's got eyes for ye, Mistress. Sure you see that?"

"Humpf, child, you got a strong imagining."

"Not so. Master Gunder'd spend all his coin just to have you
give him a smile an' you know it. Don't say you ain't noticed."

"Gunder? That silly old fisherman? Now what would I want
with the likes o' him?"

"Fish stew, fish pie, and fish soup," Jiana said, grinning.
"He'd keep the inn kitchen stocked."

"Bory, girl. That catch he made was onct in a life, I reckon.
Paid off his bar bill with it, sure, but t'weren't enow ta keep the
larder stocked more'n a Sevenstin, even with the ones I salted. Man
sits all day aside the lake drownin' squigglers three seasons a circle.
Be there for four iffen the water din't freeze over Chillmonths. If'en
I was lookin' fer a man o' me own t'wouldn't be one what sits all
day jest a waitin' fer the cork ta bob."

"He's a fine looking man."

"Looks and doin' is two different things, lass. Ye be nearin'
the age when the lads'll be eying ye fer a wife. Best ye learn what a
smart woman needs. Man's gotta have a pocket ta hold the silver he

earns to keep his house and a heart fer her alone. Find that, an' ye'll find a good life."

"The hurly's fine as new flour," Sharia said. "Can we make the bread now?"

"Good work for little hands," Aggie answered. "The two of you mix the ingredients whilst I heat the oven. Put it in those loaf pans over by the pump. Mind you grease and flour'em first so's the dark bread don't stick."

The two girls dutifully did as she instructed, but all the while Sharia kept a wary eye on Jiana's every move. Something about the other girl simply kept bothering her, and though she could not quite figure it out, she would not let up her guard.

Besides, she was sure Jiana had ruined the hurlycake on purpose.

****

"I'd rather you were with me," Jamus said as he buckled the strap on his saddle bag. "I keep thinking I'll need a Seer's wisdom with those parents of hers."

"You're wise enough in judging men," Kala said. "They are bound to be simple folk."

"Simple folk with a Wayard as a daughter? Think again, Kala. Like as not, he's a Wayard himself, and if he has half a sense he's spent the better part of his life learning how to trick people into not being able to see him for it. He's not going to take kindly to a stranger asking him questions."

"You'll find a way. You are the Rivermaster. I doubt Sorcery can actually deceive you. Besides, you have Simen on your side."

"Do I, Kala? It seemed to me my brother was not exactly my keenest support of late."

"He's worried, that's all," Kala answered. "It must be unsettling to him to see your power askew. The Master of Magiskeep should be infallible."

"Hah! Bless the Hand the day that happens. I've made more mistakes in my life than a man deserves." He sighed heavily, and reached out to gently stroke her cheek with his lean fingers. "More mistakes than I can ever fix."

Kala reached up and closed her hand on his. "Some don't need fixing, My Lord. I have found my own happiness."

"No regrets?"

"I won't lie. When you are near me, I ache for what might have been. My heart still quickens and I can't deny I still love you. But time has softened my feelings enough to let me find my own peace, even when you touch me like this." Gently, she pushed his hand away. "You need to find the same peace, Jamus. If Simen is right, it's the only way your Magic will find its center again."

"Forget you, then? That's all?"

"Forget that we can ever be anything more than friends and trusted allies. Make me one of your River's tributaries, there to use as you will, but always flowing off on its own. Water through your fingers."

"I hold the River, Kala. I am its Master."

"Then why," she asked, turning away and heading for the door, "does it mock you now?"

****

Simen offered no ceremony in opening the door to Shaidra's palace, despite Molly's warning to knock and simply wait until one of the servants let them in. "There's no point," he said firmly. "She already knows I'm here. Why pretend manners?"

Instead, he simply waved his hand, oblivious to possible illusions, letting his mirror wise senses adjust the spell to suit the surroundings. Obediently, the massive door clicked and swung open, admitting them to an expansive black marble entrance hall. Pearl tiles in the shape of diamonds broke up the darkness of the walls and floor, shimmering with an opalescent light. A wide staircase of gray stone rose slightly off to the right, and it took hardly a moment for Simen to realize that here, unlike the world outside the door, perception righted itself, the mirrored vision was somehow denied inside the structure.

Or was it? He considered a moment more, flexing his hand tentatively in the air, testing its touch on the River. Then he smiled.

The world had not righted, but simply reflected its own reflection, creating an impression of right while actually being a double deception. He would have to use care, as even a seasoned native of the Way would in such a world. A single reflection of the world posed no challenge, but a reflection's reflection needed caution. It put him at a decided disadvantage, but he could adjust. Being the Rivermaster's brother had taught him much.

Molly seemed quite at ease, her movements sure and determined as she hurried over to a door beside the stairs. "I clean for the Lady when I come. She has servants, but they don't seem to know which end of the broom works best. If she's not pleased you let me in, maybe some dusting will soothe her temper."

"I'll stand for you, Mistress. But I doubt you'll need much defense. Unless I am mistaken, bringing me here is exactly what the Lady wanted you to do."

Molly frowned, and then hurried off to work, not at all convinced he had any idea of what he was talking about.

Simen stood quietly in the hall, studying the doors and corridors leading into the palace itself, certain Shaidra had left him at least one clue to follow. She had always loved riddles and rarely spoke in plain terms about anything. The reflection of an ancient mistress of Magic who had turned her heart to Magic Unrestrained and eventually died in the flames of an angry mob, she had drawn strength from devouring a hundred other reflections of her True Self until she was almost flesh and bone. He'd often heard rumors she had even allied herself with the Black River, but there was so little difference between Shadows and those waters anyhow that he had decided it wasn't important. Like all Shadows, he would always use caution in dealing with her.

But now, simple caution seemed woefully inadequate. If he were alone in this, he would have no worry. This time, though, Shaidra had brought Jessa into the equation and the stakes were much higher. Now he would weigh every word and action a hundredfold more, and the prospect was daunting.

One tile--not a diamond but a square. Near the wall in the hallway to the far left.

Lead me where you will, Mistress. For once the lure exceeds my caution. Simen headed down the left corridor.

The door he needed to find was obvious, a golden monstrosity carved with nude figures twisting and twining around each other in lewd and impossible contortions. The handle was a woman's hand, and when he reached for it, it reached back, clamping damply on his fingers, pulling him towards it, even as he pulled against it. Despite the tug of war, the door yielded, opening into a red room beyond.

There, dressed in a scarlet gown, unfastened in the front and billowing about her scantily clad body beneath, stood Shaidra, positioned so the flickering yellow flames of the torches lining the walls cast flattering shadows on the curves of her breasts and hips. Behind her, at a long table sat seven women—all of them identical, and all of them Jessa.

Pale, even in the torchlight, each Jessa wore a flowing robe of pale yellow, her dark hair spilling loosely on her bare shoulders, her trembling mouth pulled into a tight thin line, her dark eyes rimmed in tears. As if frozen in time, each held her hands flat on the table on either side of an untouched plate of food, unmoving even as Simen met their glances with his own.

"One of them is yours," Shaidra said, smirking. "Choose the one you want and take her to bed if you wish. Try them all if it moves you. Then pick one to keep. I'll throw the rest away."

"I don't want to play your games, Mistress."

"Then take me," she said, gliding over to him with a rustle of shaenis. "I am more flesh than six of them and more woman than the one left over." She leaned in, close to his cheek, her tongue licking his ear as she whispered, "Take me, love. My body will mold however you wish. 'Tis the pleasure of pleasuring a Reflection, you know. Surely you remember."

Simen flinched away. "I remember a cold, heartless bedding. All the lust and none of the satisfaction. I am no longer of the Way, Madam. Empty reflections cannot please me anymore. Seek one of your own kind."

"Ah, you have grown so wise?" She stepped back and swept her hand at the line of Jessas. "You have until Easwin, by the outside world's clock. As there is no time in the Way, I will set a firewick for you. When it burns to its end, the Windchange will be here. Then, you will choose the one you want, and I will sever the rest from breath and hope."

"Why? What purpose will it serve you if I pick the right one? Will you then kill her too, to keep your sovereignty?"

Shaidra shook her head. "If you choose well, then I have lost…you, that is. But you are not my only quarry, and what I learn from you baits my trap for the other. Either way, I will use you to my benefit, Follyman. You have your brother's eyes."

Using me to get to Jamus. Whatever I do, she will learn something she needs to know about him. He looked at the seven women, one of them possibly the real Jessa—if Shaidra was not lying to him. *My Love. Can I sacrifice you? Can I risk Jamus' safety for your sake? Can I not?* "By my reckoning, that's not very much time, even in the Way."

"It is all I give. The Rivermaster and your Reflection are leaving on a journey fated to turn his River's course towards Darkwing's waters. I will have what I want by then or I will kill your woman. Think on it, Shadow kin. The Rivermaster's future is always first in his own hands, not yours."

"He is surrounded by deceit."

Shaidra shrugged. "And is he worthy if he cannot see through it? To whom do you owe homage? Him or yourself? You have flesh and blood, and a power nearly as great as his. Should he falter, his robes will fit you. If she dies, will you want to live at all?"

In the Way, Simen had never truly understood the power of love. In the World, he had learned it was the only power.

"By the Hand, Madam, I will choose," he said quietly. "May your hopes be damned, but I will choose."

Chapter 9

Jamus and Simen rode slowly along the northern trail, keeping to the ground both out of concern for Jamus' errant Magic and also because of the utter unfamiliarity of the terrain. Rocks seems to have strewn themselves in the most unlikely places, and tree roots grew out of unfertile soil, while the trees themselves drooped their branches from three spans away. The earth itself shifted color and texture at every turning, defying any pattern at all to the landscape surrounding them. It was as if nature itself had gone awry, unsure of what it wanted to be.

There was a small lake two spans' ride out of the village, and around it stood a cluster of little farms, all apparently deserted. A cornfield grew thick with weeds, untended for much of the season, and a thin cavel grazed on the stalks after breaking her fence to escape starvation in her pen. Seeing her, Jamus insisted they inspect the barns and sheds where they found a few hungry pigs, a starving horse, and some dead or dying hens trapped in stalls and cages.

It took until Sowin's turn for them to free all the creatures and for Jamus to assure himself there was enough food in the area to keep them.

"Soft heart for the beasts," Simen sighed as he scraped horse dung from his boot before remounting. "Ah, brother, the depth of your compassion never fails to amaze me. After all you've been through, you simply cannot harden your feelings, can you?"

"Why should I? The world has enough cynics."

"It makes you vulnerable—trusting people's goodness like that."

"You'd rather I paint everyone my enemy? I recognize enough of them already without seeing Shadows in every corner, Simen." Jamus sighed heavily. "I suppose I could be wiser, but with the River in my hand, I keep thinking I can afford to take chances."

"Until now."

"What do you mean?"

"The River has deserted you, Jamus. At least your control over its currents has gone awry. Until you regain control over yourself, you have no Magic you can depend on."

"I have you at my side," Jamus answered. "You Magic hasn't been tainted by whatever ails me. Am I a fool for putting my trust in my own brother?"

Simen shrugged. "Well, I'd be the fool to suggest otherwise."

Magwin suddenly stumbled, nearly falling to his knees in the red dirt. Jolted badly, Simen cursed aloud and yanked the reins harshly. As the black horse tossed his head angrily, his rider kicked him with his heels. "By the Blood, you clumsy oaf! You nearly shook my teeth out."

"Stop it!" Jamus ordered sharply. "The footing's bad. It wasn't his fault."

Simen roughly spun his mount in a circle until Magwin stopped dancing away from his heels. "I don't see Whim stumbling like this idiot."

Jamus reached over and snatched Magwin's reins at the bit, taking control over Simen's hard corrections. "You will not abuse a horse in my presence, Sur. If you can't keep your temper with him, then get off and walk."

"Easy for you to say," Simen growled. "Your horse is surefooted."

"You forget, Whim has his own chantings. He doesn't touch the ground when it's dangerous."

Simen paused, his eyes squinting as he stared at the silver stallion. "Magic."

"Of course," Jamus answered, soothing Magwin with a gentle touch. "You know that."

"Yes," Simen answered, his expression clearing. "I'm so used to it, sometimes I forget." He stroked Magwin's neck as if in apology, but the horse pulled away, twisting his head toward Jamus. "He's a proud one, isn't he."

"He's not forgiving, that's for sure," Jamus said. "If he holds a grudge, you're not going to have a pleasant trip."

"I never was the horseman you are."

This time, Jamus frowned. "You used to be. I was always impressed with your horsemanship, you know that. Why are you being so hard on yourself now?"

Simen shrugged. "Maybe some of your failings are rubbing off on me, brother—your Magic, and my riding, eh? Something in the air, perhaps?"

"Something in the water," the Rivermaster answered.

****

Seven Jessas faced Simen with sad smiles, identical in every respect. He studied them carefully, but even with Mirror vision, he could see no differences. Shaidra had sealed the deceptions with Master's Art, making reflections appear as real as reality itself—presuming that one of the seven actually was Jessa.

"I can assure you," the Mistress of Shadows said, as if reading his mind, "that your lady is among the crowd. I've lied in the past, but I am not lying now. There is no way I can assure you, I know. But think on this. What purpose would I have? If the woman you claim to love is not here, then I have no power over you. If I do not render her life into your hands, there's nothing at stake. And you know me well enough to know I don't gamble without gold. She is here. If you find her, she is yours."

"And what then?"

Shaidra laughed. "A bed. If you expect me to promise freedom, you are a fool. I will give you shaenis sheets to slip under if you are modest, and I will feed my own pleasure with yours. If I cannot have you for myself, I will taste you through your passions with her. This is my world and its feelings flow as I will them to."

"And if we do not want to share a bed?"

"It is my world," Shaidra repeated. "The only choice you have is among them." She gestured again towards the seven women. "One is yours to keep, the rest will be destroyed. Either way, I will win a taste of your love. I will leave you now, Follyman. Choose well."

"She's dangerous," one of the Jessas said quietly.

Simen spun on his heel to face them. "An easy observation for even a Shadow."

"I'm not a Shadow," the first Jessa replied.

"Any of us would say that," the third Jessa said.

"I love you," the fourth Jessa said.

"Good move," the seventh Jessa replied, shaking her head. "You think to win him with just a word?"

"The right word might be enough," the fifth Jessa said. "If one of us could find it. A secret word between lovers, perhaps?"

"I'll take more convincing than that," Simen answered them. "Any reflection might have overheard, or even spoken such a word in the mirror itself when she was born of Jessa's reflection."

"The wise Follyman, as ever," the fourth Jessa said. "No one can make you out to be the court fool."

"He's never really been in court to find out," the sixth Jessa said.

"My head's reeling with all of you," Simen said. "How can I possibly choose among such loveliness? A garden blooming with delicate blossoms, all the same color and variety. I need a way to tell you apart."

The fifth Jessa rose and glided over to him, the soft shaenis of her hem hiding her feet so she seemed to float rather than walk. She took his hands in hers, then spun around, sliding into his embrace with her back nestling against his body. Entwining her arms in his, she pulled herself close until his face was buried in her neck, his lips closing on her skin in an impulsive kiss. "You know me," she whispered. "I can feel it."

Simen pulled his lips tight, the kiss lingering with her scent, unmistakably Jessa's own. "If you mean to seduce me, you'll have to do better." He felt her stiffen. "Disappointed? So am I. Your body does feel good. Shaidra's done a fine job of giving you a nice skin."

The fifth Jessa pushed herself away from him. "Those are harsh words. But who's to say it's Shaidra's skin? Why not my own? I am your Jessa, you know."

Simen sighed. "I'm not at all sure of that. I still haven't tested the others." As she moved back to her place at the table, he rubbed his chin thoughtfully. "I need a way to tell you all apart." He snapped his fingers. "I have it. A necklace! If I give each of you a different color necklace, I'll be able to remember who is who." He calculated quickly, testing the air as best he could to see how many times this world reflected upon itself, adjusting his Magic until he was fairly certain any spell he cast would take a true course. Then, he spread his fingers over the table. The light shifted, glittering to sparks of rainbow colors as beneath his palms seven sets of jewels materialized on the tablecloth. Red, orange, yellow, green, blue, indigo and violet, seven necklaces lay waiting before him.

The first Jessa reached for one, but Simen stayed her hand with a gesture. "I'll put them on you," he said. "A moment of intimacy with each of you, I suppose." He smiled. "It will please me."

The first Jessa smiled shyly back, then reached behind her neck to pull her dark wavy hair out of the way.

Simen picked up the ruby necklace and moved behind her. His fingers gently caressed the skin on her neck as he fastened the clasp. He gave her nape a quick kiss, and moved to the next Jessa. This time, he stroked her hair before moving it aside to fasten the firejewels around her and gave her a kiss.

The third Jessa bowed her head at his approach, her hair falling on shoulders. The citrines glittered against her pale skin as his lips caressed as well, and she sighed at his touch.

The fourth Jessa pulled her hair up on her head, twisting it into a knot. Simen looked down at the soft skin of her nape and smiled, fastening the emerald choker around her and offering the same kiss before he moved on to the fifth Jessa.

She too twisted her hair on her head, to let him dress her in the blue sapphires, leaving her with a kiss as well.

The dark iolites slipped easily around the sixth Jessa's neck and the necklace of amethysts fit the seventh woman perfectly.

With each woman adorned, and each smiling from the touch of his lips, Simen walked back to the front of the table and faced them. "So, at last I can see the difference among you. I can only say the jewels pale against the beauty of the wearers."

"Sweet words from a Follyman's tongue, to be believed by only the fool himself," the fourth Jessa said.

"Sharp wit from my true lady," Simen answered, smiling. Then, without any hesitation he reached out his hand to the emerald-adorned Jessa. "I have chosen."

The room itself howled with Shaidra's rage followed by screams of utter agony as the other six Jessas burst into white Spellfire.

Jessa's eyes went wide as she fell into Simen's arms, her body collapsing in a scream almost as horrible as the six others fading into echoes around them.

****

Sharia kept up her guard, despite Jiana's clumsy attempts to make up for the hurlycake. Young eyes had few preconceptions about people, relying instead on intuition to form her opinions. And, the truth of it was, she just had a feeling she couldn't trust the other girl. She didn't spend much time considering it or even worrying about it. Instead, she simply watched her tongue and just about everything else whenever Jiana was anywhere near.

Mistress Jessa was no help at all. Even worse, she seemed to have formed a special bond with the girl, taking care to listen to her at the expense of Sharia's lessons. It was as if Jiana's needs for understanding the Magic were somehow greater. "If she is a Wayard, Sharia, she must be trained. You already have discipline in the Art. Surely you can stand aside now and again so Jiana can learn something."

The trouble was, "now and again" took up most of Easwin each day and often managed to devour the early spans of Sowin as well. By the time Jessa was finished with Jiana, she was either too tired or too cross to offer Sharia anything at all. "I am your Apprentice," Sharia reminded her, trying hard not to sound accusatory. "The Cup bonds us."

"Tush, child. You have a lifetime promised to you. Don't be greedy. Perhaps you should consider this trip a little vacation from your studies."

"We were supposed to learn the Scroll of Selmak, My Lady. You said it was the key to hiding Magic in the mortal world. You said the lands beyond the Rim were the best places to practice it. You said I need to learn some deception 'cause I was too…too…ingenious, or something."

"You are a clever little lass. If I said so, I meant it. Someone that smart can certainly miss a few studies, now, can't she?"

"But you said...."

"Never mind what I said. In the Keep my words have one meaning. Here they have another. Best you learn how the world makes truths instead of people."

Frustrated, Sharia took her Mistress' words to heart, letting Jiana's actions guide her own feelings for the girl. At first, she decided it was pure jealousy, the emotion she'd seen ruin more than one relationship in Magiskeep. The little commoner has certainly stolen her place in Jessa's heart and her rightful role as apprentice. But as time passed, and she grew closer to Aggie in the kitchen, she began to see something more sinister about the girl.

It wasn't just the hurlycake.

It was a tray of muffins burned to a crisp for no reason. It was a flagon of ale spilled in a tavern patron's lap when he insisted on singing a bawdy song about an ignorant farm girl. Or perhaps it was the tavern dog fleeing in pain from Jiana's sharp kick no one but she saw.

And then, there were the smiles she'd had for Simen.

He hadn't been there long, but it had been long enough for Sharia to notice. She'd heard curious giggles from behind closed doors when Jiana managed to find the Follyman alone in his chamber. When the girl would come back out into the hall with her hair in tangles, her bodice loosed, and her face flushed, Sharia would look away and wonder if Jessa had somehow grown blind.

For the Mistress of Magic had been there too. Sharia had seen her go into the room with them laughing aloud and coming back out nearly as rumpled.

With Simen gone, she'd had time to think about everything she'd noticed. What had been going on with the three of them?

"If a woman loves a man," Sharia asked Aggie one day, "does she want to keep him for herself?"

"Bory, child, you do ask strong questions at times. Any woman what loves a man wants ta own him body, heart and soul. Pity men don't see it like that."

"What do you mean?"

"Men got a bad habit o' gathering bouquets steada admiring
the single bloom in the garden, lass. It's like they can't be happy
with a rose when there's a bed o' daisies ta be had."

Sharia pushed a lock of her golden hair off her forehead with
the back of her hand and frowned. "That's like the horse that breaks
the fence to get the green grass on the other side even though he's
got a full trough of feed right in front of him?"

Aggie laughed loudly. "Couldn'ta but it better meself.
Woman might be the sweetest grain in the bin, but he has ta find a
mouthful o' somethin' else jest 'cause he sees it."

"'Tis a bitter word ye speak to the girl," a voice interrupted
from the yard door. "I ne'er threw back a good fish fer another
meself."

"If women was fish, ye'd have a basket full of 'em, an' ye
knows it, Gunder o' the Lake. Ye can't tell me ye'd be content with
the prettiest one if'en another jumped out o' the water in front o' ye."

"A woman ain't fish, Mistress Aggie. Once I set me eye on
one, t'would take more'en a jumping to pull it off," Gunder
answered, dropping a bag of flour on the counter. "Miller Bane gived
me this fer me catch. Figgered I still owed ye a meal or two an' you
had all the fish ye needed fer a spell."

Aggie nodded, her blue eyes softening just a bit at his
offering. "Kind of ye, Gunder."

"T'was thinking ye'd see it as more'n kind," Gunder replied,
pulling his cap off. He held it in his hands, crumbling the ragged felt
with his fingers as he went on, "I was wonderin' iffen ye might share
a pint with me at table."

"In me own inn? My ale?"

"I gots silver. Fishin's been good fer a change. I tole ye me
spot at the lake were a good'un. I'd take ye there ta prove it, but ye
never gots the time."

"Don't go," Sharia said suddenly, her voice edged with an
unexplained tension. Something about the man bothered her, like
Jiana, and she responded impulsively to his words.

Gunder's reaction assured her. His expression hardened and
his eyes, already too dark for a man of his coloring glared at her for
an instant, sending a chill up her spine. Then the corners of his

mouth curled up in what was supposed to be a grin, but to her looked like a sneer. "Ye won't be left ta run the kitchen yerself, lassie. Aggie an' me'd be back in a twink."

"She might fall in," Sharia said quietly, bracing her shoulders as she felt the River tickling her hand. Well-schooled in Magiskeep, she wouldn't hesitate to use her Magic if he threatened her.

His eyes dropped to her hands, and he noticed the flex of her fingers. His jaw tightened. "She might fer sure. Mebbe it's best she stay here while yer about, eh? Wouldn't want a little lady like yerself worryin' now, would we?"

"No, I don't think you would," Sharia answered, clenching her fists at her side.

She didn't relax again until he'd gone back out the door and disappeared.

"I kin swim a little," Aggie said after he'd gone.

"Don't go," Sharia repeated, sounding more like a mother than a little girl with flour in her hair. "The last thing you want to be is one more fish in his net."

****

Kala felt her own sense of inexplicable unease, despite thinking she'd done the right thing in sending Jamus off without her. She had absolute trust in Simen, of course. He was, after all, a part of Jamus himself, born of Jamus' Magic and sworn to him with total loyalty. But Simen was no Seer, and even armed with Magic, he could not judge the hearts of others who might want to do them harm.

She'd visited plenty of farm villages in her time and seen how easily pitchforks and scythes transformed into weapons in the hands of an angry mob. Farmers were a superstitious lot and had long held the reputation of knowing just how to handle any threat of Magic with efficient ease. They often had their own Seers and perhaps a Practitioner in their keep who was nothing more than a confessed Wayard sworn to protect them at peril of his own life. Unschooled in the finer points of Magic, his power would be crude but effective against even the Rivermaster if he didn't notice its presence.

But, perhaps she was worried about nothing. Surely the River would not hide from Jamus' eyes. Still she needed some reassurance, and so she found Jessa in the sitting chamber above the inn's common room and posed the question to her. "As much as I've learned about Magic, I still don't quite understand how you see it, Jessa. When Jamus met Jiana he asked her a lot of questions, but I don't think that's how he decided about her Magic. Tell me, can you recognize one of your own kind some other way?"

"If it's the Sight your asking about," Jessa answered, "the answer is no."

Kala waited, expecting more from the Mistress of the Eldentext who was usually so careful to explain everything. But the dark haired woman had already turned away. "I didn't mean the Sight. I was wondering if the River itself might reveal one of its kind—well at least to the Rivermaster."

"To Jamus? Oh, I suppose it might, if the Sorcerer didn't ward himself first. Most do, I guess. They say it's not good to practice Magic openly in Turan."

Kala's brow furrowed at the reply, not at all typical of the other woman. "I hope you're not acting on rumor, Jessa. It takes better care than that to be safe in this world of mortals. The Eldentexts make that clear."

"The texts…" Jessa said absently. She moved a small cup in front of Jiana and waved her hand over it. "There, a nice hot keldherb for you. Ah, yes, the texts. They do warn of danger to Magicians here. But there's no one else in the room right now, so I don't have to hide my power now, do I."

Kala sniffed the air, suddenly filled with a curious aroma. Distracted by the scent, she didn't respond to Jessa's comment. It was the keldherb, the steam rising from the cup, wafting the definite fragrance of delibloom in her direction. She forced her mind to concentration to counter the affect of the potent aphrodisiac on her own psyche. She needed no Vision to see the growing reaction on the girl as Jiana sipped the brew. "What are you doing, Jessa?"

"What do you mean?" Jessa asked, her tone dripping with practiced innocence.

"Delibloom for a child? What are you thinking?"

"Delibloom? Whatever are you talking about?"

"The cup," Kala said simply, nodding in Jiana's direction.

"Oh!" Jessa laughed lightly. "Just a touch of the bloom in the keldherb. I am preparing Jiana for a lesson in the Magic and I need some added passion from her for it. Nothing to worry about, My Lady Judger. I will watch over her."

"I should hope so," Kala replied. "I can't approve of your methods, but I am unschooled in the more scholarly methods of your Art. Jamus has warded her, of course, so I suppose she can't really do any harm."

"Of course she can't," Jessa assured her. "The Rivermaster's ward is a secure as it was the day he cast it." Then, she smiled. "Exactly as secure as he cast it."

Chapter 10

Simen neither questioned nor thought beyond his need, sending a Healing spell into Jessa's limp form, enveloping her in his concern, willing her breath and heart to regain their rhythms. "My love," he whispered, sinking to the floor with her in his arms as the River answered.

Darkness, and nowhere to turn. No way to know what lay beyond the reach of his arm. But she was in his embrace and in the end, that was all that mattered.

He felt the water caressing him, pulling them down, and he didn't fight the currents, all too welcoming to his Magician's body.

There was a dim light below, deep in the River's depths, beckoning.

He let it surround them, drawing them into its warmth until they dropped into the Dragon's cave where only Master's Art allowed entrance.

The Great Beast lifted its head, one great rainbow swirling eye fixing on him. "Be not Rivermaster. Why thee dare?"

"My love needs your Touch."

"Little left of what she was. Six parts dead. Seventh of flesh worth what?"

"Everything," Simen replied. "My own life, if need be."

The creature sighed. "Lovers be fools." His breath caressed Jessa's cheek and immediately, she took a deep gulp of air and several following deep breaths before relaxing into what was surely a curative sleep.

"What do you want in payment?" Simen asked.

The Dragon showed its teeth, curling its lips back as if it were trying to smile. "Ye have not half enough. Waters dark pollute my streams. Kiselor in danger be. Fool man's eyes be blinded by reflection of reflection. Mistress polish mirrors. Break them."

"It won't be easy. Shaidra is a formidable opponent."

"Swim."

"I will."

"She six parts gone. One more to die. You one only. Strength be thine. Swim."

With that, the water surged back into the cave, sweeping Simen off his feet. He grabbed for Jessa, catching her wrist as he washed past her. Then, the dark currents enveloped them.

Simen's eyes fluttered open an instant before Jessa's. She looked up at him from where she lay in his lap. "I had the strangest dream. I still so tired."

"Shaidra destroyed your six reflections, Jessa. Their energies drained yours. I Healed you."

"Then I did see the Dragon."

He nodded. Then he gently stroked the stray wisps of hair from her damp forehead. "He was generous."

"How did you know which one I was?"

Simen slid his hand behind her head, his fingers massaging her neck. "Simple really. Shaidra had spent a great deal of time layering her illusions so each of the seven of your looked exactly alike. This time there were no hints, nothing reversed in your faces at all. From the front there were no reflections at all."

"Then how?"

"She never bothered with your backs. When one of the Jessa's tried to seduce me, I noticed the nape of her neck. You have a small mole just to the left of your spine. Just there." He let his fingers trace the mark. "That's why I insisted on putting the necklaces on myself. You were the only one with the mole in the right place."

"A mole? You risked my life on the basis of a mole? What if you had been wrong?"

"Never," he said, shaking his head. "Every time I kiss your neck, it's my target. I could never mistake it."

****

The landscape had settled into patterns of rich brown earth and green fields by the time they sighted the Northern Ridges. More hills than mountains, the peaks had rounded tops, and the tree line extended all the way up the heights, broken only by one or two large stone houses, likely owned by lesser nobles. Even here, there was a loosely knit feudal system in play, with lords to keep armies and farmers to grow food to pay their taxes. Still, the little farms dotting the flatlands looked prosperous, as did the neat little village off to the east.

Jamus and Simen rode towards the main street, focusing on the search for an inn. Their arrival brought only casual glances from the locals who seemed more intent on their own business than the presence of strangers. Either they were used to visitors, or strikingly lacking in natural curiosity.

"The Broken Bucket?" Jamus said, reading the sign above a gold and brown inn near what seemed to serve as a town hall. "I'd wager there's a good story behind that name."

Simen swung out of the saddle, deftly avoiding the snap of Magwin's teeth as the horse tried to bite him. Wary of Jamus' rebuke, he ignored the attack and pulled the reins over the stallion's head to assure more control. "I'm sure we'll hear it before we leave. I think the stable's in the back. Do you want me to take Whim for you?"

Jamus nodded, but as he started to hand the silver stallion's reins to the Follyman, the horse snorted, laid his ears back, and struck with his forefoot, his teeth bared in warning. "I guess he's as fretful as I am. I'll take the horses back instead. Why don't you go inside and see if they have some rooms for us."

Simen shrugged, gave Magwin over, sidestepping another bite, and headed for the door.

Jamus stroked Magwin's muzzle. "I can't blame you, fellow. He rode worse than I've ever seen. He didn't treat you well. I wonder if he and Jessa had a falling out before we left. It would explain a lot." Magwin nickered softly and followed along obediently towards the low roofed barn.

Bad man.

'He had no right to be harsh with Magwin, Whim," Jamus agreed, thinking no more of the stallion's remark.

The stalls were large and well bedded. The stable master had a kind manner and a generous hand with the hay and grain. "Fine horses like these honor me stable, me Lord. They'll be well cared for, I thee assure."

"I don't doubt it," Jamus answered, handing the man ten gold pieces. "Use what you need for them and the rest for your own contentment." He checked the water buckets out of habit and then made his way to the inn to see how Simen had made out.

The Follyman was already seated at a table with a platter of fruit and cheese in front of him. Two flagons of ale waited as well. "Come on, brother. The beds are goose down, the sheets clean, and the fires already stoked. It looks like the food's fit for the Keep and the ale's dark. We may have chosen the best part of this adventure after all."

Jamus sink into the chair across from Simen, draping his arms over the table with in weary resignation. "It's just one more inn, Simen. I expect the cook will have a special stew for dinner or a secret recipe soup. Is our servingmaid the young buxomy type or the motherly matron?"

Simen brow furrowed. "Buxomy..." he said, uncertainly.

Jamus hardly noticed his confusion. "Low cut white blouse, I wager. Perhaps a laced bodice, snug at the waist, pushing up her breast to dare it to spill out the neckline? Is she blonde or brunette?"

"Ah, buxomy," Simen repeated, his face clearing. "She's a brunette, a wee little thing except for her chest. She leaned over when she served the ale. Close to my face."

"The usual, then. I think there must be a serving maid training center somewhere they all go to before getting hired. The lean is one of the first lessons."

"You've been in too many inns, Jamus. It ruins the anticipation." Simen took the ale with his right hand and downed a healthy swallow. "Better than the brew at the Widow's Peek, I think. Richer flavor."

Jamus took an unenthusiastic sip of his drink. "Country taste. On the bitter side. Don't think I'll drink much. I've learned my lesson too many times."

"I like it," Simen answered, putting down his mug to pluck a handful of grapes from the platter. "Maybe I'm a farmer at heart after all."

"Plants wither in your presence, my friend. If you recall, the last potted soffern you had in your room in the Keep died of loneliness within a Sevenstin, and you didn't even notice until Clouder knocked the dirt all over the floor."

"I should have insisted he clean it up."

Jamus laughed, "With what? His tail? That's how he knocked it over in the first place. As smart as he is, I still haven't seen that dog use a broom and dustpan."

Simen's face reddened ever so slightly. "Well, you always said you could teach him anything."

Jamus nearly choked on his ale. "Follyman's timing to perfection. Make a man laugh when he swallowing. Are you trying to kill me?"

"Not at all, brother, not at all," Simen answered. *Not yet, anyway.*

****

"What's wrong, Sharia?" Kala asked when she found the girl moping about in the little herb garden behind Aggie's kitchen. "The lavender alone should make a lass like you smile."

Sharia bobbed her head sadly. "My Mistress forgets who her Apprentice is."

"Jiana," Kala said simply. "She's spending too much time with her and not enough with you."

"None with me, My Lady. I tole my friend Sereise I'd be lessons ahead of her when we got back to Magiskeep, what with all the promises Mistress Jessa made to me about how grand the world was for experience. She said here the Magic was harder, so I'd have to earn every spell. But all's I've done so far is see Lord Jamus weave a traveling sphere and learned how to bake bread."

"Two skills worth something, I should imagine."

"Oh, I could maybe make a sphere myself now, not so strong as his, but one that'd work. But the bread's mortal art. Fine for the belly but not much for the mind."

"The mind can't work when the body starves. The skill will serve you well someday. But I can understand your concern. When I was a student, learning all I wanted to know of the Sight was all that mattered to me. I would have been furious is my Masters showed me how to sew a hem."

"It wasn't even the Mistress who taught me how to bake. It was Mistress Aggie."

"She's a good woman, Sharia."

Sharia traced the black garden dirt with the toe of her shoe. "She's nice. I want so bad to spell something special for her, but I daren't. People in Loren are awful superstitious about Magic, you know. Jiana oughtta be glad you and Lord Jamus saved her steada being so nasty about everything."

Kala knelt down in front of the little girl, the skirt of her green gown folding on the ground. "Jiana hasn't been nasty, has she? If it's the hurlycake, she did apologize."

"You don't gotta share a room with her. She snoops around in my pack and twists my blanket into knots. She pulled my hair and spilled the water basin all over the clothes I laid out to wear. She says she's gonna make Jessa like her steada me and she laughs when I tell her Lord Jamus won't let her do Magic when she wants to."

"Has she done any Magic?"

"No, but she says she will if she wants to."

"Lord Jamus warded her, didn't he?"

Sharia nodded, but her wide eyes looked worried nonetheless. "She says she can do whatever she wants."

"Milady Juris!" a voice called from the inn's door. "You're needed, at once. Lord Manison demands you at the Hall. It's a matter of great urgency."

Kala rose, brushing the dirt from her skirt. "Whatever could be so important?"

The messenger took a deep gulp of air, glanced nervously at Sharia, swallowed, and then said, "There's been a murder, Milady."

"What? Where?"

"At the Tallowtail. The inn where you had your rooms when you came here."

"When?"

"Sometime past Norwin last. The Lord says you are to meet him at the Hall at once."

"I'll go to the inn."

"He said the Hall."

"Seer's Vision falters from afar, Sur. I am at the King's bidding first and his command is for me to use my better judgment in matters of the law. If there's a murderer's trail to follow the scent has

already faded. The longer I wait, the less I'll See. Tell your Lord I
will meet him at the Tallowtail." She brushed past the nonplussed
messenger, casting a quick command back to Sharia. "Go tell
Mistress Jessa what you have heard. Tell her to keep the three of you
safely in your rooms until I am back. I'm going to see that Lord
Manison sends a guard to your door. Hurry now."

Manison had sent a light carriage even though the village
was not too large to traverse on foot. But Kala wanted speed and
urged the driver to hurry as soon as she climbed into the passenger
seat. The little bay horse leapt into the traces at his master's
command, crossing the main street and passing into the east part of
town in a matter of moments.

At the Tallowtail, Kala did not wait for the driver to help her
down. Despite her gown, she jumped to the cobbled street and
headed for the door, "Thank you, Sur. I'd like you to wait for me. I'll
pay a proper fee if Manison's purse wasn't generous enough."

The driver tipped his hat and smiled. "Me pockets is lined
jest fine, Milady. I'll wait here all day for ye if ye wish it."

The Tallowtail's common room was nearly empty, but the
white-faced serving maids and an equally pale barkeep were telling
witnesses to the horror lying upstairs. There a shaken constable
guarded the wooden door to a chamber of death all too revealing to
Kala.

There sprawled on the bed lay the tattered remains of a
young man. Beside him on the floor lay another body mutilated with
equal brutality. Gaping wounds gutted their midsections, and their
mouths were frozen open in what must have been final screams of
agony. The man on the bed was lashed to the bedpost by his wrist
and in his death throes, the cord had nearly severed his hand from his
arm.

The sheets and small rug on the floor were stained with
blood, and yet, the bodies themselves were white, the wounds
bloodless. Internal organs should have filled the cavities exposed by
the gashes in their bellies, but it was as if their bodies had been
emptied, leaving instead gray shells of skin and bone—hollow
remainders of what had once been human.

Kala, repulsed by the scene forces herself to study the victims, her mortal sight surrendering to the white perception of Seer's Art. Truth opened Vision.

A kiss, arousing heat dropping to a pulsing yearning tormenting his groin. Soft flesh against his body, kneading at his chest, hips pressing into him, his own heart pounding in his ears. Consuming lust and then, nearing the peak, a knife's edge of sheer terror slicing into his consciousness.

Pain, unbearable, the horror of seeing death's eyes boring into his. A knife blade down his throat, testing its metal on his tonsils. A dagger tracing his navel boring in and drawing out, over and over—not enough to kill but far more than torture.

Sweet words, laced with curses uttered in his ear, then teeth tearing at his flesh.

Agony. Fear, drowning out the desire, filling with something else.

Something else. Something lapping his blood while he lay paralyzed in body, his mind registering every second of his own death. Such darkness coiling about, tentacles plucking at his liver, curling about his intestines, pulling them out, little by little and savoring every bite.

He screamed in silence, his voice muted by the blade across his throat.

Kala screamed aloud.

"My Lady! By the Hand you shouldn't have come in here alone."

She shuddered as Vision cleared and the harsh reality of the moment returned. "I'm all right," she said hoarsely. I've seen worse." It was not entirely a lie.

"Do you know who did this?" Lord Manison asked. He had come into the room just as Kala had reeled back against the far wall, driven by the pain of her Vision. "What did you See?"

"Women. They were killed by women they brought up here to bed."

"Whores," Manison said with disgust. "Murderous bitches killed them for their money, I suppose. We'll scour the village. Bring in every loose woman until we find the right ones."

"Maybe the men attacked them first," the constable offered lamely. "I knew these two. Swaggering braggarts they was. Wedo there once took a merchant's daughter agin her will. Took a purse of sovereigns to keep her father from killin' em. And Dob cast off more lasses than I care ta name. T'weren't neither of 'em worth the sheets their lyin' on and from what I hear most women in town will be singing rather than weeping at their circles' close."

"That's a bitter condemnation, Sur," Kala said.

"T'ain't saying any more than what I know to be true, Madam. Test me if ye will and ye'll find I ain't spoke naught but true. Wedo woulda raped my sister if I hadn't come home early."

"Why wasn't he in jail, then?"

"Men like him and Dob got fat purses and they sell their daggers to rich lords like Lord Manison here."

"I've never met these…men," Manison said sharply.

"I said lords *like* you, Sur," the constable replied, not bothering to temper his remark with respect. "Some what live in the big houses hereabouts think they can do as they want no matter who gets hurt. Strong arms like these two was gives 'em power far past their pretty titles. Maybe it's about time someone stood up to that kind o' rule."

"So you think it's all right that these men were murdered like this?" Manison asked, gesturing towards the bodies as he covered his mouth with his handkerchief to stifle a gag.

"I'm just sayin' maybe they deserved it, is all."

Kala turned away from the grisly room, maintaining her composure again with the practiced ease of a well-trainer Seer. She had long ago learned to suppress her emotions in the face of all kinds of revelations. Now, though, her stomach was churning. Her words to Manison had been true enough, the killers had been women, but not prostitutes as he had concluded.

No. She recognized the work of the Shadowspawn seeking true life through the life's blood of others. She had faced Shadows before and knew their desires well. But here, in a remote village, their presence was totally incongruous. The population would hardly support the numbers they would need to kill in order to reach their goals of becoming living, breathing beings. There was nothing else here of worth to....

Jamus. His name screamed in her thoughts. And Simen too, as the Rivermaster's brother, worth nearly as many mortals.

And then the rest of it seared its possibilities into her consciousness. Jamus was here because of Jiana. What if she had been the lure to a trap keenly set by Tamor or his kin?

She shivered.

"Are you all right Madam Juris?" Manison asked, his own face still green from the horror of what lay on the other side of the door. "Perhaps we should go downstairs and have a mug of warm ale."

"No," Kala answered. "I need to go back to the Widow's Peek. I left my friends under guard and they'll be worried. I set them to fear. I need to go back and ease them from it."

Manison's eyes darted nervously toward the door. "Do we...uhm...need to do anything more about...uhm...about that?"

"A proper burial if you can find someone with the stomach for it," she replied.

Chapter 11

Jamus had considered the matter for some time before finally deciding the best course was the most direct one. He would visit a few of the shops in the village to ask about Jiana's parents while Simen would, with his best Follyman geniality, spend the day at the Broken Bucket entertaining and gossiping with the patrons. He had always been a master at uncovering all kinds of information for a song or joke. Besides, once the innkeeper saw the colorful patch sewn on the right shoulder of his tunic, there was no turning back. No longer wearing the many colored shirt of his profession, the patch had taken its place as a more modest claim. Only bards of high skill would bother to keep such a low profile, and so, whenever the patch was noticed, it usually guaranteed employment.

"Never had a patched Follyman in the inn before," Master Meekan said. "I take it ye know all the old standards? The folk hereabouts live by tradition."

"I'm a bit rusty," Simen answered. "Let me practice in my room for a bit before I take the job." With that, he headed upstairs, locked the door of his chamber, and pulled a stool in front of the mirror atop the dresser.

His hands played a pattern in the air as he spoke a chanting, *"Everendings this I see, trouble for the likes of me. Aid me in this quest anew, as I do these deeds for you. As a masque of offering, shell I wear must learn to sing."*

The mirror shimmered, his reflection wavering, then melting to be replaced by Shaidra's face. "A problem, Simen Who is Not?"

"Where is the Master? I need his help."

"He sends me first to the lesser Shadows."

Simen snarled. "Damned you be, woman, if you think I am your lesser in this. I have the Rivermaster in my hand. I could take him any time I wanted to, and believe me, I want to. One taste of his blood would give me True Life."

"And True Death an instant later," Shaidra replied, smiling too serenely for his taste. "Darkwing would destroy you."

"Perhaps an instant of Life would be worth the risk."

"You are only playing a Follyman, Serim, don't become one with idiotic remarks like that. You are Shadowsworn, bound by a promise even your sharpest desire cannot break."

Serimsimen's face dropped, his shoulders sagging. "So I am a fool to dream. Wearing this flesh is harder than I thought. It brings desires."

"Satisfy them under the covers. Surely there is a willing maid nearby," Shaidra answered. "But you did not call me to find out what to do with a woman. What's wrong?"

"I need to ply the Follyman's trade here at the inn, but I have no songs. The day he gave me to the mirrors he had sworn to never sing again. Some sort of nonsense about giving himself in service to the Hand. Penance for some sort of misdeed or other. To be frank, it was a moment to relish, being born like that out of the sins of such a self-righteous creature. Still, it does pose a problem. I cannot sing for my supper with a voice that has no knowledge of the music."

"What do you expect from me? Lessons?"

"Wisdom, at least, Madam. I would think Simen's reflection would be equipped with the talent and vocal chords to manage. I can certainly conjure a lute able enough to play itself should my fingers falter. But the tune and lyric eludes me."

"A spell then, that's what you want? A chanting giving you all the melodies a master bard would have at his disposal? Now where in all the Mirrors would you like me to find such a charm?" Shaidra asked.

"You have a Master Follyman in your keeping, do you not? Sift him. Make him give you his music. It should be a simple matter for the right hand of Darkwing, should it not?" Serimsimen said, hiding behind a mask of innocence. He knew full well taking anything from Simen that he didn't want to give would be a difficult task for even the Black Dragon himself.

"I have used my wedge to pry him once already. He will not let me use her again."

"Will he sing for her?"

Shaidra considered for a moment. Surely a well tuned love song would please Jessa in the misery of her captivity. If she could make Simen sing, and capture it in a mirror, all Serim would need to do was take the new Shadow into himself—if it would let him. "How strong are you, Sur?"

"Growing stronger each day. I have tasted blood once already—in Loren. They have not yet found the body. I was wiser than Juljessa."

Shaidra's image sharpened. "What are you talking about?"

"Rumors fly on the wind, My Lady. Or at least on fat ponies whose boys gallop them to death to bring stories to these hills. Part of the plan, I suspect, to arouse the fear among those who have not already fallen into the waters. The blood of terror feeds us so much better, you know."

"Damn, you! Stop the musing and tell me the news."

Serimsimen shrugged. "Not much except that two shells were found in one of the inns. Young men in their beds where they had not slept alone. It was the work of a clever seductress, so they say. I do believe Juljessa has perhaps taken the fledgling under her own wing. Even that mistress of deception cannot devour two in one night."

"The Follyman is not the fool in this," Shaidra growled. "Her greed will undo us, and all for an appetite she can't control. And to take the girl with her? What is she thinking?"

"Of herself," Serimsimen replied. "You accused me of as much a moment ago. If Darkwing would destroy me for such an indiscretion, does she deserve less?"

"Only that her choice was mortals saves her. Like you, she can be forgiven if the deed remains in the dark. But this has already spread to the hill farms where the water spills. We cannot afford such pollution yet. The balance of power is not yet in our hands. If fear rises too quickly, the Hags and Wayards will alert. They are wise enough in the lore of the Way to know how to dam the leak."

He frowned. "They are unschooled in Magic."

"Formal education does not match common sense, or the ancient knowing, Serim. Do not be complacent about their skill. They have no scruples about using Whitefire, nor do they practice the ceremony of asking before a sifting. Let down your guard,

underestimate their perception, and the Rivermaster will not be the first victim of their wrath. Be warned."

"Commoners," Serimsimen muttered. "To be undone by commoners."

"It has happened a hundred times before. Why else to you think we have spent so much effort driving them to the waters? Sang rumored a strange blue waterbeast to lure a dozen sightseers. Joth promised a net full of white salmon to take ten more. But it is not enough, nor is it the Hags or Windspeakers who have swum. They elude us. And they are the most dangerous."

"Give me the music and perhaps I can charm them to the lake," Serimsimen said.

"I will find a way," Shaidra said. Then, she snapped her fingers and her face was once again replaced by the vague and shimmering image of his.

Serimsimen studied his reflection for a while as it wavered in the half light instability of a reflection of a reflection. He had tasted blood once and imagined himself a little more solid. How many more would he need to feast on before he could actually make out the details of his features?

He decided he would definitely have to keep count.

****

Kala wasted no time in getting back to the Widow's Peek. Warning the Sorcerers about the presence of Shadows in Loren was critical, for the creatures would seek out Magic's blood as the shortest route to True Life. Seven Magicians, if each was a Master of one of the Seven Arts, would be enough. But a Master like Jessa, skilled in several Arts was worth even more. Jamus, of course, as Rivermaster would be the ultimate prize, but he was on the road, far from the source of danger. Whoever the Shadows were, they lurked in the darker corners of Loren village for now.

Jessa, Jiana, and Sharia were together in the room, though none too happy for it. The two girls had apparently been arguing about something with enough determination to have set off a fire in one of the beds. Fortunately, by the time Kala got back, Jessa had fixed all but the lingering scent of burned goose down and forced the two combatants to neutral corners where they sat, pouting.

"A moment more and it might have been Spellfire," she said, wagging her finger at Sharia. "You should know better than to provoke a Wayard."

"She's just a child," Kala reminded her. "They both are." She hesitated as she studied the two girls, one blond one dark, and yet they might be twins. One on either side of the Light. "Maybe you should have stepped in sooner."

Jessa glared at her. "I am not a wet nurse, Lady. There's a time when even children have to work things out for themselves."

"That may be so for ordinary children in ordinary circumstances, but not now. If ever there were a time to be on guard with your Magic, it's now."

Jessa took a deep breath to control herself. Her voice, though was edged with annoyance. "And why, pray tell is that?"

"There are Shadows nearby."

Jessa started to smile, checked it, and worked even harder to keep her tone even. "What makes you say a thing like that?"

"Two dead bodies, or what's left of them, at the Tallowtail Inn. Young men murdered Norwin last with the unmistakable brutality of Shadow's work."

"You're sure of this."

"I've spent enough time with Lord Jamus to have seen the worst of your Magic's consequences in this world, Lady Jessa. As a Seer, I was well trained in the knowledge of Magic's influence already, but my experiences with the Rivermaster have shown me more truths than I ever would have cared to imagine. These men were killed by Shadows seeking the True Life. I have no doubt of that."

"Well, then, that's a pity. I was hoping to take Jiana to the Tallowtail come Weswin. There is a traveling bard there who sings a fine tune. I wonder if he will be staying on or moving to another inn. Mayhaps the trouble will bring him here instead."

"Is that all you can say, all you care about? Don't you understand what I've just said? We're all in danger, but you and the girls particularly. You know as well as I do the Shadows will target you above all others."

"I have my Magic."

"Exactly. And so do Sharia and Jiana. Sorcerer's blood is a favored food of the Shadowspawn, isn't it? If you don't fear for yourself, then what about the girls? I doubt either one of them has the skill or experience to protect herself against something like this."

Despite Kala's vehemence, Jessa remained frustratingly indifferent. "We are doing well, My Lady. Aside from a little spat, the girls have settled in. You might take Sharia for a little walk now, if you will. I have some things I need to teach Jiana. She'll be safe with you, won't she? Sight can perceive the Darkness, can't it?"

"Sight perceives the truth behind most illusions, Madam, but it can't always penetrate the truth in the darkness."

"Well, then, if you sniff out any danger, let Sharia take care of it. She has my permission to use Spellfire if she needs to. Now go on, the two of you. Perhaps you can find something to amuse you in Aggie's kitchen, eh? Unless that lovely bard has come here."

Exasperated by the other woman's reaction, Kala nodded to Sharia to follow her and headed out into the upper hall. When they were out of earshot, she fairly exploded. "What is that woman thinking? Doesn't she understand how dangerous this is?"

"She doesn't care about anything except Jiana," Sharia answered. "They were out well past Norwin last - dancing, so Sharia told me, to some bard's bawdy tunes. 'Tis not what a Mistress of Magic should be teaching her students, My Lady. Not one so young, anyhow."

"Where had they gone?"

Sharia shrugged. "Some other inn, I guess. It's not the first time they've gone out late like that. By Easwin, Mistress Jessa's all cross and tired. But not this time. They were singing some nasty song just before Firstmeal."

Kala took Sharia's hand and pulled the girl into a secluded corner of the upper hall. She knelt in front of her, locking eyes with her in an intense gaze. "Sharia, tell me why you don't like Jiana. Tell me truly."

Sharia shivered. "You gonna See me?"

Kala smiled slightly. "Not unless you tell me it's all right."

"You oughta See Jiana. There's something bad about her."

"You said she did mean things to you."

"Uh huh," Sharia nodded. "But it's more than that. It's how she is. I just got a feeling is all."

"Does she have Magic....I mean a lot of Magic?"

"She hides it. That's what I don't understand. Mistress Jessa keeps saying she needs to teach her, but I think maybe it's the other way around."

"What do you mean?"

Sharia's eyes darted to the door of her chamber as if she needed to assure herself it was closed, keeping her words from being overheard. "I think it's Jiana that's doing the teaching. I think she's teaching Mistress Jessa bad stuff, real bad stuff."

****

Mountain Lake was, according to the all-purpose merchant and innkeeper, nothing more than a practical name for the little village. "It's cause it's near the lake is all," he said, explaining that he would have liked something more creative. "I woulda called it Ridgeview, or Overvalley meself. We're high up the slopes, you see. I mean, the lake is pretty fine and all, but there's no special ring to a name so common."

Jamus nodded. "I guess the founders thought the lake was the easiest solution."

"Easy don't bring the commerce. There's plenty of water in Lovental Province. Folks'd be looking for something more, you know? Build a nice new inn at the Overlook, people'd flock here for the Warmmonths just to breathe the cool mountain air. Bring in the silver, it would."

"It's a grand idea," Jamus agreed. "If you want visitors. Some villages like to keep to themselves."

Rogan waved his arm over the shelves, stocked with all manner of merchandise from bolts of cloth to pots of cooking oil. "Does it look like I want to keep to meself? I got the best selection of merchandise in all the Province. Been trading for near on nine circles to get it. If it's got a name, it's got a place on these shelves. Lord

Padder's been trying to get tourists up here to The Tarlet's Nest ever since I can recall. Had us a nice season or so till the trouble started."

"Trouble?"

"Strange happenings. Some say we had a Sorcerer up in the high hills put a curse on the village. People'd go off to the lake and come back all weirdy. Men'd forget their wives' names. Wives'd shun their husbands' beds, or want to spend the whole day in 'em. Not that anybody didn't like that, but," he winked broadly, "too much of even a good thing can get tiresome after a while. Didn't take more'n a short season for word to spread to the lower lands that it were a strange place to visit."

"Did anyone ever find the Sorcerer?"

"No more than a Wayard or two, but we had them since the beginning. Zanda keeps watch and they mostly just play the wind and rain for the crops. Nothing wrong in that, long as they don't bother nobody."

"I heard of a girl who was here a while ago who might have been a Wayard."

"Jiana?" Rogan said. "Sure. Little slip of a thing. Her pap has a farm up the way. Sweet little lass, at least she was. Guess she's another one that turned weirdy after going to the lake. Mistress Bonny over at the baker's said she came in one day and made all the cakes fall. Bread flattened and the dough dried, all 'cause her pap's bill was overdue and the Mistress wouldn't give her no more credit. Heard lots of stories after. Enough to make Peacekeeper Bondi tell her pap to either keep her in the house or send her away. I hear tell she had an aunt in the Lowlands and her pap sent her there."

"So she did use Magic?"

"So they say. 'T'ain't no matter most of the time here in the hills. We got farmers what call the weather and healers who chant. As long as nobody uses any of it to hurt somebody, we make do. Now, mind you, we won't hold with no Sorcerers, still. There's a difference twixt using nature's touch to do and calling on the Dragons."

Jamus checked a reaction to the remark, keeping his own voice even as he asked, "There are Dragons about?"

"Not what I said, lad," Rogan laughed. "I kin tell ye ain't had much of a rustic education, eh? From the looks of it ye probably learned all ye know from books and teachers steada the way of the Eldlore. Pity how the highers forget we common folk know a thing or two about most everything. Dragons are the Sorcerers' lords. Been so since the First Circle. Great beasts hold the Magic what flows under the world. Sorcerers worship the Scalewings and, in return, get a bit of the power when they wants it. Story's been passed down from one to another near as long as time. The Hags be our storykeepers."

"Hags?"

"Bory, lad, ye are a cobble walker, ain't ye? Never got the dirt of a country lane on your boots, have ye? The Hags be the wise women of the hills. They got the Sight. Sure ye musta heard of that?"

This time, Jamus nodded. He had not considered that even the Seers here might have their own Wayards in the Art. Certainly the Magicians had never been able to find all the children with Power in Turan. There was no reason to think the Seers of Grandisite would be any more successful. "Is there a Hag nearby I can talk to? I really would like to learn more about these Dragons you speak of."

"Zanda lives up the east ridge. Nice little stone cottage with flowers all around. Go out of the village till ye come to a wide old tree. Just round the rock ye'll see a little path, just wide enough for a one horse cart. Follow it up the hill to her door. If she asks, tell her Rogan sent ye with a basket of preserves in thanks. She gave me the name of me future wife a while back, and," the merchant grinned now, "I think I'm halfway to me wedding day. She'll welcome ye in my name. Be open with her. She's keen with the Vision and won't broach no lies."

"I'll do my best," Jamus replied, considering his options. The tradition of the Seers usually protected others from their Perception through the Vows imposed in Grandisite. As Kala had often explained, she would not Sift anyone without first asking, except in true emergencies. But a Seer without such scruples was another matter entirely. He would have to weigh whether or not to shield himself from her or allow her to see his true nature.

As Jamus left the village, he thought it through. With Magic twisting itself as it had in the last Sevenstin, attempting to weave any kind of shield against the Hag's power was decidedly risky. Yet Rogan had insisted the hill people hated Sorcerers. If the Seer exposed him, what kind of dangers would he be facing? Worse, with the River so capricious, how could he ever defend himself?

He stopped on the path, staring up at the little cottage a few paces away.

But by then, it was too late. The door opened and a middle aged woman, dressed in a simple, tight sleeved gown peered out. "Keep coming, Sorcerer. You'd be wise to finish what you've begun. Otherwise I might indeed be prompted to call out the hounds."

The Rivermaster squared his shoulders and headed for the house. "Do I need to introduce myself at all, Madam? I have a basket from Master Rogan."

Zanda laughed, and beckoned him into her home. "Did he really think his trick would work with me? Twenty circles I've been here and the Sightless still don't understand. Ah, well, I should be talking, eh? Someone with power like yours surely doesn't need to hear that."

Jamus did not even attempt to hide his concern. "You have Sifted me already. Does that condemn me in your eyes?"

"By the Hand, Sur, why should it? Condemn you and I condemn myself as well as every soul in this world who touches one of the Rivers." She grinned, pulled up a chair at the table and motioned for him to sit. "Don't be so surprised at what I know. You came to ask me about Dragons and I talk of Rivers. I may have evaded the Seekers from Grandisite, but I was not fool enough to evade their knowledge as well. I've traveled to Aberdal's Great Library more than I can count. The Masters think they have all the answers in their Hall, but fact is, what they don't have is all the questions." She set a cup in front of him full of steaming keldherb and alongside it a plate of hurlycake, fresh and fragrant.

For once, Jamus was caught speechless. To distract himself, he took a sip of the brew. His mind was reeling, but, with Magiskeep's discipline, he focused his thoughts on his main concern, Jiana.

"It's more than a wee lass you want to know about, Rivermaster." She settled herself down across from him, her green eyes studying his face.

He looked back at her, meeting her gaze directly. Auburn curls tinged with streaks of gray framed her slightly lined face. For all the world he might have been looking at Kala twenty circles from now when age had graced her with a certain quiet confidence. "Is there anything you don't know?"

"A Mage like you could trick me if he wanted to. I've little skill in sifting past more than rudimentary illusions." Then she frowned. "But you didn't even try. I See a troubled heart. Do you fear your Magic here?"

He shrugged. "A fair way of phrasing it, I suppose. It's gone awry ever since we crossed the Rim."

"Trouble's not in you, Sur. It's around you."

"What is it you See?" Jamus asked, his fingers trembling on the cup. Something prickled the hairs on the back of his neck, edging him close to fear. Was it the Magician's ancient wariness of the Sight, or something more sinister? He put the cup down before he spilled the drink.

His reaction did not go unnoticed. "Ye feel my Dragon stir, Riverlord. Mark it well. *Ye be closer to the White Waters than ye realize,*" Zanda said, slipping into the tongue of prophecy. *"But it is not the time for that. The Way is open. If ye shatter not the door, the dark waters shall flood the land. Shadows abound. They blight the land. They sitteth on thy right hand and mock the truth with reflection. Thy fear will feed their lust. Darkwing seeks the wind. Ye must not let him take flight."*

Fear surrendered to frustration. "More riddles," Jamus said angrily. "Can't prophets ever speak plainly?"

Zanda's eyes focused back on his face. To his surprise, she smiled. "It's the way of it. I'm sorry. Tomorrow's tongue speaks thus. What I perceive of the here and now is plainly spoken. Have you not found it so?"

Jamus sighed. "Until you drifted into that trance, I was actually finding you quite refreshing for a Seer. Remarkably clear and to the point."

"I wish it were otherwise. I detest the ceremony and mystic trappings the Seers of Grandisite surround themselves with. Well, most of the Seers." She winked. "The lady whose green eyes stir your heart is an exception. It hurts her not to love you almost as much as it hurts you not to love her, you know. But she is not the cause of your distress. Somehow you must sift this world on your own, My Lord. Only when you see all there is to see will your River answer as you ask. I cannot tell you more because the very forces twisting your Magic obscure my Vision as well."

"Kala spoke of darkness when she tried to sift Jiana."

Zanda nodded. "It was the same for me when last I spoke to the child. That was why I sent her away. But perhaps I was mistaken."

"In sending her away?"

The Seer slowly shook her head. "In thinking it was Jiana I sent away. Now that I have Seen your truth, I am beginning to wonder if the darkness I saw in her *was* her."

"Shadow," Jamus said, the fear clambering for a foothold.

This time Zanda nodded.

It was reply enough as a cold shiver coursed down Jamus' spine.

Chapter 12

Sight eluded her. Or light eluded her.

Kala was not sure which. Against the sacred Vow of Grandisite, she had sifted Jiana without consent, looking for some clue to her nature.

Darkness again, but worse, for when her Vision slid unintentionally to Jessa, there was even less light illuminating the Truth.

Was her Art failing her the same way Jamus' was denying him? Had she too been captured in the web of their failed love? Uncontrolled emotion was as dangerous to a Seer as it was to a Magician. Her River was no more forgiving when the Call was wrenched solely from the heart instead of reason.

But Jiana and Jessa were both sorceresses. If something in their nature or even Jamus' River had created a barrier to Vision, it would make sense that neither of them revealed anything when she Sought the truth. That idea was far more comforting, and it offered an explanation.

Yet, nothing was certain, so she decided to spend a few spans in the Inn's common room, testing her theory on someone else. It would have to be done in secret, again breaking her Vows, so as not to arouse suspicion. A Seer of her rank asking for permission to sift anyone was worthy of note in Aberdeen itself, let alone in a small village like Loren.

Selecting the right person posed another problem. Someone sensitive and aware of his own mind might feel her probes. What she didn't need was indignant rage thrown in her face and the subsequent explanations she would have to forge. The person she chose would have to be completely oblivious to the concerns of others, and totally absorbed in his own agenda. Someone like that would be far to intent on creating an impression than paying any attention to the feelings of those around him.

She sat at a table off to one side, nibbling at some slices of bread, sipping a mug of keldherb, and making the pretense of reading a rather aged book. Since few people in the village were literate, most of the patrons eyed her with a certain respectful awe, and practically tiptoed past as they made their ways to farther tables.

Then, the door was shoved open with a bang as Gunder blustered his way into the room, "Aggie, me Sweet! I gots me a purse o' silver!" He held up a small leather pouch, shaking it to make the coins jingle. "Caught me a silverhead big as a horse. Willabe is gonna skin it an' stuff it fer his wall after he bakes the innards for Lastmeal."

When there was no response from either the kitchen or the patrons, Gunder swaggered up to the bar and slammed his hand down on the polished wood. "A round fer the house, Medd. Fill 'em up on Gunder." He plopped the purse down as hard as his hand, grinning at the resounding chink. This brought a few men to the bar and raised a half dozen more eyes from the tables. "Where's Aggie? She serving?"

"Aggie's off to the miller. Lydia's in the back with the trays."

"Ah, the lovely Lydia. Iffen I cain't have me first precious, I s'pose the second prettiest lass in the Peek'll jest have to do. Set up the tankards, Medd, and keep the brew flowing till me purse runs dry."

"Ye eating?"

"Nah. I had some roast at Willabe's. Me belly's full."

Lydia sauntered out from the kitchen, her hips swaying purposefully. Perhaps twenty circles, she had already mastered all the charms a barmaid treasured to keep her pockets full of tips and favors. "So, Master Gunder, ye buying rounds, are ye? Spend all thy coin on drink and what's there to thank me for serving?"

Gunder laughed, grabbed the girl around the waist and playfully swung her around him. "Does it have ta be silver ye get from me, lass? There's more'n one way a man can gift a lass, ye know."

"And would I want such payment, Sur? I strive to be a lady."

"A lady laid be richer at Easwin in purse and body, if I have my say."

"Then say as you will, come Norwin, at the lake cottage," Lydia whispered in his ear. Aloud, she answered, "T'would not be

seemly, Sur. Take my smile at your flattery along with the ale and be
satisfied…for now," she muttered the last words under her breath as
she placed his tankard on the table.

Kala observed the pair with quiet consideration while
Gunder slapped Lydia's bottom as she passed. Surely a man like him
would not even notice her thoughts.

Sight answered the call with deliberate obedience to its
Mistress. Kala let her mind slip into the keen world of Vision, her
surroundings drifting away as she focused on Gunder, and nothing
more. The light in the room dimmed to darkness.

*Darkness. A space devoid of light, hollow and black.
Nothing, as if Sight were blind.*

Kala pulled back, shuddering, closing her eyes against the
sudden brightness of the room.

Gunder's eyes glanced her way over the rim of his tankard.
He was not smiling this time.

****

Shaidra was silent as she led Simen and Jessa to a silk and
shaenis bedchamber. A rose coverlet draped over a wide bed set near
a double window curtained in rich red velvet. A thick, intricately
patterned carpet covered the floor, and a tall mirror, framed in
darkwood, stood across from a large stone fireplace. "If you sing
your lady a love song, perhaps she will sleep more easily," she said
at last, breaking the uneasy silence.

"I have no music," Simen replied warily. With Shaidra in
command of their destiny, he was not at all sure how to react.

"You still don't trust my word? I said if you chose the right
one you were welcome to bed her. I have surrendered you to her."
She waved her hand in dismissal, "Go on, sing to your lover, or
simply ravage her at your will. Either way, I shall gain nothing but
the pleasure of knowing."

The Mistress of Shadows was not patient, Simen knew. Her
passions thrived on violence. Anything he could do to temper the
emotions of events would give him an advantage. "I have no music,"
he repeated. "I need a lute, unless you tell the winds to play for me."

"I have the power," Shaidra answered, "but I would far prefer letting you do the work." She gestured an intricate pattern over the table by the bed as Simen watched with intent interest. The air above shimmered, black tendrils curling and shaping themselves into a dark ebony lute. "It is already tuned," she said, her pale lips curling up in a satisfied smile.

Simen moved over and picked up the instrument, shaking his head. "Not for me," he said. "I fret with my right hand and finger with my left. A curious habit, I suppose but far more comfortable for my handedness. It would be an easy fix, if I could trust my Magic here."

"No deceptions, Sur," Shaidra replied. "Ply your Will. The reflections here are at my command. For the moment I will mark them true." This time she watched carefully as Simen touched the lute gently and focused his thoughts on reversing the pattern of the strings.

Shaidra paid little mind to the results of Simen's spell, for she had also focused on his method, silently cursing to herself at the ease and simplicity of his casting. There were no superfluous gestures, no incantations mouthed on his lips. His River answered his silent Will with an ease and responsiveness she could only envy. When he picked up the lute, holding the neck in his right hand as he checked the tuning, she was forcing herself to keep calm in the face of his superior Magic. The thought of admitting, even to herself, that he had bested her seethed past reason to hard resentment. It was all she could do to keep her voice steady. "Lady Jessa, set yourself on the bed. Let your hair fall loose and, for ardor's sake, undo the laces of your bodice. I don't want your lover's arousal thwarted by any strings other than his lute's once he decides to have his way with you. If your breast spill out, so much the better to tune his tongue to the proper notes."

Jessa, despite herself, blushed. Her fingers trembled as she undid the laces. To her relief, the fabric did not fall away, leaving her some sense of modesty. "As you wish, My Lady," she said meekly, struggling to maintain the illusion of composure. Inside, she burned with indignation and longed to test her own chanting against this

mistress of mirrors. Watching Simen had convinced her that the
River would answer here, at least for now.

When she had first been taken captive, Shaidra had wrapped
her in layers of reflections, denying her any sense of reason or
perception. Without either, Magic became elusive—an untouchable
force in an incomprehensible world. At this moment, though, edges
of reality were sharply drawn, and she had seen every thread of
Simen's spell as clearly as a classroom exercise in Magiskeep. How
easy it would be to sweep Shaidra to oblivion with one slender
tendril of Spellfire.

But Simen made no move against their captor, and she, sure
in her trust of his judgment, simply complied with Shaidra's wishes.

"Move over a bit," Shaidra ordered, motioning Simen to a
spot directly across from the mirror.

He too complied meekly, but his eyes caught the glimmer of
firelight reflecting in the polished surface. He deliberately kept from
looking at himself, but was fully aware of the fact that his whole
body was imaged there. Why? For some reason Shaidra wanted him
reflected in the mirror. Was she hoping to capture another part of
him there? Or— he checked his thoughts. Not so much to capture a
new reflection but rather to aid an old one? She had not brought him
into the Way without sending something to replace him. Already he
had seen Gunder here and his Shadow in Loren. If there were another
Simen riding at Jamus' side, was there some secret he needed to
assure his place? He fingered the lute idly. The music, of course.
What was a Follyman without a song? Now he knew the game. The
rules slid to his side of the board. "What shall I play, Madam? A
true courtier's song, or something to arouse my lady's passions?"

Shaidra licked her lips. "Something to inspire lust, Sur.
Bring the bitch to heat if you will, or yourself. It doesn't matter
which one fires first, as long as the flames ultimately consume. I like
my blood well roasted."

Simen diverted his glance from Jessa's stricken expression,
his lips sealed tight against a retort to the demeaning remark. He
forced a smile. "Well, then, a bawdy ballad." He tested the strings,
strummed a chord and began to sing.

"Pretty little sparret,

fledgling from the nest
Testing wings against the wind
blowing at her breast.
Little bird of daring,
nothing in her head,
Soft and downy bottom
feathering my bed.
I shall pluck thy plumage,
till thy breast is bare,
Nestle in the crevice
and the pillows there."

He winked at Jessa, pretending to tease her. But she read something else, and nodded back. He was changing the song—a note here and there, and a word or two, no more, but enough that anyone who'd heard it before would notice the difference. Apparently, Shaidra had not.

"Pretty, pretty sparret,
snared within my net
For the spans of Norwin,
ye shall be my pet.
Sing thy song sweet sparret,
plead your feathers back
I shall not restore them,
such purpose do I lack.
Plucked thus I may use thee,
as desire demands,
Play your supple body
with my hungry hands.
When Easwin arises,
and I've had my fill,
Take the offered silver
and fly off at thy will.
Sparrets are for taking
as the hunter's prey
Tasty in the darkness,
useless in the day.
Pretty, pretty sparret,

> *snared within my net*
> *For the spans of Norwin,*
> *ye shall be my pet."*

He finished the song with a flourishing arpeggio and a leering grin as Jessa pretending to shrink away as he advanced. "Well, little sparret, are you ready for me?"

Her eyes darted over to Shaidra who was breathing heavily, her brow dotted with sweat. "The lady...," she said, deliberately leaving the rest unfinished.

"Madam," Simen said sharply. "At least give us the illusion of privacy."

Shaidra started, then spun on her heel and fled the room, leaving them alone.

Simen sank down on the bed beside Jessa, his shoulders slumped. "I pray to the Hand it worked."

Jessa's hand slid into the belt of his breeches, tugging at the lacing. "It worked, My Lord. Perhaps not exactly as you expected, considering the circumstances." She kissed him full on the mouth, her lips opening to his. "It definitely worked." Then she lay back and urged him down on top of her.

****

Serimsimen picked up the lute and imitated the reflection he'd seen in the mirror. All during Simen's singing, the Magic of the Way had absorbed itself into the pores of his insubstantial body, filling it with Simen's music and Simen's song until he could duplicate both on instinct alone. Watching and probing, he had gathered a dozen more songs, strummed a hundred more chords and memorized enough to trick the keenest critic. Now, as he looked at himself in the mirror, he saw an exact duplicate of the real Simen. It was perfect down to the last detail.

He tested his voice, *"Pretty, pretty sparret, snared within my net - For the spans of Norwin, ye shall be my pet."* It too was perfect.

The joy of it was that he would earn a silver or two at the inn, a remarkably satisfying bonus. Aside from having True Life, the Fleshers' need for material possessions was the other difference between them. At last one half of his desire to live would be fulfilled once he had a coin in his purse. The other half would have to wait until, as Shaidra had promised, he would feast on Simen's blood.

He dressed in the colorful tunic of the Follyman, admiring the well cut fit at the waist and shoulders. The elegance and style were more evidence of the real Simen's position and worth in the world, firing even fresher envy in his reflection. The smooth shaenis lining of the garment aroused new sensations in the skin he wore, rousing unexpected and incomprehensible pleasure. New feelings indeed, and all the more reason to wish for solid mortality to replace the shades of his own existence. Confidently, and with a surprising sense of anticipation, he picked up the lute and headed down to the common room.

A small crowd had gathered in anticipation of some entertainment. The common room had tables and chairs for about fifty, and half were filled with simply dressed men with about ten women joining them. From the looks of the females, most were wives, but several were glossed in too much paint and frills to be anything but paid companions ready for an evening of drink and a Norwin between the blankets. Serimsimen recognized two of his kin laughing in the darker corners of the room, keeping to the shadows out of habit, as they explored the world of fleshers to discover the weaknesses and secrets their Riverlord needed to complete his conquest. It was altogether a satisfactory audience for his first performance.

He strode to the empty floor in front of the fireplace and strummed a chord. As the eyes of all turned in his direction, a shiver of excitement coursed through his body, settling in a quiver in his stomach. It took him a moment to regain his composure, so he fumbled with the lute's tuning to cover his nervousness. He was so intent on the deception that he did not notice as Jamus came in the door to sit at a table by the window.

The music came with unusual ease, falling from Serimsimen's fingers in rhythms of curious complexity. The audience murmured restlessly, until one more elegantly-clad man raised his voice. "Don't ply your high art, Follyman. This is no highlord's hall where the ladies swoon at pretty figures. Give us a song a man can sing or at least remember for a span."

Puzzled by the remark, Serimsimen shrugged and transitioned into the opening notes of the sparret song. As applause erupted, he grinned, pleased to have made the right choice. Then, he began to sing.

Jamus frowned. He had never seen Simen holding his lute with his left hand dancing on the frets while his right plucked the strings. Perhaps the instrument was borrowed as he had certainly not brought one in his traveling pack. If it was, the explanation was simple, for his brother would respect a fellow musician's treasure and not toy with its configuration. He relaxed at the thought, only half listening to the song as the barmaid placed a tray of meat and vegetables on the table in front of him and poured a hefty flagon of ale.

Zanda's words had unnerved him more than he'd realized. He'd left her house with far too many questions unanswered, promising to return the next day when both of them had sorted out the essence of her Vision. But the fresh air and even a ride through some of the mountain passes had done little to clear his head. So, he had headed back to the inn in hopes of talking it all over with Simen, relying on the Follyman's keen knowledge of the Way to sort out some of the possibilities. Instead, he found Simen entertaining the villagers with a bawdy song.

> "Sparrets are for taking
> as the hunter's prey
> Tasty in the darkness,
> useless in the day."

The words were wrong. Simen should have sung, "*Pleasure in the nighttime, forgotten in the day.*" Jamus' shook his head, focusing on the music, the melody and harmony even to his ear not quite as it should be. He stole a quick glance around the room, noticing a few other patrons shaking their heads and frowning as well, then bending to whisper to their tablemates as the song rolled to a conclusion. A good round of applause answered the final notes, but even that was dotted with a few mutters of discontent.

"T'were a strange singing of an old song," one of the rustic workmen said aloud. "Where ye be from, Follyman that ye mangle the words of the Eldenlay?"

Serimsimen's mouth twisted as he searched for an answer. His memory of Simen's singing had been flawless, of that he was certain. "I learned the song from an eldersinger, Sur. If anyone's knowledge of the lyrics is wrong, I suspect it's yours."

"T'ain't jest his memory," another man said. "It's mine too. I learnt that song from me grandpap and it weren't as ye recalled it."

"I am from a distant land," Serimsimen said uneasily. "Perhaps my people have their own version of the Eld."

"The Eld be the word of the Hand in Turan," the man replied. "The winds sing the words to all who walk the land. They be the same from Easwin to Weswin by the blessings of the Great Circle."

"Country superstitions," one of the dark corner women said, interrupting. "I have traveled far enough from here to know the music of Windchange itself. This Follyman sang as I have heard in Valleyvale, far to the south of the greater Provinces. Perhaps, as it is said, the Hand does not reach below the boundaries of the King's domain."

"Blasphemy!" a third man, well dressed and older than the others, cried. "To speak of a godless world is to deny the Dragon. I would sooner hope the winds twisted the words in the ears of this bard's master than to insult the Scalewing."

"The winds then," the woman replied, smiling too sweetly. "But rest assured, I have heard this Follyman's version before. But, let us not debate. No matter what the words, I cannot fault his voice and talent with the strings. I, for one would find much pleasure in hearing more of his music."

With that, another round of applause broke out, bringing the grin back to Serimsimen's face as he strummed a few chords and began another song.

Jamus toyed with his ale, spinning the golden brew to the rim of the tankard until the foam nearly spilled. What Eldersinger had taught Simen a new set of words to the song? Magiskeep's borders held no such teacher. Unless…his mind paused…of course, the Great Library, Jessa, and a hundred old scrolls filled with the Eldenlore. It was an easy answer, and comforting. If Simen had learned new words to old songs in the ancient texts, all suspicion fell away. If he hadn't....

Chapter 13

Sharia sat tightlipped and silent by the window, gazing out in pretended interest at the alleys behind the inn. All the while her ears and frustration burned at the giddy laughter punctuating the close-headed conversation between Jiana and her Mistress, Jessa. Repeatedly ignored by the other two, she had decided it was better to sit in the room with them, catching bits and pieces of their lessons together than flounce off in a pout to the kitchens to learn how to bake one more kind of bread or to brown a duckling to perfection. Besides, despite the pleasure of cooking with her own hands, Magic could just as easily prepare a fine meal with far less time and effort.

The Cups of Magiskeep had not destined her to be a kitchen drudge, but rather a Mistress of Magic, full robed in the Art of Comprehension. Jessa owed her something, and she did not intend to sit idly by while another student stole the privilege from her. "My Lady," she said, keeping her voice steady. "I would like you to impart some of your knowledge to me today. I am your Apprentice and have a claim to at least some of your time."

Jessa looked up, more surprised than annoyed by the intrusion. "No one has denied your joining us, Sharia."

"I would prefer learning about the Runes of Shelock rather than how to best convince a man to come to bed with me, Mistress."

Jessa grinned, "So you have been listening. Then why do you complain? Apparently I've kept nothing from you."

"You're not teaching the Art of Magic," Sharia said. "That's what I want to learn. If I wanted to master the art of seduction, there's a whorehouse two streets away."

Jiana laughed aloud, "Well, well, the little lass has learned a thing or two since she's been here. Isn't this the girl who thought babes were conceived with a kiss? Seems to me you've grown up, little Sharia. Maybe we should take you with us the next time we go out so you can learn the pleasures spreading your legs, eh? What do you think, Jessa?"

Sharia blushed despite herself, gritting her teeth to hear the other girl so familiar with her Mistress. "I'm not as eager to sell myself as you are, Jiana. I may be inexperienced, but I do know right from wrong."

Jiana held up her hand in mock blessing. "Oh, the virgin speaks. How honored I am to be chastised by the most pure." Then she laughed derisively. "At least this time the moral lesson comes from lips that have a rudimentary understanding of what they're talking about. I was growing weary of the constant ignorance. I should think your Mistress would be proud to know you actually have learned something since you've been here."

"Now, now, Jiana, don't be too hard on her. Sharia's led a sheltered life in the Keep all these circles. I've neglected too much of her worldly education in favor of dusty tomes and scrolls. If she prefers the Runes of Sherlock to bettering her womanhood, I am as much to blame as anyone."

Instead of replying, Sharia moved back towards the window. Shaking her head, she slid along the wall as if cringing away. "You are not to blame, Madam. I am, for being so arrogant as to think I knew better what to do than you do. I can clearly see I am outmatched. Forgive me."

Jessa frowned slightly, then nodded deferentially. "Why don't you go downstairs and play with your friend Aggie, Sharia. I am sure she will find some way to amuse you with less…ah…mature entertainment. I'm afraid Jiana and I have offended your sensibilities."

Without a word of reply, Sharia rushed out the door. Her breath came in harsh gasps as she ran down the stairs and into the kitchen. "Mistress Aggie, do you know where Lady Kala is? I have to talk to her right away."

"The lady went to the Town Hall less than a span past, child. She should be back soon. She told me she wanted me to show her how I tend the potter's herbs in the sun shed out back." Aggie reached out a hand to steady the heaving girl before she dashed out of the inn. "Here, now lass. Calm thyself. Ye looks like ye are being chased by a savage tark. Here now, Aggie's kitchen's a safe haven. I have me cleavers ever at the ready."

Sharia managed a weak smile as she let herself be pushed onto a wooden stool by the counter. "I've seen awful," she said, panting. "Just awful. I'm sure of it."

"Not Jiana again was it? Did that girl torment you again? I thought ye two had settled matters between ye."

"No. But I need to tell Lady Kala. She'll know what to do."

Nearly on cue at the mention of her name, Kala opened the door from the garden. "Mistress, I'm back. If you have the time, I'd love to see the shed."

Sharia rushed to the Seer's arms, forcing Kala to grab her or collide with her. The little girl gulped hard, then said, "My Lady. If it's not the black Dragon at work, then some other curse has taken us all."

Kala instinctively put her fingers on Sharia's lips to silence her. "That game is over, Sharia. I told you at Easwin we wouldn't play it again." She smiled indulgently and glanced over at Aggie, shaking her head. "A silly riddle game we played winds past. Sharia just gets so caught up in it she forgets to separate it from the real world. Poor little child, such a vivid imagination. I'll take her outside into the fresh air and try to explain again. Come on, little one. The sunshine will do you good." Still keeping her hand close to the girl's mouth, Kala ushered Sharia outside to the far side of the garden, where no one could possibly hear them. "Have you forgotten the lessons of the Keep so easily, Sharia? The Dragon, the river, anything of the Art are not for common ears."

"I'm sorry, My Lady, truly. But I was so afraid."

"Of what?"

"Mistress Jessa."

"Jessa? Dear little one, of all the people in the world I've ever met, Lady Jessa is the least frightening."

"She's been talking sex with Jiana all day long. It's so mean what they say about making men want to lie with them."

Kala knelt before the girl, gently rubbing her hands to soothe her. "I'll admit that's not the nicest thing for you to hear, but perhaps the Lady feels Jiana needs some lessons in proper behavior I'm sure she knows best."

"You don't unnerstand. There's more." Sharia swallowed
hard again and went on, "I interrupted them and told Mistress Jessa I
wanted to go on with my studies. At first she just laughed, but then
she said maybe it was her fault I wanted to study to study Sherlock,"
she made a warding gesture with her hand and continued, "steada
woman stuff." When Kala did not react, Sharia's voice took on a
pleading tone. "Don't you see, My Lady? It's not Sherlock, it's the
Runes of Shelock. That's the most sacred texts of the Art of
Comprehension. Mistress Jessa would never, ever say that wrong,
not even if she was making a joke. Shelock, blessed be the name, is
near holy as the Hand to the Sorcerer. It's the key to Magic."

Kala gripped the girl's hands. "You're sure of this?"

"Every Prentice in the Keep knows it, My Lady. It's the very
first lesson of the Art. If Lord Jamus was here, he'd tell you.
Mistress Jessa would never make such a mistake. Why, it's
like…like blasmaphe."

"Blasphemy," Kala corrected distractedly. "A sin against the
very values of Magic. Nothing the Jessa I know would dare. Come
with me, Sharia. I'm not well schooled enough in the ways of your
Keep to understand all of this. But with Jamus gone, we'll need
someone else to advise us."

"Where are we going?"

"To find a mirror."

****

Kala moved to the mirror in Jamus' room, letting Vision
pass into its surface instead of merely looking at her own reflection.
It took a moment for her eyes to See, but soon, instead of her room, a
chamber in Magiskeep appeared before her. She breathed a sigh of
relief when she saw movement, and recognized Salene, seated at a
desk writing something in a book. "Talk about luck," she said aloud.
Then, she reached out and rapped the mirror sharply with her
fingertips. Salene started, turned and peered back at her. When Kala
rapped again, she got up and walked over, her intense blue eyes
seeking into the reflection as well. "Salene," Kala said, "I need your
help."

"By the Hand, Kala, I never expected to find you there. Jamus, perhaps. What's wrong?"

Kala found it hard to concentrate on keeping the image of the other woman in place, her own face constantly threatening to take its place. "Can you spell something to make this easier? I'm having trouble seeing you."

Salene smiled and gestured with her hand, her image suddenly becoming solid and secure. "I'd step through, but as you know the Way between is not always hospitable. The last thing I want to do it get lost in one of its corridors."

"This will do. When Jamus told me he'd chanted this mirror so he could keep in contact with you, I took the chance it might work without him here."

"He's not with you?"

He's gone north to find the girl's family. And that's the problem. I need a Sorcerer's advice and counsel."

"What about Simen or Jessa?"

"Simen's gone with Jamus and…well, Jessa is part of the problem. Sharia's here with me. Maybe she can explain things better than I can." Kala pushed the girl forward. "Just look past your own face, Sharia. Lady Salene is on the other side."

Sharia nodded, stood for a moment and then curtsied quickly. "Mistress. Well met on this day."

"Well met as well, Mistress Sharia. Where is your Master?"

"Lady Jessa is in her rooms, keeping close company with Jiana, the Wayard girl Lord Jamus came to see. She's acting really strange. Both of them are, My Lady. At first I thought it was fine, just kindness on my Master's part, but now I'm not so sure."

"Sharia's convinced something is wrong with Jessa," Kala said.

"It's more than that, Lady Salene. Just today, a little while ago, she called the Runes as Sherlock's, instead of Shelock's." Even as she said it, the girl shuddered.

"Are you certain?" Salene asked. "You didn't hear her wrong, did you?"

Sharia shook her head. "Never, Madame. She's been talking about…about bedding men and all with Jiana all Easwin, ignoring all the study spans we were supposed to have. She's broken her bond with me ever since she and Master Simen rode off for a day at the lake."

"They came back together?" Salene asked.

"Yes, My Lady…but…she wasn't the same. She started paying all kinds of attention to Jiana and forgot all about me."

"Kala, have you used your Sight there in the village?"

"I have, but it's failed me more than once since we've been here. When I tried to See Jiana, it was all darkness. Yesterday, I used Vision to sift one of the locals and it was the same. Simen has a theory about it," Kala added, somewhat reluctantly. "I don't exactly hold with the idea, but he insisted Jamus' feelings for me were interfering with his Magic, so I suppose the same might be true of my Vision."

To Kala's relief, Salene seemed to take no notice of the implications. "Are you saying something was wrong with Jamus' Magic? Tell me."

"It didn't work…at least not the way it was supposed to. He tried to light a fire and snow fell on the wood instead."

"And Simen blamed it on his love for you."

Kala nodded. "Exactly."

"Kala, right now, while we are together, I want you to sift Sharia. Give her permission, lass. It's my command."

"All right," Sharia said nervously. "Go on."

Kala turned her gaze on the girl, letting her mind See beyond the confines of her eyes. *Innocence, wonder, and the brightness of Easwin flooded her thoughts. The world opened in front of her like a vast and glorious adventure of color and sensation. Golden currents of gentle streams lapped at her feet, rubbing against her legs like little kittens begging for attention. She felt the urge to reach out to grab at the sun, as if she could actually hold its light in her hands, reveling in the warmth and joy of its life-giving grace. Beyond, a long road stretched ahead, lined with graceful brellums offering numerous paths on either side with tantalizing flowers and plants to pluck or study. The horizon seemed endless and beautiful. She gasped at the wonder of it all. And then, from the corner of her eye, she spied a Shadow, dark and looming,*

somehow threatening to dim it all to nothingness and her heart
dropped, caught in a hollow of despair and worse, fear. She forced
herself away, her own eyes wet as she heard Sharia's sobs of misery.
"Sharia's right, Salene. Something is terribly wrong. I saw a Shadow
threatening her."

"The Shadows treacherous," Salene said. "They can take on
the appeance of those we know. Jamus has always said the
Reflections of the Way can hide in the familiar. Perhaps it is not
Jessa there with you. Sift her, and if you find only darkness, then I'd
suspect that's what may be happening. No true Mistress of
Comprehension would ever mistake Shelock's name. The Runes are
sacred to her Art and one of the first lessons a child of the Keep ever
learns. It's near to blasphemy to speak of them in common tones."

"That's what Sharia tried to tell me."

"You're in danger, Kala, and right now, without Jamus or
Simen, the only person who can protect you is that most perceptive
young lady. Sharia, dry your tears and pay close attention to me."

Sharia swallowed a sob and straightened her shoulders. "My
Lady?"

"Can you cast Spellfire?"

Sharia's mouth dropped. "It is forbidden! Magic
Unrestrained is against the Vow!"

"It is the only weapon you have against the Shadows, Sharia.
If you are right about your Mistress and Jiana, you are in grave
danger. Can you cast Spellfire?"

"I don't know, Madame. I've never tried."

At that, Salene laughed. "Blessed be. The one child in all of
Magic who has never cast Whitefire is now left the sole protector of
an entire village. You do understand how to cast Spellfire, don't
you?"

"Aye, Mistress. I need to let my feelings call the River
instead of my head."

"Exactly. But you must be strong with them. Get angry, or
afraid, if you must. Don't stop to think. If there are Shadows in
Loren, they will attack quickly. You don't have time to sort through
a chanting to stop them. Scream out to the Magic if you must. Do
you understand?"

Sharia nodded. "I think so. I read a lot about it in Master Seneth's class. It always made my stomach all wobbly inside."

"The Lady Kala is depending on you, Sharia. I'm trusting you with her life and...well, I might even be trusting you with Lord Jamus' life. Kala, is there any way you can warn him?"

"Not unless we ride out after him. I'm not even exactly sure where he's gone."

"Zanda might know," Sharia said. "Mistress Aggie said she knows everything."

"Come back to the mirror at Norwin, Kala. Tell me what's happening. I may not be able to come, but Sarn and some of the others might be willing to risk it. By the Blood, if Magiskeep had an army, I'd send it."

"Is the danger so great?"

"Look about you, Madame Juris. Use your Sight. I'd wager pretty Mistress Jessa and her Jiana are not the only dark spots in your Vision."

Kala shuddered as the image of the murdered men leapt into her head. Now, she was beginning to wonder how many more bodies still lay undiscovered in the houses and fields of the Province. Shadows rarely stopped at one victim.

****

Flushed with pride at the sustained rounds of applause, Serimsimen sat back down across from Jamus and downed a second pint of ale. "Drink up, brother. Celebrate my success with me."

Jamus pushed his own tankard aside and shook his head, "You know better than that, Simen. One drink is more than enough for me."

Serimsimen waved at the barmaid who was more than eager to attend the inn's newest star patron. "Fill me up and my brother too," he said. "It's a fool who refuses a free drink in honor of another."

Jamus put his hand over the rim of his tankard and shook his head. "No more. You, of all, should remember what happened last time I had too much to drink."

"A headache and a sour stomach are small price to pay for the pleasure in between," the Follyman replied. "Drink up and enjoy."

Jamus leaned back and studied Simen's face carefully. How could his brother so easily dismiss the incident with Casla back in Magiskeep? He'd played the lute with the wrong hand, sung an old familiar song with the wrong words and now he'd forgotten such a failing. It made no sense. He'd always felt he was looking in the mirror when he looked at Simen. Now it was as if he was looking at himself, instead of his reflection. "The song you sang, Simen. You changed some of the words. Where did you learn the new version?"

Serimsimen coughed in mid-swallow, spewing ale onto the table. "It's how I learned it."

"Obviously, but not how it's supposed to be sung."

"Artistic license," he replied. "I felt it needed a little more spice here and there." His brain was reeling from one tankard too many and the growing fear that somehow he had been tricked by the true Simen's Reflection. He'd sung the song exactly right and yet it had been wrong. "Didn't you like it?"

"It had a decidedly sharper edge," Jamus replied. "Not quite what I would expect from you, though. I've more often heard you soften a bawdy lyric when the audience is mixed."

"Aside from the graybeards in the audience, I didn't have too many complaints. Seems a goodly number liked my version."

"Ah, yes, the patrons in the shadows, over there," Jamus gestured towards the darker corners of the room."

At the mention of shadows, Serimsimen swallowed hard. "What are you suggesting, Brother?"

Jamus' fingers played a weave under the table. He had to focus every thread, fighting against the alien currents swirling ever deeper around him. But he was beginning to recognize the reflections now, twisting his own spells to reverse themselves in a River that seemed to be flowing from the Way of Mirrors. "I have bound you, Simen," he said at last. "Master's Art to keep you under my control."

Serimsimen leaned in, his voice dark, "You are not Master of our River."

"There you are wrong, Shadow. I am Master of the Way and see the deceptions as well I as see you. Now, let us politely make our excuses and go someplace where we can be alone. I'd rather not make a spectacle here until I better understand everything that's been going on."

Serimsimen started to raise his hand, then blanched as he felt the sharp edged coils of Jamus' spell holding him. Even the slightest thought of defiance sliced a dagger of pain into his body. He cursed under his breath, rose from his seat, and let Jamus guide him out of the inn.

Once in the street, out of earshot of the inn, Jamus took Serimsimen's arm and pulled him around to face him. "Now, tell me, my friend, just where is my brother?"

****

Jessa stirred in her sleep and Simen put a reassuring arm around her. For the last span, he had not felt Shaidra's presence. She had lost interest once their lovemaking had ended. He would have denied her even that if Jessa had not insisted--her need for his love the only assurance she could find in their captivity. Now, alone together, as much as he longed for her, he needed to think with cold rationality.

His Magic worked here, and Jessa's would too. At least here in the palace of reflected reflections, neither one of them would have to make any adjustments in casting a spell. But, conquering Shaidra in order to escape the palace would set them both back out in the world of the Way where everything was in opposition.

He had already proven himself capable of coping with it by taking on his true identity as a child of the Way. But Jessa? It wouldn't be as easy for her. To cast every spell in opposition would require concentration and if there were an emergency she might not have the time to think. If only Jamus were here. Certainly a Master of the Way would have some solution. It was, after all, simply a matter of reflections.

"Jessa?" he said, shaking her gently. "Wake up. I need to talk to you."

She opened her eyes. "Talk? I was dreaming of something more interesting."

"We need to get out of here. Shaidra and her Shadows are trying to take over the world outside this reflection. We need to stop her."

"How, Simen? She has as much, perhaps more, Magic than we do and it is her realm."

"She's not as powerful as she wants us to believe, my Love. Mirror Magic cannot defeat the reality it reflects. In here, in her palace, her Magic is reflection of reflection and the two of us can easily defeat her. Outside, it may be stronger, but never the match for the Truth of the River. There's a problem, though."

"Of course there's a problem," Jessa sighed. "As Jamus keeps telling us, the River is full of riddles."

"We're in the Way of Mirrors, Jessa, and outside this palace, everything is reflection—reality reversed. If you cast a spell of fire, it will end up as snow."

Jessa frowned. "So before I can use any of my Magic I have to figure out how to do it backwards?"

Simen smiled. "Simply and precisely put. That would be fine if you had the time to think it all through, but if any of Shaidra's minions decide to attack us, I doubt you'll have time to think. Just reacting by instinct could be useless at best and dangerous at worst."

"So I can't risk using Magic?" Jessa frowned even more as she considered the possibilities. Then a trace of a smile lifted her lips. "If I had a mirror to chant through, wouldn't it reflect every spell I cast?" Her eyes started to sparkle now with the idea. "Think about it, Simen. In a reflected world my spell would be reversed, but cast through a mirror, it would be reversed again."

"Not through a mirror, my Love, but off a mirror. You'd need to cast your spell into a mirror and then send that reflection where you wanted it to go. I don't think...."

"Three mirrors then," Jessa insisted. "In a pendant hanging at my neck. Cast the reflection of this land into one, let true be reflected into the second mirror. The false reflection from that mirror hits the third which then sends out the true intent of my spell. All we need to do is angle the facets in the pendant so when I first send the magic it follows the right path. I can face whatever I'm trying to chant that way and the pendant will send my power where I want it to go."

Simen shook his head more in wonder than denial. "Crystal Amulet twisting truth to new directions. It will deserve a place in Senital's vaults when we get back home."

It took the better part of what might have been a day in the mirror's world to fashion an amulet that worked. They'd taken the pendant Jessa already wore, transformed it into crystal, and then began to align its facets. A scorched curtain by the bed, a shattered vase and a pile of snow turning to soot in the corner of room remained as testimony to their various experiments. Between them, with Jessa's superior skill at Comprehension and Simen's peculiar talent with reflections, they managed to create a powerful stone the Mistress of the First Art could use to warp her Magic to suit the world of reflections she would face outside the palace gates.

"I have to aim it perfectly to get the full effect," she said at last, peering through the amulet. "But even Spellfire sent close to an adversary can be damaging. And if the target's big enough, I'm sure to hit part of it."

"You're confident enough in using it, then?"

"With a man of Mirrors at my side and this, how could I not be confident? Besides, I'm rather tired of this room and the confines of Shaidra's hospitality. What I need is some fresh air and a chance to stretch my legs."

Simen laughed, took her hand and pulled her to her feet. "A woman eager for adventure. Who else would I want at my side? Come on, then, let's bid Mistress Shaidra farewell and be off." He opened the door to the room, and, keeping Jessa protectively behind him, stepped out into the hall.

Shaidra had set guards outside, but they were mere Shadows who fell at the first breath of Spellfire from Simen's hand, wisps of their insubstantial being drifting towards the ceiling.

As the couple made their way down the hall, Shaidra herself marched up the stairs towards them. Her face was set with determination, but her steps faltered, proving Simen's conviction that she knew her Magic was no match for his.

"Madam," he said quietly, "move aside and let us pass. I would rather leave you here to rule your kingdom than destroy you, but the choice is yours, not mine."

Shaidra started to raise her hand and snapped it back against her breast an instant later. "You are more perceptive than I thought, Sur. You have proven yourself against me already. I will not challenge you here." She turned sideways to let them pass.

As she watched the Magicians head for the palace door, she smiled. "Not here," she whispered. "But out there? Magic turns on itself in my realm, Sorcerer. Out there, I have the upper hand." She waited until Simen and Jessa were outside and then strode up the stairs to her own chambers. There, she changed her gown into a soft brown traveling tunic with leather leggings, picked up her pack and slipped out the back door of the palace to the stables.

****

The Lady Jessa and Jiana had spent the day deep in study, excluding Sharia once again. But the young sorceress had taken a seat in the corner of the room, pretending to be deeply engrossed in a volume of Eldentales she had found tucked away in Jessa's pack. It would have been one of the texts an apprentice would study with her Mistress, but it was forgotten now as Jiana's interests strayed far from classical education. Whenever Sharia heard parts of the conversation between the woman and girl, it seemed they were far more interested in male anatomy and how men liked to use women for their pleasure.

"Out by the lake," Jessa said. " Are you sure?"

"Not too far," Jiana said. "It's an old inn, but very popular with the travelers who wander in from the wastes. Far from town so no one notices much what goes on there. Whisper Grove they call it."

"Lots of men?"

Jiana laughed then stole a quick glance over to the corner where Sharia was sitting. "More than enough, and hungry too," she said, her voice dropping to a murmur so the other girl could no longer make out what she was saying.

Sharia leaned forward, pretending to stretch, but it was useless. She couldn't hear any more.

The day dragged on into dusk, the Windchange promising a moonless night. Frustrated with the strain of listening to what Jessa and Jiana were saying and bored with the puzzling language of the ancient tome, Sharia had drifted off into a doze. When she woke up, the room was empty. The other two Sorceresses were gone.

She got up and hurried out to find Kala. The Seer was in the Inn's common room, eating a light meal. When she saw Sharia, she beckoned. "Come, have a bite to eat. It's going to be a long night."

"Lady Jessa and Jiana are gone."

"I know," Kala answered as Sharia sat across from her. "Up to no good, I imagine. I saw them leave a span ago. "

"I sent a Sifting with Lady Jessa," Kala said. "It will help us find out where they've gone. It wasn't as strong as I'd like. There is something Dark in your false Mistress' heart that seeks to deny my Sight."

"I overheard them talking about an inn near the lake," Sharia replied. "The Whispering Grove. They were talking about the men who go there." She lowered her eyes, blushing. "They said some other things about men, too, My Lady. Should I try to tell you?"

Kala smiled, reached across the table and took Sharia's hand in hers. "No need, Sharia. I can tell even without the benefit of Sight it's not anything either one of us needs to hear again. If we're right about the two of them, they are Shadow, and nothing they say is meant for honest hearts to hear."

"You know a great deal about Shadows?" Sharia asked.

"More than I'd like to and less than I want to," Kala conceded. "What I lack are the weapons to defeat them. For that, I need your Magic."

"Spellfire," Sharia said softly. "I don't know if I can."

"It won't be easy," Kala said. "You'll have to surrender every vow you've ever made to your River."

Sharia nodded. "Magic Unrestrained, anger driving the Power through my hand. Will surrendering to the lust to destroy. The very opposite of all Magiskeep teaches." She closed her eyes, and began to rock slowly back and forth, caught up in the spell of an

Elden chant, *"Ancient rage against the foe. Takes heart where heart must never go. Fury's fire, destruction's might, sent to rend the endless Night. Shadow's fear and Shadow's end, With this weapon, Light defend."*

Shaken by the intensity of the girl's trance, Kala squeezed her hand, "Sharia? Come back to me."

"Hungry Shadows bloodlust born to the Darkness ever sworn. Let this hand with fire fill. Their corruption ever kill. Close my heart to gentle deeds. Wrath is all it ever needs."

"Sharia!" Kala almost shouted.

The girl opened her eyes, her lips twisted in an ugly, cruel grin. "I am ready, Madam Juris, to exact justice if you so command."

"Sharia, what have you done?"

"Called the River," Sharia replied. "I didn't spend all that time reading the Eldenlore without learning something." Her eyes glittered, cold and hard. "I could not depend on calling the Spellfire any other way. It's not my nature to either cruel or passionate enough. For now, consider me your sword, My Lady. All you need to do is point me toward the enemy."

Kala shivered in the face of Sharia's claim and Sight came unbidden. *She fell into an abyss of darkness, heavy and suffocating all around her. Too wise in the ways of Vision to fight, she let the black air envelop her, controlling her breathing so she would not panic.*

Too much like Jamus' cave in Cowltop, too much like the Shadow of Tamor, too much like the beating of dark wings in the night air. Too much like hate, grief, regret, vengeance, pain, rage, deceit, and all the memories she abhorred. The little golden haired girl danced in the darkness, reveling in its power, her eyes like soulless arymis, her lips twisted in a scowl. Gone was innocence, gone morality, all replaced by overwhelming fury. She shuddered again as the world righted, the Vision fleeing before her own indomitable Will.

Yet around Sharia, the trace of Vision lingered and Kala knew how dangerous the girl had become. Worse, she looked somehow darker, even more like Jiana than she had before—sister to Darkwing's daughter.

"Come, then, Sharia. Let's go find these Shadows. Perhaps it is time to put them back where they belong."

****

Simen wasted no time in leading Jessa out of the palace, but once they were out the door, he hesitated. "Follow close behind me Jessa, and don't question where I step. Everything out here is reflection. For me, as a child of the Way, it's not hard to see the reality. For you? If it worries you too much, look through your amulet as we go along and you'll soon learn to trust me."

"I need no lessons in trusting you Simen. It's my eyes that need to learn not to trust. Go ahead. I'll stick close."

Despite her attempt to reassure him, Jessa found the surroundings completely disorienting. After just a few steps into the yard, she took hold of Simen's hand behind his back and let him pull her along. She tried to deny what she saw as they made their way out into the wasteland, ignoring a boulder that appeared on her right as Simen seemed to dart into it, but it was nearly impossible. Finally, out of a desperate frustration filling every footstep, she lifted the mirrored crystal to her eye with her free hand and peered through it.

Though still a bit distorted by being reflected three times through the gem, the world suddenly righted itself. Or, at least the path Simen was choosing righted itself and his decisions began to make sense. Her gait became steadier as her confidence in him swelled. Now, like a dance partner at the ball, she let him lead, her own eyes ignoring all but his broad back, his hand in hers, and the movements of his body directing the movements of hers.

They walked like that for what might have been a span when Simen stopped. "It's not far now. I remember this path. The cabins are just over the next rise."

Jessa nodded, realized he couldn't see her and said, "Rise or fall, Simen? One way or another, I'll follow you. Are the cabins chanted too?"

"Like Shaidra's palace, it seems. A welcome break from the reflections out here. They afford the residents a little respite from the deceptions. We'll find true friends there."

As he'd predicted, they made their way over a small rise and soon were on the porch of the main cabin.

It was Gunder who met them at the door and ushered them inside. "Welcome back, Lord Simen. I see you had a good fishing expedition of your own. That's the prettiest catch I've ever seen."

"Lady Jessa," Simen offered, introducing her as he led her into the cabin. "Mistress of the First Art of Magiskeep, and the woman I love. Jessa, the former residents of Loren, captured as we were by Shaidra's traps. From what I've seen, she's planned to take the whole village and replace everyone with Shadows.

"To what end?"

A base for the Darkness itself, or a Kingdom of her own?" Simen said. "Who's to know for sure? I haven't quite figured out if she is focused on her own conquests or is subject to Darkwing. In the end, it doesn't matter. She's stolen the lives of these good people and imprisoned them here. We need to get them all back home."

"And jest how does ye think ta do that, Master? Jest how powerful is thy Magic?" Molly asked.

"It's not my Magic that matters. It's Shaidra's. And hers is all based on the Way of Mirrors, my birthplace. Reflections never have the strength of the reality they copy. Most of you have already learned to navigate outside these walls, challenging the reflections with your own perception of the truth. All we need to do is pursue the truth and we will conquer her."

"How?"

"Take me to the gateway, and I'll do the rest."

"Where be that?"

"Wherever you came into this world. You left by the lake, didn't you?"

"Sure it be," Gunder agreed making up a story quickly to cover what had actually happened. "I was anglin' fer a nice big brownyfish and fell inta the water. Next thing's I knowed, I was in the wastes, flat on me face in the sand."

"I were takin' a bath in Lillypond and ended up on a sand dune on me backside," Michah said.

Soon it was clear all the captives had similar stories, all connected to the lake or one of its side tributaries. But where was the lake? There was no such water in the Wastes. Simen was wondering whether his theory was right, when one of the villager spoke up. "Sandy Mount. I climbed it onct. From atop I could see all kinds o' row mounds o' sand leadin' ta littler hills. Ne'er much thought about it then, but iffen I coulda drawed a map it woulda looked like the streams an' ponds o' home. Iffen we's lookin' fer the reflection of water…"

"Sand,"Payton agreed. "But there ain't no way in. I mean ye kin fall inta a lake, but a pile o' sand? Ye climbed it and still ye was here in the Wastes. Ye shoulda falled through back ta Loren, eh?"

"There has to be a door," Simen told them. "Some place in the mount that's different from the rest. How far is it from here?

"Two spans walk iffen ya know the path. Four iffen ya gotta sorts it."

"I don't need to sort. The rest of you? "

"Most of us is good on the trails," Molly offered. "Gunder an' me go out all the time lookin' fer a way out. Ya think ya knows one, then?"

"I can find it if anyone can. Pack all the belongings you want to take out of here with you. Any weapons too. I doubt Shaidra will let us go quietly. Lady Jessa and I have Magic to protect us, but there's naught wrong with a sword or bow in times of trouble."

"I gots me a whole quiver o' arrows," Farrel said. "Tried a bit o'huntin' out in the hills. Ain't had a whole lot o' luck but I learned ta shoot straight."

"Good," Simen answered. "We may need the distraction. "Let's be be on our way. Hard to say when the sun will set, but I'd rather be looking for that portal than wasting time here talking about it."

Chapter 14

"I'll ask one more time," Jamus said softly as he propelled Serimsimen out into the street, looking for an alley where they could talk without being overheard. "Where is my brother?"

"Here," Serimsimen replied, trying for all he was worth to maintain his composure. Even Shadows knew fear when it came to Magic. He could feel Jamus' Power surging in the River even without any command from him. "Don't you recognize me?"

"I recognize a fraud. You made too many mistakes, Shadow. I'd cast you to ashes right now if I didn't think you had information I needed. You have two choices. Either tell me what I want to know without pain, or wear a Spellfire collar on your neck and tell me to avoid its sting."

Serimsimen shuddered now, his body trembling despite all his efforts to appear calm in the face of the threat. To answer Jamus was to defy Darkwing. To deny Jamus was to suffer torture beyond imagining. It was a choice of no choice. "He is with Mistress Shaidra, in the Way."

"And just who is Shaidra?"

The question bolstered Serimsimen's confidence. Knowledge was a sort of power. He would have to play his hand carefully. "Mistress of all Reflections. The Way belongs to her."

The answer was a mistake. "I am not a fool. I am a Master of the Way myself, Sur, and I've traveled its halls more times than you might dare count. If this Shaidra were indeed its guardian, I would have met her a long time ago. Now, one more time, Who is Shaidra?"

Serimsimen bowed his head in defeat. "She holds a hall of her own, blessed by Blackwing himself. She does his bidding when he so commands. The rest of the time, she chants for herself."

"And now?"

Serimsimen shrugged. "The Dark Lord knows what she's doing, but the idea was hers. To command a village—a province--in the world of mortals would be a useful tool. Call it an experiment if you will. She takes men in and replaces them with their reflections."

"To what end? Simply to control a village in one of the far Provinces? It doesn't make much sense."

"You're here, aren't you?" Serimsimen watched for Jamus' reaction. He smiled when he saw the Rivermaster start. Once again he tried to press an advantage. "Ever the prey, Kiselor? Would you sacrifice yourself to save the innocents?"

"There's never a need for sacrifice when the River's at my hand, Shadow," Jamus replied evenly. Don't underestimate me."

"It's not my estimation you need to worry about. I am just a reflection sent to take your precious Simen's place. You can banish me in an instant with your Spellfire as you've already said. But what then will happen to my reflection? That's what your brother is, you know. We are connected by the Way's chantings."

Jamus had not considered that. If what the Shadow was saying was true, resolving the abductions was not as simple as it seemed. "How many villagers have been taken?"

"Twelve, at my last count," Serimsimen answered. "Add your Follyman and that woman of his and it makes fourteen. Fourteen lives in your hands."

Jamus raised his hand, surrounding Serimsimen in a silvrin sphere, binding him to impotence. None of his dark intent could escape, and if he tried to use Magic, the spells would reflect back on him. "Come with me, or go your own way. Until I choose, it makes no difference."

Gritting his teeth and all too aware of his captivity, Serimsimen seemed to shrink into himself. "I will wait for you at the Inn while you seek out the girl's parents. If I can sing a song or two to earn a drink, I'll drown my sorrow in ale and leave you to your mastery. I want no part in the rest of it."

Jamus watched the imposter go back inside and then he went to the stables.

Soon he was on his way to the hills where Jiana's father's farm lay. The stableman had pointed him to the trail, admitting that he knew very little about the family except that the girl was a suspected Sorceress.

"Take care, when ye go," he'd said. "We don't hold with the Magic here. It be a good thing the girl's gone, but ye need to wonder where her blood come from. It's said the Magic passes down from the parents."

Jamus smiled at that, thanking the man for the warning. He had no fear of Magic, of course, but he still needed to be careful.

He rode for a full span as the sun warmed the air, the clear blue sky promising a good day to make such a journey. The trail divided by a tall oaker tree and he took the left fork. Soon tall mountain pines lined the path as the trail grew steeper. Whim's powerful hindquarters carried them easily up a steep grade and when they paused at the top, Jamus saw the little farm spread out below. The house was nestled against a cliff, with a barn off to the right. A few rustic sections of fencing seemed broken and neglected around it. The fields of corn were wilted, and what looked to be a vegetable garden was overgrown with weeds. A skinny cow was grazing on a dry patch of grass while a few chickens scratched in the dirt nearby.

As they rode down to the yard, Jamus could see at least one far too-thin horse with its head drooping out of a ramshackle stall. As much as he wanted to meet Jiana's parents, the sight of the pathetic animals drew him to the barn instead of the house.

Hungry.

"I know, Whim," he said as he dismounted. He opened the barn door, and nearly drew back, his nose assaulted by the smell of decaying flesh.

One horse lay dead in his stall, starved to death. Two more were so emaciated they were barely able to stand, and a third was lying in a pile of manure, groaning.

Jamus wasted no time and hurried first to the stricken horse's stall. He knelt and the creature's side, laid his hand on its neck and sent a chanting of healing and restoration. *The air grew heavy with Master's Art. Jamus was drawn down into the waters but just as he reached for his Power, a vicious current swelled against him, spinning his body around. He was enveloped in crystal clear streams reflecting his image, reflecting the animal, and finally, threatening to reflect his Magic.*

Mirrors, the Way, the River trapped in Reflection. Shaidra's world, leaking into his own. He adjusted quickly before he killed the horse with a Healing and instead Willed it to die under his hand.

Willed pain, Willed pain, Willed starvation, Willed its breath to cease and its heart to falter.

The River leapt to his commands, reflections whirling about bouncing off one another. The horse took a deep breath, its taut skin softened as new flesh covered its bones. Then, with a snort of relief, it struggled to its feet, leaving the Rivermaster on the floor of a filthy stall, spent and unable to stand himself.

*****

Even in the dark, as they walked along the winding trail to the Whispering Grove, Kala could feel Sharia's confidence in her newfound power increase. The girl had seemed to age ten circles in a span, and she'd lit a maglit torch with a simple wave of her hand as if it were the simplest spell she'd ever cast. She was not Jamus, of course, but Kala was finding an unexpected confidence in her presence. What was making her uneasy was what they might face once they reached the inn.

"Don't hesitate, Sharia. I'll do all I can to assure you if what we suspect about Jessa and Jiana is right. I'm going to need to depend on you judgment too, though. You know far more about Shadow Magic than I do."

"I'm still a novice in that skill, My Lady. Yet I am convinced that this Mistress Jessa is not my Master. As for Jiana? There is something Dark about her, I know it. And yet, I feel a strange connection now and again when I am near her. It worries me a little."

"I don't need a lack of confidence from you now, Sharia."

"I'll do what I must, Madam Juris. When the time comes, not before."

Kala nodded. The Inn was in sight now, its windows shining with the light of lanterns inside the common room downstairs. Above floors, one or two windows showed candlelight but most were dark some even with the shutters closed.

They paused at the door, each woman taking a deep, steadying breath. Then, the stepped inside. The room was nearly empty, except for one lone man at a table sipping a cup of keldherb and the innkeeper himself, stationed at behind a polished wooden bar.

"Well met, my Ladies! Welcome to the Grove. Warm food and bright lights on a dark night. What brings ye here so late?" he called out, beckoning to them. "More pretty faces to charm me? What have I done to be twice blessed on the same day?"

"Twice blessed?" Kala said moving over to him. "Tell me, Sur, have you other such ladies in the house?"

He grinned at her. "Women of beauty, yes. The term 'ladies' may not apply." He winked. "Ye do appear of another sort."

"These women, where are they now?" Kala asked.

He gestured towards the staircase. "Last room at the far end of the hall. Said they wanted privacy and quiet for a nice evening with their companions."

"They're not alone then."

"Perhaps I have not judged them fairly, but I do not think the men were their husbands. Whether money passed hands or not I do not know, but I hold no ill will against a woman what needs to earn her keep, however she does it."

"Not worried about your Inn's reputation, then." Sharia said smiling sweetly at him. "I take it your Inn caters to the miners and a rougher sort."

Kala was surprised at the girl's forwardness, taken aback now to see she had physically matured even more since leaving the main village. When she saw how the innkeeper's eyes widened at Sharia's remark and then how he smiled back at her, she nearly laughed. Had her mission not been so serious, the circumstances might actually have been quite entertaining. "Men such as that do make for a good business," she said at last.

The Innkeeper snapped out of his fixation on Sharia. "Ladies such as ye need not know such men, indeed. Now, can I get ye some food and drink?"

"The women may well be the friends we've been searching for," Kala said. "If so, we have important news for them that cannot wait. We'll just go up to talk to them."

"I dare say they said they didn't want to be disturbed."

"Oh, they won't mind us," Sharia assured him as she led the way up the stairs. "Stay behind me, Kala," she hissed under her breath. "If one of them strikes, I don't want you in the way."

The room was at the end of a long hall. The thick wooden door muffled the sounds inside, but it was unlocked. Putting her finger to her lips, Sharia pushed it open.

Kala gasped.

Jessa was poised over a man bound and gagged on the bed. Stripped from the waist down, he was writhing against his restraints, his eyes wide with horror as the shining blade of her dagger descended to his belly. Jiana, half naked, sprawled on the carpet over another panicked victim who was bound to the leg of the bed and a nearby chair. She was distracted by Jessa's blade and didn't even turn to look when the door opened.

All Kala heard and saw in the next instant was Jessa's vicious snarl and the falling dagger and then the room erupted in a blinding white light.

Jessa screamed as the Spellfire struck her, shattering first her arm holding the blade and then coursing up into her shoulder before her entire body shuddered and exploded into a shower of white sparks. Black coils of smoke spiraled up with dizzying speed as the Magic enveloped her form, searing her to oblivion.

But Sharia had wasted no time watching the results of her attack. Instead, even as Kala gaped at the destruction, she threw coil after coil of Spellfire charged ropes around Jiana's body, a fraction away from touching her, building a menacing cage around the other woman to hold her at bay without killing her.

Jiana's face twisted into a mask of fury, her dark eyes burning as she faced her attacker. "Shetark, daughter of a rimsnake, how dare you intrude?"

"Get off him slowly, Jiana. Move too quickly and the bars will touch. You've seen what Spellfire can do to Shadows. No need to kill yourself yet."

Jiana got up, moving in slow motion as Sharia's fingers played in the air. Once she was on her feet, she stood absolutely still within her prison.

Only then did Sharia turn her attention to the two victims. More aware than she realized of the curious reflections shimmering within the Magic this close to the lake, she instinctively cast a spell of binding, freeing both men in an instant. "Put on your clothes, go home, and tell no one of what happened here," she said. "I can as easily end your sad lives if I need to in order to promise secrecy."

The man on the bed gulped and nodded. "No need, Sorceress. Ain't got words ta tell nobody anyhows. Who's gonna want ta believe it?"

"I thank ye fer me skin," the second man said. "An iffen a word bond is all I needs ta keep it, ye gots it from me. Asides, cain't say I'd be more'n shamed ta tell it." He pulled up his pants, grabbed his tunic from the floor and with only one quick, shivering glance at Jiana, ran from the room. His equally-shaken companion followed close behind.

"Why didn't you kill me too?" Jiana asked through tight lips.

Sharia studied her carefully. Jiana had matured, much as she had, her girlish body rounded out to womanhood, as if somehow the two of them were linked in some way she did not understand. "I need to know who you are."

Jiana laughed. "Ever the fools, these Sorcerers. Answers always matter more than practicality." Then she paused dramatically. "Oh, I nearly forgot. You've murdered your Mistress of the First Art, haven't you. Too bad there is no one but your own poor skill to lead you to Comprehension now. I'll tell you what. If you want to know who I am, I'll play a game with you. Four guesses and if you fail, I'll touch these bars and you'll never know, now, will you."

"Can you Sift her?" Sharia asked leaning close to whisper into Kala's ear.

"Darkness, that's all," Kala said. "I'm sorry."

"How much does she look like me?" Sharia asked then. "I've changed. Has she?"

Kala's brow furrowed in concentration as she studied both young women. Curious that now, even with the new age difference, they still looked so much alike. Magic had matured Sharia, while Jiana still remained a young girl. Jiana's hair was dark, Sharia's light, but feature for feature, they might have been twins. Strange she had never noticed that before. "She could be your sister."

"Or my reflection," Sharia said. "Those ancient texts I read speak of the One True Reflection from the end of the Way."

Now it was Kala's turn to become teacher. "Lord Jamus spoke of that. It is the test of the Waymaster to meet his true reflection and conquer it. His was named Suman and he carried him in his heart for a long time before he finally accepted that part of himself. It is said the True Reflection is the exact opposite of the True Self. Either the Waymaster conquers it, or it conquers him."

"The she is my Darkness," Sharia said and Jiana's snarl confirmed it. "Much as you would like be to believe you would sacrifice yourself for no reason, I doubt you will ever touch those bars of your own volition, Jiana. You see, I know myself well enough to know I would give my life for a just cause. You, on the other hand have no such scruples. So, tell me, my Shadow, just why you are here?"

"To have you take me as your own," Jiana replied.

Kala shuddered. Suddenly the utter blackness she had Seen every time she had tried to Sift Jiana made sense. Who else but the Black Dragon's spawn, Darkwing's Daughter, could be so defiant to the light of her Vision--the Black River, the White River's reflection. If Jiana were so, what did that mean of Sharia? For the first time, she found herself studying her young companion with more than casual interest. It made no sense. "She's not your True Reflection, Sharia, no matter what she claims. How can she be? You would have to have a dreadful capacity for evil in your heart, and as much as she'd like to believe that, I simply cannot."

"Nor can I," Sharia agreed readily. "So I either have a liar in my snare or an imposter who has taken on my image for some other purpose." She turned back to Jiana who was struggling now to keep her body still. It seemed to be getting harder and harder for her. "So, Shadow. I ask again," Sharia said, "Just exactly who or what are you, and why are you here?"

*****

It took Jamus longer than usual to recover from the horse's Healing. The need to reverse the intent of his spells had worn him in both mind and body. Now, though, with a new understanding, he was able to restore the other horses to better flesh and do the same for all the neglected animals on the farm. He filled mangers with sweet hay, feed buckets with careful measures of grain, and water troughs with fresh clear water. A wave of his hand cleaned and bedded the stalls with new straw and set the barn to some sense of order.

He took more time than he needed, avoiding what he expected to find in the house. When he finally approached the door, he was almost reluctant to open it. The sight inside confirmed his worst fears. On the bed lay a desiccated corpse of a woman, her belly gutted, her body contorted in dreadful pains of death. She was dry skin draped over bones as if all the fluids of her body had been drained away. Her graying hair was the only hint of her age for the rest of her was too wrinkled to tell any of her story. She had been stripped naked and bound to the bedposts with sharp twine that cut into the little skin she had left.

The corpse was not the only tale to tell. On the floor lay a pile of clothing, stretched out in the shape of a man's body. There were rusty stains on the chest of his shirt, the fabric slit open by a sharp dagger Beside the man was an empty tray and a pitcher that may have held water. His right sleeve, now empty, still wore a fieron shackle, chained to a ring bolted into the ironwood framing of the house itself. He had been held prisoner, left to starve with only enough rations to sustain him for a Sevenstin at best.

He had been of the Magic. Jamus was certain of it, for there was a faint residue of ash on the clothes, the sign the body who had once worn them had faded to the oblivion of the River's promised end for all who called its name.

He knelt by clothes, moved the shirt a little, and found a piece of parchment under it. The writing was faint, smudged charcoal somehow pulled from the fireplace off to the right. *"Killed her mother, little girl. So much blood. By the Hand, why leave me. Drink only enough to fill her belly and then go. So hungry. Need water. My girl, Jiana."*

It was a pitiful message. A mad raving, or perfect sense?

This was Jiana's home. Was that her mother, and the pile of clothes all that remained of her father? By his name, he had been Touched by the River, a Magician whose body would vanish to mere dust after his death. Had his own daughter left him to die after drinking enough of his blood to give her one half the True Life a Shadow sought?

His own daughter.

Or something else—something wearing his daughter's skin.

Jamus tried to close his mind to the thought. It was over for the man now, and the woman. He'd come too late to save them. Caring for their animals and giving them a proper resting place was all he could do to make amends for the Shadow's offenses.

Until he was sure, it would have to be enough.

The efforts of carving a tomb in the cave beyond the house, burying the remains, and then setting the house itself to right, taxed him more than he expected. He had to test each chanting to see if it demanded truth or reflection in the distorted world of the little valley. Whatever was corrupting the Magic in Lovental reached beyond the lower village even here into the wilderness. He would have stayed to rest in the house before heading back, but his nerves were on edge and he was starting to worry about those he had left behind in Loren.

After assuring himself all the animals were well tended for the night, he headed back down the trail towards the southern village. He had to warn Kala.

Only the darkness of Weswin in strange terrain kept him from lifting Whim's strides to speed the journey along.

*****

Jessa stumbled and nearly fell, her head reeling. Gunder turned just in time to catch her, calling out to Simen up ahead of the group. "Hold up, Master. Yer Lady's a might faint. Mayhaps we need ta stop fer a mite."

They'd been walking less than a span, but even Simen was finding it hard to keep his focus. Since they'd left the cabins, the reflections had seemed to be twisting and turning on themselves, sometimes reversing to reality and then reflecting back. He hurried back to Jessa. "What's wrong?"

Supported by Gunder's strong arms, she was finding it hard to stay on her feet. "I don't know, Simen. It's as if something suddenly was pulled out of me, torn from my very being."

"Magic?"

"Or the loss of it," she said, taking a sip of water from the flask he offered her. "I'm feeling better now. It was just such a shock."

"Are you sure you can go on? We can stop for a while if you need to rest."

She shook her head and patted Gunder's arm. "If this gentleman will lend me his hand for a bit more, I'll be fine, really I will. We don't have time to waste sitting around here while the sun drops in the sky. The last thing we want is to be out here in the dark."

Simen squinted at the sun which seemed to be just hanging in the sky where it had been for the last two spans since they'd decided to leave the little settlement in search of the portal. "I've had no sense of time since we stepped out into this wasteland, " he said. "For all I know, it might be night already and that sun just a reflection of the real one fallen long below the horizon."

Jessa straightened, stretching her back. "All the more reason to go on and an inspiration for me. Another challenge to Comprehension to keep my mind busy and my body awake. Let's get going before I have to decide whether Easwin will be Weswin before I even notice."

Simen smiled, "A sense of humor is a good sign, My Love." He kissed her lightly on the cheek, much to Gunder's embarrassment, and headed back up to the front of the group.

They hiked for another span before the mountain loomed suddenly in front of them, appearing, it seemed, out of nowhere in the vast expanse of sand and rocks.

"There," Molly pointed. "That's the mountain, I'm sure of it. I remember that cluster of rocks off to the left. Well, they're not really on the left as I found out when I tumbled over them."

"The portal must be somewhere in the mound," Simen said as they drew near. He was about to cast a spell to see if he could discover anything when the sound of galloping hoofs spun him around. "Get behind me!" he shouted to the others as he saw Shaidra and a group of mounted warriors riding towards them.

Jessa leapt to his side holding her amulet in front of her. "I'm ready, Simen. I hope two Magicians will be enough."

Simen threw up his hand, casting a barrier of shimmering bars in front of them. Shaidra just managed to rein her horse to a stop before she hit it but two of her soldiers met it head on, horses and men screaming and writing as the potent Magic sliced them to strands of dark smoke. "Shadows," he whispered to Jessa. "Spellfire will be enough. We just need to keep them from getting past us."

The words had barely passed his lips when Shaidra raised her hand, ready to signal an attack. "No one leaves my kingdom without my consent, Follyman. Surrender now, or face my army."

"Twenty do not make an army, Madam. And Shadows do not fare well against Spellfire. Already two have fallen to my Magic. How many more will you sacrifice?"

In answer, Shaidra cast her own spell, one Simen could not easily sift. A shield of dark smoke surrounded each warrior and when the first rode forward at her command, he and his horse easily passed through the barricade Simen had set. Fabin, one of the refugees, recklessly rushed forward with his axe to swing at the attacking knight. With an almost casual ease, the warrior swung his huge broadsword at his enemy, slicing his arm. The only thing that saved Fabin was a blast of icicles from Jessa who had reacted desperately to his defense and sent a chanting without using her amulet.

The warrior laughed and started to swing again, but this time it was Simen who sent the killing Spellfire at him as the others pulled Fabin, moaning and bleeding, into a protective circle.

Torn now between healing Fabin and defending against the warriors, Simen hesitated and it was all Shaidra needed to see his weakness and send in the rest of her troops.

The Wastes erupted into a full scale battle. Jessa, amulet in hand, began sending blasts of Spellfire into the fight as Simen, the choice made for him, joined in the defense.

A black horse screamed as its legs were scorched from its body by Magic, and as it fell, Gunder lopped off its rider's head with his axe. The Shadow's body writhed on the ground, groping for its weapon as a second later Spellfire tore into it, sending it to ashes.

Two knights headed for Jessa at the same time, but she held her ground, sending measured bolts of white-hot flames first to one and then the other a fraction before he trampled her. Simen's hands were full of Magic, searing three warriors with one wide swath of power and a fourth as with a spear of flame as it headed towards Molly.

The air exploded with the energy of Magic Unrestrained.

"Simen!" Jessa cried, "Shaidra! Stop her!"

Simen spun from the melee to see Shaidra raising her hand, about to direct a chanting at the small group of women shielding three children behind them. He threw up a silvrin shield in front of the group as blue flame shot from Shaidra's fingers. The spell hit the silvrin surface and reflected back to the sender, hitting her square in her stomach. She screamed and doubled over, stricken by her own Magic. One of the knights grabbed her horse's bridle, pulling it along behind him as he fled back towards the palace. All but one of the remaining Shadow warriors spun their mounts and followed behind their wounded mistress.

The last knight, caught in full charge when his commander was struck, could not stop his horse and together they plunged full force into a small crevice in the mountain's side and simply disappeared.

Five of Simen's group lay wounded on the ground. But the battle had been won.

And, they had found the portal back to Turan.

Chapter 15

Jiana was finding it harder and harder to keep from squirming inside her prison. The girl's body had a life of its own, it seemed, perhaps fueled to the hope of True Life by the taste of the man's blood. Sandu had been a minor Mage, of little consequence in the River, but even small Magic mattered to a Shadow seeking feast. All she needed was one more drink of Sorcerer's blood to gain the gift her kind desired. Wearing the girl's skin had tempted her with a longing to feel warmth in her limbs and all the other sensations of living. Now, a Sorcerer stood before her, a perfect victim to her wiles if only she could play her well. All she needed was one sip of blood, one swallow of precious fluid from Sharia and it would be done. Then, only the Breath of the Dragon would be her enemy.

All she needed to do was play the part. "I am Reflection, no more," she said. "Your darkness, as you say. You are not whole without me."

"I am content without you," Sharia countered. "I don't need you."

"Ah, but my Lady, already you have used me—to good end if destroying the false Jessa served you well. It was she who taught me to seek sustenance from those poor men. It was all her idea."

"There were other victims."

"They were hers, Sharia, not mine. Yes, I was with her, but even I, your Darkness, was appalled by what she did. Despite my nature, your good nature shines even in your opposite. I was horrified to see her feast."

"And yet you came here, and from all accounts were ready to join in her murdering ways," Kala said. "All I see in you is black intent, nothing more."

"Have you Searched Shadows before, Madam Juris? Often the Light is denied by Reflection's power. This land is cursed by Reflections. Surely you have noticed."

Kala shook her head. "I do not Touch the River as Sorcerers do."

"Then I will tell you. I am not the only Shadow here. And since I am not the only person you have Sifted since you came to Loren, then I am sure you have seen Darkness in others as well."

To that, Kala nodded. "I thought it strange."

"Lady Jessa is not the only one deceiving you."

"Who else?"

"Half the village by now, if the Shadowmistress has her way."

"Shadowmistress?"

"The Lady Shaidra. She claims Blackwing as her father." Jiana shivered quite deliberately. "She is a powerful Sorceress."

"A Reflection of the Way?"

Jiana shook her head. "I know not, My Lady. She commands a kingdom of her own in the Way and she's the one who took Mistress Jessa."

"And what of Master Simen? He and Jessa rode out of Loren together."

"She would want them both, I suppose."

"Master Simen rode with Lord Jamus to the mountain village," Sharia said. "If he's not the real Simen, then Jamus is in danger."

"Lord Jamus is a Master of the Mirrors," Kala said. "If anyone can take care of himself, he can. Besides, there's no way to warn him from here. Dealing with Jiana is about all we can do."

"Give me your hand, Sharia," Jiana pleaded, extending hers as far as she dared. "My Darkness will become your strength. Virtue has no value against the Shadows. You've already had to chant simply to use Spellfire. Together, we would need no words to cast against Shaidra's army."

"How can I trust you?" Sharia asked, shaking her head. "You've tormented me ever since I met you."

Jiana's eyes filled with tears, hard-drawn from a soul with no heart. Fortunately, the skin she wore had once had feelings. "Jessa's doing, not mine. All I wanted was a friend. She corrupted me with her lies. I am, after all, still a child, easily deceived."

Sharia hesitated, studying the girl. It was true, she was still a child while she herself had matured with the River's Power.

Deception indeed, for if Jiana were her True Reflection, why was she
still so young? Yet, her knowledge of the Way was limited by what
she had read in the Elden texts. It would be wise to be wary.
Accepting Jiana would give the other girl's strength and an edge of
indifferent cruelty useful should a battle against the Shadows face
her. But it also meant a sacrifice of her own virtue and values which
she could only hope would be strong enough to overcome Jiana's
desires to own her body.

"Why should you fear me?" Jiana asked. "I am merely one
moment in your life when you peered into a mirror with your own
anger. I was once a part of you. All you would be doing is taking
back that moment."

Sharia looked at Kala, but the Seer could offer nothing. Sight
eluded her in the face of Jiana's Darkness and all she really knew of
the Way of Mirrors was what Jamus had told her. The Masters of
Grandisite rarely spoke of Reflections. "It is your decision, Sharia.
The Juris has no advice for you."

Sharia nodded now and raised her hand. Extending it to
Jiana, she banished the bars of Spellfire.

Jiana reached out with her left hand to grasp Sharia's right
hand. Her lips curled in a smile as their fingers touched. Then, with
a flash of silver, she struck at the Sorceress with a dagger concealed
in her right hand, slashing the sleeve of Sharia's gown, drawing
blood in her forearm. She leapt, her mouth agape.

Kala screamed a warning too late.

But Sharia had not entirely played the fool. Her whole body
exploded with the white flame of Spellfire, the Magic searing out of
her skin.

In midleap, Jiana could not pull back as the deadly power
engulfed her. She screamed now, the Magic tearing her apart,
sending sparks and ashes into the air as she twisted and writhed in
agony. Black smoke enveloped her, swirling in a desperate attempt
to hold itself to the skin she wore. The effort was futile. A whirlwind
of black shadow bolted upwards as the body fell to the floor. In one
last horrendous cry, the Shadow Jiana was no more, leaving the
remnants of the real Jiana's form lying crumpled on the floor.

Outside the inn, the sky rumbled, thick, dark clouds covering the full moon and passing over its face on huge beating wings. There was a screech of rage as a heavy wind rushed over the roof, shattering slate shingles as they fell to the earth below.

A huge clap of thunder roared once in the whipping wind.

Daughter.

And then, there was silence.

*****

Jamus was nearly blown off Whim's back by the sudden blast of wind. He looked up to the sky, for a moment imagining he saw wings brushing the moon aside. But he had no time to sort it all out. He was passing the lake and as the water whipped itself into waves.

The world tumbled into chaos as a huge black horse and rider bolted out of the waterfall, charging at them in full fury. Dark flames shot from the rider's hand, his cries of rage echoing against the cliffs.

Jamus clutched at the reins, but Whim had the bit in his teeth and an answering rage pulsing in his muscles. He leapt at the attacker, teeth bared, hoofs striking to kill. Thrown back in the saddle, off balance, Jamus had to hold on with both hands, until he could catch up with his mount's furious lunge.

He ducked just in time as within a fraction of a second the Darkfire seared past his head. With no thought beyond panic, he raised his own hand to let a bolt of Spellfire, charged with his surprise, explode out towards his attacker.

The white flame struck home. The dark rider screamed once and, plunging to the ground, seemed to burst into a shower of dark cinders and then simply vanish. The horse, untouched by the fire, collided with Whim, but its substance was so insubstantial, it passed through and past the silver stallion's body and continued to gallop with long, frantic strides out into the mountain passes.

Whim trumpeted again, this time in triumph, spinning around to watch his fleeing opponent. But Jamus felt no satisfaction. Instead, his stomach turned with the sickening stench of Spellfire and a disconcerting queasiness born of having faced the utter emptiness

of pure Shadow. Worse, as the stallion turned, he saw a deep pit
burned into the rocks once at his back where the Shadow's Darkfire
had struck, and he shuddered, remembering how close the flames
had passed to his cheek.

He stroked the silver stallion's neck, urging him around to
face the waterfall again. He had no way of knowing if the dark rider
had come upon them by mere chance or by design. Either way, he
did not intend to be caught unprepared again.

Then, he paused. Spellfire had worked perfectly. Magic
Unrestrained had not twisted upon itself as his other Powers often
had since coming to Lovental. Yet, even now, as he attempted to
weave a shield around them, his chanting opened even more space
around, making him all the more vulnerable. Again, it was exactly
the opposite of his intent.

Exactly the opposite.

Reflection.

He tested the air, weaving a thread of blackness towards the
left of the waterfall. He nodded in satisfaction as a shimmering
thread of silver streamed out to the right. As long as his Magic
required thought instead of being driven by the pure, elemental force
of Magic itself, he would have to weave it backwards to force it to
his Will.

Heat for ice and ice for fire—a simple equation, once a man
understood it.

But that meant his enemies already did understand and
worse, they had taken a strong foothold in his world. Now he was
certain the danger lay near, for the dark knight who had attacked him
from the waterfall was more than likely a guard to the gates of the
Shadow's kingdom.

Whim danced restlessly beneath him, tossing his head and
snorting.

The air had stilled again, the moonlight streaking silver light
from the sky reflected perfectly on the lake's flat surface. And
beyond, the waterfall shimmered too, a nearly perfect mirror.

Then, from its wall of water, another rider emerged—this
one riding a silver stallion.

Whim trumpeted a challenge and the other horse replied as it burst into a gallop, seeming to cross the surface of the lake without a splash. The rider, dressed in a royal blue tunic, raised his hand and Jamus, too slow to respond, had to rein Whim hard to avoid the Spellfire.

Whim fought the bit for the first time in his life, rearing and spinning to face the other horse. Black tendrils reached up from the lakeshore, grasping at his legs, and as he danced away, one of the coils wrapped around Jamus' leg, yanking him from the saddle. He fell into the shallows, Magic flying from his fingers to cut off the bonds as the horse and rider crashed into the shore.

The rider leapt from the saddle and rushed at Jamus, fully prepared for physical combat now that his Magic had failed. He slammed into him and struggled to pinion him in the water.

The two stallions met chest to chest, bodies colliding in grunts and fury. Whim spun and kicked his enemy full force in the ribs. The other horse spun back and lashed out with vicious hoofs as Whim darted to the side. They whirled again to face each other, a match in size and power, heads lowered, front hoofs pawing the earth, their heads snaking at each other, teeth snapping.

Jamus pounded his fists into his attacker's body, breaking the hold on his neck, rolling over to gain some leverage in the fight. He was a poor wrestler, but desperation served in place of skill as he managed to free his hand. Only moment, a moment was all he needed. Reflections. He had to fight the reflections.

The stallions reared and struck with their forefeet, but Whim was the wiser of the two and as the other horse went up, he feinted another rear and struck in low instead, crashing into his opponent's exposed belly, sending the other horse reeling backwards. The silver imposter lost his footing in the mud and he fell over backward as Whim struck at him again.

Jamus' head cleared long enough for him to send a blast of Spellfire again, this time striking the other Jamus in the chest. The Reflection screamed in pain, twisting away in a futile effort to escape his doom.

Whim pounded the other horse with his sharp hoofs until he heard Jamus cry out, "Enough, Whim! Enough." The enraged stallion stepped aside as his master sent a bolt of Spellfire into the fallen horse's body as well.

With a helpless moan, the horse's body melted into black smoke, blending with the clouds of darkness swirling from where his master lay. Then both simply vanished into the sky passing into wisps of clouds in the moonlit sky.

Bad dark gone. Whim kill.

"Yes," Jamus said. "The Reflections are gone. You did well." He was still gasping for air and starting to shiver from the cold and wet.

Bad dark. Not like Whim. Not like Best One. Different.

Jamus started. What did the horse mean? Had they been mere Reflections, when they had touched there should have been a joining. Instead, there had been a battle. Deceptions, rather. Something created out of a chanting he did not yet understand.

He looked at the lake again, backing away lest the black tendrils reach for him again. The waterfall still shimmered, its face reflecting the shoreline almost as if the water falling from it were solid and still. He shivered again, and without a thought cast a spell of drying only to find himself drenched in even colder water. Magic still turned on itself as it had so many times since he'd been here. But it was worse here at the lake and he forced his mind to think in reverse, drying his chilled body with a casting which might have drowned him in another place.

Whim nickered, and moved over to him. *Best One cold. We ride now. Find warm.*

Despite his Magic, Jamus was still cold and as he swung up into the saddle, he had to agree with his horse. What he needed was a warm fire in a protected place. Out here, in Norwin's spans, he was too easy a mark for whatever might emerge from the night air.

As they rode around the bend in the lakeshore trail, he saw the welcoming yellow lights of an inn up ahead. He nudged Whim into a trot and soon arrived in the stable yard of the Whispering Grove.

****

As Simen knelt to Heal one of the villager's wounds, he thought he saw a flash of silver vanish into the portal, but he was too absorbed in sorting out the complexities of Healing in reverse to take much note. The wounds were fortunately not too serious, and by guiding Jessa to work her own Magic backwards as well they managed to do a fair job of curing at least enough to make them all fit to travel again. With everyone ready to move off, he gathered them together.

"I will test the portal first. There's no point in risking everyone if it's not the way back to Loren."

Gunder stepped forward, bold for the first time in his life. "No, My Lord. Not you. If anything should happen to ya, who's gonna take care o' the rest, eh? Yer lady's fine but she ain't got the way ya gots. Let me go. 'T'won't be much ta lose iffen I don't make it safe."

Reluctantly, Simen had to agree. "Go on, then Gunder. If it's safe, put your arm back through and wave to us so we'll know."

"Better I wiggles me fishin' pole through back atcha," Gunder said. "Don't wanna lose me arm jest in case the door ain't kind, iffen ya knows what I mean."
With that, he marched resolutely to the crack in the wall where the dark warrior had disappeared. He saluted once with his fishing rod and then stepped in, vanishing as the knight had.

Simen held his breath, but it only took a moment before Gunder's pole emerged from the cliff beckoning to them. He smiled, bowed to Jessa and said, "Lead on, My Lady. I'll take up the rear just in case one of Shaidra's minions decides to come back. With you in front we'll have Magic at both ends."

Jessa nodded. "Let's all hold hands in a line, just in case. We don't want to lose anyone." Reaching out, she grasped Molly's hand in hers and when she was sure the rest had joined together, she stepped into the sand.

The Way beckoned on both sides, calling with voices Jessa thought she recognized, but ahead, she could see the moonlight shimmering on a lake. Resolutely she pushed forward and in ten steps plunged through the ice cold waterfall to stumble onto the rocks beyond. Gunder's strong arms grabbed her, dragging her to the shore as the others, gasping and sputtering in the icy rapids, followed.

Last out, drenched and coughing, Simen fell to his knees on a boulder. Gunder took his arm and pulled him back to his feet. "Couldn't warn ya. Figgered getting' ya all's back out were more important'n worryin' bout ya getting' a bath, eh? Asides, there's a good inn jest a little up the path wid a warm fire ta dry us all off."

"Should have expected it," Simen said, his teeth chattering with the cold. "It was too hot and dry on the other side. You're sure we're back in Lovental?"

"Lived here all ma life," Gunder replied. "Fished the lake a hunnert times. Knows ev'ry rock like a brother. We're back."

A little tentatively, Jessa cast a drying spell, but when she saw a shower of snow threatening her fingers, she snapped her hand back. "Reflections command here too," she said. "I think the inn's the better answer. Is everyone all right to walk?"

Murmurs of agreement answered. "I needs me a nice hot mug o' keldherb," one of the men said.

"Whispering Grove's jest up the way," Molly said. "They brew a fine pot."

They headed up the trail to the inn with Simen keeping a wary eye on the lake behind them. Until he found a way to close the portal, he needed to keep watch in case some of Shaidra's warriors might follow them.

*****

The guests of the Whispering Grove were cowering together in a far corner when Jamus came in. The stench of Spellfire still filled the air.

"Where are they?" he demanded as he hurried toward the stairs.

"Last room in the hall," the innkeeper replied, gesturing vaguely to the left.

Jamus was running now, taking two steps at a time into the upper hall. Weaving a quick sphere of protection around himself, and readying his hand to cast an attack, he flung open the door.

Kala knelt beside Sharia, who was sitting weeping on a stool by the bed. On the floor lay the withered body of what once might have been a young girl.

Jamus hand dropped to his side as he let his shield fall. "You figured it out," he said flatly.

"Sharia did," Kala replied, stroking the young woman's head. "Jiana tried to…to kill her."

"Shadow," Jamus said. "A murderous monster thirsting for blood. She'd already killed Jiana's parents. One drop of Sharia's blood and it would have taken more than mere Spellfire to destroy her."

"Mere Spellfire? That Magic is the most frightening thing I've ever seen and you tell me it would not have stopped her?"

Jamus shook his head. "We'd need a Dragon once she had True Life. You did well, Sharia."

The girl looked up, her eyes red with tears. "I killed them both. I mean…even though they were Shadows, all the time we've been here, I thought they were real. It was all I could do to raise my hand against them. Do you know how hard that was?"

Jamus gritted his teeth, holding back his own pain. He knew too well how it felt to end another's life, even if it were bred from the Darkness itself. In the end, Shadows like Jiana were not so different, for all they wanted was life, little more. "It's the hardest thing you'll ever do, Sharia, and I'm sorry you had to be the one to do it. I should have been here. I was a fool to leave you alone with Jiana."

"There was no way for you to know," Kala said quietly. "Even I was deceived."

"From the first moment we came here, I should have known," Jamus answered. "Everything pointed to this place being tainted by reflections. I'm a Waymaster. It's my responsibility to know. I should have come back here as soon as I figured out Simen was a fraud. Instead, I wasted time in the hills."

"Jiana's family," Sharia asked, her voice steady now as she regained her composure. "You said she murdered them."

Jamus nodded. "Slaughtered her mother and left her father chained up to starve to death. She couldn't kill him outright. He was a Magician, her first drink of chanted blood. If she'd killed him he would have vanished, taking all the power with him. So, she simply fettered him and let him suffer."

"I'm glad I killed her then," Sharia said, straightening. Then she looked at the dry skin on the floor. "But why did she have a body to leave behind? Jessa's Shadow didn't leave one."

"She stole the real Jiana's body for her own," Jamus replied. "Despite her name, the poor girl never inherited her father's power, so she was an easy victim—the Shadow's first kill. It's not much consolation, but she probably died quickly. The Shadow would not want a damaged skin to wear. "

Kala got to her feet, her body rigid. "How you have changed, Rivermaster. To be so callous about a young girl's murder. I expected more of you."

"Practical simplicity of a lesson for a young Apprentice," he said, shrugging. "A broken heart learns too little. We'll take her body home to lie at rest and give her our tears then."

"And now?"

"Now I have a lost brother and Mistress of the Keep to find."

"Not much worry there, My Lord," Simen said from the door. "As soon as I heard what happened, I knew I'd find you here."

Kala was about to hurry over to greet the Follyman, but Jamus took her arm, pulling her back behind him to shield her with his body. He'd already played the fool once with Serimsimen. He wasn't going to take any more chances. "Downstairs, Brother. Pick up a lute and play me a tune. Then I'll decide who you are."

Simen started to laugh but checked himself in the face of Jamus' icy stare. He knew Shaidra had been at work on this side of the waterfall and Jamus had every right to be suspicious. "It will take me a while to set the strings. I fret with my right hand, you know."

Jamus relaxed at that. "Your Reflection failed on that count, Simen. Your little ploy worked. How did you get him to change the song?"

"Shaidra," Simen replied. "It's a long story."

"We'll make time," Jamus said. "How did you get back?"

"Through the waterfall. It's a portal to her world."

"Then we need to close it. I've already had my fill of visitors from Mistress Shaidra." When he saw Simen's frown, he added, " Another long story. I take it you didn't come back alone."

"Jessa and a group of villagers are downstairs trying to warm up by the fire. It was a cold and wet return."

"How many of you?"

"Twelve villagers, Jessa, and me," Simen answered.

Jamus nodded. "Then we still have Reflections to deal with back in town. Jessa's is gone, yours is waiting for me in Mountain Lake."

"What are you going to do?"

"It all depends," Jamus answered. "When I met my duplicate from Shaidra's realm at the lake it was clear it was no ordinary Shadow. If it had truly been from the Way as soon as we touched we would have merged. Instead, it had a physical form of its own, Magic engendered." His mouth twisted in a wry grin. "Like you, my brother. Far more dangerous than mere Reflections. You and I need to ride up to the mountains to deal with Serimsimen. Can we keep the villagers here until I decide what to do with the rest?"

"I think so," Simen said. "They spent enough time with Shaidra to know how dangerous she is. Jessa and I should be able to convince them to listen to reason.

Simen's prediction proved true as the villagers were ready to accept Jessa as their leader while they waited for the Sorcerers to return. The Whispering Grove welcomed the unexpected bounty of so many guests and Jamus made sure there were denerets enough to cover every expense with plenty left over.

As he and Simen made their way to the stables, Kala caught up with them. "I'm coming with you."

"I don't think we'll need the services of a Juris," Jamus said.

"Jiana's body needs proper ceremony and this Seer needs to understand what's been happening here. Call it duty if you will, or call it my own insatiable curiosity to see Magiskeep justice at work, if you will. I am going with you."

Jamus smiled now. "I guess you are, then. I know better than to argue with you once you've made up your mind. I hope I live up to your expectations."

"You usually do," she replied, slipping her riding gloves on her hands to find something to do with them instead of strangling him. As usual, he had completely turned the argument to his side with infuriating ease. "You were planning on taking Jiana's body back for burial."

"I said I was," Jamus answered. "We've already packed it on one of the horses. It's not as dignified as a proper wagon, but we don't have time to waste. The sooner we resolve this the sooner I can close off the portal."

Silenced again by Jamus' answer, Kala moved over to Flax's stall. "I take it I can ride her?"

"It would be best. We have Pebble for Jiana, so all four horses are used to Magic. We can easily lift strides and be in Mountain Lake by Windchange. I know the trail now and the sun's already up."

He made good on his word as soon as they left sight of the inn, for the horses were eager and the sky was clear. Had the journey been for less serious purpose, Kala would have enjoyed soaring through the bracing wind. But her mind was in turmoil. Despite her Duty to the Provinces and all her oaths to Turan's justice, once again she was throwing her trust to Sorcery, knowing full well it was the only answer to the threats to Lovental. How many times had she denied the Vows she had made in Grandisite for the sake of Magiskeep's Lord? Now she was at his side again, trusting his judgment instead of her own.

He had disturbed her with his cold assessment of what had happened back at the inn. He'd treated Sharia with indifference, not sparing her feelings after the horror of the killing she'd done. The girl was shaken and he hadn't cared for an instant.

She shivered. What if he were not the Jamus he claimed to be? With so many Shadows already on the land could he be one too? What was the reality in this twisted land?

The next time they landed, she nudged Flax up alongside Magwin. "Simen, is it truly Jamus?"

"Who's to say I'm who I claim to be, Kala? You could well be asking my Reflection, you know."

"Sift me if you need, to, Madam Juris," Jamus said from up front as he reined Whim to a halt. "I'm frankly not surprised you asked. I tested Simen when he came to the inn. No reason I deserve any less suspicion. I swore I'd never lie to you."

She felt Sight beckon, the urge too great to ignore. There was no barrier between them, no ward, no deception on his part. That, in itself should have been enough, but the Light would not be denied.

Jamus, in the Rim, tormented by a nightmare. Jamus, in her arms. Jamus facing her justice in an angry village. Jamus, astride a silver Dragon. Jamus, the Rivermaster, a man hardened by battles she had not seen, death slipping too easily from his hand in the face of Darkness. Jamus, the man she once loved, still loved, and now feared. Power surrounded him, ruled him, and cursed him.

"You are the Jamus, the man I once knew and know no longer. I'm sorry I questioned you."

His face softened, his grey eyes warming as he studied her. She had Seen too much. "It's all right, Kala, truly. You had every reason to be suspicious considering all that's happened. There are still challenges to come. I hope I can depend on you to help when I ask."

Kala stiffened, "Was there ever a question of that, Jamus?"

He smiled. "Only one of many questions I've faced since I've come here, My Lady. Every corner I've turned has had one." He pointed up the trail. "The farm is just up ahead. I'll tend to the animals while you and Simen go on to the base of the cliff. You'll find Jiana's mother's grave there. Her daughter should lie with her."

With that, he rode off to the barn, leaving them behind.

Simen found the grave easily for Jamus had set it with beautiful flowers and a stone inscribed with both Lorna's and Sandu's names. He carefully spelled a new grave beside it and gently laid Jiana's thin body in it.

"We need to wait for Jamus," Kala said, her eyes wet with tears. "She was such a little girl."

Simen nodded and with an easy gesture, chanted a lute in to his hand. His left hand strummed the strings idly, testing their pitch. As he adjusted the tuning keys with his right hand, he said, "The

Shadows have no mercy, My Lady. All that matters are their own desires." He tested a chord and began to play a haunting melody.

Jamus walked up the slope to meet them, as Simen began to sing:

> *High on a hill*
> *in the ancient of days*
> *The wind blew the dust*
> *of tomorrow away*
> *As time took all memory*
> *off on its wings*
> *And rains fell in teardrops*
> *our sorrowing brings.*
> *Let hearts sigh with grief*
> *for the ones who are gone*
> *Yet even without them*
> *our own lives go on*
> *The winds take the dust*
> *of the ones we did love*
> *And carry it off*
> *to the heavens above.*
> *So sing we of heartbreak,*
> *and all of its pain*
> *For those we have lost*
> *to see never again.*
> *The winds take the dust*
> *of the ones we did love*
> *And carry it off*
> *to the heavens above.*

His voice trailed off to a mere echo in the valley, the last note lingering in the air as if it never wanted to let go.

Kala swallowed hard and lifted her hands up over the grave. "The Light be gracious to those who seek it. The Light give solace to those who mourn. The Light grant peace to soul it embraces. Circles end at their beginnings. May the Light grant us all its blessings."

With that, Jamus closed the grave as more flowers sprung up from the freshly turned earth and a third name appeared on the stone. "It is enough," he said. "We have work to do." Then without a backward glance he headed back down the little trail as Simen and Kala followed silently behind.

Chapter 16

"So how long do we hafta wait afore we go back home?" Tara asked as she brushed the crumbs of bread from her skirt. The Whispering Grove had welcomed the travelers with enough food and drink to satisfy three times their number.

"We need to wait for Lord Jamus to come back," Jessa replied. "He knows what to do with any reflections who may have come through the portal."

"Ya think there's more?"

"It would make sense. If all of you disappeared from your villages, don't you think someone would have set up an alarm? But when we arrived at Loren, no one said a thing about anyone's being missing."

"Ya mean Mistress Shaidra sent reflections ta take our places?"

Jessa nodded. "Most likely. We know she wanted control over Lovental. What better way than to fill it with her servants?"

"So there's a 'tother one o' me back home?" Gunder asked. "T'ain't what I call a blessin' on the world."

"Stop it, Gunder," Molly said sharply. "If it t'weren't fer you haf of us'd be brainsick by now. Ya weren't there fer long but ya made us all hope agin jest by takin' charge. An' yer the one what went first through the sand. When we needed a leader, it was you what stepped up."

Gunder stared down into his ale, swirling the mug nervously in his hands. "I ain't so much a man as I'd like ta be," he said. "Fish all day an' ne'er get a bite more'n a little wriggler. 'T'aint got the brain ta work at much more."

Molly moved over to sit beside him. "Man ain't got ta be the best at ev'rythin', Gunder. All's that matters is he be the best when he needs ta be. Ya proved that already." She laid her hand on his, stilling the cup.

For the first time since he could remember, Gunder felt himself smiling.

*****

The Tarlet's Nest was abuzz with activity when Jamus, Simen, and Kala arrived. Serimsimen's entertainment had drawn more customers than Rogan had seen in seasons. Now, the pretender Follyman was singing a rollicking ballad, setting the whole room to stomping and clapping along.

Even Jamus' arrival did not squelch the festivities for Serimsimen simply looked his way and went on with his music. But then, he eyed Simen and lost the beat for a few measures.

For his part, it was all Simen could do to keep his jaw from gaping open to see himself performing in front of an enthusiastic crowd. "Am I really that good?" he whispered to Kala who had stopped in her tracks at his side.

"Better, I think," she replied softly. "He is good, though."

Jamus, oblivious to the impressive performance, strode into the center of the room and raised his hand. Serimsimen's hand fell away from the strings as his voice choked and the room fell still. "Steal a man's music and you steal his soul, Follyman. I'm not sure my brother would approve."

"Ask him," Serimsimen said hoarsely, his eyes darting about the room for some escape.

Simen hesitated. Seeing himself standing there helpless in the face of Jamus' wrath choked back a response. Something about Serimsimen's expression tugged at his heart. This Reflection was, after all, not much different than he himself had once been. "Just what is it you want from me, Shadow?"

"Take me," Serimsimen said, holding out his hand. "We should have met at the end of the Way, not here. Ask the Waymaster. He understands."

"Jamus?" Simen asked.

"If he is your True Reflection he has a heart as black as the Dragon itself, Simen. Take his hand if you must, but be warned. If his Will is stronger than yours, my Spellfire will consume you both. I don't want to lose you."

"How do I know what to do?"

"Look at me," Serimsimen pleaded. "Am I a monster? My hands play your music, my voice sings your songs. How can such beauty be as evil as the Rivermaster claims? I've harmed no one and look at these people here. If anything, I've made their lives better."

"Deceit can be quite charming," Jamus said quietly. "Even I was taken in by your lies for a while."

"Please," Serimsimen repeated, reaching out his hand. Suddenly, he lunged for Simen and swept him into his embrace. As he did so, his clothing changed to match Simen's exactly. The two tumbled to the floor wrestling.

Jamus raised his hand as though to unleash the Spellfire he had used to control Serimsimen, but then realized the danger to Simen and instead pulled it back, afraid the violence of the tussle might release it, killing them both.

A True Reflection would have melded at once with Simen's body, but like his own duplicate at the lake, this one had form and substance quite capable of inflicting some serious damage in a fight.

The two Follymen were evenly matched, struggling against each other, each trying to gain advantage. One struck the other hard on the chin as the other fought to grip his opponent's neck. They clawed and grunted desperately, trying to pin each other to the floor.

Jamus raised his hand again, this time with a bolt of energy slicing between the two opponents, sending each sprawling to the side. Just as quickly, he threw out silver coils of Magic to bind them and then, with a snap of his arm, pulled them both to their feet to stand, sweating and panting. They looked exactly alike.

"You were right, Jamus, he is a liar," the Simen on the left gasped.

"Not Reflection," the Simen on the right hissed between labored breaths. "Something else."

"Shaidra's creation. Dragonspawn," Left Simen said. "Dangerous."

"I don't understand," Simen on the right replied. "Not from the Way."

"Not the Way," the other Simen said. "Shaidra's world."

"Send him back."

"Destroy him if you can't."

Jamus studied the two men. They were alike in every detail. The room had fallen silent, the patrons cowering behind the tables and counters, their wide eyes staring at Magiskeep's Master, all too aware they were in the presence of power beyond anything they had ever experienced. Even country superstition had not prepared them for this confrontation. "I think," Jamus finally said, "the villagers need some entertainment." He waved his hand and in it appeared a beautiful lute. He handed it over to Left Simen. "Play the Bonnylay for me, Brother. Only the most skilled can do it well, and I'm sure you're up to the challenge."

Left Simen smiled and tested the strings. Then, without hesitating, he began to play the intricate tune. His right hand danced on the strings flying along accenting the melody with strums of quick harmonies. It was a masterful performance, worthy of the best of Follymen and even the stunned crowd broke from their fear with a round of applause and cheers.

"Now, you, Sur," Jamus said, handing the lute to Right Simen.

"I can't."

"Play for your life," Jamus ordered sternly. "Now!"

The Follyman shrugged, put his left hand on the frets and began the tune. It was, at best, a fair rendition. Now and then he stumbled with the more difficult passages as the people groaned with each mistake. Clearly, he was not the lute's master, for it had mastered him.

Left Simen grinned triumphantly. "So, now we know the true Follyman."

"Yes, we do," Jamus replied as he sent a coil of silver strands, pinioning Left Simen in an inescapable snare.

"What? Why?" Left Simen cried, struggling futilely against his imprisonment. "I played the tune!"

"My true brother plays the strings with his left hand, not his right," Jamus replied. "Bonnylay is one of the hardest pieces ever written for the lute. He's told me more than once how it's the only piece he's never mastered with a right strung lute." Jamus looked over at the real Simen who was breathing heavily, relief washing his face. "You've almost done it, Simen. Mastered the piece right-handed, I mean. I few more circles practice and you might even manage to earn a round of applause."

Simen smiled for the first time since he'd entered the inn. "I
was afraid, Jamus. I wasn't sure you'd know me." He twirled the
lute in his hands, chanting the strings to suit his left hand. Then, as if
to prove himself to the murmuring crowd, began again to play the
Bonnylay, this time with such skill and passion the music took on a
life of its own. The room hushed, every eye focused on his flying
fingers as the music soared to a final cadence. Then they people burst
into cheers and applause whistling and stamping their feet
demanding more. Serimsimen had entertained them. Simen had
captured their hearts.

"Now that's my Follyman," Jamus laughed, pulling the
cords tight around the imposter. "You may have learned your lessons
well, but the true artist plays from his soul. Since you don't have
one...." He shrugged. "Come, my Shadow. We'll take you back out
to the lake and let you decide your fate. You can either go back to
your mistress or die. It makes no difference to me."

Eyes fixed firmly on the floor, Serimsimen let Jamus' Magic
drag him from the room as Simen began to play another song for the
insistent villagers.

*****

Another four winds had passed by the time Jamus, Kala, and
Simen returned to The Whispering Grove. Jamus had sent
Serimsimen back through the portal and then chanted the waterfall so
nothing else could pass through from the other side. He had decided
not to close it completely until the rest of the villagers were safely
back home and their duplicates dealt with.

"We need a way to indentify the true villagers," he said after
he'd explained what had happened at The Tarlet's Nest. "I don't
want to make any mistakes in case people get mixed up."

"I can sift them," Kala said, "but if they end up tumbling
about as the Simens did, it won't be easy."

"It has to be something the imposters cannot see," Simen
said, remembering how Jessa's mole had saved them both in
Shaidra's palace. "You saw how quickly my imposter changed his
clothes to look like mine. They'll mirror every detail if they have the
chance."

Jamus nodded now, "All of you, turn around. I'm going to put a mark on the back of your neck. It's nothing permanent, but enough for now to make sure we know who you really are."

In the end, as far as Mountain Lake Village was concerned, the marks mattered little. The nine villagers who had been supplanted by Shaidra's reflections easily took their proper places as soon as Jamus, Simen, and Jessa trapped their imposters. It was a sorry band of Shadows who trooped to the waterfall and vanished back into the desert that was Shaidra's kingdom.

"I almost feel sorry for them," Jessa said. "The world beyond is so barren compared to this one."

"It doesn't have to be," Jamus countered. "Clearly Mistress Shaidra has the power to change it. She'd have no need to conquer Turan if she would use her Magic to make her own paradise."

"She's too much Darkwing's daughter to think of creating something instead of destroying," Simen said. "I'm not even sure she has a heart of her own." Shaidra's need to see his and Jessa's intimacy had told him a great deal about the wasteland Sorceress.

"The Black River colors her Magic," Jamus said. "She is a powerful mistress not to be underestimated."

"But we're done with her, aren't we?" Jessa asked. "Simen and I fought her off at the portal and once you seal it she has no way out."

"There's always a mirror somewhere, Jessa," he answered. "Though I doubt she'll be looking for one anytime soon. She's had enough of Spellfire."

*****

Easwin's first breath set Jamus, Kala, and the three remaining villagers back down the trail to Loren to deal with their imposters.

When Payton's Shadow put up a battle in the front yard of his farm, Jamus solved the contest with one sliver of Spellfire, restoring order and Payton's rightful claim to the little ramshackle hut. "You, know, Sur," Jamus said as he studied the broken fence rails in the cow pen, "there is a lovely little farm up past Mountain Lake that needs a good hand to care for it. As far as I can tell, the owner has no heirs. I asked about it in the village, and no one there seemed interested. I could put in a word for you if you'd like."

Payton, who'd fallen on so many hard times in the last circles, nodded and smiled. "Can't tell from lookin' at me place here, but I'm a good farmer. Ain't got the luck to beat the drought and the milk fever though. I could use a fresh start."

"I have jurisdiction in this Province," Kala said. "As long as no one objects, I'd be pleased to make you caretaker of the farm. When we're done in Loren I'll go back with you and get things settled."

The sudden spring in Payton's step assured Kala she had made the right decision.

Now, only Molly and Gunder were left of the refugees.

"The Widow's Peek," Molly told him. "I was the serving maid there."

"I shame ta say I spent many a span there meself," Gunder agreed. "Too many of 'em sopping up ale an' tellin' fish tales. 'T'ain't likely even a good reflection of me'd do much better."

Jamus bit back a rebuke and simply nodded. "The Widow's Peek then. And as I've told the others, do exactly as I tell you. Kala, keep a close eye on things for me. I may need your Sight."

There were few patrons in the little inn when they arrived, but as Molly had predicted, her reflection was there, sidled up to a table where The Other Gunder sat, playing dice with three of the village's rowdies.

"Morgin and Tavner," Gunder said under his breath. "They ne'er gave me the time o' day, let alone diced wid me."

Clearly the men were close friends, laughing and shouting each other down at each throw. Aggie carried a steaming platter over to their table, giving The Other Gunder's hair a quick tousle as she set the food down. "Finest fish ye e'er caught, Gunder, me lad. I added a bit o' dillyweed jest like ye like ta flavor it. Ye lads want another round ta go with yer meal?"

The Other Gunder puffed up at that. "Fill the mugs and bring a pitcher, Aggie, me dear. I's payin' fer ma friends here so's keep us filled, eh?"

Gunder shrank back from the door. "I ne'er had two denerets ta rub together," he said dropping his gaze to the floor. "Caught nothing but lakeweed, an' they all usta laugh at me. Look at him what's there is ma place. Likes I should be the one go back through the falls and let Loren have a better man'n me."

Molly took Gunder's arm and squeezed it hard. "That Molly over there ain't got no taste fawning over that braggart," she said. "A better man knows it ain't what ya says or how many fish ya catch what matters. A better man knows how ta be kind, how ta jest sit an' see how pretty the sun shines on the water. A better man don't need ta tell the world how good he is, 'cause the world knows already. Master Jamus, pin that Molly's wandering hands to her hips where they belong and throw her back inta the lake. An' while yer at it, if she's so hot on that big mouth fisherman, tie him to her line and send 'em both off ta Shaidra."

"I want ta talk ta him," Gunder said. Before Jamus could stop him, he walked over to the table. The Other Gunder and his friends looked up, their eyes wide. "I wanna know," Gunder said, "what kinda bait ya used ta catch that fish, an' them." He waved his arm towards the rowdies.

"Wriggle worms and ale," The Other Gunder said as his clothes changed to match Gunder's exactly. "A good put deneret makes friends easy."

"So it's got naught ta do wid who you is but what ya kin pay?"

"Man's measure's in his purse."

Molly's Imposter rubbed her hip suggestively against The Other Gunder's shoulder. "Gold and silver make a soft bed. Makes a man too, I kin tell ye that."

Molly, at the door, could not contain herself. She marched over to the table to confront her reflection. "Woman's a fool what sells herself fer coin when she gots a chance fer somethin' better'n life."

Molly's Imposter threw her thumb in Gunder's direction. "What? That? Ya wanna live a life drudging here at the Peek cleaning tables jest so's ya kin support a pupling what soaks his empty line in the lake all day an' comes home empty handed? Let him put his soggy bottom in yer bed an' cold fingers on yer breasts? Give me a purse o' denerets ta keep me warm any day."

Molly braced her hands on her hips and glared at the other woman. "Give me a man what's got a heart an' puts me first over hisself an' I'll be glad ta earn all the silver we need ta keep us warm."

Molly's Imposter sauntered over, not bothering to match her rival's clothes, even though she struck the same impudent pose. "I got's me pride. 'T'ain't the woman's place ta earn the bread. Man's gotta pay his way under the blanket."

"I ain't no country whore," Molly countered. "Don't know which mirror ya come from but it sure ain't' one in my bedroom."

Molly's Imposter laughed, but in an instant, her face twisted into a snarl and she slapped Molly hard across the face.

It was all the distraction The Other Gunder needed as he leapt up from the table, lunging at Gunder. The two rocked back against the counter, locked in a wrestling match.

Once again, Jamus was faced with a choice, but this time he waited. This was a battle Gunder needed to wage on his own, one chance to prove himself to himself more than to anyone else. Instead of interfering between the men, he chanted quickly to pull Molly's Imposter aside, silencing her enraged screams with silver bonds of Magic.

Gunder managed to free his casting arm, taking a wild swing at his opponent. The Other Gunder ducked the first blow, but Gunder was quick to throw again, this time hitting him squarely on the chin.

The Other Gunder was spun back against the edge of the table, dazed. Gunder dived at him, head low, meeting the other man's belly with his head, knocking the wind out of him. The Other Gunder grunted and doubled over as Gunder grabbed the back of his neck and held him upright.

"No man buys ma place," Gunder hissed. "It ain't fer sale." He balled his hand up into a fist and struck hard, one blow to the belly, the next to the chin again and then he let his foe crumple into a heap on the floor.

Only then did Jamus step in with his silver bonds. "I'll take them both to the portal," he said. "I think you and Molly need to stay here to explain everything to the village. Somehow, I think the two of you have a lot to talk about." Another wave of his hand erased the marks on Molly's and Gunder's necks, the last assurance he needed to know he had made the right choices.

"Me Lord," Molly said, "I thank ye. Truly I does."

"No thanks needed for a wrong well righted," Jamus replied.

Kala smiled at the couple. "I do hope you call on me when the time comes to make bond between you," she said. "I would consider it a singular honor to officiate at your ceremony."

Molly blushed, and Gunder's color nearly matched hers as he leaned over to kiss her on the cheek.

*****

Molly's and Gunder's imposters meekly trailed along behind Jamus and Kala on the trail back to the lake, resigned, it seemed, to their fate.

Once on the shore, however, The Other Gunder balked. "There ain't no water back there, Mi Lord. How kin a man fish the sand?"

"Complain to your Mistress, not me," Jamus replied. "If she has power to give you solid form, she had power to change sand to water."

"Not wid a heart all dried up like a ol' wrinkled surlep," Molly countered. "Wouldn't surprise me ta find there ain't even no blood in her veins, cold as she be."

"Then teach her," Kala replied. "You are reflections bred from two people who have learned to love each other. Teach your Mistress what that means."

"Worth a try, I s'pose," The Other Gunder sighed. "'T'ain't likely this fine lord here is gonna show no mercy."

"Reflections are deceptions," Jamus said simply. "A trick of the eye, a glance at the impossible. There is no way to trust you on this side of the portal." He was about to send them into the waterfall when the face of it exploded with galloping horses and riders.

He threw Kala behind him, shielding her with his body, and slashed his arm across in front of himself, throwing a shimmering silver barrier across the full expanse of the lake.

The first rider nearly crashed headlong into it, his horse rearing at the last instant to spin on its hind legs before dumping the rider in the water as it fell on its side.

The other riders managed to yank their horses aside as from the attackers one rider emerged, a beautiful raven haired woman astride a coal black charger, snorting and pawing at the water, sending up plumes of white froth around them. Dressed in onyx armor over a purple tunic, the woman raised her arm to salute Jamus as her horse danced under her.

"Rivermaster. I simply could not let you go without saying farewell. I had hoped to catch you unawares, but that was not to be." She dropped her hand and stared for a long time at Kala. "The Juris, Seer of All Things. I expected you to be taller."

Kala stiffened, squaring her shoulders as she stepped out from behind Jamus to face Shaidra. "I am tall enough. Stature comes from within, not without."

Shaidra laughed. "A sharp tongue. I am glad to know I did not underestimate the woman in the mirror. I think you would have liked your Reflection, My Lady. She really is quite talented in word and skill. Too bad. She'll have to wait for another day, I suppose."

All the while, Shaidra's eyes were studying the barrier Jamus had set, looking for a flaw.

"Art of the Waymaster," Jamus said at last. "Not an easy weave to conquer, even for a Mistress of the Way like yourself. We've reached a standoff, but with two Rivers at my command, I do believe I have the upper hand."

Shaidra's dark eyes glittered, the intricate threads of silver and gold intertwined in the shield reflected in their depths. She knew it was hopeless to even try to broach them. "Next time, Rivermaster," she said. "Give me my servants and we shall go home. You've won this battle. Wear your smile on the way home. There will be another day."

Jamus nodded to The Other Gunder and his Molly, who then waded into the lake, following Shaidra and her little army as they headed back to the waterfall. The crystal surface seemed to part to let them through as they disappeared into the world beyond.

Kala let out a puff of air. "I thought she was going to attack."

"She was," Jamus said. "One more second and that first knight would have reached us. The Hand be blessed I've learned to weave so fast. Though I must admit the curious nature of reflections in this place did give me an advantage."

"How so?"

He grinned lopsidedly. "When I saw that knight charging all I had to do was want, more than anything, for him to kill us both. Panic threw the Spell after that."

Kala started back, staring at his face. "I should believe that?"

He shrugged. "I promised I'd never lie to you, Kala, but that doesn't mean I'd never keep a secret."

*****

Sealing the waterfall portal was a simple matter. First Jamus narrowed the channel so the water crashed against rocks as it descended from the cliffs above, churning the once clear waters to white foaming rapids.

Then, behind the falls he set a Chanting, weaving one reflection upon another until even he could not sort them out.

For all intents and purposes, it would take a greater Sorcerer than he to ever open the portal again. Somehow, he suspected even the Black Dragon himself would find it a challenging puzzle.

They made their way back to The Whispering Grove to get Sharia and then head back to Mountain Lake where the others waited.

As Norwin drew, near the moonlight reflected off the waters of Lovental in bright beams.

For the first time in months, it was a beautiful sight.

Dreamchaser

Chapter 1

"Boy ain't worth a rimrock speck's far as I'm concerned," Samil grunted as he pushed the stack of leather back up on the shelf. The old leathermaker had been running his shop in Magiskeep for more than forty circles and was held in high esteem by most of the Keep. His word was nearly always final when it came to judging the young men of the village. Now, his words could not be ignored. "I put up with a passel o' poor lads in me time, but I never yet met one with his head so empty."

Josep sighed heavily in the way old men weary with the weight of decision often did and shook his head. "So ya thinks the lad'll suit the stables? The critters of Magiskeep ain't all so kind's ta look out fer little fools, ya know. I gots a barn full o'wee ones without a lick o'sense in their heads."

Samil laughed. "Then the lad oughtta git on right fine wid 'em." Then, he wrinkled his brow in genuine concern. "I don't know what else ta do wid 'im, Josep. His poor Ma'm's hardly got two denerets to rub together."

"Nobody's ever gonna starve in Magiskeep," Josep replied quickly. "All ya gots ta do is speak ta Lord Jamus about her an'.... "

"Ne'er do that," Samil answered nearly as quickly. "The lady's far too proud fer that. She sews and takes in washin' fer the coin an' does right well by her little family. Jebe, though, is her hope. The coins he brings in from 'is prenticin' is what makes her smile." Now, the old leatherworker shook his head too. "Lad's been a trial fer her, though. He's had six masters since the first o' Warmmonth, and now that the Chill season's turned, I'm gonna have ta let 'im go too. 'E's ruint six hides over the last Sevenstin and I cain't afford ta keep 'im on."

"So you 'spect me ta take 'im ta the Lord's stables?" Josep asked, scrubbing his hand through his gray hair.

"'Tis the law, ain't it? Kur Jamus claims he'll take in any soul what needs a place."

"I don't think Lord Jamus meant stray lads for stablework. He spoke most 'bout welcoming the hungry or them without a home inta the Keep if need be."

"The lad's as proud as his mother, an' twict as quick ta take offense iffen ya offer charity. He'll take a job."

Josep considered this for some time. As master of the Keep's stables, he certainly had need for young strong lads to do the chores his old bones no longer relished. Magic eased his burden somewhat, but often the horses would not abide spells in place of a human hand to feed them or scrape the pasture mud from their coats. Even Whim, Jamus' gifted silver stallion, preferred personal handling despite his own Magical abilities to care for his own needs. But, taking on an inept boy whose every effort had seemed to turn duskits to rimsnakes was another question. As he'd told Samil, he had a barn full of young horses, all still silly with the foolish shenanigans of foals who could not comprehend the need to watch where they put their hoofs and teeth. The last thing he needed was a lad as undisciplined. "I s'pose I kin talk ta the Lord hisself."

"That'd be a good thing," Samil replied as he stitched a seam in a pair of walking boots one of the sheepmen had left in his care. "I'll keep the lad till Easwin next an' iffen ya don't call, I'll haf ta send him home. I cain't keep him more'en that."

"Fine, fine," Josep replied absently, already tumbling a hundred explanations to Jamus over and over in his head. As close as he was to Magiskeep's Lord, he still found himself tongue-tied when it came to discussing matters of business.

He mumbled to himself all the way back to the Keep's stables and was still mumbling when he walked in and nearly crashed headlong into the Lord of the Keep himself, who was just finishing up one of his regular inspections of the young stock.

Jamus' steady but gentle hand on the old man's chest was all that diverted the collision. "Sur Josep, if I were any less of a man, we'd both be on the floor right now. What in all of Turan is distracting you so?"

Josep took a step back and looked up into Jamus' grey eyes, shrinking slightly under their perceptive study. "I gots me a problem, M'Lord."

"That even I can see," Jamus replied, laughing a little. "Is there something I can do?"

Josep cleared his throat. "If yer willin' ta take in a cursed little lad who ain't got a skill ta his name, I guessed ya kin," he said at last. "Boy named Jebe been at near ev'ry shop in the village since the crops was in an' cain't seem ta find him a place. Samil ... ya knows, the leatherman ... he seems ta think the boy'd do right here. I gots my question 'bout that, but knowin' how ya gots the likin' ta take in strays .... "

Jamus laughed aloud now, not even trying to hide his amusement. "Do you really think you need to ask? I seem to remember circles ago how you took in a stray from the Rim and welcomed him as your son. If I should ever do any less in the rest of the circles of my life, I'd be less than the man you helped me become. Bring Jebe here and teach him whatever he can learn. If he proves a poor learner here, we'll find something he can do well in the house proper."

The old Stablemaster grinned. "I ain't never been wronged by ya, lad, and I ain't been now. Seems ta me ol' Jeamel, Becca, an' me done right by the lessons we done tried ta teach ya, fer sure."

"Lessons of love, I think," Jamus replied. "If it hadn't been for all of you, I never would have…." His voice broke off, the words unnecessary. The pain of his past life was best forgotten now. He quickly changed the subject. "I see Flax's foal is still not behaving himself."

Josep straightened as he brought himself back to the business he knew well, "Mischievous little critter. He bites and kicks awful an' keeps skitterin' in an' out o' the stall worse'n his pap. He done 'herited yer Whim's Magic but ain't got the ounce o' common sense ta go wid it. Jest Laswind he done broke inta the grain bin an' iffen I hadn't stopped him he woulda et all the sweetfeed. He'da colicked good, I tell ya."

Jamus walked back over to the big box stall where the troublesome foal was housed with Flax. Even the golden mare seemed tired of her offspring's antics, for she stood off to one side hardly paying any attention at all to the little creature who had sprawled out on the straw with his long legs stretched every which way. His coat shimmered with a mix of metallic color, at first appearing as gold as his mother's and then seeming to shift to the silver he had inherited from his father. His well-shaped head bore a clearly defined white star which was the only part of his coloring to keep itself fixed as he snored in his sleep.

"He looks innocent enough now," Jamus said softly, leaning on the stall door.

"'Bout the only time he is," Josep sighed. "Even Flax loses her patience wid 'im. He nips her ev'ry chance he gits. Soon's the weather breaks, I'm gonna haf ta wean him ta give the poor lass a break. He's a mite big fer his age so'd I figger he kin hold his own wid the yearlings. Maybe some o'them'll teach him some manners."

Jamus nodded. "It's often the best way. Sometimes horses sort out what we can't." Then, the Lord of Magiskeep gestured slightly with his hand. "In the meantime, I'll put a bit of a weave on our problem child to keep him from playing his little escape games. Be careful, though. When he realizes he can't use his talent, he might be a bit cranky. Just stay out of the way if he throws a tantrum."

"Ya spelled 'im?"

Again, Jamus nodded. "Simple Magic, Josep, but a spell to keep our little fellow in line."

Josep grinned. "He'll be afired, fer sure. T'won't be ta his likin' not ta have his way. It's take a load offen me mind, though. I cain't keep me eye on 'im all day."

With that, Jamus left the stable and hardly thought at all about what he'd left behind. Whim's firstborn had taken on his father's magic and none of the great silver stallion's intelligence, it seemed. For now, the Lord of Magiskeep had little patience for such things. Bestowal was near, and he had a list of promises to keep.
*****

Jebe arrived at the great stables of Magiskeep wearing his best clothes. His mother had insisted he dress well, despite the lowly position he was taking. The Keep, she told him, was the hold of Lords and Ladies, and no son of hers was going to be seen there in common rags.

As soon as Josep saw the boy, he knew there was trouble ahead.

Jebe walked along as if in a dream, his head cocked to one side, his hazel eyes constantly looking upward as if searching the sky. Now and then, he tripped over a cobble or some other slight obstacle in the path. Only then would he focus on where he was going, and then, a cluster of dark blond curls would fall over his forehead so he would have to brush them away with his thin little hand. He was a little fellow, slender and pale. His square cut green tunic hung loosely off his shoulders as if it were at least a size too large, and his boots wanted to swallow his legs into their hastily polished leather. In them, he tripped on the sill of the stable door and then, tumbled into the building to land in a heap on a bale of straw in the aisle.

"Grand entrance fer a stable lad," Josep remarked. "Yer early enow so no one but me's seen ya, though. Come on, git to yer feet and brush the straw offen yerself. Then go inta that little room over there." He gestured toward his own quarters. "Change inta some work duds. I got some ol' britches in there close ta yer size and a blousen that'll suit. I onct had a lad here 'bout yer height. Good thing I keep some o' his things about fer me lads."

"Sir?" Jebe asked as he pushed himself off the bale and rose unsteadily to his feet. "Me Mam says I'm ta dress well fer the Keep."

"Stable's a stable, no matter where it be," Josep replied. "Ya wears yer dress clothes on the way here iffen it'll please yer Mam, but change inta somethin' harder onct ya gets ta work."

Jebe shrugged and tottered off to change as ordered. When he reemerged, he wore the rustic britches and top as well as a less dramatic pair of boots far more suited to the job at hand.

Josep eyed him critically, taking in his thin shoulders, trying to decide just how much work the boy could do. "Here, lad, kin ya lift that bale o'straw over there?"

Jebe shrugged and reached for the bale nearly as large as he was. He hefted with all his might, managing to lift the burden about a foot off the floor before he collapsed with a gasp to let it fall back out of his grip. "It's pretty heavy, Sur. I can move it a little."

"Aye, lad, a little. Tell ya what. We'll open the twine an' ya kin carry it a bit at a time over ta the stalls I tell ya. Me mares need beddin'. The stalls done bin cleaned already while the ladies is out in the sunshine. All's they need is fresh straw. Now look here. Ya see this aisle?" The old man pointed to two rows of stalls. When Jebe nodded, he went on, "All the horses is out. Ya need ta put a bale o' straw in each o' them stalls and use the fork ta spread it out nice and even. Then, ya gots ta fill the water buckets with fresh water. Do ya think ya kin manage?"

Jebe gulped and nodded, clearly not at all sure he could handle the work. But, Josep's encouraging smile gave him enough confidence to try. "I'll do my best, Master Josep, I promise."

"Good lad," Josep replied.

Left to his own devices, Jebe managed to cut the twine with the knife he found hanging on the wall and then carted the straw to the first stall. Soon, he was hard at work spreading the fresh yellow stalks evenly about the floor. The aisle held twelve large stalls, and it took him nearly a three spans to bed them all. The straw had been stored at the far end of the aisle, so by the time he reached the opposite end of the row, he had carried armful after armful along the aisleway, dropping debris all along the way. By the time he was ready to tackle the water buckets, the aisle looked nearly as well bedded as the stalls themselves. Still, he pressed on, filling the larger buckets in the stalls by using a smaller one he could handle. This, he had to fill from the pump near the center of the barn. Water sloshed from it with every trip, soaking the straw on the floor with every step he took. With the job finished, the stalls were ready and waiting, but the lane between was a total, soggy mess.

Coming back to inspect his new employee's work, Josep groaned at the sight. "Bory, lad, ya made one grandy mess here. Din't ya think ta sweep afore ya drowned ev'rythin'?"

Jebe's brow furrowed. "You didn't tell me to sweep, Sur."

Josep shook his head. Common sense, it seemed, was not Jebe's best skill. Now the floor would have to be cleaned with the pitchfork and barrow. Had the straw still been dry, it would have been an easy matter to sweep it into the stalls themselves instead of having to cart it out to the manure pile. "Yer right, Jebe," he sighed. "I din't tell ya ta sweep. Well, ya learnt a lesson, then. Now ya gots ta pick up all the wet and tote it out to the dungpile. I cain't bring the mares in till yer done, neither, cause the wee ones might slip in the aisle."

"I'm sorry, Sur."

Josep waved his hand in dismissal. "Ya's entitled ta mistakes, lad. Jest learn how ta fix 'em. All's ta worry 'bout is the critters. I don't need no apologies as long as naught ya do hurts one o'them."

"I'd never hurt a horse," Jebe protested, his voice pitching up in alarm.

"Din't say ya would a purpose," Josep replied, "but what's ya gots ta remember is that ev'rythin' ya does here is fer the horses an' ya gots ta think o' them first. Ya gots ta use yer eyes an' yer brain ta watch out fer 'em." He pointed to the hay fork Jebe had left leaning up against the wall. "Now see there? That fork's in the aisle 'stead'a hanging back up in the toolroom. All that's got ta happen is fer some nosy foal ta start a pokin' at it on the way in ta the barn. S'posin' he pushed it over an' it fell with them sharp points a'stickin' up, eh? One o' the wee ones or his mama could step on it."

"Oh no!" Jebe cried, his eyes widening. "They could really get hurt!"

"Horseman's eyes'd see that afore it happened," Josep said, wagging his finger for emphasis. "What ya gotta learn is horseman eyes, lad."

"I will, I will." Jebe nodded vigorously, and for once, he really believed it.

In fact, over the next Sevenstin, he actually did learn. Under Josep's watchful guidance, he managed to clean and bed his twelve stalls without a single mistake, and soon, the old stableman began to trust him. True to his word, Jebe worked hard and concentrated on every task during the day, but even so, he was not quite as successful with the other stable lads.

Josep had four boys and one girl working for him in addition to Jebe, and most had chosen horsemastery as their vocations since they had reached eight circles. Jebe's presence as a rejected apprentice from the village did not sit well with them. He was not a horseman by birth, nor a horseman by choice and so, in their lofty opinion, was not a horseman by right.

Seng, the oldest of the boys had already spent three circles under Josep's tutelage and considered himself an expert horseman. Though he had never even ridden one of the creatures, he was full of advice on training since had had observed Lord Jamus at least a dozen times. Magiskeep's Master had trained nearly all of the Keep's mounts to saddle, and was recognized as one of the most skilled horseman both there and beyond the Rim. Lord Delran, the esteemed breeder from Telma Province had often sent his more difficult animals to Jamus when his trainers were unable to make any headway.

"He's got a soft hand, he does," Seng remarked when assessing Jamus' technique. "Horses like the soft hand."

No one ever questioned Seng's expertise, at least not among the stableboys. The fact that he'd never swung his leg over a horse's back didn't seem to matter. He was older than the rest of them, and a lot stronger, with teenage muscles already filling out his arms.

Jebe, though, was not the kind of boy who accepted words above deeds. As foolish as he might have been with his own clumsy body, his mind had a keen perception for sense when it came to words. And so, on one of those days when Seng was holding forth with a longwinded speech about just how a frisky young colt should be taught to accept the saddle, Jebe interrupted. "How are you to know all that, eh, Seng? You ain't ne'er been astride a horse since I been here. Where'd you learn to ride?"

Seng sank back into his tunic for just an instant and then puffed back up with false bravado. "I bin here long enow ta know what's right and what ain't," he said. "I seen the Lord Sagari straddle Coranth wid me own eyes. An' I was here when Lord Jamus first put the girth ta Whim. Kin ya say the same?"

"There's a mighty big difference between seein' and doin'," Jebe replied. "It's kinda like pushing the barrow full of dung to the pit. It looks a lot easier than it is."

Seng's face reddened and he clenched his fists at his side. "Ya callin' me a liar?"

Jebe shook his head. "I'm just telling you riding is one of those things you got to do afore you know what it's all about."

Now, Nobby rose to Seng's defense. Nearly six inches shorter than the older stableboy, Nobby was still an imposing lad, with a stocky build beneath a shock of flaming red hair and a temper to match. "If'en ya knows so much, s'pose ya tells us how many times ya bin in the stirrups, Li'l Runty. I don't see no shine on yer britches."

Jebe shrugged. "I've ridden once or twice. Thing is, I don't make no claim to be an expert like Seng does. All's I know is it's harder than it looks."

Torrem, the middle lad who usually hung back in this kind of battle chewed his lip thoughtfully and then offered, "I always figger a man kin stand behind what he says. It's like Josep always tells us, 'It ain't the talkin' but the doin' what counts.' Maybe we could find a doin' to settle this without drawing blood."

"Hey," Jevin piped in, "that ain't so bad a idea. Tomorrow's Sevenday an' all's we gots ta do is the Easwin chores afore we gets our own time. Mebbe we kin sneak out ta Hidden Pine an' Seng kin show us he knows what fer."

"Yeah," Nobby agreed quickly, "whatta ya say, Seng? I'd be right proud ta give ya a leg up onta any critter ya've a mind ta straddle. 'Bout time L'il Runty got put in his place. He's bin mollying up ta Josep long enow. Might be good fer him ta larn who's the better'en this barn, eh?"

Sila, the only female in the group, usually held her own but this time, she'd keep quiet for a lot longer than anyone expected. With her mahogany hair cropped short and her tunic as rumpled as the rest, she hardly looked out of place among her cronies. She was tougher than anyone besides Seng, and when she spoke, everyone listened. Now was no exception. "I says if we're gonna make this'en a fair test, we oughtta pick two of them three circle colts Lord Jamus sent out ta the Pines. They ain't never had no saddle on 'em an' he said he'd decided they was goin' fer the dray steada the saddle. That way it won't matter none if'en one o' these big talkers messes up. Larning ta the harness is a whole other thing than ta the leg."

"Good idea," Torrem agreed quickly. "That makes it a fair test right sure, an' without no danger we'd be ruinin' one of the prize colts the Master be sending to Lord Delran."

Seng cleared his throat nervously, his dark eyes darting from face to face, hoping to find an ally who might join him in finding a way out of the challenge. Instead, he saw only eager anticipation. "I don't want us ta git in trouble wid Master Josep. If'en the L'il Runty gits hurt, there's gonna be Shades ta pay."

"Who's gonna know?" Nobby asked.

"If'en we goes out ta Hidden Pines, nobody's gonna see us," Sila said. "An' iffen we all swears a Riveroath ta keep secrit 'bout it, who's gonna tell? Jebe, ya knows what a Riveroath means, dontcha?"

Jebe swallowed hard and nodded. "I got a touch of the Magic."

"Fine fer 'im, an' Jevin, you Sila, an' me," Seng replied, "but Nobby an' Torrem ain't Riverblood. What's ta hold 'em to the swearin'? Somebody gits hurt an' they ain't gonna hold up under the Master's quizzin'. I say it ain't a good idea lessen we kin all Riverswear."

"H-m-m-m." Sila rubbed her chin as she considered the problem. "We gotta do a bindin' then. We ain't got much Magic by ourselfs, but mebbe iffen we join up we kind weave a net."

"It might work," Jevin agreed. "That way we all be holdin' ta the oath the same."

Reluctantly, Seng nodded and Jebe, who was totally sorry he'd ever questioned Seng in the first place, shrugged. "I guess. I never really said I could train a horse better'en Seng, though. I jest wanted to know how come he figgered he could do it so good himself."

Nobby wagged his finger in Jebe's face. "A man ain't got no right ta question another man lessen he kin show hisself ta be better. You take back what ya said right now, or ya take up the challenge. Leastwise that's the way I sees it."

Seng brightened. "Yeah, that's the way of it. Ya takes back what ya said an' ya don't gotta do nothin' 'cept lissen ta me when I tells ya somethin' from now on."

Jebe considered this for a moment, then decided having to listen to Seng was far worse than breaking his neck. "I ain't gonna back down on what I said. If Seng is so good at training horses, then he can show us. If that means I gotta do it too, so be it. That's the way it's gotta be."

And so, it was settled. In two more days, the truth and the lies would somehow be resolved.

At least, Jebe hoped so.

Chapter 2

Despite the turning to Sowin, the Sevenday held the chill in the air, denying the fact of Chillmonth's end. There was a brisk breeze with the wind's change, making it even colder.

Jebe's work tunic was barely enough to keep him warm on the long hike to Hidden Pines, but he didn't say a word. The others had woolen jackets and hats to protect them. Jebe's mother had not had enough money to buy him a new coat after he outgrew his last season's one. Since he was going to be working inside the leather shop, she hadn't worried too much about it. Now, with his job at the stable, he had grown used to shivering and pretending it didn't matter.

Hidden Pines was, on foot, a full span from the Keep proper, set in a meadow surrounded by lofty pine trees and thick brellums. Horses pastured there during the cold seasons were protected from the harsh winds by the pines and found shelter under the brellums. The long grasses provided good forage for all but the last of the Chill days, and the running stream along the pasture's western edge never froze. Josep carted huge round bales of hay out during the latter part of the season and these assured the animals plenty of forage until the Green month's turn brought new life to the land.

This circle, Jamus had decided to pasture six young horses in the Pines, hoping the time away from the Keep would help them build strong bones and hard muscles for their future lives in the harnesses of the farmers and carters of Telma Province. Stall coddling and small paddocks were not for these animals.

As the sun passed second span, the stableboys and Sila reached the fences of the pasture full of the excitement of the upcoming challenge. Once there, they made a pile of all the equipment they had carried with them for the test and then settled under one of the sheltering brellums to discuss strategy.

"Before we begin," Sila said, "we must set the bond." The language of Magic fell easily from her tongue as she let herself fall into the accent of the Keep. "First we must join hands and then, speak the words of promise in the name of the River. Those with the Art must call the River with Will and voice. The touch will bind us all together with the Magic as witness."

The six of them linked hands and waited for Sila to tell them the rest. Jevin and Seng had spent enough time in study to recall most of the chant, but Sila was in charge after she had dared to search the Great Library that Easwin to find the exact phrases they would need.

"Now then," Sila told them, "I will say a line and you must all repeat it together exactly as I say it." She cleared her throat and began the ancient liturgy,

"I to the River make my call,
River one, the River all-
wisdom, truth and honor fair.
River, in thy name I swear.
Now to thee I promise make,
word is bonded not to break.
Till my circle close its end,
on my vow can thou depend."

There was a rustling in the branches above them and for a brief instant the air grew thick with Magic's presence. It was not much of a call, but more than enough to make them tremble from something besides the cold.

"There, it be done," Sila said. "Ya caint break yer word now or ya'll haf ta answer ta the River itself. T'ain't a thing I'd be wantin' ta do."

"Fair enow," Jevin said as he got to his feet. "Now let not waste no more time talkin' 'bout it an' git to it astead. I brung headcollars fer the critters. Torrem brung the ropes an' Nobby gots some grain in case we gotta catch 'em. How we gonna pick which ones ta ride?"

"We'll pick the two biggest," Nobby replied. "That way we knows they is strong enow ta take a rider. No sense in riskin' a wee babe ta this. I figger the size oughtta tell us which ones is growed enow."

"Good," Torrem agreed. "Now, who picks?"

Jevin poked his own chest with his thumb. "Me, Sila, an' you. Nobby's too close ta Seng and the contesters ain't the ones who should."

Seng shrugged, trying hard to appear nonchalant, even though his heart was pounding. Jebe nodded nervously, hugging his arms around his thin body in a vain effort to warm up and hide his shivering.

It took less time than anyone had expected to round up the two biggest horses from the little herd. As soon as the animals saw the people, they trotted over ready to nibble on whatever treat they could find. Well-handled as foals, the big bay mare and nearly as big young chestnut stallion willingly accepted the head collars and allowed themselves to be led to the fence so the boys could mount.

Gulping back his terror, Seng moved over to the chestnut and climbed up to the top rail. Not to be outdone, Jebe scrambled up the rails beside the mare and took a deep breath before swinging his leg over her back.

Unbroken horses often react differently when first mounted. Some buck and plunge, trying to rid themselves of the strange creature attacking their backs. Some run off, trying to escape while others simply stand stock still as if so confused they have forgotten how to even walk.

Fortunately for Jebe, the mare was one of the latter.

Unfortunately for Seng, the stallion was one of the first kind.

As soon as he felt the weight on his back, the chestnut exploded into a leaping frenzy of fear and anger. Only his long legs kept Seng on the horse's back through the first few bounds, but after one more, it was clear he and the stallion were about to part company. He grabbed the horse's mane and began to scream for help. All the yelling did was panic the horse more.

Jebe, astride the frozen mare clutched with all his might, praying she would not join her herdmate in the fray. He could feel her heart pounding under his legs and felt her muscles tense under his seat. For what seemed an eternity, he watched in horror as Seng flopped about and then, as if in slow motion sailed up and through the air.

Rid of his burden, the stallion squealed, kicked up his heels and took off across the pasture, racing like the wind to return to his friends near the stream.

Instinct set the mare's legs on fire. In one bound, she bolted. Jebe cried out, his voice drowned in the wind of the gallop as his mount raced off, heading for the far pines and the fence.

"Stop 'im!" Nobby yelled as he leapt the fence and ran over to help Seng to his feet.

"What happened?" Seng asked, shaking his head painfully.

"Dontcha know?"

"I cain't remember nothin'. Did I show ya how ta ride?"

"Sure, sure, Seng," Nobby replied worriedly. Then he called, "Jevin, can ya still see'em? If anythin' happens to that horse we's gonna be in big trouble."

"If anythin' happens ta Runty we's gonna be in bigger trouble," Sila told him.

"They's crost the stream an' she's still a-runnin'." Jevin said. Then with sudden inspiration, he grinned, "What say we leave 'im?

He's Riversworn so he can't tell nobody what we done. If we jest go back ta the Keep, who's ta know?"

"What if he gits hurt or somethin'?"

"Like I said," Jevin replied. "Who's ta know?"

The mare was not ready to stop. Jebe clung to her like a burr, some instinct telling him how to shift his weight with her every move. Then, he saw the fence looming in front of them and he pulled hard on the rope attached to the mare's collar. She lifted her head and then, in one plunge, lifted her body with it and soared over the top rail.

Jebe felt them leave the ground and closed his eyes. When he opened them again they were on the ground and heading for open country.

*****

Jamus always looked forward to Sevenday, for it was the one time during the Sevenstin when he knew no petitioners would approach him. This day, he had saddled Whim well before Sowin and ridden out to the Rim to check the spells holding the mountains' chantings out of his kingdom. The silver stallion had been fresh and frisky in the cold air, ready for a long run once they were past the fences of the east pasture. Now, after nearly three spans of riding, he had settled into a long smooth walk and Jamus was enjoying the pleasure of his freedom.

Too many spans spent inside the walls of the Keep had worn his patience more than he realized. The Chillmonths had been colder than usual and several snows had turned paths and trails to ice. Though he might have spelled Whim's hoofs so they wouldn't slip, the shifting winds and icy air ruined the thought of pleasant rides. Magic again could have made journeys easy, but somehow, using the River to deny nature ruined the whole idea of riding out to escape the burdens of his position. Instead, he had waited, grumbling about the weather with all the other horsemen of the world. Then, on the first day the season's change scented the air, he had saddled up and headed for the farthest place from the Keep he could manage in a ride of a Windchange.

He patted Whim's silver neck and sighed. "If this was all I could do for the rest of my life, I think I'd be happy." The stallion nickered softly and Jamus laughed. "I'm not sure what you just said, but I'm hoping you were agreeing with me."

Suddenly, he reined to a stop, his eyes squinting in the Sowin sun. There, off to his left, was a madly galloping horse with a small boy clinging desperately to its mane and crying for help.

One dig of Jamus' heels sent Whim into a long-strided run after the pair. It was a matter of moments before they were alongside the runaway. Jamus reached over and snagged the boy's tunic. "Let go! I have you. Let go."

Jebe forced his hands to break their white-knuckled grip on the mare's mane and felt himself swing through the air to land safely in Jamus' lap. Then, Whim slowed to a trot and finally halted, waiting for his rider's command. The mare ran on for a bit, then stopped too, her herd instinct overriding her fear. She nickered and made her way back to the stallion, lowering her head to nibble on the grass nearby.

Jamus shifted Jebe into a more secure spot in front of him and said, "Well now, if I'm not mistaken, you are Josep's newest stable lad. Jebe, isn't it?"

Gulping in huge gasps of air, Jebe struggled with his hoarse reply, "Aye, my Lord."

"Just what was it you were trying to do, lad? That looks like one of my dray horses."

"Aye, My Lord."

"And you were riding it?"

"Aye, My Lord."

"Was there a reason for this?"

"I can't say, My Lord," Jebe replied nervously. "I ... I be Riversworn."

Jamus shook his head in resignation. "This smells of pranks, Jebe. If you're Sworn, I guess I can't insist on your telling me the rest of it, but I certainly can see your part of it. Did you take the mare out of the pasture?"

"No, My Lord ... leastwise I didn't mean to. She jumped the fence."

"With you on her back?"

Jebe nodded.

"You are quite the rider, young Sur. That fence is over four feet."

"I don't know how to ride. I just... well ..." The boy was close to tears. "I'm sorry, My Lord, really, I am. I done a bad thing. I coulda hurt the horse."

At that, Jamus smiled. "Of all the things you might have said to me, Jebe, that is the one thing I wanted to hear. Now come on, let's get down and have a look at your mount to make sure she is all right. With a little Magic and a good horseman to look after her, I'm sure she will be just fine."

And indeed, aside from being lathered and winded, the mare did seem just fine despite her adventure. Jamus ran his hand down each of her legs, instructing Jebe on just how to check for heat or swellings. Then, he straightened. "You'll have to be punished, lad. Just because there's no damage we can see doesn't mean you haven't harmed her. What you did was wrong."

Jebe swallowed hard and shivered under Jamus' gaze. "I know, My Lord." This time he couldn't stop his tears and he began to cry freely. " Me Mama is gonna to really be sad. She was so sure I was gonna do good in the stable. I never shoulda listened to Seng and Nobby. I shoulda just walked away like Mama taught me." He moved over to the mare and buried his face in the horse's massive shoulder. "I'm so sorry, girl. I coulda hurt you bad. I'm jest no good is all. No good. I always mess up everything."

"Stop it, Jebe," Jamus said softly. The boy's pain ached in his throat as he went on, "Don't say that about yourself. You made a mistake."

Jebe looked up at him, his eyes red. "I always make mistakes. I ain't good at nothing."

"You stayed on that mare's back, didn't you? Bory, lad, I'm not sure I would have been able to. I should think with the proper training, you'd make a fine rider. My stable could use a young lad who doesn't weigh too much to back my young horses. Do you think you might be interested?"

"Me? After what I done?"

"Show me you know how to make amends, and I don't see why not," Jamus replied. "Take a good look at your horse and tell me what you need to do."

Jebe studied the mare, his wrinkled in concentration. He'd never really cared for a horse before beyond leading the animals in and out of the barn, but he had seen Josep and the others, especially Jamus. Whenever the Master of Magiskeep had ridden, he'd hidden himself in the loft of the barn and watched. "Well," he said finally, "she's awful wet. She needs to be dried off. I kin walk her, but I ain't got no brushes or laving cloths to rub her. An'," he added, as his enthusiasm built, "she oughta have a sip or two of water while she cools. I seen Josep sponge down a lathered horse like this, and then give him a nice hot oat mash fer his belly. She'd like that." The mare lowered her head to the boy and he stroked her nose. "She'd really like that. But we're out in the middle of nowhere." Then he brightened. "I kin lead her back to the Keep. The walk'll be good for her. Maybe Josep would let me put her in one of the side stalls. I could sit with her to make sure she was OK."

Jamus laughed. "It's a long walk back to the Keep Jebe. There's a Keeper's cabin not far from here with a little barn. Suppose you and I go there and see if we can find a nice bucket of oats."

When Whim shoved his nose into Jamus' shoulder, nearly knocking his master off his feet, Jamus added, "All right, all right, Whim ... two buckets of oats. One for you and one for your lady friend."

Jebe coughed a little and reached for the mare's rope, his hands trembling with the cold. "I'll take care of her. I'll take good care."

Jamus frowned now, angry at himself for not having noticed how cold the boy was. "Jebe, where is your jacket?"

Jebe shrugged. "I ain't got one. I growed out of my old one and Mama didn't have the money to get me a new one. The stable's warm. It's all right."

Jamus shook his head. "It's not all right, Jebe." He gestured easily with his hand and in an instant, the boy was wrapped in a thick soft wool coat. A warm cap protected his head and a pair of thick gloves covered his hands.

Jebe grunted in surprise and cowered back, struck by Magic's sudden touch.

"Don't be afraid, lad," Jamus said quietly. "Let the River hold you. The hand of Magic is kind to its children."

Jebe nodded hesitantly. The coat felt wonderful. It was almost as if the fabric itself was generating warmth. "This is the best coat I ever had. Thank you, My Lord." Then he gathered the lead rope in his hand, stroked the mare's nose again, and waited for Jamus to show him the way.

It took less than a quarter span to reach the little cabin. As Jamus had said, there was a small but sturdy barn in the side yard, with four spacious stalls and an ample supply of hay stacked in the shed to its left. Built of logs fitted together by human skill rather than Magic, both the barn and the cabin had borne the weather well over the circles. "Nathin, the stablemaster before Josep took over in the Keep, built cabins like this in four places around Magiskeep," Jamus explained. "They're all fairly near the far pasturelands and this one's on the way to the Rim. Nathin never felt completely comfortable sending horses out to fend for themselves in the fields, so he would have one of his men stay out here during the harsher seasons. Later, when Josep earned the mastery, he kept most of the animals closer to the Keep and these cabins were hardly used. He stocks them all for travelers or emergencies. You can never tell when a field horse might need some special care and not be well enough to travel back to the Keep."

"It's nice here," Jebe said as he urged the mare into a stall. She was a bit nervous being inside after so much freedom and wasn't at all sure about the bucket hanging in the corner. Jebe soothed her, "It's all right, lass. That bucket won't hurt you. I'm gonna put some nice hay right near it so you're gonna have to go near it if you want to eat."

Jamus watched with interest as the boy took a good flake of the fragrant hay and let the mare sniff it. Then, when she took a bite and reached for more, he moved slowly into the stall and lay the hay to the right of the bucket. "I don't want it right under," he explained to Jamus, "'cause if she lifts her head and hits it, it's gonna scare her again." He smiled as the mare moved cautiously over to the corner, lowered her head, and began to eat. "Should I rub her first before I put on the cooler?" he asked.

Jamus nodded. "A bit. But don't try to put the cooler on by yourself. As far as I know, she's never worn a blanket. I'm taller than you are, so I can swing it up on her more quietly. When you've rubbed her down, you hold her rope and I'll do the rest."

"You don't have to help me, Sur. She is my responsibility."

"You're a good lad, Jebe," Jamus said, grinning. "I'd like to keep you safe and sound so you can learn how to handle some of the young horses for me. If you want to do that, you'll have to listen when I tell you what to do. Agreed?"

Jebe's voice was serious as he replied, "I promise, Master Jamus."

They spent the next span settling the mare into her new surroundings. She did shy away from the cooler and Jamus taught Jebe how to teach her to accept the strange object on her body. Whim, across the aisle, watched the activity with great interest, as if he too had a stake in the affair. When Jamus was satisfied that the mare could be left alone, he spelled an oat mash for Whim and a mix of less rich oat hay for the mare, then bolted the stall doors. "She's been on grass all season," he explained to Jebe. "Too much grain now isn't good for her. Now, I think we should go in the cabin and get some food for ourselves. Are you hungry, Jebe?"

The boy shrugged. "I got to watch the mare. You said she was my responsibility."

"And you said you would do whatever I told you to do. The horses will be fine here. You've done all you needed to do to take care of your mare."

"She ain't my mare, Master Jamus. I just took her."

"A master horseman needs a mount, Jebe. If you're going to learn to ride, you need something to practice on. You've already shown you can stick on her back. Besides, now that she knows she can jump the fence I don't think we can trust her out in the fields without someone to watch her. I'll see that she is properly trained to saddle and then she will be your horse to care for. She's pretty big for you, but I know she's bred to have good sense. Once she understands her job, she will be a perfect horse for you to learn on."

Jebe's face, lighting up more and more with each of Jamus' words, burst into a huge grin. "She'll be my horse?"

"I think she already is," Jamus said, laughing as the mare pushed her nose over the stall door to nuzzle Jebe's curls. "What will you name her? We can't keep calling her 'mare.'"

Jebe thought for a long time. "Skybound," he said at last. "I'll call her Sky for short."

"Skybound," Jamus repeated. "That's an interesting choice."

Jebe nodded. "She's a good jumper an' I already near touched the sky riding her, so that's a good name."

Jamus smiled. "Come on, Master to be. If Josep hasn't stocked the kitchen with anything we like, I'll Call a few dishes from the Keep kitchens to fill our bellies. Then, you and I are going to have a nice long talk."

True to his word, Jamus chanted a feast from the kitchens. Vegetable soup, thick dark bread, a roasted chicken, two huge baked taroots, and thick slabs of ballycake. Sweet surlep juice, a pitcher of milk, and a pot of steaming keldherb rounded off the meal. Noven always understood when food disappeared from his tables, and though he always grumbled about it, Jamus knew he always made extra whenever the Lord of the Keep was away just in case. This time, he would know Jamus was sharing time with a guest and soon the gossip would begin. "I'll have some explaining to do when we get back, Jebe, so you'd best eat every bite. I want you looking well fed when I give you back to Josep."

Jebe stared down at his heaping plate and sighed. "I never had so much food, My Lord."

"I can see that," Jamus replied. "You're far too thin. Does your mother stock a good kitchen?"

"Mama's a real good cook, but sometimes food is hard to come by. She takes in washing and does some sewin' for folks, but that don't bring in the denerets. I give her all the money I earn."

"So she has no other job?"

"She usta, afore I was born. She usta be a steward in the Keep, but onct she had me, she had to leave."

"She hasn't tried to go back?"

Jebe chewed a mouthful of bread, washed it down with a swallow of milk and shook his head. "She said she couldn't. She said she left under… under trying circumstances and it weren't safe for her to go back. She said she wouldn't be welcome."

Jamus frowned. There was no reason he could think of to keep the boy's mother away from the Keep unless there were someone there she needed to avoid. As Master, it was his duty to make sure no one in his household ever felt threatened or uncomfortable. "What about your father, lad?"

Jebe shrugged. "I ain't got a pa. Mama never talks about him."

Now things began to make some sense. The boy was, by name, clearly of the Magic in some small way. Since the River flowed through the male line, his father must have been a Magician. Who? If he could assess the boy's skill, he might have some clue. "You have some Magic, Jebe. Do you know how to use it?"

"No. I never done nothing like the Magic at all. Mama tells me I got some, though. She says sometimes it just takes a while to grow into it."

"Your mother is right, Jebe, but that doesn't mean you can't hurry it along. I could help you if you like. After we eat, let's talk about it."

Jamus sat back and studied the boy as he ate. Small for his age, Jebe had the coloring of more than one of the Keep's mages. He would have to do some investigating once they got back to the palace. Jebe's mother needed a job and there was no reason for her not to have one. If one of his mages was denying her that right, it was up to him to find out. "What's your mother's name? She must have been in the Keep when I was still there."

"Lurela," Jebe said. He straightened his shoulders proudly. "I be her only son and I be near nine circles now. That's almost a man. When I'm growed, I'm gonna take good care of her."

Nine circles. Then, Jamus was still a Prentice. He couldn't recall the woman's name. Then again, he'd never paid much attention to women in the Keep back then. He'd spent too much time hiding from Siamel. Besides, he wouldn't have had the foggiest idea about who might have been sleeping with whom. At that thought, he chuckled to himself, remembering his innocence in such matters. It had gotten him in a lot of trouble more times than he cared to count.

Now, though, it all mattered. If indeed Jebe was the son of a mage in his palace, then both the boy and his mother had been sorely

wronged. It was not the way of Magic, but more importantly, it was
not the way of his rule.

They ate, talking of the village, horses, and Jebe's dreams.
By the time the boy took his first bite of bally cake, he was laughing
and perfectly at ease with the Lord of Magiskeep.

"We need to test your Magic," Jamus said at last, when he
was certain the boy was completely relaxed with him. He didn't want
fear or nervousness to block the River as it often did when children
were faced with questioning by the Prentice masters. He remembered
his own initiation into the Way of Magic and how intimidating it had
been. In the end, his Magic had flowed easily and he had been
accepted as a student. How many children had failed, though,
because they were too frightened to call upon the River?

The first test was simple-a matter of Illusion. Jamus reached
into the pocket of his tunic and pulled out three balls of different
colors. These, he laid on the table. "Now, Jebe," he said. "I want you
to look at these three balls. Two of them are quite real, but the third
is an illusion I have created. Can you tell me which one that is?"

Jebe screwed up his face as he studied the balls.

"Don't try too hard," Jamus told him. "Just look at them and
let your mind See what it will. If you think too much the River will
not answer your call."

"But I thought you had to think to do Magic," Jebe replied.
"Mama told me the first Art is Comprehension."

"It is," Jamus answered patiently, "but here I am trying to
find out if you can feel Magic's flow. You can't call on something
you don't know in your heart, Jebe. It's a matter of believing. If you
need some kind of proof, or logic to find the Magic, then for you it
will never exist. Trust that it is there, waiting for your call and only
then will it answer."

The boy looked confused but did as Jamus instructed and
simply waited, his eyes focused on the balls just expecting to know
the answer. Suddenly, the blue ball seemed to waver, its contours
becoming fuzzy for just an instant. As soon as he concentrated there,
however, the ball became solid and sure again. Totally at a loss now,
he chewed his lip and then said, "The blue one, I think."

Jamus smiled. "Excellent, Jebe. How did you know?"

"I didn't. I just guessed. I thought … I thought for a second
that I saw something, then it went away."

Jamus nodded. "It went away as soon as you thought too
much about it. Trust your instincts, Jebe. This is what I am testing
you for, not whether you understand what's happening. Now, I want
you to take one of the balls without touching it. Decide on either the

red one or the yellow one. Once you choose, you must want the ball in your hand more than you have ever wanted anything in your life. Do you think you can do that?"

It was a test usually reserved for much younger children. Usually the object was a piece of surlep candy or a toy the child desired. Jamus was not certain the test was valid with someone as old as Jebe who had already learned to control such emotions, but it was worth a try.

Jebe focused on the red ball, wishing it were in his hand. When nothing happened, he glanced worriedly at Jamus and shifted uneasily in his seat. Would the Master send him from the Keep if he failed here? Surely the Lord of Magiskeep would not want to bother with a fool who had the name of Magic and no power to go along with it. The other boys had been right. He was just Li'l Runty, the clumsy stable lad nobody wanted. How dare he think the Keep would accept him when nearly every master in the village had declared him worthless?

Stupid ball. It was all that lay between him and his dreams.

The red ball lofted into the air and before he knew what was happening, Jebe raised his hand to catch it.

Chapter 3

Jebe's more formal testing in the Keep itself was a dismal failure. Despite every effort on Joria's part to get the boy to offer a simple illusion after her careful instructions, he showed no sign whatsoever of being able to control the Magic Jamus had detected.

"He has no talent for the Art at all, Jamus," the Mistress of Illusion repeated in answer to Jamus' insistence she try again. "He has kinship with the River, but no sense of Call. He's best off in the stable tending the horses. I've heard he shows some interest there. He certainly has none for my lessons."

Jamus sighed. He had hoped Jebe could gain a Prenticeship and earn a place in study. It was a far more suitable choice for a boy whose mother needed respect in the palace. Still, even with Jebe a mere stableboy, the Lord of Magiskeep fully intended to bring her back to her rightful position. Jeamel had agreed to take her on as one of several housemistresses whose jobs included supervising the maids who cleaned and organized the upper floors of the house. Though Magic could easily maintain the whole of the Keep with a single thought, Magicians had long ago learned that men thrived on physical accomplishment and often preferred using their hands to wash and sew rather than to weave spells. Besides, there were many of the Magic whose skills were so limited their calls to the River went unheeded. For them, serving the Masters and Mages was a way to share the Magic's Gifts while still maintaining their own pride as useful members of the community.

Jebe, it seemed, would have to be one of them. Fortunately, he seemed perfectly content with the prospect of earning his keep with the horses instead of in the classroom.

Seng, Nobby, Sila, Torrem, and Jevin were another matter. When Jamus and Jebe had returned to the stables astride Whim, they were all gathered in the tack room making a grand show of polishing the harness. In reality, they had been nervously discussing the disaster in Hidden Pines and trying to decide just what to do.

When Jebe's horse had jumped the fence, they had run after them in a vain effort to stop the mare's mad running. Although they had pretended not to care what happened to the boy, none of them really wanted to see him get hurt. The mare was too fast, though, and since they had no horses of their own to give chase, all they could do was try to keep sight of the pair in case Jebe fell off. They headed for the hill just north of the pasture to get a better view. Then, Nobby made it to the top of the hill before the others and saw the very end of Jamus' exciting rescue. But, the group's collective sigh of relief at the news offered no real reassurance. Though a Sevenstin had passed since the adventure, with no consequences, they were still not satisfied. Not a one of them knew exactly how solid their Riveroath actually was.

"Iffen he tells the Lord what we done, we'll all be sacked," Nobby said.

"He ain't gonna," Seng replied. "He swore like the rest o' us."

"He ain't Keeptaught, though. Who's ta say he's got ta abide?"

"Mebbe we should ask 'im," Sila suggested. "Soon's the Easwin chores is done, s'pose we bring the li'l Runty in an' put it too 'im."

The others agreed quickly. Then, they hurried off to care for the horses before Master Josep noticed them.

Jebe had mastered cleaning all the stalls in his aisle within a span. Gone was the loose straw and spilled water, for he had managed to gather enough sense and skill to carry a full bale to the barrow to wheel it to each stall. Now, his were the best-bedded horses in the entire barn, and Josep made careful note of it. "Good work, lad. It does me good ta see the mares an' the wee'uns have sech a good home."

Jebe grinned at the compliment. "I like to see the babies all nestled in the fresh straw, Sur. They sure sleep a lot."

"They's growin', lad. It takes a heap o' work ta grow's much as they does in so short a time. Wears 'em out."

"All but Flax's little shimmer colt," Jebe said. "He's always frettin' or botherin' his ma. Sometimes she looks like she don't want him with her anymore."

"Aye," Josep replied, " he's a terror, 'e is. His pa were full o' the mischief when he were a wee'un, but this fella's got it all over on 'im. Lord Jamus had ta spell 'im ta keep 'im in the stall steada meltin' in the aisle all the time getting' in ta trouble."

"He's spelled?" Jebe asked, his eyes wide with wonder. The all too elusive Magic still fascinated him.

"He is," Josep said. "I'd wager it's why he's frettin' so at the door. He cain't figger why he cain't get hisself out when he wants ta. Makes 'im mad, I reckon."

"He just wants something to do," Jebe answered. "He's bored in there. You see how happy he is when he and his ma is out in the paddocks? He wants to be doing things instead of being penned in."

"H-m-m-m-m." Josep rubbed his grizzled chin thoughtfully. "Ya might be right at that, lad. We cain't leave him out more, though, not whiles the weather's so chill."

"Do you think I could play with him a little?" Jebe asked hopefully. "We got that shed across the lane where sometimes the Lord works the big horses when it's raining out. If I took Shimmer over there, it wouldn't be so chill and I could teach him how to lead real good. He'd like that."

"Shimmer?" Josep said. "Is that what ya calls 'im?"

Jebe grinned sheepishly. "I didn't think Flax's Colt was much of a name, Sur. Until he gets a right proper one from Lord Jamus, I thought Shimmer would do."

Now Josep grinned. "If'en Lord Jamus agrees, I think it's the right name. As ta yer idea, ya'd best ask the Lord yerself. He's took ya on as prentice as far as training the beasties goes, an' ya already got Sky ta train. It's up ta him whether ya kin work the wee'un."

"Me ask?" Jebe said nervously. "I thought you'd... "

"'Tain't me place ta come between Lord an' prentice, Jebe. Ya gots ta larn ta stand up fer yerself."

Jebe gulped and nodded. As kind as Jamus had been to him, the Lord of Magiskeep still was an imposing figure in his eyes. Still, Josep was right. If he were every going to learn, he would have to do the asking himself.

Sowin's turn signaled the end of chores and Jebe hung the fork up on the wall next to the barrow and then reached out for Sky's lead rope and halter. He was checked by Seng's voice behind him. "What'd ya tell Master Jamus?"

Jebe spun to face the four other stablelad and Sila, blocking his path out of the little alcove at the side of his aisle. "I didn't tell him nothing I wasn't supposed to. I swore the same oath as you."

"So we're s'posed ta believe ya, Runty?" Nobby said, sidling up a bit closer. "I say ya ain't Keeptrained, so ya ain't holden ta the Riveroath."

Jebe stiffened a little at that. "Lord Jamus had me tested by Mistress Joria. He said I was of the Magic enough to earn a Prenticeship."

"Tested, eh?" Sila asked, peering at him. "Then how comes ya ain't wearin' prentisgrey, eh? Ya got yer school tunic hid away whilst ya muck stalls?"

Jebe's face reddened. He shifted a little uncomfortably in his brown woolen tunic. "I didn't make it this time. Not yet. Mistress Joria said I was maybe too young yet."

"Pah!" Jevin sniffed. "You gots near eleven circles behind ya. Most Prentices start after only seven. It ain't yer age, it's yer talent what stopped ya. Ya ain't got no Magic worth a lick, I reckon. Yer no better'n the rest o' us, an' yer a whole lot less. Leastwise we got skill in horsetendin'. Yer still lugging buckets."

Now Jebe bristled. "I'm gonna be a horse trainer like Lord Jamus. He's gonna teach me."

Sila laughed derisively. "First yer gonna be a Mage, now a horse trainer. What other kind o' dreams an' fibs ya gots in that head o' your'n, Runty? Ya gonna tell us yer gonna be Lord o' the Keep next?"

"Nah," Nobby mocked. "Next he's gonna tell us he's gonna be a horse."

"At least then he'd have more sense than the rest of you," a voice said from the shadows of the aisleway.

The group froze as one. Jamus' voice was recognized by everyone in Magiskeep. The River gave tone and power to every syllable.

"Now," he went on, "suppose you tell me what's going on here. For some strange reason, it looks as if five lads are ganging up on one, or do my eyes deceive me?"

Sila, braver than the rest where matters of quick invention came into play, turned to face the Keep Lord. Her face wore a look of complete innocence. "Four lads and a lass," she said, her lips curling up into what she was sure was a charming smile. "We're just having a little chat with young Jebe here."

Jamus hid his amusement. Sila may have been a stable lad in Josep's eyes, but she certainly had no trouble exercising her woman's wiles now. He pretended to be softened by her demeanor. He bowed slightly, "I am Sorry, mistress. I had thought you were threatening my prentice trainer. such a thing would, of course, concern me greatly, both as his teacher and as the Lord of this Keep. I don't mind childish pranks now and then as long as no one gets hurt, but I won't hold with cruelty to man or beast. I remember well how it feels to be tormented by those who should be friends and compatriots."

"We was talkin' friendly like," Nobby said quickly.

"Well, I could ask Jebe himself about that," Jamus replied quietly, "but I would never ask a man to defy a Riveroath."

The group gasped, unable to hide their surprise at his remark. Sila recovered first. "My Lord, whatever do you mean? There's been no swearing here."

This time, Jamus shook his head sadly. "Don't lie, madam. Dishonesty does not suit my stables. Do you think the River keeps secrets from me, her master? Her waters fill my ears." When Sila made a move to reply, he held up his hand to stop her. "No, I don't expect you to tell me about it. You have sworn to keep silent and so you shall. As I said, I have no problem with childish pranks, no matter how ill conceived they might be. Making foolish mistakes is part of growing up. It's the motive behind them I question. Jebe is here under my protection. He has a right to expect you to treat him well."

"What d'ya want us ta do, me Lord?" Seng asked. Older than the rest, he had seen Jamus deal with those who defied his law and wanted no part of it. The money he earned here was more than enough to keep his mother and sister well. He couldn't afford losing his place, and he knew Jamus wouldn't hesitate about sending him away if he didn't cooperate.

"I can't force you to be friends," Jamus answered, "but I can insist you all act with respect towards each other. If you must, talk only about your work here when you are together, or wait until Master Josep is with you before you share anything else. Before you speak, think how the words would sound if you were hearing them instead of saying them. One day, Jebe will be a Master Trainer here and you may be doing as he tells you to. Keep that in mind."

"He weren't lyin' 'bout the trainin' then?" Jevin asked.

"If that's what he told you, it's true. If you recall, I tested each one of you when you came to see if you had a natural leaning towards riding. If you also recall, all but Sila fell off as soon as the horse I asked you to ride began to move. The lady here managed to keep her seat until Pebble began to trot, if I remember correctly. Jebe, on the other hand, sat a galloping mare and a four-foot jump over a pasture fence with no trouble at all. Now, it would seem to me either he was extremely lucky, or extremely able. I happen to hope he is able. "

"He din't fall off?" Torrem said. As soon as he finished, he clamped his hand over his mouth as Nobby glared at him.

Jamus laughed. "It seems being Keeptaught doesn't promise the silence of the Riversworn. No, Jebe did not fall off. And, once his mare stopped running, his first concern was whether or not he had hurt her with his foolishness. Now, I don't need to know just why or how he happened to be astride an unbroken three-circle mare from my pasture, but I can well imagine the rest of you do. Let us just say it's done and leave it at that. The point is, Jebe proved himself and that earns him a chance to learn to ride unbroken horses the right way."

Seng bobbed his head up and down. "That's good. That's good, me Lord."

"Let's consider this done as well," Jamus said. "By the sun, I see it's nearly time for midmeal. Why don't you five go on up to the Keep and tell Jefir in the kitchen that Lord Jamus would like you to have a master's feast today. Tell him it is thrice commanded. Can you remember that? He'll understand."

When the other lads and, of course, Sila had gone, Jamus directed his attention to Jebe, who had sunk down on a bale of straw. "Are you all right, Jebe?"

"I'm fine," Jebe answered. "Are they gonna leave me alone now?"

"I think so. You have to understand, Jebe, sometimes people are cruel when they are afraid. You were new here, and they knew from the start I had a hand in your coming." Jamus sighed and raked his fingers through his dark hair. "In a way, it's partially my fault. I should have explained you weren't here to push someone else out of a job. I've never had more than five lads here at a time. I can only imagine what they thought when Josep took all that time helping you learn your job. Maybe it's best if you start your new position right now. Then it will be clear you have your own place here that's different than theirs."

"You mean I won't be a stablelad no more?"

"I'll talk to Josep right away so someone else can have your aisle."

"No. I mean, please, no, My Lord," Jebe protested. "I like taking care of the mares and babies. Besides, Shimmer needs somebody to walk him and keep him busy when he's about to get into mischief."

"Shimmer?"

Jebe shrugged. Then he went on breathlessly, "Flax's colt. Josep said if you said it was all right, I could take him out and walk him and things when he started to fret in the stall with his Mama. Josep said if you said it was all right we could call him Shimmer and I could help train him and he would be a good horse. Josep said...." He cut off quickly when Jamus raised his hand.

"Josep said all that, did he?"

"Well, almost. He said I was to ask you."

"And you did. That's good." Jamus rubbed his chin thoughtfully. "Shimmer is a good name the way his coat keeps shining from silver to gold. And you may be right about his needing to be kept busy. As Josep may have told you I had to spell him to keep him out of trouble. I'll tell you what, Jebe. We will take Shimmer out today and you will see if you can handle him. If you do well, then we can discuss your plan."

Jebe's face split into a wide grin. "That'd be grand, My Lord. Just grand. Can we do it now?"

Jamus nodded, and together, they headed for Flax's stall.

As was his habit, Shimmer was pacing the wall, his little head tossing every time he passed the door. The outlines of his body wavered now and then as he fought against Jamus' Magic with his own, but he couldn't break free. As Whim's creator, Jamus understood the essence of the stallion's little son far too well. He had woven a stelin net to keep the colt in line and had no intention of loosing it until the young horse had learned some manners. He was more willful than his father and so far had shown little of the great stallion's natural common sense. Now was as good a time as any to see if he had inherited anything of worth besides his beautiful coat.

With Jamus' approval, Jebe carefully opened the stall door and, with rope in hand, approached the colt. Shimmer snorted and Jebe waited, letting the rope dangle casually in his hand. "Come on now, Shim, you've seen a rope before. Remember when Josep had me lead you behind your ma? Now don't be silly." The colt eyed him warily, and then lowered his head. "That's a good fellow," Jebe said softly, slowly walking over. He reached out and snapped the lead on the little halter. Then he stroked Shimmer on the neck. "Do you want to go for a little walk? We're gonna go and have some fun learning all kinds of new things." The shining colt seemed to understand, for as Jebe headed for the aisle, he pranced along at his side as if happy to be on some grand adventure.

With Jamus keeping close watch, they made their way across the stableyard and into the training shed. All the way, Shimmer's head twisted from side to side as he took in all the new sights and smells of the strange place. Paddock-raised, he had never been out into the yard. Still, he kept himself under control and only shied once when a stray breeze sent a pile of leaves swirling in a far corner of the yard.

Once in the shed, Jebe turned to Jamus. "I figured I should lead him all around in here first before I do anything else. He should see it's a safe place to be. It's hard to learn if you don't feel safe."

"Good," Jamus replied, smiling. "That's exactly what I would do."

Shimmer fussed a bit on his tour, but Jebe's soothing words and gentle touch reassured him. Soon the pair were marching along as if they had been working together for days instead of less than a span.

Jamus showed Jebe how to teach his pupil to move away from the pressure of his hand by at first pushing against the colt's shoulder with his hip at the same time. "If you watch horses in the field, you'll see how they herd each other with their bodies. You have to pretend to be a bit of a horse yourself when you begin. Shimmer will understand what just your hand means later."

They worked for less than half a span and then Jamus ordered them to stop, explaining how young horses could not be expected to concentrate for very long. Then they headed back to the barn.

Once Shimmer was safely back in his stall, Jebe looked hopefully at his master. "Well, did we do good enough to let me try?"

Jamus leaned on the stall door to watch as the shining colt sank into the straw for an apparently much needed nap. "Promise me that you will only work him when either Josep or I am close at hand to call if you need help. Later, perhaps, when the other lads have thought about what I said to them, you may handle him when one of them is nearby. You must remember, he is still just a baby and if something goes wrong, you can't be sure how he will behave. It's important you have another horseman around to help you so neither one of you gets hurt. Do you understand?"

"Aye, My Lord," Jebe replied eagerly.

"Now then, didn't you and I talk about working Skybound today? I hope you haven't forgotten her."

"I never would forget her," Jebe said. "She is my horse. I groomed her before. If she didn't lie down in her stall, she should be all clean so it won't take me long to get her ready."

In short order, Jebe was in the shed with the bay mare, carefully settling into her saddle. The Sevenstin before, they had carefully taught her to accept the tack, then weight on her back, and finally a rider. With Jamus walking at her head, Sky had learned to walk along with her new master on her back. Now, she was ready to try it without a leader to follow.

She was a quick learner, and as before, Jebe's quiet handling and encouraging words seemed to reassure her. She let him guide her a bit with the reins as they walked along, following her head as he pulled it a little to the left or right, testing her reactions. At last, he tugged back carefully and said, "Whoa." When she stopped, he patted her on the neck and swung off on to the ground. "You are a good girl. That's enough for today, I think." He slipped her a surlep candy from the pouch at his belt. "My Lord, I would say it's time to stop. She's done everything I asked."

"Excellent choice," Jamus agreed. "When you are finished grooming her, give her two flakes of greenhay and be sure her water bucket is full. Then you and I will share midmeal. Later we'll go out for a short ride in the fields. I want to watch you trot Pebble. You will need to practice your balance if you are going to do much more with Sky than just walk. Young horses need skilled riders. If you can't keep your seat where it belongs, it will make it hard to teach your lady anything at all."

With Jebe working hard to follow his instructions, Jamus went to Whim's stall, opened the door, and settled himself on the stallion's manger. Whim nuzzled his arm and then went back to contentedly pulling out mouthfuls of hay while Jamus watched. "So just what goes on in that head of yours, my friend? Do you dream dreams like I do? I know you have a big heart and more sense than most men I know, but what secrets can you tell me?"

Like little one. Good hands.

Again, the stallion nuzzled him, and Jamus scratched him under the chin. Whim stretched out his neck and almost seemed to smile. "So, is the lad worth the time, eh? I know he touches the River, I've seen it. And yet, in the Keep, the Magic denied his call again and again. Why? He's the son of a Mage, and, I'd wager, not one of the lesser ones. I could feel the River reaching out to him. What is his talent, I wonder? If I could find his father, perhaps I'd have a clue." Then he sighed. "I don't suppose his mother would be particularly willing to tell me. Then again, I am the Lord of Magiskeep."

Whim snorted. *River waits for call. Know when time.*

One more riddle and this one from a horse.

*****

The far borders of West Village boasted no elegant homes. Instead, the dirt streets, though well-tended, were lined with modest cottages and a few little shops. Jamus had offered more than once to use Magic to improve his subjects' lives, but time and again, he and the other Masters of the Keep had been refused. Here, as nearly everywhere in Magiskeep, people preferred the freedom to succeed or fail on their own skills instead of on the River. Assured that no one would starve or suffer from plagues because of Magic's protections, the commoners went about their daily lives relying on Turan's Way and the grace of the Hand rather than the grace of the Rivermaster.

Still, Jamus felt a nag of guilt every time he came here. The palace and Keep proper were richly furnished, and his charges there fed only the best food and drink. It had never seemed right to him that some should prosper purely because of a favor of birth while others had to live by wit and sweat alone.

"It's what we wants, me Lord," Becca had always told him. "Them what ain't got but muscle and brain ta give'em what they needs wants ta use 'em. Ya think about it. A Master like yerself could have most anythin' 'e wanted, jest by thinkin' on it. But, ya don't. Ya don't use yer Magic so much."

"Rule and Vow deny it," Jamus replied. "Magic is not to be used freely without good purpose."

"An' why do ya s'pose them Rule an' Vow come inta bein', eh? Them Eldenmages weren't no fools, I tell ya. They knowed the truth o' how a man's gotta work fer what he gits or he ain't gonna be happy."

"I never thought of it that way," Jamus replied. "I was always taught they were to deny the use of Magic Unrestrained."

Becca frowned in confusion at that. She had never really learned enough of the Magic to quite understand what he had said. She simply countered with a typical Becca solution to every problem. "Here," she said, "set yerself down and have a nice plate o' me hot stew."

Jamus chuckled to himself, remembering. And he remembered too her lesson. Jebe's mother might be living in the smallest cottage on the street, but it was the cottage she had earned herself. He would be wise not keep that in mind.

He went to the door and knocked.

A small face appeared at the window, peeking out from behind a pretty yellow curtain. Two wide eyes stared at him in utter surprise. Then the face disappeared and he heard scuffling at the door. A moment later, the door itself swung open as a slender young woman curtsied deeply to him. "My Lord. I am honored to have you at my house. Please come in and feel welcome at my hearth."

Jamus extended his hand in the formal greeting and lifted the woman from her curtsey. "Mistress Lurela? I hope I've not come to the wrong house." He was startled to see how young she looked-no more than a girl just passing into her twenties. Jebe was nearly eleven circles by his reckoning. How could his mother be so young?

"I am Lurela," she said softly, her voice musical and sweet. Then her face sharpened in alarm. "You're not here about Jebe, are you? Has something happened to him? I worry about him with those big horses."

"Your son is fine. Be assured I won't let anything happen to him as long as he is in my employ. He is a fine lad with a special gift for horsemastery. Someday, he'll be a trainer. Fine horsemen can earn a good living anywhere in Turan, you know."

Lurela sighed with obvious relief. "I'm glad. He's had so many jobs already and he's only but twelve circles. Poor lad."

Twelve. Older then, than even Jamus had guessed. "I thought Jebe told me he was ten."

"Oh, he would," Lurela said quickly. "He doesn't know when he was born. I was near wee lass myself, just past thirteen circles. You don't think a lad would need to know that, do you?"

"Thir... " Jamus began. Then he shook his head. No wonder hardly anyone in the Keep recognized Lurela's name. She must have been one of the minor maid's helpers who came and went with little notice. "I've come to ask you about that," he said finally.

Lurela's face grew darkly serious, her deep violet eyes hardening with every word. "And why would that be, My Lord? What does it matter now?"

"Jebe has the Magic, My Lady, and the River always concerns me. I sense a definite connection in him to some secret shore I can't quite understand. If Jebe has potential, it's my duty to see it realized."

She shrugged. "He seems right happy in the stables. Why don't you just let sleeping tarks lie?"

Jamus studied her for a moment. Her hair was dark - almost black - and she was a little slip of a thing. That might explain Jebe's being so small for his age, but it didn't explain his coloring. What mage did he resemble? His hair was dark blond, his eyes hazel. Certainly his father might have been any one of a dozen golden Sorcerers in the Keep. Then again, who would have been so bold as to bed a mere child who'd just barely become a woman? He shuddered to think of any man in his charge with so little moral compunction.

There would have been Sagari, of course, but that really didn't make much sense. The River had been potent in the former Lord's veins. If Jebe were his son, there would be no question of the boy's skills in Magic. Inheritance from a Master of such Art was guaranteed in Turan's Way.

"Who is Jebe's father?" Jamus repeated evenly. He would not use the Voice of command here. Lurela would have to tell him of her own free will.

"It were a childish mistake made by two, My Lord. I've paid for it and he has probably forgotten. Let it be."

Jamus sank into a chair by her little table and traced a pattern on the wood with his finger. The bright curtains at the windows and the colorful quilt on the beds against the east wall of the little two-room cottage did little to lighten his mood. Normally, he would have enjoyed seeing the attractive little home Lurela had made here for her son. But there was a poison tainting it. "It's not right, Mistress. The boy's father has a responsibility to the both of you. Don't you see that?"

"I see my home, and a son who smiles when he comes in that door. I haven't seen you smile once yet. Is that the price Magic makes you pay? If so, I don't want that for Jebe."

"The River may not will it so."

"Then let the River name his father, for I will not."

This time, Jamus did smile. Without realizing it, Lurela has solved the problem for him.

Chapter 4

Salene put the last book on the new bookshelf in Jamus' study and stood back to admire her work. It was the first bit of woodworking she had ever tried and, though the result was not perfect, she finally decided it really wasn't that bad after all.

The pinewood had been easy enough to saw once Master Saraban showed her exactly how to measure each piece. But then, when she had begun to fashion the joints together, somehow one whole section became lopsided, as if all the boards had been different lengths.

"A fraction here, a fraction there," Saraban had told her, "may not seem to make much difference at first, My Lady. But think of this. Each little bit at one end of a board is magnified at the other end of a board, and the longer the board the more it matters. Here now, make your shelves shorter, and put braces in between." Then, he taught her how to straighten and adjust the corner joints to correct most of the problems, until, at last, the shelves had the semblance of being squared.

Now, even with a slight tilt to one of the lower shelves, the whole case looked sturdy and fit well in the corner by the window. She was particularly pleased with the finish-a dark wood stain overlaid with a silky varnish she had sanded and layered at least three times. Watching the wood color and feeling the surface smooth beneath her hand had been such a pleasure, she was already considering refinishing one of the study tabes in the Great Library.

Magic, of course, would have been easier, and even Master Saraban had asked why she wanted to do the work by hand. "It's not the usual task of the Lord's Lady," he said.

"And I am not the usual Lady," Salene replied, smiling. "I suppose I could be spending my time sewing shaenis coverlets." She laughed. "I'd wager they'd be even more crooked than the bookshelf, though. I wanted to learn something new, Master Sor, something challenging. It's not enough to run the household and teach a class or two, especially with all the servants to do the real work. A person needs to accomplish something with his own two hands."

"Indeed," Saraban replied, rubbing his own hand lovingly over the polished top of a chest of drawers he had fashioned. "I could Magic this and have as fine a piece, but it would never be mine."

She sighed. "Magic's Gift is sometimes a curse, Sur." And then she thought of Jamus and her heart ached. How many times had the River taken him unbidden, as if it were his master instead of the other way around? How many times had he told her how he wished to be free of the Power consuming him? And how many more times would it be before the Magic would take him from her forever?

That was why she had made the bookcase for him in the first place. It was as if putting it here, in the room where he spent so much time wrestling with the River's secrets, there would always be a small part of her for him to hold on to.

"Salene?"

She spun in surprise, caught off guard by Jamus' sudden arrival. "Oh, Jamus. I didn't expect you yet. Weren't you going into the Village?"

He nodded. "I already did." Then, he peered past her, his eyes brightening as he notice the bookcase behind her. "You made that?"

She grinned. "I did. No Magic, either. Sor taught me everything I needed to know. It's not perfect, but the books haven't fallen out yet."

He walked over and laid his hand on the top shelf. "The finish is beautiful. How many times did you sand it?"

"Three," she replied proudly. "By then the final coat lay so smoothly I couldn't believe it."

"I like the design, with the shelved divided like that. We can arrange the books into categories that way. What do you think?"

"You really like it?"

"Have I ever lied to you?"

Now, she had to pause for a moment. His words rang back in her memory to circles past, when he had made a promise to her of unquestioned honesty. "No," she said at last. "Then again, sometimes you do tease me."

He laughed. "I'm not teasing now, my Love. I really do like the bookcase." Then, he settled himself down in the chair by his study desk and leaned back. "Tell me, Salene, do you remember a little serving girl by the name of Lurela who was here in the Keep some twelve circles past?"

"Lurela," Salene repeated. "Tiny thing, dark hair and lovely violet eyes?"

He nodded.

"She was quite a seamstress, if I recall. She once mended the sleeve of my favorite dress so well I never even thought of using Magic to mend the weave. She left, I think, around the time I myself left the Keep. I can't quite be sure about that. I was not exactly clearheaded about what was going on beyond my own concerns."

"She is Jebe's mother."

"How could that be? Why, Jamus, you said Jebe was nearly eleven."

"He's twelve."

"Twelve? Than that means she was hardly a woman herself."

"She'd just passed thirteen circles," he answered.

"By the Blood! She was a baby! Who was the father?"

"Lurela won't tell me that. She did say, though, they were both too young. Jebe has Magic, Salene, so it had to be one of the Mages here... one of the Prentices?"

Salene dropped down on to the bench under the window. "How are you going to find out?"

This time, Jamus smiled. "Magic knows its own, Salene. I should think you and I can certainly discover a way to let the River reveal the truth." He stretched his arms over his head, rocking back even more in the chair. "We do have a Seer to consult, and a certain Crystal at our disposal. All we really need beyond that is a set of suspects and the right questions."

"Prentices from twelve circles past," Salene said thoughtfully. "Your classmates would fit into that category, you know."

Jamus' face betrayed no reaction. "That's true, as would Prentices from the class before mine."

"What about the NewMages during that time? Would any of them have been young enough to play the fool like that?"

He straightened again and dropped his hands on the desk. "Possibly, but NewMages would not so easily frighten Lurela into leaving the palace. The Oath is still too strong in their hearts to let them threaten her. No, I'd think it would be a Prentice still wrapped up in his own selfish pursuit of power. Someone like that would thrive on the excitement and find it a challenge to assure his own anonymity in the affair. Prentices think they have something to prove."

"You've not forgotten much of your childhood, have you."

"None," Jamus told her. "I keep it with me always to remind myself to be humble. Sometimes, when the Power surges in my hand, I look at the floor like I used to and remember how hard it is to suffer at the hands of someone bigger and stronger than you are. Then, the River listens and obeys."

"It must be hard to fight sometimes, Jamus. I've felt the strength of the Magic in you. To think of it trying to do its Will without your say... " Salene's voice trailed off. She could hardly conceive of how it must be. To tell him otherwise was a lie, and she believed his promise had to work both ways. "I can't imagine what it would be like."

"It is as it is," he replied. Then, he slapped his hand down decisively on the desk. "But, I didn't start this conversation to solicit your sympathy for my problems, Love. What we need to do is come up with some kind of plan to find Jebe's father. Who keeps records of all the Prentices of any given Circle?"

"Joria has the Journals. I can ask her."

"Good. I know the Prentices of my class, but those of the Circle prior and the Circle after? Strange. You'd think I might have known some of them."

"Once a Prentice flies the Cup, his whole life is centered on his Master. Before that," Salene said, letting a smile tug at her lips, "didn't you say you were looking at the floor?"
*****

Jamus arrived early at the stable the next Easwin, on the pretense of having important business to attend to with Josep. While the business was real, its urgency was not. The claim was merely an excuse for his visit to see how effective his lecture to the stablelads had been.

He found Jebe in his aisle wrestling with an unusually heavy bale of straw. As the smaller boy tried to lurch it into the barrow for the third time, Nobby noticed and hurried over to give him a much-needed hand. "That's a big'un," he said once the bale was settled. "Don't know why the baler sometimes throws 'em that size. I wisht it din't. Near always takes two ta lug 'em when they's so heavy."

Jebe smiled warily. "I was gonna take another one when I couldn't handle this one. That's what I always did afore."

"No need o' that, Jebe," Nobby replied. "If'en ya gets one too big agin, ya jest call me. Kin I ask the same o' you if'en I gets a job what's too big fer me?"

Jebe nodded. "I'd be glad to help you, Nobby."

Nobby grinned now, openly and kindly. "Yer not sech a bad fellow, Jebe. Not sech a bad fellow at all." Then he jogged back to his own aisle across the way, whistling an old country song.

Jebe stood for a little while before pushing the barrow off to the stalls. Then, whistling his own version of the same song, he went back to work.

Jamus, watching from the shadows by the tack room, smiled.

"Don' know how ya done it," Josep told him later in his office, "but ya gots them lads ta git along. They's all bin helpin' each other this Easwin like I never seed afore. Chores'll be done a span early, looks like. What am I gonna do with the lads then?"

"Maybe they'd like to learn how to ride properly," Jamus said. "I'd be glad to teach them."

"Ain't a bad notion," Josep said. "Ya could use I mite more help takin' that stock ta Lord Delran come Newseason. I figgered ya'd be takin' Jebe, but young horses kin be a trial fer only two herders. Mebbe one o' the other lads'd suit? Do ya think?"

"I was coming to tell you I'd like to make the trip in the next three Sevenstins," Jamus replied. "I think at least one of those lads might be able to master enough skill to go along with us by then. Could you manage here with only four lads while we're gone?"

"Ya leavin' Sarn in charge o' the Keep agin whilst yer away?"

Jamus nodded. "He's the best man at managing things. I may not like him, but I can't fault his abilities. People certainly do listen to him and respect his opinion. Salene will be here to temper his decisions, if necessary, so I don't see any reason why not. Why did you ask?"

"Ah, naught but he likes ta ride a lot more when yer not here is all. Fair hand with the horses too. Kind o' surprises me. Jest that he ain't so good doing the drudge work like saddlin', groomin', an' coolin'. Need a lad jest ta tend 'im, ya see. Four'd leave me one more short with 'im hangin' 'round."

"I didn't know Sarn liked horses."

"O' 'e likes 'em all right, an' strange ta say, they likes 'im too. I seen 'im ride an' ta tell the truth 'e ain't no master up there astride. But the weird o' it is the horses seem ta know what 'e wants 'em ta do no matter how bad 'e asks. 'E ain't ne'er hurt one, neither. Rides 'em gentle all the ways home so they come in all happy an' full 'o theyselves. I usta jest give 'em ol' Pebble 'cause I figgered she'd ne'er hurt 'im, but now, aside from the stallions, I give 'em whiche'er beastie needs ta be out fer some exercise."

"Well now," Jamus said thoughtfully, "this is all very interesting. Sarn's never been one of my favorite people, but a man who's good with horses must have a spark of decency in his somewhere. Too bad I never had the chance to notice it."

"Yer 'is rival, Me Lord. 'E figgered all long ta be Master here onct Lord Sagari was gone. Ya ask Mistress Joria if'en ya don't believe me. Then ya comes along an' from the first 'e knows ya got more Magic'en anyone. It's jest like the lads here wid Jebe. I knows ya seen it, 'cause elsewise ya wouldn'ta done nothin' about it. They was jealous o' 'im jest like Sarn were jealous o' ya."

"Did Sagari ever hint he'd name Sarn?" Jamus asked.

"They usta ride together afore ya come. Tight as Lastseason boots they was. The ya come along an' Sagari spent all that time showin' off what a grand kind man 'e were by takin' in a stray from the Rim, an' Sarn got left in the dust. T'weren't no big thing to nobody but Sarn, I reckon. Cain't say nobody but me mighta even noticed."

That would explain a lot, Jamus thought. From the first, Sarn had resented him. Still, explanation could never undo all the misery he had suffered at Sarn's instigation. He had been the leader among the Prentices and had given no quarter where Jamus was concerned. And it was for that very reason Jamus had appointed him to take his place whenever he was away. It might seem strange to the rest of the Keep who well knew of past animosity, but Jamus placed the good of the kingdom well above his own feelings. If the Keep should ever be in danger, Sarn would not hesitate to use whatever force or Magic was necessary to defend it.

"I said, jest why does ya always leave 'im in charge anyhows?" Josep asked, interrupting Jamus' thoughts. "Seems ta me the Lady Salene'd do the job jest fine."

"Sarn's not afraid to be cruel," Jamus replied. "The Keep might need that if there's trouble."

Josep rubbed his grizzled chin and peered at him. "Them's strange words ta be comin' from ya, lad. Firstwise, I don't think I ever seed a cruel bone in yer body an' yer doin' a fair job o' runnin' the place. An' nextwise, I ain't particular seed nobody tryin' ta do the Keep in."

"Salene and I have enemies, Josep, the kind who'd stop at nothing to destroy Magic's sanctuary. Some of them have powers even I can't reckon. And as for my cruelty, I can assure you it's often all I can to do keep it reined in."

"Ya hides it good," Josep replied, laughing a little. Then he shook his head. "Ya sure ain't the wee lad what first come here wid Sagari, that's certain. I cain't say I'm all pleased wid what ya become, but ya ne'er done me or mine wrong. Yer a good man, Me Lord, a good man, an' don't ya fergit it."

Jamus smiled. "I respect your opinion, Josep. Still, Sarn will be in charge when I leave. In the meantime, I'll go into the village and find you a lad or two to help out while we're gone. I suspect if I paid him well enough, Master Tam in the livery could manage to find some competent handlers. Maybe he has a lad who's used to waiting on the gentry who could act as Sarn's groom."

"Tam runs a good stable, but it ain't up ta Keep standards," Josep sniffed.

This time, Jamus laughed. "Your standards, you mean. You don't need to serve dinner off the floor in a barn, you know. Tam's horses are well fed and well cared for."

"I s'pose I could train 'is lads ta do it right. Be a bit o' work undoin' all their bad habits."

"I knew you could," Jamus agreed heartily. "Then it's settled. I'll take Jebe and one other lad with me, bring you two from Tam, and head out to Lord Delran's Keep without a worry."

Josep simply nodded. Somehow he didn't believe a word of it.

*****

Magiskeep was noted for breeding fine horseflesh and the main stables were full of superb saddle animals. Still, it was not an easy task for Jamus to find five mounts both quiet and tolerant enough to accept the clumsy stable crew in a group lesson.

It wasn't that the horses were not well-trained enough, but training was not the only requirement. Pebble, the sturdy brown mare nearly anyone could ride with confidence was an obvious choice, as was Flutter, a large spotted pony who let children hang off his tail whenever he visited the village. But the last three were a question in his mind. Certainly Redwin was quiet enough, but like Toggle, he had never really been ridden by a raw beginner. The last horse was Whim himself, the one creature in all of Magiskeep Jamus could entirely depend on. Yet, the silver stallion did have an individual sense of humor and Jamus was not completely convinced he might not decide to pull a prank if he were bored or bothered by the whole experience.

He matched Sila with Pebble and Nobby with Flutter, paired Jevin with Redwin and Torrem with Toggle, and finally, bold Seng with Whim. They made for a motley bunch, but the humans were eager to try and the horses interested in the new adventure.

"Jebe," Jamus said, "I'm expecting you to act as my second eyes. If you see anyone getting in trouble, let me know at once."

The arena was large enough to accommodate ten riders at once, so the young students had plenty of room to learn to maneuver their mounts. Still, horses seemed to be going in all directions including backwards when Jamus first tried to explain how to steer. More often than not, someone would tug the reins back instead of to the side and their mounts would respond accordingly, much to the frustration of the rider. Jebe finally took charge of the far end of the ring, issuing supportive advice whenever someone managed to walk by.

Jamus patiently explained over and over exactly how to sit in the saddle, how to hold and use the reins, and just exactly how to encourage the horses to go forward. Of all his pupils, Nobby quickly proved to be most able, with a good sense of balance and control.

Seng, on the other hand, had little concept at all of how to communicate with his horse. At first, Whim put up with his constant tugging and his rocking in the saddle every time they began to move. But gradually, the stallion began to show his displeasure. He swished his tail, then laid back his ears, and once or twice simply refused to move at all even when Seng let go of the reins completely. "'E don't want ta lissen ta me," Seng complained. "'E's jest a stubborn ol' mule, 'e is."

"I wouldn't say that if I was you," Jebe warned. "Whim is very proud. You shouldn't insult him."

"'E's stupit," Seng insisted. "'E don't do nothin' I tells 'im too."

"You gotta tell him right," Jebe replied. "Stop pulling so hard on the reins. If you want him to go left put your hand out to the left side and give him a nudge with your left heel the way Master Jamus showed you."

Seng grunted and gave the stallion a kick with his heel. Whim answered with a kick of his own, nearly unseating the already unbalanced boy. Seng grabbed the horse's mane and groaned, "I hates this. I hate ridin' and I hates this big ugly beast. 'E's dumb an' stubborn like a mule."

Suddenly, Seng was on the ground, falling straight down into the sand as Whim simply melted out from under him to reappear a short span away, his head lowered, his front hoof pawing the sand in annoyance.

Jamus managed to keep a straight face. The sight of Seng and saddle bottom down in the dirt was almost too comical to bear but by turning away and coughing, he succeeded in hiding his laughter.

Jebe, though, reacted at once, hurrying over to Seng. "That were a mean thing he did to you, Seng. Are you all right?" When Seng grunted and nodded, Jebe looked straight at the stallion and wagged a finger at him. "You should be ashamed of yourself, Whim. 'Tis not nice to be cruel to someone who's just learning. If you want to show how smart you are, then show it by being a good teacher instead of throwing a tantrum. Smart folks know how to be kind 'cause they got the brains to understand how hard it is to learn something new."

Whim stared back at him, his head sinking lower and lower with each of the boy's words. Then, he shuffled quietly over to Seng and nuzzled him ever so gently on the shoulder.

"That's better," Jebe said. "Come on, Seng, I'll help you put the saddle back on him and get back on."

"I ain't riding that monster agin," Seng replied, close to tears. "'E hates me."

Again, Whim nuzzled him gently and nickered softly.

"No he don't," Jebe said. "He's sayin' he's sorry. Look, Seng, you gotta get back on or you're never gonna be able to ride 'cause you'll always think you can't do it. I'll walk along beside you if you like. All you got to do is go one time around the ring, all right? Just one time and then you can get off."

Jamus listened with interest, staying out of the situation. Clearly something important was happening and he didn't want to interfere.

Dusting off his wounded pride, Seng clambered to his feet. "I ain't real good at putting the saddle on," he said.

"I can show you," Jebe said as he undid the girth and then hefted the saddle up to Whim's back. The horse was far too tall for him, however, and he couldn't reach. "Well," he laughed. "I could show you if'en I was taller. I think we need to take him over by the mounting steps so I can reach. Do you want to lead him?"

Cautiously, Seng took the stallion's reins and tugged. This time, Whim followed obediently.

Once back in the saddle, Seng listened intently to every word of instruction Jebe gave him and after one turn around the ring, decided he would try another. Soon, he was back in the lesson itself, carefully obeying Jamus' directions and managing quite well on his own.

Nobby was the only one of the five who was able to trot a bit by the lesson's end. When they were all back on the ground, and the horses groomed and fed, Jevin and Torrem decided their careers in the saddle were over. Nobby, Sila, and Seng all decided to try again, telling Jamus they would like to learn how to ride well enough to take horses out to check the far pastures instead of walking. When Jamus agreed, they went off to evenmeal, chatting happily, quite pleased with themselves.

"I was proud of you, Jebe," Jamus said as the boy topped off Whim's water bucket. "You were very kind to Seng."

"I wanted to laugh," Jebe admitted. "He looked so silly setting there on the ground like that, and Whim was only trying to teach him a lesson. But he was so embarrassed, and maybe a little scared. I didn't want to make a fool out of him, even if he did deserve it."

"I'm not sure I could have treated him so well myself."

"Oh, you woulda, Sur. It was just I was closer." Then Jebe did laugh. "Whim sure has a mind of his own. I think he taught Seng more right then than anybody did during the whole ride."

"I suppose he did," Jamus replied, laughing a little too. "He has very strong opinions about things."

"Shimmer is just like him," Jebe said. "Why, if Whim didn't love you so much that he wants to do what makes you happy, he and that son of him would be making all kinds of trouble here in the barn. I could just see it now. Master Josep would be having a fit."

"He would indeed," Jamus agreed, remembering too well how often one of Whim's disappearing tricks would drive Josep to distraction. He was suddenly glad he had put such a strong weave on the little colt. Then, he thought for a moment. "Jebe, how do you know so much about what Whim thinks?"

Jebe shrugged. "Sometimes I just knows, that's all. I guess maybe I figure what I'd be thinking if I was him, that's all. Horses ain't much different than people."

"I see," Jamus replied, but something nagged at the back of his mind. As natural as Jebe's talent with the horses seemed, there was also something uncanny about it.

Something quite uncanny.

Chapter 5

Master Tam's livery stable was clean and orderly, despite Josep's claim to the contrary. In fact, in many ways it rivaled the Keep's barn. The horses were well-fed and well groomed, the stalls clean and the aisles, though lined in wood instead of cobblestone, were well swept.

"Two lads, eh?" Tam replied. He squinted his green eyes into thinking slits, scrubbed his hand along his red beard and seemed to have a hard time puzzling out the request.

"Twenty denerets a day to cover the loss of their help," Jamus offered, knowing full well the lads would have only earned half that. Tam would be making a ten deneret profit even if he had to hire two more boys to replace those Jamus needed.

"Cain't say as I got two lads to spare," Tam said.

"I wouldn't ask if I didn't need lads who knew something about horses," Jamus answered, avoiding the issue of offering more money. "Josep has a lot of young stock right now and I don't want to risk novices. I thought you could find a few lads in the village yourself more easily. But, if that's not the case, I can just… "

"No, no, My Lord," Tam broke in quickly. "I gots two youngins in mind what wants a job. I dint take 'em on yet 'cause it's still not the full season. I reckon I kin hire 'em now an' when the leasin' starts up in Newmonth, they'll be full ready ta do me a good job with the customers. Tell ya what. Ya gives me two more denerets fer the trouble they'll be, and I'll lend ye Mat an' Arv fer yer barn. They's my two best. Arv usta groom fer Lord Sarkem down in Southreach afore he come ta the village. 'E knows what side o' the horse ta put a saddle on, I tells ya. As fer Mat, he's a good hand an' he works hard. Ol' Jospep'll be lucky ta have 'im."

"Fair enough," Jamus said, knowing full well Tam had gotten the best of the bargain. The liveryman had earned a nice profit and could teach two new workers all they needed to know before his busy season began. "I'll expect the lads at my barn come Sevenstin next, then. Here's half the money now. I'll send the rest just before I leave."

"So, yer takin' stock ta Lord Delran, eh? What's he lookin' fer? I gots me a few real good palfrey's fer sale. If'en he needs ladies' horses, these is the best."

"Not this time," Jamus replied, "but I will tell him. I have some young work stock he's been waiting for. We bred them for the harness. I'm going to be interested to see how he likes them."

"Aye. The Lord has a fine eye for the beasties, 'e does. I went wid Lord Sagari onct ta see 'is barns. Misery traveling through them damn mountains, but I tell ya, the trip were worth it. Some o' the finest stock I seen. Some even better'n Magiskeep's. Ya do yerself right proud if'en he likes what ya bred, My Lord, right proud." Then, he motioned to one of the stablehands who had been standing in the feed stall, listening. "Wyam, why don't ye go get the chestnut mare ta show Lord Jamus here. If'en he looks at her, he might put in a favorable word ta Lord Delran fer me. I'd be mighty pleased ta have her sold 'crost the Rim. Gives man a good reputation, ya know?"

Jamus had to admit the mare was pretty, with a big white star and four white socks. She seemed quiet too, and Tam assured him she was well-mannered under saddle. "Lord Delran might really like her," he said, stroking the mare's silky muzzle. "I might be able to take her with us, especially if the new lad I'm training works out."

Tam grinned. "Take her, an' ya kin have back the two denerets extry ya gived me. I'll settle on twenty a day an' the price ya git fer Lacy here. Fair?"

"Fair," Jamus agreed. "Have this little lady ready to go when I send for her and we'll see if Turan is ready to do business with you."

Wyam patted the mare's neck and reluctantly led her back to her stall while Jamus and Tam made the final arrangements. He had wanted to hear every word they were saying.
*****

Salene had narrowed the list of suspects to Jebe's parentage down to five--three boys from Jamus' class of Prentices and only two more from other classes. "I had a long talk with Jiala and Siamel," she explained. "Those two know more about who had been a virgin back then than anyone in the whole of the Keep."

"Boys too?" Jamus asked with a hint of surprise.

Salene laughed. "By the Blood, my Love, if I didn't know better, I'd think you were still an innocent yourself. You know those two mistresses better than most. How can you even imagine they wouldn't know such a thing? They've tried to bed every eligible man in the Keep at least one time between them."

Jamus felt himself redden. "Aren't you overestimating those, ah, ladies?"

She laughed and kissed him lightly on the cheek. "And this is why I love you so much. If there is a way to think better of someone, you will always find it. Well, I must disappoint you this time, Dear One. Jiala and Siamel knew the intimate histories of every man in the Keep. So, here is the list." She handed him a vellum scroll.

"Jeimer, Soren, Sarn, all from my class. Jogat and Selm from the class before," he read. "An interesting list. You're sure about this?"

"Siamel insists it's right. She is certain about the Prentices from your class. It seems she kept records."

"Records?" He shook his head. "I wonder how my page reads?" Salene grinned. "Very well. You know, Siamel may have teased you more than once, but all in all she really did have a pretty high opinion of you."

"I doubt that."

"Well, she did." She took the scroll from his hand and put it on the tabe. "Now what do we do with these names?"

"If Kala were here, we could have a Truthseeking, but it's not a matter important enough to call her. The Sorcerer's Crystal will have to do."

"And do you propose traipsing around the Keep with the Stone interrogating people? Even if you are the Lord of Magiskeep, that would certainly raise questions about your sanity."

"You could always tell everyone I'd traveled the Way of Mirrors one too many times," Jamus teased. "Then I'd have an excuse."

"Don't joke about that, Jamus. It's one thing I don't find very funny."

"Well then, if that's not an option, I guess you will just have to walk around the Keep with the Crystal asking questions. Maybe no one will notice." He tried to keep a straight face but failed miserably. Then, he became serious. "I think a direct approach would be more fitting. None of these men will refuse a command to appear before us, especially if I call the Seven to sit. I certainly think the gravity of the problem warrants public recognition, don't you?"

"It began as a private affair, Jamus. Two children, after all."

"And the child has now become a man. The time eventually comes when a man must answer for what he's done. I don't expect him to pay for the deed itself if Lurela doesn't demand it, but he certainly has to answer for his misuse of power afterward. Someone drove that girl from a good position here in the Keep and sent her to the streets to fend for herself and her child. There is a price to pay for that."

"So you've already thought out the punishment?" Salene asked. "Something fitting, I presume?"

"A season in the village, working with his hands instead of his Art. I'd like him to learn humility. In truth, there's little one Mage can do to punish another and in the end it would really be a question of whether or not he would honor my commands. I would hope he would offer Lurela some kind of recompense and publicly admit his part in chasing her from the Palace. Either way, I'm going to see she has her job back. Neither she nor Jebe will ever want for anything again."

"Jamus, why have you taken so much of an interest in this boy and his mother?"

"You said it before, Salene. He is the child I was. I need to try to make his life better. I don't want to fail this time."

*****

With the Sevenstin passed, Tam's two lads arrived at the stables, ready and eager to work for the Keep proper. Jamus provided Josep with ample funds to pay them well, hoping to encourage them to learn their jobs before he left, but there had really been no need. The prestige of the opportunity was more than enough incentive. Arv was a keen learner who had forgotten nothing of the skills he had learned with Lord Sarkem and Mat's strong back was matched by a quiet hand with the young horses. Josep was pleased, and Jamus delighted.

Nobby, Sila, and Jevin all had learned how to ride, but Nobby was still the star pupil. He had learned to canter Flutter by the third lesson and was totally confident in the saddle.

For Jamus, the decision was now easy. "Nobby, I would like you to come with Jebe and me when we take the horses to Lord Delran. Will your parents allow it?"

Nobby's eyes widened. "Me Mam an' Pap always says I gotta do like the Lord says."

"I'd feel a lot better if we had their permission. You're not a man yet, even though you hold down a man's job."

"Me Mam kin write ya a letter sayin' it's all right," Nobby said proudly. "She learnt her letters afore I was born. Would that do?"

"That would do just fine. Have her send it on tomorrow if you will. We will be leaving the day after at Easwin. You will need to pack some extra clothes but don't worry too much if you forget anything. I don't hold back on Magic when it's really needed. Bring whatever makes you feel comfortable, but keep the pack light. You don't want to overburden Flutter with all kinds of extra weight."

"Aye, Me Lord," Nobby agreed happily.

With Nobby off to tell the others, Jamus turned to Jebe. "I already spoke to your mother, Jebe. Now that she is back in the Keep, I took it upon myself. You did want to go, didn't you?"

Jebe fairly squirmed with delight. "I sure do, My Lord. Sky will enjoy the trip too."

"You can't take Sky, I'm afraid. She is still too young and inexperienced. The trip through the Rim is dangerous, even when you know the way as I do. I think Redwin would be a better mount for you. He's strong, fit, and clever. I'm sure you can handle him."

"Reddy's a good one," Jebe agreed. "I'd be proud if he'd be willing to let me ride him. If he says it's all right, I will."

Jamus paused, puzzled by the strangeness of the boy's remark. This was the second time Jebe had hinted of something beyond ordinary communication with the horses. "How will he answer you, Jebe?"

"In my head," Jebe answered easily. "He talks in my head."

"Are you sure, lad?"

Jebe nodded. "I hear him, My Lord. Whim talks too. Sky doesn't say much yet. She's too young, I guess. But Whim has a lot to say. He talks about everything if I ask."

"Show me, Jebe," Jamus said.

The boy shrugged and led Jamus over to the stallion's stall. "Hello, Whim," he said. "Lord Jamus wants me to talk to you."

Whim snorted. His dark eyes met Jebe's and his seemed to nod his head.

"He says, 'Tell Best One Whim like sweet.' Whatever that means."

Jamus laughed and nodded. "It doesn't take a Beasttalker to tell me that. Here, give him one of these surlep candies. He likes them."

Jebe held out the treat and Whim delicately took it from his palm. "He says, "Sweet good. Whim like. Best One fix hole in big mountain.'"

"What?" Jamus asked, startled by the comment.

Best One know. Cruel Hand almost fall in hole in mountain.

Jamus caught his breath, remembering well the day he and Sagari had ridden out to the Rim and the then-Lord of Magiskeep had almost ridden into a rift at the mountains' edge. Jamus had sealed the chasm a fraction before Coranth reached the edge, and never told anyone a word about what had happened. Could Sagari be the Cruel Hand? He had been harsh with the horses at times and Whim had not liked him at all. Who is the "Cruel Hand, Whim?

Whim stamped his foot and snorted again. *No like remember. Bad master to Best One. Whim glad gone. White One glad too. All fourleg glad.*

Jebe frowned. " What does he mean, Sur? It's confusing. Something about the fourlegs?"

Jamus shook his head at the wonder of it. Either the boy was a Beasttalker,or he had a most vivid and impossible imagination. Yet he had heard Whim himself, and so, it seemed, had Jebe.

"If I understand it, Jebe, Whim is talking about the Lord Sagari. Apparently the horses really didn't like him."

"Neither did my mother," Jebe said. "She said the Lord didn't want her in the Keep."

Sagari? But that would be impossible. If he were Jebe's father, the boy would have inherited far more power than even this. Master's blood was strong. "Did she say why, Jebe?" he asked.

"No. She just said he didn't want her there."

Suddenly, things began to make sense.

*****

"The Masters are not keen on having a Gathering for this," Salene told Jamus when he returned to his study. Dressed more formally than usual in her royal blue shaenis gown, it was clear she had not made the request of the Seven as mere equal, but as Mistress of the Keep. "They will do so at your command, but not willingly."

Jamus sighed. Sagari never would have been questioned. Then again, he had made a point of not emulating Sagari in his role as Lord. Always, he had encouraged independent thinking and responsibility on the part of all his Mages. If this was the price he had to pay, so be it. "If I'm not mistaken, we can dispense with the formal hearing after all and focus our attention on just one person. Sarn."

"Sarn? Why him above all others? I know you don't like the man, but to accuse him of this?"

"The pieces fit, Salene. Josep told me Sarn was Sagari's favorite before I came to Magiskeep, so we know he'd be watching out for him. Jebe's tells me his mother said it was Sagari who didn't want her in the palace anymore."

Salene nodded. "Then Sagari could be the culprit."

"No. As I've said before, the blood runs strong in Masters. Jebe has talent, certainly, but not enough to be a Seven Arts mage. I

told you once I found out just what it was he could do, I'd have a
better understanding of who his father might be. Now, I know."

"Sarn was Apprenticed to Jorn. ReCreation is not one of the
worthiest Skills. Besides, didn't Joria already test him for that?"
Salene asked.

Jamus shrugged. "She tested him for all Seven Arts and
found none. I'm not surprised. The boy's a Beasttalker."

Salene's blue eyes registered her shock at his claim.
"Beasttalker? ` Whatever makes you say such a thing?"

"Jebe told me things about Whim no one else in all of
Magiskeep could ever know. I'm truly ready to believe he talked to
that horse of mine."

Salene sat down suddenly, her slender hands gripping the
arm of the chair. "Are you sure? That would be a powerful skill."

Jamus knelt beside her. "As sure as I can be. It was truly
amazing."

"But Sarn.... "

"Josep tells me Sarn has an uncanny way with horses
himself. Did you know he loved to ride? Josep says when I leave the
Keep he spends a great deal of time in the stables."

"I had no idea, though I do remember when he was a boy
how he wanted to be a stablelad. That was until he was tested and
Prenticed." She thought for a moment. "That's right. He and Sagari
used to ride together all the time. Now I remember. Sarn was young,
then, not yet eleven. It stopped when you came, but by then, Sarn
was a Prentice and it just seemed to be the natural course of things."

Jamus rose and walked to the wide window to stare out into
the pastures beyond. "It would explain everything, Salene, even why
Sagari was the one to scare Lurela into leaving the Keep. Can you
imagine the scandal if the boy he'd once chosen as his heir had
fathered a child by a commoner? A serving girl, no less? Better to
chase her away as if she were shamed instead of one of his pets.
Sarn's noble blood, as I recall. Born of a Lordmage and a
landowner's wife."

"Surely Sarn knew what happened. What's his excuse for
not recognizing the lad now that Sagari's dead? He should have
made amends."

"I think," Jamus said, turning back to face her, his grey eyes
iced with determination, "that we should ask Sarn that, don't you?"

"I'll call for him."

Salene headed for the door, but Jamus checked her. "Not
now. Tomorrow Jebe's going with me to Lord Delran's. There's no
reason to complicate his life yet. Let him have this trip while he still

sees himself as a common boy. I need all his sense and concentration on the journey."

"All right then. While you're gone I'll see what I can find out. Sarn will, I'm sure, be pleased with all the attention."

*****

Easwin brought warmer weather. Jamus rose early and met Sarn in the Audience Chamber as they had planned. The towheaded Mage had changed little from their days as Prentices together. He was still as arrogant as ever and rarely disguised his contempt for Jamus despite their respective positions. Jamus never pressed the point, choosing instead to disarm the other man's dislike of him by always taking the better role. This day was no exception.

"I'm depending on you, Sarn. I doubt my mortal enemies are ready to cross the Rim, but I have no doubt the Shadows have no barriers between them and Magiskeep."

"Are you expecting an attack?" Sarn asked. He had already changed into a gold threaded tunic of green as a mark of his status as acting Lord of the Keep. When Jamus had taken no notice, he had been disappointed. Every advantage he could have over his rival delighted him, and every counter Jamus made was frustrating. Now, though, Jamus' warning intrigued him. Defending the Keep from enemies might well give him more lofty status than simply as a substitute. The Mage with the greatest Magic was not necessarily the rightful ruler of Magiskeep--the best man was.

"There's always a danger. I have traveled the Way often enough to disturb reflections there and more than once I've encountered Shadows in Turan. It may have some kind of connection to how often I touch the River, but I really don't know. If you have any concerns, remember, Simen is here and he knows the habits of Shadows. Please keep him in your confidence."

Sarn smiled slightly, the corners of his mouth turning up in what might have been a sneer. "Consult a Follyman? Not precisely good precedent for Master of the Keep."

"In Turan, the Follyman is often the wisest of men and the only one who dares speak the truth."

"This is not Turan," Sarn returned. "In Magiskeep, wisdom is reckoned by Mastery. I hold a Five Arts Medallion. What medal does the Follyman wear beyond his buttons?"

"A mirror," Jamus replied easily, "and you would do well to remember that. Simen is of the Way, and until the day you can claim mastery of the mirrors yourself, you will only see half the truth of this world."

Taken only slightly aback by the rebuke, Sarn shrugged. "And many men never see any truth at all." Then, he bowed. "I will respect your wishes, My Lord."

"Good. There are a great many things about the River we all have to learn, Sarn. The wise Mage will always be her Prentice."

Sarn might have agreed had the words come from anyone besides Jamus, but his resentment was far too deep. Once more, he put on the pretense of listening while his mind pursued other paths. Still, Jamus had entrusted him with the rule of the Keep, and for that, he was pleased. Without Jamus' virtue to watch over his every move, he was free to do as he pleased.

He could hardly wait for Jamus to be on his way.

*****

It took the full span to ride out to Hidden Pines since Jamus dared only one lifted stride towards the end of the journey. Nobby was still too green in the saddle to risk riding the wind, for he had not spent much time outside the ring. Although Flutter was a solid, experienced Mage's mount, the boy's skill warranted more care. Only after Jamus was sure Nobby would follow his instructions to the letter did he attempt to shorten the journey. But then, Tam's mare, not Magic-bred, was quite unsettled by the strange mode of travel. She nearly broke away, flailing against the lead rope so hard she almost pulled Jamus from his saddle. Whim's skill at keeping himself under his rider was about the only thing that saved him from a nasty fall.

Once they grounded again, Jamus rubbed his chafed hand on his knee, and laughed. "I don't think we'll try that again. Mistress Lacy doesn't seem to like it very much."

"She's scared," Jebe said. "She liked Master Tam's stable. She's been sold fives time since she was a filly and thought she had a home."

"Lord Delran is a kind master," Jamus assured him. "If we insist, I know he will find an even kinder home for her. He never sells horses to people who won't treat them right."

"She's still scared," Jebe said.

"How ya know that, Jebe?" Nobby asked. "How ya know?"

"She told me," Jebe replied.

"Ya kin talk ta her?"

"Jebe has a talent," Jamus said, reining Whim to a stop. "I didn't want to tell anyone while we were still in the Keep. Being a Beasttalker like Jebe is a rare gift indeed and there would have been far too many there who would have wanted to study him. Now that you know, we all share a secret."

"I'll make a Riveroath not ta tell," Nobby offered. "I kin keep a secret."

"A man's word is all I need, Nobby," Jamus answered.

Nobby drew himself up proudly in the saddle. "I promise, on me name, Sur. Yer secret's safe wid me."

"That's more than enough for me," Jamus said. "Come on, then. Let's see if our horsemen's skills and Jebe's Magic can convince that little band of youngsters to come with us into the Rim. I'd rather not spend a wind trying to round them up."

Whether inspired by Jebe's persuasive abilities, or Whim's stallion determination, the young horses fell quickly into line, linked by the leads Jamus had strung together. Had they not been traveling through the Rim, he would have felt no need for ropes, but he had to be sure none of the herd would wander from the path he chose. Passing through the Illusioned mountains was difficult enough without worrying about stray horses with no sense of the dangers lurking behind the Magic.

Nearly a span sooner than he had expected, Jamus reined Whim into the rocky pass at the Rim's eastern edge. Behind, the two riders flanked the six nervous animals, trying hard to encourage them even with their own confidence in question.

The Rim simply waited to swallow them.

Chapter 6

Illusions abounded at the beginning of South Rim Pass, hiding the entrance from mortal eyes. Only a skilled Mountman or a Magician would even notice the trail as it wound its way among huge boulders and scrub pine. Jamus, though, raised in the mountains and bred of the Magic, hardly cast a second look as he reined Whim into the first opening. Behind him, he heard Jebe gasp and Nobby call out a quick cry of protest.

"Yer headin' fer a cliff, me Lord! Look out!"

Without turning his head, Jamus answered back, "Don't trust your eyes, Nobby, trust mine. Magic plays tricks here. I know where to go."

Jebe, though none too certain himself, nudged Redwin forward. "Whim ain't gonna hurt himself, Nobby. He's too smart for that. All we gotta do is make our horses follow him and we'll be fine."

Jamus chuckled to himself. He would have preferred the boys simply listen to him, but if Whim were a better leader, so be it. Besides, most of what Jebe said was true. The stallion was as keen a traveler in these mountains as any. His kinship with the Magic was so complete, he knew exactly where to place his hoofs. He had carried Jamus safely through the range before, and Jamus was sure he could to it again now. Still, it was the southern pass they wanted this time as the trail was wider and would be easier travel for the young horses. There were shorter routes to Lord Delran more suited to Whim's clever feet, and it was likely the silver stallion would choose one of them if left to his own devices.

That was evident when they came to the first crossing, and Whim balked. A little frothy stream lay ahead while to the right lay the beginning of Hill Trail, the quickest path to Cowltop at the Rim's center. Three times, the stallion spun right as Jamus steered left.

"He wants to go the other way," Jebe said as he watched from his position at the head of the string of horses. "He says it's not so far."

Exasperated by the horse's stubbornness, Jamus gritted his teeth. "Tell him we need to take the long way for the baby horses. They are too foolish to climb the hill." As soon as he said it, Whim relented and strode off to the left as Jamus wanted. "Good, job, Jebe. You told him well."

"I didn't tell him nothing," Jebe said. "You did."

"I did?"

"Uh huh. He understood what you said. You gotta trust him more, My Lord. Sometimes all you gotta do is explain things."

Jamus didn't laugh at that. Beasttalking was still new to him and too often he forgot its power when other things were on his mind. He needed to remember to listen. Fool, he thought. You don't half believe in yourself yet, let alone Jebe. When would he ever remember to just listen?

Best One forget. Whim here.

Jamus smiled to himself, reassured that the stallion was still willing to talk to him despite the insult of his forgetting.

"How much more afore we stop fer a bit?" Nobby said, startling himself with how loudly his voice echoed against the rocks. "Me bottom hurts."

Jamus hadn't thought much about either boy's stamina when he had proposed the trip. Nobby had, after all, just learned to ride. He sighed. He had hoped to be at the clearing by Norwin's change. From there, they would have had enough time to reach the campsite at Rimcenter at Weswin. Stopping now would delay them until past dark. Still, there was no point in making the boy suffer. "A little way further, Nobby. There's a stream just ahead where we can water the horses. You can get off there and walk around a bit."

The stream was several feet wide, with clear, clean water running over the red rocks. They lingered for a half-span, Jamus' patience not allowing any more time, for the sky was growing cloudy and the last thing he wanted was to be caught on this trail in a storm. By the time they had remounted and organized the line of horses, the wind was picking up. Soon after, spatters of rain began to fall.

Without even thinking, Jamus cast a protective spell over the group, shielding them all from the wet. The River leapt to his hand with eager anticipation, fueled by the Rim's Magic as the rain began to pound down in earnest.

Though they were dry and comfortable in the Sphere, the ground at their feet soaked up the water churning itself into slippery red mud wherever the sand gave way. Rain poured in sheets along the Sphere's surface, making it nearly impossible to see where they were going, and it was all Jamus could do to make out the trail.

Finally, he was forced to lead the band under the sheltering ledge of the mountainside to wait until the worst of the weather passed.

As luck would have it, the delay cost them the better part of Sowin, and they did not reach Rimcenter until well after Weswin. By then, the horses were tired and hungry, the boys completely worn out, and Jamus' temper on edge. It did not make for a pleasant night.

"It's all my fault," Nobby said as he squatted next to Jebe by the fire. "If'en I hadn'ta whined an' made the Lord stop back there by the stream, we'da bin here long afore."

"You didn't make it rain," Jebe said. "That's what really slowed us down."

"I ain't gonna say nothin' tomorrow, no matter how sore I git. I'm jest gonna keep my mouth shut an' keep ridin'."

"Master Jamus is gonna know, Nobby. He ain't gonna let you do that. He's too kind a Lord for that. Best you be honest with him an' tell him when you're tired. Far as I know we ain't got no special time we gotta be at Lord Delran's. Better we all get there in one piece, eh?"

Nobby chewed his lip thoughtfully. "I ain't never knowed nobody like Lord Jamus afore, Jebe. Even me Pap ain't bin as nice ta me as 'e has. I wanna do good fer him."

"You are, Nobby. He wouldn't have asked you to come elsewise. This is a big job we're doing. It took Lord Delran, Lord Sagari, and Lord Jamus a whole lot of circles to breed these horses."

"Them?" Nobby asked, pointing at the young drays eating the hay Jamus had spelled from the Keep to feed them. "They don't look so special."

"Lord Jamus says they are mixed from Magiskeep's best runners an' Lord Delran's finest work horses. They wanted to get stock what would do for Lord and Ladies who wanted to ride in big fancy carriages what weighed a whole lot an' still wanted pretty beasts in front. You watch them move an' you'll see how nice they go, all like dorsetts bounding. But they're real strong too. I think they could work all day a ne'er pull a hard breath."

"You knows a lot about horses," Nobby said. "How come?"

Jebe drew his shoulders back proudly. "Lord Jamus taught me, an' Josep too. I'm gonna be a horsemaster, like I said."

"Do ya think I kin too?" Nobby asked a little shyly. "Me Pap says I ain't never gonna amount ta much. But he sure were proud Lord Jamus wanted me ta come along. Me Mam said maybe I could learn somethin' useful. It'd be grand if'en I learnt ta be a master."

"You got a good way with a horse, Nobby, and I'll be glad to teach you all I know. Maybe even Lord Jamus would too, if you ask him."

"Me? Ask him?" Nobby nearly cried. "Bory, Jebe, 'e's the Lord o' the Keep! The likes 'o me ain't got a right ta ask him nothin'."

Jebe grinned. "Seems to me I said the same thing myself to Master Josep not too long ago, and, as I recollect, it all worked out pretty good. If a Li'l Runty like me can talk to him, I sure figger a big fellow like you shouldn't have no trouble."

"Oh, Jebe," Nobby laughed. And then he punched his new friend in the arm. When Jamus came back to the campfire, he found the two boys engaged in a friendly wrestling match.

"Call it a tie, lads, and come on over for your evenmeal. I snitched some cavel roast and vegetables from the Keep's kitchen a mite ago. You'd better eat it while it's still hot."

The boys giggled and crawled over to where he had spread the feast. Then, after a satisfying meal they bedded down on the soft sand and fell quickly asleep.

Jamus sat by the fire a while watching them and listening to the rush of water in the stream. For once, he felt at home in the Rim, his own past fading. The boys were making it easy to forget.

*****

Salene was beginning to feel like a spy. With Sarn in charge of the Keep, it was hard for her to find time to see him alone, so she had taken to keeping watch as he made his rounds. The trouble was, she didn't want him to notice.

However, her lurking in the stairwell finally paid off when she saw him pass Lurela in the upper hall as the woman was taking some linens to one of the guest rooms. The moment was brief, but revealing. Lurela paused in midstride, her eyes wide, her face ashen. Sarn reddened, started to reach out his hand, then drew back as if stung, spun on his heel and hurried off.

Salene followed him, knowing full well the maid would tell her nothing since she had already refused to talk to Jamus. She found Sarn at the end of the hall, standing in confusion as if he had forgotten just where he was going. When he saw her, he shrank back.

She motioned to the door at his back. "We'll talk," she said.

Inside the Mage's study, Sarn cast a furtive glance around to make sure they were alone before he said anything. "What's she doing here?"

"Working, for me," Salene answered. "Shouldn't she be?"

"She swore she'd never come back here."

"And who told her not to?" Salene asked. "Did you?"

He shook his head sadly, a quite unexpected reaction. "She hates me, you know. I tried to tell her I was sorry, but she wouldn't listen. She kept blaming me."

Salene pretended ignorance. "Blaming you for what?"

Sarn's eyes fired. "You know perfectly well. Don't think I don't know what's been going on behind my back! Jamus and...and...my son! How do you think that makes me feel? There he is, Lord of the Keep, playing father to my boy? And his mother won't let me near him!"

Salene's heart lurched. This was something she never would have expected to hear...not from Sarn. "Jebe is your son? You admit it?"

Sarn sank onto a bench and dropped his head in his hands. "I've always admitted it, or wanted to. But Sagari wouldn't let me. He said it would shame me, shame him, and shame the Keep. He said she was just a common drudge, not a fitting mate for me. I was a fool...too young and stupid to realize what I'd done. Oh, it was fun conquering her, telling her how much I loved her just so I could get her into bed as if she were some kind of prize. But a baby....By the Blood, a baby. But Sagari said it didn't matter. He said he could fix that. He said he would, too, if I tried to go with her."

"What? He threatened her?"

Sarn gulped and nodded, looking up at her, his eyes wet. "He told her if she said anything he'd get rid of the baby and make sure she would never have any more. And, he told me I'd better do as he said too, or he'd fix everything."

"In Sogol's Name, how could he?"

"He wanted me to be his heir, Salene, and he didn't want any...'encumbrances' he called them...in the way. Up until Jamus flew the Cup, he swore he'd give the Mastery to me."

"And you believed him? You are only a Five Arts Mage, Sarn. The Mastery needs Seven."

"I would have learned. For that, I would have learned Compassion and Elevation. A man can change."

Salene shook her head. To think of Sarn with the open heart Compassion required or the high morals of Elevation was nearly beyond her capacity. And yet, up until a moment ago, she had also never believed he had any feelings at all beyond himself. "Sagari's gone, Sarn. Why haven't you made it up to Lurela since?"

"I tried. More than once, but she won't have any part of it. She says she's done just fine without me and Jebe doesn't need a man like me as his father. Sometimes I'd just go to her house and sit across the way, waiting until the boy came out so I could at least see him. I even went to the shops in the Village where he was prenticing to buy things. It was hard when the masters complained about how clumsy he was, but what could I do? Then, he came here to the Keep. Have you seen him with the horses, Salene?" Sarn's face lit up.

"He's a real wonder! He took to the saddle so fast. And Jamus chose him to go with him across the Rim! Jebe, the smallest lad in the place."

"Does Lurela know how you feel about her…your son?"

Sarn shrugged and sank back down. "Who knows? She won't even talk to me. I wouldn't be surprised if she's already left the Keep now that she knows I'm still here."

"She is here under Jamus' command and his protection, Sarn. If she leaves, I have the right and duty to bring her back, whatever it takes."

"I'm in charge while Jamus is gone, Madame, and I will not have you tormenting that woman, even if it is by his command. Leave her be."

This time, Salene's eyes fired, and even Sarn felt himself falter under her glare. "You are not Lord of Magiskeep, Sarn, and it would be best you remember that. Jamus' law reigns here and my hand upholds it. Defy me and you defy him. Lurela will remain in the Keep, and by the Hand, if I have anything to say about it, she is going to talk to you face to face about this." Then she softened. "She will talk to you, Sarn. She has to, for her sake, for yours, and for Jebe's. I can hardly believe I'm saying this, but that boy really deserves to know you are his father."
*****

Easwin brought more clouds, but no sign of rain. The travelers made good progress through the early spans of the day with Jamus insisting they stop at least twice to let the young horses rest. "No sense in pushing them too hard," he said. "Nobby, why don't you get down and check the gray mare's leg for me. It looks a little puffy."

Grateful to be out of the saddle, Nobby knelt at the mare's side and ran his hand along her tight tendon. "I cain't feel nothin', me Lord."

"Lead her off a ways and then trot her back towards me, would you? I just want to be sure she's all right."

When the mare trotted sound, Jamus nodded and waited until Nobby was back in the saddle. "Good job, lad. You handled her well. I'm glad it was just my imagination about that leg."

"You could heal her if she was hurt, couldn't you, Master?" Jebe asked, concerned.

"I could, but even with the best of Healings, it takes a while for the body to recover fully. Injuries and illnesses affect us in ways hard to explain. Magic may cure the physical damage. It doesn't repair the spirit."

"So she'd still be sick?"

"In a manner of speaking, Jebe. She'd need a good rest, that's for certain, until all her strength and faith in her leg were back."

"I thought Magic could fix everythin'." Nobby said. "It ain't so?"

"No. Magic is only a part of Turan's power. Sometimes, if the Hand wills it otherwise, Magic can't fix anything at all."

They rode on for a long time in silence as both boys considered Jamus' words. To them, Magic had always been the answer to everything. It was a lesson their parents had taught them from the beginning. Now to hear otherwise from the greatest Magician in all the land was disturbing.

For Nobby, especially, it was frightening. His father had told him there would be no danger on this trip because he was going with Lord Jamus. The Rim was the source of nightmares, vicious tarks, and black demons who ate little boys. His grandfather had warned him never to sit in the mountains' shadows lest the evil eat his soul. And all the village taletellers, even his uncle Wyam, blamed the Rim every time someone suffered bad luck. He'd only come because of Jamus, daring the adventure because the Magic would protect him. Hadn't Jamus made a shield from the rain and provided food already? They'd heard a tark snarl from the rocks above and Magiskeep's Lord had sent a bolt of fire to frighten it away. Magic could fix everything. It had to. It simply had to.

Midmeal and Sowin passed, each span a journey past rocky cliffs and narrow canyons. Then, at last, the terrain seemed to ease. They had passed into Turan's side of the Rim and by Sowin's turn of the next day, would be out into the foothills and free of the range's illusions.

Jamus was feeling surprisingly tired himself. Keeping an eye on Jebe, Nobby, and the horses while still sifting his way through the mountain's tricks was taking an unusual toll on him. More than once, he had let Whim choose the turning, relying on the stallion's perception rather than his own to find the safe way. He reined to a stop and rubbed his eyes wearily. Then, he turned back to see how Nobby was faring.

It was the only thing that saved him.

The arrow flashed from the rocks above, thudding into his shoulder instead of his chest. Jamus grunted in pain as another missile hissed out and plunged into his thigh, knocking him off balance. He clutched in vain at Whim's mane and then, with an agonized cry, slid from the saddle to land in a crumpled heap in the rocks at dirt below.

Jebe cried out as an arrow whizzed past his ear and as he yanked the rein, Redwin reared. The boy tumbled off, landed hard, and rolled down a little hill to crash into a pile of scrub bushes at the bottom. He heard yells from above and another thud, as if someone else had been hit.

"Get 'em afore they bolt!" a harsh voice ordered.

"He's over here! Under the big silver horse! Should I finish 'im off? 'E ain't dead yet."

Whim screamed.

Jebe scraped his way up to the top of the shallow ridge and peered over. Five roughly dressed men, mounted or leading tough little mountain ponies were rushing about, snatching lead ropes and trying to calm the panicking horses.

One man, dark bearded and burly was advancing on Jamus, his blade drawn. But Whim would have no part of it, and the stallion charged, his head snaking out, his teeth and hoofs slashing the air. The man leapt to the side but the stallion spun as quickly, blocking him again and again.

"Divil," the man spit. "Augie, git over here an' help me. This big hoss is gonna kill me."

"Git away from him, Bonder, an' mebbe Toady kin git an arrow in 'im."

"Whim," Jebe whispered. "Look out!"

The stallion spun again and vanished in a wisp of silver mist as the arrow sailed past to split the tree branch behind him. Then, he reappeared, more furious than before, his heels lashing out to send the men reeling back.

"'E's Sorceled, I tell ya!" Toady cried.

The last two men had gathered the scattered horses, including Redwin and Flutter.

"Leave the big'un an' the Sorcerer too. 'E won't make it nohow out here in the mountains. Asides, Toady put some o'his special potion on least one o' them arrows" one of them said, laughing. "The Sorcerer won't make it tha night."

"I'd feel better if'en I'd slit 'is throat," Bonder snarled. "Only good Sorcerer's one 'at's sure an' dead if'en ya ask me."

"Well, I ain't askin'," the one called Augie said.

Whim pawed the ground furiously, but stood his post just in front of Jamus, protecting him from any more attacks.

The man called Toady, stepped over to where Nobby lay, and kicked the boy with his foot. "Ya hit him awful hard, Augie."

"I had ta. 'E was gonna turn aroun' an' he mighta reconized me."

"Ya mighta killed 'im."

"Nah, 'e's got a hard head like 'is Pa."

"Where's the other one?"

Jebe shrank back into the bushes, not daring to breathe.

"Who cares? Wyam says he's too stupit to know nothin'. 'E ain't gonna be able to do nothin'. I say we leave 'em an' git ourselfs outta here."

"What about the silver beast? 'E'd fetch a fine coin in Lebardese. They likes 'em fiery."

"Yeah, an' I likes meself alive. Ya wanna take 'im, ya go git 'im. I ain't goin' anywheres near that hetark."

"Git his saddle. It fell off when 'e made like fog. It oughtta fetch some." Toady inched his way over to the saddle, and snatched it away just an instant from Whim's next charge.

Jebe heard more scuffling. Then the sound of hoofs clattering on the rocks.

Then silence.

Whim snorted. *Go kill. Hurt Best One. Whim go kill now.*

The voice sounded in Jebe's head. "No, Whim! No! Stay here. Jamus' needs you. I need you! Stay here."

Best One be sick. Jebe help?

Jebe scrambled back up the hill, peered over, and when he saw none of the men, got to his feet and ran over to where Whim stood, his great body shielding Jamus' prone form.

Jebe's breath caught in a gasp in his throat.

The arrow in Jamus' right thigh had shattered at the shaft, but the one lodged in his left shoulder, just above his heart, quivered with each gasp of his ragged breath.

Blood was seeping into the red sand beneath him.

Chapter 7

"Nobby, Nobby, you gotta wake up. We gotta do something! Nobby!" Jebe shook Nobby's shoulder desperately, until at last the other boy stirred. "Wake up, Nobby!"

"Wha...?" Then Nobby groaned. "Oh, me head. Me head."

"They hit you, Nobby. And they took the horses. Master Jamus has been shot...shot with arrows and he's hurt awful bad. We gotta do something!"

Wincing and holding his head in his hands, Nobby slowly sat up, letting Jebe hold him steady. "I seen 'im fall, Jebe. An' I seen this bad lookin' man ride up an' then, somethin' hit me hard an' I fell off. Where's Flutter?"

"Gone. They took 'im an' they took Reddy and they took all the horses 'cept Whim. Whim wouldn't let them take him. He was gonna kill them. But there was five of them, Nobby and Master Jamus... Master Jamus...." Jebe's voice trailed off into a sob. "We gotta do something."

Together, the two boys staggered over to where Jamus lay. Nobby sank down, his legs giving way, while Jebe knelt at Jamus' side. Gently, he touched Jamus' right arm and shook it. "My Lord. Can you hear me? Please, My Lord?"

Jamus moaned and his eyes opened. "Jebe," he whispered hoarsely. "They didn't hurt you."

"I'm all right. Nobby's got a big bump on his head. You're hurt awful bad. Can you heal it?"

"No. We need help, Jebe."

"Where're we gonna get help?"

"Lord Delran. A Healer. He has a Healer." Jamus struggled with the words, his tongue stuck in his mouth, his thoughts spinning. "Whim," he said thickly. "Whim knows."

Silverhair. Jebe heard it in his head.

"Will you take me, Whim?"

Go, now.

"Nobby, Whim is going to take me to get help. You're gonna have to stay here and tend Lord Jamus."

"Me? I don't know nothin' 'bout healin', Jebe. What am I s'posed ta do?"

"Well I don't know nothing about healing neither, but I do know something about riding.

Whim's gonna take me for help and you gotta stay here. You do whatever you can to make him comfortable, all right? You do whatever he says. I'm counting on you, Nobby."

Now, Whim insisted.

"We'll go as fast as we can, My Lord. I promise," Jebe said, squeezing Jamus' arm with his little hand.

"On the wind," Jamus muttered. "Tell him on the wind."

Whim moved over beside a big boulder so Jebe could mount and then after waiting for the boy to lace his fingers in his mane, galloped off.

The wind seared Jebe's face. Suddenly, the earth dropped away below as the stallion's stride lifted. Jebe clung like a prickleburr, using every ounce of muscle and courage to stay with the tremendous leap. The icy air ripped at him and just when he thought he would have to let go, they grounded, a full span beyond the foothills of the Rim.

Again. Far to go. Again?

"Yes," Jebe said aloud. "Again. As fast as you can. Again."

And they lifted stride again, covering spans to Delran's.

*****

Salene felt the Magic shudder. Once. Twice, a surge, and then, nothing. Vainly she stared out the west window of the study, trying to see beyond to the Rim.

The door opened. Simen.

"Something's happened to Jamus," he said.

"I know," she replied. "I felt it."

"The whole of Magiskeep did," Simen answered. Salene turned to face him, her eyes startled as always to see how much he looked like Jamus. The same grey eyes, the dark hair, the chiseled face. But Simen usually wore a warm smile. Today, his face was grim. "Where is he?" he asked.

"In the Rim. Perhaps out, by now. He was taking horses to Delran."

"Ah, yes. Jessa told me. I didn't talk to him before he left. Which pass was he following?"

This time she shook her head. "I don't know. Whichever was best for the stock, I suppose. He had two boys with him. Jebe and Nobby. They're good lads, but very young, and neither of them has any Healing. If he's hurt... " She shuddered.

"I'll go. I can get to Cowltop through the mirrors, but after that, it's pure luck to find them."

"Delran's would be better. Go there, Simen. Tell him something's happened. He can send out search parties. He'd know where to look."

"What's going on?" It was Sarn this time. "The Magic cried."

"We think something may have happened to Jamus." Salene replied uneasily. Telling Sarn was like loosing a rimsnake to the duskit's hole.

"I'll get some men. We can go after him."

"No, there's no point in it. By now he'd be near the far side of the Rim. There's better help from Turan than from us. Lord Delran will know what to do," Salene said.

"Fine, that's just fine. And how do you propose we let Lord Delran know he needs to do anything at all, eh?" Sarn asked, "I don't see any messagebirds around here ready to take on the task of telling him. Do you?"

"I'll go to him through the mirrors," Simen told him.

Sarn stiffened. "At your Will, or mine?"

"Does it matter?"

"In Jamus' absence, I am Master here. Journeys through the Way are not so freely taken, you know."

Simen drew himself up to his full height. A head taller than Sarn, he glared down at him. "I will go whether you approve or not, Master Sarn. Where Jamus is concerned, you are of no concern to me."

To his credit, Sarn stood his ground. "I only meant perhaps you should not go alone. If there are enemies around, it wouldn't be wise for you to go without some help."

"Lord Delran is well armed, Sur," Salene explained, "and he has a most competent Healer. Until we know what the situation really is, one skilled Mage should be sufficient. Besides, taking others through the Way would only slow Simen down, as does this pointless interference of yours."

Sarn bristled, but wisely held his temper in check. "Go, but swear on your life you will ask for help when it is needed. I don't want to lose you and your brother at the same time."

Simen smiled and bowed slightly. Then he hurried from the room to the mirrors.

"Thank you, Sarn," Salene said. "I thought for a moment... "

Sarn took her hand in his. "I am not a total fool, My Lady. Simen may not be Jamus' equal, but he is certainly my better, as you are."

"So you did it because you were afraid of us?"

"Let us say, fear, respect, and love hold hands together, My Lady." He lowered his head and kissed her hand lightly. When he looked back up, he was smiling. "Let me know as soon as you learn anything. I want to know… for the sake of the Keep."

Then he glided out of the room, looking every inch the Lord of Magiskeep.

Salene stood dumbfounded. Then she ran out the door, hurrying to find Simen before he entered the mirrors.

He was at the door of the mirror room when she caught up with him. "Take me with you," she panted, out of breath from the run and her own emotion. "If Jamus is hurt, I need to be there."

Simen studied her for a moment. "I can't, Salene. You know I can't, especially if Jamus is hurt. You knew that a few minutes ago when I told you I was going. Why would you think differently now?"

"It's Sarn. He, he frightened me. He already thinks he's Lord of the Keep, Simen. He thinks Jamus is dead."

"Sarn frightened you?" Simen asked. He might have smiled at that had she not looked so stricken. "Salene, Sarn is a charlatan compared to you. You have more Magic in one hand than he has in his whole being. I've never seen you like this. Did you feel something more in the River than I did?"

She sighed. "Nothing, Simen, and that's the worst of it." Then Simen did smile and she couldn't help herself. She smiled back. "I suppose I am acting like a fool. It's just that, for a moment, back there, after you left, Sarn was… he was acting and talking exactly like Sagari."

Simen lifted her chin with his hand. "Sagari's dead, and by the Blood, no one will ever treat you like that again. You know it, and I know it. This thing… whatever it is… with Jamus has shaken you more than you want to admit. If you want me to stay, I will."

"Jamus needs you."

"I'd take you if I dared, but the Mirrors aren't safe for you without Jamus beside you. He's awakened too many shadows already. They'll leave me alone, because I'm one of them. But you're flesh and blood."

She shivered. "You'll find him, won't you? And you'll bring him back safely?"

"If it is to be done, I will do it, My Lady. I am even less without him than you are. Now let me go. There may be no time in the Way, but here the winds pass and each one may make a great deal of difference." He started to open the door, paused, and then added, "As for Sarn, remember your lesson to the Prince. A good deed can always be done twice." Then, he winked and entered the chamber.

*****

"Whadda I do, whadda I do?" Nobby kept repeating, wringing his hands in anguish. After Jebe had left, Jamus had drifted back into unconsciousness and lain silent and still. There were no blankets to be had, nothing, for the thieves had taken all the equipment along with the horses. Nobby's paltry little jacket barely covered half of Jamus' chest, and the boy was already trembling in the chill air.

Nobby felt in his small leather pouch and realized his flint was there. Pap had always told him to carry his flint and his knife. He'd remembered. Now, all he had to do was gather up some kindling and start a fire. That took some doing, for much of the wood around was still damp from the rain. Eventually, he found some dry twigs and larger branches, enough to get the blaze going. Soon the air around them warmed, and Jamus began to stir.

"Me Lord, I made a fire."

"Good," Jamus mumbled. "Feels good."

"Me Lord, I don't know what else ta do. Ya gots ta tell me what ta do."

The boy's plea roused Magiskeep's Lord. He opened his eyes and slowly began to focus on his surroundings. What had happened? Arrows, that was it. He had to get rid of the arrows. They were poisoning him. How? The boy couldn't possibly pull them out. He could feel the barbs digging into his body, severing tissue, killing him. Think. Focus. Magic. Call the River. You can't heal yourself, but you can change the enemy. "Nobby, Nobby, can you hear me?"

Nobby leaned close. "I hears ya, me Lord."

"I'm going to use my Magic on the arrow in my shoulder. When I tell you, pull it out, quickly. There won't be much time. I can't hold the spell for very long. Can you do it?"

"Aye, me Lord."

The River stirred, sluggish to his call, but it did stir. Transformation, simple, child's play. Why was it so hard? Concentrate. The barbs were smooth now, then gone. "Pull, Nobby, now!"

The boy took hold of the shaft and yanked. He fell backwards as the arrow pulled clean and free. Jamus gasped as a spasm of pain wracked his body.

Blood, if the barbs had still been there, it would have killed him.

Nobby was crying. In his hand the arrow reformed, the plain straight shaft filling out again with the three cruel fieron barbs, sharp and bloodied. He dropped it as if it were on fire.

"Nobby, you have to do it again. The one in my leg. The same way."

"No," Nobby sobbed. "I cain't. I cain't hurt ya like that. I cain't, Me Lord."

"Nobby, you're the only one who can. Please. I'm counting on you."

The boy crawled back over, his face streaked with tears. He sniffed hard and nodded.

It was harder this time. He was tired, his shoulder throbbing in agony. He called and the River answered her Master. "Now, Nobby, now."

Nobby pulled, sobbing in near hysteria, his whole body trembling. The arrow flew to the side, slipping out of his hand. He scrambled back over to Jamus, terror in his eyes. "Yer bleeding bad. I gotta do somethin'." Jamus groaned, too lost in his pain to answer.

Nobby thought quickly. He pulled out his knife and cut the fabric of his shirt, tearing it into strips to use as a bandage. Hurriedly, he bound the cloth around Jamus' thigh, pulling it tight. The bleeding nearly stopped.

Jamus' pain eased a bit, enough to let him talk again. "My shoulder."

"I ain't got no way ta bandage it, Me Lord. Mam says…Mam says eightleg webs works good. I'm gonna look fer some."

"Eightlegs… " Jamus whispered hoarsely to himself. "Creepy crawly eightlegs, climbing on the wall. Two legs, four legs, double that and all." Stupid song. Where had he heard it? Mother maybe? Mother, that was it. In the cabin by the waterfall. She used to sing to him. He hummed the tune, the notes jumbling one on top of another. Mother was a Healer. She'd know what to do.

Nobby knelt beside him, his hands full of sticky strands of silken webs. There were hundreds of them around, woven by the eightlegs to catch the insects brought out by the rain. He pressed them into the wound, sobbing each time he touched it and Jamus gasped.

"It worked, Me Lord. It worked. Ya ain't bleedin' half so bad now."

"Are you all right, Nobby?"

"Me head hurts awful bad. They hit me."

"Poor boy. Poor little boy. Come here." Jamus held out his good arm and Nobby let him pull him close. One more time. That's all. Can't Heal myself, but I can Heal him. Please. He's such a little thing. So brave. So afraid. So like me.

The water was soft, sweet to his plea. Not commanded, but answering willingly. No time to make a shield to ward himself from the Compassion. Nobby's pain seared into his head, adding to his agony. It was nothing, really. Nothing compared to what he'd already suffered. Then, the world flashed white and the pain in his head was gone. Nobby sighed and nestled against him.

The fire flared once, then settled to a healthy flame keeping them both warm.

*****

Four strides and Whim landed lightly in Lord Delran's yard. Jebe was too out of breath to call out, but the stallion's frantic trumpeting brought grooms and the Lord himself scurrying out of the stables.

"Bory, lads! What have we here?" Delran bellowed.

Whim wore no halter or bridle, but he stood stock still as Joss approached. "It's Whim fer sure, My Lord. But who's this on his back? Poor lad looks all done in." Josep's son reached up and tried to pull Jebe down, but the boy clung to the horse's back.

"J...J...Jamus," he muttered, his teeth chattering.

"Come on, lad, come down from there," Delran urged. "You can't talk while you're shaking like that."

Jebe let Joss catch him as he half fell. Whim nickered, and pawed nervously, upset by the delay. *Tell Silverhair need Heal. Best One need Heal. Whim go. Tell now.*

"Lord Jamus' been hurt bad. He needs a Healer. He sent me."

"Joss, saddle Magwin and take Cloudstrider with you. Go get Jern at once."

Whim go. Fast on wind. Say now. Tell Whim where.

"Whim's going to go… Master Jamus said so…" Jebe improvised quickly. "He said Whim could bring the Healer faster."

"How will the stallion know where to go?"

"Master Jern's over at Lord Margston's," Joss said. "Three spans south of here. Whim's never been there."

Make picture.

This was going to be hard. How could Jebe tell them without revealing his secret? "Lord Jamus said… he said if you tell Whim what it looks like, he can find anything. It's how…how they fly together."

Delran frowned but answered evenly. "South of here. That way." He pointed. "About three spans ride. It's a huge stone house. Earthstone, not blustone, mind you. Black fences all around. The house is on a little hill, not far from the Green Lake. Straight south, mind you. Nothing much in-between. The road's straight with plenty of trees on either side."

Whim snorted and vanished in a flash of silver mist.

"I've ne'er seen the likes o' that," Joss said, whistling.

Delran simply shook his head and looked down at Jebe. "Where is Lord Jamus, lad?"

Jebe waved his hand in the general direction he had come. With Whim in the clouds, he had no idea where or how far they had traveled. "In the Rim, somewhere. I lost my way."

Then he started to cry.

Delran knelt beside him and put a comforting hand on the boy's shoulder. "It's all right, son. What's your name?"

"J...Jebe."

"Well now, Jebe, maybe if I ask you some questions we can figure it out, all right?"

Jebe swallowed hard and nodded.

"Do you remember anything Lord Jamus said when you first went into the Rim?"

Jebe thought hard. "He said something about the South trail. We was going along fine."

"Then what happened?" Delran motioned to Joss and whispered hurried orders in his ear. Joss ran off to the barns, calling for grooms and riders.

"We stopped for the night by a nice stream. Then we rode off again. I remember passing this big weirdy rock. It looked like a face, I think. That's when I heard a tark, but Master Jamus scared it off."

"Good, Jebe. That's Old Face. I know that boulder. You were nearly out of the most dangerous part of the Rim then."

Jebe nodded and went on. "We rode for like near a whole wind and then... then somebody shot a arrow an' it hit Lord Jamus here." He slapped his shoulder. "Then there was another one an' it hit him in the leg an' he fell off. Reddy reared an' I fell too. There was five of 'em. Five! They were gonna kill Lord Jamus but Whim wouldn't let them. They hit Nobby on the head and took everything. They took all the horses, and the saddles an' everything. Excepting for Whim, 'cause he wouldn't let 'em. Whim was mad. They tried to shoot him too but he disappeared. They said I was too stupid to kill so they didn't try to find me. They..."

"It's all right, Jebe," Delran soothed as Jebe gulped in big breaths of air. "We'll find them. You say there's a Nobby with Jamus?"

"Nobby's a lad, like me. He only just learned how to ride. He's bigger than me, but I can ride better so I come here with Whim. Whim told me he knew where…" He snapped his mouth shut, hoping Delran wouldn't notice what he'd said.

The old Lord was too wise to acknowledge the boy's slip for now. There were far more pressing concerns. Joss pulled the team and carriage up beside them. "Will Whim take Jern directly to Jamus?" he asked.

"He will, I think," Jebe answered. "He's awful worried."

"I hope Jern understands him as well as you do. He left so fast we didn't have time to send a message with that horse," Delran returned.

"I think Jern will get Whim's message, Me Lord," Joss said. "Somehow that stallion always makes hisself understood. Asides, when he sees what horse it is, he'll know who he's comin' fer." He reached down and swung Jebe up in the seat alongside him.

Delran climbed in the back along with one of the grooms. There were eight armed men riding beside them, their eyes wary, their hands ready at their weapons. Jebe eyed them nervously.

"We need them, lad," Delran said. "If there are thieves about, I don't intend on becoming their victim myself. Besides, once we rescue that Lord of yours, we'll need someone to track the villains down."

Just then, Simen burst out of the house, running at full speed toward the carriage. Delran's face whitened. "Lord Jamus! I thought…!"

"Not Jamus," Simen panted. "His brother. I came by the Way. He's in trouble. The Magic stirred. Do you know where he is?"

"The Rim…," Delran sputtered, his voice trailing off.

Joss clucked nonchalantly to the team, sending them off at a brisk trot as Simen climbed aboard. "Hello, Master Simen. I was wondering who'd come first from the Keep."

Simen reached out and gave Joss a playful nudge. "Don't play games with me, Joss, me lad. You're just as surprised as anyone. Still, it's glad I am it's you at the reins. I don't think there's anyone this side of the Rim who could get us there faster."

"'Cept Whim," Jebe said timidly.

Simen leaned forward. "Whim? Where is he, Jebe? Isn't he with Jamus?"

Jebe shook his head. "He's gone for the Healer."

"We sent Whim to get Jern," Delran explained. "I don't exactly understand how it happened, but it did. No point in discussing it now. I sent messengers after him so if he doesn't get the Healer my men will. I didn't want to waste any time, so that's why we've set out too. One, the other, or all of us will find Jamus sooner or later and get him to safety. Jebe says they were waylaid by horse thieves and Jamus was hit by arrows."

Simen thoughtfully rubbed his own shoulder. "No wonder," he said to himself. The pain had been distinct, but he'd dismissed it at first. Now it made perfect sense. "How long will it be?"

"Nearly two winds to the Rim, I'm afraid," Delran said. "We can push the horses, though. These are my best team. They can run all day."

"Whim brung me in four bounds," Jebe said.

"Then let's hope Whim finds Jern," Simen replied. Four strides on the wind, he thought. Jamus could hold on at least that long.

Chapter 8

Lord Margston raised his glass to toast his new son. "To ye, Jern, for bringing my son safe into this world."

"Your wife is more responsible than I, My Lord," Jern replied.

"My wife is indeed a rare jewel," Margston began, but he was interrupted by a loud shout from outside.

The shout was followed by a crash, then a series of thumps with more, angrier, and louder shouts. The house shook.

Margston pushed himself back from the table and was headed for the door, when it burst open with a thunderous crack.

His mouth fell open.

A huge silver horse was shoving its way into his dining room.

Only slightly less startled than his host, Jern leapt to his feet. A fraction later, he settled himself enough to speak. "Uhm, My Lord. Do you happen to have a spare saddle and bridle I can borrow? I… uhm…well I think he's come for me."

"Bridle…" Margston sputtered. "Horse… here…"

"I really do need the tack right away, Sur," Jern replied calmly, even though his heart was thudding in his chest. By the Blood, what was Whim doing?

"Gant, go get the equipment. By the Hand, Jern, can't you take that… that beast outside? Really, I find it hard to believe you need to ride him in here."

Jern grimaced and headed for the door, motioning Whim to back away. The stallion obeyed reluctantly. "Well, no, My Lord. It's just that… well, he gets a bit impatient sometimes, that's all. Maybe he's hungry. I… uhm… I had to be going anyhow."

Before the shocked Lord could ask another question, Jern bolted from the room. In a matter of seconds he had the saddle girthed and the bridles sized and buckled to Whim's head. Then, he had one of the servants give him a leg up.

As soon as his seat touched the saddle, the stallion spun and headed into the last light of Sowin. A moment later and Jern's breath was taken away as they lifted into the shifting wind.

"By the Hand," Margston muttered as they disappeared. "That Healer is the strangest man I've ever met."
*****

Six strides, seven. Jern lost count. All he knew was that it was dark, he was cold, and Whim was bound and determined to take him somewhere.

Suddenly, they grounded and this time, the silver stallion did not lift himself again. Instead, he slowed to an easy trot. Up ahead, Jern saw the faint glow of a campfire.

"So, this is where you want me, eh, fellow? All right then."

The horse stopped a few feet from the burning logs.

Jern jumped off as soon as he saw Jamus lying there. There was no doubt now as to why he had been called so dramatically.

"For Sogol's Sake, I hope I'm in time," he said.

Nobby whimpered in his sleep, then woke with a start. Without even thinking, the boy threw his body protectively over Jamus. "Go 'way! You leave 'im be!" He pulled out his little knife and held it out, towards Jern's face. "I'll cut ya! I will! Ya leave 'im be!"

Jern drew back to let the boy see Whim behind him. "Whim brought me, lad. It's all right."

"Whim?" Nobby asked, straining to see into the darkness. The stallion nickered and stepped into the ring of firelight. "Who you be? Where's Jebe?"

"I don't know who Jebe is, Sur, but I do know Whim and he came to get me. That's Lord Jamus you're protecting. I've come to help." When Nobby did not relent, he went on. "My name is Jern. I am a Healer. Please, let me Touch your Master."

"Me Lord?" Nobby shook Jamus gently. "Me Lord?"

"Nobby," Jamus said weakly.

"Ya knows a Jern?"

"Jern. Good man."

"'E's here."

Jamus' eyes opened. "Jern," he repeated.

The Healer knelt at his side, his hands trembling. "May I Touch you, My Lord?"

Jamus nodded almost imperceptibly then slipped back into semi-consciousness

Jern took a deep breath, sealed himself in his protective weave and placed his hands on Jamus' chest.

The river cried-not so much in pain as in Sorrow. Tired, so tired. And afraid. Not for its own sake but for the sake of those it longed to protect. The innocents. He'd promised to keep them safe. It was a lie. He'd promised never to lie. Now he had and he suffered for it.

The waters wept. The currents twisted and turned in their anguish of grief for innocence lost. It wasn't fair. They weren't ready yet.

Jern reached out. Groped into the waters, trying to find the answer. Not your fault-the world's.

His shoulder screamed. His thigh was on fire. More than price paid.

Not your fault. You can't change the world. Not even the River can change the world.

How many times? How many times? I've been hurt so many times.

Like stelin, must be tempered by the fire. Again and again until it will not bend or break. Blood must flow in the River.

Below, the Dragon bellowed.

Jamus writhed beneath his hand.

The fire flared.

And it was done.

Jamus' breath was regular and deep. Jern wiped the sweat from his brow, rocked back and took his own deep breath of the cool night air. It had never been like that before, but already he had learned to expect the unexpected from the Rivermaster. Nothing was as it seemed with him.

"Mister," Nobby asked. "Are ya all right?"

"I'm fine, Nobby," Jern replied. "And so is your Master."

Eyes wide, Nobby looked at Jamus and saw the wounds already disappearing. "Ya Healed 'im?"

"I did."

"Why ain't he awake?"

"He won't be, for a while yet. It will take a few days for him to recover his strength. It's the way of the Magic."

"I don't know nothin' 'bout Magic 'cept what me Mam an' Pap tole me."

Jern looked at the boy and frowned. "You're shivering."

"I had to use me shirt fer a bandage an' Lord Jamus needed a cover so I gived him me jacket. It's all right. The fire's good. I kin add more wood."

"No," Jern said. "There's no need of that." He played his fingers in the air and Nobby felt a soft woolen jacket cover him. A moment later, a blanket covered Jamus who now lay on a fur covered pallet. "We need shelter too," Jern continued. His hand wove a roof of pine boughs over their heads and walls covered with more branches on either side. He added more blankets and cushions next, making sure Nobby was well settled. "Are you hungry?"

Nobby stared at him in wonder and barely nodded.

Jern waved his hand again. "I don't have much food at my house, but surely some bread and cheese will do. Cups for water, I think, and a pot to brew some keldherb." The food appeared at once. Not a feast, but more than enough to satisfy.

Nobby pulled off a hunk of good brown bread and chewed it while he watched Jern prepare a potion.

"I like Magic," Nobby said.

"It has its benefits," Jern replied. "I don't use it all the time, though... not like this. You understand that, don't you?"

"No. If'en I had Magic, I'd use it all the time."

"That'd be wrong, Nobby."

"Why? If'en ya gots Magic, ya kin do whate'er ya wants. Why'd that be wrong?"

Jern sighed. He was just a boy. How could he understand? It always looked so easy to those who had no Magic, and that is what had once nearly destroyed the world. It was the very cause of Rule and Vow and the source of conscience in the Mage's mind. But there was more, so much more. Magic took away a man's pleasure, stole his satisfaction, and cheated him of struggle. Magic lessened the soul if a man let it, and broke his will. It was all a lie to say he was master. The River mastered him. Then he looked back at Jamus. How must it be for him? "Having what you want doesn't always make life better, Nobby. Sometimes being alive is all about wanting."

"I don't unnerstan'."

Jern laughed. "Why should you? You're still just a boy. Why should you even have to? Nobby, haven't you ever wanted anything more than you could stand it?"

Nobby shrugged. "I wanted ta work, ya know, ta be out on me own, 'steada making me Mam haf ta worry 'bout me all the time."

"You are working now. Is it as good as wanting to work?"

Nobby wiped his nose on his sleeve. "It's harder than I thought, an' this sure ain't been good. I liked thinkin' 'bout it a whole lot more, that's fer sure."

"Then you understand a little, Nobby. Doing something with the Magic is just never quite as good as you think it's going to be."

"Oh." The boy hesitated for a long time. Then he said, "I guest it's like larnin' ta ride. If'en yer bottom ain't sore, then ya don't feel like ya done nothin' at all."

Jern laughed. Nobby's comparison was better than he ever could have invented himself. "You're a smart lad, Nobby."

"He's a good lad too," Jamus said from the shadows.

"Well now, you're awake at last, My Lord," Jern answered, smiling. "Just once, I'd like to meet you standing up on your own two feet having no need of anything from me except my sparkling conversation."

"What fun would that be?"

"You're right as usual, Master Jamus. There is no fun when there is not some crisis or other to attend to. What pleasure could there ever be in leading a normal life?"

"Thank the Hand you don't live one, Sur, or I would be well dead by now. Where's Jebe?"

Jern grunted as he poured a cup of keldherb. "Just who is this Jebe I keep hearing about? First Nobby and then you, asking me about the fellow. He must be must be special if he's so important."

"'E's my friend," Nobby stated firmly. "An' 'e went off on Whim ta find Lord Delran."

"Delran," Jern said. "I should have known he'd be in the thick of it. Well, unless I'm sadly mistaken, your Jebe should be coming along by Easwin or so on the morrow with Delran in tow. Since I had the best horse, I got here first, that's all."

"Whim brung him, Master Jamus," Nobby said proudly. "Jest like Jebe said he would."

"With borrowed gear," Jern explained. "I had to use one of Margston's saddles. They'll be the foolcap to pay for it too, I fear. I left on a rather strange note. Did you know that stallion of yours likes to use the front door?"

"He was in the house?"

"Interrupted a fine meal too, mind you. We were just about to taste some of Margston's best wine, and there he was."

Jamus laughed, then coughed and Jern hurried over. "Don't be too jolly, my friend. You're not well yet. Lying about on the ground half bled to death is not the best thing for a man's health."

"You're a Healer. Why don't you fix me?" Jamus asked, his voice tinged with amusement at Jern's too sharp concern. "Don't fuss, Jern. I'll be fine now. I've been wounded enough times by now to know I'll recover."

Jern tucked the blanket around his patient and clucked his disapproval. "Always throwing yourself about in the Rim. You'd think a man of your intelligence would learn from his mistakes."

"If I'd made any, I would," Jamus returned. "We were ambushed. The Hand only knows how they knew we were coming."

"They stole all the horses," Nobby said. "They knocked me in the head an' stole ev'rythin'.""

Jern called the boy over and examined him. "You have a bump, there, Nobby. Does it hurt?"

"It don't no more. Master Jamus made it better."

"You Healed him? In your condition?"

Jamus shrugged and snuggled deeper into the blanket. "I had a spare moment or two."

"A less than perfect job," Jern said, gently massaging the lump on Nobby's head.

"I was... distracted," Jamus returned.

"It don't hurt," Nobby repeated. "Asides, what am I gonna show Jebe if'en I ain't got no bump? Man's gotta have somewhat ta show fer bein' hurt, ya know?"

"Why, yes, he does," Jern replied. "As long as it doesn't hurt anymore, I think you should be right proud of that bump, Nobby." He took the pot from the fire and poured a cup of keldherb. He carried it over to Jamus and helped him sit up so he could drink. "You amaze me still, Jamus. Half dead and you found the strength to Heal him. How?"

"He needed me. He was afraid."

"And you. Weren't you afraid too?"

"I have the River, Jern. When the time comes, she'll take me. Until then, it will be as it will be."
*****

The horses pressed on hard, their muscles pulsing with the endurance of seasons worth of training. Jebe had fallen asleep, and Simen had taken him into his lap, wrapping him in a fur robe from the back of the carriage. He and Delran had talked long and hard about what had happened, piecing together Jebe's story with conjecture and common sense.

"It had to be someone who knew they were coming. If they were ambushed where I think," Delran said, "it was the only spot, and too perfect for chance."

"Did anyone from Turan know Jamus was on the way?"

"How could they? I didn't even know myself. We'd agreed it would be sometime near SeasonTurn, but that was about all. The weather here has hardly broken and I had no idea what it was like east of the Rim in the Keep. I would have thought perhaps another three Sevenstins."

"Then it was someone in Magiskeep."

"Jebe mentioned names. Did you recognize any of them?"

Simen sighed, "No. But I can't say I know everyone in the Kingdom, especially the mortals."

"They didn't seem to use any Magic."

"They didn't have to. Arrows are as fine a weapon as any against a Magician. The secret's in the surprise. No man can defend himself from an attack he doesn't expect."

"Pray to the Hand Lord Jamus is alive," Delran said.

"He is, My Lord. Surely I'd know otherwise."

"Do you think that stallion of his really did find Jern? It'd be a wonder if he did. I swear, it was incredible to see the boy with him. The horse acted as if he understood every word he said."

"He did, my Lord. Jebe is a Beasttalker," Simen replied.

Joss flicked the reins to urge his team on. "Does me Pap know that?"

"I doubt it," Simen replied. "Jamus hasn't told many people yet. He said he didn't have sufficient proof to declare it to the Gathering, so he was keeping it quiet. I don't suppose it matters much here. It seems to me you would all cherish him instead of poking and prodding him like some kind of experiment or other they was they would in the Keep."

"A Beasttalker," Delran repeated. "A wonder indeed. What a treasure he would be in my Keep. I have so many horses that need a kind ear. I've been taking in strays from all over Telma, you know. There are so many that have been abused by fools who think a horse is just a bauble to be shown off, used up and thrown away. They're hurt, frightened or even worse, enraged by what's happened to them. To think of being able to tell them it's all right, that I am going to give them a good, safe home for as long as they need it…"

"Perhaps, when this is all resolved," Simen said, "Jebe could stay with you for a while. Jamus might consider it."

"What about the boy's parents? He's such a wee lad. Surely they'd have something to say about it."

"Jebe's mother works in the Keep. If you'd have a place for her, I'd wager she'd be willing to come to look after him. He had no father to speak of and I doubt she'd object to leaving Magiskeep. As I understand it, she has no love of the place."

"Would Lord Jamus let him stay with me?"

Simen grinned. "My brother is no Sagari, My Lord. He'd never stand in Jebe's way if that's what the boy really wanted."

"There's the Rim," Joss said, pointing ahead. "We gotta head a mite Southerly ta hit tha pass. I gots ta give the team a breather agin an' let'em have some water. It'll be a right quick stop, like tha last ones, I promise."

Jebe shifted a bit in his lap and Simen flexed his left arm experimentally. He hadn't thought about it much recently but now, he realized his pain was gone. He smiled. "It's all right, Joss. There's no need to hurry anymore. Jamus is fine. The last thing you want to do is show up to rescue him now with a team of lathered and lagging horses."

"How do you know this?" Delran asked as he swung stiffly out of his seat to stretch his legs. "Jebe said he was arrowshot. A man doesn't just recover like magic from... " He checked himself. "I've Turanded again, haven't I. Forgotten just who I'm dealing with. Then I pose the question again. Just how do you know he's all right?"

"We're more than mere brothers," Simen began, checking himself nearly as quickly as Delran had. Some things were just better left unexplained. Telling Lord Delran how he was Jamus' reflection freed from the Way of Mirrors was one of them. "We've a special kinship, Jamus and I, and the Magic speaks to us. When Jamus was first hurt, I felt it. My pain's gone. His is too."

"He's been Healed?"

"I'd say the silver stallion managed to convey his message quite well, My Lord. Unless, of course, some other Healer was wandering aimlessly about the Rim and just happened upon them."

"Bah," Delran puffed. "No Healer in his right mind would be wandering those peaks. Rim's really bad out this way. Tarks prowling about and so many tricks that if you don't know every inch of the trail, you're like to fall off a cliff and break your neck. Sorcerers made it that way so the mortals'd keep their noses out of the place. Aren't but a few Mountmen I know who'd dare those foothills."

"The thieves did," Simen said.

"Aye, and I've been thinking on that. Whoever they were, they knew Jamus was coming and they knew the trail. Unless I miss my bet, I'd say there's a force behind the scenes here worth investigating."

"You have an idea who it might be?"

"I've an acquaintance a piece north of here worth talking to. He's the kind of man who makes his money selling horses and his reputation buying them back for half price when the seller realizes what they're really worth. Lebard and I don't exactly get along. I've spent my lifetime earning an honest living, and he's spent his earning a living, if you get my meaning."

Simen nodded. "The coin's more important than the truth, I take it."

"He'd sell a horse with three legs to a poor old farmer and tell him the beast'd work better that way because he could dance between the rows. Worst of it is, he's such a glib talker the farmer'd believe him and buy the critter. Man like that gives horse dealers a bad name."

"And you think he'd steal Jamus' stock?"

"Bory, lad! I can't imagine what Lebard'd do if he laid hold of some good horses for a change. Why, he'd a like go all the way to Aberdeen to sell them to the King himself for half the treasury!"

Simen mulled the information over for a bit as Delran climbed back into the carriage and sat next to him. "But the trail. How would Lebard know enough about it to send those killers safely in?"

The carriage lurched forward as Joss set the horses into an easy jog. Delran wagged his finger. "He has a Sorcerer of his own, at least that's what I say. The man calls himself Eagen. He'd not Keepbred, mind you, nor Turan, but he's Sorcerer."

Simen remembered the story Jamus had told him of his honeymoon and Erlik. "There are other kinds of Sorcerers in this world, My Lord. You may well be right."

"Aha! I thought as much. That would explain it all. With his Sorcerer, he scried out the Rim trail and set up the ambush. He's probably already lined up buyers for the horses. Those lads must be cursing themselves for not managing to take Whim too. He'd fetch a purse or three of gold." Delran rubbed his hands together with keen delight. "Tell me, Simen, are you a fair magician yourself?"

"Passing," Simen replied. "Not up to Jamus' standards, but adequate."

"We do have a span or so yet before we reach that brother of yours. Let's say we spend the time discussing just how to bring Master Lebard his just rewards, eh?"

Simen leaned back in the seat, tucked the robe snugly around Jebe and smiled. "I would enjoy that conversation, My Lord. Do go on."

Chapter 9

Salene breathed a sigh of relief as soon as the River caressed her with its whispered assurance. She had been half-asleep, resting her eyes from reading a book in the sunlit warmth of the conservatory. Weswin's change, with the soon to set sun, had lulled her into a drowse and opened her mind to dreams.

It was already dark in the Rim. Turan's sun had passed over the Western peaks and left the mountains in shadow.

The waters lay still, silent-waiting.

Far above, on a rocky ledge, a great brown hetark hissed his displeasure at being denied his meal by a scavenging rimhawk. He knew there was prey below, lying helpless in the sand, but nearby, an orange light glowed and flickered in the darkness. He had felt man's fire before and wanted no taste of it now. He, like the waters, would wait. Sooner or later the flames would die and he would seek his quarry. He could smell the fresh blood and he slavered.

The wind sprung cool, eager in its early hours, feeding the fire, sending sparks to the sky.

Beside it, a mist hovered, golden, shimmering in the building light. The voice was but a breath in the mounting breeze, yet its words were clear, "My son. I am here."

Someone sighed and moaned.

"Just but call and I will come."

Suddenly, the golden mist was supplanted by silver, swirling and insistent, a force determined to command the scene.

It was then the River whispered, "All is well. The Lord is free, and the waters sing."

Salene roused with a start, her face beaming, her eyes alight with hope for the first time since Jamus had left. He was alive, and safe. The Magic had spoken.

Gently, she closed the book, rose from her little bench and stretched. How she loved this room with its plants and cobbled walkways. In the Chillmonths, this and the Greenrooms offered sweet reminders of the Warmmonths in the Keep when fields were colored with wildflowers and the brellums with green. Now, it offered solace in ways she had never expected.

Sarn never came out here. He was too caught up in the day-to-day business of the Keep to bother with plants and pools. To him, Magiskeep was a great toy to toss and turn in his hands until something broke and he had to be called on to fix it. Jamus had long ago learned most of the Mages and Masters were far better at doing their jobs than he was at supervising them, so he left the palace to manage itself. Now and then there were a few disputes to settle, as there always would be whenever men tried to work together, but for the most part, he had little to do. Salene too found herself little involved in the normal running of the household, leaving the details to Jeamel and his staff. The old houseman was more than competent and knew every square inch of the palace so well, not even a speck of dust out of place would escape his notice or care.

Today, though, she had been busy. Lord Sarkem and Lady Delise of the Southern hold had announced a visit. Normally, this would have caused little disturbance of the Keep's daily routine, but with Sarn in charge, the event had mounted to a major complication.

First, of course, he had demanded the Recordscholars dredge up every bit of information on the guests the Keep had ever stored in its tomes and scrolls. Then, he insisted the Ceremonial Steward research the proper protocol according to the rank and station of the guests and their entourage. Tameer, in the kitchen, was plagued with Sarn's orders to stock his larder with Southern delicacies and kegs of three-season amberwine. He had even invaded the stables, charging Josep with reserving ten of his best stalls for the guests' horses by relegating Magiskeep's stock to the second barn for the duration.

While Jamus would have merely announced his guests' visit, Sarn declared it and demanded reports from every quarter of the house on their progress towards making it perfect.

Soon, the upstairs maids were grumbling, the downstairs stewards were muttering, and even old Jeamel had stormed out of the Main Hall to pout in the scullery for most of Easwin. By Sowin, Salene had had enough and retreated to the serenity of the indoor gardens to find some peace. Then, the dream had come and all of Sarn's foolishness didn't matter anymore. She was refreshed and her husband was safe. Sarn was just a pebble to the Rim.
*****

Jern warmed a new cup of keldherb and stoked the fire. Nobby had at last fallen asleep after nearly talking the Healer to a circle's end and Jamus was drifting in and out of sleep himself. Though free from pain and well Healed of his injuries, the suffering seemed to have taken a serious toll and he needed several more days of quiet before Jern would pronounce him fit again.

Whim too had finally relaxed and, after nibbling with little interest on the scant grass scattered about the area, he had finally settled himself a little way off from his master and dropped his head to drowse. Here in the Rim, he would never lie down as he might in his stall in Magiskeep, for he was ever listening with one wakeful ear to the sounds of the night.

The hetark yawned, bored with his long vigil. The fire was not dying and the new twoleg joining the others did not look either weak or sick. Stretching his lean body to its full ten- foot length, the great mountain cat padded off and up the slope in search of easier prey. Even the horse below smelled of Illusion and he wanted no more of it. His keen feline senses wasted too much valuable energy sifting him through the mountains' tricks. The last thing he wanted to do was eat some.

Jern had other considerations to ponder. The most important was just what he was going to feed his patient and the boy at Easwin. His stock of food from his own cabin was already used up, and skilled as he was at most Magic, charming a meal from the Rim was not his strong suit. To think, he had left a fine meal at Lord Margston's to ride into the cold night air just to starve to death.

Margston. What had been on that table? There was, as he recalled, a roast boar and a fair sized cavil haunch. Bread and cheese, of course, for no table in Turan was ever without either. A platter of taroots roasted golden brown, and greenlings fresh pulled from the cold garden filled a platter near the pitcher of calidew. A feast fit for a Lord's celebration of a new son. More food than Margston and his one guest ever could have eaten. And with Jern so strangely vanished, certainly too much food for one man.

Jern smiled. He gestured once, and brought the roasts. Another movement filled the depression near the fire with the bread, cheese, and vegetables. Then, a final call settled the calidew just to the edge of the little shelter. Margston's kitchen would be bare at sunrise, but Jern decided it was his due. The Lord had never paid him for bringing the baby safely into his mother's arms and he had left with an empty stomach. The food was not denerets, but it would suffice.

He leaned back against the rock and looked up at the sky. The stars looked so bright against the blackness of Norwin. To think, just spans before, he had been soaring with them in the night, flying on the wind astride a great silver stallion. He glanced over at Whim and nearly laughed. To look at the horse now, his lower lip drooping, his hind leg cocked as he snored, who would ever believe he had such magnificent power and so much Magic. It defied reason. Magicians themselves had no ability to work the Magic on themselves. Sorcerers could not fly unaided, and yet the horse had managed quite easily. Could animals know secrets men didn't?

"Jern?" Jamus whispered his name as if almost afraid to say it.

Jern moved over beside him and touched his shoulder reassuringly. "I'm here."

Jamus seemed to sigh. "I was afraid I'd dreamed you. We talked before, didn't we?"

Jern put his hand on Jamus brow. He had a fever. "We did, Sur. You don't remember?"

"We talked a lot, about the River, Nobby… "

"That's a fair summation. You do remember, then," Jern replied, puzzled by Jamus' confusion now. "Why are you asking?"

"She was here… my mother. She wanted to take me with her, but Whim wouldn't let her."

"Jamus, I really hate to say this, but you're not making much sense. You shouldn't have a fever either, so none of this is really making much sense. Was it all some kind of dream? Have you had a nightmare? I can't cure that, you know, but I can listen." Jern adjusted Jamus' blanket and then settled himself down on one of the cushions.

"Just before you came, Jern, she was there, by the fire. I saw her."

"Your mother."

Jamus helplessly shook his head, knowing full well how hard it all would be to explain. "The golden woman of the River who claims to be my mother. Damn, you'll think I'm crazy or delirious, I suppose, but she was here. And she was calling me."

Jern thought for a moment. "You did say something about how when the time came she'd take you. Did you mean her? You just said the River, as I recall."

"I think I was dying, Jern. Not close to dying, but actually dying. Those arrows, were they poisoned?"

"It's possible," Jebe replied, feeling Jamus' brow again. "It would explain the fever. When I Healed you, it was very strange. I didn't sift for any kind of poison, actually. I just Touched you to cure the wound."

"It's not gone."

"I can see that. I can clear most of it from your blood, but I can't undo the damage it's already done." Jern Touched Jamus again, first on the shoulder, then his thigh, letting his Magic reach out to seek the alien substance flowing through Jamus' veins. He felt the heat, and let it sear into his own body, taking it on as his own. Compassion consumed it, softening its pain, and sealing it in the cooling waters of the River. It was simple, easy, something he had learned so long ago he had forgotten exactly how to do it.

Jamus sighed. "That's better. My head's clearer now. I was starting to think I was losing my mind."

"I was an idiot not to think about it myself," Jern said, raking his hand wearily through his thick blond hair. "I must have been more unsettled by that ride here than I realized. And here I thought I was so worldly and sophisticated about the whole thing."

"You saved my life, Jern. That took some doing."

"To leave you to die all over again from something I foolishly overlooked."

"Well, I'm still alive. That's twice I owe you my life, I think. Or three times, if we add past experiences."

"I failed miserably the first time too, as I recall," Jern replied.

"I never would have made it to Tulene if not for your Touch, Jern. You're far more skilled than you realize. You have to stop doubting yourself. The Magic denies the Mage who can't accept his own Mastery."

"It doesn't deny you," Jern said quietly. "You run from it every chance you get and still it leaps to do your bidding."

"Who told you that?"

"The River. When I Healed you. I didn't understand then, but I do now. You don't want to be the Rivermaster."

"Would you, Jern? Would you want your life controlled by the River's and Turan's needs? Every way I turn I'm forced to face the Magic's riddles. She never leaves me alone, even when I try to escape her." A sob caught in his throat. He'd never said this to anyone, not even Salene. To her the River was a rival. To him, a curse.

"Magic is a wondrous thing, My Lord. It frees us from want and assures us life. Yet those of us who have it wish we didn't and those who don't wish they did. Perhaps the Seers were right-Magic is Turan's bane," Jern replied sadly.

"Or its salvation," Jamus answered. "I've seen the darkness too, Jern. That's the worst of it. If I deny the River, then the Shadows will have nothing to stop them."

Jern shivered. "The fire's burning low. I'd better add more wood."

Jamus raised his hand and the flames freshened, fed by his power. "I can keep it burning all night."

Jern was even colder now. The weight of Magic's presence chilled him to his very core. "The Eldenlore speaks of Shadows and the Circle's close," he said. "It's all just legend."

"No. Truth, Jern. I've seen them. They want this world for their own, to keep it in darkness where they can savor the blood of men. It's all true, everything you've ever read, everything you've ever heard, every nightmare…"

"Stop it, Jamus. This isn't you talking. It's the fever." Jern said, as if words could soothe Jamus' distress. He pulled out a pouch from his belt, dropped some powder into the lukewarm cup of keldherb and held it for Jamus to drink. "You need to rest, My Lord."

Jamus sipped the brew and lay back. "The fever speaks the truth too, Jern. Remember that," he said softly. Then, he closed his eyes and fell asleep.

Like stelin, tempered by the fire, not to bend or break.

Still the fire burned brightly, as if his hand still stirred its spirit.

*****

Easwin found Delran and his men a span from the Rim trail where they believed they would find Jamus. The rest of the journey flew by as the horses also seemed to sense they were nearing the goal and quickened pace of their own accord.

As soon as they saw Jern and the shelter, Simen leapt from the carriage and hurried over to where Jamus lay. Delran inched himself stiffly from the seat and limped over to the young Healer, while Jebe, still sleepy eyed, let out a squeal of delight and bounded towards Nobby who was just finishing off a joint from the boar.

Delran clapped Jern heartily on the back nearly knocking the slender Magician off his feet. "Well, well, lad, you made it! I should have known, I should have known. Master Simen was convinced, but I'm not ashamed to say I had my doubts. Never held much store in the Magic when muscle and brain would do as well. Now lad, come on, tell me everything. I've brought a nice little keg of amberwine along and we can talk over a cup, eh?"

"Bory, My Lord," Jern replied, a bit nonplussed by Delran's enthusiastic greeting, "the sun's barely up."

"What's that to men who have so much to celebrate?"

"You haven't even looked at my patient yet, Sur." Jern protested. Then he lowered his eyes. "I nearly bungled it, My Lord."

Delran's gaze darkened, and he squeezed Jern's shoulder with his strong fingers. "What are you saying, lad?"

"One of the arrows was poisoned, and I overlooked it. Thank the Hand it was the one in his thigh and not the one near his heart. He'd bled so much it had leeched most of it out, but there was still enough left... "

"Come now. You did find it. And, you Healed him."

"Only because my patient is a wiser man than I, I'm afraid. Had he been a mortal to begin with, you'd be bringing amberwine to his grave."

"By the Blood, Jern, don't you understand anything? If he had been mortal, you never would have been here in the first place. Nor would I. He would have perished and the boys too. Only the fact that he is the Rivermaster even gave you the chance!" Delran assured him. "Think on that, Sur, instead of what you see as your failing."

Jern smiled weakly. "It seems to me someone told just about the same thing last night. Poor consolation for a nearly fatal mistake."

Simen had finished examining Jamus and moved over to the other two men. "He's asleep. He didn't even stir for my touch. His heart's strong, though, and his breathing's regular. Aside from the time he'll need to regain his strength, he's fine."

Jern simply stared at the Follyman, his eyes riveted on his face. When Simen reached out to take his hand in thanks, he shrank back without knowing why. "I... I don't know you, Sur."

"I am Lord Jamus' brother."

"No."

Simen realized in an instant that Jern had sensed his true identity. Compassion had honed the young Healer's perception, even to the point of realizing he was in truth, Jamus' reflection brought to flesh and blood. "By the Will of the River, I am, Sur." Then he laughed, trying to disarm the tension before it shattered Jern's composure completely. "Jamus would tell you if he were awake, but since he can't, I guess you will just have to trust my word as a child of the Rivermaster's family."

The words registered and Jern gulped and nodded. "I thought... I was given to believe Lord Jamus had no brothers. I can see the resemblance in you, Sur. It does seem I was mistaken. How is you're here with Lord Delran? It seems a curious coincidence."

"Like my brother, I can travel the Way," Simen replied.

Again, Jern nodded mutely, his suspicions confirmed. This man was of the Way, not a mere traveler. "I've heard that can be dangerous."

Simen smiled. "No more so than the Rim, apparently. When the Magic surged at Jamus' agony, I knew I had to find him. Lord Delran's was the obvious place to begin looking."

Delran sensed there was something more going on between the two men than idle conversation, and he sensed too it was time to change the subject. "Well, we are all here now, though, by the Hand, I can hardly believe it all myself. May I again offer the wine to toast the reunion?"

This time, Jern decided to accept. He could use a stiff drink.

"And then Whim just flew!" Jebe said, as Nobby grinned broadly to hear the story again.

"Jest like we done when we first left the Keep?" Nobby asked.

"Bigger and higher and longer even," Jebe replied. "I was scared, I tell you. It was all I could do to hold on."

"I was scairt too," Nobby said. "Lord Jamus was awful sick, Jebe, an' I din't know what ta do."

"Looks like you done just fine," Jebe replied proudly.

"I made tha fire. An' then Whim brung Master Jern."

Jebe stroked the silver stallion's soft muzzle and fed him another surlep from the store in Lord Delran's carriage. "Master Joss knew what to bring, didn't he, Whim? Joss is Josep's son, Nobby, and now he works for Lord Delran. When the Lord found out we had to come here all he did was say one word to Joss and in a flash, all these men and horses and everything was all ready to go. Joss did it all himself."

Nobby whistled in admiration. "'E mus' be a right powerful. There ain't no lad in th' Keep Master Josep would let do that."

"He's right fine a sure. Master Josep musta taught him good. You see how lucky we are, Nobby, being right there learning from the master? If we do good maybe can get jobs like Joss . Think on it, Nobby, working for a grand lord and being all responsible for the whole barn!"

"It'd be grand, sure as thinkin'," Nobby agreed. "Me Mam an' Pap'd be real proud. Do ya really think it could happen, Jebe? Do ya? It'd be like a dream comin' true, a dream, ya know?"

"It sure would," Jebe agreed.

*****

Sarn stepped back from the mantel and cocked his head to more critically eye the balance on the flower arrangement Jeamel had just replaced. "It's still not perfect," the young Mage said. "I would have liked a deeper pink in the lollies. Are you sure these were the best in the Greenrooms?"

Jeamel gritted his teeth, forced a solicitous smile, and offered a formal explanation. "Jerban picked the best he had. He said these were bred from the Keep's own stock and none in all of Turan could compete with them."

"The Lady Delise likes pink, Sur, not pale… peach." Sarn spit out the word as if were bitter on his tongue. "What do you think it will look like to her and her husband if the most powerful Keep in all of Turan cannot provide her one simple pleasure?"

"Then Magic 'em if that's what'd please ya, Me Lord," Jeamel replied sharply as he waved his hand in disgusted dismissal. "Make 'em pink as a baby's bottom fer all I cares. I'm done wid 'em an' done wid this whole place!"

"You are the Housemaster, Jeamel. You have duties," Sarn said firmly.

"I ain't no more, Sur." Jeamel bowed sharply. "As of now, I ain't Housemaster no place but at me own hearth."

"You… you can't just walk out," Sarn sputtered. "There's work to be done, details seen to. For Sogol's Sake, man, we have guests coming!"

"Well, I tell ya what. Maybe Missy Tasra kin find ya a nice pretty pink tunic ta wear an' ya kin greet the Lord and Lady fer yerself, 'cause I ain't doin' no more fer ya 'bout it." At that, Jeamel spun on his heel and headed for the Keep's huge ironwood door.

Sarn snarled and raised his hand. A bolt of green fire shot from his fingertips, slashed past Jeamel's ear and shattered a statue just to his left.

Jeamel froze in his tracks and the every servant in the Hall fell to shocked silence.

"It ain't the way o' the Keep," Jeamel said, his voice trembling with emotion.

"I told you to stay. I am the Lord here now. You are Magiskeep's Housemaster."

"No," Jeamel repeated, and he reached for the door handle.

Sarn raised his hand again, but a woman suddenly rushed past him. "I ain't working here no more neither," she said, standing squarely in front of his outstretched fingers.

"Me neither," a lad called from the right, to be joined by voice after voice as one after another, the servants all began to rebel.

Jeamel swung the door open and marched out, his knees shaking, his face pale.

Behind him a crowd of resolute maids and menservants followed in complete silence.

Sarn stood open mouthed. Then he dropped his arm and let his hand hang loosely at his side. There was nothing left to say.

Chapter 10

The pebble had become a boulder and now, a mountain.

When Salene entered the Great Hall, she shook her head in amazement. A shattered statue lay in shards beside the huge door hanging open to the fresh breezes of Easwin. A bouquet of lovely pink lollies dangled in disarray from a tilted vase on the mantel of the great fireplace and there was not a servant to be seen. Worst of all, there was the taint of Magic in the air.

"Jeamel!" she called into the Reception Room. "Jeamel, where are you?"

"Gone," someone answered from the small study chamber to the north of the hall.

Salene went to the doorway and stood, leaning against the darkwood frame, trying to appear relaxed despite her sense of foreboding. Sarn was slumped in a chair by the ashes of a spent fire, a goblet dangling from his limp fingers. "What happened? Did you use Magic out there?" She pointed towards the Hall.

"Jeamel was walking out on me. I needed to stop him."

Salene straightened, her Master's ire sparked by his careless response. "It is not the Way of the Keep to use Power against our own, no matter the provocation."

"I was under the impression the Lord of the Keep established the law here," he replied, taking a sip of his drink. He gestured towards the decanter and cup on the table nearby. "Would you like to join me? The wine was for the guests, but I decided I should taste it first. It's very good. Fruity, the way ladies usually like it."

"You are not the Lord of Magiskeep, Sarn. And even if you were, it would not be your right to defy the Elden Decrees against using Magic to intimidate a servant--or anyone--into obeying you."

"Jamus named me in his absence."

"To keep his Vow and protect us against the Shadows. The only shadow I've seen is the one you've cast over this place. Your pride and arrogance have ruined circles of harmony among our people," Salene replied angrily. "What did you think you were doing?"

"Upholding the honor and dignity of Magiskeep," Sarn answered. "Sarkem and his wife are important people in the Southern Lands. We owe ourselves better than common grace in welcoming them here."

"And just what do you suppose Lord Sarkem and his Lady could ever possibly do to benefit us that you have to alienate a man as loyal and worthy as Jeamel for their sake? By the Blood, Sarn, this is Magiskeep, hold of the Rivermaster. There is no greater force on the face of Turan. What could we even dream of gaining from even one mortal?"

"Admiration," Sarn said quietly. "Or better, fear. How will they respect us if they don't see us as their betters? Wealth and status are all people understand, Madame. Power comes from having more than those you rule. Do you think they would respect us if they tasted water in our wine or ate a morsel of burned meat at our table?"

"Men are not judged by their tables, nor are they valued for their clothes or the content of their purses. They're judged by their deeds and the value of their word. Haven't you learned anything from the Masters here?" Salene asked. Her fingers were white as they gripped the doorframe, using it to steady her temper.

"I learned from the best Master of all," he answered.

The name caught in her throat. "Sagari," she said hoarsely.

"He knew better than anyone what made men respect him." Sarn studied his hand as he flexed his fingers in front of his face. "Power is the only thing people care about in the end, Salene. Jamus thinks he knows another way, but he's wrong. Why do you think he left me here in his stead? He knew if we were threatened, I wouldn't hesitate to use the Magic."

"We weren't threatened, Sarn." Salene said, moving a bit into the room.

"We were. By humiliation."

"Humiliation? You nearly killed a man to avoid embarrassment? Damn you, Sarn, what kind of a man are you?"

"A Sorcerer," Sarn answered, and then he poured himself another drink.

*****

Joss rested the horses a full wind, then harnessed his team and prepared the carriage for the trip back to Delran's Keep.

Four of the guards had remained with the party, while the others had gone off to follow the track of the ambushers. Just before the group was ready to leave, one messenger reported back. "My Lord, we followed the trail to Blue Valley Pass. It seems the thieves drove the horses there. If so, your guess about the horses being taken to a Northern hold would make sense. Dougal wants to know if you would like us to keep tracking them to the end of the trail or whether we should go back to the Keep."

"Follow the track until you're sure they've gone to Lebard. I don't want to stage a raid unless we're certain. Get Tomas to make a map of the area. He has a keen eye and a good hand for it. He'll know the details we'll need."

The guard saluted. "Aye, My Lord. Tomas will want to know if you plan a full attack or more subtle approaches."

Delran stole a glance at Simen, who was helping Joss settle Jamus in the back seat of the carriage. "Let us propose a subtle beginning with a more direct conclusion."

"Very well, My Lord," the guard replied. Then he reined his lean-legged horse back up the trail and sent him into a long strided gallop. Keen riders like Delran's men, mounted on some of the finest horses in Turan could cover the foothills and valleys west of the Rim in a wind and the Lord expected news almost as soon as his slower moving party made it back home.

Simen seated himself next to Jamus and waited for Jern to climb in alongside them. "Well, brother, I hope you're fit enough for the trip. It's going to take at least two winds."

Jamus leaned back in the seat and sighed. "I had hoped to arrive at Lord Delran's under different circumstances, but I guess this will have to do."

"The Hand be blessed we have you at all. According to Jern your circle was perilously close to its end."

"The Hand be blessed I had Jebe and Nobby with me, Simen. Jebe knew Whim would take him for help, and Nobby had more presence of mind than most men I know. He built that fire and kept me from freezing to death."

"They're good boys," Simen agreed. "I should think Magiskeep will offer them more than common thanks when we get back."

"That would be quite a difference for Jebe," Jamus said thoughtfully. "Don't you think it's ironic? Here all the time I've been trying to find a way to make that boy's life better and all I had to do was nearly get myself killed. By the Blood, if I'd thought of that sooner I could have spared the poor lad Sevenstins of misery."

Simen's mouth dropped open and he simply stared at Jamus. Then, his face broke into a wide grin. "Sometimes I wonder whether or not I really am your true reflection, Sur. Unless it is possible a Follyman can be reflection of himself."

"What? Do you think I spilled all my wit into that mirror, brother?" Jamus laughed. "How many times do I have to tell you I only gave you half of it."

"Half a wit is better than none," Simen replied, trying to keep a straight face. "Does that mean between us we are of one mind?"

"If your mind is intending to get those horses back that were stolen from me, then indeed we do," Jamus answered. "I'd rather do that than waste time coddling myself all the way back to Lord Delran's."

"No talk of that, My Lord," Jern said as he settled himself on the seat. "You will need more than two winds to recover your strength."

"While the bandits sell the stock and we lose track of them?" Jamus replied contentiously. "Whim can take care of me well enough if I go after them."

"In Sorem's Name, Jamus," Simen replied with a heavy sigh of exasperation, "why do you always insist on doing everything by yourself? Here you are, surrounded by friends and watched over by a more than competent contingent of soldiers and you still think you're the one who has to fix everything."

"Because I can, Simen. With one finger, I could change the course of Turan's Way if the River Willed it. Why should I risk the lives of dozens of men when I don't need to?"

"Because dozens of men are willing to risk their lives, My Lord," Jern said crushing the last herb in the cup before adding water to his potion. "Once more, Sur, you forget the lessons of Wizardchase and the Mages' Vow. Men must do for themselves, you know that. Here, look at yourself. If Magic were the natural way of things, why didn't my Healing restore all your strength and vigor? The River knows better than you do, My Lord. Magic cannot be the spirit of man without destroying his spirit."

Jamus took the cup Jern offered him and drained it. "I seem to be surrounded by philosophers. I might as well surrender then, since it's impossible to win any points in a philosophical discussion. Besides, I'm feeling sleepy again." He yawned and closed his eyes.

Jern took the cup from his limp fingers and shrugged. "Jaroot and a touch of palion do have a way of ending even the most philosophic of discussions, don't you think, Simen?"

Simen nodded as the carriage began to move. "Effective, Sur, especially where Jamus is concerned. I really think he would have tried to ride out of here if he'd had the chance."
*****

Bayard Lebard's Keep lay nestled in a narrow valley between two green hills more than a wind's ride north of Delran's Keep. A wide, well-cared for road led in from the Western

Provinces, leading up to a broad tree lined drive in front of a granite and wood mansion. Lebard had gone to great expense setting up a huge walled yard in front of the main entrance with covered walkways to the right and left leading off to ruggedly constructed barns. Again, no coin had been spared to build the barns to be attractive and almost elegant.

Lebard had learned long ago the nobility of Turan was more impressed by setting than content, and he contended he could sell almost any nag if he had the chance to present it well to the customer. He had a full complement of grooms whose sole job was to clean, trim, polish and otherwise prepare his horses for sale. Their skill at dressing a horse for presentation was so good, it was said a client had once brought in a gelding to sell to the master and later, he had bought his own animal right back after it had been rubbed to a shine by Lebard's handlers.

It was not that every horse Lebard sold was bad. He often had worthy stock. The trouble was, just as often he had horses of questionable worth and was willing to misrepresent them to unsuspecting buyers if he had hope of making some money.

Too many of his clients were not horsemen, but rather moneyed gentry who only wanted to look good riding in fancy carriages or astride a dancing hoofed steed. They had no sense of quality beyond what their eyes could see. A slight limp, a crooked leg, or even long teeth revealing too many circles mattered little. If the horse had a proud carriage and good color, it was marketable and Lebard never missed the chance to sell such creatures to the vain lords and ladies who sought them.

Delran was his bane. The true horsemen of Turan much preferred making the more difficult journey to his southern hold to find quality animals guaranteed to be sound and fit. Never once had he heard of a client dissatisfied by the elder lord's offerings. To make matters worse, Delran had some sort of arrangement with the Sorcerers beyond the Rim to breed his animals with their stock and to trade with them as well. He had fields of fine mares of his own along with at least five prize stallions noted for breeding beasts with stamina, grace, and beauty.

Now, he had heard the rumor of a new cross of horses that Delran had conspired to obtain and had decided to stop the competition dead in its tracks.

He had a contact in Magiskeep and when word had come across the Rim from his wandering cadre of well-paid mountmen, he had ordered the ambush.

It paid off better than he had expected. Not only had he gotten the five young horses of the new line, but he had also acquired three other quality saddle animals.

"The mare's a beauty," he said to Augie as the brigand led the mare past him one more time.

"She is, ain't she," Augie agreed. "'Pears ta me she weren't one from the same stock as the big'uns, eh?"

"No. She's saddle bred and quiet enough to be a lady's palfrey. You know, with the flashy chestnut and the pony, I do think I have a fine family's set here, don't you think?" Lebard rubbed his hands together greedily. He had already donned his burgundy formal coat and fastened his silver studded belt around his ample middle in anticipation of some arriving customers. Grinning, he slapped his feathered velvet flatcap on his head, taking surprising care not to mess his hair, which had been dressed and curled into a wreath around his head. Then he hooked his fingers in his lapels, jutted out his chest, and cleared his throat for an experimental sales pitch. "Yes indeed. Here we have an elegant set of mounts for the entire family. Whose head would not turn to see the lord and lady ride by on shining horses the color of the sunset with their precious lordling trotting alongside on a perfectly mannered spotted pony? You would be the envy of your neighbors, my friends, and rightly so. What say you? For a mere sixty gold, you can become the talk of the town. And for another twenty I will throw in the beautiful saddles and bridles as well."

"Sixty gold?" Augie gasped. "Sur, you can get that much?"

"Why... why...," Lebard sputtered, realizing too late he had played a poor hand in front of the thief. "You can well imagine it won't be easy, Augie. These beasts have had a hard crossing and will need some good food and tender care before they're worth that kind of coin. I'll probably have to put half that much into their bellies before I can even offer them for sale. Then, my men will have to spit and polish them to a shine. Add their wages on and I'll scarce make any profit at all."

"Mebbe I oughta try ta sell 'em meself," Augie said thoughtfully. Somehow the twenty denerets apiece he had agreed on no longer seemed quite so attractive.

"Come now, Augie," Lebard countered quickly, making up for his blunder with style. "Look at yourself. Dear lad, do you really think anyone would give you seventy golds for anything you had to sell?"

Augie tried to wipe the red dust of the Rim off his scuffed boots by rubbing them on the back of his legs one at a time, but all he did was dirty his leathern trousers even more. His homespun shirt and leather vest were well worn, but he was so comfortable in them he'd never even consider trading them for even a square of Lebard's velvets. "I could try, me Lord. Ya cain't fault a man fer lookin' fer a fair profit."

Lebard cleared his throat. "I'll tell you what, Augie. I'll give you twenty-five apiece instead, and another five for each set of tack. That's nearly twice the usual price for the stock you bring me."

"I'll be thinkin' on it," Augie replied. "What about the young'uns? They's the ones ya wanted in tha first place. Ya tole me thirty fer them. I might like a mite more, ya know."

Lebard sighed. "Thirty five and not a copper more. They are green and hardly even broken to the halter. I'm going to have to train them to harness before I can even show them."

"They's lookers. Considerin' their size, I was thinkin' more like forty-five."

"Forty-five?" Lebard gasped. "Do you think I am one of your marks, Augie? Why, that's robbery, plain and simple. Pressed, I'd close at forty and that's the end."

"Forty it be," Augie agreed quickly. To him it was a King's ransom.

To Lebard, it was pocket change. The drays would fetch even more than the saddle horses, he'd decided. Carbit could break them in less than a Sevenstin and have them ready to drive. He knew the tricks of the trade better than any trainer Lebard had ever hired. The fact that Delran had fired him for being too cruel only added seasoning to the whole affair. To think, he had Delran's horses, Delran's trainer, and Delran's profits all in one bundle. It was too perfect.

On the hill just to the south, Tomas jotted down his last notation just as the chestnut mare was led back into Lebard's barn. He had found the vantage point by sheer luck and mountman's sense learned from circles of wandering the Province on his own. Now, in Lord Delran's employ, he had developed a keen sense of loyalty to his new master and an equally keen sense of contempt for any of his former class who chose thievery over honest work.

Even at this distance, he recognized Augie by his black shaggy head, broad shoulders and stubby legs. That would mean Toady, Bonder, and Dickel were not far behind. Word was, there had been five bandits and he knew four. The best part was that he also knew exactly where those four spent most of their time. He folded the scrap of vellum where he had drawn the map, tucked it into his pouch and made his way back down to where Dougal and the others were waiting.

"I got good news for the Lord," Tomas told them as he remounted his horse. "The horses are all there, just like he figgered."

Dougal grinned. "A nice piece of work Tomas."

"Aye, and ye'll be glad to hear I also know the culprits. T'won't be more than a day's exercise fer us to take 'em when the time comes. And I, fer one, intend to ask Lord Delran fer the honor of leading the charge."

"Someone you know, Tomas?" Riv asked.

"Yep. Old friends. Real old friends."

*****

The Keep was eerily silent as Salene made her way out through the empty kitchens. Apparently loyalty to Jeamel far outweighed loyalty to Mages and Masters, for there was not a servant to be found on the ground floor. Soon, at Windchange, the Prentices and teachers from the upper levels would be coming down for midmeal. The Dining Hall had been set and ready, and there were all kinds of pots and platters set out as well in the kitchen itself, but there would be lots of hungry mouths this day.

She considered remedying it herself with some quick weaves, then changed her mind. To do so would only cover Sarn's mistakes. This time she wanted him to reap the consequences of his actions. Certainly, his Magic could prepare a feast if he wanted it to, but she doubted he would even think of it on his own. Let him suffer the consequences.

Josep was in the stables, as were his lads, sitting idly on bales of hay. When she arrived, he nodded to her, but did not rise.

"I'm surprised you're even here, Josep," she said as she collected her gear from the tack room.

"I cain't make the horses pay fer a Lord's stupidity," Josep answered. "Be assured, me Lady, the animals will be well cared fer despite Master Sarn." He gestured to one of the lads to help her.

She quickly shook her head. "No, Sur. Please. I am fine doing it on my own. As far as I am concerned I don't think one of you should lift a finger to help anyone who claims himself to be above you until all of this is resolved."

"Now, me Lady, I don't recall either you or yer husband ever once claimin' ta be above the like o' me."

"Nonetheless, it is a matter of principle, Josep." She walked Shadow into the aisle and hefted the saddle on the gelding's back.

"Well, at least tell me where yer goin', Me Lady," Josep said. "I don't hold wid havin' ya jest ridin' out o' here wid no by yer leave. If'en somthin' should happen ta ya, I'd at least like ta know where ta look fer yer remains."

Salene started laughing. Soon, Josep joined in, as did his lads, breaking the tension completely. "I am," she finally said between giggles, "going to see Jeamel and offer him at least my apology. Since I can't speak for Sarn, I doubt he'll come back to the Keep, but I would hope, for my sake he might consider it."

"'E won't come lessen Sarn knows 'is place."

"And I don't blame him for it, Josep. Sarn will find out soon enough he's played the fool. Once he does, I'm not sure just how he'll try to fix it. In the meantime, I'd like Jeamel to know he has at least one ally with Power."

"I don't think he ever doubted it," Josep replied, wiping his eyes with his sleeve as he slipped into the accent of the Keep. "I'd wager they'll be a few more Mages who agree with you as soon as they find out."

"Indeed there will," Salene replied as she led her horse out into the yard. "And, I should think it will be an extremely interesting afternoon once they do." Then she swung up into the saddle and headed out to the streets.

As Sowin drew near, Sarn busied himself about the second floor guest chambers putting the finishing touches on the walls. He spelled a tapestry of a lord and lady riding out into the countryside on the wall beside the dresser and then stood back to admire his handiwork. The maids had done most of the work cleaning every surface and making up the bed with fresh sheets and a lovely down comforter covered in a pink floral shaenis dust cover. He had added a portrait and the tapestry as well as a small arrangement of lollies .

"This isn't so hard," he said to himself, quite pleased with the effect. His Magic had played easily into his hand setting the place to right, and he was beginning to think servants really were a waste of time when the River was just a Will away.

Still, the Lord and Lady would need someone to tend their needs when he was not available during their visit. So he had enlisted several of the younger fourth circle Prentices to act as hosts in his stead.

Joella and Joreen, the twin sisters who had hoped by now to be among Jiala's charges, were delighted to accept the role of ladies in waiting, especially since it meant they could cast off their Prentice grey and wear gowns instead. Sant, Jestin, and Skit were equally pleased to assume position as housemen since it guaranteed them spans out of the classroom and a chance to play the Magic without the watchful eyes of a Master checking their every move. Sareth, still

one of Sarn's closest friends through all the circles since their mutual
Prenticeship, welcomed the chance to act as second in command.
While in number, the group hardly matched Jeamel's staff of nearly
a hundred, Sarn was confident Magic would make up the difference,
at least as far as his guests were concerned.

As the wind changed, he realized he had seriously
miscalculated.

"My Lord," Senteen, one of the lesser Mages said as he
bowed over and over, "there is no food prepared for midmeal, and
we have a troop of hungry young Sorcerers to feed."

"So feed them" Sarn replied, impatiently. "Surely you and
your cohorts can conjure a meal from the kitchens."

"My Lord, to use Magic for such mundane purpose... and so
freely, I might add, is against the common law of the Keep."

"All right then, send some of the women into the kitchens
and have them prepare the food. I certainly have better things to do
myself than worry about such trivialities."

"My Lord, none of the women know how to cook, at least
not well enough to feed the whole Keep," Senteen protested, his head
still bobbing. "I really don't know what we shall do."

"By the Blood, man, can't any of you fend for yourselves?
Must I do everything? Look, the larders are full and there is certainly
more than enough food about to satisfy even the hungriest lad. Let
the mages care for themselves and the Prentices as well. I would say
learning how to conjure a meal for oneself is a much needed lesson
for any Magician. Whatever would happen to them should they find
themselves alone on the road, eh?" He waved his hand in dismissal,
"Go on, now, hurry off and tell them I have so commanded. I have
other matters to attend to."

Once the skinny little Mage had left, Sarn went back to
selecting a belt to go with his tunic. Appearance was, he decided,
everything--and he wanted to look absolutely perfect for his first
presentation to the outside world as Lord of Magiskeep.

Chapter 11

"We're not going to be able to keep him in bed as long as he needs," Jern said as he prepared another potion for Jamus. "By tomorrow, he's not going to drink any more of these potions unless we can force him to. You'd better think of some way to satisfy him about those horses, or we are in for one battle none of us can win."

They had reached Delran's Keep by Weswin's change, put Jamus to bed and sat down for a hot evenmeal. Now, over the cups of Keldherb, the three men were discussing strategy.

"As I see it, we've only two issues to deal with. We need to get the horses back, of course, and we need to bring the culprits here to face Jamus. I don't think any other options are open. If we take them to the King's justice, there's no guarantee they can be proven guilty of anything more than horse theft...and while that is a substantial crime, we can't forget they nearly killed a man," Delran said. The silver haired Lord shook his head sadly. "Somehow, I don't think Jamus can afford to accuse them in open court, even if Kur Kala is the Judger."

"Kala," Simen repeated. "I had nearly forgotten she would be called in on this if it became public. I think, gentlemen, we need to take the law into our own hands in this case, as Delran has suggested. Turan's justice is not prone to serve Sorcerers well, I fear, no matter who wields it."

"Then it's back to plan A," Delran replied, pouring himself another cup of keldherb.

"There was a plan A?" Jern asked. "When did this come about?"

Simen laughed, "We didn't just talk about you on the way to the Rim, Sur. It did cross our minds we would be forced to take some kind of remedial action. I must admit, I was not too fond of plan A, but after having seen how badly Jamus was hurt and, in the absence of a viable plan B, I agree with Lord Delran."

"So tell me," Jern said. "Or, I should say you will tell me after I drug our Rivermaster back into submission, just what exactly 'plan A' entails." He headed for the stairs and Jamus' room. "I'm all ears."

Upstairs, Jamus was already waking from another induced sleep. The cure was working more slowly than he would have hoped. His shoulder was stiff and unresponsive to his commands, while his thigh ached with the urge to flex. Then, when he tried to move, he found it simply required too much effort. To make matters worse, Jern was back with another one of his potions.

Jamus inched up on the pillows, his grey eyes wary. "What did you bring me this time, Jern, purple palion to do me in altogether?"

"My Lord! Such ingratitude. Such mistrust. I am appalled."

"Of course you are, Jern. Don't think I don't know what you're up to. The lot of you are conspiring to keep me in bed while you run off and have all the fun chasing down the brigands. Damn it, I deserve a piece of them, you know."

"And you'll get it, rest assured." Jern offered him the cup but Jamus waved it away. "Sur, Rivermaster or no, you do not have the strength yet to do much more than rest, so you might as well give in. Until your blood builds itself back up, you'd pass out if you tried to walk ten feet."

"So I'll just do five at a time."

Jern grinned. "That would be interesting, I must admit, but as your Healer, I can't permit it. Besides, those boys of yours would have me drawn and quartered if they thought I wasn't taking proper care of you."

"The boys," Jamus mused, "seem to keep cropping up in this. How are they getting on? Jebe told me Joss was going to take him out to the pastures to see Rowen, Delran's big stallion. Did he go yet?"

Jern paused. Despite Jamus' claims to the contrary, he still was not fully aware of what had happened, or how long it had been. They had only just arrived at the Keep. Didn't he know that? "Not yet, My Lord. There hasn't been time yet."

Jamus frowned. "How long have we been here? Two days already?"

Jern shook his head, "A wind, no more."

"I must have been dreaming. It's all so confusing."

"You were very sick."

"A wind," Jamus repeated as if he didn't believe it. "I could have sworn... Simen. I need to see Simen. Would you send him up here, Jern?"

"Drink this and I will."

Jamus took the cup and drank the brew. Almost at once, he closed his eyes and fell back asleep. Jern waited until his breathing was deep and regular and then he went back downstairs.

"He wanted to see you," he told Simen when he reached the bottom step. "I gave him the brew, though, so he's asleep again. I'm a bit worried. He doesn't seem to know what day it is. He thinks we've been here two days already."

Simen flexed his shoulder, felt the Soreness, and sighed. "Maybe it's your drugs, Jern." As soon as he said it, he knew even he didn't believe a word of it.

"If anything, they should clear his head," Jern replied. "He dismissed it by saying he'd been dreaming. Could that be all there is to it?"

"I'd like to think so," Simen answered. In his heart, he knew differently. Shadow-spawned as he was, he was all too aware there was no time in the Way. "Let me know when he's awake again and I'll go talk to him. Maybe I can ease his mind. We are brothers, you know."

"And strangers in Turan," Delran said. "Which is exactly why I still say you are the only one who can do it."

Simen rolled his eyes. "I may be a Follyman, but that doesn't mean I am a fool, My Lord. I'm not sure I can be the horse trader you need."

Jern cleared his throat. "I would like to be filled in, if you please. I feel as if I've walked into a party without my invitation."

"Lord Delran proposes I simply ride into Lebard's Keep and get the horses back."

"Now, Simen," Delran chided, "that's not exactly what I propose and you know it. I want you to ride Whim into Lebard's and trade him for the saddle horses. Once he's there, we can use him to bring the rest of the herd out."

Jern held up his hand. "Now wait a minute. You're going to trade Whim? I don't think Jamus would stand for that."

"Whim is, uhm, untradable, Jern," Simen told him. "There's no way Lebard could ever keep him there once he decided to leave. He does have his own Magic, you know."

"All right," Jern said, "but that doesn't get the other horses out. Explain that to me."

"If Whim can get out without being seen, he can get back in," Delran explained. "He goes in, finds the missing horses, and comes back out, fetches someone to open the gates and that's the end of it."

"Have you been drinking some of my potion?" Jern asked. "I'll admit Whim has shown some decidedly clever thinking of late, but just how do you expect him to figure all this out?"

"I suppose," Delran said, smiling, "we will just have to get someone to explain it to him."

*****

As soon as evenmeal was finished and the adults had left the dining chamber, Delran's houseman had hustled the two boys off to bed. Nobby, worn out from his long vigil with Jamus and a far too exciting ride back to the Keep, fell asleep as soon as he lay down. Jebe, on the other hand was too full of curiosity about the place to settle down. Finally, after thoroughly exploring their room, he sneaked out into the upstairs hall.

It didn't take him long to find the back stairs. In a matter of minutes, he was out of the house and making his way to the stables.

Whim was, for once, happily settled into a roomy box stall with a manger of good sweet clover hay. That did not stop him from nickering and marching over to take the surlep Jebe had snatched from the kitchen on the way out.

"Ya oughta be in bed, Jebe," Joss said. Whim's call had roused him from his own cot and he'd come to investigate.

"I brought him a treat. I figured he deserved it."

Joss laughed. "He's had four already, the beggar. Big as he is, he's like a baby when it comes to sweets."

"He won't get sick will he?" Jebe asked, horrified to think he may have fed the horse one too many of the fragrant fruits.

"Nah," Joss said. "I've seen him down seven at a time from Master Jamus' hand. Surleps ain't colicky lessen a horse finishes a basket of 'em."

More?

Jebe laughed. "He wants more."

"You know that?"

Jebe nodded. "He told me, just now."

"You really kin talk to 'im?"

"I think so. Master Jamus thinks so too. He says I'm a Beasttalker. I only talked to the horses so far, but don't you think I oughta be able to hear what the other animals is saying too if I want to?"

Joss thought about it a bit. "It do make sense, Jebe. We ain't got many critters 'round the Keep proper aside from the horses." Then he smiled. "Lessen ya think a cat'd have a fine word er two."

"I dunno. I never met a cat afore," Jebe said.

"Well," Joss replied, "I cain't say as I'd expect a cat ta make much sense anyhows. But I sure would be fun ta try. I wonder where Li'l Sergeant is. He's the chief barn cat. Best grainsnatcher hunter I ever did see. He's probly patrollin' the grain bins right now. Come on, them little furly thieves do their work at night an Sarge likes ta sit there waitin' ta ambush 'em."

The two boys headed for the feed room. Sure enough a tough looking gray and black striped cat was crouched behind a feed sack, his eyes intent on one of the bins near the corner of the room.

Joss held his finger to his lips as the cat's tail switched. Then, Sergeant simply sat up and yawned as if the whole affair had bored him completely. "Go on, Jebe," ask 'im somethin'," Joss prodded.

"Whatcha doin', Sergeant?"

My duty. As is proper. You scared the robber. I was waiting and you ruined it.

"He says we ruined it. He was waiting to catch a robber."

No matter. It will come again. It is a fool to think it can escape me. I am all see, all hear, all know. What do you want, twoleg?

"He wants to know what we want, Joss. What do you want me to ask? He's kinda unfriendly."

Busy. Work. Twoleg cannot do. Allwise must do for the clumsy foot. Tell Joss the cream is good. I like meat too.

"He says the cream is good and he likes the meat too."

"He oughta. Mistress Morrie up at the house saves it fer him and the other furries near every day. She says a hungry kit won't hunt. Ask Sarge if that's true."

Before Jebe could even form the thought, the voice answered in his head. *No hunt for hunger. Hunt for pleasure, hunt for duty, hunt for pride.*

Jebe screwed up his face as he tried to Sort it out. "I think, he says yes. He says he doesn't hunt because he's hungry."

"Can you really hear him, Jebe?" Joss asked again, excited.

I sleep Joss foot when door open. Tell him I purr when the sun hits window. Then I sleep on warm blanket without him. He laughs. I laugh too. He work. I sleep.

"Does Sergeant sleep on the bed with you Joss, on your feet? And does he purr when the sun comes up?"

"Yeah, darn little rascal wakes me up near ev'ry Easwin wid that big roar in me ears. Wait a minute, did 'e tell ya that?"

Jebe nodded.

"I ain't ne'er told nobody that. The boys here'd think I was all soft if'en they knew. Ya gots ta keep that quiet. Will ya, Jebe?"

Joss be proud I pick bed. Not like all twoleg.

"He says you should be proud he picked your bed, Joss. He says he doesn't like everyone."

"The li'l devil thinks a lot o' hisself, don't 'e," Joss grinned.

I am allwise. Think is no question. When Jebe chuckled, the cat swished his tail again and turned back to his vigil at the bin. *Young talker have much to learn. Maybe better to listen.*

*****

Magiskeep's kitchen was a disaster, as was the Dining Hall. Once they had been given free rein to get their own food, every Prentice, Mage, and Master in the Keep had conjured up some version or another of his favorite dish. While the results were mixed with more than a few hunks of burned cavil, everyone had had a grand time experimenting. Unfortunately, no one even thought of cleaning up afterward.

When Sarn, in search of another pitcher of amberwine, came upon the scene his heart dropped. "Sareth, get in here!"

Sareth ran into the Dining Hall and skidded to a stop just before running into a table still full of dirty dishes and debris. "By the Blood, what happened in here? Was there a ground rumble or something? I didn't feel it where I was."

"I wish it had been. No, Sareth, this is what remains when Magic is left to its own devices without a Lord commanding it." He sighed heavily. "I suppose you and I will just have to clean up."

"How?"

"Magic, of course."

"But I don't know where anything belongs. We can't just go putting things any old place, Sarn."

Sarn rubbed his chin thoughtfully. He had no idea himself just exactly how to set things right. He could certainly clean the linens and wash the dishes, but what to do with them afterwards? He could perhaps rearrange the whole setup, but if the servants ever came back there would be the Rim to pay for it. "For now, let's just clean everything and stack the dishes and linens on the tables."

"What about the kitchen?"

That posed an entirely different problem, for the food would have to be more carefully stored. Perhaps one of the women would know. Salene would. But she had ridden out of the Keep at least a span before, on some kind of errand she had concocted to avoid seeing him. Damn. Just like a woman to desert a man when he needed her most. Like Lurela when she had left and taken his son from him. "I'll take care of the kitchen. I'll figure it out. It can't be that hard if a woman can do it."

*****

Salene's arrival in the village had practically shut down every business in the area. Word of what had happened in the Keep had spread like the winds themselves and everyone wanted to hear what she was going to do about it.

"Jamus put Sarn in his stead to run the Keep," she explained to the third crowd of Sowin. "It's not my place to override his decisions. He made a mistake. For the sake of the peace, I think it would be wise for us all to remember a man has the right to be wrong once in a while."

"But Me Lady, he insulted Jeamel an' made him ta be the fool. That ain't jest wrong, it's like puttin' a dagger in 'is heart."

"Please," she said, trying to quiet the protests. "You must remember Lord Sarn was raised of a noble family. He's never learned the way of the common folk."

"That ne'er stopped Lord Jamus from comin' ta the village ta talk wid us. What makes Sarn think he's so special?"

"He doesn't understand," Salene insisted. "I don't agree with him, nor do I support what he did, but that doesn't mean I can't forgive him. He simply doesn't understand."

"So who's gonna teach 'im, eh?"

"I think he will teach himself. What the servants have done by leaving the Keep is a good lesson for your Lord. Soon enough he'll realize there's more to running that palace than mere Magic can control. Just be patient." Though the crowd was not satisfied, she rode on again until at last she reached Jeamel's and Becca's little cottage.

Jeamel himself opened the door for her. "Come in, Me Lady, come in!"

"I wasn't sure you'd want to see me, Jeamel."

"An' why not? I cain't say I kin think of a single reason why not."

"I am of the Keep, Sur," she said.

"An' so is I, Mistress," Jeamel replied. "Ya don't think I ain't still the houseman there, I hopes. When Lord Jamus comes back, ya'll see right quick who makes the decisions 'round there."

"I thought you might come back before that."

"Why? So that yaller haired pompom kin tell me I'm stupit? Ain't likely, Me Lady. Long as Sarn is up there givin' orders, I is staying right here. Leastwise in me own house all I gots ta lissen to is me wife, an' there ain't no doubt but she's always right."

"Oh, Jeamel," Becca said as she escorted Salene to the table. "Ya do go on so. Here now, Me Lady, ya sit yerself down an' have a bite ta eat. Seems ta me me love left the Keep afore the midmeal was prepared, so I doubt ya et yet."

"I'm not very hungry."

"Bory, Lass, ya takes after that husban' o' your'n. Near ev'ry time he drops by he says he ain't hungry neither an' afore he's gone I gotta fill his plate twice."

Salene nearly laughed. She'd heard all the stories from Jamus about how the woman had always shamed him into eating something whether he'd wanted to or not. She'd also hear what a good cook Becca was and how wonderful everything had always tasted. Now, she was certain she was going to find out for herself. "All right. I suppose I could have a bite or two. But don't go to any trouble."

"Trouble? Why I was jest settin' out midmeal as it was. We're eatin' a mite late today 'cause o' what happened. Right now I'm waiting on some sweet powder from the village. I done run out jest as I was ready ta top off the surlep pie." She looked up and out the window, "Oh good, here comes tha lass now."

Again the door opened, but this time Lurela walked through with a bag in her hand. When she saw Salene, she almost bolted, but Jeamel's hand stayed her. "Don't ya go runnin' off, Missy. When the Lady o' the Keep comes ta my house, I 'spect me other guests ta be polite."

Lurela handed the bag to Becca and curtsied. "Madam. It is a pleasure to have you here."

Salene waved her quickly to her feet. "I don't usually expect people to bow to me, Lurela. Neither my husband nor I stand on ceremony. It is a pleasure to see you as well."

"Jeamel and Becca were kind enough to invite me here to stay while my son was away. They didn't feel it was good for me to be alone in my cottage."

"I see," Salene replied, suspecting there was far more to it than that. "I hope you didn't feel you were in any danger."

"Damnation if'en she weren't," Jeamel cut in. "That pompom was makin' noises like he was gonna make a issue out o' her bein' back up at the palace. I figgered he wouldn'ta dared do nothin' if'en she was wid me an' Becca."

"Sarn threatened you, Lurela?"

"Not in so many words, Mistress. But he does want Jebe. I think he believes if I were gone when my son came back the boy would have no choice but to go to him for comfort."

Salene gritted her teeth. So, Sarn's grief over losing Lurela was not real after all. She had to admit he had done a masterful job of pretending to be concerned for the woman. "Just why does he want Jebe so badly, Lurela? He doesn't need to be saddled with the responsibility of a child to take care of."

"Why does a man want a bauble for his buckle or a fine-blooded horse to parade around on, My Lady? Tell me that and I'll tell you why Sarn wants Jebe. Don't you remember how Sagari bragged when he brought Lord Jamus home from the Rim? I was still at the Keep that night. You'd think he'd conquered half of Turan. And everyone fawned on him for it, tellin' him how wonderful he was to have been so kind. That was the night Sarn bedded me for the last time."

"Was that when Jebe was conceived?"

Lurela shrugged, "Then, Greenmonth before, who knows for certain? I was too young to notice the signs until it was too late. All I remember is Sarn strutting out of the room telling me he never wanted to see me again." She sighed. "I started to show by Warmmonth. By then, Sarn was struggling to regain Sagari's favor. That's why he told him he was the father. The rest, I think you know already."

"Sagari drove you from the Keep," Salene said. "And did Sarn ever try to make amends?"

"Not until after Jebe was born, and even then just so he could try to take him from me. Once he saw Jebe's hair and found out he was of the Magic, he began bothering me all the time. I moved into the cottage mostly because it was near Master Lorry's and he swore if Sarn showed up there he'd kill him. I guess Sarn believed him. After that he stayed away. The other day, in the Keep, was the first time I'd seen him in circles."

"But you stayed anyway."

"My Lady," Lurela said nervously, "I was there by Lord Jamus' commandment and he had my son. What else was I to do?"

Salene was speechless. But Becca had a voice and used it sternly. "By the Hand, girl, Lord Jamus'd kill hisself afore 'e hurt that lad o' your'n. What do ya take 'im fer?"

"A Lord of the Keep," Lurela replied softly. "Like Sagari. He wanted to murder my son before he was even born."

"Damn Sagari, lass," Jeamel told her furiously. "Jamus ain't nothin' like 'im. Nothin'! Yer little lad is a safe wid him as 'e is in yer own arms. Ya mark my words on that, Missy. Safe as in yer own arms."

Chapter 12

The conspirators had definitely decided on plan A. That, of course, required Jebe's assistance. At Easwin, when he and Nobby finally rolled out of bed, the boys found themselves greeted by Delran as if they were heroes.

"Well, lads, you do my house honor enough by being here. And now, to find you so cheerful after spending the night in my beds delights me even more. May I interest you in a Firstmeal of your choice? Mistress Morrie will prepare absolutely anything you would like."

"Anythin'?" Nobby asked, his eyes wide. "I always like flatcakes with surlep syrup and bangleberries in 'em. Me Mam makes the best in the whole world."

"Noted and agreed, Sur," Delran said, bowing slightly. "Mistress Morrie may not make them up to your mother's standards, but she will do her best, I promise you. And you, Sur Jebe. What would you like?"

"The same as Nobby, I guess. My mother never made me flatcakes 'cause the flour always cost too much. We'd have meal and milk usually, but I think I'd like flatcakes."

"Then flatcakes for two it is. We will offer milk as well as some lovely fresh melonade to wash them down. I have a lovely table over here by the window for the two young gentlemen if they would care to sit." Delran's blue eyes twinkled as he pulled out a chair for Jebe.

Jebe squared his shoulders and strode over, trying hard to look dignified. Nobby followed suit and soon the two were seated at the round wooden table as if they were two lords. "Did Master Simen and Master Jern eat already, My Lord? I wanted to ask how Lord Jamus was faring."

"Even now the two Masters are with the Lord, Sur. I'm sure you can ask them as soon as they come down. Would you allow me to sit with you for a bit instead?"

Jebe flushed. "You're asking me?"

"Of course, Sur. A man of honor always asks another man of honor for permission before imposing on his society."

Jebe chewed his lip nervously. "I'd be glad to have you join us, My Lord. I guess we can think of something to talk about."

Delran chuckled and sat down across from Nobby. "I've spoken at some length with Jebe, but I've not had the chance to talk much with you, Nobby. You said you worked in Master Josep's stable at the Keep, didn't you?"

"Fer near two circles now, Me Lord."

"I'd judge you a good worker then, for Master Josep does not tolerate slackers. Have you decided on your ambition yet? Do you intend a career in horses?"

Nobby nodded enthusiastically. "I'm gonna become a horsemaster. Jebe says iffen I ask Lord Jamus mebbe he kin teach me like he's teachin' Jebe. Me Mam an' Pap'd be right proud iffen I was ta take a mastery like that. Pap says I ain't gonna be nothin' worth much, but I figger I kin show 'im iffen I git the chance."

Delran's heart dropped to hear the boy talk of his father that way. He had lost a son himself ten circles before and could not have imagined even thinking of him as anything less than a complete success in whatever he tried. The boy had been talented, true, but Delran would have encouraged him and loved him even if he had never even tried to make his own way in the world. How sad to hear of a father who could think otherwise. "I shall speak to Master Jamus on your behalf, Nobby, if that would be all right. If he doesn't have the time to train you, I'm sure we could find a way to help you here. I have several masters who are keen to find bright young Prentices."

"Here? Me?" Nobby said, his mouth having a hard time closing.

"Certainly. Your actions in the Rim more than proved you have the right kind of intelligence and courage to take on such a task. Why, any Lord would be proud to have you in his employ."

Nobby's face split into a huge grin. "Ya hear that, Jebe? Ya hear that? Iffen Master Jamus cain't teach me, I kin larn here. I'm gonna be a master. I really am!"

"That's wonderful, Nobby," Jebe agreed, delighted at his friend's good fortune. Assured of his own place in Magiskeep, he reveled in this second stroke of good luck. "When Lord Jamus got hurt, I guessed it was just about the awfullest thing that ever happened. Now, it's turning out real good. Real good."

"Thanks to you and Nobby," Jern said as he pulled out a chair to sit. "Lord Jamus is feeling much better this Easwin and wanted me to thank you both again. I thought perhaps by tomorrow he'd be fit enough to have some guests and he said the first people he wanted to see were you two lads."

Simen came to the table and swung himself into a chair, sitting down heavily. "What do we have to eat? I swear, arguing with that brother of mine certainly gives me an appetite."

"A dispute?" Delran asked.

"It's all right, My Lord. We both have thick heads and thick hides. Neither one of us drew blood." Then Simen grinned. "Besides, with Jern on my side, Jamus was outnumbered."

Jern patted the pouch at his belt. "I do have strong methods of persuasion."

Simen took a flatcake from the pile, poured the thick red syrup on it and took a bite. Then, he looked at Delran, who nodded. "We have to ask you to help us, Jebe. We want to get the horses back that were stolen, you see, and we need you to do something for us."

"Are you gonna get Reddy back too, and Flutter?"

"We plan on getting all the horses. We have a good idea how to do it, but we need Whim to do some of the work. Do you think you might be able to talk to him for us?"

"I can try," Jebe said. "Sometimes Whim doesn't want to listen, though. Maybe Lord Jamus could tell him."

Simen looked at Jern for help on this one. Jern shrugged, "Lord Jamus does not entirely agree with all of the plan, Jebe."

"Is Whim gonna get hurt?" Jebe asked worriedly.

"Oh no, not at all. It's just that if the plan is really going to work, we may need more help from you, and Lord Jamus is concerned about that."

"I can take care of myself," Jebe said proudly.

Delran nodded. "You have proven yourself quite a capable young man."

"I told Lord Jamus I would watch over you," Simen added. While that was true, Jamus had been none too happy at the prospect. Jern's drugs were still strong enough to quiet his protests but he knew they would have to act soon, for the Lord of Magiskeep was getting stronger every span.

"Whatcha want me to do?"

"You and I are going to ride to Master Lebard's where the horses are, Jebe," Simen explained. "You will pretend to be my son. We think the Master will be more likely to believe the story I'll tell him if I have a boy with me. Then, while he and I strike a bargain, you will find out where the drays are being kept."

"And Whim? What's he supposed to do?"

"Allow himself to be traded," Simen said. "He must pretend to be the kind of horse Master Lebard would be willing to trade for Reddy, Lacy and Flutter, you see. Then, when it's dark, he can simply vanish and come back to us."

"But what about the other horses? How we gonna get them out?"

"That's where it gets a bit tricky. You see, we will need someone who can ride Whim back into the Master's yard. Someone who is very clever, and very quiet. Someone who can open the gate so the horses can get out. Then Whim can lead them home where they belong."

"I can do that," Jebe said.

"There might be some danger."

"Whim won't let anything happen to me. You shoulda seen him in the Rim, Master Simen. Those men wanted to… to kill Lord Jamus and Whim wouldn't let him get near him. I won't be scared if I'm with him."

"I wish Jamus had your confidence." Simen sighed.

"Lord Jamus didn't see Whim. I did," Jebe replied. "He were a right scary sight, Sur. They wanted to take him, 'cause they said he'd be worth a lot of money too."

"That's good to hear," Jern said. "That makes it all the more likely Lebard will find the trade attractive."

"A horse like Whim could fetch ten times what those other horses are worth," Delran said. "If Simen presents this right, Lebard will be convinced he's made the best deal of his career. I just regret one thing."

"What's that, My Lord?"

"That I won't be there to see the look on his face when he finds Whim gone the next day."
*****

Lord Sarkem and Lady Delise arrived just after Easwin's turn. Sarn's little entourage of mock servants greeted them at the door, took their luggage, and then one of the little ladies escorted them to the Reception Room. Since Josep had taken their horses to the stables, on the surface, there appeared nothing amiss.

Sarn greeted them with proper courtesy, and settled down for a long conversation while he waited for Sareth to conjure up a proper meal. They had decided to serve the guests Firstmeal there instead of the Dining Hall to avoid the problems, and had already set the table with the finest silver.

"I thought we'd be eating with the Mages," Sarkem said as he noticed the settings. "This is most unusual."

"While Lord Jamus is away, I have made a few simple changes," Sarn explained. "I thought, since we have little acquaintance, it would be nice to relax here with some peace and quiet so we may converse."

"Oh well," Lady Delise said with obvious disappointment. "I suppose I will have time to visit the kitchens later then."

"K...kitchen?" Sarn asked nervously.

"Why, yes. The last time I was here I had such a delightful time sharing recipes with Mistress Nell and Master Tareem. I had planned on preparing a meal for them this trip. I had a new way of searing and braising pettifowl I wanted to show them. I packed my spices just for the occasion."

Sarn cleared his throat. "Well, I, uhm, don't know if there will be the opportunity for that, My Lady. We have an unusually large number new Prentices this season and the cooks have been terribly pressed."

"All the more reason for me to visit the kitchen, then," Delise said smiling. "While you men are discussing business, I can lend a hand."

Sarn fumbled with the decanter of amberwine, nearly spilling the brew on the floor. Worse and worse, he thought. This was going to take more doing than he had expected. "I am sure your husband and I will conclude our business quite quickly, Madam. I am not a man to dwell on decisions."

"We have the Sevenstin, My Lord," Sarkem said. "I understood Lord Jamus might even be back before we had planned on leaving. While I do certainly respect your right to offer me judgment, I would not be adverse to having him confirm it."

"Oh, Lord Jamus had a change of plans. He is, I believe, staying over at Lord Delran's for a short sojourn. I wouldn't expect him back for at least... well, two Sevenstins."

"This is but grand, husband," Delise said, clapping her hands together. "You were so right in telling Tyron we might stay on here for a while. He will not expect us back. You see, Lord Sarn, Lord Jamus and my husband have many common interests. But, what has been even more wonderful have been all the things we have shared with the household staff here. Both Sarkem and I are avid gardeners, and," she laughed, giving her husband a playful poke, "my darling mate also has a fondness for doing some of the remodeling around the house all by himself. Your workers here are a treasure store of ideas and assistance. We are so looking forward to sharing our visit with them."

Now Sarn knew he was done for. There was no way to remedy this. "Some of my staff are on holiday," he offered lamely. As skilled as he normally was at lying, this was still not easy. "It is near Bestowal, you see, and I thought, with Lord Jamus gone and all, it would be nice to give them some time with their families."

Lady Delise's face dropped. Then she perked back up. "Well, it's no surprise then that your kitchen staff is so overburdened. How fortunate that I am here. Perhaps I should hurry on over now to see if I can be of any assistance... "

"No!" Sarn nearly shouted. Then he forced himself to be calm. "No, please, My Lady, not this Easwin. You must be tired from your long journey. My cooks would be quite upset to impose upon you so soon after your arrival. They are proud workers, you know."

"And rightly so," Sarkem said firmly. "The Keep has the best servants in all of Turan, I'd wager. Madam and I have crossed the Rim many times and in no noble house have I ever met such talented, wise and fine people as those who grace the halls of this Keep. Why, any Lord would count himself lucky to have but half this staff."

"Yes, yes, any Lord would," Sarn agreed half-heartedly. Then he took a huge gulp of amberwine. It would not be the last hard drink he would have to swallow that night.

He just hoped he could remember where Jeamel lived.
*****

Whim was eager to be off once Jebe explained where they were going. *Worry friends. Good we get. Whim be smart.* He had a first not understood why they wanted him to be kind to Master Lebard, but then, he caught on and decided playing a trick on the man who had masterminded the robbery was a grand idea.

Simen had an uneasy feeling about the stallion's willingness to play along, for he knew Whim had a mind of his own. He was too much Jamus' horse to be so complaisant. Still, without a squadron of men and the possibility of someone's being seriously hurt, this seemed the better alternative. Besides, there was a definite poetic justice in the solution. Cheating Lebard out of something he himself had stolen did a lot towards revenge for Jamus' suffering.

Four guards rode along with them, but they would hide in the hills around Lebard's Keep while Simen and Jebe rode in alone. Meanwhile, a larger contingent of armed men had set out after Augie and his friends. Their task was to bring the criminals back to Delran's Keep where Jamus would be given the chance to decide what to do with them.

Whim wanted to *windwalk,* or so Jebe told Simen. But the guards and their mounts posed a problem.

"I'm not as skilled at lifting strides as Jamus is," Simen replied.

"Whim says that's all right," Jebe answered. Mounted behind Simen, he hooked his hands tightly into the follyman's belt and added, "Whim says he can help."

Before Simen could answer, the ground dropped away. The guards were superb horseman and all their skills were tested at that moment, for their mounts surged into the momentous leap with excited energy and it was all they could do to keep their seats.

When they grounded, Simen groaned. "The Hand defend us against the beasts if ever they should claim the world. Next time, please, have Whim give us a warning."

At that, the stallion tossed his head and squealed. A moment later they were in the clouds, and half the distance to Lebard's had been crossed.

"Does he know where we're going?" Tomas asked breathlessly.

Jebe giggled. "Whim says you know and so he does too."

"Then pray to the Hand I made no mistake in my map," Tomas said, clutching at his gelding's mane in anticipation of the next bound. "Bory, I hope I drew it right."

He had. Within the next two strides they were settled on the far slope of the hill just south of Lebard's hold. It was absolutely perfect.

Simen had dressed Jebe in a pale blue tunic, a child's replica of his own. Both were stylish and perfectly cut, obviously well made of quality fabric. The follyman wore a sword, belt and dagger, as well as leather gauntlets to compete his appearance as a former knight only recently retired from his wanderings.

Once he and Jebe crested the hill, a bell began to ring in Lebard's Keep. By the time they reached the gate, there was a footman to greet them. He held Whim as Simen dismounted and lifted Jebe to the ground. Then he escorted them all to a finely set table under a canopy by the side of the walled yard where Lebard showed his sale horses to customers.

Lebard himself, dressed in a modest velvet tunic of dark burgundy rolled his way over to his guests as soon as they were seated. "Welcome, Sur, welcome. I have an idea in my head you have come to do business?"

Simen nodded and was careful not to get up at the dealer's approach. He wanted to make the clear impression he was of noble blood and not at all used to standing for commoners like Lebard. "I have, Master Lebard. I have heard you are a dealer with a fine selection of mounts. I am interested in doing some trading with you."

"Trading? I am not much for trades, My Lord. Cash is my preferred method of business. However, I am not adverse to listening to offers. Just what is it you wish to trade?"

Simen gestured towards Whim. "My stallion. I have only just married and in acquiring a wife and son...." He put his hand on Jebe's shoulder for a moment and then went on, "I find myself possessed of a war mount I no longer need. While he is a fine animal, what reason could a landowner have of such a creature? I would be pleased if you would consider trading him for some more suitable family mounts."

Lebard pretended indifference, but his eyes betrayed an almost animal lust as he studied Whim. The stallion raised his head and arched his neck as his silver coat shone brilliantly in the sunlight. And yet, despite all his apparent fire, he stood docile and obedient to the footman's every command. "He is a fair animal. If he is sound, I would consider a trade."

"Come now, Sur," Simen replied. "I am not totally ignorant of his worth, nor of his value to you. A horse like Streaker there could command a solid price to the right buyer. I myself have neither the time nor the inclination to find the right buyer, and so I offer him to you."

"And what makes you think I'd want him? I don't have much call for war mounts here."

Simen laughed. "Come now, Sur. You'll take him to Aberdeen and the King's guard will be fighting with each other to buy him, if the King himself doesn't outbid them. Were I in need of the money, I'd take him myself. But my wife is a wealthy woman and I love her far too much to leave so long as to make that trip."

"So, then you will trade him to me for what?"

"Three other horses would suit me fine. Something a family would look good on when we travel to town."

"Papa?" Jebe asked, as he started to squirm in his chair.

"Not now, Doren. Your papa is talking to the man."

"Papa, I wanna go play. I'm tired of sitting here. Can I go play?"

Simen smiled indulgently. "I am sorry, Master Lebard, but I'm afraid Doren here has not yet learned to be patient. Do you think it would be all right for him to have a look around your yards? He really is a good boy."

Lebard smiled too, his eyes constantly glancing over to Whim as if the stallion were already in his barn. "Roger, would you please escort young Master Doren here on a tour of our yards? Please watch out for him so he doesn't stray into any of the paddocks. As fine a horseman as I think he is, I cannot vouch for the behavior of some of my young stock."

A servant in burgundy livery snapped to attention and then held out his hand for Jebe to hold. "Come, Sur. I will be glad to show you some of the best horses in all Turan."

"You got any big ones? I like big ones."

Lebard laughed. "Show him the new stock, Roger. They should impress him."

Jebe trotted off at Roger's side chatting happily about nothing at all the way precocious children were prone to do.

Simen managed to hide his grin. The boy was certainly playing his part well. Now, he had to do the same.

Lebard instructed one of the grooms to go to the stables and in short order a trio of skinny bays was paraded into the ring. While the dealer extolled their virtues, Simen pretended interest. Then, he shook his head. "Frankly, Sur, I would like prettier horses. My wife favors chestnut mares. I've never been partial to redheads, but you know women."

"Chestnuts, h-m-m-m." Lebard considered for a moment. Then he called the first groom over. "The new mare and the young stallion with her. Bring them next." He turned to Simen. "I had some new horses delivered just the other day. So far they've been well mannered, and they certainly suit the bill as far as looks go. I must be honest, though. I've not had them in the yard long enough for my trainer to work with them so I'm not sure how well they ride. The men who brought them assured me they are good mounts."

As soon as Redwin and Lacy were led into the arena, Simen found himself losing his composure. Here at last was undeniable proof of what had happened in the Rim. It wasn't that he had ever questioned it, but somehow, seeing the stolen horses dug at the wound, making it bleed anew. His own shoulder caught in a spasm of pain and he nearly gasped.

"Are you all right, My Lord?" Lebard asked, concerned. He would have hated to lose this particular customer so close to making the deal.

Simen took a deep breath and nodded. "An old battle scar, Sur. Sometimes, without warning, it reminds me of why I gave up my life as a knight. I will be fine in just a moment."

Just then, Jebe came bolting along the walkway with Roger running breathlessly behind. "Papa, Papa! You oughtta see them. They got five real big horses in the back in a real pretty pen. You wanna come and see, Papa?"

"No, Doren, not this time." Simen took a few more steadying breaths, glad of Jebe's diversion. He shot the boy a warning glare a mere fraction before Jebe turned to look into the ring. It was a good thing, for Jebe nearly gasped himself when he saw the chestnut pair. "Did you see anything else interesting, son?"

Jebe shrugged, "I seen a pretty pony. All kind of red and white spotted. I'd like a pony like that, Papa."

"A pony," Simen said with obvious interest. "Do you have a pony, Master Lebard?"

Lebard smiled again. If he could throw the pony into the mix, he would save himself at least one horse. All he had to do was convince the pony was a far better choice for the Lord's family than three full sized horses. Quickly, he knelt in front of Jebe. "You liked the pony, lad? He is a pretty little fellow."

Jebe nodded. "I like him a whole lot. If he were my pony, I'd feed him surleps every day."

"Perhaps, if you ask very nicely, your Papa would get him for you. What do you think?"

Jebe grinned with childish glee and looked up at Simen. "Papa, I like the pony. Would you get him for me?"

It was absolutely perfect. Simen let his face melt into a look of fatherly affection. "If Master Lebard can part with him. A fine pony like that is very special." Then he looked over to the horse dealer and winked. "Could you bring yourself to part with that pony, Sur? I should think my stallion would just about cover the cost of him and those two chestnuts down there."

Lebard squeezed Jebe's arm in congratulations and rose to his feet. He extended his hand. "It is sealed, My Lord. The horses are yours. I will give you the tack as well since I feel I have the slight advantage still."

The shook on the deal and in short order, Redwin, Lacy and Flutter were back in the hands of Magiskeep. Redwin was fairly dancing as Simen mounted and even little Flutter seemed eager to be off. Lacy was still wary, having found herself once more displaced. After all, in the Rim, Jamus had made a promise to her. Still, Redwin's happiness was contagious and as they headed for the gate, she two dared a dance step or two.

Then, Redwin saw Whim in the hands of a stranger and nearly stopped. Whim glared at him, his dark eyes boring into the other horse. Simen felt Redwin shudder and then pick up pace. As Whim was led to the barns, they headed for the hill where Delran's escort waited.

Whim did not even nicker a farewell.

Chapter 13

Sarn found Jeamel's house after two spans of searching. No one in the village seemed to know where the houseman lived despite his high reputation. The truth be told, no one wanted to tell Sarn where Jeamel lived, but the temporary Lord of Magiskeep was far too proud to even consider that possibility.

When at last he came upon the cottage, it was by sheer luck and Jeamel's very obvious presence in the front yard tending the greenlings sprouting in Becca's flowerboxes. He hardly looked up as Sarn dismounted and tied his horse to the hitching post.

"Master Jeamel," Sarn said, stepping on to the cobbled walkway, but daring to go no farther.

"My Lord," Jeamel replied evenly.

"I have come to ask you to return to the palace."

"An' why would I do that, Me Lord?" Jeamel asked, slipping back into the village accent.

"Because Magiskeep needs you, Sur."

"An' what about 'er lord, eh? Seems ta me ya don't need nobody, Sur. I figger from the way ya was actin' ya knew how ta do it all yerself."

Humility came hard to Sarn. It was not among his skills. Still, he tried hard this time. "I was wrong, Jeamel. Running the Keep is not about issuing orders. It's about knowing the people there and meeting their needs. You have been doing it a long time and doing it well. I should have known better than to question you."

Jeamel peered up at him, trying to find deceit in the young Magician's face. "Are ya tellin' the truth now? Ya ain't got the fairest reputation in that, ya knows."

Sarn paled. "I don't know what you mean, Jeamel. I am, if anything an honest man."

"As a lad ya wasn't an' I ain't quite sure tha man's much different. Ya lied ta Lady Salene 'bout Lurela."

"What?"

Jeamel wagged his finger in Sarn's face. "Tell ya what, me Lord. Ya do right by Lurela, an' jest mebbe I'll come back ta work fer ya."

"Do right? What do you mean, marry her? Bory, man, we don't love each other. As much as such a thing might benefit the woman, what kind of life would that be for her?"

Jeamel shook his head. "I'da ne'er wish sech a curse on th' lady as ta be saddled wid the likes o' ya, me Lord. Nah, that's not what I mean. What I mean is ya stands up in front o' the whole o' the Keep an' admit what ya done. Ya admit yer the lad's father, an' ya admit ya ain't done kindly ta the lady. Then, ya makes a promise, right there in front o' witnesses that she an' her boy gots nothin' ta fear from ya an' that yer gonna protect them no matter what."

Sarn's color did not return. The demand overwhelmed him. To think of facing such an ordeal completely unnerved him. "Isn't there something else you'd settle for?"

"Nothin' less. I'll give ya til Lord Jamus comes back to do it, though, 'cause when he does, I'm gonna tell 'im ev'rythin' an' I doubt he's gonna be as kind ta ya as I is."

"And in the meantime?" Sarn asked hopefully.

"I come back ta the Keep an' you stay outta me hair. I hear one word from ya 'bout flowers er anythin' that ain't yer business an' the deal's off."

Sarn grimaced. He had well underestimated these commoners, that was for sure. At least Jeamel had given him some time to find a way out. He extended his hand. "So be it, Sur. Is it sealed."

*****

Once Tomas had made sure Simen was safely into Lebard's complex, he had headed out to meet the other group of guards. The lifted strides had put him well ahead of schedule, so when he reached the appointed meeting place he was able to rest his horse and take a much needed rest himself. Since they had gone to find Jamus in the Rim, he and the other men at arms had been riding nearly non-stop. Last night had been the first time they'd had to relax.

But, the fact was, for Delran, he and the rest of the guards would have done almost anything. There were few men in Turan who garnered that kind of loyalty. Delran had, in his youth, served in the King's army and earned a high reputation for bravery, integrity, and sheer combat skill. When he retired to Telma Province and his horse farm, he was followed by several of the men who had served under him. These guards were their sons and relatives, taught by the patriarchs of their families that Delran was more than worthy.

And Delran himself assured their devotion by treating every single one of them as his own son. He saw to it they were well paid, well fed, well sheltered, well clothed, and above all respected. He knew their individual talents and encouraged them. No man was ever belittled or criticized and more often than not, especially in matters like the hunt for Jamus' ambushers, rarely questioned. Once he told Dougal, Riv, and Tomas what he needed them to do, he left them to their own devices, standing ready in case they sought his advice, but otherwise not interfering. He trusted them to do the job, and in return they did it willingly and better than any man could ever hope.

Riv, Dougal and Tran arrived just before the half of Sowin had passed. They had ridden hard, but Delran's horses were bred for it. So it took only a half span for the group to gather a second wind and then head out for the little village of Mudlake where Augie and his friends spent their money.

Mudlake was settled on the shore of a mountain fed pond with the annoying habit of going dry for no apparent reason. In the wet season or dry, the water level varied with no sense or logic, as if it were as enchanted as the Rim. The trouble was, the lake was nowhere near the Rim and instead seemed to be fed from the smaller mountains to the north of Telma Province. Some declared those hills too were chanted, but no one had ever been able to prove it. Still, it was enough of a rumor to keep the village population down and isolate the place from more civilized areas.

It was a perfect hideaway for anyone who really didn't want to be found.

Unless Lord Delran's men were looking for him.

Dougal had spent circles in the place as a boy, since his father had established a profitable tavern there, and he knew every square inch of the town. There was no place to hide from his eyes.

Augie didn't even try. He was too drunk to notice the leather clad riders or the quality of their horses. If he had, he wouldn't have been able to run anyhow. He couldn't even see straight.

Bonder and Dickel were hardly in any better shape, and Gerd, the fifth robber, had already passed out. The money they had earned from Lebard was half-spent on women and ale.

Only Toady had kept his wits about him, for as a master bowman, he had a strong urge to keep his hand steady and his eye clear. It didn't do him much good, for in the safety of the village, he had unstrung his bow to work on the grip and had only his dagger at hand.

The brigands were in the very tavern Dougal's family had owned. When the guard burst in, it was a pitiful contest. Augie simply stared. "Whatcha wan' 'ere, lowlanders? Ya ain' welcome."

"We don't expect welcome," Dougal answered.

"Go 'way," Bonder mumbled. "Ya ain't wanted."

"We don't need to be wanted," Riv replied, taking out a length of rope. In one swift, economic motion, he grabbed Bonder's right hand and twisted it behind his back. He lashed the rope to his wrist and clutched Bonder's left wrist in almost the same motion and lashed it as well.

In short order, Dougal tied Augie the same way, while Tran took Dickel.Tomas made short work of tying up the unconscious Gerd, and then turned to face Toady. The bowman's mouth was dropped in surprise, but instinct had drawn his blade. He did not intend to be taken without a fight.

Toady's eyes narrowed as he watched Tomas approach. With his partners bound, he knew he was outnumbered by Delran's guards, but he also knew they were men of honor. And men of honor could often be outwitted by deceit. He held his dagger loosely with his left hand and in his right, he took one of his poisoned arrows. "What right ya got comin' in here an' strong armin' me friends?"

"We take no quarter with thieves and murderers," Tomas answered quietly. He had shifted to an easy two-legged stance, perfectly balanced to move in any direction. "I'd rather not fight you, Toady, but I'm taking you with us to Delran's Keep for a judging."

"Judgin' fer what? Not gittin' drunk like the rest o' them?"

Tomas shook his head slowly, his eyes never leaving Toady's face. "For stealing nine horses in the Rim and leaving their master for dead. We followed your trail and saw Augie there bargaining with Lebard." His gaze flicked to Toady's quiver hanging on the chair. "I would also add, that the fletching and shaft of the arrows used in the ambush match yours exactly."

At that, Toady lunged, his blade flashing. He feinted left, to meet Tomas' quicker parry. The guard spun onto his right foot and brought his knee up into Toady's stomach, but the bandit pulled in his gut and avoided the worst of the impact. Again, the blade slashed and again Tomas countered, his own dagger crossing and locking onto to Toady's at the hilt. His had a curved guard on the handle, designed for just such encounters, and he hooked the metal around his opponent's hilt, twisting, trying to wrench the weapon from his grip.

But Toady was too experienced to fall for it and reversed the direction of his thrust, sliding his blade free. They broke and crouched facing each other again, dancing to and fro, looking for an opening.

Tomas rocked back, his heel hitting a nearby chair and for a split second he faltered. It was all Toady needed. He dived in, the dagger cutting up, towards Tomas ribs. Tomas threw himself to the side, at the same time bringing his own blade out to meet the other man's attack. But it was not the dagger Toady intended to use to strike the fatal blow, for even as he slashed with it, his right hand whipped in with the arrow.

Tomas was not so easily tricked. As before, he hooked Tomas' dagger in his and blocked Toady's arrow arm at his wrist. As quick as he was the barb nicked his arm, but the blow knocked the arrow from Toady's grip and sent it flying across the room. Then, he spun right with his whole body, still keeping the blades locked.

Toady grunted as Tomas' left foot hit his knee and it buckled, sending him to the floor, the dagger sliding from his grip as he fell. In the next instant Riv was behind him, lashing his hands behind his back. The other guard pulled him to his feet, and whistled with admiration at Tomas. "Not bad for a Keepbred warrior, Tomas. I'm impressed. I bet Toady here is too."

"Bah," Toady spit, "I coulda took 'im iffen my foot hadn'ta slipped."

"Yeah, yeah, that's what the loser always says."

Tomas rubbed his arm tentatively then wiped the blood from the arrow scratch on his breeches. "I guess I'm getting a little slow in my old age."

"You're tired," Dougal replied as he dragged Augie over to join the group. "We all are. I'm going to be damn glad to get this garbage back to the Keep so I can take a nice long nap."

Finding a wagon and team in the town proved easier than they expected, particularly when Delran's silver did most of the bargaining. They loaded the prisoners in back, none too concerned about their comfort, and headed back to the Keep, Riv driving, and Tomas taking the point. The journey back took longer than the one out, but none of the men really cared. They'd captured their quarry and satisfaction was enough to keep them entertained the whole way.
*****

Weswin's turn brought the cover of darkness to the hills above Lebard's Keep. Simen, Jebe, and the remaining guards had set up a fireless camp in a grove of trees just below the summit of the hill. They had brought food from Lord Delran's kitchen and a skin of calidew in deference to Jebe. Now, they ate and waited for some sign from the silver stallion.

"Will Whim let us know when he's coming?" Simen asked.

"He's busy," Jebe replied. "I don't know what he's doing, but it has something to do with some other horses. He says he'll be along soon."

As if in answer to the boy's remarks there was a swirl of silver mist near one of the pine trees and from its center, Whim materialized. *Now we go. Watchers eat. Pay no mind to horses. Come. Much to do.*

"He wants me to go now," Jebe said, getting to his feet.

Simen stayed him with a hand on his arm. "You be careful, Sur. Remember what I told you. Don't take any chances."

"Yes, My Lord," Jebe said. Herold gave him a leg up and without a word, he rode off into the darkness.

Whim's hoofs made no sound, even as they crossed the rocks.

"He'll be all right, My Lord," Bergan said as he gathered up the remains of the meal. "He's a resourceful lad."

"The stallion'll take care of him," Herold agreed. "I know horses and that one has a temper. If anyone tried to hurt the boy he'll be on them like a rimsnake to the duskit."

"I hope so, Herold," Simen replied with a sigh. "I certainly hope so."

Whim trotted slowly down the incline and then, eased to a long strided walk. *Ranger and Flurry in barn. Jebe free?*

"Why, Whim? We're only supposed to get Master Jamus' horses."

Silverhair be master. Not this twoleg.

"They're Delran's horses? Here?"

The stallion snorted.

"How do I find them?"

They tell. Go. Hurry.

Jebe slid to the ground and ran into the barn. The lanterns were dim but he could make out a long aisleway with stalls on either side. "Ranger? Flurry?" he whispered.

A horse nickered from the far end. *Here. Flurry.*

He headed for the sound and found himself face to face with a leggy black mare with a broad white star on her forehead and sprinkles of white spots on her rump. "Flurry?"

Flurry be. We go home?

Jebe shrugged and opened the stall door. The mare immediately walked over to a stall across the aisle and nudged the door latch. Jebe opened that door as well to release a plain brown colt with one white sock. Then, with the two horses close behind, he headed back out into the yard.

Whim was already heading for the back paddock where the drays were kept. He had the gatelatch nearly undone when Jebe arrived. The boy unhooked the restraining chain and then climbed up on the fence to remount.

Suddenly a harsh voice rumbled from the shadows to his right. "What's goin' on there? Hey, you. Whadda ya think yer doin'?"

A bulky figure emerged from the darkness as one of Lebard's stablehands headed for the gate. Silent and deadly as a great tark, Whim spun and kicked sharply with his back hoof, hitting the man square in the belly. With a great grunt of air the man gasped and collapsed in a heap, the wind completely knocked out of him.

Jebe slid on to Whim's back and heard only one word in his head, *Run!*

The herd took to their heels, clattering out of the alley, into the yard and beyond to the hills.

Behind them, they heard the shouts of angry men and the ringing of Lebard's bell, echoing through the valley.

"By the Blood," Simen cursed, "they've caught him."

"Not likely, Sur," Bergan called down from the hill. "They're well ahead of them." Then he skidded his way down the slope and ran for his horse. "Come on, mount up, lads, we'll have a fight on our hands."

Simen leapt up on his horse and headed for the trail. "Not if I can help it," he shouted. "As soon as the boy's past, get out of the way."

The freed herd galloped up the hill and raced past the campsite. Just behind, Whim ran with Jebe astride. As soon as the pair was clear, Simen urged his horse into the center of the trail and raised his hand. From his fingers shot a bolt of white-hot Spellfire at the boulders to the side just out of sight of Lebard's men. The white flame burst upon the rocks and slashed into the ground, exploding shards and dirt to ricochet off the surrounding rocks creating a landslide down the slope. Bombarded by the debris, Lebard's men fell into panic.

"Slide! Look out! Run fer it!"

Simen whirled his mount and galloped after his confederates.

Walk on wind. Whim said calmly.

It was all Jebe could do to cry out a warning. "Hold on, we're going to the clouds!"

Horses and riders soared into the sky and in a moment vanished from the scene as below Lebard's men scattered in total chaos.
*****

"What do you mean you had to let him go?" Jamus shouted as Jern cowered by the bed. The Lord of Magiskeep had awakened and there was nothing the Healer could do but tell him the truth when he asked to see Jebe. Now, Jamus was on his feet, pacing the floor in a rage. "Damn it, Jern. The boy's my responsibility. I promised his mother I'd protect him, not send him off into a warly's nest."

"Simen will take care of him."

"Simen is not me."

"He's a part of you. He is your reflection," Jern replied.

"Who told you that?"

"No one had to, Sur. I am not as unschooled in the River as you may think."

Jern's answer calmed Jamus a little. "Simen is the better part of me, Jern. The person who smiled and loved as a child. I was neither. And it's because he that best part of me that I worry about Jebe. Simen doesn't have the ruthlessness to protect him."

"Don't underestimate him, My Lord. Sometimes love is far more dangerous than hate. Have you ever seen a mother protect her young? Simen will not let anything happen to that boy."

"I told you to wait until I was better. In a day or so...."

"In a day or so, you'll be strong enough to walk downstairs and not much farther. Look at yourself now. Your hands are shaking and you're ready to collapse and all you've done is crossed the floor of this room. By the time you were ready to ride out to Lebard's those horses would have been in Aberdeen."

"And what would be the loss, eh, Jern?" Jamus replied tiredly, sitting down on the edge of the bed. "Would the loss of few horses been worth Jebe's life?"

"It was nearly worth yours."

"To them. To those hopeless men who value silver over everything. But not to us, Jern. We're supposed to be civilized and human." He dropped his head in his hands. "The River wants revenge, you know, and I have to deny her. It's not the way here in Turan." Then he looked up. "But if Jebe gets hurt, if they so much as bruise him, I swear by the Rim those waters will not be denied."

Jern shivered. "He's with Whim, Jamus. If Simen isn't enough, doesn't that stallion make up the difference? He walked right into Margston's house to get me and must have passed at least five guards to do it."

Jamus' brow knit in confusion. "Into the house? You told me this before, didn't you?"

Jern nodded. "You had a fever then, so I'm not surprised you don't remember. That's how I got to you in the Rim before everyone else. Whim issued a personal invitation. He showed up at Lord Margston's Hold, marched into the dining room, and made it absolutely clear that the only way he was leaving was with me on his back. Then, we practically flew to you."

"The house," Jamus repeated as if he still couldn't quite grasp the concept.

"The dining room, actually," Jern said.

Jamus stared at him, and for an instant the Healer thought he saw a twinkle in his ice grey eyes. "Bory, Jern, I certainly hope he didn't eat anything. His table manners are atrocious."

Jern choked. Then, for the first time since they'd met, the two men began to really laugh.

*****

Sarn heard the sound of dishes in the kitchen and cringed. Someone had cleared the Dining Hall while he had been in the village, but it was still too soon for any of the servants to get word to return. The thought of more Prentices and Mages running rampant with the Keep's food completely unnerved him. He ran to the door and shoved it open. "What in Sorem's Name do you think you're doing?"

Salene, her arms covered with flour and the Lady Delise, her hair wrapped in an apron looked up in surprise. "Preparing Evenmeal for over a hundred, if we've counted right," Salene said.

"I've never quite tried so much all at once," Delise added, "but the soup's nearly ready and I think the stew will go around twice. If," she laughed, "they even ask for seconds."

"Oh, Delise," Salene chided playfully, "with your stew they'll probably want thirds. You should taste it, Sarn. It's delicious."

Sarn's mouth worked silently for a moment before he found his voice. "Madam, this is not proper. You are a Lady."

Delise waved her wooden spoon in the air, dismissing his concern. "Nonsense, Sur. I told you I love to cook! Why this has been so much fun. When Lady Salene and I came down here and saw the mess.... Well, it was just obvious someone had to do something."

"I have servants to attend you," Sarn offered lamely.

"Oh, my, lovely little things too. They were just darling enough to set the tables for us. They were so cute, all excited to be doing something brand new. Do you know Joreen had never set a table in her life before today? I had to show her the proper order for the silver." Delise clucked in disapproval. "Things like that, any lady should know."

Salene smiled and bent her head to study the dough she was kneading. With her Magic and Delise's sense of organization, the two women and managed to clean up the Dining Hall and kitchen in less than a span. Then, Delise had set the young Prentices to work. It had been quite a sight watching the children scurry about carrying dishes and linens without a single idea what to do with them. But the Lady had soon set them straight and the Dining Hall at least looked welcoming.

"Serving may prove a bit of a challenge," Delise said, "but now that you're back we had some extra hands. Salene has decided to spell the food to the tables to save time. Perhaps you could oversee and pour the drinks?"

"I... " Sarn began, and faltered. "What about the children? They could serve."

"Dear me, no," Delise stated firmly. "In the first place they are far too small to carry the trays. Besides, they need to sit down and have a nice hot meal. They've already done far too much."

Sarn peered around. "I don't see them anywhere. If they're not working now, I don't see why they couldn't eat early and then help out."

"Delise clucked again. "But the little dears are working. The ladies have gone off to the Greenrooms to find some flowers for the tables. I told them to find as many different colors as they could." She giggled. "I thought that would keep them busy."

"Flowers," Sarn muttered under his breath. Flowers had been the start of all the trouble.

"I do hope they find some yellow and red ones," Delise went on. "While the air is still so chill outside, I find bright flowers really make everyone feel so much better. Don't you think, My Lord?"

"Ah, yes. Bright flowers, lots of color."

Delise smiled benignly. "You are such a clever man. I am surprised you gave so many servants the same day off without thinking of the consequences. But then, you are a man, and only the temporary Lord here. I shouldn't expect you would have thought about all of this. I'm sure you have a great deal more important things to think about."

"We've got them, My Love!" Sarkem called triumphantly from the door. His was holding a large basket of freshly dug taroots. His arms, face, and shirt were covered with dirt. Behind him trotted Skit and Jestin, each carrying another basket. "Until Jestin here told me, I had no idea we had to dig the fool things up. I'm sorry it took so long. My men and I worked as fast as we could."

"It's fine, My Dear. Lady Salene can simply conjure them into the stew. You can do that, can't you, Salene?"

"Oh, absolutely," Salene replied hitting the dough even harder with her hand to keep herself from laughing. The stricken expression on Sarn's face when Sarkem came in had nearly broken her resistance. She had vowed to take all this seriously for Delise's sake. The woman was one of the kindest, most open people she had ever met and she certainly did not deserve laughter. But the fact was, the whole situation was ludicrous. She raised her hand and the taroots flew to the countertop, their skins peeling away in midair. They seemed to slice themselves and then hop, already half steamed, into the cooking pots. "There," she said soberly, "that should do it."

Delise clapped her hands in delight. "There, Sarkem, my Sweet, did you see that. Magic has its place after all! Adhering to Rule and Vow is certainly laudable, and I don't fault you one moment for it, but what good is having Magic if you never use it?" She looked at Sarn and smiled, shaking her head. "My precious husband refuses to use his Power, you see. Being a mortal myself, I simply can't understand it. Now, mind you, I don't want him using it all the time. He takes such great pleasure in doing things with his hands, you see, but once in a while, especially to solve one of those problems that has no other way around? What could be the harm?"

"Only in need," Sarkem said as he rolled up his sleeves to wash his hands in the basin by the sinks. "If any other deed be done, then deeds had best be left undone."

Delise sighed. "There he goes again, quoting the Elden Law. Perhaps Sarn here could talk some sense into you while we're here," she said. "He looks like a man who wouldn't hesitate to raise his hand."

And too quickly, Salene thought, hiding another smile. She could see Sarn's face redden and relished his discomfort. "You are right, Lady Delise. Sarn is a man of action. Why that's the very reason Jamus put him in charge to drive the enemies out of the Keep." She let herself smile now, directly at Sarn.

His expression told her he understood completely. "I've not always used my Magic wisely," he said keeping his voice steady, "but I have learned from my mistakes. Magic indeed has purpose as Lady Delise points out, but as Lord Sarkem suggests, it should only be used in direst need, not frivolously. It takes some Mages a while to really understand that."

"Power of any kind is a great responsibility," Salene added. "The wisest man takes care not to abuse it, whether it be for Magical ends or for mortal."

This time, Sarn frowned. There was something else behind Salene's words, he was sure of it. She had looked directly at him, her blue eyes cold, piercing into him. He had felt the chill from Jamus' gaze more than once, but Salene's struck him in the heart and he felt it thudding. What did she know? Jeamel couldn't have gotten word here so soon. Then again, Salene had ridden out earlier in the day. Could she have gone to the village? He began to worry now. Any advantage he might have in avoiding his promise to Jeamel would be lost if Salene knew about it. He Willed himself calm and hoped his expression masked his real feelings. "I have never considered mortal ends, My Lady. I've had little contact with anyone except Magicians since I was a boy sent here by my parents."

"But the servants," Delise interrupted. "Surely you have communed with the servants of the Keep. So many of them are mortals."

Sarn shrugged. "I was a Prentice at six and in lessons from then until Master Jorn took me as Apprentice. Surely I spoke to the servants, but to commune? No, My Lady, except perhaps on the rarest of occasions, I never communed with them."

Salene gritted her teeth. If bedding one wasn't communing, she had no idea just what was. Was she supposed to feel sorry for him now, hearing of his monastic life as a child of the River? She hadn't been raised any differently herself - more so as the daughter of the Lord of the Keep. But it had never been her choice to walk in the rarified air of nobility Sarn pretended to. Like Jamus, she had kept her roots in the people the Keep protected, never forgetting that they, not the Mages, were the true soul of Magiskeep. Did Sarn actually believe what he was saying, or was it just one more lie added to his ever-growing pile?

Delise smiled sadly. "How much you missed, My Lord." Then, she brightened. "But come now. It's nearly time for Evenmeal and the bread's not done. Here, My Lord, you can make a fist, can't you? Magic may bake it in the end, but no one should ever miss the satisfaction of pounding out his misery on a knot of dough."

Sarn grinned feebly, walked over to the counter, and, with a grimace, slammed his fist into a pile of the dark dough. Delise was right. There was satisfaction in beating on something.

Chapter 14

With Jebe riding triumphantly on Whim at the fore, the band of horses and guards arrived at Delran's Keep in the bright moonlight of Weswin.

When Jamus saw them through the window, he grabbed Jern's arm and insisted the Healer help him downstairs. Though he had to use the doorframe for support, he was standing in the main entrance of the house when Jebe dismounted and ran up to the wide porch. "We got'em back, My Lord! We got 'em. You shoulda seen Whim. He did everything just perfect!"

"The Hand be thanked you're back safely," Jamus replied, kneeling down to meet the boy's eyes. "I was worried about you."

"No need for that, My Lord. I was with Master Simen and Whim. What coulda happened?"

Jamus laughed. "You are right, Sur. What could have happened? Here now, help me up and walk with me over to that big smart horse of mine. I'd like to thank him." He winked as a handful of surlep candies appeared in his hand.

"You don't gotta go to him, he'll come here," Jebe said.

"Don't even suggest it," Jamus replied, waving the horse back. "If I let him come up to the house here, who knows what he'll try back in Magiskeep? No, I think Whim had better stay away from the porch." With Jebe's help, he got to his feet and made his way over to the horse. Whim gently took the candy from his hand and chewed it thoughtfully, savoring every bite.

"He really likes that, My Lord. He says sweet hards are his favorite."

"Sweet hards," Jamus said. "That's what he calls the candy?"

"Beasts don't have all the same name for things we do, Sur. They give a thing a name according to how they see the thing. Sometimes it makes it hard to understand what they mean, but Whim's pretty good about making sure we understand."

"I guess he is at that," Jamus agreed, stroking Whim's neck. "If you're not too tired, do you think you could take care of him for me tonight, Jebe?" Jamus asked. "I'm really not strong enough yet to do it myself and he deserves special care."

Jebe beamed. "I'm not tired, My Lord. Come on, Whim, I'm gonna make you a special mash with surleps in it. Joss showed me how to do it right." As he walked off, he continued talking. "What's that you say?" he said. "Oh, you want lots of surleps? Now, Whim, too many will make you sick. Don't argue with me. Lord Jamus says I gotta take care of you and I'm gonna do it right."

Jamus smiled.

"The lad's a fine horseman," Delran said as he walked up the steps. "Simen tells me he's a Beasttalker."

Jamus paused. "Simen was speaking out of turn, My Lord. That's something I've yet to determine."

"My Lord, I think you already have," Delran said, surprising himself for being so forthright with the Rivermaster. "A boy like that could have a worthy career working for someone who truly appreciates and needs his talents. Magiskeep has your hand, My Lord. Don't you think Turan deserves his?"

"And what are you suggesting?" Jamus asked as they headed back into the house.

"I'd be glad to take Jebe on here as an apprentice trainer-- Nobby too. I've already spoken to him about it. I've a place for their parents here in the Keep and would be glad to set them up in the free lands if they'd like that more."

"Jebe's mother is single," Jamus explained. "There are circumstances about his birth…" He stopped. What to tell Delran? How much did the man need to know? "His father is a Mage in the Keep, My Lord. There is some question about how it all happened and until it's straightened out, I'm not sure it would be wise to make any commitment on his behalf. I'll tell you what. You ask Jebe what he thinks about the whole thing. After all, in the end, it's his life. If he wants to come, I'll do my best to convince his mother it would be to his benefit. As for her, she's had a hard enough life already. I intend to keep her under my protection."

"You could protect her here, My Lord, as I would." Delran took a deep breath and lowered his voice, "Jamus, that little boy deserves a family. I lost my daughter circles ago and my heart still aches for her. I'd take Jebe's mother into my house if she'd let me, and care for her as if she were mine. By the Hand, I swear it on my life." He pleaded now, a grieving father longing for all he had lost. "I'd treat him as my grandchild."

"He is not mine to give," Jamus replied, putting a comforting hand on Delran's shoulder. "But I won't stand in your way if Lurela agrees. Know, though, you will have to answer to me if anything should ever hurt her here."

"Only after I answer to myself," Delran stated firmly. "My life on it, My Lord. My life and the honor of my whole Keep."

The pledge was powerful, for to a Lord like Delran, honor was more precious than life. "I'll talk to her on your behalf," Jamus repeated. "It's all I can do."
*****

Lurela returned to Magiskeep with Jeamel. The housemaster decided to keep her in the downstairs halls so he could keep an eye on her in case Sarn wanted to plead his case. Still, duties did not allow him to watch her every second and when he went to the kitchens to try to settle a dispute between Lady Delise and the returning cooks, she was left alone in the Northern Wing.

Sarn took the opportunity as soon as she was alone and watched as she carried a pile of dirty linens into the maid's chamber at the far end of the hall. Silently, he made his way to the door, listened for voices and, hearing nothing, pushed his way inside.

Lurela's back was to him. "So, you're back," he said.

She stiffened but did not turn around. "I have work to do."

"And so do I," Sarn replied. "Obligations to fulfill, so I'm told. To my mind, nothing of importance except to those who wish to humiliate me."

Lurela turned. "Is that all that ever matters to you, Sarn? Whether or not you've been humiliated?"

"I have my name to uphold, Madame. You'd never understand about that. You weren't born with one of your own."

"My parents were married, Sur, and loved each other dearly. I had a happy childhood under their roof until they were killed in a fire. My name was given to me by my mother, after her mother. I would say it is at least as worthy as yours."

Sarn advanced into the dimly lit chamber, his fists clenched at his side. "I am of noble blood, not the spawn of gutter slime."

Lurela held her ground, but her eyes darted to the side, looking for an escape. The shelves blocked her on the left, and Sarn had filled the space to the right. She clutched the bundle of linens close. "My father was a carpenter."

"Sawdust and splinters. And your mother took in washing, her hands red and raw from soap scum, while my mother stitched shaenis pillows. A name means nothing when it's born of dirt and filth," he said, his voice low.

"And Jebe? What of his name?" Lurela asked, trying to keep her voice calm.

Sarn stopped. "It depends on where he lies. On a straw pallet, in some dirty little hovel, his name is nothing. But put him on a velvet couch, and his better half rises to the tongue. He is mine, Lurela, and he deserves better than you can ever give him. With me, he'll learn to touch the River. With you, more soapsuds and muddy rinse water."

"And what will the Rive give him in the end? Will he be like you, Sarn? Will he be bitter and cruel, with no heart for anyone but himself?"

Her words hit hard and Sarn's shoulders sagged. "I have a heart, Lurela." He moved in closer and lifted his hand to touch her cheek. She cringed away, but he let his fingers stroke her soft skin, ever so gently. "You were so beautiful and so innocent. I wanted you, then, because I thought... I thought perhaps, just once, it would be different. Siamel was so hungry, and the others... they had all done it before. But you...." He sighed.

Lurela's back was pressed against the little table, the edge of wood cutting painfully into her spine. His breath was warm against her neck and she could hear his heart. "Leave me alone, Sarn."

"Why?" He leaned nearer, pressing his body against her, his hand reaching down, stroking her waist. "Don't tell me you've forgotten? Don't tell me you haven't wondered what it would be like to be with me again. You see my face in our son, hear my voice on his lips. He's part of me, Lurela. The best part of me. Why won't you let me have him?"

"You'll never have him, never," she cried, pushing against him with all her might.

He laughed, and took her arms in his hands, pinning her in his grip. "And do you think you can keep him? When they find out what he is, they'll lock him up in the halls and study him like some kind of ancient relic to be prodded and scried."

Her eyes widened. "What are you talking about?"

He grinned. "Oh, I have ears, Lurela. Don't think I don't know what Jamus believes. He thinks the boy's a Beasttalker. Do you know what that means? He's an oddity, a freak, a creature of the Eldenlore. Why do you think the Lord of Magiskeep spirited him away? He has him now, and he has his Magic. Jamus is no fool."

"He told me he'd take care of Jebe," she protested, her voice hoarse with fear.

"You trusted him, just the way you trusted me so many circles ago. Still so naïve, to trust the word of a Sorcerer." He shook her a little. "Wake up. The Rivermaster thrives on the Power of others, and relishes the taking of it. The boy belongs to Jamus now. Unless..."

Lurela's heart skipped. Could this be true? Jeamel, Becca... they spoke so highly of Jamus, but they were only commoners. What did they know of Lords? Sarn was bred of nobility himself. He understood. "Unless what, Sarn?"

"You're his mother. The Gathering and the Keep would not deny you a request. Stand up for the boy. Tell them, he must not be the Rivermaster's pawn. Tell them he needs a Master who won't exploit his talents. Tell them…" His eyes met hers. "Tell them he needs a father."

She trembled in his grip, afraid to try to break away, and afraid not to. There was something in his eyes she couldn't read. It was as if he'd veiled his thoughts from her. "You'll claim him?"

He nodded slightly, his lips parting. He lowered his lips to hers and whispered, "As my son, my heir, whatever pleases you."

His mouth brushed hers and she shuddered. Despite everything, she was drawn to him, all the circles of pain forgotten.

Sarn played the spell carefully. He could not afford to lose her now. He made his kiss light, almost as if he were afraid she would not respond. But he knew she would. He had learned the Fifth Art from Siamel and was a much a Master as she. He Manipulated coils of the weave, netting her reason, stirring her emotions. She would not resist.

But Sarn was no fool. Taking her now would spoil the plan. If she believed she was included in the bargain, she would never stand in front of the Keep and give him the boy without expecting him to take her too. No, she would have to believe Jebe was the way to win him, not part of winning him. He let go of her arm with one hand and placed his finger on her lips, breaking the contact. "Not now. Not until it's settled. Once Jamus surrenders his claim, and Jebe is freed to me, then we can begin again. But we have to think of him first. Jebe has to come first."

Breathing heavily, Lurela nodded.

Sarn smiled and turned away, leaving as silently as he had come.

Lurela leaned back, put her hands on the table, closed her eyes and tried to steady her beating heart. Jebe would come first, and then, Sarn.
*****

Easwin brought more riders to Delran's Keep, and with them, a cart full of cursing thieves.

"We should have gagged them, Tomas," Dougal repeated for the hundredth time since they'd left Mudlake. "Foul mouthed bunch of garbage like this doesn't need to spoil the Lord's Easwin with all this noise."

Tomas rubbed his arm and shrugged. "You should've thought of it sooner. It's too late now."

"Bory, Tomas," Dougal countered, "I've been telling you for the last two winds. Who've you been listening to?"

Tomas shook his head. "I'm tired, Dougal. I guess I just didn't listen at all."

Dougal rode up alongside his friend. "Are you all right? You do look kind of pale. I thought you took a nap while you were waiting for us on the ridge."

"The ridge?" Tomas asked, confused. "Didn't we meet in town?"

Riv reined the team to a stop. "Are you losing your memory in your old age, Tomas? You were on the ridge way ahead of us. What's wrong with you?"

"Tired," Tomas repeated.

Dougal grinned. "Well, Riv, remember, he did have that fight in the tavern."

"Fight? It looked more like a Ridgy Dance if you ask me. Hardly enough to put a sweat on a man. I think old Tomas is just getting soft."

"Tell you what Tomas," Dougal said, "why don't you just go on up to quarters and take yourself a nice nap while we deliver the goods to the Lord."

To Dougal's surprise, Tomas nodded and rode off, his body slumping in the saddle.

"Do you think he's all right?" Tran asked.

"He is acting a bit strange," Dougal replied. "Look, why don't you go on up with him just to make sure. Maybe he did more up at Lebard's than we knew. Riv and I can take the wagon to the house. Lord Delran has plenty of men up there to deal with these characters."

Riv drove the wagon to the main gate of the house. Billing, the guard there called in to the yard. "Call the Lord. Tell him we've some rubbish to dispose of."

"Ya gots no right!" Augie whined from the cart. Finally sober, he had complained for the last three spans of the trip and wasn't about to stop now.

Toady had given up, all too aware they were in a hopeless situation. He intended to rely on Delran's reputation for fairness and generosity. He was sure there was a way to get the stolen horses back and planned on saying so.

Bonder, Gerd and Deckel had never been the spokesmen for the group and chose now to let the other two speak for them-at least until things started going the wrong way. Then it was every man for himself.

Five pairs of hands unceremoniously tugged the prisoners out of the wagon and then pushed them into the front yard of Delran's great stone house. Their legs weak and wobbly from the long ride and too much liquor, the thieves stood uncertainly, staring at the broad wooden door.

When it opened, they all wished it hadn't.

The first figure who appeared was the last person they ever wanted to see. Though in the Rim they had not really gotten a good look at his face, his clothing, bearing, and coloring were something all of them recognized now.

"It's him," Augie whispered. "The Sorcerer."

"He oughtta be dead," Bonder replied. "I knew I shoulda slit 'is throat. I knew it."

""E is dead," Toady said. "Nobody coulda made it through me boderb. It's some kinda trick."

Simen walked out behind Jamus and stood a step away, ready to support Magiskeep's Lord should his strength fail.

"Damn, I tole ya it were a trick," Toady exclaimed. "See? There's two o'em!"

Delran moved to the front of the porch. "Who are these men, Riv?"

"Tall ones' Augie, Sur. And then," he pointed, "we have Toady, Gerd, Bonder, and Dickel. These are the men attacked Lord Jamus in the Rim and stole your horses."

"Ya ain't got no proof," Augie protested.

"This man was seen at Lebard's trading the very animals taken from the victims, My Lord. He and his… friends were tracked to Lebard's. The arrow pulled from Lord Jamus' body matches the ones this man had in his quiver." He pointed at Toady. "Furthermore, My Lord, I do believe you have a witness."

Delran nodded, and gestured into the house behind him.

Jebe, shuffled out, his eyes lowered. He moved over next to Jamus. Magiskeep's Lord squatted down beside the boy and put his arm around him. "Do your recognize any of those men, Jebe?" he asked.

"Uh huh," Jebe said. "That one, with the shaggy hair was in the Rim when the horses were stolen. He kept yelling at everybody. And that one," he pointed to Bodner, "had a knife and he was gonna kill you. He said so, right there. But Whim wouldn't let him, so that one," now his finger indicated Toady, "tried to shoot Whim with an arrow. But Whim was smart and he disappeared. They knew he was magic then, so they got scared. I guess they run off then. I hid behind the hill so they wouldn't see me."

"Stinkin' brat," Augie hissed. "I knew we shoulda taken care o' 'im too."

"Yer the one what said he was too stupit to do nothin'," Bonder accused. "Ya said none of 'em was gonna git out 'o the mountains alive. They sure look alive ta me."

"That arrow had the boderb on it," Toady grunted. "Ain't no way 'e's still breathin.' It's some kinda trick, I tell ya."

With help from Simen, Jamus pushed to his feet. "Gentlemen, I take it you're not disputing what this boy says?"

"If'en I had the chance, I'd kill ya agin, Sorcerer," Toady snarled.

Augie focused his attention on Delran. "What's it worth to ya anyhows, Me Lord? The Sorcerer here's alive. It 'pears we ain't done 'im no harm. Jest what's it worth to ya ta git them horses back, eh?"

Delran kept his expression sober. "You could return them?"

Augie puffed up a bit at the question, sure now he had piqued Delran's interest. "I got my ways. I stole 'em onct, din't I? I figger I kid jest as easy steal 'em agin. Him what gots 'em knows they ain't legal bought and sold, so he ain't gonna kick up no fuss if'en they jest kinda disappear agin, ya know?"

"Oh," Delran replied, nodding, "I certainly do know. Certainly." There was going to be no complaint from Lebard, that was for sure. The dealer knew better than to challenge Delran for recovering his rightful property. Besides, with Flurry and Ranger back in the barns, there was ample evidence to prove Lebard guilty of their theft, and Delran had full intent to do so.

"Well, mayhaps we 'ere kin strike us a bargain, then. What say ya lets me an' my boys 'ere go an' fetch yer stock an' we jest call it even, eh?"

"H-m-m-m-m." Delran rubbed his chin thoughtfully. "That would be an equitable solution, were your only crime the theft of the horses. The problem is, Sur, you seriously injured Master Jamus here and young Nobby. You terrified Jebe, and left the three of them to the mercy of the Rim. Now, as much as I love my horses, I love these people more."

"'E's a damned Sorcerer!" Bonder cried.

"He is a man, first, Sur," Delran countered, "one of the best I have ever known. Magic does not lessen him but rather makes him greater. He has more power than I could ever dream of, and yet he doesn't victimize with it. You have muscle and courage, more than most, I would wager, yet you hurt others for your own gain. Does that make you worth more than Lord Jamus?"

"Whatcha gonna do to us?" Augie asked, thinking now might be the time to plea. "If'en we brung the horses back, that is."

"There's nothing for you to bargain with, Sur. We already have the horses back. My men went to Lebard and retrieved them."

Augie's face fell. He dropped to his knees. "I ain't bin doin' right, I knows that, me Lord, but I don' know no other way ta earn me keep. Thievin's in me blood. Look, ya gots yer stock back an' the... the Lord here don' look none the worse fer wear. What say ya jest give me a whuppin' er somewhat an' call it square, eh?"

"No," Delran replied. "I've only two choices. The first is we hold you for a Judging in Tulene. Lady Kala will be there within the next two Sevenstins, I believe. But, the penalty for horse theft is often death in this Province, for a horse often is a man's only means of survival. Add to that the charge of attempted murder, and I don't think the Lady will look too lightly on you." He paused dramatically. "But, I am Lord of this Keep and that grants me the right, under the King's Law to dispense justice as I see fit. But, it was not I who was wronged. Those horses were not yet mine. They still belonged to Lord Jamus. It was also his body that suffered under your attack. Therefore, I think it fitting he be the one to pass judgment on you."

"No," Augie gasped.

"Please, me Lord," Toady whispered as all five criminals fell to their knees to join the plea.

"He's a Sorcerer," Bonder whimpered. "He ain't got no right. Please, me Lord."

"I have said it," Delran proclaimed. "Lord Jamus, these men are yours to do with as you will."

Jamus hesitated for one brief instant, and then a smile spread across his face. "So be it, Lord Delran. Gentlemen, you condemn me as Sorcerer, believing that makes me something you have a right to destroy. I think it fitting that I, freely admitting to my Magic, teach you a lesson about my kind. Justice and right are as important in my Kingdom as they are here, perhaps more so. As Lord Delran said, when men have power, all must be done to assure no one be harmed by it. And so, I plan on assuring that no one will ever be harmed by your power either."

"'E's gonna kill us!" Bonder whined, cringing back.

Jamus raised his hand.

The heavy weight of Magic descended on the yard. The five condemned men gasped, finding it hard to breathe in the thickened air.

Simen watched, amazed as the threads of silver from Jamus' fingers snaked out to the five bowed bodies and coiled about them, weaving an intricate pattern. Five at once, and all the same, silvrin spheres with the threads knotted, and locked in such complexity, even he, who had watched it all, would never be able to sift them. But these were not ordinary Spheres of Protection as he had so often seen Jamus weave in times of danger. No, these were somehow different, and when he realized how, he gasped.

Magic lifted its heavy hand.

Augie looked down at his body, saw no change and looked up. "What'd ya do ta me?"

"Filthy Sorcerer," Bodner shouted, but then wincing, he clapped his hands to his head and his own shouting pounded into his ears. No one else seemed to notice.

Toady clambered to his feet as the bonds slid from his hands. He reared back and struck at the nearest guard, but the blow fell short a good foot and his hand bounced back to slam into his own chin, nearly knocking him back off his feet. He stood stunned.

"A gift of life to you, from my Magic," Jamus said quietly, his soft tone issuing more authority than a King's proclamation. "I have given you each a Sphere of Protection. Around you lies a spell which no force except Magic can break. Normally, I would give someone such a Sphere to protect them from danger on the outside. You see, the spell is created so harm cannot pass through. A person so protected could still be Healed, or loved, or held with kindness. But anyone or anything intending to hurt him would not be able to pass the barrier."

"Yer protectin' us?" Gerd asked, mystified.

Jamus shook his head. "No, Sur, I am not. Men like you don't earn my protection. But the world has earned protection from you. I have given you Spheres bred in the Way of Mirrors, Spheres reversed in their purpose and couched in reflection. They are not meant to protect you, but rather to protect the world from you. From this day until I decide to release you, you will live in your prisons. But take care, for their walls will tolerate no evil from you. Any harm you try to inflict on someone else will be reflected on you instead. Speak words of hatred, and they will ring in your ears alone. Strike at a man, and you will only strike yourself. And Toady, I would take great care with my arrows if I were you. You may hunt the duskit for your dinner, and even practice at a target, but if you raise that bow against a man or beast in rage, greed, or revenge, then you had best prepare to take the arrow yourself. It will turn on you and strike as straight as you aim it."

Toady gulped.

"Be warned," Jamus said, "the Spheres grant you no immunity from attacks by others on you."

"K-kin I defend meself?" Bonder asked, trembling.

"If your cause is just," Jamus replied. "I have no reason to let you die at another's hands without good cause. The Sphere will reflect the intent of your heart. All you need do is act according to the laws of this land and you won't even know it's there."

"How'em I gonna live?" Augie moaned. "I don't got no way ta earn me keep."

"I think," Jamus said, "that Lord Delran is owed some recompense for this crime. Perhaps, you could pay him for his trouble by working here in his Keep until you learn the value of hard labor. My Lord, surely you have a barn or two in need of a good cleaning."

Delran, barely recovered from the Magic's presence, straightened his shoulders and shook himself back to reality. "Five strong men could be very useful around here, My Lord. Since these men can no longer be a threat to anyone, I will be pleased to have their muscle at my disposal. Riv, suppose you escort them to the workers' quarters...the Brellum House, if you please. It hasn't been used in circles and could stand a good dusting. Billet them there and see to it they have provisions. Send Tanner to watch over them for the time being. Come Easwin tomorrow, we'll hand them over to Baylor. He'll find plenty for them to do."

Simen watched as the five were escorted away. Then he said, "You amaze even me, brother. It would take a Master of your equal or better to untangle that weave. I've never seen the Way used better. Where did you ever learn such a trick?"

Jamus sighed. "It's a variation on a weave Sagari once used, I'm afraid. It's sad to think I have once again become his Apprentice."

"Never," Simen replied. "He could never be great enough to be your master." He smiled now. "I did as you asked and called Salene by way of the Mirrors. I told her you were well and that we'd be on our back before the close of the Sevenstin. So you think you'll be strong enough to travel?"

"If I could convince Jern, I'd be on my way within the span. Tomorrow, though, should be fine. Lord Delran, would you lend us a carriage for the trip back? If Jebe and his mother decide to take you up on the offer to come here, it would be good transport. If not, I'm sure Lady Salene would love to come back with me for a visit when the season turns."

"My Lord, I'd be pleased to give you a carriage."

"Thank you, Sur. I'm not quite up to riding the whole way back to my Keep. Besides, I think Nobby would appreciate the soft cushions. I'll let him drive." Jamus replied.

"I meant what I said about giving him a position here too," Delran reminded him. "I've been impressed by both those lads beyond words. Do you have more like them in Magiskeep?"

Jamus laughed. "To hear Josep tell it, he has a stable full of them."

"Well, if his son is any indication of his judgment, then he probably has. I'd find work for any he wants to part with, you know. Turan has need of fine horsemen to run its stables."

"I'll remember that," Jamus said. "I was wondering...."

A shout from the gate interrupted them. "My Lord! My Lord! We need the Healer, now! It's Tomas! He's fearful sick!" Tran called as he ran up the walk.

"Jern!" Delran called into the house.

The young Healer was there in an instant, his belt pouch in his hand. "Take me to him."

Tran ran off with Jern close behind. Jamus frowned. "Isn't Tomas the one who led the guard to Augie?"

Delran's face was grim. "He was. He's a fine, strong young man. I can't imagine what could be wrong. Where's Dougal?"

"He went to the kitchens to see if Morrie could make something special for his men," one of the other guards said. "He said after a long ride, they needed a good meal."

"Go get him," Delran ordered.

In short order, Dougal was on the porch. "Tomas was the one who captured that Toady," he said, when Delran asked him what had happened at Mudlake. "They got into a bit of a tussle, but aside from getting scratched by one of the bowman's arrows, Tomas got the best of him, easy."

"One of the arrows?" Jamus asked, his face paling.

"Aye, me Lord. It were just a scratch."

"Simen, come with me. We have to get to Tomas at once. Jern's going to need help."

With Simen at his side, Jamus limped off. Delran motioned to Dougal and hurried after. "Lord Jamus," he called.

Jamus replied with one word, "Boderb." It was enough.

Chapter 15

Jeamel finished fixing the latch on the cabinet and straightened stiffly. "I don' like the looks o' it, Me Lady. Sarn's been walkin' 'round all puffed up. Ya'd think wid what he's gotta face afore the Keep 'e'd be a mite bit humbled. If'en ya ask me, I'd think 'e's up ta somewhat."

Salene handed the Houseman a small hammer and sighed. "Simen tells me Jamus will be home within the Sevenstin. Maybe we should just wait and let him resolve this. If Sarn has some trick up his sleeve, I'd just as soon not deal with it."

"'E's so damn smug, is all I say. It ain't natural fer a man what's gotta admit what he done." He tapped a rivet back into place. "There, that's fixed. So, ya gonna talk ta Lurela?"

"You really think Sarn's done something to her?"

"She's bin avoidin' me an' done gone an' moved back ta her li'l cottage. Becca's plumb sick wid worry 'bout the girl."

"Lurela's taken care of herself for circles, Jeamel. I'm sure she'll be all right. But, I'm just as concerned as you are as to why she left your house. She seemed quite happy to have the company. She didn't say anything?"

"Jest somewhat 'bout not wantin' to be beholden to no friends o' Lord Jamus," he replied as he packed up his tool kit.

"The girl hardly knows Jamus. He only met her when he found out she was Jebe's mother, and then only to reassure her. She had no trouble giving him permission to take her son across the Rim. Why would she think differently now?"

"I'ma tellin' ya, Mistress, it's Sarn's doin' fer sure."

"If it is, Lurela will never tell me, nor will Sarn. He's too skilled a liar."

"Ain't ya got some way ta tell what's true an' what ain't?"

Salene nodded, "The Sorcerer's Crystal. Jamus and I were going to use it before we found out Sarn was Jebe's father. I brought I up from the Vaults before he left. Sarn will recognize it, though. It's well known in the Keep."

"Clear gem, ain't it? No color?"

"Clear, yes. Why?"

Jeamel smiled and tapped his head with his finger. "Ya e'er see them crystal pitchers Mistress Jiala puts her brews in? Ya kin see right through 'em."

Salene frowned. "I have Jeamel, but they aren't made of the same crystal as the Stone. They have no magical powers."

"Dint say they did. But I figger if'en ya puts some plain ol' water in one of 'em an' then drop a clear stone like that one inside, who'd see it? I 'member onct when the Mistress was workin' one o' her charms, she lost a diamond. She was real mad, an' said one o' my maids musta took it. Ya know what? I found it, there in one o' them pitchers o' hers, jest layin' there in the water. Only ya couldn'ta seen it lessen ya knowed it was there."

"Jeamel, you amaze me."

"It ain't but good sense, Me Lady. All's a man's gotta do is see what's 'round 'im in the world an' he gots answers ta most ev'ry problem."

Salene smiled and headed up the stairs to Jiala's study. The Mistress of Manipulation was not noted for being one of the more generous Masters in the house, but where Jamus was concerned she was usually more than willing. Even before he had become a Master himself, she had tried to take him as her own, in both mind and body. Salene may have married him, but that made little difference to Jiala. Anything she could to ingratiate herself to him, she did willingly.

That made it doubly hard for Salene to ask for her help. She always felt like a grainsnatcher in the claws of a cat whenever she visited the Fifth Art's Mistress. Now was no exception.

Salene was counted a beautiful woman, but compared to Jiala, when she chose to ply her feminine skills, the blonde Lady of the Keep felt like a shadow. Today, Jiala was in rare form. She had dressed in a low cut crimson gown of shimmering shaenis. It fit her slender body like a second skin, falling to a full but clinging skirt slit up to the thigh. "Ah, dear, Salene," she said, welcoming her rival with pretended sincerity. "It's always so good to see you. I was just on my way to a class."

"Dressed like that?"

"Of course. It's impossible to teach the lure of my Art unless I can demonstrate its effect. There are two young men in a class with seven pretty girls. I thought it was time I made it quite clear what kind of temperament a Master of my Art must attain. I already see one or two who seem to have a talent."

Salene clucked in disgust. "So you will seduce the boys and teach the girls just how a woman can torment a man?"

"Oh, Salene, always so proper. It's a wonder you can keep that husband of yours satisfied. I keep telling him, if he ever tires of you, I will be glad to remind him what a pleasure love can be."

Salene bit back the worst of a retort, keeping her response more even instead. "I am sure he appreciates your concern, Mistress."

Jiala's eyes widened in surprise. "What? No attack? Has marriage so mellowed you? I would have expected at least some insult."

"Marriage has made me even more aware of Jamus' worth, Jiala. And, whether you believe it or not, I suppose he really would appreciate your lust for him. You see, he understands now how much of a burden his Power really is. Being Rivermaster is as much torment for him as it is a temptation for you. It's never been Jamus you've wanted. Both you and I have always known that. But be warned, Mistress, Jamus knows it too. One day, perhaps, when the River has her way, he may indeed come to you. If so, I will have no say in it."

Jiala moved to the window, her auburn hair catching the sunlight, making a halo around her head. But she was not being worthy of the crown, and she knew it. "How quickly you can disarm me, My Lady. To hear you say such a thing chills my heart. How can you even think of losing him?"

"Because one day I know I will. You may be the mistress of seduction here in Magiskeep, but out there, where the River rules, you are nothing. Magic wants Jamus and neither you nor I will be able to stop her when the day comes. It breaks my heart to even speak of it." Salene's throat constricted as her voice trailed off.

Jiala turned. "I'm sorry. It's been so long, I'd forgotten what love is really like. But, you didn't come here to tell me this. You came for something else, I'm sure. A favor, perhaps?"

"To borrow one of your crystal pitchers, that's all," Salene replied, her voice hoarse.

"A pitcher."

"Yes."

"No reason?"

"None to tell you now. Suffice it to say, it would please Jamus if you'd lend me one. I would conjure one of my own, but this time I'd prefer one with no magic in its weave."

Jiala laughed. "I think you're baiting me, Mistress. Are you concocting some sort of potion of your own?"

"In a manner of speaking," Salene replied. "Let us just say I am preparing a truth serum."
*****

Jamus' leaving the house left Delran with the two boys who were far too excited by events to even think of midmeal.

"Didja see'em, Jebe? They was the ones what attacked us!"

"They was, Nobby."

"That's real bad, Jebe. Real bad." Nobby shook his head sadly. "The big one, that Bonder man." He shook the hem of Delran's tunic. "Me Lord, I gotta tell ya. I jest gotta."

Delran moved away from the window where he had been watching for some sign from his guards at the gate. "What is it, Nobby?"

"That one they calls Bonder. I seen him afore. He was in the village, wid me uncle Wyam."

"Your uncle, Nobby? Are you sure?" Delran asked.

Nobby swallowed hard and nodded.

"Wyam," Jebe said. "That's the name I heard'em say in the Rim. The one I couldn't remember, My Lord."

The last piece of the puzzle had fallen into place as far as Delran was concerned. There was an informant in Magiskeep and now that they knew who it was, Jamus could handle the matter from there. "You are indeed two of the finest and bravest lads I have ever known. A man like me would count himself lucky if you would come to work for him."

Nobby grinned. "Ya askin' Jebe too?"

"I am." Delran said. "Jebe, Lord Jamus has given me his consent to ask you if you would like to work here. He told me about your mother and how she would need to agree. All I want to know now is if you would be interested."

Jebe chewed his lip thoughtfully. How many times had his mother told him she wanted to leave Magiskeep? How many times had he heard her cry herself to sleep in the little drafty cottage? "I can't leave my mother," he said.

"You wouldn't have to, Jebe. Your mother is welcome here too." When Jebe still hesitated, Delran put his hand on the boy's shoulder. "Come with me, Sur. I have something to show you."

He escorted the boy to the south wing of the house where Jamus had been staying. The bedroom there was light and airy with wide doors opening onto a terrace in the Warmmonths. There were four rooms set together. Along with the bedroom was a huge bath with a tub and sink with fresh water pumped in from outside and a huge fireplace. A lovely sitting room adjoining the bedroom was furnished in rose-tapestried furniture and thick rich carpets. Another room, now used for storage, lay off to the side, but it might have been some sort of workroom.

"These were my daughter's rooms," Delran explained. "I house special guests like Lord Jamus here now. If your mother came, they would be hers."

"My mother, here? In these rooms?"

"I've missed the sound of a woman's singing, Jebe. When my daughter was killed in the avalanche, I lost the greatest treasure in my life. Her mother had died when she was born and I had to raise her by myself. I've not been able to find someone willing to stay here with me since. My Keep is too far from civilized Tulene, and too close to the Rim for any woman I've met. Morrie and Lesa stay because their husbands are part of my guard. The other men's wives have homes of their own on my farmland. So I'm left here in this big house with no one to talk to. I'm an old man, Jebe. Having you in the house reminded me of what I might have had if my Deana had lived."

"You'd keep your word? Mother would live here?" Jebe said.

"I am a man of honor, Sur. Here." Delran pulled an amber ring from his finger and put it in Jebe's hand. "In Turan, when Lords make a pledge, they offer a token. This is my token. Your mother and you are welcome to live here in this house for a long as you wish."

Jebe stared at the ring, his mouth quivering. "But I ain't got a token to give you back, Sur."

Delran smiled. "You don't need one, Jebe. You're not yet making a promise. Remember, your mother must decide this too. All I ask of you now is to tell me if you would like to do this."

"I would, My Lord, I would. Why, it's like a dream come true!"
*****

Jern's forehead was slick with sweat. No matter where he Touched Tomas, all he felt was a vast emptiness, as if the River had abandoned him. Desperate, he pulled open his pouch and searched vainly for some tonic or herb to restore at least a little of the man's stamina.

The guard's skin was a sickly blue gray and his breathing so shallow it was hard to tell if he breathed at all. "I don't know what else to do," the Healer said. "The poison's done too much damage." Then, to his horror, he heard Tomas gasp and fall limp. He dropped his ear to the guard's chest and listened. Then, tears in his eyes, Jern pushed up from the bed, shaking his head. "It's too late."

Jamus had just arrived and heard the Healer's words. He moved quickly to Jern's side. "Stay here, Jern, and don't leave me, no matter what. Simen, take hold of me, around the waist."

Jern clutched Jamus' arm. "What are you doing? He's dead."

"The River owes this man a debt," Jamus said, placing his hand on Tomas' chest. "And for once, she is going to pay because I command it." He felt for Simen's fingers at his belt as if to reassure himself. "Simen, I need you with me. I'm not sure if I'm strong enough yet to do this alone."

"I'm here," Simen told him, tensing his muscles. He knew the River well enough to be ready.

The waters were hot, burning at first with fever, then as icy as the Norreaches. They spun and roiled, confused and tortured by pain. Power seemed to flee, just up ahead, then below, as if it too had no direction.

But Jamus plunged down, ignoring the turmoil, his Will set on a course to the deepest waters. Simen steadied him, pushing him on when he faltered, and holding him back when he dropped too fast into the raging currents.

Images swirled past. An arrow, laced in blood screamed by, unaffected by the swirling waters. Another, sharp barbed tore into Jamus' shoulder and he screamed, his voice drowned in the savage rush. Simen held hard, despite Jamus' trembling, Willing his strength to sustain them both.

Deeper they went, as a third arrow lodged in Jamus' thigh and a fourth nicked his arm. He twisted in pain, but forced himself on, refusing the waters' demands, and ignoring the pain.

"For Tomas' sake," he whispered to himself. "For a man who would willingly give his life."

Suddenly, they hit bottom, and stood at the cave's entrance.

And when they walked in, Tomas already lay at the Dragon's feet.

"He's not yours," Jamus said, his voice wracked with pain. Blood seeped from his shirt and from his breeches where the arrows had pierced him, and his arm throbbed. "Give him to me."

The great rainbow Dragon raised a sleepy eye and yawned. "You ask?"

"No," Jamus replied. "I am not asking. I am commanding."

"Command? Rivermaster not fly. Dragon not be commanded."

"You owe this man for my life."

The Dragon rose on its haunches, then stretched its massive head down, cocking it to peer at them with one spinning, mirrored eye. "You trade?"

"What?"

"This meat for you? You trade? I be hungry. Take one for other."

Jamus straightened. The arrow in his shoulder twisted as he moved and another slash of agony rocked him back into Simen's embrace. But the Follyman held firm. "If you so wish," Jamus replied.

"No, Jamus," Simen cried. "You can't!" He let go and pushed himself in front of his brother. "Here, take me instead. I'm the same size. I'll fill your belly just as much as he will."

At that, the Dragon opened its great jaws and a low rumble came out, almost as if it were laughing. "Size no matter. Is what is. Rivermaster be Magic."

Jamus clutched Simen's arm and tried to pull him back, but Simen was stronger and wouldn't budge. "Simen, don't do this. It's not your bargain to make."

"Not mine? Who better to sacrifice himself for you, Jamus. You gave me life. All I'm doing is paying my debt. The world can do without me. It can't do without you."

"Follyman be wise," the Dragon said, wearing its Dragon grin with obvious amusement. "Pah, all be River taste bad. Other twoleg like this," it said, poking Tomas with one huge claw, "be sometime sweet."

"You said you'd trade," Jamus insisted. "Leave him be. I told you you could have me."

"Dragon lie."

"You can't," Jamus said. "It's not the Way of the River."

The Dragon lay down again, dropping its head on its forefeet as it studied him. "Rivermaster lie. So do Dragon."

Jamus caught his breath. "Lie, how? I haven't lied."

"Not say afraid to die."

Jamus felt his heart drop. His shoulder was on fire. Every moment in the Rim came back to him in an instant and with it, the fear. The River had come for him, her voice calling and he had tried to run. He'd lied when he'd told Jern he was ready for death, and he lied to Nobby and to Jebe when he said he could protect them. It had all been a lie in the end, and the Dragon knew. "I am afraid. I'm afraid of this Power I have and where it will lead. The River wants my life and I'm afraid to give it to her."

"Good."

"Why? A man can't live in fear."

"Rivermaster can no live without. Danger be all around. Must fear death to live. River be life."

"I... I can't let her have me."

"Then fear her. Fight her. Make her do Will. Be master. But see fear. Only when fear death will you live."

"And Tomas?"

"Not hungry now. Go."

There was a burst of rainbow light and they were thrown upward, spiraling and spinning in cascades of color.

Simen heard Jern's voice from a distance and then, in his ear.

"Simen, help me. We need to get Jamus to lie down."

Groggily Simen opened his eyes. The room was brighter than he remembered. Jamus was behind him, leaning against a bedpost, groaning. Tomas moaned, and his chest heaved.

Jern gasped. "He's breathing. How…?"

"The Dragon…" Simen whispered, and then he too collapsed on the floor.

*****

"By the blood, I'll be out of beds if this keeps up," Delran exclaimed as the guards carried Simen into a bedroom and settled him on the bed. "I'd thought Jamus was Healed and now you bring both him and his brother back in even worse condition. I tell you, Master Jern, I am having serious doubts about you lately."

Jern checked Simen to be sure he was just asleep. Wearily, he rubbed his forehead and sighed. "Do you have any really strong wine, My Lord? I could use a drink."

"Of course," Delran replied, suddenly concerned for Jern's condition. "I hadn't realized how pale you were. Come, here, sit down." He pulled up a chair and pushed Jern into it, surprised at how weak the Healer seemed. "Lad, what in the name of the Hand happened? I'll be putting you to bed next."

"Tomas died, My Lord."

"Dead, Tomas? The Hand be cursed for it. The poor lad. He was a fine man, a fine man."

"But he's not dead now, Sur."

"What? How can that be? A man doesn't die and then not die."

"This one did," Jern replied weakly. "His heart stopped. But Jamus would not have it. He ordered me out of the way and Touched Tomas himself."

"Impossible. Even the Eldenlore denies such things."

Jern sighed heavily. "It seems the Eldenlore is mistaken, My Lord. I was there, I saw it."

Delran sat now, his face nearly as pale as Jern's. His hand trembled as he reached for the decanter of fullseason wine, the strongest brew in his Keep. He poured himself a full goblet and another for Jern, placing it on the table beside the Healer's chair. He took a big gulp of the rich drink, coughed a little, swallowed, and gulped again. "How, Jern? How could this be?"

Jern's head sank into his chest as he let the emotions of the past span overwhelm him. He had warded himself with Healer's stelin when he'd first Touched Tomas, protecting himself from the guard's anguish. Even when Tomas had stopped breathing and he'd felt no heartbeat, he had blocked himself from grief, wrapped in the shell Compassion demanded of its disciples. A man could not Heal if he could not understand, and too often, emotions refused the Touch. Sometimes, indeed, a Healer might let his patient's illness overcome him, but never when it was stronger than a man's Will.

But Jamus had used no ward. He had faced Tomas' agony with no shield, and, in doing so, had faced his death as well. He and Simen, together, had held death in their grip, and let it take them with it to the depths of Turan's soul.

Jern knew it. For in the Healing, he had seen them drop to the floor and when they had, he had run to them, panicked by their stillness. And when he had put his hand on Jamus' neck, he'd felt no pulse, no breath, no life. And there was none in Simen either.

Instead of one man dead, he saw three, and ward or no, his heart broke.

But Magic too was in the room, its heavy hand pressing ever down, humbling his shoulders and buckling his knees until he too was on the floor, unable to move. It was then he heard the waters themselves rushing in his ears and, for one brief instant, he thought he heard a deep rumbling laugh as if some great creature had found something amusing in the tragedy.

The rest was a blur. He could recall voices, and he remembered somehow rising again. He knew Jamus had moved, for Simen was not longer behind him, but in front. And then, he saw Tomas' chest heave and the room seemed to explode in a rainbow of sparking light.

He raised his eyes and looked at Delran. "It was the Magic, My Lord. Magic as I have never known it. I can't even conceive of what, or how, or why it ever could have happened, but Jamus seemed to know exactly what he was doing. That was the most frightening thing of all. His eyes were like ice and his voice was so sure. There wasn't a moment's hesitation. He put his hand on Tomas and simply... simply Healed him."

Delran shook his head. "And paid a dear price for it too from the looks of him. Both he and his brother. And you too, Jern. You look as if you've aged a lifetime."

"I feel it, My Lord," Jern replied as he took a long draught of the wine. "A Mage thinks he understands his craft, and though he knows he has never reached its boundaries, at least he's sure he knows where they lie. Then, in one moment, his whole belief is shattered. I've been such a naïve fool."

"Jern, don't question yourself. Jamus is Kiselor, the Rivermaster. The Magic will do things for him it would never do for another."

"I'm a fraud, Delran. Just a fraud. I know so little. When Jamus first came here, wounded with Sagari's Spellfire, I couldn't cure him. Then, in the Rim, he was poisoned, and again I failed to discover it until it was almost too late. Now, Tomas..."

"Even I know a Healer cannot do everything, Jern. When my daughter was injured in the avalanche, no Healer in the world could have mended her and saved her life. The mortals who were here in Turan then, couldn't even ease her pain. She died in my arms, weeping in agony, and on that day, I vowed I would never need to feel so helpless again. It was then I began to search Turan for someone gifted in the Art. By the Blood, I even contacted Sagari and pleaded with him to send someone to me across the Rim. But he refused. Then, I found a young man with clear blue eyes and a heart so full of compassion, I wished him to be my son. That man was you, Jern." Delran's voice nearly broke as he went on. "Never once have you failed me, boy. And you've not failed me now. No man can give more than he has to give. We both know that. How could I ask for more?"

"But what if I do have more to give, My Lord? What if it's my ignorance keeping me from the River's deeper waters? I've never been trained in the Keep. All I know I learned from wise women in the forests of Turan who hide from mortal eyes for fear their Art will condemn them in the eyes of the law-Sirala, Jeda...herbwomen with the River in their blood."

"And do you want more, Jern?"

Jern took another drink of the wine. "I do, My Lord. I want it all. Today, I learned how much more there is."

"Then why not go to Magiskeep? Surely you can learn there."

"Magiskeep."

"Why not, boy? Jamus isn't Sagari. He will find a Healer to take your place here in the Province until you return. How long would it take? A circle? Two? Jamus said you were gifted." Delran's eyes were bright from both the wine and the idea. "When you came back, we could build you a keep of your own, small, at first. You could teach there. Think of it, lad. Turan has Healers, but how many of them are like you, unschooled and afraid? What a blessing it would be for them to find a place to learn."

Jern considered this between two more sips of his wine. The more his thought about it, the better the idea seemed. By the time he had drained his goblet, he and Delran had already picked a spot to build his keep.

By the time he had drained his second goblet, both he and the Lord were quite drunk.

Chapter 16

Salene knew the Sorcerer's Crystal was not the gift of Seer's Vision. While Kala was able to sift the truth of anything a man might say, the Stone could only sift the truth of what a man might be. It had the ability to defy Illusion and reveal the true nature of spells and weaves, but with men, all it really could do was reveal their souls. She recalled how she had once viewed Jamus through it when he was still a boy and seen the Rivermaster he was destined to become. Jamus himself and looked through the crystal facets at Sagari and seen such twisted hate within the Master, he had at last found reason enough to kill him. Powerful though the gem might be, it would never tell her whether Sarn was lying, but it would tell her exactly what he was.

She placed the Stone in the borrowed pitcher, poured in water and was delighted to discover that Jeamel had been right. The Sorcerer's crystal simply vanished. Unless someone knew it were there, to the naked eye, it had become invisible. Experimentally, she held the water up before her eyes and glanced around Jamus study. Then, she smiled. Her little crooked bookshelf, seemed to glow within the Crystal Vision. Every loving stroke of her hand on the wood seemed to shimmer as if the case itself had a life of its own. The very sight of it filled her heart with such passion and longing she ached, thinking of her husband and how hard she had struggled to learn the secrets of woodworking just to make a gift for him. Had the bookcase a voice, it would have whispered his name and sung of her devotion.

Salene laughed and put the pitcher back down. Magic was indeed a wondrous thing, but in the end, its power was nothing at all compared to the wonder of human love.

The very nature of her Art, Compassion, proved that again and again. How often had a Healing depended more on the Healer's heart than on his skill? She had come to believe a Mage's talent was only limited by his capacity to care.

And it was, she thought, the very reason Sarn had never Mastered the Sixth Art.

*****

Despite his weakness from Tomas' Healing, Jamus was determined to leave Delran's Keep the next day. With a carriage, he could relax while Nobby drove. The journey itself would be far less stressful with Simen along to help sift the Rim's illusions, and, if he tired, Whim was more than capable of taking the lead.

Still, Delran had reservations. "My horses are fit and strong, My Lord. Nobby is an excellent hand but I'd feel much better if I sent my own driver."

"We can manage," Jamus insisted. "Remember, we have a Beasttalker with us."

Delran smiled, but still persisted. "I'll send Joss with you. It's high time the lad saw his father again. Then, if Jebe and his mother decide to come here, he can drive them back. He's been through the Rim before and knows at least one of the trails well."

"I won't send Jebe back without an escort who is well-versed in the Rim's illusions, Sur. Simen can ride back here with them and then return to the Keep through the mirrors... if Jebe decides to come, that is."

Delran nodded. "I've made my pledge to him. The decision is in his hands."

"And Nobby?"

"The boy seems thrilled with the idea," Delran said. "From what he's told me, I think his parents will be as thrilled to agree. I'll offer them a farm here if they want to come too, but I'm not sure they'll be interested."

"Nobby's father is a craftsman," Jamus told him. "He's not likely to give up his shop. Farming is not an easy alternative."

"It would be just as well. Nobby's an independent lad who wants to make good on his own. He'd be well cared for here."

"Perhaps even better than he is now," Jamus said. "I didn't feel his parents worried as much about him as they did about the coin his work brought into the house. As long as I was paying him well, they hardly cared that he was going into the Rim. It was sad, really."

"I'd be glad to send them a Prentice fee for my having the lad if that will help."

Jamus shook his head. "No need of that. If Nobby wants to come here, I'll see they're paid for his loss. The money doesn't make any difference to me, but if it makes a difference to Nobby, I'll pay it gladly. I owe him much more than a few denerets a Sevenstin."

So, it was settled. By Easwin of the following day, the little party was packed and ready to go. Joss took the reins for the first part of the trip, instructing Nobby on the art of driving Delran's sensitive and well-trained horses. Jebe rode Whim, while Simen rode Redwin. Flutter trotted happily along behind, delighted to be the extra horse for a change.

Jamus settled himself in the back seat of the carriage and rested, letting his mind wander.

"You are so still. Why do you not call?"

Jamus sighed. "I have no need of you. Leave me alone. I'm tired."

"I am here to help. My strength to your will, my power to your hand, my answer to your call."

"I don't need you."

"Your weakness betrays you, my son. Let me restore you. All you need do is raise your hand."

"No. I will not use the River for something I can do myself."

"It is so easy. I am here for you, my son. My blood is your blood. My breath your breath. My heart your heart."

"Leave me. I didn't call you."

"I am here, nonetheless. You need no call. The Dragon sings for you."

"The Dragon laughs at me. He knows the truth. I'm nothing without him."

"You are the River."

"I'm nothing."

He awoke as the sun began its descent in the east. The mountains' shadows lengthened, covering the foothills in purple. Joss pulled the horses to a stop, "We should camp here, My Lord. Tomorrow, by Sowin, we'll be in the Rim."

"And from there, Magiskeep," Jamus said. "It will be good to be home."

*****

Sarn had wanted to refuse Salene's request, but he knew better. No matter what he wanted to believe, she was still the Lady of the Keep. He had been avoiding her ever since he had spoken to Lurela, uncertain that he could keep his secret in the presence of the keen-sensed Healer.

Instead, he had spent his time with Lord Sarkem, pretending interest in the Lord's farm to the South and his need for water. They pored over maps together, trying to decide if diverting a small creek would serve the purpose, and traveled to the Keep's own fields to see how Magiskeep's farmers dealt with irrigation. Despite his reasons, Sarn learned how crops were rotated, and how hard the farmers worked to see the Keep was well fed even during the Chillmonths. He saw corn stored in huge round bins and dug taroots from the cold soil. He marveled at the warehouse full of grain and saw the dried herbs and greens hanging in the rafters. Never one to have noticed before, he saw the fatted cavil tended in the barns and even found himself wondering as a new calf took its first look at the world.

But, he was still Sarn. Nothing would ever change that.

Now, he warded himself with stelin determination and headed for Jamus' study where the Lady waited. He had left Lord Sarkem and Lady Delise at Evenmeal, promising to return with at least a small decision about the creek. "I have to consult Lady Salene, My Lord. She is Jamus' voice while he is away. If he isn't going to be here soon, perhaps she and I can give you an answer to your request."

The excuse sounded reasonable, and gave him a good reason to be with Salene. Now, he took a deep breath and carried through with the pretense. "Madame, I did want to see you this Weswin."

"Oh?" Salene replied. She was seated at Jamus' desk, a half eaten Evenmeal pushed to the side next to a pitcher of water and a goblet. "I thought it was I who sent for you."

"Fortuitous circumstance," he answered. "I would have come regardless. Lord Sarkem and I have been discussing his farm."

"How interesting. I didn't know you knew anything about the subject."

Sarn smiled as a father might when indulging a rude child. "I know a great many things, My Lady. I've made a habit of learning all I can."

Salene had known him far too long to believe a word of it. Still, this was the very reason she had wanted him here. "How satisfying that must be. Jamus has always said knowledge is the key to ruling well. It's why he's spent so much time in the villages. How much better to rule a people you know than strangers."

"Ah... yes," Sarn agreed, caught a bit off guard. "A Lord should know all he can about his Keep."

"The people, especially," Salene said. "The servants..."

Sarn held up his hand. "If you're going to lecture me about the unfortunate misunderstanding between Jeamel and me, please, spare me. I've spent enough spans already paying for that. He is back here now, and content. Let it be so."

"I wasn't just thinking about Jeamel," Salene replied, lifting the pitcher to pour herself a goblet of water. "Lurela has returned as well. Have you seen her?"

Sarn shrugged. "She's still avoiding me. I've no intention of intruding on her life if she doesn't want me to."

Salene held the pitcher up, pausing in her pouring, as if his words had stayed her hand. "Jeamel believes you owe her something."

"So, he's told you."

"He has," she said, peering nonchalantly through the water at him. "It's my understanding you will be paying her before the Keep when my husband returns."

"Sooner, if it pleases Jeamel," Sarn spat. "He'd have me confess my crime to all in hearing and apologize. I'm not the one who's done wrong. Rather, I've had wrong done to me."

"That's not exactly what I've heard."

"You've heard incorrectly, Madame. I was in Sagari's power then, and in the lady's power since. What would you have me do? I am just a man."

Salene looked at him through the crystal's facets and her heart lurched.

All she saw was Sarn, no more, no less. And Sarn alone. There was nothing more to him, as if his very essence were so totally immersed in his sense of self there was no room for anything else. He was empty of hope, of passion, of anything beyond his own need to be. Even his Magic swirled about his hands as if it sought to defend his own being and nothing else. She saw desire for power, not for the sake of power but for the sake of self-satisfaction, and ambition, to rule because ruling defined him and filled the void that was his soul. She would have wept if he suffered from his loneliness, but he relished it, content with his selfish existence.

At last, she understood why Jamus had chosen him to rule the Keep in his absence. No man in all of Turan would defend the Magic better - to Sarn the Magic was the key to his existence. He relished the touch of the River, for it defined him, filled him and gave him his identity. Through it, he thrived, depending on its presence to keep him company. Without it, the emptiness of his life would overwhelm him and he would have to face the pitiful shell he was without it. No heart but the Magic. No soul but the Magic. No man, none at all. Just Sarn.

"You are more than man, Sur," she said at last, controlling her emotions with ultimate care. Now was not the time to reveal her disgust. "You are a Magician, a Master in this house. If the Magic cannot live in honor here, then where is its rightful place in this world? Whether it was Sagari's Magic or yours that betrayed Lurela, you are the one who must make amends. Give her her respect back, at least."

"And my son? What of him?" Sarn asked, his mouth quivering as if he were about to cry. "My boy?"

"I'd say that's all up to Lurela, and even Jebe himself," Salene replied coldly.

Sarn worked his mouth silently as if at a loss for words. He thought quickly. "I can understand your mistrust, My Lady. I've made so many mistakes. But can't a man learn?"

"A man would learn, Sur. I'm just not sure you can." She put the pitcher down, took a sip of water and leaned her elbows on the desk. "You needed an answer for Lord Sarkem, I believe? Something to convince him you had come here of your own accord instead of at my bidding?"

"How…?" he was genuinely surprised she knew.

"As I said, Sarn, a wise ruler knows his servants. They are the eyes and ears of the Keep."

So she had spies. It would do him well to remember that. "Lord Sarkem would like to divert a small creek South of the Keep in order to furnish water to his fields. Since is the Keep's land, he came to ask permission of its Lord. I cannot give it without your consent, as you speak for Lord Jamus."

"Tell Lord Sarkem my husband is expected back before the Sevenstin ends. As I have not examined the particulars myself, I cannot speak for him. The Lord is welcome in this house for as long as he wishes to stay, so if it would not be inconvenient to him, I am sure the True Lord of the Keep would be glad to entertain his request."

"He has consulted me," Sarn said firmly.

"The True Lord," Salene repeated.

Sarn bowed. "As you say, My Lady." Then, he turned on his heel and left.

Salene sighed took several deep breaths. Then she looked at the pitcher. What would she see if she could look at herself through that eye of truth? She shuddered and closed her eyes.

Perhaps it was better not to know.

*****

When the rolling pastures of Magiskeep came into view, the horses quickened pace of their own accord.

"Whim's glad to be home," Jebe said laughing. "He wants to walk on the wind so we get there faster."

"Tell him it doesn't work well with carriages," Jamus replied, "but if you and he want to go on ahead and tell Josep we're coming, it's fine with me."

"Kin I go too?" Nobby asked. Since they had left the Rim, he had been riding Flutter and the pony seemed as eager as the silver stallion.

"Only if Simen goes with you."

"It would be a pleasure," Simen answered. "I doubt you and Joss need my protection at this point."

As the horses and riders lifted stride, it was all Joss could do to hold his team in check. "They wants ta run, Me Lord."

"Then let them, Joss," Jamus answered. "The road between here and the Keep is good enough."

"Me Pap'd have me head if'en I brung 'em in hot an' sweaty."

Jamus laughed. "I can fix that, Joss. What's the good of Magic if I can't use it once in a while? Just pull them up at the West gate and I'll take care of the rest."

Joss grinned a let out a whoop. The team burst into a gallop.

Whim landed lightly in the stableyard with Flutter and Redwin a pace behind. Josep, out raking the lane, looked up, masking his surprise with a pleased grin. "So, yer back. Where's th' Lord?"

"A bit behind," Simen replied as he swung out of the saddle. "He's coming by carriage. We had a few difficulties at Delran's and he was too tired to ride."

"Carriage, eh? Cain't say as I've e'er seen him in one. 'E drivin'?"

"No." Simen hid his smile. "Delran sent a driver. Good man. Ought to be able to help you out while he's here."

"Ain't got no time ta waste wid some Outworlder. 'E kin care fer Delran's stock but he'd jest better stay outta my hair. Here now, ya lads, Jebe, Nobby, whatcha standin' there fer wid yer mouths hangin' open? It 'pears ta me ya got mounts ta care fer. Now hustle too afore I fill yer positions wid them what's willin' ta work fer a livin'."

The boys nearly tumbled off their mounts in their hurry to obey Josep's orders.

"It ain't natural fer Jamus ta come back like that, Master Simen," Josep said as soon as the boys had gone. "He ain't hurt, is he?"

"He was, Josep. They were attacked on the way to Delran's. Jamus was wounded by some arrows. He's better now, but still hasn't fully recovered his strength."

"'Tis a long time fer 'im ta be ailin'."

"There were some unexpected complications. But, he'll be fine, especially now that he's home where it's quiet."

"Cain't say that fer a fact. Bin a few upsets here since you bin gone. Gonna be a bit more from what I hear from Jeamel. I sure hope Jamus is fit enow ta deal wid it."

"He'll be fine," Simen said, not at all convinced. He had been hoping Magiskeep's tranquility would restore Jamus' energy. He had been strangely silent on the way back, and not once had he chosen a path through the Rim's illusions, leaving all the decisions to Simen and Whim. Well-acquainted with Reflections, the mountains' deceits posed no problem for him, but he would have felt better if Jamus had shown at least some interest.

"When they comin'?" Josep asked, shading his eyes to peer down the western lane.

"A span, no more. We left them just out of the Rim. Delran's horses are fit and fast. They'll make good time."

"Run'em so far and they'll be blowin'. No man better be bringing beasts what be blowin' inta my yard," Josep said. "I don't hold wid sech nonsense."

"This man won't," Simen assured him. "I'll go tell Lady Salene we're back." He headed for the house to leave Josep waiting impatiently behind.

At the West gate, Joss reined the team back to a walk. Jamus raised his hand and gestured slightly. The sweat melted from the horses' coats and their breathing steadied. "I'd give them a polish too," Jamus said, "but your father'd be suspicious."

"They t'weren't very hot nohow," Joss said. "They coulda run all the way an' hardly caught breath."

"No sense in taking chances, Joss. I don't want you to lose even a mite in your father's eyes. Walk the rest of the way."

"Aye, me Lord," Joss replied as he clucked the team along.

The drive was short, and soon, they too were in the yard.

Josep dropped his rake, wiped his hands on his breeches and simply stared.

"Hello, Josep," Jamus said, breaking the silence. "I think you know my driver. If you'll excuse me, I'll go on up to the house and leave you to get reacquainted."

Joss didn't even bother to hide his feelings. He leapt out of his seat and ran over to his father. "Pap! Bory, Pap, it's so good ta see ya!"

Josep's eyes filled with tears and he opened his arms to envelop his son.

Jamus looked back and smiled. Home was even sweeter than he remembered.

Chapter 17

Nestled in Jamus' arms, Salene lay in bed wondering what it would be like to live without the capacity to love. How cold a world it must be and how empty. She snuggled closer, and Jamus moaned a little in his sleep. She felt his heart quicken against her hand. Gently, she shook his arm. "Jamus? What's wrong?"

His eyes fluttered open, his breath caught. "Dream," he muttered. "Just a dream." He pulled her close, his breath warm against her cheek. "Not wrong with you here."

She kissed him and let her lips linger on his. "I missed you."

"So you said."

"I can say it again, can't I?"

"Always, Love. It's what brings me back," he answered.

"What were you dreaming about?" she asked, settling her head on his chest under his chin. She could still hear his heart pounding.

"The River. She's after me again. I keep trying to run, but there's no place to go. She wanted me in the Rim, and almost had me this time. If I'd died…." His voice trailed off.

"I don't understand. Doesn't being Rivermaster mean you command those waters? Why don't you just tell them to leave you alone?"

He sighed. "I try. They won't listen, at least not all the time. Salene, it's as if the Magic demands I use it, whether I want to or not. The more I deny it, the more it demands of me."

"You're tired, My Love. Weak from your injuries. Let me Touch you. I can help."

"No!" he cried rolling away from her. "Don't you see? That's what she wants. She wants me to need her. I have to do this on my own to prove I don't. She has to understand I'll call because I want to, not because I have to."

Salene wanted to reach out to comfort him, but she held her hand. His torment wracked her body as if she felt his pain. "All right. I'll wait. I'm used to waiting."

He got up from the bed, wrapped himself in a woolen robe and sat down again across from her. "I'm sorry, Salene, truly I am. But I have to do this alone. I promised I'd share everything with you…" He paused and the Dragon's laughter echoed in his ears. "I can't share this. It's between me and the River."

She crawled over and wrapped her arms around him. "That doesn't mean I can't still love you, does it?"

He smiled, and kissed her hard. "Perhaps we should discuss it." He lay her gently back against the pillows, and pressed his body to her. "Or, perhaps not."

*****

Lord Sarkem rolled out his map and pointed, "Here, My Lord. Do you see where the stream diverges? I want to send the eastern branch just ten spans farther south, That way I can use it to keep my greencrop watered."

Easwin's sun was filtering in through the western window of the Mage's study, lighting the table where Sarkem had laid the map for Jamus to examine.

"What's downstream?" Jamus asked.

"A small pond, here," Sarkem pointed. "But I've already thought of that. Once the stream passes my field, I'll set it back to its original bed. The only thing that will be affected are the brellum trees along here." Again he pointed. "There's very little other vegetation of note along the banks for that stretch."

"It sounds like a reasonable idea," Jamus agreed, "but I'd really feel a lot more comfortable about it if I saw if for myself. When do you need an answer?"

"I'll be planting within the month, My Lord, but I won't need the water right away. Once the seedlings take and the weather warms, though, that land gets dry."

"So there's enough time for me to visit the site before I give you permission."

Sarkem nodded. "Indeed, My Lord. I would be pleased to have you as my guest. I never expected you want to take the time."

"I should think it's my duty as Lord of the Keep," Jamus replied. "If I don't take an interest in the needs of my lands and subjects, what kind of a ruler would I be? Shall we set a meeting for Sevenstin next? I'm sure I'll be fit enough to travel then."

"I heard of your injuries, My Lord. I'm glad to see you're recovering well. I heard it was quite serious."

Jamus shrugged. "Serious enough. But I had a skilled Healer and the luck of two very brave and clever young men with me, so it worked out better than a man might have hoped."

"I suppose you know Lord Sarn had some difficulties here while you were away?" Sarkem said, leaving the question hanging.

"Lord Sarn makes his own trouble, I'm afraid," Jamus replied. "And yet, he is the ablest man here to protect the Keep for me."

"He is an interesting man. Quite intelligent, actually, but not at all wise in the ways of men. I'd thought it was a skill taught here in the Keep."

"The Sixth Art requires it," Jamus answered, "and Sarn is but a Five Arts Mage. I suppose since he's had no need to acquire the skill, he simply hasn't bothered."

Sarkem rolled up the map and tucked it into its carrying pouch. "My wife and I ask your leave to return home this Sowin. We've already stayed longer than we'd planned."

"You don't need my permission, Sur. I don't stand on formalities like that. I'll see that Josep has your carriages ready."

Sarkem bowed, despite Jamus' remarks, and left.

Alone in the study, Jamus considered the Lord's words. Sarn was, perhaps wiser in the ways of men than anyone suspected, provided those ways could serve to his benefit. Within the span the Seven Masters would sit in full audience to the Keep, ready to hear Sarn confess to his part in Lurela's life.

He had to wonder just how Sarn planned on getting out of it.
*****

Though Jamus had made the call to the Gathering less than formal, most of the Seven Masters chose to dress in their official robes. Jired in his yellow gown and Seneth in a purple knee-length tunic entered together, deep in conversation. Joria followed soon after, taking her seat in the second chair on the platform and arranging her long grey robe so its skirt wrapped around her body. Jiala fairly floated in, her crimson gown flowing suggestively about her legs, hinting she really wore nothing else underneath the soft shaenis fabric. Sarena in white and Savel in pale blue entered separately and walked to the far chairs with such quiet serenity, much of the crowd in the Great Hall dropped their voices to whispers as if talking might somehow disturb the Sixth's and Seventh's Masters contemplation. Jamus and Salene entered last, she in a simple gown of royal blue laced with silver and he in a long coat of royal blue over a pale blue shirt and grey dorrsettskin breeches. The silver stallion crest on his chest shimmered in the maglits as he walked, and the hall fell into such a hush, the sigh of several ladies brought giggles and more than a few poking elbows.

Jamus seated Salene in his ornate ceremonial chair in the center of the row, and stepped down to the floor to take a simple wooden chair from the audience for himself. Again, this brought a murmur from the large crowd of mages, servants and villagers who had managed to squeeze into the Hall. Outside, as often happened, there was another crowd in the Keep's front hall and more outside on the steps and front yard of the palace.

Jamus set his chair to Salene's left and then turned back to face the people. "I've appointed messengers to carry news and testimony from these proceedings to the people outside this Hall," he announced. "I must apologize that we don't have room for everyone inside. I hope to remedy that for future events. I'd just not expected to yet have need of the extra space. If anyone here wishes to speak or have more information after the Gathering has sat, I will be happy to meet with you myself to clear up any matters of concern."

There was a smattering of applause at that. He waited, then went on, "Today, as has been agreed, Master Sarn of the Five Arts has been summoned to offer testimony in regard to his actions here in the Keep. As the matter concerns Mistress Lurela and her son, Jebe, both of whom are here under my protection, it is my duty to speak on their behalf." He looked down and nodded to Lurela who sat next to Jebe in the front row of the audience. "Mistress, is that acceptable to you?"

Lurela rose, "I don't know, My Lord."

The crowd murmured.

Jamus looked puzzled for an instant, but recovered quickly. "If you have reservations, My Lady, I will be glad to step aside. You're welcome to appoint another spokesperson, or, if you wish, you make speak for yourself."

"There's no one here to speak for me," she said. "I'll let you take my part, but I'd like to be able to speak for myself if I disagree with anything you say."

Salene touched Jamus' arm reassuringly. He nodded. "Very well. Please, then, don't hesitate, even if it means interrupting. This matter solely concerns you and your son, and you have every right to speak your mind."

"Oh, I will, My Lord," she replied.

Jamus beckoned to a door to his right. "Please tell Master Sarn to come in."

Dressed in an elegantly-styled mid-thigh tunic of rich kelly green laced and embroidered in gold, Sarn swaggered into the room. Salene was a bit surprised at this bravado, considering the circumstances, but Jamus seemed unimpressed. Still, she knew he was on guard, for she saw him square his shoulders and then settle to a quiet, passive posture as he took complete control of himself.

"Master Sarn, unless you here deny it, it is true that you are the father of Lurela's son, Jebe. We are not here to condemn you for that act. What we are here to consider is what happened afterward.

At some point, Mistress Lurela was driven from her position her in the Keep and left without employment to support herself and her child in the village. The question of that and what you have done since in regard to her and her son are at issue."

"I am Jebe's father," Sarn replied, making a great show of looking over at the boy with an apparently warm smile. "And, I much regret not having spent time with him as he has grown up. But it was not my doing, I fear. Lord Sagari had much to say about the matter and did his best to see I was not allowed to see either the boy or his mother."

"It's true," Lurela agreed. "Lord Sagari threatened me and forced me to leave the Keep. He didn't want Master Sarn's reputation tainted by my claims."

Jamus raised an eyebrow at her quick defense of Sarn. This was not what Salene had led him to expect. "Lord Sagari had been gone now for nearly two circles, My Lady. Does his threat still matter so much that Master Sarn could not have made amends for the past?"

"What for? Jebe and I've been getting along fine." She looked over and smiled at Sarn. "But now, the lad's becoming a man and needs a father to look after him. The past be best forgotten if my son can now find a place here at his father's side."

"Lass, what are ya sayin'?" Jeamel shouted from his seat in the second row. "'E plumb scairt ya t'other day! An' ya claimed he ain't had a kind thought fer either on o' ya."

"Master Jeamel," Jamus said, interrupting, "Have you a stake in this that you speak so freely?"

"Yer damned right I does," Jeamel replied. "I be the one what demanded this Gatherin'. T'ain't my way ta stand by an' watch a lady bein' abused by a man, no matter whether 'e wears a Medallion or not. Missy Lurela's bin stayin' in me house wid me an' me wife fer nigh on three Sevenstins. I took 'er in ta keep 'er safe from that... that scoundrel." He pointed at Sarn. "Pears ta me somewhat happened here that ain't right ta make 'er speak up fer a man what she hated not so long ago."

"I misjudged him, that's all," Lurela countered. "What I believed was indifference was merely his fear I would reject his offers to care for his son as a father should. Jebe needs his protection now."

"I have given mine to you both," Jamus replied. "Surely the Lord of Magiskeep would suit instead."

"Never," Lurela said softly.

There was an audible gasp from the assembly as Sarn smiled and puffed himself up.

Jamus kept his composure, much to Sarn's disappointment. "Madame, you seem to have reservations. I would like to know why."

"You want to take him from me. You want Jebe for your own purposes, to use his powers for your own needs. Do you think I don't know how you are... all of you?" She glared accusingly at the Gathering. "You'll take my boy from me and teach him to hate me for being a mortal."

Salene half-stood, "Lurela, you can't mean this! Jamus would never..."

"Liar!" Lurela cried. "You're no better than the rest. You pretend to care, but all he is to you is some kind of trophy! Sarn's his father. He cares about him. You don't!"

Salene fell back in her seat, shocked by Lurela's passion. Damn Sarn, she thought. He's gotten to her.

Jamus though, did not flinch. "He is your son, Mistress. It is your choice."

"No!" Jebe shouted, leaping to his feet. "No, Mama, no! It ain't so. Lord Jamus ain't like that, he ain't!"

"Jebe, be quiet. This isn't for you to decide. Haven't I always done my best for you?"

"You have, Mama, but you're wrong now. It is for me to decide. I got a chance to be something and I ain't gonna let anybody, even you, take it from me."

"They've lied to you, Jebe," Lurela replied patiently, as if he were still a small child. "The Mages have lied."

Jebe reached into his pocket and pulled out Delran's ring. He held it up for her and everyone to see. "This ain't a Mage's word, Mama. It's a man's, and there ain't a much better man in all of Turan. Lord Delran gave me this as a sign of his promise. He wants me to work for him, to be his horsemaster. He's got a place for me there and a place for you to, if you want it. Look at this ring, will you? It's worth more than you'd be able to earn in five circles. It's mine, whether I go to him or not. I wanna go, Mama, more than I ever wanted anything in my life." He paused and took a deep breath. "But I ain't gonna go without you."

"Jebe..." Lurela began, then her voice faltered.

He looked at her, tears filling his eyes. "I wanna go, Mama. It's like I been running after a dream all this time, and now, I finally got a chance to catch it. He's a real fine man, Mama. He has a big house and the prettiest room in the world there for you. You wouldn't have to work no more if you didn't want to. I could take care of you. Don't you see, Mama? It's my dream."

She stared at him, her own eyes wet with tears. "You've grown, Jebe. You've become a man overnight."

He shook his head. "No I ain't Mama. But I ain't a little boy anymore either. Master Jamus trusted me with his life and I couldn't let him down. It's the first time anybody trusted me like that. But Whim and me, we did the right thing, and that's when I knew I could do most anything if I really tried."

She reached out and stroked his cheek with her hand, wiping away a tear. "Of course you can, Jebe. Of course you can."

"You can do anything you want here in Magiskeep too, son," Sarn said, moving over to the boy. "I'll see to it."

Jebe glared up at him. "Can I make my mother cry like you did? Can I make her wash clothes until her hands is all red and raw and she's so tired at night she can't even sing me a song before I go to bed? You did that, Master Sarn. You want me to be like you? I'll tell you what. Suppose you come with us across the Rim to where people don't care about Magic, and then tell me what I can do."

Sarn stepped back, clearly startled by the boy's words. "I... I... I belong here, in Magiskeep, and so do you."

"Why? So's you can pretend you got a son? Will that make you feel good? When people really care about other people, they care all the time, not when looks good. Lord Delran, he understands that." Then he looked up at Jamus. "And Lord Jamus, he does too. He cared about me before he even knew anything about me."

Sarn looked pleadingly at Lurela, but her gaze was focused on her son. Slowly and subtly, he began to play his hand, working the weave of his spell. With Jebe the center of attention, he hoped no one would notice.

Jebe had turned to face the Gathering. "Nobody ever thought I could do anything. Do you know what that's like when everybody thinks you're nothing? Then I came here, and Master Josep let me make mistakes and never got mad. And Lord Jamus, Lord Jamus, he told me I could become a horse trainer. Me! He said I was good with the horses. That's the first time anybody told me I was good at anything. If I'da had a real Pap, he woulda told me I was good, like my Mama did, but I didn't have no Pap. So Master Jamus, he told me instead. Don't ya see? If Master Sarn wanted to be my Pap, how come he didn't tell me I was good?"

Lurela's eyes glazed as Sarn's weave clouded her reason. "He never had the chance, Jebe. I wouldn't let him. I made him stay away."

"See, Jebe?" Sarn said. "It's not my fault, it's hers."

Something was wrong. Jamus sensed it even as Sarn spoke. He stared at Lurela, letting his mind seek beyond her words. Nothing.

"My fault," Lurela repeated. "You…" she faltered.

Sarn worked his fingers, but this time, Jamus noticed. He raised his hand.

Salene gasped. "Jamus, what are you doing?"

A silver thread darted from Jamus' fingers, coursing through the air like a fishing line. It struck something halfway between Sarn and Lurela, and snagged, the hook taken.

Sarn's mouth dropped open as his hand was jerked up, his fingers half pointing, half curled in the workings of his weave. His gaze darted nervously from Jamus' hand to the place where the thread had snagged. Then, his eyes widened in horror as the weave he had cast about Lurela slowly became visible to even the mortals in the room.

This time, the murmur rose to an angry buzz.

Jamus stood placidly, letting his own spell expose Sarn's lesser Magic. The River answered his commands with willing ease, so all he really had to do was think of what he wanted. Yet, he let his fingers play the air, for the sake of the assembled Mages. It would, he decided, not be wise to let them see how adept he had really become.

But Salene knew, as did Joria, who watched the subtle dispelling of another Master's Art with grim satisfaction. The Mistress of Illusion was not easily impressed, yet now her heart ached to see how far removed Jamus was from the small boy who had once hidden himself in her classroom to avoid Sarn's torments. If ever justice was done, it was now.

The web around Lurela shimmered and like ice melting in the morning sun, seemed to sparkle into drops of water and then, simply slide to the floor where it vanished.

Lurela blinked and her eyes focused. "By the Hand...my son, Jebe, what have I done?"she cried.

"Fallen prey to a chanting, Mistress, nothing more," Jamus replied soothingly. His voice was to gentle, so melodious that it seemed it carried the Magic's voice in its tones. And indeed it did, for with it, he evoked Compassion to ease the shock she might suffer once she realized what had happened. "It's all right now. You're free. There's no more to be said."

"I have a right to speak!" Sarn shouted as he broke from his own state of shock. "You don't understand! It was the only way I could convince her to give me my son! Don't you see how much I care about him? She wouldn't listen to reason. What was I supposed to do?"

"Enough," Jamus said quietly. "It is enough."

Sarn's mouth snapped shut and he stood, muted by the ancient words of command and Magic's hand clamped over his mouth.

"Mistress Lurela, I will ask no more of you. What Master Sarn has done is my responsibility now. He has wronged you, certainly, but by using Magic to do so, it's no longer up to you to have any part in this. I will promise you justice will be done."

Lurela's lower lip quivered, but she did not cry. "I am sorry, My Lord. I didn't know what he was doing to me."

Jamus held up his hand to stop her from saying any more. "From now on, your life is your own to live as you please. Jebe has been offered a position with Lord Delran and the Lord has graciously offered you a place there too. If you wish to stay here in Magiskeep, you are welcome here under my protection. Your choice, Madame. Use it as you will."

"Mama," Jebe said, "the Lord's Keep is beautiful. You'd like it there."

"Do you really want to go, Jebe? Do you want to leave Magiskeep?"

Jebe nodded. "I want to catch my dream, Mama."

Lurela smiled and turned back to Jamus. "My son and I will accept Lord Delran's offer, My Lord."

Jamus smiled back. "Jeamel, please escort the Lady and her son to my study. Give them refreshments and your hospitality until I come to discuss the arrangements. I still have business here to attend to."

Jeamel grinned and led Lurela and Jebe from the chamber.

Then, Jamus looked at Sarn and shook his head. "I'm disappointed in you, Master Sarn. I thought you'd learned your Prentice lessons better than this. I won't fault you for trying to get your son, but I do have something to say about how you tried. Master Jorn, Sarn was your Apprentice. Is this what you taught him?"

Jorn, caught off guard by the question, cleared his throat and rose. "No, My Lord. Rule and Vow are sacred in my study. The Third Art does not accept such behavior."

"H-m-m-m-m," Jamus rubbed his chin thoughtfully. "Well then, Mistress Jiala, Sarn has been judged Master of your Art as well. Perhaps we have seen one of your lessons here?"

Jiala's fingers gripped the arm of her chair, her knuckles white. "The lesson is mine, My Lord, but under these circumstances, I would never condone its use. Such weavings are a private matter. But to force a woman to give up her child? Never, My Lord."

"Is there a Master here who doesn't believe Sarn has done wrong? Anyone? Speak up, please."

The room was silent.

"I chose you as my surrogate, Sur, because I knew how much you valued the Magic. I knew too that you'd stop at nothing to defend it in my absence. What I misjudged was how much you value the Magic over the rights and well being of others. If you are ever again to sit in my place, it's something you're going to need to learn. Once already this month, I passed judgment on those who would use their strength against others. I was, quite frankly, pleased with the sentence I set on them." Jamus lifted his hand. Magic descended on the Hall. Those of mortal blood felt a crushing weight pressing down on them, sending some of them to their knees. Masters, mages, and Prentices felt the River too, but for them, it was a comforting arm enveloping them.

To Sarn, it was sheer terror. He saw, with vivid clarity, a complex net of silvrin threads lashing out at him. He raised his arms protectively, but the cords stopped just short of his chest and spun themselves into in indecipherable pattern, forming a sphere all around his body. Then to all but his keenest Mage's sight, they disappeared. "What... what have you done to me?" he asked, his tongue finally loosed from its muting spell.

"Protected the world from your Magic," Jamus replied. "Consider yourself warned. I've neither taken your Power from you nor mitigated it, as I might well have. Instead, I have channeled it. The inside of the sphere you wear is born of the Mirrors, and like a mirror, it will reflect back upon you. Cast a spell, and you cast it on yourself."

"But, what if I need the Magic?" Sarn sputtered, his whole body shaking. "Sometimes... sometimes a man needs Magic."

"The weave allows the River to seep through, as long as its purpose is noble or necessary. But the selfish cast, the convenient cast, will come back to you instead."

"How... how will I know if it's right?"

Jamus shrugged. "I suppose you'll just have to learn. Rule and Vow, Sur. Obey both and what can you fear?"

"I don't know how," Sarn sobbed.

"Learn," Jamus repeated. Then he looked away and addressed the crowd. "Two days from now is the Feast of Bestowal.

It is common practice for the Mages of the Keep to grant favors to any mortals who wish it. Master Sarn, Lady Salene, and I will hold audience here in the Great Hall to hear our requests. The Seven Masters are welcome to sit with us as well if they so choose. Otherwise, I'm sure they'd be happy to sit the privacy of their studies if some of you have requests you'd prefer to handle that way. The Keep's kitchens will be open for anyone who needs food for his table. May the Hand guide your hearts to true requests, and may the River have power to grant them."

He reached out his arm for Salene. She rose and kissed him lightly on the cheek. "I have a request of my own, My Lord. One best considered in private."

Jamus reddened as the whole Hall burst into good-natured laughter. Then Salene took his arm, smiled coyly and let him escort her from the room.

Far below, the Dragon laughed too.

Epilogue

Easwin of the Day of Bestowal brought the villagers out into the streets at first light. Most had gifts to exchange with friends and neighbors. Merchants opened their doors and invited customers in for refreshments or special free offerings. The woodworkers had made small toys for the children, the seamstresses had fashioned scarves or decorative collars, and the bakers had cut cookies and mini ballycakes. There were songs and dances, parties and earlenmeals in nearly every street.

Master Tam had decorated several ponies in ribbons and bows. He and three of his stableboys then led the animals into the village square to give the local children rides.

With the master away, Wyam was left in charge and had settled himself in the livery office where Jamus found him.

"My Lord," Wyam said, leaping to his feet when the Lord of Magiskeep entered. "I din't expect ya. Master Tam's not 'ere right now."

"I did want to see Tam," Jamus replied. "I have the money for the mare he sent to Lord Delran." He waited and watched, looking for some sign from the stablehand.

Wyam did not disappoint him. "Ya gots the mare there?" Wyam asked nervously.

"Does that surprise you, Sur?"

"I... well...I mean I heard there were a mite o' trouble. Word 'ere is there's bandits in them mountains."

"We were attacked, I'm afraid. In fact, I was almost killed."

At that, Wyam blanched. "By th' Blood! 'E promised 'e wouldn't hurt no one! Damn that Augie. I shoulda knowed." Then, he seemed to take a gulp of air as another thought hit him. "Nobby! L'il Nobby. Is 'e all right? They din't hurt 'im did they?"

"One of them hit him on the head. He might have been killed."

Wyam dropped to his knees. He was close to sobbing. "The Hand curse me fer a fool. Please, me lord, tell me the boy's all right."

"He's fine, Wyam. We were both blessed by the River in that. You're not denying your involvement?"

Wyam shook his head helplessly. "How kin I, me Lord? I near sold yer life an' me li'l coz out fer twenty silvers. I swear, I din't want nobody hurt. Augie, he tole me he was gonna take the horses whilst ya was sleeping. 'E said ya was gonna haf ta make camp jest west o' Li'l Peak an' iffen he waited, ya'd be off guard middle o' Norwin. 'E swore ta me they'd be no hurtin' or 'e'd fergit it. 'E swore."

Jamus looked down at the man, considering his words carefully. "Why did you believe him, Wyam? Augie doesn't exactly have an honorable reputation."

Wyam stared at his hands. "Man believes anythin' when 'e needs the money, me Lord. Twenty denerets may not seem like much ta a Lord like ya, but it's a fair purse ta me."

"To what end? Why should it matter to you? It's hardly more than a week's worth of ale."

Now Wyam looked up, his brow furrowed. "Ale? 'T'weren't fer ale, me Lord. I gots me a family. Wife an' a li'l girl. Look, Me Lord, I earns a fair wage 'ere, an' Master Tam's a fair man, an' me an' my family don't want fer nothin'. Nothin' 'cept a pretty rocky horse me girl seen in Master Jobin's shop. Didja ever have yer li'l girl want somthin' so bad an' know ya ain't got the means ta git it fer her? Mara talked 'bout it near ev'ry night, tellin' me how she wanted ta play like she was her pa. Wid Bestowal comin', Augie was like a gift o' the Hand. It were wrong, I knows, but me li'l Mara..." He choked back another sob. "Jest onct, I wanted ta give her somthin' want she wanted, steada jest what she needed."

"You bought it for her with the money?"

Wyam shrugged. "Cost me twelve o' the twenty, it did. I used the rest fer a bluegem pendant fer me wife, Lila. She's got a real pretty blue eyes and a grand smile when she's happy. You shoulda seen her when Mara got her horse and then I gived her the gem. Grin'd like ta split wide open. I tell ya, it were the best thing e'er was."

Jamus studied the man for a long time. If he were lying, he was truly talented at it. "Where is your house, Wyam?"

"Eastalley. I gots green shutters on the winnows."

"What you did was wrong, Wyam, but if you're telling me the truth now, I will consider that in my justice. I'm going to your house, as is the custom for the Keeplord on the Day of Bestowal. Stay here. Your word will decide your fate," Jamus said as he left the stable and headed out into the streets.

Despite his being dressed in a rustic green tunic and simple leathern leggings, a number of the villagers recognized him. But, they kept their greetings simple, well aware it was a day when their Lord often walked among them as an equal, keeping the tradition of the day when no man counted himself better than another.

There was a little cottage on Eastalley with green shutters, just as Wyam had said. When Jamus knocked on the door, it was opened by a bright, blue-eyed little girl with flaxen hair and a happy smile. "Welcome, Sur," she said, bowing politely. "'Tis a right pleasure ta have a guest at the door. Would ya like ta come in?"

"Is your mother home, Mara?"

"Mama!" she called inside. "There's a man 'ere what knows me name."

At once, a woman appeared next to her. Her blond hair was tied into a bun, accenting her plain features, but her blue eyes sparkled as much as her daughter's. Around her neck she wore a simple pendant set with a small bluegem. "Sur? Do we know ya? Yer right welcome on this Day."

"I'm told there is a fine young horsewoman here who needs a proper riding dress to wear and a blanket for her steed to ward off the chill of Norwin."

Mara squared her shoulders and lifted her chin in a quite royal manner. "I be the woman," she said, "and Moonbeam sure could use a coat. Ya got one?"

"Well," Jamus said, "I just may, but first I have to see Moonbeam to make sure it will fit."

Lila nodded. "Come in then, Sur, in the spirit of Bestowal."

Jamus stepped in. The cottage was indeed small, with perhaps two rooms. Apparently, Lila and Wyam had their bedroom in a little chamber in the back while Mara's cot was set near the fireplace in the main room. There were a table and some chairs and a sitting couch, as well as two chests of drawers arranged about the room. A counter off to the side provided a place to prepare meals and a cupboard sat near the door. Near Mara's cot stood a beautiful rocky horse carved out of pinewood and colored with silver paint. It had a nice leather saddle and bridle and a long silky mane and tail made of real horsehair. "This be Moonbeam," Mara said proudly. "She looks like Lord Jamus' stallion but she be a girl. Ain't she a looker? Do ya think yer blanket'll fit?"

The toy horse did bear a remarkable likeness to Whim, and by the arch in its neck, Jamus was sure Master Jobin had intended it to be a stallion. But Mara's imagination had its own perception and he had no reason to doubt it. "She is indeed a beauty," he said. "She is decidedly a fine horse for a fine lady." He looked over to Lila. "Madame, if I may, I would like to offer a gift to your daughter."

Lila looked puzzled. "Certain, Sur, but I don't see no bundle. It must be a wee gift."

Jamus smiled now. He raised his hand and gestured slightly. A soft blue blanket trimmed in silver with the name "Moonbeam" embroidered in the back corner covered the toy horse. Then, an elegant riding dress appeared on Mara's bed, complete with a feather trimmed hat and a pair of soft dorrsettskin boots.

Lila gasped. "Yer a Mage."

"I am, Mistress. Now, if I may." He raised his hand to her and in her arms appeared a lovely blue shaenis gown. He gestured towards one of the chairs where a blue man's coat materialized on its back. Then, on the table a feast simply seemed to arrive as if set there by unseen hands. "The Lord of Magiskeep would be pleased to accept the pleasure of your family's company at his table tomorrow for evenmeal."

"Ya speak fer the Lord?" Lila asked.

Jamus smiled. "I am the Lord, Madam."

Lila was about to drop to her knees, when he reached out and took her arm. "No one bows to me, especially not today. I've met your husband and found him to be an honest man. The Keep needs honest men."

She smiled. "'E's a good husband an' a good father, right sure. How come ya knows 'im?"

"I think I'll let him tell you that in his own way," Jamus replied. "I'll be going now. May the Day bring you joy."

Lila extended her hand in farewell. "May the River protect you, Me Lord."

Jamus hesitated. The River had already protected him. Then, Mara, who had run into her parents' room emerged wearing her new dress. "It fits perfect," she cried. "Look, Mama! Ain't I the perfect lady? I can really ride Moonbeam now! Thank ya, Sur. I wish...I wish the River gives ya ev'ry dream."

Dreams, where the River flowed. He nodded to Mara. "Thank you, my lady. May you ride well."

On the way back to the stables, Mara's words rang in his head. To her, to her mother, the River was a blessing. How could he see it as a curse? Their pleasure in his Magic and his satisfaction in giving it were immeasurable. Perhaps it was all simply a matter of perspective. As a child, he had heard his Power called a gift. How had he strayed so far from the person he once was? It was time to remember.

"Me Lord?" Wyam asked, interrupting his thoughts. "Didja see me Mara and Lila? Ain't they the prettiest ya e'er laid eyes on?"

"You're a lucky man, Wyam."

"I ain't so. Not after what I done. Ya promise me ya'll take 'em under yer care, won't ya? If'en I gots ta pay fer what I done, it ain't fair they gotta pay too."

"They won't pay, Wyam, nor will you beyond your own guilt. This is the Day of Bestowal, and I am blessed with the power to gift as I choose. To you, Sur, I bestow mercy and a promise. As long as you uphold a promise in return to me, you and your family will have the gift of my Magic. If ever you have want, you are welcome to come to me. There's no more reason for you to make bargains with dishonest men to answer your daughter's dreams," Jamus said.

"Me Lord, why? I done a real bad thing."

"Love drives men to foolish deeds, Wyam, and a mistake is no reason to ruin a family. I'm not a vindictive man. Unlike you, I have the Power to choose my way in this world with neither need nor want. Forgiveness is a simple gift for me to give. Take it and learn its lesson," Jamus replied, and as he did, he realized he had answered some of his own questions as well. It was time to accept at least one small part of the Magic. "Go home, Wyam. I'll send one of the men from my stable to tend things here until Master Tam returns. You need to be with your wife and child today."

He left the stunned Wyam and headed back to the Keep. There were still more promises to make.
*****

Windchange, and with Weswin, Jamus rose from his chair in the Great Hall and stretched. Sarn had left a span before, while Jamus still had a half dozen people waiting. But at last, for the first time since Sowin's turn, there were no petitioners in the door. There was also a pile of gifts at his feet. "I don't know why people feel they have to bring me things," he said, holding up a handmade quilt a woman from the village had given him. "I enjoy doing things for them."

Salene caressed a lovely carved falcon one of the craftsmen had give her in exchange for a simple Healing of a sore shoulder. "It is the Day of Bestowal, Jamus. I don't know that the rules say we're the only ones who can give gifts. Besides, it makes people feel good."

"I really don't need anything," he sighed, "when Magic offers me more than I need."

She laughed and held up the falcon. "Will you never learn? Could your Magic carve this? How many times have you said Magic is no replacement for the treasures of the heart?"

"It just seems so wrong for me to accept something like this from a woman who has to labor all day just to keep her family fed," he replied, showing her the quilt. "Look at these stitches. They're so fine and perfect. She must have taken Sevenstins to make this."

"And that's exactly why she gave it to you, My Love. It's her small way of expressing her love and appreciation for her Lord. You're very special to these people, Jamus, whether you want to believe it or not."

"Sometimes I wish…" he began. Then he shook his head. "Well, it's better than being pursued by the River, I suppose. It is a beautiful quilt."

"Perfect for our bed. Shall we go try it out?" she teased.

"Later," he answered. "I still have one more gift to bestow."

*****

Jebe was in the stable, finishing up the Weswin chores. He and his mother were packed and ready to go, but he had insisted on spending the better part of the day in the barns, caring for the horses and talking to Josep and Joss.

Now, as he filled Shimmer's water bucket, he let the little colt nuzzle his shoulder. "You're gonna have to be a good lad, Shim. No annoying Master Josep with your pranks. He really likes you, you know, but he worries all the time that you're gonna do something to hurt yourself."

Shimmer good for Jebe.

"I know you're good for me, but you have to be good for Josep and Jamus too. I'm going away and they're going to take care of you from now on."

Want you.

"I'm going away, Shim. I have to. Lord Delran's gonna give my Mam a grand place to live and I'm gonna be a Master myself. You have to stay here." He buried his face in Shimmer's glistening neck and hugged the colt with all his might.

Jamus had come into the aisle a moment before. Now, he moved over to the stall. "Jebe?"

Jebe looked up, his eyes red. "My Lord? I'm almost done here. Did you need something?"

"I was thinking, Jebe. A Horsemaster and Beasttalker like you needs more than a plain brown mare. Sky is a lovely mount for you now, but when you get older, you'll need a horse to mark your station. It occurred to me, that Shimmer here needs a proper master of his own. Do you think you might be willing to take him with you when you go to Lord Delran's? I wouldn't worry about him if he were with you."

Jebe's eyes widened as his mouth dropped in surprise. "Shimmer with me? You mean it?"

"You'll have your work cut out for you, Jebe. It's not easy training a young horse, especially one as clever as he is. But, if you succeed, there'll be no other horse in Turan like him."

"'Cept Whim," Jebe replied, grinning.

"Not even Whim," Jamus answered. "And that's because Shimmer will be your horse."

"Aye, My Lord, mine." Jebe said, stroking Shimmer's neck as the little horse shoved him with his head, trying to find surlep candies in his pockets.

Jamus had given the last gift of the day.

It was more than enough.

*****

The golden light glowed softly in the darkness. From its heart, a figure gradually formed, her arms outstretched, her hands raised in supplication. "Come to me, my son."

"No," Jamus replied, his voice calm, "I'm not ready to be yours."

"Why do you flee? I am everywhere."

"I'm not running anymore. It's just not time."

"You will come, then?"

"Later, when the riddles of my life have answers. Until then, you will have to wait my call."

"So easy. You need but whisper."

"You will wait."

The light faded.

"Jamus? Are you dreaming again?"

"Nothing," Jamus replied. "It's all right. I understand now."

"She was after you?"

"She is me, Salene. At least a part of me. I kept running, thinking I could get away, but you see, it's impossible for a man to escape himself. The River is my blood. One day, the two of us will be one. For now, though, we've reached an understanding."

"I don't want to lose you."

"You won't," he answered, taking her into his arms. "Not for a long, long time."

This time, the Dragon smiled, then dropped its head and fell back asleep.

*****

Alone in his room, Sarn tried one more time to sift the thread of Jamus' weave. It was all a hopeless jumble. He sighed and pulled the covers up under his chin.

He'd simply have to wait. The Lord of Magiskeep could not possibly live forever.

Cave of Shadows

Chapter 1

Lord Sarkem's Keep, Greenhope, lay some ten winds to the south of Magiskeep's palace in the grasslands bordering the Great Wastes. Using the area's somewhat warmer climate, the Lord had carved out an agricultural empire supplying many of the kingdom's smaller keeps, as well as the main Keep and villages, with fresh produce during the greater part of the circle.

Many claimed his gardens were enhanced by Magic, but the truth was hard work, sweat, and an enormous amount of study and knowledge were the real charms to his success. He had taken circles of cross breeding and grafting to invent new strains of fruits and vegetables well-suited to his soils and growing seasons. Sweet surleps flourished in his orchards along with cherries, pears, solfruit, and caliberries. Corn, balbeans, tomerats, peppers, onions, greenings, and taroots filled his fields, growing full-flavored in the sunshine of warm Sowins. He prided himself on growing the best of every known variety and was never afraid to experiment with new ones.

Now, he had planned a new field of sweetling corn in some of his farther acreage. The problem was water was scant and for a good crop the land needed better irrigation. So he had petitioned the Master of Magiskeep to allow him to divert one branch of a healthy stream bordering his Keep in order to use its water in his furrows.

He had visited Lord Jamus to make his request, but the Master had delayed a decision on the plea until he himself was able to survey the land in question. Now, as he had promised, Jamus was making a visit to Sarkem's Keep. The message had come by way of a red message bird and Sarkem had immediately begun to prepare.

Greenhope's main house was more practical than elegant, constructed mostly of wood with many levels in order to facilitate air circulation in the warmer clime. Furnishings were simple yet comfortable with plenty of chairs and couches so people could sit and relax in nearly every room to take advantage of every direction a breeze might take. Lady Delise kept her home filled with flowers, freshening tasteful bouquets every day. She had an extensive flower garden of her own and a large greenroom so that even when the

winds chilled her outdoor beds, she could still smell the soft
fragrance of lollies, dailies, roses, and purplets whenever she wished.

To honor her guests, she took special care to air and prepare
the grand guestroom on the second floor. On the large mantel above
the white marble fireplace, she set an arrangement of peach and
yellow lollies to complement the pale beige comforter and linens of
the chamber. She hung new drapes on the huge double-windowed
door which opened out onto an expansive balcony overlooking her
flower garden. Then she had her servants move chairs and a table
there in case the Lord and Lady wished to sit out in the sunshine.

"Everything's ready, my dear," she told Sarkem when he
came in from his fields. "I'm sure Lord Jamus and Lady Salene will
be comfortable here. I've prepared two other rooms as well for any
attendants they might bring."

Sarkem laughed. "I doubt the Lord will bring servants. You
know him as well as I do. Do you really think he'll come attended?"

Delise smiled back at her husband. "Friends, perhaps, but no
servants certainly. The Lord is the most unassuming man I've ever
met and his wife is at least as modest. I'd imagine they won't even
want our servants to wait on them while they're here. Still, I've told
everyone to treat them with honor and respect. They are, after all,
patrons to this land."

"Aye, and I'm hoping the Lord sees it as I do. If he refuses
to let me divert that stream, I'll lose all my hope of my new corn."
Sarkem raked his fingers through his dark, silver-laced hair. "He's a
hard man to read. It's as if he guards his thoughts when you talk to
him, never revealing a hint of more than exactly what he wants you
to know. And yet, I never have the feeling he's being anything but
completely honest. It's just as if there is another person inside him
working through whatever problem he's facing at exactly the same
time."

"He must have a great deal on his mind," Delise said as she
rearranged one of her bouquets to balance the colors. "To think of
being responsible for all those Mages and mortals at the same time
with Magic ever a temptation. Why, how many times have you told
me how hard it is sometimes to keep yourself from simply chanting
one of your precious plants instead of letting it grow naturally to see
how it turns out? And you have perhaps a tenth of the Magic he
holds. Can you even imagine how hard it must be for him?"

"He's bound by Rule and Vow more than any man I've ever
known, My Dear. While I'm sure obeying those precepts must be
hard, I could never even imagine his breaking them without good

cause. Magiskeep is lucky to have him as its Lord, and the River is blessed he's its Master."

Delise untied the gardening apron from her slender waist and folded it neatly. "You sound as if you worship him yourself, husband. I didn't know you were so in awe of the man."

"I'm in awe of all he represents, My Love. And I am always in awe of a man of principle. Come; let's see if our watchers have any word yet. By my reckoning, the Lord and Lady should be here within the span."

Together, husband and wife walked down the broad wooden staircase of their elegant country estate. Though large, the house was simply designed with natural woodwork and plain cream-colored walls of plaster. The couple preferred practicality over pretense, furnishing room after room with neutral tones of browns and blues, letting Delise's flowers bring color and beauty to each setting. Earthstone fireplaces and exposed wooden beams leant an almost rustic air to the place while wide latticed doors and windows invited the outside air and sunshine into every corner. This far South of Magiskeep proper, the seasons brought far less change, and through most of the Circle it was easy to enjoy the weather either outside or under the great house's slate roofs.

The weather favored the outdoors for nearly the full circle. Even Chillmonths were sunny and warm enough for midmeals outdoors and green fields of hardy crops.

And so it was that Sarkem was able to foster crops of all sorts of vegetables, using the cooler months to harvest greenings and root bulbs while his Warmmonth crops lay dormant. He was the prime supplier of grain to the Keep's villages and farms. His were the oats and hay nourishing the main Keep's herds of horses and he took pride in offering only the best to his customers.

In a word, Sarkem was a farmer, born and bred to the land. Seeing a small sprout poke its head through the tilled earth delighted him beyond measure, and he thrived on the scent of wet dirt after a precious rain. But he loved to experiment as well, and the new corn field was his latest venture. "If I can just get the water to it," he said, "I'm sure this crop will bring new meaning to sweet. Just think of it, Delise. Why, we can make all kinds of tasties to please the children."

"Corn candies?" Delise asked teasingly.

Sarkem chewed his lip thoughtfully. "Indeed, an interesting idea, my dear. Do you think you could come up with a recipe?"

Delise laughed as she often did at her husband's fertile inventiveness. "If you want a recipe, Sarkem, then I shall create one." Her dark eyes twinkled mischievously. "Pink, perhaps, shaped like little hearts?"

"Pink?!" Sarkem gasped, caught by her joke. "Pink? What in the name of Sorem are you thinking, woman? Pink corn candies? Little boys won't even look twice at them."

"Who said I'd make them for little boys?" Delise teased, pretending to be serious. "The last thing little boys need are sweets. Now little girls?"

"My dear, if you had a little boy you'd think again." Sarkem broke off quickly before he finished the sentence. His face fell, stricken by what he had almost said. He clutched his wife's hands in supplication and drew her close. "Please, my love, forgive me. I didn't mean to even mention such a thing."

Delise shook her head, trying to keep her tears back. "I know, I know. But, we can't pretend it doesn't matter all the time, my love. How hard it is to want a child so much and yet to have no hope of ever having one."

"We can still hope, Delise. No one has ever said it would be impossible."

"I've lost one baby already, My Lord. To think of losing another just to fulfill our hope is too dreadful a thing to even consider. I dare not dream."

Sarkem nodded, remembering too well the agonizing grief of watching his only child, a tiny baby boy, gasping for air as he died in his mother's arms a few minutes after his far too early birth. The Healer could do nothing, even with Magic flowing from his fingers in visible, desperate streaks of Compassion. It was as if the River itself had chosen to deny the couple the one thing in the world they both longed for more than anything else.

And indeed, according to Delise, it had, for she was totally convinced her very life was under a curse driven by the River's dark intent. Though Sarkem had tried again and again to convince her otherwise, she refused to share his bed out of her fear. "There is nothing wrong in dreaming, My Love," he said now. "Perhaps Jorl has changed his mind about it?"

Delise shook her head. "Our Healer still believes in the curse. He tells me I dare not risk another pregnancy as long as the waterfall blocks the sunlight from that cave. The darkness within denies me life within my body."

Sarkem held back a sigh. Her words made Jamus' visit all the more important. If there was any way to divert the stream so it would both water his fields and change its bed near the granite rocks where the cave lay, he was more than ready to do it. But, he would have to be careful. The Lord of Magiskeep was not likely to act based on one woman's superstitions or one husband's desire. "And how does our Healer know this great truth, Delise? Eldenlore? The tales of old women at their looms?"

"Jorl is a wise man, Sarkem. Don't mock him. He is Keepbred."

"Being Keepbred doesn't give a man common sense. He was there in ages past, long before Lord Jamus was Master. It stands to reason there is much he has never learned."

"Then you think Lord Jamus might have some knowledge of the curse Jorl doesn't have?" Delise asked hopefully.

"He is the Rivermaster," Sarkem replied, kissing her lightly on her cheek.

For the first time in Sevenstins, Delise eyes sparked with anticipation. "I would so love to use our bed again."

"Not more than I," Sarkem said, shaking his head and pulling her into his embrace.

But Delise stiffened, and after a moment, he had to let her go. "I'm sorry," she whispered hoarsely. "Not yet. Not now. Not until the sunlight breaks through."

Sarkem took a deep breath to steady himself. Then, he simply nodded and turned away. One way or another, he would find a way to divert that water.

Until then, Greenhope's halls would remain empty of children's laughter and two longing lovers dared not even share a bed.

****

Jamus and Salene had left Magiskeep on horseback with first light. Because they had spent so much time apart in the last month, they chose to ride naturally for at least the first two full winds of the journey, saving lifted travel for Weswin's turn when darkness would overtake them.

The morning had been sunny and warm, unusually so for so early in the Newseason. The horses were delighted to be out, heading in a new direction away from the Keep, as ready for adventure as children on a jaunt to Silver Lake. Whim pranced along the trail for the first span, jouncing Jamus about with every stride while his master simply laughed at his energy and let his tall body relax in perfect balance with the stallion's capers. Flax, far more mindful of her mistress, simply lengthened her generous walking stride to keep up with her trail mate and saved a few jogging steps for starting at flutterbys and the one or two duskits bouncing across their path in search of tender sprouts.

"I'm still not comfortable about your leaving Sarn in charge again while we're gone," Salene said as they reined their mounts to a halt by a little stream for a drink. "After what happened while you were at Lord Delran's, I should think you'd have second thoughts about it."

Jamus shrugged. "He's still under my weave, Salene. He certainly can't do any damage with his Magic while we're gone."

"As I recall, a good part of the damage he did last time had little to do directly with his Magic," she countered. "Perhaps you should have chanted his personality as well."

He laughed now. "You said yourself Sarn and his Magic are one being. The man is nothing without his Power. Forcing him to use his Art only with pure purpose should be more than enough to keep him in check. Besides, I won't be so far away this time. Joria or Sarena will send a callbird if things go awry."

"I still would have felt better if Simen were there."

"Jebe and his mother needed an escort to Delran's," Jamus explained patiently, even though he had told her all this before. "Besides, this will be a good lesson for Sarn. He's never had his Magic controlled before. I expect he's going to learn a great deal about doing things for himself for a change."

"So, you left him in charge to learn a lesson at the expense of everyone else in Magiskeep? Why does he matter so much? I've never seen any love lost between the two of you."

"Sarn has the potential to be the strongest Mage in the Keep," Jamus replied as Whim dropped his head to the water and took another long drink. "Someday, when Magic needs a defender, he needs to be ready."

"Why? You're the Rivermaster."

Jamus lowered his gaze to the water, diverting his eyes so he did not have to meet hers as he answered, "There will come a day when I will not be given the choice of defending Magiskeep, Salene. When the Darkness rises, the Rivermaster must love Turan first and all else after."

"Including me," Salene said softly. "You'll be the River's then, won't you…no longer mine."

He nodded sorrowfully. "It's Magic's Way, not mine. Salene, if I had a choice…," his voice trailed off.

Salene struggled to keep her composure. "I know it will happen one day, My Love. By then, perhaps I'll be ready - resigned to my fate. Not now, though. We have time. Surely we have time."

"As long as the Dragon sleeps we have all the time in the world."

Whim took that moment to begin pawing playfully in the water, cascading great splashes up onto his belly and his rider.

"By the Blood," Jamus gasped as a slap of icy liquid hit him in the face. "He's trying to drown me." The horse pawed all the more furiously, catching Salene and Flax as well in his game.

The golden mare snorted indignantly and sidestepped out of the water. Salene laughed as she brushed a wet lock of hair from her forehead. "A good thing it's not a mud puddle, my dear. All you are is soaking wet. The sun will soon dry you off."

Jamus tugged at the stallion's reins and the great silver horse reluctantly pulled up his head and turned away from the grassy bank. "He did that once to me in the dead of Chillmonth. Bless the Hand for Magic that day. Otherwise I would have been an ice block by the time I got back to the fireside to dry myself." Whim tossed his head and snorted as if laughing at his own prank. Then he let Jamus steer him back to the trail and this time stretched out into a contented walk to continue the journey to Greenhope.

They chatted of memories then, recalling all sorts of small adventures they had shared, laughing at foolish mistakes and trying to find excuses for them. To Salene, it was the perfect ride, a chance to have Jamus all to herself without worrying about either Magic or title. He was now only her husband, the man she loved.

To Jamus, the journey was a pleasant escape from those same forces. It had been as if Magic had been trying for so long to keep him and Salene apart that to be free of it, even for the few spans of this trip, was more satisfying than he had ever expected. The soft breeze of Easwin rustled in the brellums along the trail, whispering nothing of consequence, as if even nature knew this was time to leave the Rivermaster in peace. "I'd forgotten," he said quietly, "how beautiful being alone with you could be."

Salene started at his remark, frowning slightly before answering. "Has it been that long?"

"Longer than it ever should have been," Jamus replied. "Something always seems to interfere in our time together. Now, it's so quiet, I can hardly believe it."

Salene brushed back a lock of her golden hair and smiled at him. "Then I should take the opportunity and use it well. I wish I could think of something clever to say right now. It seems the perfect moment."

"Tell me a dream," he said.

"What?"

"A dream—one of yours. We're always talking about mine … at least every time the River taunts me with one. We never talk about yours. What do you dream about, my Love?"

"Days like this, I think," she answered thoughtfully. Then she added, almost shyly, "And a family."

He started now, more surprised at his reaction than to her words. A family. Children of their own. Something he was ashamed to admit he had hardly considered in all their time together. Surely Salene had mentioned it before and he knew as soon as she mentioned it now how much it mattered to him. He'd always loved the children of the Keep, taking them into his own care as if somehow he could make up for losing his own childhood by assuring them theirs. But a daughter of his own? Why hadn't he thought about it more? There'd been no reason not to. It was a perfectly natural wish and one of the reasons for getting married in the first place. And yet, something had denied him the pleasure of such a dream. Something dark and obscuring had kept those thoughts from his head, filling him more with the moments of now or the future of Circle's End rather than all that might happen in between. "Do you just want a girl?" he asked at last.

"One of each, don't you think?" Salene replied, as if she hadn't even noticed how long it had taken him to answer.

The truth was it hadn't taken long at all. Jamus' thoughts had soared through his brain as quickly as the River itself flowed to his hand. What seemed an eternity of reflection had passed in an instant, and Salene was none the wiser about his insensitivity. "Two at least," he agreed quickly. "A boy for me to teach to ride and a girl to spoil silly. I mean, isn't that what fathers are supposed to do for girls?"

This time, it was Salene whose mind raced. Sagari had certainly never spoiled her, and she suddenly realized neither she nor Jamus had any idea at all as to what a proper childhood should be. To all intents and purposes, both of them might as well have been orphans. "I don't know, Jamus…" she faltered now, the charm of the conversation paling in harsh reality. "How would I know?"

He nudged Whim closer to Flax and took the golden mare's bridle in his hand, guiding her to a stop. Then, he reached out and gently gripped Salene's arm. "We can learn, Salene. It isn't as if there's no one in Magiskeep to teach us. Becca, Josep, good people, people who know how to love children as they ought to be loved."

"It's not fair," she said, choking back her tears. "I love you so much and yet the thought of being a mother to your children scares me. It's wrong, Jamus. It's wrong. You, more than anyone I know, deserve better."

"There is nothing better," he answered, leaning over to kiss her softly. "Don't you think every couple worries about it? Children are such a precious, fragile treasure, my Love. Living, breathing beings with needs and wants all of their own. If raising them were easy, then there'd be no Sagaris or Sarns in the world."

She shivered slightly. "Ugh. To think of having a son like Sarn."

"With you as a mother, that could never happen," he assured her. "You wouldn't let a boy grow up not understanding how to care about others."

"How can you be so sure?"

"The River blessed you with a heart, Salene, and Compassion never fails its children."

"So that's why you married me, eh," she answered lightly, trying to recapture the easy pleasure of the ride.

"I married you," he said, "because I have never loved anything in this world more than I love you."

For now, it was more than enough for the both of them.

Chapter 2

Sunlight faded into the first breath of Weswin, and as Sarkem had predicted, his guards spotted two riders cresting the hill to the north in the lengthening shadows. As soon as the call sounded in the valley, servants hurried to the dining room of Greenhope with laden platters and pitchers of fresh calidew, setting a festive table for master and guests.

Sarkem's head groom, Dom, checked his awe at Whim's appearance, and took the silver stallion's reins from Jamus with confidence. Sarkem had tried to explain about the horse, but words had hardly prepared the stableman for reality. At nearly eighteen hands, Whim was an imposing presence, and far more magnificent than any horse Dom had ever seen. Still, from the moment he took hold of the bridle, he knew he would have no trouble caring for the animal. The stallion obeyed his slightest direction and behaved with impeccable manners.

"He has some, ah, peculiar habits," Jamus said, stroking Whim's neck, "but he's usually on his best behavior when we're visiting. If you keep his manger full of good hay, he should be fine. If, though…he does happen to get out of his stall, just let me know. I don't want him causing any trouble while he's here."

"Oh, 'e won't git out, ne'er you fear, me lord," Dom assured him confidently. "We has good double latches on the doors. Lessen somethin' gives way, 'e'll stay put, 'e will."

Jamus nodded and gave Whim a warning stare. "Good, Sur. Then there should be no difficulty then. None at all." Whim lowered his head as if in agreement and let the man lead him away.

Lord Sarkem hurried down the stone walkway to the yard, his arms wide in greeting. "Lord Jamus, Lady Salene, what a pleasure to have you here. I told Delise you'd be here by Weswin. I knew you'd want to be off the trails before dark."

"We lifted only the last few strides," Jamus explained. "It was such a beautiful day we just enjoyed the rest of the ride." He offered his hand in greeting. "I'm honored to be so welcome here, my Lord."

Sarkem grinned. Nearly as tall as Jamus, he met the other man's gaze with warm sincerity. "Thank you, my Lord. My wife and I are delighted to have you and Lady Salene here at last. It's a chance to repay some of the hospitality you've shown us."

"Oh," Salene laughed, "so you want me in your kitchen, do you? It seems to me the last time you visited us, you ended up playing the servant."

"And loving every minute of it," Sarkem answered quickly. "Delise has talked about it nearly every day since we left. Our cook, Lydia, has had the devil of a time keeping her out of the kitchen. She seems bound and determined to cook evenmeal for our entire keep at least once a Sevenstin though Lydia will have none of it. I'm hoping your visit will temper her desire just a bit."

Salene shook her head. "Far be it from me to discourage a Lady from soiling her hands in common labor. Both Jamus and I believe status is in name only, not deeds. If Lady Delise wants to scrub pots, I'll be more than happy to join her myself."

Sarkem groaned. "Now I've two of them in my house! The Hand preserve me. Lord Jamus, please don't tell me you want to clean my stables while you're here."

Jamus flexed his arm experimentally. "I could use a bit of manual exercise, My Lord." Then he noted Sarkem's stricken look and grinned. "Then again, I would prefer good field dirt under my feet instead of manure this trip. I am extremely interested in this new strain of corn you're planning to cultivate."

Sarkem sighed with obvious relief. "We can ride out to see it at Easwin's turn after the ladies have filled our bellies with food. Come on, now, the both of you. Spend at least this night with my wife and me as proper lords and ladies should. Lydia and her fellows have prepared a fine evenmeal for us all and fully intend to serve it most formally. I think we should humor her, don't you?"

Lady Delise greeted her guests in the main entry hall, her dark hair and eyes shining above the demure neckline of a pale yellow gown perfectly fitted to her slender body. She curtsied formally, extending her hand in an equally formal greeting. "My Lord, My Lady, welcome to Greenhope. May your stay be a pleasure for us all."

Salene stepped forward, took Delise's hand and urged the other woman to her feet. "I am honored by your greeting, My Lady, but I hope it's the last formality between us while we're here. You and I have stood together up to our elbows in flour. I should think the friendship we entered that day will last longer than the bread we baked."

"I should hope so," Delise replied, smiling. "The bread was gone in less than a span. I've never seen so many hungry youngsters. You'd think they hadn't eaten in days."

Salene laughed as she pulled off her riding gloves and tucked them into the pockets of her riding skirt. "They'd cooked for themselves for at least that long, I'm afraid. I'm not at all sure they had eaten anything worth remembering."

"The kitchen was a mess," Delise agreed. She gestured towards the dining room door and walked beside Salene as they made their way across the hall. "From the looks of it, you may be right. There was more ruined food on the floor and counters than in their bellies. Did you ever find out what that concoction spilled all over the oven was supposed to be?"

"Corn bread," Salene replied. "Except one of the more ambitious children had invented the recipe using green corn instead of meal. She'd added milk and eggs with several scoops of sweetsop, trying to make it more like a cake. I'm not sure what the finished product looked like, but considering the slop in the oven, I'd say she ended up with a pan of rather interesting soup."

"Did she eat it?"

"Poor dear had enough to give herself a bellyache. Sarena told me she and about a dozen other youngsters ended up in her chambers by Norwin. It wasn't a pretty sight."

"Poor little ones," Delise replied. "They're lucky they have someone as kind as Mistress Sarena to care for them."

"Sarena is a wonder with the children," Salene agreed. "At times I really envy her."

Delise offered her guests a tray of small appetizer pastries filled with tender meats and cheese. "You surprise me, Mistress. I've seen you in the Keep. The children worship you."

"Worship is not quite what I'd like," Salene sighed. "They talk to Sarena, tell her secrets, and ask her advice. She's their friend, not their Mistress as I am. I just don't have her talent with children."

"Nonsense," Jamus interrupted. "You just don't have the opportunity she has. Seven Arts status doesn't offer much contact with the younger children, that's all. If you had a PrePrentice class of your own you'd understand."

"I'd fumble all over myself, tongue tied and helpless," Salene replied. "Sometimes I really worry about what I'll do when I have a child of my own, if I'm so incompetent with others' children."

Delise put down the tray and paused for a moment, her eyes unfocused as she thought of her own empty life. "Don't you think the Hand blesses mothers with enough love to make up for incompetence, My Lady? It seems to me if you have love the rest will follow."

"I do hope so, Delise," Salene answered. She pulled a chair away from the table and sat wearily, as if the turn in the conversation had somehow drained the energy from her. "It's a big responsibility."

Delise sighed. "And one I long for, Madame. Sarkem and I have been married for nearly four circles now and we've yet to start a family."

"Now, now, My Love," Sarkem said quickly, moving to Delise's side and pulling out a chair for her as well. "It will happen soon enough. Jorl has told us we just have to be patient."

"Jorl?" Jamus asked. "Is he your Healer? I seem to remember that name from the Keep."

"He is indeed," Sarkem answered, "and as fine as man as you'd ever want to meet. When Delise lost our first baby, he took such good care of her I hardly saw a tear. He said then it was the River's Will sometimes for such things to happen."

"He was wrong," Delise said quietly. "It was my fault. I never should have gone to the waterfall. You know it cursed me."

"Foolish superstition," Sarkem chided. "We had a picnic, nothing more. It was pure coincidence. The waterfall had nothing at all to do with it."

Delise shook her head. "Jorl knows of the cave's secrets. He told me the trip cursed our baby, Sarkem, and you know it as well as I do. I've been barren ever since."

"Now Delise."

"You know it, Sur. Don't tell me you don't believe it as well as I do!" Delise said a bit too loudly, slamming her palm down on the table for emphasis, setting the silver rattling.

Jamus grabbed for one of the flower vases, catching it an instant before it toppled over on to the linen cloth, as his hostess stopped in wide eyed horror at her own outburst.

"Please, darling," Sarkem pleaded, "don't do this again. I thought we'd settled the matter long ago."

"It's not," Delise fumbled for words. "It's just... Oh, I am so sorry. I don't know why I should have said anything"

"It's my fault," Salene cut in quickly. "I'm the one who mentioned children. I had no idea it would upset you so. Please forgive me for bringing up such a sensitive subject."

Jamus hid any reaction to Salene's apology, acting as if nothing at all unusual had happened. "Have you ever noticed how easy it is to open our hearts among friends? I count us all lucky to carry no shame for anything we say or do when we're with those we love."

Delise gulped and simply stared at him. Sarkem moved over and took her trembling hand in his. "We've wept ourselves dry over this, My Lord. There's no reason to mention it again."

"I've told you before, Sarkem, there's no need of formality between us." Then, Jamus sat down across from Delise and added softly, "If you want to tell me more, please don't be afraid. I've never met a person in my life who doesn't deserve to be heard. Perhaps there's something I or Salene could do to help?"

Delise's fingers closed tightly on her husband's hand. When he nodded, she said, "I lost our baby two seasons, nearly three seasons past. It was but a Sevenstin since Sarkem and I had taken a trip to the waterfall. I didn't know it then, but there is a tale of Eldenlore telling how the caves behind the falls are chanted with an ancient curse, promising death to follow in the footsteps of those who tread their rocks. There is a lovely little path there and it was such a hot day…near the end of last Fullmonth, you know, so I coaxed Sarkem to walk with me there, behind the falls where the mist was cool and sweet." She paused again, collecting her thoughts. "I remember the water hitting my face, like a cold kiss on my cheek- -the kiss of death."

"Delise, please," Sarkem pleaded gently. "You don't have to say anything more."

"But I must," Delise said, her voice hoarse with unspent tears. "Not speaking of it doesn't change the fact. Do you think by keeping silence we might somehow alter the dreadful truth? I killed our child, Sarkem. My foolish desire to walk in the Cave of Secrets murdered our baby!" The tears flowed now as she wept, dropping her head in her hands.

Jamus shook his head. "The River does not grant curses like that," he said. "I've never heard of such Magic."

"Listen to him," Sarkem said, gently placing his own hand's on his wife's gently prying her fingers from her cheeks. "Do you hear the Rivermaster? There is no curse."

Delise shook her head. "He's wrong. The Elds spoke of the cave and even Jorl told me it was so. He said there could be no other reason for me to lose the child."

"There are hundreds of reasons," Salene broke in. "While having a child is the most natural thing in the world, it's also far more complex than most people realize. The Hand does not always bless a conception with a baby, My Lady."

"I am cursed," Delise insisted. "I can't have any more children."

"I don't know much about Jorl," Salene said, "so I will not condemn his judgment, but I would be more than willing to Touch you myself to see if that's true. I've known many a woman who has lost her first babe who has gone on to mother many more."

"You'd grace us with your Gift?" Sarkem asked, holding Delise's hands tightly as if he was afraid she might simply vanish from him if he let go.

"I consider it my duty," Salene answered. "If the Mistress of Magiskeep cannot serve her people, then she is a poor helpmate to her Lord. Tomorrow, I will do all I can to help you, My Lady."

"And I," Jamus said, "intend to find out all I can about this cave of yours. If there is any hint of truth at all to the Eldenlore surrounding it, then I can't ignore it."

Sarkem shrugged. "I don't hold with such nonsense myself, but I see no harm in investigating. Besides, the stream I've told you about is fed in part by the falls. You might want to see them anyhow."

"Tomorrow then," Jamus agreed.

A servant entered just then, carrying a tray of hot food. Delise, somewhat consoled by Salene's promise, rose and gestured to the table. Soon, the party settled in for the feast and talk turned to more pleasant subjects.

While the Cave of Secrets was not forgotten, its presence quickly faded into the background, where it lingered, waiting in the shadows.

****

Jorl stirred another of his herbal brews as he sang an old folktune, struggling to remember the exact words. "Mist on the meadow, covered with dew. Where came the flowers of every hue." He grimaced. "Blood of the Masters," he muttered, "that can't be right. Why can't I remember the cursed words? Was it really that long ago?"

A hundred circles? More? How many winds had passed since he'd crossed through the mist and given his life to the Darkness? Had he already given his life? He remembered that as badly as he remembered the words to the song.

He was a sorcerer of the True River, not a minion of the Shadows. Didn't he see his reflection in the mirror every Easwin?

Yet who was to say what was reflection and what reality? He had wandered the mirrored way too many times to believe any of it anymore. Somewhere along one of those deceptive corridors, the madness had overtaken him, stripping him of reason and logical perception. He'd lost his sense of direction and found himself trapped in a mirrored room where each vision reflected back upon itself in endless repetition.

He remembered screaming, but not much more. The rest was a blur.

When he was silent again, he'd found himself in the cave behind the waterfall, lying on a pile of leaves set there by unseen hands.

"Darker darkness is thy pay, seeker of the Mirrored Way," the voice had said. He remembered those words vividly.

"Who are you? Where am I?"

"Where you do not wish to be, safety where you cannot see. Keeper of the dark am I, from my realm you cannot fly. Everendings ever be, unaware, you seeketh me."

"I traveled the Way of Mirrors, not your realm. I am a magician of the River."

"Many rivers waters pour. You have found the last of four. Now you touch the waters here, soul of darkness, black as fear. Shadow all that's left of you, Everendings Will you do. Better life within the dim, than eterne upon the brim, caught between thy final breath and the quiet peace of death."

"What are you saying? If you intend to kill me, then do it," Jorl had shouted into the darkest corner of the cave, his voice shivering along with his body.

"Live or die, it matters not. You are not the prey I sought. Find me soul of purity, sacrifice it unto me. Blood I seek then of one more, Master of the Rivers Four. He is still yet unaware of the destiny he'll dare. Lead his path unto my door; yours shall be life evermore."

"Why do you speak in riddles?" Jorl said, struggling to keep his composure.

"Riddles are the Magic's way, in the dark and in the day. Everendings ever be, no more shall I tell to thee."

With that, the sunlight had suddenly streamed into the cave as if some great barrier had been lifted from the opening behind the falls. Without thinking beyond the moment, Jorl had pushed his way out into the fresh air of Easwin. What day it was and how long he had been lost didn't matter so long as he was free from reflection and shadow.

But was he free?

The dark words haunted him night after night, turning dreams into horrible nightmares.

Then, he had discovered Delise's pregnancy, and on impulse had mentioned the beauty of the waterfall and the peaceful coolness of the cave.

She and Sarkem had gone there.

The child aborted soon after, the first sacrifice to the Shadows.

For Jorl, with all his herbs and potions, the first part of the bargain had been easy.

Then, he had planted the seed of rumor in Delise's ear, suggesting the cave itself had been the fault instead of his "healing" brew.

The rest he had left up to fate and a few more clever suggestions - intimating perhaps Sarkem need Jamus' approval before diverting the stream to irrigate his crops.

Now, at last, with the Rivermaster in Sarkem's Keep, the rest of the bargain seemed ready to be played out. Jorl was sure the Darkness itself had had a hand in bringing all the right elements together, but it really didn't matter to him. His prize, "life evermore," was too great a treasure to care how it came to be.

****

"I need to talk to Jorl," Salene told Jamus as they prepared for bed. Delise's dinner had diverted the conversation from the painful topic of her lost child, but the thought of it had never left Salene's mind. "It's rare a Keep trained Healer would lose a baby under his care, you know. There's usually something that can be done."

Jamus nodded as he pulled off his tunic and laid it on a chair. "It seems strange to me too. And all the talk of a curse from a Keep Magician is just as bothersome. I won't deny the possibility of such a thing, but you'd think he would have investigated himself instead of spreading more rumors about. It's strange - his name seems somehow familiar, but I just can't seem to place it."

"He could be ancient, my Love. There were Magicians even before Sagari, you know." Salene laughed. "The circle did not begin at his Mastery."

"I just never thought much about it before," Jamus replied. "I know plenty of Magicians left Magiskeep and traveled to Turan, but it just seems strange to think of any I've never met still here in my kingdom. This hold is not remote enough to warrant solitude. Surely he'd still have ties back to the Keep, or even an occasional need to consult one of his former masters."

"Unless he left on less than perfect terms," Salene said.

Jamus considered this for a moment before replying. "Joria is one of the eldest Mages in Magiskeep. If I could talk to her about it, she might remember something. I could go back by the Way and ask her. I'd be there and back before Sarkem or his lady even noticed."

"Is it really that necessary?" Salene asked, trying to hide her real concern. He always seemed to be running off into his secret worlds when they were together. It was as if he didn't really want to be alone with her. But she didn't want to be the nagging wife. Such behavior defied her principles. Why then, did she have to bite her tongue now? "What I mean is, perhaps once you meet Jorl all your questions will be answered. He sounds like a curious enough fellow."

"I'd still like to talk to Joria first." He began to move the large floor mirror in their room opposite to the one on the dresser. As a Waymaster, he no longer needed four mirrors to enter the Way, and in essence, could even enter through only one. But that technique required more Magic than he wanted to use right now. All of Delise's talk about curses and the Eldenlore had left him wary. Better to not call attention to himself, especially in the Way, where the Darkness was his equal.

Salene bit back another protest and instead sank down on the bed, draping are arm suggestively over the pillow. "I'll be waiting for you, then," she said at last, her voice warm and, she hoped, welcoming.

He hardly acknowledged her as he lined the mirrors up so each reflected into the other, opening the vast eternal corridors of the Way of Mirrors. Then he simply stepped through.

Salene sighed and let her body go limp. Perhaps, if she just pretended he'd said goodbye, she could stop herself from crying.

Chapter 3

The Way was eerily silent, as if even it were sleeping in Norwin's breath. Jamus, though, was not deceived. He had too well mastered the mirrored halls to drop his guard. Each journey into the passages brought increased risk, for his presence stirred the Shadows' interest and lured them to him in hopes of stealing his life or seeking his favor.

That was, in fact, what he believed eventually drove most travelers mad in the end. Either that or another possibility—one far more daunting.

He'd studied much about the Way in the Eldenlore and read every account he could find in the Great Library and in Senital's vaults. And, every now and then, the tales hinted of a more sinister danger than mere madness.

In bringing Simen to reality, he'd already seen the truth of some of his theory and in his gain of mastery had even suffered to conquer his own demon, Suman.

Both those events had led him to read the ancient texts more carefully, and time and time again, he'd found related phrases. *"Sporath was no longer himself. It was as if one Jurb had entered the Way and another emerged. Sabesa was no more the woman she had been before her last maddening journey."* Too many coincidences? Or the reporting of a disturbing reality?

He'd met enough reflections here to know how much they wanted to be free of the mirrors and granted life in the real world. Just suppose, in all those Eldentales, that is exactly what had happened. Could reflections have emerged in place of the Magicians? If so, every word of the ancient texts made terrifying sense.

And so it was he journeyed the Way with careful steps, his eyes searching every corner for possible ambush.

Still, he was a skilled traveler, and now he made his way quickly to Magiskeep's portals, entering the palace's mirrored room within minutes of leaving Greenhope.

Joria, seated by the window of her study, hardly even bothered to look up when Jamus opened the door. "So, you're back already, My Lord? I was wondering how long you'd trust Sarn alone here."

Jamus grinned at the grey-haired Mistress and moved over to the window himself. Gazing out into the fading light of Weswin, he shrugged. "I didn't come back because of Sarn. Still, I suppose it won't hurt to ask. Has he done anything I should know about?"

The Mistress of Illusion looked up now, and smiled. "He has been a perfect gentleman, I'm afraid. It's so out of character for him the whole palace is buzzing with gossip. I've never seen one of your chantings provide so much entertainment."

"I didn't want anyone bored while I was away," Jamus replied, barely managing to keep a straight face. It was too easy to enjoy the idea of Sarn's suffering. "But, I've come to ask you a question, Joria, a name, actually."

"You came back here for a name? My Lord…," Joria stopped in midsentence and simply stared at him. Then she shook her head. "You left Salene and your hosts to ask about a name? I certainly hope, Jamus, that this name you seek is more important than your duties as Lord of Magiskeep."

"What do you mean by that?"

"Where did you leave your wife at this span, Sur? It's late enough to be in bed."

Joria didn't need to say anymore. The implication of her words was painfully clear. Jamus sat down heavily beside her on the end of the bench. "I've done it again, haven't I."

"It sounds to me as if you have," Joria answered quietly. "You pursue your curiosity—the Magic again, I'd wager—and leave your wife to fend for herself. How many times do you intend to desert her, eh? She deserves more."

He rubbed his brow and leaned back against the windowsill. "I didn't think about Salene. I just thought about the puzzle I was trying to solve. She should have said something."

"Why? Have you ever listened? Blame the River, or blame yourself, Jamus, but don't blame her." She shook her head again and sighed. "So what is this name of such importance? The sooner I give you an answer, the sooner you'll go back where you belong."

"Jorl," he said simply.

"You didn't need to come back here for that. You've already heard his story. It's one of the first a PrePrentice ever hears."

"If you recall, I was a latecomer to your classes, Mistress. Sagari didn't think I was worthy, even after I passed the Testings."

"All the more reason you should know the tale then, My Lord. It was circles ago, perhaps ten before Sagari became Master here. Jorl was Prentice then, though no one quite knows why. He was inept in every art, and one of the worst students the Keep had ever seen. Only his name and an ingratiating personality managed to keep him in his classes. Why the lad couldn't even manage to hold an

Illusion past first challenge. He had a smile, though, and a laugh
worth ten chantings."

"So you tried to teach him anyhow?"

"I tried, Seneth tried, and every other Master tried. Then, at
last, the Gathering met and decided Jorl wasn't worth the effort. We
were about to place him in the village when the River twisted in its
course on his behalf."

"Are you sure it was the River?" Jamus asked. "It may be
important for me to know for sure."

"I have no other explanation," Joria said. "A Gathering for
the Call is a formal ceremony, with Masters' toast. Every one of the
Seven Masters had his cup, including Jeress, who was Mistress of
Compassion then. We had already made our decision about Jorl
when the most extraordinary thing happened. Jeress told me later she
was about to take a sip of her amberwine when her cup began to
shake in her hand. She said she tried to hold it steady, even
considered a spell to check it, but the cup defied her efforts. In one
sudden spin, it wrenched itself from her grip and flew to the far
corner of the room where it hovered. One of the lesser mages tried to
retrieve it, but the cup danced away again and again. Then, the
young, failed magician entered the room to hear his fate and the
River spoke. Jeress' cup sailed into Jorl's hand as surely as Sagari's
leapt to yours."

"But it wasn't a Choosing. No cup flies before that night,"
Jamus said.

"I saw what I saw, My Lord, and the Gathering agreed."

"Had Jorl shown any talent at all for Healing?"

Joria shrugged. "No more than for any other Art—until that
moment, at least. Afterwards, though, when Jeress accepted him as
Apprentice, his skill seemed to blossom. He showed a sudden and
amazing capacity for Touch. It was the only Art he ever mastered."

"But surely Comprehension?" Jamus began.

But Joria shook her head. "The man didn't have the vaguest
concept. It's the strangest thing I've ever seen, and the very reason
we always tell the story to the PrePretentices. It motivates them to
believe in their own talents, no matter how limited they may be."

"I'm sorry I missed that lecture," Jamus said.

This time, Joria laughed. "You never needed it, My Lord.
For you, the Magic always flowed freely. It's as if you are Jorl's
complete opposite."

Jamus stiffened at her remark. Reflection? Could it be? Then
he shook the thought away. The Way of Mirrors tended to warp his
thinking into its patterns instead of logic. Jorl was Prenticed circles

before he'd even been born, and though the Way defied time itself, he doubted it could twist it so completely. Still, he was confident he'd know as soon as he saw Jorl whether or not there could be any connection at all between the Healer and the Way.
But confidence in the Way was a dangerous thing.

****

The journey back to Greenhope was an easy passage, as quiet as before, at least until Jamus reached the final corridor.

And then, it wasn't so much a sound as a sense of presence nagging at him as he moved along. It was as if something was watching him from the dim light to the side, but each time he turned, no matter how quickly, there was nothing there. Whatever lurked in the darkness would dart away, as quickly as a Shishadow. Yet Jamus knew it wasn't one of those harmless little creatures, for this being was grim and determined. Its invisible glare bore into his being, sifting his intent, its questing licking at his internal Sphere, probing for a weakness.

"If you want an answer, just ask," Jamus said aloud, keeping his eyes on the corridor ahead. "You should know by now I'm not a complete fool in the Way. I didn't come here unprotected."

Silence was the only reply.

"You've followed me before," Jamus said. "I've felt it. Show yourself. There's no point in hiding."

Nothing again.

Jamus shrugged his shoulders and made his way into Greenhope's room. Then, he slipped into the lone mirror back into the bedchamber.

Behind, in the Way, a tall figure slid out of the shadows. It was an exact replica of the Rivermaster himself—his perfect reflection.

Jamus' features were so perfectly imitated, the difference between man and image were virtually indiscernible. To see them side by side, even Salene would be hard pressed to notice any difference. Now, the figure wore the blue and silver tunic of the Keep's Master, with the silver stallion crest on the right, instead of the left, marking him as a creature of the mirrors, but all he needed was a change of clothes. He stood, looking at the room where Jamus had left and carelessly raked his left hand through his dark hair.

"Use the right," a voice hissed from an even darker corner of the Way.

The image quickly dropped his left hand and used his right instead. "I forgot."

"Fools forget and fools die for it. Be the Master, not his mate. Dost thou desire true life?"

"I do."

"Then remember. Deny thy nature. Assume his in all but the Shadow's way."

The image nodded and walked back into the darkness to wait.

****

"So, you're back," Salene said, obviously struggling to keep her voice even. "It wasn't easy explaining to our host and hostess why you missed both earlenmeal and midmeal."

Jamus blinked in the Sowin sunlight streaming in from the wide window of their room. Clearly the journey in the Way had taken longer than he'd thought. Usually when he returned from such a trip, hardly any time at all would have passed in the real world. But, there was no time in the Way, and apparently the mirrored passages had played a new game. "What time is it now?" he asked.

"Well into Sowin," Salene answered. "Nearly Windchange again. Why were you gone so long?"

"I'm not sure," he said, sitting down on the edge of the bed. "I only went to the Keep and then came straight back. This has never happened before. Usually, even when I'm in the Way, I have some sense of time…at least I think about it. I wonder if that's the difference. It never even occurred to me until now."

"Well, I wish it had," Salene said.

He looked up at her, noticing for the first time how strained she seemed. "I'm sorry."

Her shoulders sagged. "No, I'm sorry, Jamus. I don't know what's wrong with me. I've been acting more like a nervous shetark than your wife these last few days. I keep promising myself to understand how hard this must all be for you and still I can't help myself."

He got up and took her in his arms, holding her close. "If you felt any other way, I don't think I could stand it, Love. You're the one who keeps bringing me back, you know. Every time the River tries to take me, to lure me into one of its secrets, the fact that you're waiting for me to come home tempers my idiocy."

"Idiocy?"

"What else would you call leaving you?" He felt her laugh against his chest and smiled. "That's better. Now, do you want to hear what I found out about Jorl?"

She pushed a little away and looked up into his face, her eyes moist. "Was it worth the trip?"

"Joria told me all the PrePrentices knew the story. He's the one the cup flew to without a Bidding."

"Of course!" Salene moved back now, her face brightening. "The Healer with no Mastery! Why didn't I remember? It's one of Compassion's better tales—something I shouldn't have forgotten."

"You're long past your PrePrentice days, Salene, and you certainly haven't been teaching any of the younger children in quite some time."

"I suppose," she said thoughtfully, "but if I had remembered, I could have saved you a trip. Now that you've told me, the story's as clear in my head as if I'd heard it just yesterday. But up until now…it's strange. It's almost as if something had made me forget."

"Perhaps its Greenhope's aura," Jamus said, laughing. "This place is so warm and beautiful, who would want to remember an old school tale?"

She laughed again. "It's a wonder you noticed. You've hardly been here long enough to see much. I was going to take a walk in Delise's flower gardens before evenmeal. Would you like to come?"

He grinned, bowed and extended his arm. "My lady, nothing would please me more than to escort the most beautiful woman I know into the gardens…unless she'd prefer…" he nodded briefly at the bed.

"Flowers now, pillows later," Salene said coyly. "You made me wait. Now it's your turn." At that, she took his arm and marched resolutely to the door.

****

Jorl stirred another herb into his cup and then sat down beside his fire to sip the brew. He was always cold, no matter how hot it was outside. The sunlight just wouldn't penetrate his bones, as if the Shadows were inside of him as well.

"Another sacrifice I find, one of even greater kind. Child of Rivermaster be, second sacrifice to me."

"What?" Jorl straightened in his chair as the voice hissed out of the fire.

"Give me, give me, life anew, this I shall demand of you."

"I don't understand. I've given you the Lady's child. That was the bargain. Now he's here. Isn't that what you wanted?"

Jorl heard a wet, smacking sound as if the creature were licking its lips. *"More is wanted, needed yet. Rivermaster owes a debt. Pain to suffer so must he, Everendings ever be. Stirs a life within her womb, everdarkness be its tomb. Child of Rivermaster be, second sacrifice to me."*

"Lady Salene is pregnant," Jorl said, shaking his head. "And now you want her child too? Does it ever end, all this killing?"

"Blood is mine to feast upon—theirs or yours, it shall be gone. Choice to make is yours to do. Drink of them, or drink of you?"

Jorl shivered. It was not the first time the Shadow had threatened to kill him if he refused its demands. There was too little in this alliance for his benefit. "I'll give you her child, if that's what you want. But she is a Healer herself, and protected by the Rivermaster. It's not going to be easy."

"Rivermaster shall be mine, then his woman shall be thine. Easy prey I give to you, simple in the end to do."

"If you have him, why do you need his child? I thought he was all you really wanted."

"Rivermaster come to me, suffer, suffer, this must be. Strong in Magic, strong in will, I must torment him until neither River nor his hand answers to his heart's command. Break him, break him this I must, turn his River into dust."

Jorl swallowed hard, trying to check his fear. The Shadow's voice chilled him beyond anything his fire could do to warm him and he was trembling. The creature intended to capture Jamus in some kind of trap and then force him to submit to its will by whatever means necessary. And he, Jorl, a Healer of the Keep, was going to help.

It was either that, or die.

****

"I trust your appetite is better, My Lord?" Delise asked as she laid a plate of cheese and fruit on the table for evenmeal. "Lady Salene said you'd not been feeling well last night, and that's why you didn't share meals with us today."

Jamus nodded. "I am sorry, Mistress. Usually, Salene's Touch is more than enough to make me feel better, but I guess I was more tired than I realized this time. It's not so long since my mishap in the Rim, you see, and sometimes, when I do too much, I still feel a bit weak."

Sarkem sat down at his place and unfolded his napkin. "That's exactly what your wife said, Sur. I keep telling Delise even Magic's cures have their limits, but she seems to think a Healer's Touch resolves everything."

"Oh, but it doesn't," Salene said quickly. "It would be dangerous if it did. I could restore health completely, if necessary, but it would ultimately be as much illusion as anything. Far better the body heal itself in the end. Touch takes away pain, begins the mending, and assures life, of course, but nature is the better healer."

"And how long does nature take?" Delise asked. "A lifetime?"

"It depends on the patient's will," Salene told her. "Some people just never seem to choose to recover."

Delise stared at her. "Are you suggesting that I chose this?" Her voice drifted off on the question.

"I don't know, My Lady," Salene said, "but I do intend to see Jorl to find out. Jamus and I have discussed this curse and both of us are suspicious there's more to it than it appears."

"Jorl is a Healer of some note," Jamus said, "and Keeptrained enough not to be misled by old tales and legends. When can we meet this Healer of yours?"

"We've invited him for evenmeal," Sarkem replied, "though he has a notorious reputation for forgetting the time, I'm afraid. I just sent Galia to fetch him. He's probably stirring up one of his potions and gotten so involved he didn't even notice the sun."

"I love the man dearly," Delise said with a sigh, "but he is so absentminded about keeping appointments and such. You'd think time meant nothing to him."

"He's not a young man, my dear," Sarkem said. "As a matter of fact, I'd wager he has far more circles passed in his life than he appears. Were he not such a good Healer, I'd have lost patience with him long ago."

It was just then the door to the dining chamber opened and there, dressed in a disheveled robe of pale grey, stood Jorl. Tall and thin, with straw colored hair, his darting hazel eyes seemed to take in every inch of the room in several quick glances. "Oh my, oh my," he said nervously as he rung his thin hands. "I've done it again. I was out in the garden and I found a patch of delfweed at its peak. Early for delfweed, you know. I was just so taken by it I had to harvest. Dear me, by tomorrow the blossoms would have opened and we just couldn't have that, now could we, my lady?" He had moved over to Salene and kissed her hand.

"No," Salene said, peering down at his bowed head. "Delf loses much of its potency once it flowers."

Jorl lifted his gaze and smiled at her. "You see, I was right. When the Lady of the Keep agrees, how could it be otherwise?" Though he was gawky and appeared awkward, he glided over to

Jamus and offered a welcoming hand. "Once I harvested what more could I do but hang it in the herb loft, eh? It would never do to let it lie there even a span."

"It spoils quickly," Jamus said, returning the gesture. "Good herbs need careful tending, I'm afraid. Do you use delf often, Master Jorl?"

"Oh, 'tis a wonder it is," Jorl replied. "Nothing better to soothe the stomach and ease cramps. Did you know it mixes well with sandel, though? Together the herbs are a marvelous tonic for restoring strength and energy after an illness. If you'd like, I can prepare you a brew with my fresh delf. It might serve you well, My Lord."

Jamus' expression hardened. "I did not give you leave to Touch me, Sur. Have you so forgotten your Keep Vows?"

Jorl shrugged. "Healer's Sight comes to me unbidden, My Lord, and just as often unwanted. I cannot ask leave when the River simply gives. The only thing I can do is learn when to shut my mouth."

Jamus smiled slightly. "A wise lesson for any man."

The Healer straightened. "You have been ill, My Lord?"

"An injury," Jamus said. "I'm recovering well."

"My brew would speed your way," Jorl said. "Tomorrow perhaps? If I blend it this Norwin, by the time you arise, it should be full potent. You won't regret it."

"If my Healer agrees," Jamus said, nodding to Salene, "then I would be grateful for your brew, Sur."

"How wise of you to defer to the lady," Jorl laughed. "Whether as Healer or as wife. We men must always surrender to a beautiful woman."

"I am flattered, Master Jorl," Salene said, "but you won't win me over with mere words. While I have no reason to doubt your skill with herbs, the Lord of Magiskeep is under my care. I will judge your medicine as I would judge any other."

"I'd have it no other way, My Lady," Jorl replied. He vowed silently to be even more cautious than he'd first planned. If it meant he'd have to spend all of Norwin hiding his more potent brews, so be it. By the time he needed them, he hoped to have Salene's and Jamus' full confidence and trust. Until then, he would have to make no mistakes.

"I saved you some surlep derries," Delise said, offering Jorl a plate with the glazed fruit.

Jorl grinned. "And this is why I was worried about being late. Mistress, you are a wonder to remember how much I love these before a meal." He took one of the dainties and slipped it into his mouth, savoring its flavor as he licked the juice from his fingers.

Jamus watched the Healer pull out Delise's chair and then seat himself beside her. She leaned over to him as he whispered something in her ear. Then she laughed and nodded to the servant at the door to begin the meal, all the while keeping her full attention on Jorl's remarks. Jamus escorted Salene to her seat beside him and then sat himself across from his hostess. She was happier and more relaxed than she'd been since they arrived. Whatever comfort Jorl's presence brought her seemed the ideal cure. But as Jamus watched, he had an uneasy feeling nagging far back in his thoughts. It was almost as if he'd met Jorl before—or at least someone exactly like him.

Chapter 4

Jorl's house was set aside from the main mansion at his choice. He'd had Sarkem build him a small cabin in a grove of brellums just out of sight of the stables where he could have his privacy yet still be readily available should anyone in the Hold need his Healing Touch.

Just south of his back gates were several trails winding their way into the foothills of the Shadedmounts, the hills bordering the southern boundary of Sarkem's tilled lands. For the most part, the paths appeared overgrown and unused, but in truth, Jorl traveled them often, visiting secret ridges and, of course, the caves. There, through crystal pools and polished stone walls, he found endless entries into the darker passages of the Way of Mirrors where those he considered his allies waited for the sacrifices he would offer.

It had been nothing at first. A child had contracted a wasting disease with little hope but the River's strongest power as a cure. Jorl had taken her from her parents and carried her to his cabin, knowing full well his Magic could do nothing. The lie had been easier than he'd expected, and the child lighter to carry to the cave at the edge of the waterfall.

Her screams, though, as the darkness closed in on her to devour the small life left in her frail little body, had echoed in his ears for Sevenstins after.

By the fifth offering of blood, his ears had learned to be deaf to the cries.

The remains of Delise's child had appeared to be a simple gift. But though he had left the wailing behind him in Sarkem's Keep, far from the caves themselves, that had not made witnessing the dark feast any easier in the end.

Whatever delight the Shadows felt as the innocent blood fed their desires, Jorl had suffered tenfold in opposition. The feast tormented him, for as much as they were Shadow, he was reflection of Shadow, and their pleasure was his pain.

To think of doing it all again was unbearable. "Why must you take the Rivermaster's child? It wasn't part of the bargain," he said as he settled himself beside a still pool of brackish water lying in a crevice of rocks just beyond his cabin. "I've given you everything else in due order. It's not fair to change your demands."

"Fair is not my River's way. You shall do what I shall say."

"Don't you understand how much pain I suffer because of your lust? Giving you Delise's child nearly killed me. If this is the path to my eternity, then I'm not ready to follow it."

"This time torment not for you. Gives another one his due. Rivermaster shall be mine, and his blood shall be my wine. Everendings ever be, his life my eternity."

Jorl stirred the water in disgust, ending the contact with the gesture. So, it was Jamus the Shadow wanted, and Jamus who would suffer the agony of this dead child.

Jorl sighed with relief. He long ago learned it was impossible to deny the Shadows whatever they wanted, for the nightmares they inflicted in retaliation were too terrible to face. But, compared to the torture he had suffered at the last sacrifice, he would have traded ten nightmares.

He consoled himself with the knowledge that Jamus was a strong, vibrant man far better equipped to meet the Shadows' demands than he ever had been. Besides, if he could convince the Lord of Magiskeep to drink his delfweed brew he would be even more fit. The combination of herbs really did have a healing magic of its own. Not only did it restore energy, it enhanced it, giving the patient sharper senses and greater strength. He'd used it often himself, especially after his visits to the cave. Sometimes it had been the only thing keeping him alive.

He hiked back to his cabin, his arms full of various wild roots he'd dug to cover his real intent. When he got there, Jamus and Salene were already waiting in his garden.

"You have a wonderful collection of herbs here, Sur," Salene said. "It appears the climate favors them all."

"Greenhope affords the best earth and the best weather in all of Magiskeep, Mistress," Jorl said, putting his burden down on the garden table by the door. "Nearly everything I plant seems to grow on its own. Come, come, though. Admiring another garden in Greenhope is like looking at sand in the Rim. The real interest lies within. Please, come in and see what a Keep Healer has learned from the world."

If Jorl had cleaned house for his visitors, it was hard to tell. Pots of all sizes and shapes lay haphazardly around the main room which served as kitchen, dining, living and work area. A wide counter, set off to the side, was layered in piles of dried herbs, mixing bowls, and tools. Only one chair sat vacant, the others covered with scrolls or pieces of fabric vaguely resembling clothing.

Jorl hastily swept a pile of parchment to the floor and gestured for Salene to sit by the fire. Then he pulled up the lone clean chair for Jamus and seated himself on a stool nearer the counter. "I've so many ideas, it's hard to tell where to begin or where to end. Do you use many potions in the Keep, My Lady?"

"A few," Salene said, "but most of my Healing relies on the Touch. I've not run across many ailments Magic cannot define. You prefer herbs, I take it?"

"Oh, yes," Jorl answered. "The River is indeed kind, but nature is kinder. Besides, with herbs, I can offer solace to those who wish or need to care for themselves. Magic requires my being there. Herbs don't."

"That's true," Jamus agreed. "Many of our village healers rely on nature's cures. It's often only when they fail that our Keep Masters are called."

"Ah, the village healers," Jorl sighed. "Far too set in their ways to accept the Magic, I fear. You'd think in Magiskeep it would be different. When I traveled to Turan beyond the Rim, of course, I expected it, but here?"

"You've been to Turan?"

"I am nigh passed four hundred circles, My Lord. A man of my age might well have traveled there and back ten lifetimes. Actually, it's only been some ten circles since I settled here in Greenhope. For my old age, of course." He winked. "The Hand's blessed me with long life. I've tried to use it well."

"And you're happy here?"

"Content is a better word. Being happy requires more effort than I'm willing to put into life. I have a home here, and the freedom to do as I please."

Jamus nodded. "No better life indeed." He glanced at Salene. "Except it lacks love. You've never wanted a family?"

Jorl shivered and seemed to shrink into himself as he rubbed his hands near the fire. "Not here, surely. Not so close to the Caves. Hasn't Lady Delise told you of the curse?"

So, there it was at last, and by Jorl's reaction, Jamus was certain the man believed what he was saying. Until that moment, the Healer had been every inch a Keeptrained Magician, confident and adventurous. Now, though, he cowered at his very words and even seemed to revel in the chill of them like a talespinner frightening children before bed. "The Lady mentioned something."

"More than mentioned, I should wager, if I know the Lady," Jorl replied. "That's why you're here, isn't it?"

"That and your potions," Salene said quickly. "You did offer to help Jamus, after all."

Once more Jorl's posture straightened as his whole face brightened. "Aye, that I did." He bounded from his stool and began to busy himself at the counter, humming tunelessly.

Jamus shook his head as he looked over to Salene. She responded in kind, her eyes pleading with him to temper his actions. If Jorl was as mad as he appeared, no words from the Lord of Magiskeep could alter things. Far wiser for them to play the fools now and simply listen to his rantings. "And what do you mix with your delfweed, Sur? You did say sandel?"

"Sandel and sage, My Lady, that's all. The three together a marvelous tonic. Here." He carried a vial over to her. "Sift it, if you please. You'll find more delf than anything. It's the proportions that make the difference, you know. Something in the sandel joins the delf, at least that's what I've been able to find out so far."

Salene studied the brew for a long time, sifting for weaves and deceptions. She held it up in the firelight, well within Jamus' sight, letting him cast his own seeking into it, using more subtle and perceptive analysis. The blend was exactly as Jorl had described it. "It looks fine," she said.

"Will My Lord drink some then?" Jorl asked, crouching into a little bow. "I'd be honored to do him service by restoring some of his strength."

Jamus took the vial from his wife's hand and sipped. Spans of weariness slid from his body and he felt his muscles surge with eager energy. An instant later, the stronger feelings passed, but he felt fitter and stronger than he had since leaving for Delran's Keep.

Instinctively, Salene reached out, Touching him as he nodded giving her consent. She smiled at once. "By the Hand, Jamus, it worked. This is amazing."

Jorl grinned and danced a little jig. "I told you! I knew I could teach the Keep a thing or two if I had the chance! Fly me the cup and then say I'm a freak, will you? I've waited four hundred circles for this!"

Salene felt Jamus tense under her hand as her own jaw dropped in surprise. Was this all Jorl had wanted? Some sort of validation in the eyes of Magiskeep? Madness was far too moderate a word to describe this.

"The Keep would be most impressed," Jamus said, more easily than Salene anticipated. "Are you willing to give us the recipe for the mixture, or would you rather bring it to the palace yourself? Either way, I would be most pleased to recognize you for it."

Jorl stopped in midwhirl, his eyes widening in surprise. "You would? You'd stand my name before the Gathering?"

"It's worthy of recognition, Master Jorl. I see no reason why not. I can't say the Mistress of Compassion may not want further study of your remedy to be sure it has no detriments in the long term but I would be willing to trust your judgment in that regard. You've used this for circles already, haven't you?"

Jorl pulled out a vellum scroll and unrolled it on the counter. He beckoned to Jamus. "Here are my records from the first. Nearly forty times in the last ten circles, I've used it, I have. Here are the names and the reasons. Every one of these people is alive and well here in Greenhope. Ask them if you question me."

"I'd never question a man of integrity," Jamus replied evenly. "I cannot, however, speak for the Gathering. Your documents will be welcome as evidence."

"Are you not the Master?" Jorl asked, frowning.

"Men need freedom to do as they please," Jamus answered, smiling.

But Jorl did not hear his own words echoing back at him. He was lost in the shadows of his inner thoughts. "The Rivermaster is the River's voice. He is the Magic's word, the heart of its worth. His beginning is the Magic's head and his end the Magic's destruction. How can they not listen?"

"It is not the way of my Keep," Jamus said quietly, as if trying to soothe Jorl back to his senses.

"It will never work then. Never." Jorl's hazel eyes cleared in instant after he spoke, as if something had jolted him back to the present. "They won't believe me if they don't accept your word, My Lord."

"Then we shall have to convince them, won't we?" Jamus picked up the scroll and handed it to Salene. "We can talk to these people and listen to their stories. Such testimony would hold great weight before the Seven Masters."

"You'd do that for me?"

Salene gently rolled the scroll and tied it with a golden band conjured from a stalk of delfweed. "You have created a wonderful medicine, Master Jorl. I do this for the sake of Magiskeep as well as for you."

"You will make a beautiful mother," the Healer said, smiling at her.

"When I am so blessed, I hope I will," she said.

Jorl winked at her. "You are blessed now, My Lady. Didn't you know?"

Salene felt Jamus' grip tighten on her arm. "What are you talking about?"

It was all Jorl could do to keep his feet planted so as not to resume his mad little dance. "You carry the Rivermaster's child, Mistress--a daughter fresh in your womb and not much more than twelve Sevenstins grown. Let your husband Touch you and he will know I speak the truth. The Hand willing, before the next Fullseason ends, you will be a mother."

Salene nodded. "It is so. I'm surprised you know."

Jamus smiled. "We have known for some time. We've told very few people beyond the Mistresses of the Keep."

"No secrets from me," Jorl grinned. "No secrets at all."

****

"Pregnant!" Delise cried as soon as Salene told her of their conversation with Jorl. "Not here. You must go home at once. Didn't Jorl tell you about the curse?"

"He mentioned the cave," Salene said, "but somehow we never heard much more. Jamus will be spending more time with him, though. I'm sure he'll ask."

"He must, he must," Delise insisted. "In the meantime, you mustn't leave the grounds here."

"I have to visit the village and some of the farms. There are questions I need to ask."

"No. It's not safe."

"I'll be just fine, Delise. Jamus would never let anything happen to me or our child."

"Your Lord cannot control the curse, My Lady, no one can. I've felt its power. Jorl tells me of its danger."

"Jorl is not half the Magician Jamus is," Salene interrupted. "My husband is the Rivermaster, and much as I may not like it, he and the Magic are one. This curse you believe in can only be sourced from one place—that same River. It can't possibly defy him."

"I wish…," Delise faltered. She slumped down onto a garden bench, her head dropped into her hands. "Your husband. You have so much faith in him."

"Isn't that as it should be?"

"Sarkem, I love him dearly, but in this, he's not been the hand I've needed. It's not that he hasn't been gentle, even kind. But, it's the understanding he lacks. He's never quite believed the waterfall had anything to do with this."

"Lord Sarkem and I are of one mind, then, My Lady," Salene said, sitting down beside her. "Does it matter so much if he believes you or not? Isn't his strength enough?"

"Strength cannot replace compassion, Mistress."

Jorl—Salene thought, taking her time to reply. Too much of a coincidence to be anything else. But was it honest? From what Jamus had told her, Compassion was Jorl's only talent. Could Manipulation be among his talents as well? She shook the thought away. Jorl was charming, in his own curious way, but she sensed no unusual skill in him. Madness, perhaps, or mere eccentricity. "He loves you, Delise. Whether he believes in the curse really doesn't matter. Jamus and I don't always agree. Still, no matter what, we can depend on each other when it matters. You and your husband share the same kind of love. You can't discount that."

"He doesn't understand, not like Jorl."

"Don't be deceived. Compassion is an Art, not a reality. Jorl is a Magician, trained to offer you both the comfort and the words you seek. To him, they are simply the tools of his Art, no more." Salene took the other woman's hand. "I am a Mistress of Compassion myself, well schooled in these things. Trust what I'm telling you. All Jorl is doing is practicing his trade, nothing more."

"He cares about me."

"The Sixth Art," Salene insisted. At her feet, the shadows of Weswin's turn seemed to be creeping along the pathway, even as she watched. She shivered. Never before had she thought of her Art as a danger.

Why did the shadows seem so dark?

****

Jamus pulled off his tunic and slid into the bed next to Salene. "Now everyone knows about our child—a girl."

"Maybe it's time," Salene replied, kissing him lightly on the cheek. "Soon I'd not be able to keep it a secret anyhow."

"We haven't talked much about it," Jamus said. "What's it going to be like being parents?"

She sank into his embrace. "It won't be just the two of us anymore. Not many more nights like this, alone."

"Well then, perhaps we should make the best of it," he said, kissing her.

She put her hand against his chest and pushed him away. "After we talk, my Love."

He sighed and leaned back against the pillows. "Jorl. I knew that man would have to come between us sooner or later."

She crawled up to lean against the headboard. "He worries me, Jamus. It's as if he has some kind of strange hold over Delise. It's not natural, even for a Healer. I could understand her gratitude or even a sense of dependence upon him, but certainly not to this extent."

"Do you think he's chanted her?"

She shook her head. "I don't think he has the skill. It's this curse he talks about. For some reason, he's persuaded her it is the ruling force in her life.

"Sarkem doesn't believe in it."

"That's the worst of it. She's questioning his love for her because he doesn't. It's not Jorl's place to come between them, Jamus. Compassion's Rule denies the Mage such behavior. A Healer has no such right."

"Are you suggesting it's my duty to intervene?"

"I don't know. If Jorl were in the Keep itself, I'd have no doubt. Here, though, considering how many circles have passed since his Mastery there, is it really your responsibility? What law demands a Magician uphold his Vows?"

"None I know of except morality itself." He rubbed his chin thoughtfully. "Even the Rivermaster can't discipline the Wayward. I worry though."

"About what?"

"When I was in the Way, I felt that presence again, as if I was being watched. Why here? I could understand in Magiskeep, but not here, so far away."

"Do you think there's some connection to Jorl?"

"Too many coincidences always make me wonder, Salene. We both agree he's mad, but do we agree on why?"

"His resentment of the Keep and they way he was treated there."

This time, he shook his head. "No. I think it was the Way. When I first saw Jorl, it was if I recognized him somehow. But it wasn't because I'd seen him before. It was something else, something about his very nature that seemed familiar. He's a Way Traveler, Salene, I'm sure of it. But more, I'm growing more sure he's been tainted by the Reflections there."

"Mad from the Way of Mirrors?"

"It's something we don't really understand, but all the stories I've heard about it certainly do suggest there may be something to it. If so, then I have to be careful in dealing with him. The Way and the Shadows are kin."

She gripped his arm. "Shadows? Here?"

He nodded wearily. "Everywhere I am, I'm afraid, although this time, I'm not so sure my presence inspired them at first. This cave Delise so fears may well be their doing."

"If so, then the talk of a curse may not be mere fantasy after all."

"I'm not taking it lightly."

Now she shivered again as she had in the garden and here, in the safety of his arms, it worried her even more. "What are you going to do?"

"I can't ignore them. They mean to destroy the River."

"Please, not this time. Leave them to their own for once, won't you?"

"I would, My Love, if I thought their presence was no threat. But the darkness intends to conquer Magiskeep and all it stands for. That means you and…and our child are in as much danger from their purposes as I am. I can't stand idly by while they play whatever game it is they've planned. If there's a way to stop them, I have to."

"So, once again, you and River ally against me?" She leaned her head against his chest. "My own curse for marrying you, I suppose. I'm sorry I can't give you my blessing, My Love, but I won't even try to stop you. Just promise, no matter what, you will remember my love for you."

"How could I possibly forget it?"

"In the Way, all things are possible," she replied.

Chapter 5

Jamus and Sarkem rode out to the southern fields as soon as they finished earlenmeal the next day. The morning was sunny and warm, promising the Warmmonth's break. Whim checked his pace to let Sarkem's chestnut gelding keep up alongside so the two men could have a conversation.

They talked of horses, of course, and then crops, leaving the more personal topics of wives and children behind in Greenhope's great house.

Once they crested the last rise before the rolling peaks of the Rising Mountains, Sarkem reined to a halt and pointed at a freshly tilled field to the left. "There's where my sweetling corn's to be planted if you grant me permission to divert the stream." He pointed to the right. "You can just make out where the bed runs now. It passes beyond this ridge to the west a bit, but the land there is too rocky to farm. If I can just send a new tributary east, I can irrigate my fields. Once the new channel passes my crops, it will join back up near the little lake I showed you on the way here."

"And there's enough water so dividing the current brook won't matter?"

"That's for you to decide, My Lord. You'll see the falls and the stream's source once we reach the foothills. As far as my studies go, I think there's plenty of water. Still, it is your Kingdom and its welfare is in your hands."

Jamus smiled. "I'm not much of a farmer, Sarkem, but I do have a passing acquaintance with rivers. Let's hope the secret of this one doesn't elude me."

They rode along the trail through a grove of mountain pines and then into a rocky outcropping bordering a rushing brook. A full twenty spans wide, the water churned white as it battered itself against granite boulders strewn along its banks. They had to shout to hear each other over the sound of the rapids.

Sarkem moved his horse to the front as the trail narrowed and wound itself around a sudden, steep cliff. All he did was point ahead as he let the gelding pick its way among the rocks.

Then, up ahead, the waterfall took command of the scene with its own dramatic presence. Cascading down a cliff of some hundred feet, a torrent of water surged out from above and spewed down in roaring white foam to a deep, wild pool at its base.

Jamus had no trouble making his decision now. He turned to Sarkem and nodded. "You have your corn," he shouted.

Sarkem grinned. "Shall we go back now?"

Jamus shook his head. "I want to see the cave."

Sarkem shrugged and nudged his horse along the bank, following a narrow path up the slope. Finally, they reached a flat plateau a few spans from what appeared to be an equally flat surface where the falls seemed quieter.

Greenhope's Lord dismounted and tied his horse to one of the scrubby evergreens along the bank. "In there," he said.

Jamus dismounted as well, leaving Whim loose with the reins tied to the saddle. The stallion moved over near the other horse, dropped his head, and stood, ready to wait patiently for his master to return.

It was an easy walk to the cave entrance and, as Delise had said, once they were inside, it was delightfully cool and quite beautiful. The sun shimmered in through the curtain of water falling over the entrance, lending a delicate light to an almost surreal atmosphere.

The cave itself was full of stalactites, dripping from a ceiling extending up twenty or more spans. There were several chambers, the widest opening to the left of the first. Behind it there lay a narrow aperture not much larger than a small study room and another chamber about three times its size. The walls behind each of these appeared to be solid, suggesting the cave extended no further. Aside from some scattered rocks, all the chambers were empty.

Jamus was a little surprised. He had expected at the very least some sort of deep pit or echoing tunnel to lend a sense of danger or uncertainty to the place. But instead it was light enough to see into nearly every corner, and nothing at all seemed to be hidden anywhere. Lying in the few sandy patches between boulders there were some curiously striped stones, worn smooth by circles of being tossed about in the white waters above.

Jamus picked one up and put it in his pouch before turning back to the entrance. "From what Delise told us, I would have expected more," he said. "Why did she call it the Cave of Secrets?"

"It's Jorl's name for the place," Sarkem replied.

"And he gave no explanation?"

"Sometimes our Healer doesn't make much sense to me. When Delise lost our baby, he kept insisting it was because she had come to these caves. Tell me, My Lord, do you, as Rivermaster see anything here to blame? I'll admit, my Magic is limited, but I can't sense a thing."

Jamus let his own senses sift the very air of the caves, searching for some hint of illusion or any kind of unnatural deceptions. Then, he reached out with the River's Will, letting the golden waters seek for darkness. Nothing. The caves were no more than they appeared. "I can't find anything extraordinary either, Sur. I'm beginning to believe this curse is just one of Jorl's delusions. If he's wandered the Way of Mirrors too many times, as I suspect, his judgment is not to be trusted."

"You think he's mad?"

"Or close to it," Jamus replied. "There's enough sense in much of what he says to make me wonder, and not enough to convince me of anything."

"What should I do? He is my Keep's only Healer."

"He is a gifted Master of his Art, but you'd be wise to question his intentions here. While Salene and I are in Greenhope, you've nothing to worry about. Still, I'd feel better if you had another Healer to consult with once we're gone. I'll have someone sent from my Keep as soon as possible."

"And my wife? She trusts Jorl completely."

"For now, leave it alone. I'll talk to Salene. She has a talent for making other women see sense no matter how their hearts are twisted." Jamus peered around the caves one last time. "There's nothing wrong here, My Lord. We might as well go back."

They headed back to the main house well after Sowin's change, visiting the orchards and grain fields along the way. By the time they reached Greenhope's door, Jamus had granted Sarkem permission to divert the stream, and urged the Lord to plant at least one more field of ambergrapes. "The climate here certainly favors them, Sur, and the markets in Turan beg for fine wine. I don't see any reason Greenhope shouldn't earn a place on the vintners' shelves there."

"Is it wise to trade beyond the Rim, My Lord?"

"I know a number of Turand Lords who'd be discreet partners for you, Sarkem. I think you'd enjoy the challenge, and they'd certainly enjoy the wine. Why not let someone besides Magicians reap the benefit of your harvest?"

"Why not indeed?" Sarkem said, grinning.

****

Later, when Jamus and Salene had settled back in their rooms, he pulled off his tunic and dropped his pouch on the floor. It landed with a thunk on his bare foot.

"What in Sorem's name do you have in that?" Salene asked, laughing as he danced on his good foot. "It's your own fault for carrying fieronstones about, you know."

Sitting down hard on the footstool, rubbing his instep, Jamus grinned in embarrassment. "Actually, it was more of a souvenir I forgot I'd collected." He pulled the striped stone out and tossed it on the bed. "From the falls."

Turning it over in her hands, Salene examined it. "Interesting coloring. Sandfire and quaretz, I think. Smooth, as if it's been tossed about in the stream."

"Probably worn down by the falls," Jamus told her. "It's the only thing of any interest I found in the caves."

"Nothing else?"

"As far as I can tell, they're completely empty. I can't figure out what might have inspired Jorl's curse."

"Perhaps you should ask him, then," she said, putting the stone on the small table by her pillow. "He's completely chanted Delise with his tales. I can't get her to be even the least bit reasonable about any of it."

He sighed. "I was hoping I could avoid confronting Jorl about all of this until I'd studied the matter more myself. The trouble is, aside from those caves, I haven't the faintest idea where else to look. At least if I talk to him again, I might get some clue as to where to start."

"I'm going to the farms and village," Salene said. "Jorl's been here long enough that the people know him. I'd think they'd have some opinion on the curse, don't you?"

He slid over to the bed and settled himself beside her. "The people always have opinions." He closed his eyes. "Sometimes I just wish we didn't have to listen to anyone but ourselves."

****

Jamus found Jorl in the forest, not far from his little house. The Healer was leaning up against a tree, muttering to himself. He held a handful of wet pebbles, as if he'd scooped them up from a nearby pond, and the hem of his tunic was dripping. His hazel eyes were glazed and staring, the muscles in his neck tense. "They won't be quiet. They won't be quiet."

"Who are you talking about, Jorl?"

"Dark voices in the night."

"Shadows?"

At the word, Jorl stiffened, his eyes focusing on Jamus' face. "Is that what they are?"

"They may be. Don't you know?"

Jorl shook his head. "They come in my dreams. It's the only time I ever hear them. I can never really see. It's just voices." The lies became easier as he told them. He was beginning to think that if he kept at it, he'd actually believe them himself. "I don't know why I have nightmares like that. I've never done anything to warrant it."

"You've traveled the Way, Jorl. That's enough, you know."

"The Way? What Magician of my circles hasn't? Mere curiosity, mind you, nothing more, and certainly not often." A hundred times a hundred, he thought, until I forgot I needed to come back.

"Once can be a mistake," Jamus said. "All you have to do is stir the wrong reflections."

"No one ever told me."

"Few people know."

Jorl pushed away from the tree. "Why did you come to see me again? Didn't I answer all your questions yesterday?"

"I never asked you much about the curse. It puzzles me. I visited those caves with Lord Sarkem and didn't see anything curious about them. What did I miss?"

Jorl improvised quickly. "You didn't see the runes?"

"Where?"

"In the second cave, down low, in the far corner. They're very faint and unless you know just where to shine the light, they're easy to miss. I could show you."

Jamus hesitated, weighing the risk. Going to the caves with a possible madman who spoke of shadows in the night certainly edged near stupidity. But, he'd been behind the falls already and nothing had happened then. Where did necessity end and foolishness begin? Still, it was a riddle, and riddles needed answers. He had his Sphere to protect him, set in a stelin weave not even the Darkness could broach. Besides, he was on guard now, and for once, ready for an attack. "I'd like to see them, Jorl. When can you show me?"

Jorl bobbed in a series of quick bows. "Now, My Lord. Now. The sun's fresh and the wind young. I have a pair of sturdy mountain ponies if you'd like to leave your horse here. My trail isn't as clear as the one Sarkem took you on. A big horse might not fit though some of the passes."

A short bit into the ride, Jamus was glad he'd not ridden Whim. The trail would have posed no real challenge to the great stallion with all his Magical abilities, but his rider would have spent a great deal of effort trying to explain it all to his companion. The shaggy pony negotiated each turn and narrow pass with ease and needed no chantings to make his way through the rocks. That left Jamus free to talk of other things and further try to sift his way through Jorl's personality.

The Healer remained much of a puzzle. Despite circles of life beyond his training in Magiskeep, he carried himself as a Keepmage, and spoke with the dialect of his youth. It was clear his education there had been complete and lasting, and yet an alien aura clung to his manner and his beliefs. Magic and the River repeatedly denied such things as curses where Magic itself took charge over the Mage's Will. Though it was true Magic could be left to act on its own, a skilled Master always had the power to loose a weave. Some were more complex than others, requiring more than the simple talents of a Healer like Jorl, but few could defy the Rivermaster's Art. If there were any truth at all to Jorl's stories, Jamus was certain he could unravel the secrets.

They approached the caves from the opposite side of the rushing stream. The trees were sparse among the rocks with just enough bare ground around them to tether the ponies. The entrance to the caves behind the falls was narrower too, and far more confining, matching the entire trip from Jorl's cabin.

Jorl led as they climbed single file along the slippery rocks and into the cave. "I know you were here before, My Lord, but your eyes did not see then. Let me open them for you."

Instead of replying, Jamus followed the Healer warily, letting his Sphere expand around him to shield him from any possible ambush.

But the cave was as empty and spare as it had been on the visit with Sarkem.

Jorl beckoned towards the larger inner cave. "In there. I'll show you. It's down close to the floor in the far corner." He ducked past a stalactite and knelt in the sand. "Here, carved in the rock. Do you see now?"

Jamus closed in and squatted beside him. "It's too dark in here to see clearly." He raised his hand lifting with it a glisten of silver light illuminating the space.

The Healer brushed his hand over the rocks, marking the spot where a series of curious runes were carved into the stone. "Eldenscript. I'm no master of it, but I know enough to understand the meaning. 'New life ends in shadowed walls. Death flows rapid in the falls. Endings here shall ever be.' It's clear, isn't it? When Delise lost the child after she came here, I knew what it meant."

Jamus peered at the markings. Why had Jorl translated it that way? Such words of Darkness set him on guard. "From what I know of the Eldentongue, there's never an exact meaning to any word without the others next to it. Here, you see the marks for 'life' and 'death' as you've translated them, are nearly identical. How can you know which is which?"

Jorl's eyes glittered in the silver light and he tapped his nose with his index finger. "Reflections, Sur, reflections. Do ye not see with eyes of the Way?"

Jamus' sphere hardened as he stiffened. "I see with eyes of the Rivermaster. Truth and the Way are not kin."

"Ye are foolish to believe so, My Lord. Look again with mirror eyes. On Reflection Truth relies. Thus the image thy eyes see, all that Truth shall ever be."

A cold chill coursed through Jamus at Jorl's phrases, the rhythm and rhyme all too familiar. "Where did you hear that?"

"My words, My Lord. None other."

"Not yours," Jamus replied. "Don't lie to me, Jorl. You've traveled the Way many times, but don't be too confident of your ability to deceive me with its weaves."

"I hear what I hear, Master Jamus. Let's go back out into the sunlight to discuss this." Jorl shivered. "It's too cold in here for my old bones."

Jamus waved his hand over the carved stone, copying the runes onto a parchment materializing in his hand. He followed Jorl out the opposite side of the cave to the clearing beside the falls where he and Sarkem had rested their horses. The sun was brighter there, and warmer, but he noticed the Healer was still shivering. "Sit here, Sur," he said, gesturing towards a log in a patch of sunlight. "I'll brew some keldherb if it will help."

Jorl shook the offer away. "No need, no need," he said, his teeth chattering. "The light will warm me soon enough. It's the darkness that chills me."

Again, Jamus alerted. Too many coincidences. "Are you often cold, then?"

The Healer nodded. "Hard to warm my reflection, you see. All those mirrors stand so cold and still. I can't quite escape the visions I see there. You've traveled the Way. Surely you understand."

"I've Mastered the Way, Jorl. Tell me how it holds you and perhaps I can help."

"No help anymore, My Lord. I've forgotten which is which. How can a man tell what he is when he sees himself in so many mirrors, eh—the smiling fool, the wayward lover, the raging warrior, the soul of virtue, or Shadowspawn itself? Too many journeys, I fear. I've lost my way."

"At the end, a man finds his True Reflection, and with it peace in the way. I could take you there."

Despite the sun, Jorl's shivering increased. "I don't want to go back." Then, his eyes cleared, he steadied and seemed to shake off his fear. "Look at the runes again, My Lord. Maybe you're right after all. I may have misread them. Here in the daylight, I find it hard to believe that beautiful waterfall with all its rainbows could be so deadly."

Jamus glanced up to the falls where the sunlit mist had dissolved into a prism of color. Then, he looked back at the parchment. "There's something missing. Do you see this last line? It bears no end mark."

"I've never looked for more," Jorl said, his brow furrowing as he studied runes. "Do you think something more may be buried under the sand?"

"It's possible. If you're ready to leave, we have to cross back through to get to the horses. We can dig around a bit."

"You dig," Jorl said, wrapping his arms around his body and rubbing as if to warm himself. "I don't want to stay in there any longer than necessary. The cold...."

Jamus nodded and headed back into the opening. Jorl followed from several paces back, moving slowly back into the dimness within.

As soon as he knelt by the back wall, Jamus noticed how the sand had piled up against the wall, so he brushed some aside and soon revealed more markings. There appeared to be only two more lines of writing, for the end mark was etched deeply after the second. He was about to chant the markings on to his parchment, when the cave darkened as if the sun had slipped behind some clouds.

"Master of light, pursuing the dark? Beware the strike of the shadowing tark."

"Not now, Jorl. No more of your riddles," Jamus answered as he finished his spell, satisfied as the letters appeared clearly on his parchment. He rose and turned.

"Now in the darkness the Master is prey, endings of freedom and endings of day."

It was not Jorl.

The entrance to the inner cave was filled with a black presence, blocking the light from outside and blocking an easy escape.

"Who are you?"

"Everendings ever be, ask and ye seek misery."

"Why do you your speak in the Dragon's way? Who are you?"

The presence laughed. "Does it matter, Rivermaster? You belong to him now."

"You have no name of your own then?"

"Naboth will do if it means so much for you to have a name for your death. I suppose even the Rivermaster needs to name his enemy to conquer fear. Pity it was so easy to trap you, though. The blood is fresher after the chase."

Jamus raised his hand.

Spellfire shot from his fingers, straight at Naboth's voice.

But the Whitefire splattered against a black wall, scattering into sparks, some bouncing back so Jamus had to dart behind a stalactite to protect himself from his own attack.

Naboth clucked disapproval. "Now, now, Sur, losing your temper serves no purpose. Do you really think I'd be vulnerable to your pathetic Magic? I've planned this far too long to fall for that."

Jamus squinted into the shadows beyond the entrance. It was as if there were a thin black transparent curtain hung over the opening. Through its weaves he could just make out the shape of what might be a man. "What do you want from me?"

"Still you ask the obvious. Blood of blood, Sorcerer. You are the Black Dragon's cup. Your blood grants immortality and cherished victory."

"Never."

Naboth reached out, through the veil, his arms long tendrils of black snakes, striking towards Jamus.

But as soon as they touched the rim of Jamus' Sphere, they hissed and screeched, smoking and coiling back.

"Behola!" Naboth cursed, gasping in pain. "Damn you, Flesher. You chant against me."

"I too have planned," Jamus replied evenly.

"Then we stand a match," Naboth answered.

"So then?"

"So then, you rot in there until you are ready to surrender to me," the Shadow answered, turning away in contempt.

Jamus flung himself at the creature.

The instant he hit the darkness, pain seared through his limbs despite the Sphere's futile intent to protect him. It was as if the dark weave met and simply needled its inky threads between the silver, stabbing into his sinews with agonizing ice.

He was pummeled backwards, stumbling in torment against the cave wall.

Then, with a groan, he fell, writhing in tortured misery.

The last thing he heard before he fainted was Naboth, laughing in triumph.

Chapter 6

Through a haze of returning consciousness, Jamus heard muffled voices.

"They'll notice he's gone if I go back alone."

"You're not going back alone."

"But you said you'd keep him here. I don't understand."

"Foolish little man. If you weren't still useful to me, I'd drink your blood and teach you the way of the Shadow. I told you I'd planned. Behold." There was a rushing sound, too much like the rustle of Dragon wings for Jamus' taste.

He struggled to regain his senses, his teeth chattering as circulation slowly restored itself into his trembling muscles. He was so very cold, even into the pit of his stomach.

Finding one small reserve of energy, he called the River, and when the answer came in a surge of warmth into his limbs, his breathing steadied. He peered through the veil to the outer cave and the new found air puffed out of his lungs in a gasp.

There, next to Jorl, stood a perfect replica of himself, wearing the royal blue tunic of his station and dorrsett leather breeches cut exactly as his were.

"Shadowspawn," Naboth continued, grinning. "A reflection captured in the Way just for this purpose. As soon as our...guest...wakes up, we'll dress this one in his clothes and send you both back to your Keep."

"No!" Jamus cried, pushing to his hands and knees.

"And why not, Rivermaster?" Naboth asked. "He is your duplicate in all but one detail-his obedience to my will. He will not taste blood without my command, and until I tell him otherwise, he will act on your behalf in all matters of concern."

"They'll know."

Naboth waved an admonishing finger. "He has been watching you a long time, Rivermaster, and knows your secrets. Look into his eyes and you'll know I speak the truth."

Jamus shook his head, trying to deny Naboth's claim, but it was futile. Those eyes watching him in the Way, that presence he had sensed so many times now all made perfect sense. And he, through his own complacence and foolhardy confidence in his own Magic, had fallen into the trap. How much had Naboth planned? How long? If anything could be said of Shadows it was that they were patient. After all, they had eternity. "My wife...the Masters. They're not blind."

"Your wife is with child, and as I understand it, the Flesher females are not of soundest mind when they are so burdened. But..." Naboth sighed heavily. "We will soon relieve her of that burden."

Jamus' heart lurched. "What are you talking about? You have me. What more do you need?"

"Blood of thy blood, Rivermaster, and thy Will broken for the Dragon's feast. Do you think we are ignorant of your trickery and lies? You've defeated his minions before with your River. But this time, as you've already felt, your waters will deny you solace. The Dragon demands sacrifice."

"Leave my wife alone. I'll do what you want."

Naboth shook his head. "You must break, Chosen One. You must grovel in defeat at the Dragon's feet. You must plead for mercy, not for the sake of some female who has sotted your reason, but because of your own need for it. You don't yet understand how much he loathes you and your kind. It is not a matter of conquering. It is a matter of crushing."

The River surged, raging to his Will, all its Power rippling in his hand. He was the water, and he felt its Dragon stir. "I cannot bow to the Black Master. My River is the heart of Turan's Way. It's my duty to see the Circle does not close in darkness."

"So, the Sorcerer speaks now instead of the man. This is what I'd hoped for. Conquest means little if the foe is not a worthy adversary. I'll break man and Sorcerer both, mark my words. Until then, fight your fear, Flesher. I have other business to attend to." Naboth deliberately turned his back and spoke to Jorl. "Take the Shadow with you back to your Keep. Do all you can to assure his masquerade. You know what else to do."

"I do your will," Jorl replied. "The clothes?"

Naboth nodded and gestured towards the black veil. Suddenly, Jamus felt the clothes being stripped from his body, despite the Sphere. Curious, he thought. Naboth's powers could touch his belongings, but not him. He watched as his Shadowdouble transformed into an even more uncanny likeness, looking for all Turan as he had when he'd ridden out of Sarkem's Keep that Easwin. There was more to it, though, for the creature had learned to mimic his gestures, raking its hand through its hair and shrugging its shoulders in the same nonchalance he often wore. He shuddered.

"Are you cold, My Lord?" his double asked. "I must say you are a fine specimen to look at, but I would think you'd be more modest."

Jamus nearly covered his nakedness with his hands, then thought better of it, preferring to act as if it didn't really matter. "I am what I am, Sur. Can you say as much?"

The Shadow laughed. "I will be what I will be. Looks now, mortality later. When I have feasted on the blood my my thirteen, or perhaps tasted of your wife, then who will say you are and I am not?"

Jamus wished his words were riddle instead of truth. "If you pretend to wear my identity, you'd be wise to act accordingly. There are many who can sift your deception."

"Little by little, I will change your world until The Jamus the Dragon created will be The Jamus the world worships. My Master has accounted for your limits and the weaknesses of those who follow you. Despair, He Whose Name is Mine. Your circle belongs to me now."

Arrogance, Jamus thought, *the one quality I've fought against all my life. If I can only foster it in him, perhaps someone in Magiskeep will notice.* "Hah," he spat, accenting it with a crude gesture he'd never used in his entire life. "You think you better me? Sorem be damned if that's so. Go on, play your game. I'm not defeated yet."

The Shadow cocked its head, taking in Jamus' reaction. "I haven't often seen you crossed. Good. Now I have the final piece to your nature. Thank you for accommodating me."

Jamus started back as if he were upset by what he'd done. "No....I'm....that's not how I am."

Naboth laughed again clearly enjoying the show. "Come, my friends, I'll set you on your path. We'll leave the Rivermaster to consider his fate alone for a while. It's said the solitary mind works demons in the dark."

As the three figures walked out of the cave, Jamus leaned back against the rocks, his confidence sagging with his body. The cold stone against his skin jolted him to awareness of his nakedness. The River rose to his hand, transforming some of the sand on the floor into a brown tunic, leathern leggings and boots. He sighed. The black barrier could not keep his River out, at least, despite its apparent ability to keep him in. He sent out a thin beam of Magic to test it again and watched as the spell bounced back. Then, he slumped to the floor and began the laborious task of trying to sift the barrier's weave.

****

Naboth, Jorl, and The Jamus made short work of the trip back to

Jorl's cottage, navigating the trails with Magic added to the ponies' sure hoofs. Once there, they set to inventing the best story to take back to Sarkem's Keep.

All went well with the plan until The Jamus encountered Whim.

The silver stallion would have no part of him, first shying away from his hand, then turning to back to challenge him. His sharp hooves pawed the earth as he lowered his head, shaking it angrily, ears flat back. He snorted and The Jamus backed warily away.

"He knows I'm not his master," The Jamus said.

"Nonsense," Naboth replied. "Talk to him. He's only a dumb beast. You startled him, that's all."

The Jamus held out his hand. "There now, good fellow. Take it easy. We've work to do together." If he hadn't been quick enough pulling his hand back, he might have lost it to Whim's savage teeth.

The stallion snaked his head out again a second later sending The Jamus reeling back through the gate.

"Well," Naboth said, shaking his head, "we seem to have a problem here. Never mind. You tell them back at the Keep that the horse went lame and you left him here with Jorl to be tended."

"But what about going back to Magiskeep? Surely I'll need to take him then."

Naboth grinned wickedly. "The lameness couldn't be cured, even with all of Jorl's tending. It happens, even in the best of worlds. A broken leg refusing to mend at Magic's command? An injury discovered too late? Jorl had to put him down in the end, that's all. We can't have the beast ruining our plan."

"Get rid of him now, then," Jorl said. "I don't want to have to deal with that devil if I can avoid it. I'm no horseman."

Naboth raised his hand, pointing it deliberately at Whim.

But when the blast of black fire seared out, the stallion simply melted into a mist and vanished.

Naboth frowned, then cursed when Whim appeared again off to the right outside the corral in a clearing beside the house. "Damn the River, he's chanted. I should have known. Had I sifted him, this never would have happened." When one more bolt of fire failed to hit its target he grunted in disgust. "Curse the beast. Leave him. The best we can hope is that he wanders off in search of his true master. I'll send my own Shadowbeasts to hound him. That should keep him occupied as long as we need."

The issue settled, they packed a knapsack with several of Jorl's potions, tied them to one of the ponies' saddles and The Jamus set off for Sarkem's Keep.

"Remember," Jorl called after him, "use the whole vial in her drink. It should take a Windchange, no more. I'll be ready."

The Jamus waved an acknowledgement and headed up the trail.

"Now, my Lord," Jorl said, "would you care to share my hospitality? I've a fine cut of cavil to roast."

"Don't bother," Naboth said. "I like my meat raw."

Jorl grimaced. "So be it. I'll cook mine, though, if it doesn't offend you. Have you a taste for wine?"

"Do as you will. As long as you are still flesh, you must act accordingly. I will supply the wine from my River's cellar. The common brews of this land are far too frail for my taste."

They settled to the erratic dinner, the candles making dim light in the cottage against the blazing fire Jorl insisted on stoking. "I'm always cold, it seems. Is the Dragon like that?"

"The Dragon is the Dragon," Naboth answered, licking the blood from his fingers as he lay a cavil bone on the table. "There is neither heat nor cold in his realm. You feel the emptiness while you linger in that mortal skin you wear. When you give it up, you'll have no need of fire."

"I don't intend to give it up soon," Jorl said. "As Mage, I have the choice of the wind my circle closes."

"So you say."

"The bargain struck gave me sovereignty. You said so yourself."

"Words of the Way, Flesher. Did you study them in the mirror?"

"You still need me."

"Aye, that I do, and the Dragon strikes bargains in reality and reflection. Your life is your own, as long as you do his bidding."

Jorl shifted uncomfortably in his chair. "This is the last deed I was to do. Once it's done I was promised secrets of the Darkness. You said I could rule in Magiskeep when I knew them."

"You will rule when the Keep falls to the Shadows. Don't think the Dragon will surrender enough strength to you to defeat the Keep's River by yourself."

"You've great confidence in your plan. Suppose Lord Jamus doesn't break? As long as his Will survives, his River will command Magiskeep."

"There are more Wills than his ruling that River," Naboth answered. "Seven Masters rule Seven Arts. One at a time we will twist them to the Black Dragon's Way. Like you, they have ambition, grudges, weakness, and ignorance. These are the weapons we use against them. Once seven wills fail, will the One stand against them?"

"Jamus is strong."

"He is a man, nonetheless, and men stumble."

Jorl took a sip of the thick, rich wine and considered his own situation. He was in far too deep to see any way out of his covenant with Naboth and the Shadows. Why, then, did he clutch at the faint hope Jamus might somehow escape this fate? He hated Magiskeep and all it stood for, and yet there was something about its Master tugging at his conscience as if somehow he owed the man loyalty. Was it Jamus himself or what he stood for? He shook the thoughts away. He was a grown man now, not the child warped by Rule and Vow in Magiskeep's classrooms. What had they ever done for him except ridicule his peculiar talents? Damn Jamus and his kind. "It will be a pleasure to watch him fall," he said at last.

****

Spans of study revealed nothing about the barrier-not one single thread of its weave.

Jamus sank back in frustration rubbing his eyes in exhaustion. He'd even tried touching the darkness again, and, as before, he was thrown back in piercing pain as soon as his fingertips reached it. If enduring the pain was the secret, he would have risked all and passed through. But with the pain, there was a physical force as well, pummeling his body back, so that even if he dared, it was still an impossible task.

He had to find another way out.

The cave walls and ceiling, though high up, were all impenetrable rock. He tested now and again with his Magic, and even considered using Spellfire to blast a hole in the mountain. But a short attempt at a tunnel proved Naboth had thought of the same thing, and had extended the barrier on all sides instead of just at the door. The White flames had sparked back, as they had done before, nearly hitting him.

"Fine thing," he muttered. "Wouldn't Naboth be delighted coming back to find out I'd killed myself with my own stupidity."

It was Naboth's move then, not his. Idly, he swept the sand away from the runes, deciding to study them while he waited.

There was really nothing else to do.

****

The Jamus arrived at Greenhope shortly before evenmeal,

making his excuses for the day with the story of Whim's injury and an interesting visit to the falls and caves.

Salene was confused by his story of the stallion's lameness, but kept her tongue until they were alone, wisely deciding to avoid discussing the horse in front of their hosts.

"So the runes did speak of a curse, just a Jorl said?" Delise asked again. Though The Jamus had already told the story once, she seemed to need reassurance.

"Indeed," he answered. "It's just as I told you. I can't say I'm ready to accept it yet, but the words do indicate Jorl was not as mistaken as I'd thought."

"Words alone do not make a curse," Salene said. "You, of all people should know that, Jamus. There's something more you're not telling us."

He shrugged. "It's just a feeling I have. This time, there was something in the air I couldn't quite sift. I'd need more proof, of course, something tangible to convince me one way or another, but for now, I'm satisfied to consider it a possibility."

"The Rivermaster's Magic would penetrate any weave, wouldn't it?" Sarkem asked.

"If my Magic were all Turan had to offer, it would," The Jamus said. "But I'm not familiar enough with the Shadow's Art to be confident about sifting its secrets."

"Shadows," Salene said, shivering. "You think they have a hand in this?"

"The runes suggest it."

"Shadows," Delise said thoughtfully. "I thought they were creatures of myth."

The Jamus sighed. "I wish it were so, Madame. I've seen enough to know better."

Without thinking, Sarkem raised his hand to intensify the Maglit sconces on the wall, filling the room with a flare of bright, silver light. "I toast the River's shining," he said, raising his goblet. "May the waters rise to the Rivermaster's hand, and his life inspire the Keep."

The Jamus smiled. The wish was more than he had hoped for.

****

"I really don't feel well," Salene insisted when The Jamus tried to kiss her in their bedroom.

"Let me Touch you then," he said, stroking her cheek.

She nodded.

The Jamus placed his hands on either side of her neck, and she closed her eyes as he began to massage her. "Strange," he said.

"What?"

"Your skin is soft as cavilcream. I never noticed before."

"For shame, Sur, you break your Healer's Vow by getting personal with your patient."

He nearly drew away, but then he saw the smile on her lips and relaxed. "I am sorry, Madam. But when a Healer has so luscious a patient, it's hard to remember a promise made so many circles ago."

Salene started to laugh. Then she grunted and clutched at her stomach. "Oh! Jamus, please, something's wrong!"

He made move as if to help her, then reeled away as if suddenly wracked by a spasm of his own. "By the blood," he gasped, his chest heaving, "not now, not now!"

"Jamus!" Salene cried, fighting to keep from doubling over as she stretched out her hands towards him. "What is it?"

"My wound," he panted, "the pain. Damn that Jorl and his tonics. I'm dizzy, dizzy....so tired...."

"Help! Somebody!" She screamed now, loud and long.

The door opened. "My Lady?"

"Get help, Maggie," Salene cried to the frightened serving woman. "We need the Healer, now!"

Maggie raced away. An instant later, Delise appeared with Sarkem at her heels.

By now, The Jamus had collapsed on the floor, his eyes closed in pretended unconsciousness.

Delise rushed over to Salene. "My poor dear, what's wrong?" Her mouth gaped open. Already the crimson stain of blood was seeping through Salene's nightgown between her legs. "By the Hand, the child."

Salene looked down and moaned. Then she fell back onto the bed trying to knot herself into a ball is if somehow she could hold back the inevitable.

On the floor, The Jamus fingered the empty vial in his pocket and smiled inwardly. He let Sarkem roll him over and lay still as the striped stone on the bed table. So far, everything was perfect.

Chapter 7

Jamus woke from his doze with a start, all his senses alert, the River charging to his hand. Something too terrible to contemplate had happened, churning the waters to a near frenzy. He heard thunder outside and could tell, from the nearly impenetrable darkness in the cave that the sky outside was thickening with clouds. He could feel Magic's turmoil and let it fill him with his own, strengthening his Will to stelin intent.

Let Naboth come. Whatever he had done, the Rivermaster would not yield.

The Shadowlord arrived as if on cue, his clothes dripping from the storm. "Your skies bellow, Rivermaster," he said, shaking the water from his black hair. He swept his hand over his burgundy cape, drying it with a casual spell. "The clouds burst too quickly even for me. I shielded too late. It should please you to hear that."

"Any time you suffer pleases me," Jamus answered.

Apparently, Naboth had dressed formally for the occasion. With arrogant flair, he whipped off his cape to reveal a black and burgundy velvet tunic falling to his knees with a border of gold brocade. He posed for a moment, as if considering what to say next. "You are so sure of yourself, Flesher. It will please me to shatter your certainty."

"The River upholds me," Jamus replied.

"We shall soon see. The Healer does not travel on the wind as I do, and your storm will slow him even more. But when he comes, we will test your mettle."

Jamus forced himself to settle back, sitting on one of the large rocks by the wall. "Tell me, Naboth, did you ever have a life before you gave yourself to your Dragon? Surely, you were once at least the spirit of a man."

"Once. So many circles past I can't even remember. I lived a wretched life of want and misery. Once I'd learned to kill I found solace."

"Good men rise above their circumstances."

"Oh, so you are one to judge? A man of privilege and power cannot ever begin to understand the torment of an empty life. We shall see how you maintain your virtue when you are broken and wanting, Master of Magiskeep. You are brazen now, content with your Magic and confidence. But how will you fare when a season passes? Or the second? How bold will you be after a circle of your own company and no one to affirm your worth?"

"I've been alone before. I've wrestled with nightmares too."

"Hah," Naboth spat. "I'm not talking about imaginary demons. I'm talking about the kind of demons that prey upon a man's mind until he goes mad. I'm talking about your own thoughts, your doubts, your guilts, and above all, uncertainty. These you cannot escape, and when they are your only companions, even Waymadness would seem relief."

Choosing to ignore the threat, one he would prefer not to consider yet, Jamus took another course. "Like Jorl?"

"You think he's mad?"

"I think he's traveled the Way too many times."

"Has he now?" There was something strange in Naboth's tone, hinting of another secret he intended to keep.

Jamus pressed him. "He doesn't act like a Keep trained Magician, but I've traced his history and know full well he is. I find it hard to accept how far he's strayed from the precepts he was taught by Magic's masters."

"Perhaps he's learned to be wise in his circles in the world."

"It's not wisdom; it's a denial of some very basic beliefs. By rights, without them, the River should not even answer his call."

"He is a pitiful sorcerer," Naboth said. "Perhaps his lack explains it."

"No. He's wandered too far."

"So you say. But the Way has riddles even you've not solved, I think." Naboth looked out at the falls. "Time in your world passes and still he's not here. Whatever your Jorl may be, he is certainly slow of foot."

"Can a master of eternity be impatient?"

Naboth spun. "Hungry, that's all. Even I anticipate a feast." Once more, for no reason he could fathom, Jamus shuddered.

****

Jorl had made it to Greenhope's main house in a matter of minutes once he was called.

He had been fully prepared, for he knew exactly how long it would take for the potion in the vial to work. He had told The Jamus to put it in Salene's drink at evenmeal, and counted the spans since. He was pleased to discover he'd nearly been perfect in his calculations.

When he arrived in the bedroom, Salene lay moaning on the bed, soaked in blood. The scene was flavored with drama, for The

Jamus lay unconscious on the floor with Sarkem cradling his head in his lap while Delise wailed helplessly at Salene's side. Two maidservants were doing their best to comfort the stricken ladies, but there was little they could do to ease anyone's suffering.

Jorl took immediate charge. "Get me some warm water, towels and a ceramic basin. Sarkem, get some men to help you drag Lord Jamus out of here. And you, Maggie, take Lady Delise to her rooms. Here." He handed the maid a small bottle. "Give her five drops of this in some water. She'll fall asleep quickly. Stay with her. If she stirs before Easwin, dose her again. I'll be in come daylight to tend her."

"And Jamus?" Sarkem asked.

"Jamus later, his wife now. Put him to bed somewhere as well. Brew some keldherb to give him if he wakes. Tell him his wife in safe in my care. Now go."

It took him the better part of two spans to care for Salene. She had lost the child, just as he'd intended, and he placed its remains in the bowl, covering it with a towel as he set it aside. Then, with surprising gentleness, he cleaned Salene and, with Emila's help, changed her nightgown and the bedding. When they were done, Magiskeep's mistress was lying in a restless doze on fresh sheets as if nothing at all had happened.

Jorl Touched her quietly then, doing all he could to ease the rest of her pain and heal any damage the miscarriage might have done. "Her body will heal," he said, "but I can do nothing to cure her mind."

"She needs her husband," Emila said. "She can't bear this alone."

"If he's not well, his weakness will only add to hers. You stay with her and I'll go take care of him. Then, I'll properly dispose of this." He picked up the towel covered bowl. "T'will be treated with respect, I assure you. Comfort the Lady with that if she wakes." He did not notice the faint wisp of silver mist drifting away from the bowl as he carried it off. Somehow, he had forgotten the River always claimed her own.

The Jamus was an easy matter to resolve. A quick Healing Touch restored him to consciousness and a sip of an energy potion brought him to his full senses.

"By the Hand, Jorl," Sarkem said, "your powers still amaze me. Have you been so able with Lord Jamus' wife?"

Jorl hesitated, as if reluctant to report in front of The Jamus. "She is well, My Lord."

The Jamus sat up. "And the child?"

Jorl shook his head. "It was too late. There was nothing I could do."

The Jamus balled his hands into fists and pounded the blanket. "Why? Salene is strong and there was no reason for her to lose our baby."

"The curse, somehow the curse," Jorl replied quietly.

"Nonsense. Lady Salene never went to your caves," Sarkem said. "Are you telling us the curse follows the husband as well? If that were true, every woman in Greenhope whose man has gone to that stream should be barren."

"It must have been something else. You didn't bring anything back from the cave, did you?"

The Jamus started to shake his head, then stopped. "The rock. By the Blood, I brought back one of those strange striped rocks and gave it to Salene. You can't mean to tell me the curse came with them."

Jorl sighed. "The rock was tainted, My Lord. A poison for sure."

The Jamus groaned.

Sarkem sank down on the edge of the bed. "I find this hard to accept, Sur, but, what can a man like me say now? Two children of the River's blood have been lost and in both cases those caves have somehow been involved."

The Jamus struggled for words. "The runes, I saw the runes. Bory, I should have listened to Jorl from the first."

"Go to your wife, Master, and stay with her. There's no point in weeping alone over what's been done."

The Jamus climbed from his bed and left the room. Sarkem sat staring at the floor. "If the caves can defeat the Rivermaster, what can I do? This is my land, and on it, I have a danger to my people."

"Destroy the caves," Jorl said. "Even small Magic should be able to close them off. Seal the entrances so no one else can ever wander in."

"I don't want to go there," Sarkem said. "I never want to be near those caves again."

"Such Magic can be done from afar, My Lord. Surely you can conjure a simple spell like that. Lord Jamus would probably be quite eager to help you. You can go to Overlook and cast from there. Seal the doors, Master, and end this threat."

Sarkem nodded. Then, he got up and plodded to the door. "I have to go to apologize to my own wife," he said.

Only when he was alone did Jorl smile. He stole a quick glance at the mirror in the corner of the room to survey his appearance. It really was remarkable how real he looked.

****

If anything, the storm grew worse as the wind reached full change. The darkness was solid and intense, turning even the bravest of lanterns to mere halos of light as travelers caught out in the dark fought their way to shelter.

Jorl's little mountain pony trudged along, its body twisted as it tried to turn its rump to the wind. The Healer prodded the beast with his heels, trying to urge it to a faster pace, but the animal was wise enough in the ways of the mountain trails to mark each step carefully.

By the time Jorl reached the clearing near the falls, he was soaked to the skin and nearly frozen. Teeth chattering, he slipped and slid his way into the cave, holding the bowl close to his body so as not to drop it.

"At last," Naboth said, rising from the cushions he had conjured to make himself comfortable. He'd lit the room with glowing yellow lanterns to ward off the darkness just enough so he could see Jamus and now, Jorl. "You've brought it?"

Shivering, Jorl nodded. "It went as we planned, My Lord. Exactly."

"Bring it to me."

Nearly stumbling, Jorl offered the bowl to the Shadowlord.

Naboth pulled off the towel, and grinned. He moved over to the black barrier and held out the bowl for Jamus to see. "Do you know what this is, Flesher? Eh?"

Jamus did not answer. He clenched his teeth, fighting to control a sweeping sense of dread.

"Blood of thy blood, flesh of thy flesh, life of thy life," the Shadowlord intoned. "*End of life, of life anew, Sacrifice I take of you. Be the Shadow's endless breath, given at the price of death.*" He raised the bowl to his lips and drank.

Someone's horrible scream drowned out the sound of his sickening slurps, and Jamus realized it was his own as he collapsed in the sand in more pain than the black barrier could ever have inflicted.

****

Darkness, complete, and with it something stabbing at his heart. Every fiber burning with Spellfire intensity.

Not Spellfire, though. Too dangerous here. What then? Grief.

He'd never felt it before. Not like this.

How must it be for Salene? The Hand preserve her.

"Don't despair, child of my being."

The voice was soft, warm, and comforting, wrapped in a dim golden light in the farthest corner. "No hope," he answered hoarsely. "It's too late. He's won."

"Thy blood is my blood, Lord of the River. Have you forgotten? The child is no more, but does hope die with her?"

"A daughter."

"No more. I am the River's Will. She is mine now."

"No, I saw him...." His voice trailed off.

"The Magic is not flesh, my son. Can you not remember?"

Little comfort there. What had once been his child had vanished in the way of Magic long before the blood had touched Naboth's lips. "In the end, it doesn't matter. He killed my daughter and I can't do anything about it. And Salene?"

"She lives."

"With pain greater than mine could ever be. I can't help her here."

"Then leave."

"How? I can't pass that barrier. I could stand the pain, for her sake, but it tosses me back like a leaf in the wind. It defies my Magic. Tell me how."

"This, I cannot, child of my waters. Find the tapestry and repair the weave. Bear your grief in reason instead of rage."

"Damn you. Riddles again. Not now. I have too many tears yet to spend."

"While he laughs."

The golden light faded into the darkness, swallowed, it seemed, but agonizing reality.

Jamus woke.

Naboth was gone again, and Jorl too. The only possible satisfaction was that the storm still savaged the outside world. Since his Art was its source, it was possible neither dark mage would have been able to protect himself from the rain. Little revenge, but little was better than none.

****

Feverish, Salene tossed against her pillows, her mind reeling with hundreds of thoughts jumbling into a pile of madness. Jorl's drugs had eased her pain and healed her body, but nothing could soothe the torment of loss.

She opened her eyes and saw The Jamus, sitting on the edge of the bed, not even looking at her. Was she so repulsive now in her

failure? Would he ever forgive her? Worse, did she deserve
forgiveness? "Jamus?"

He turned slightly. "What is it, my love?" The endearment
seemed almost as afterthought.

"I'm sorry."

"Sorry?" He sounded as if he didn't know what she was
talking about.

"Our baby. I'm sorry I lost her."

"Oh, that." He started to get up, then sagged back onto the
mattress. Be the reflection, you fool. Play the part or they'll know.
He would care for her, support her, love her, no matter what. The
child mattered to them. Show it. "It's not your fault, Salene, not your
fault. It's mine. I should have listened to Jorl."

"The baby" The words choked in her throat.

"Please, Salene, my love, please, don't blame yourself. By
the Hand, if I could just undo it all."

"You don't hate me?"

"Hate you? Why should I hate you, my darling? You are the
most precious, most wonderful thing in all my life. It's not your
fault, it's mine. I let my arrogant pride deny the curse and in my
stupidity I brought it to you. I'm the one who killed her, not you."

"No, not you. Never you." She sat up weakly, her hand
fluttering to his shoulder. "Hold me. I need you."

The Jamus slid over and took her awkwardly in his arms. "In
Sogol's Name, I never thought anything could hurt like this."

Salene began to weep, burying her faced in his chest.
The Jamus rested his head on her golden hair and sighed. Naboth had
not told him how boring this part of the plan was going to be.

****

Jamus sat in the darkness for a long time, letting his grief
pour out in tears and sighs. It was as if he was purging himself all
emotion until he was a hollow shell without a heart.

How easy to be empty. There was no pain, no memory, no
thought.

But there had to be thought. Reason and logic were the
River's law, the even keel to sail her waters. If she were to be his
defense, he must be her captain.

Think.

What had she told him in the dream? Bear your grief in
reason, not in rage. Find the tapestry and repair the weave.

Riddles and more riddles, and yet in riddles lay the answers. If he was charged with repairing a weave, then there must be some way to reach it.

It couldn't be the black barrier, though, for all his efforts to sift it had been in vain. Whatever weave patterned it was beyond his Comprehension.

Then where? Someplace, there had to be a Magic he hadn't yet detected.

He looked around his little cave, letting Mage's eyes perceive illusion, but again, he found none. Then, his gaze lowered to Jorl's runes and he reconsidered. Already the words had revealed a small part of Naboth's plan, and certainly they had been a useful lure to draw him into the trap.

The storm outside had subsided to a heavy, steady rain. As the stream began to overflow its banks, water began to seep into the caves, gradually increasing into its own little rivulet. The black barrier did nothing to stop the flow and soon, it was running into Jamus; cave pooling at the base of the far wall.

"Fine thing," he muttered. "If I don't die of Naboth's torture, I can drown instead.

With hardly a thought, he raised his hand. "It is enough."

The ancient words of command touched the dark skies and the rain softened while the winds began to ease.

The pool, despite the continual flow from outside, stabilized, and then, amazingly enough, began to diminish.

Jamus focused his attention there. The water was draining out, somewhere. Then, he caught his breath. There had to be a hollow beneath the stone.

Jamus dropped to his knees and began to dig away the wet sand. Though a layer of the striped stones and a pile of sticks and other debris washed in during earlier floods, he found the channel.

The space between the rocks was narrow, but as he dug, Jamus soon opened up a space he could squeeze through. He peered down, using threads of Maglit to illuminate the hole. There, at the bottom lay a pool of water, settled now with a mirrored surface reflecting the light from above.

The Way.

Hardly considering any danger, Jamus dropped his feet down into the opening and let his body slide into the pool below.

The surface rippled in the silver light as he slipped through and under.

"Come to me."

"Here, Master. This way."

"No, over here."
"Don't listen to her. This is the way out."
"She's a liar. Come to me."

He fell solidly into a room in the Way.

Above him, the pool in the cave shimmered a span above his head, offering a way back into his prison. The only other way out was a single mirror, glowing with the unsteady light of another realm within the Way. He could clearly see there was no route to Turan's reality from here. Still, the misty image of trees beyond the reflection promised more than the caves he'd left. He stepped into the mirror, and into the water.

A moment later, Jamus' head broached the surface of a fern edged pool in the middle of a forest glen.

Pale sunlight filtered in through the thick branches of elms, brellums, and oaks, rising like sentinels on all sides. Somewhere, not far off, a tarlet trilled, and a shy duskit darted to cover under a feathery brellybush.

Jamus waded to shore, waved his hand over his body to dry himself and smiled, pleased to know at least his Magic worked according to his Will in this place.

Scanning the area, he could see no trail, no sign of any kind of path through the dense trees.

"Hello! Is anybody here?" His voice echoed back, unanswered. Strange. He'd never found an exit room in the Way without at least one person in it. Every world he'd ever visited had been peopled. Besides, if this were part of the weave he had to solve, there had to be someone with the answer to the riddle.

Right, left, forward, or behind. With no full sense of the sun, there was no way to be sure which direction he would travel.

Still, it wasn't the cave, and free for now of Naboth's trap, he could make his own choices.

He closed his eyes and let his other senses lead his feet. Then, he began walking right, letting fate guide him the rest of the way.

****

"We're going home tomorrow, My Lord," The Jamus said when Sarkem met him on the stairs at Easwin. "Salene needs another day of rest, but no more. Neither she nor I want to be here any longer. At least Magiskeep can afford us a measure of comfort with our own beds and society. Sarena is Compassion's Mistress with a talent far beyond mine for Touching wounded spirits. She may be able to help my wife."

"And who will help you, My Lord? Don't ignore your own pain. Believe me, I know how foolish that can be."

"I won't ignore it, Sur, but I won't dwell on it at Salene's expense. Right now, she's far more important than I am." He raised his hand as Sarkem started to protest. "Don't worry. I have confidents in Magiskeep myself to whom I can turn. I'll find comfort there too." The Jamus paused, as if thinking. "I was wondering if we could impose on your generosity once more, though. Salene certainly can't ride back home and with Whim injured, I am without a horse myself. Could we borrow a carriage and team for the trip?"

"Did you even need to ask?" Sarkem replied. "I have a fine team and a carriage with a ride as soft as silk. Take both, and keep them as long as you need. It's a small payment for all I owe."

"You owe me nothing except an end to all of this."

"You mean the cave?"

"I thought we could ride out before Sowin and do double duty with that stream," The Jamus said. "We can divert the bed to water your fields and put an end to the cursed caves at the same time."

"Your Magic would be welcome, My Lord," Sarkem said. "I'm not the Master you are."

The Jamus shook his head. "You shall do the honor, Sur, not I. With me beside you, the River will grant you all the Power you need. But this is your land, and your keeping, not mine."

"Come then, Master Jamus, if you've an appetite, we'll share earlenmeal and then ride out. I'm eager to be done with this. Delise has spoken of nothing else since Lady Salene fell ill. I can't really blame her. Had I listened to her when she…we lost our child, perhaps you and your wife wouldn't have suffered the same fate."

"You were lax in this, Sur, and unfeeling. But poor judgment should not condemn you for the rest of your days," The Jamus said coldly, catching Sarkem completely off guard. "Pay for your indiscretion now. Let your hand bury the curse forever, and with it, all memories of its existence."

"I'll never forget it. How can you?"

"By shutting it away in the darkness, Sur. What man cannot see, man cannot remember. It will take some time, I admit, but the darkness will ease the pain in the end. You'll see."

"Strange to hear you talk that way, My Lord."

The Jamus stiffened. "What do you mean?"

"To speak of darkness as an ally. It's not something I'd expect from the Rivermaster."

"Ah. But you see what I meant, don't you? Once those caves are closed, the curse will be shut forever from the light of day, that's all."

Sarkem frowned, puzzled by Jamus' quick defense. "I understood, My Lord. It was just the way you'd put it, that's all."

The Jamus relaxed a little. "I'm sorry." He raked his fingers through his hair and sighed. "I guess I'm more upset than I realized."

"Of course, of course. I, of all, understand. But let's not waste time sharing regrets. I'll send Dane to saddle the horses and we can go as soon as the sun's high enough to light the ravine trail."

The Jamus nodded bleakly. But once Sarkem had gone, he walked over to the counter and poured himself some amberwine, raising the goblet in a mock toast. "To you, Rivermaster, and your new life in eternal darkness. Let us see how long you bear your pride without the sun to fire your courage." Then he downed the drink in one gulp and poured himself another.

Chapter 8

How far he had wandered mattered more than how long, for time meant nothing in the Way. But fatigue and frustration were unaffected by the Mirrors' Magics, and Jamus' steps grew slower and slower as he trudged along, weaving an uncertain path among the towering trees.

After a while, everything had begun to look exactly the same and even the shadows appeared to twist in different directions at each turning. Strangely, though, they neither lengthened nor faded as he journeyed on, hinting of time's perversion in this world.

Each effort assured him he was passing through reflection, rather than reality, lingering in some sort of mirrored existence.

That might well have explained how tired he felt as well, for meeting Magic face to face in every direction wore at Jamus' senses as his own Will involuntarily sifted the alien Power. It was, he decided, even worse than crossing the Rim with all its Illusions. At least there, the Magic was of his River. Here, it was bred of some other source.

Just as he reached the brink of exhaustion was ready to let his body collapse against a tree trunk for some rest, Jamus spotted a faint wisp of smoke rising ahead between some thinner branches. He took a deep breath to steady himself and headed for the alluring sight, hoping it was not just another deceit in the midst of the endless forest.

There, etched in startling contrast to the vertical tree trunks, sat a little stone cottage surrounded by bright red and yellow flowers and a wide patch of emerald green grass.

Jamus made his way up a cobble walk to the door and knocked.

"Come in, come in, Rivermaster. I were wonderin' when ye'd reach my door. If ye are fair tired, then ye are right on time. Elsewise, the Sights have underestimated thy skill."

"Well, I'm past tired, so I'd say your 'sights' knew me better than I did," he replied, pushing open the door.

There by a weak little fire in a huge stone fireplace sat an old, silver-haired woman dressed in a scarlet robe wrapped around her thin body. At her feet lay a brindle tark, its great head dropped on its front paws, its amber eyes half closed as it noted Jamus' entrance.

The Rivermaster froze at the sight of the great mountain cat. "Is he tame enough for me to come in?"

"She," the old woman corrected, "does not eat Sorcerers of the Right Rivers, if that's what you mean. Do you have faith enough in thine to risk it?"

Jamus considered. His River had sent him here. He walked into the room.

The tark yawned and closed her eyes.

"You know my name, My Lady. Would you grant me yours?"

"Aye, My Lord. Taba has accepted ye as worthy, and so shall I. I be Keldra, Seer of the Caves."

"The caves? This looks like a forest."

"To eyes what want to see, it is what they will. Have ye truly escaped thy prison or are ye but in another chamber?"

Jamus' weary legs gave way at her words and he sank to the floor. "Another dream, then."

"Naught but the reality ye make, Rivermaster. The Black Dragon is no easy foe. Did ye think to flee his trap so simply?"

"Then this isn't a way out."

"I did not so say. It is here ye must riddle, as thy Lady already told ye."

Jamus sighed. He let his body sag onto the rag rug on the floor, ignoring the tark's interest in his new posture. He had no strength at all in his body. "I can't answer any riddles. I can't even think."

Keldra slowly pushed to her feet. She took a blanket from a nearby chair and stiffly made her way over to Jamus. "Then sleep, son of Magic, and let peace restore thy energy. It be too long since ye rested. Rest now in the haven of my house. Here there be no darkness, here no grief." She rested her skinny hand on his head, her bony fingers gently stroking his hair. "Naught shall harm thee. Sleep."

Jamus closed his eyes, and for the first time in many circles, he slept, untroubled and at ease.

Purring mightily, Taba settled against him, her supple catframe fitting neatly into contours of his body.

****

The journey back to Magiskeep in the carriage took nearly twelve winds, for Sarkem's horses had half the stamina of Magiskeep mounts and far less tolerance for Magic aided travel. Salene spoke little during the trip, offering little more than a few polite apologies for her silences.

To The Jamus, it was a blessing. The less he had to talk to her, the less the risk of making a mistake. Luckily she hadn't bothered to ask about their horses and had let them settle her in the carriage under a soft blanket without a whimper of protest. She'd even slept both Norwins of the trip in the seat, preferring the close quarters of the vehicle to the ground and the stars she usually enjoyed while they were on the road. "I don't want the skies to see me," she said, by way of explanation, and The Jamus had nodded wisely as he went off to sleep by himself.

But he really didn't sleep, for it was not his nature. The darkness invigorated him, heightening his senses to every scent and sound. While she slept, he hunted, quenching his thirst on the blood of dorsetts he could ambush, or on careless duskits too young and ignorant to leap away at the first sound of rustling in the bushes. He cursed the barren landscape otherwise, promising himself he would remedy the lack of settlements between Sarkem's hold and Magiskeep's. Human blood would be far more sating, and the next time he took this trip, he wanted to be able to feast better.

Still, the animal's flavor eased his hunger pangs and moved him inches closer to his reality, the ambition of every Shadow, no matter how anointed by the Dragon. True, he had been chosen especially and promised more than most, but he knew his Master's capricious Will and had no intention of trusting his vows. He was on his own in the end and would do all he could to assure success.

They arrived at Magiskeep during Evenmeal, so old Josep was not there to greet them at the stableyard. The young hand who took care of the team and rig knew better than to ask questions of the Keep's true Lord and simply took the reins as The Jamus helped his stricken wife out of the carriage and up to the palace.

The Main Hall was equally empty, with most of the servants eating in the Dining Hall or off to their homes. The Jamus and Salene slowly made their way up the main staircase and to their bedroom, where he tucked her into bed. "I'm going to find Sarena, my love," he said gently. "She'll know what to do."

"There's nothing to do," Salene replied. "She can't bring back what we've lost. This emptiness has no fill, Jamus."

"She'll know," he repeated. As he shut the door behind him, his lips curled in the familiar smile. As long as he could keep her at a distance, he stood a chance.

Sarena was in her rooms, but it took The Jamus a few extra minutes to find her. So used to the Way instead of reality, he kept turning in the opposite direction in the halls, mistaking left doors for

right ones. Once he'd oriented himself, he took a deep breath and
knocked.

"Come in," a warm voice said from inside.

"Sarena? I need your help."

Seated at her tabe, the Mistress of Healing was reading from
a thick tome, her dark hair spilling on the shoulders of her demure
white gown as she turned her head from text to the herbs beside it.

Pity, The Jamus thought, *to cover her soft skin with cloth. So
much beauty should be flaunted, not draped with bedsheets.* He
licked his lips.

Sarena looked up and half rose. "My Lord! Jamus. I didn't
know you were back."

"We've just arrived," he said, pushing his lust back to
pretense. He told her the gist of what had happened, letting his words
run quickly together as if he had to push them out to avoid
confronting the sense of what he was saying.

Sarena rose quietly, her whole manner calm and assuring.
"You need help, My Lord. Here, sit down. I have some herbs to calm
you."

"Not me. I'm not the one. Salene needs…"

"You first, Jamus. The Healer cannot Heal when he suffers.
"Here." She handed him an earthen cup. "Drink this."

Taking the cup, he held her hand in thanks, not noticing how
her eyes widened in surprise. "Thank you, My Lady." He pretended
to sip, then put the brew down. "I'm all right, really I am. I have the
River to hold me. The Waters soothe me better than any brew you
might offer, Lady. I've failed with Salene, though. She keeps
pushing me away."

"It's harder for her," Salene said. "She's lost a part of
herself."

"It was my child too."

"In her body. As Compassionate as you may be, My Lord,
it's not something a man could ever really understand. Stay here is
you wish, and finish the tonic. I'll go take care of your wife."

With Sarena gone, The Jamus poured the drink out into one
of the herb plants she had potted by the window. Then he examined
the book she had been studying seeking some sort of clue to her
recent interests. It would be important to find out how her mind was
working now. Of all the mages, she and Joria would be the hardest to
manipulate. Savel, for all his high and mighty purpose, was naïve
enough to fall for lies and the others, he'd been assured, had hidden
ambitions to prey on. The two women, though, were paragons of

virtue and wise in human perception. The Dragon's trickery would have to be keen indeed to sway them to his side.

Sarena had been studying energizing potions, reading about how to restore strength and vitality after a Healing. He grinned again, his teeth sharpening involuntarily. Jorl's brews would certainly interest the Master of Compassion. Magiskeep's outcast had clearly surpassed the teachers in this matter. Bargaining power? It was worth a thought.

Definitely worth a thought.

****

Jamus started to roll over only to find himself blocked by a heavy pile of furs. He was about to push them aside when he felt them move and heard a low rumbling sound. He started back as his eyes came into focus on Taba's huge body stretched out next to him.

"I've ne'er seen her take to anyone the way she's taken to ye, Master Jamus. Ye truly be the one I seek."

Jamus sat up slowly, trying not to disturb the mountain cat. "There have been others here? Where are they? I saw no signs of any other houses."

"Naught of this world, lad. And all have taken to the weave on the quest. So far none be returned. My cottage is the only one here, but beyond lie hundreds. I am but the stopping point before the tapestry. It is thy destiny to go forward still."

Jamus shook his head trying to clear his thoughts, to make some sense of her words. "I'm afraid I don't understand you, Madam."

"Ye aren't supposed to, Sur. 'Tis part of the riddle." She pointed to a back room. "In there lies the door. As ye already know, that pool in the cave was not a way out, but a way in. Ye are deep in the shadows, Rivermaster, and must go deeper still before ye can leave thy prison."

"But I will escape?"

She shrugged her shoulders. "That is for ye to say, not I. Three have gone before ye and not returned. I know not what fate befell them. Perhaps they chose to stay. Perhaps not. Yet still the weave lies open and the tapestry undone. Until the threads are tied, who is to say whether the world so woven will be the world or naught. Solve the riddle and thy Kingdom is saved. Fail and the tapestry unravels."

"Even your explanation is a riddle," he sighed. "I suppose I should have expected it. It's never easy in the Way."

Keldra laughed. "I've prepared a stew for ye. From the looks of ye, food has not been on thy mind of late. How long did the Shadows hold ye?"

"No more than the passing of four winds, as far as I can tell," Jamus replied. "But time in the Way…"

"Days now, My Lord. Near a Sevenstin has passed in thy world."

"My wife?" he asked hopefully.

"While ye slept I scried for thee. She is well in body, but her spirit mourns."

"I should be with her."

"She thinks ye are."

"The Shadow. He's with her, then. Damn."

"She is safe, for now. Even if ye were by her side, it would not matter. The grief she bears is too lonely to share. She will deal with it best in solitude and your Shadow prefers it that way. He has other duties."

"You know the Dragon's plan?" Jamus asked as he took a bite of the stew. Not as good as Becca's but tasty enough to fill the gnawing in his stomach. He'd not even realized he was hungry. Each bite seemed to heighten his senses and bring back some semblance of normality to his feelings. His own grief lay deep under layers of other, more pressing thoughts, as if the River were drowning it in its own needs, insisting on his full attention. It was just as well. Such pain was almost impossible to deal with.

"Whether I know or not matters little. I cannot tell ye more, for it is part of the secret ye must discover."

Something nudged his elbow. Jamus looked down as Taba shoved her head into his arm.

"She wants a bite of stew," Keldra said. "If ye feed her, ye'll ne'er be rid of her affection."

Jamus rubbed the tark's head until she began to purr. Then he offered her a spoonful of stew. "I'm honored she wants it," he said. "She's a magnificent creature."

"Her sister is in your world."

"It she as beautiful?"

"A perfect reflection," Keldra replied, winking. "As I said, ye have a friend for life."

Jamus smiled. Having a tark as a friend might well be worth something.

After feeding him a large slab of berry pie and a cup of sandelwine, Keldra led Jamus to the back room. There, on the wall, hung a huge tapestry. Woven into the pattern was Magiskeep's palace, its silver and blue towers bright against a graying cloudy sky.

Jamus' heart lurched at the sight of his home, so vividly portrayed. Had there not been a flaw in the lower right corner, near the stables, he might have believed he could step into the image to enter the Great Hall. "Who made this?"

"It is the Way, Rivermaster. 'Tis as much mirror as the pool ye entered. But see where the weave is not yet tied and the threads ready to unravel? It is up to thee to finish the tapestry at thy Will. Go, therefore, and make the mend as ye choose."

Jamus stepped towards the image, watching it begin to shimmer as he neared. An instant before he stepped through, Keldra laid her bony hand on his arm. "Be warned, Lord of Magiskeep, this is true reflection, unlike some ye have met before. Whate'er ye do there be truth for thy world."

"Truth or the reflection of truth? Mirrors reverse the images."

Keldra grinned a toothless smile. "Perhaps ye be wiser than the Dragon thinks, Waymaster. It is all up to thee." Then she gave him a healthy shove and he fell through the tapestry into the new world.

****

Sarena comforted Salene as best she could, all too aware there was really little she could do. Physically, she was Healed, but emotionally, she had not yet paid the full price for her loss.

"Jamus wants to help you, Salene."

"I don't want him near me. Don't you know what might happen? Suppose we should make love again? We can't, you know. We simply can't."

"There's no reason to think that."

"I'm cursed, Sarena. As soon as Jamus gave me that stone the curse of those caves fell on me. Do you think I want to kill another child? I've no right, no right at all. If I keep him away from me…" her voice choked.

"You're the guardian of your own life, Salene. It's not for me to tell you differently, but I find it hard to accept the idea of a curse. Does Jamus?"

Salene nodded. "Before we left, he and Sarkem went out to the falls and sealed the caves lest someone else fall victim to the evil there. Don't you see? The Rivermaster himself knows I'm tainted now. How can the Lord of Magiskeep risk his heir to my womb? Better he should find himself another mother for his children."

"No, Salene, you can't mean that."

Salene pounded the pillow with her fist. "I do, Sarena, I do. My poor little baby. I killed her. Why should I be allowed to kill another?"

Healing's Mistress dropped her hands helplessly at her side, powerless to offer the right answer. When the herbs she had given Salene began to work, Sarena left her asleep and went to Joria's chambers.

The grey robed sorceress was ready for bed, turning in early as she often did. Sarena's story roused her to intent interest. "Both Jamus and Salene believe in a curse? This is beyond my comprehension. Are you sure?"

"Not completely," Sarena told her. "I've only heard Salene admit it directly, but Jamus hinted of it when he first told me what happened. If he did block off those caves, I'd have to think he didn't dismiss it."

"This defies the very logic of the Keep. I can almost picture a rebel like Jorl accepting such a thing, but not Magiskeep's Lord."

"How well did you know Jorl? I'm too young to remember much about him."

Joria settled down in her rocker and tented her hands. "I was but the new Master myself when his talent was discovered. He'd been in my classes and nearly convinced me it'd be a mistake to plan a career as a teacher. I couldn't teach him a thing. Jeress was Mistress of Compassion then, and, as you know from the stories, her cup flew to his hand completely unbidden. After that, his talent for Healing flowered like the dailies in Greenmonth. There was nothing he couldn't cure. Rumor had it he once even brought a villager back from the dead."

"Impossible."

"So you said before Jamus' hand Healed Becca."

"It's not the same. He's the Rivermaster."

"Aye, and Jorl is a Master Healer beyond any I've ever seen before or since. The Gathering insisted on testing him and did so again and again. He was considered a freak of the River's caprices and everyone wanted to study him."

"He must have been very popular."

"Quite the contrary. If he was invited to an affair, it was as an oddity or conversation piece. He had few, if any, friends and plenty of people who wanted to use him for their own research or amusement."

"You couldn't have been so cruel."

Joria sighed. "I was too young and uncertain of myself to be outright cruel. Instead, I avoided him. As my only failure, Jorl was a blot on my precious reputation, so I pretended he never existed. I tell you, Sarena, what I did to that man was worse than the insults inflicted on him by the rest of my companions."

Sarena smoothed her gown with her hands and leaned back in her chair. "I wonder how I would have treated him if I'd been Mistress then. He would have been my rival. I never remember Jeress' mentioning him."

"She and I were nearly as close as you and I," Joria replied. "She acted better than I only because he held her cup. She did the least for him a Master could for an apprentice and left it at that. She was as relieved as I when he ran away from Magiskeep."

"No one tried to find him?"

"He disappeared in Norwin after a most embarrassing Evenmeal of answering questions before a collection of Lords and Ladies Sagari had invited to the Keep. When Jeress found his rooms empty the next Easwin, she never said a word about it. It wasn't until Weswin next when Sagari called for him again that anyone else noticed he was missing. By then, it was impossible to follow him."

"A Sorcerer who wants to be lost is lost for certain," Sarena said, quoting an Elden adage.

"Aside from Sagari, who'd lost his parlor pet, I don't think the rest of the Keep really cared. By then, Jorl had grown so bitter he was far from pleasant company. He'd taken to spending spans in the back corners of the Library reading all kinds of Eldenlore on Magic Unrestrained. I wouldn't be surprised if he did believe in curses with all that nonsense in his head."

"That doesn't explain Jamus and Salene."

"As I recall, when Jorl wanted to be charming, he could be quite persuasive. With Salene so vulnerable, she might easily fall under the spell of his words. Jamus, though," Joria frowned. "You spoke to him. Is he as irrational as his wife?"

Sarena shrugged. "He says not, but I'm not convinced. No matter what he says, Salene is his anchor in that River of his. With her adrift, he's forced to swim alone in those waters, and it's all he can do to keep from drowning. Besides, he's still suffering from the aftereffects of his injuries in the Rim."

"Then he'd be as easy mark for Jorl as well."

"I'd like to meet this Healer. A man capable of such influence would be interesting company," Sarena said.

"Then you should," Joria replied quickly. "I'll tell you what. Once Sarena is a bit better so you feel it's safe to leave her, you and I will go to Sarkem's Keep and see him. I, for one, would be grateful for the chance to make amends and you might learn something from him."

"Be it so," Sarena agreed. "Even the Mistress of Compassion can be a student now and again. It may well be he can teach me a thing or two."

"Let us hope he doesn't manage to convince us of his curse. I'd much rather live my life in ignorance of such things."

"Ignorance is the Mage's bane, Joria."

"Then let it be blessed," the Mistress of Illusion replied. Then she poured each of them a full goblet of amberwine.

Chapter 9

Jamus landed face down in a pile of dirty straw and dung heaped beside Magiskeep's stables. At least, it looked like his stable, though the hanging air of neglect and sloppiness bore little resemblance to Master Josep's meticulous premises. Still, the buildings and yard looked familiar, and when he scrambled to his feet and idly waved away the filth from his clothes with a casual spell, he was sure he recognized several of the horses' heads poking out of the stalls.

Redwin nickered softly, and Jamus walked over to the chestnut, his hand outstretched. The horse shied away, backing into the corner of his stall. Jamus whistled in disgust at the reek of urine and then grunted when he saw the horse's scruffy coat and too long hooves. While he looked reasonably well fed, his eyes were dull and he showed no sign of muscle or care.

When a quick survey of the rest of the stock showed similar conditions, Jamus wasted no time in remedying the situation. As foolhardy as it was to risk so much Magic such a new and untested place, he couldn't stand seeing the horses in such misery. One spell cleaned and bedded every stall, put fresh water in the buckets and slicked ill-kempt coats to reasonable polish.

Then he set out to find Josep.

But the old stableman was not there. In his place was a bedraggled fellow lounging about the offices with a mug of calidew in one hand and a plate of cheeses in the other. "Oh, Me Lord, whatcha want, eh? I kin saddle ya up a pony iffen ya wants ta ride, though ta be fair I cain't say I gots a sound one fer ya."

"I don't want to ride, Sur," Jamus replied. "What I do want is you off your lazy backside taking care of my horses as is proper. Where is Josep?"

"Eh? Josep? Ya knows right well ya sent 'im packin' Sevenstins ago, Me Lord. Ain't but one too many times 'e called ya on ridin' too hard as I recall." He laughed. "T'weren't a pretty sight—Josep all huffed up an' ya yellin' at 'im like a fishwife. Gotta pay ya the due, still 'cause ya din't use no Magic 'gainst 'im like the last time. What a woozy that were."

"Enough," Jamus commanded, almost too startled by the man's demeanor to manage to take control of the situation. "You seem to have mistaken me for someone else. I never dismissed Josep."

The man peered at Jamus' face for a long time, his bleary eyes scanning every feature. "Ya ain't one o' them backwalkers, is ya?"

"Backwalkers?"

"Yeah, the ones what think everything's opposite o' what it is? Ya know from the mirrors? Lord Jamus said sooner or later one what looks like 'im was gonna show up an' then there'd be the divil ta pay."

Once again, the man caught him off guard. Clearly this world of Keldra's tapestry had rules of its own he knew nothing about. "You've met backwalkers before, have you?"

"Course. They all start off in me dung heap over yonder. Yer too clean to have come by that way, though. I figger you be Lord's Illusion then, sent ta torment ol' Donni fer the hell o' it. Keepmaster's like that. Bit of a pranker, 'e is. Most times 'e don't mean no harm, but I seen 'im be right mean off an' on." The man stretched out his hand and touched Jamus' shoulder. When he met solid flesh, he started back with a gasp of surprise. "Bory, I ain't seen no 'lusion done so good afore. I heard the Lord's got the Power ta do 'em fine, but I ain't ne'er expected it so good. Ya be a right proud chantin', Sur. Right proud."

"This too is common here?" Jamus asked, trying to learn as many rules as possible before going any further.

Donni rubbed his stubbly chin. "Ya sure are fresh ta Magiskeep, ain't ya. 'Tain't no holds on Magic hereabouts, ya see. Since 'lusion's the lowest it's most used, ya see. Know a few Sorcerers what keeps ta their rooms all the time jest lolling about whilst they send their images all over ta do their errands."

"It must be a very strange way to live, encountering such beings all the time."

"Who's ta say what's strange when it's common, eh? Ya gits used to it. Most o' the greater mages don't bother wid sech nonsense. All's they do is charm what's they need." He gulped down a mouthful of calidew and wiped his mouth with his sleeve. "It's kinda hard on us mortals a times, watchin' them git what they want whilst we gots ta sweat fer our'n, but if'en a man's clever enow, he kin git hisself a patron an' take life easy too."

"Like you do?"

Donni poured himself another mug of calidew. "I gots me a job here, 'cause the Lord favors me, yeah. The work ain't hard, an' I got all I want ta eat."

"The work's not done well. The horses are ill cared for."

"I don't hear Master Jamus complainin' none."

"Perhaps that's why he sent me. Did you ever think of that?"

"Well now, that is a riddle, ain't it. Considerin' he was the one what tole me not ta do more'en feed the beasts twict a day. Said he was gonna see to it a lad did the heavy chores an' I wasn't ta lift a finger more meself."

"And has he sent the lad?"

"Aye. Wee slip of a thing. Cain't push but a quarter barrow at a time. Takes him till well after Sowin ta pick the stalls. Does a paltry job o' it, but he's the lad the Lord sent, so I ain't complainin' none."

Jamus sighed. For now, he had taken care of the worst of the problem here and with the horses clean and comfortable, he saw no point in pursuing the issue with Donni. He'd heard enough about this world to feel relatively confident at this point. The fact that he didn't have to hesitate in using his Magic was decidedly reassuring. He'd felt the River leapt eagerly to his hand and sensed the waters ever ready to answer his Call.

Strange, he thought. Even thought Donni had called the Lord of the Keep by his name, Jamus, he had named him Keepmaster, not Rivermaster. A curious oversight or simply a matter of some tradition here? The Eldenlore claimed there was but one in each Great Circle so privileged to the title. Could it be that even in the worlds of the Way, there was still but one Rivermaster? If it were so, he had a distinct advantage to press and plenty of options.

The prospects for solving Keldra's riddle suddenly seemed quite bright.

****

        "I told you I left Whim back at Sarkem's because he was lame," The Jamus repeated to Josep, not even trying to hide his exasperation. "There was no point in dragging Flax back with us either. The carriage made best time without her."

        "If'en Whim's hurt he'd best be cared fer here, an' ya knows it, me Lord. I cain't figger what coulda happened ta him that ya couldn't fix, though, 'specially knowin' how he's kin ta the River."

        "I can't explain it myself. My Healing did little. I tried to sift the source but his Magic seemed insistent on contradicting mine. I finally had to let Jorl resort to his herbs and poultices."

        Josep frowned. As far as he knew, Whim and his Magic were part and parcel of Jamus'. Unless something totally inexplicable had happened, none of this made any sense. "It ain't like ya ta leave Whim behind, me Lord, and knowin' what I does 'bout ya and that stallion, I cain't hardly believe sech could e'er happen. If'en yer coverin' fer some secret or other, it's fine by me, but I ain't partial ta havin' my horses left fer no good reason."

        "Whim's in good hands," The Jamus replied, trying to stay calm in the face of Josep's questioning. It had never occurred to him that servants in the Keep would dare question a Lord. Worse, Josep's questions hinted the stableman knew things about Whim The Jamus would sooner keep secret.

        "Good hands ain't my hands," Josep insisted. "Ya knows as well as me 'e ought ta be home here if'en 'e's poorly. Matter o' fact, lame or no, I be surprised he ain't come home on 'is own."

        "I told you he was lame," The Jamus said, gritting his teeth.

        "You know as well as I do that makes no difference to him," Josep answered, slipping into the accent of the Keep to mark his seriousness. "It might be better if you were at least honest with me, My Lord. These horses are my responsibility."

        The Jamus' temper flared. "I don't like being interrogated, Sur, nor will I tolerate it. Until you learn better manners in dealing with me, I think it would be best for you to turn your duties over to someone less contradictory. Frankly, I've had enough of your insults."

Josep drew himself up, his own temper nearly matching his master's. "So, it's come to that, has it? Lord's arrogance has finally come to the fore, eh? Well, mebbe it's better if'en I go. T'ain't likely me belly can take much more or yer righteous indignation anyhows." He dropped the pitchfork on the floor, spun on his heel and left, not even bothering to look back.

A bit shaken, The Jamus let out a relieved puff of air. Care of the horses was not of much significance in the greater scheme of things. He'd soon find a man from the village to take Josep's place, preferring to avoid Keepmen in case the story of Whim's nature was well known. All he really needed was someone to feed the beasts and keep the place relatively clean. Certainly, the animals didn't really need much more.

He resolved to settle the matter as soon as he'd finished with the first step in Naboth's plan to twist Magiskeep until its sunshine fell into shadow.

Once back in the palace, The Jamus put on a sorrowful face and headed for Mistress Jiala's study. Manipulation's Master was at the head of the list because of her reputation and ambition.

Jiala and Siamel, her Apprentice, were together when he arrived, putting a crimp in his initial advances. Perhaps, though, it might be just as well, for as soon as he saw the women he was tempted to move far more quickly than he was supposed to.

They simply took his breath away. Both had cascades of auburn hair and sparkling green eyes set in creamy faces as lovely as any he'd ever seen. No amount of watching from the shadows could ever have revealed the true beauty of the women, nor could it have tested the ache in his groin at the sight of them. But, he quickly reminded himself, he was supposed to be Jamus, and that meant he would have to control his urges and pretend he was not at all stirred. "My Lady, I need your advice."

Jiala tossed her hair back from her bare shoulders with her slender hand and frowned. "This is a bit unusual, My Lord, but these are unusual times. I've heard of your loss. I am sorry."

The Jamus tried to take his eyes off her cleavage, all too visible in the deep neckline of her crimson gown. She certainly knew how to dress well. He focused on her eyes, almost losing himself in them as well. "Thank you for your concern. I was just, well, it's difficult to discuss this, but Salene's being…." He paused as if too embarrassed to go on. He acted as if he was gathering his courage before going on. "It's just that since our loss, Salene's been keeping me at a distance. I mean, I can understand she'd be upset about what happened, but that's no reason to keep me out of our bed, is it? A man has needs, you know."

Jiala stole a glance at Siamel, who shrugged. "And just what would you have me do, My Lord?"

The Jamus shrugged himself. "A chanting, perhaps? Some Manipulation would be most helpful. If you could just sway Salene's determination a bit?"

Jiala did not hide her surprise. "You want me to use Magic on your wife?"

He waved his hand quickly. "Nothing grand, mind you. But I just thought one woman would know far better what to do to another woman than I would."

Jiala folded her arms across her breast, adding to her cleavage with the gesture. "You've caught me completely off guard, Sur, and I must say I'm surprised to hear such a request from you. Suppose you give me some time to think about this and I'll see what I can do to help."

The Jamus bobbed his head nervously. "Thank you, thank you, My Lady. I'd be most grateful, most grateful." He backed towards the door. "I'll be awaiting your decision. Thank you so much." He slid out into the hall and waited until he was out of sight before straightening and letting himself smile one more time.

"Mistress, I can't believe what I just heard," Siamel said, shaking her head.

"Apparently, our Lord and Lady are having some very serious marital problems. I must admit, though I would have thought Jamus would be better able to handle his sexual frustration better than that. He's always been most, ah, controlled about such things."

Siamel laughed. "A prude, you mean, and more modest than any man in the Keep. He still blushes, you know."

Jiala chewed her lip thoughtfully. "I know. Whatever happened in Lord Sarkem's Keep must have made some drastic changes in his thinking. I've heard severe trauma can change a personality, though. If it all was so dreadful, why should the Rivermaster be immune?"

"This bodes well for you, My Lady, unless you no longer harbor your particular hopes."

"Now, dear Siamel, whatever would give you an idea like that? You know as well as I do our Art never quite feels satisfaction when its desire remains unfulfilled. We shall have to find remedy."

"For Salene's behavior?"

Jiala shook her head, the corners of her full lips turning up ever so slightly. "No, Apprentice, remedy for my desire. Now, if you are a good little girl in the meantime, perhaps I'll be willing to share."

****

Once in the Palace, Jamus was nearly as appalled as he'd been in the stables. While things appeared clean and tended, he could taste Magic in nearly every corner. Illusions abounded in vases of flowers on the mantels, Transformation shimmered in cushions on the couches, and Manipulation marked both pieces of furniture and the occasional maid lounging about.

"Madria," he heard a voice call from upstairs as one of the maids rose slowly from her doze. "Madria! I need you up here, now with a fresh pitcher of calidew."

"Aye, Mistress," Madria answered. "Ya wants I should carry it up, or jest bring it to the stairs. Me feets is a bit sore yet."

The voice sighed loudly. "To the stairs will be fine. I'll chant it up."

The maid grinned and headed out to the kitchens without the slightest trace of a limp.

When she returned with the pitcher, Jamus approached her. "I'll take that up, Mistress. Who was it who called?"

Madria bowed slightly. "Lady Jiala, me Lord. Didst ya not recognize her call? I shoulda thought, considering how close ya is, ya woulda."

"Where we're together we usually don't speak quite so loudly," Jamus replied, assessing the situation quickly.

His assumption proved accurate when Madria winked broadly. "I'd say not, Me Lord." She playfully poked his shoulder with her finger. "As a fact, I'd say ya don't even talk much at all, eh, 'specially when ya gots other business on yer minds?"

"Exactly," he answered, taking the pitcher from her and heading for the steps.

Once on the second floor, he realized at once that the rooms were set exactly the opposite to those in his Magiskeep, for the door to the small study was on the right instead of the left. Jiala's door was open, so he walked right in, wishing in instant later he'd been more discreet.

She was only partially dressed, wearing nothing more than a thin shaenis camisole, just barely skimming her thigh, with its straps threatening to slide off her shoulder if she took a deep breath.

Which is exactly what she did when she turned and saw him.

The garment behaved exactly as predicted, exposing her breasts.

Instead of covering herself, she smiled. "So, you did change your mind after all. Do I need to tell you how much that pleases me?"

Jamus swallowed hard and shook his head, locking his sphere to stelin and praying hard he could keep from blushing. The charade was getting more and more complex as he went along and trying to figure out all the rules could well prove his undoing if he let his emotions run away with his reason. "You don't have to tell me a thing, My Lady. Your actions are perfectly clear."

She glanced down as if suddenly aware of her nakedness, made a halfhearted effort to pull the straps back up, but when she shrugged and they fell again, she didn't bother. "It will save you some time, My Love. You always did say you couldn't understand why a woman's clothes were so bothersome to take off."

"Uhm, yes, too many laces and layers."

She sidled closer, licking her lips. "I've adopted a new approach. Lets you get to the goods without all the extra wrapping." He forced himself not to take a step back. "You're not some package from Market Square, My Lady. You shouldn't talk about yourself that way."

Her lips pursed into a pout. "The last time we played, I was a whore from Till's Tavern, as I recall. It was fun. You don't like that game anymore?"

"I, ah, wasn't thinking of games this time, Jiala. I just brought you this." He thrust the pitcher of calidew into her hands. "And I just came to ask a question I'd forgotten before."

Her pout intensified. "So you are still leaving then. Going to Sarn and that precious Jorl of his down in Greenhope." Then she brightened. "I know! You came back to ask me to go with you after all!"

His mind raced. "No, not this time. I plan to make just a quick trip there and back. How would we ever find time to enjoy ourselves?"

She clutched the pitcher to her chest with one hand and tickled him under the chin with the other. "Ever the tease, aren't you, Jamus? So just what was it you wanted to ask me?"

"I wanted to bring you a present. I just thought it might be nice if it was something you really wanted."

Her hand dropped far too low as she leaned in to kiss him full on the mouth. "Only one present," she said, caressing him. "Though if you promise to take a dose of Jorl's energy potion before you give it to me, it will last a lot longer. I'd like that."

Jamus felt his sphere tighten, holding back his response and the allure of his Magic with grim determination. His skin felt too hot and his pulse was racing. He steadied his breath. "A promise," he replied, pleased at how even his voice sounded. "Now, I really do need to go. If you'd just let go of me."

She squeezed one more time and then laughed. "I still love the way you blush, My Lord. After all this time, you just can't seem to hide your feelings." She kissed him again, lightly, on the cheek. "You are such a dear."

Back out in the hallway, Jamus leaned against the wall to steady his knees and worked on several more long, steadying breaths. The waters here were almost too deep for him, and his efforts to swim were falling far short. If he kept it up like this, he would drown for certain. He needed help.

Joria.

Surely the old mistress couldn't be much different than her counterpart in Magiskeep. She, of all the mages was rooted in reality. As Mistress of Illusion, she was most aware of the deceit of reflections and rarely let herself stray from her even, logical self. She was a rock in the River, and he could cling to her.

If he could find her.

Even with the reversal of rooms, she was not in her chambers. Instead, he found a younger Mistress there, who told him Joria had left her Mastery some months before, as he should have well known. "I didn't say I didn't know she'd gone," he explained. "I just asked if you knew where she was now. I needed some information."

"I can help you, Sur. I am her successor."

"No. It was all before your time, Madame. A question about Master Jorl, nothing I could find in the chronicles, either. I'm going to see him soon and Mistress Joria once knew him."

"Oh," the woman said. "Then I suppose the best place to look for her is in the village. I heard she took a cottage near the East Gate, far from the rest of the rabble. If she's not there, try the village school. For some reason she took it upon herself to teach the mortals there, though what she hoped to gain by that, I'll never know."

Gain? Nothing, Jamus thought. Nothing but the satisfaction of knowing she was doing good for someone else and the joy of working with children.

He was about to head out to find the old Mistress when another of the maidservants intercepted him. "My Lord, the Hand be Blessed you are still here. You've got to come quickly, the Lady is overwrought again and no one can stop her. She needs your warding, Sur."

"Who...?" he started to ask, but the maidservant had already hurried on ahead and there was little he could do but follow.

They ran up two flights of stairs to one of the chambers in the West Tower. At the door, the maid stopped, and called in. "I have him, Gira. Can you see to it she doesn't fire the door?"

"It's all right," a voice answered from inside. "But hurry. She's quiet now, but won't be for long."

The maid opened the door and ushered Jamus in.

The room was in chaos, with scorched blustone on nearly every wall, a smoking dresser lying toppled in a corner, and the rugs and furniture tossed and turned. Another maid stood, her arms outspread is if she were trying to guard something, but when Jamus neared, she backed away.

His heart caught in his throat.

There, huddled in a miserable heap against the wall below the window, was Salene, her eyes glazed, her hands trembling.

The stink of Spellfire was unmistakable.

Chapter 10

The Jamus and Naboth had no hope of conquering Joria. While Sarena might be tricked, the Mistress of Illusion would not fall prey to their deceits. She had too keen a sense of Illusion and all its relative Arts to accept lies, no matter how well the Shadows disguised them.

They had instead, decided to convince her to leave the Keep, but even that would not be easy. After visiting Jiala, The Jamus decided to sow the first seeds with the Mistress of the Second Art. "Madame," he said as he entered her study without bothering to knock, "I've grown worried now about the village. Have you been out recently?"

Joria's brow furrowed in annoyance. "You're acting strangely, Sur. Have you been wandering the mirrors again? I worry, you know. I've told you again and again it's not the answer to your miseries here."

"Strange? I just asked a simple question."

"Aye, and as far from what really matters as any I've ever heard. To talk of the village now when your wife and you have suffered such a loss smacks of evasion upon evasion, My Lord."

"Call it what you will, Mistress, but I can't spend all my days tormenting myself at the expense of this Kingdom. I thought if I did something constructive it might make it easier for me."

She stared at him for enough time that he had to struggle not to cringe back. He could almost feel her gaze lighting the darker corners of his being, searching for his true identity. "You've sealed your Sphere so well, I can't even find you anymore, Jamus. Shutting yourself off from your friends and the loneliness will drive you mad. You won't even need the mirrors."

He laughed nervously. "Sealed only until I'm sure I won't break, Joria. It's the only thing holding me together."

She nodded. "So what is this about the village?"

"Ignorance, I'm afraid. Since my visit to Sarkem's, I've thought a lot about what ignorance can do. That curse—who knew how dangerous it could be? I mean, the Lord and I have sealed the caves so no one will ever enter them again, but how many children died before they saw the sun because no one knew enough to question?"

"Do you really believe there was a curse?"

"I've nothing else to believe. I know, I know, it goes against the very Laws of the River, but every fiber of my being refuses to ignore the evidence of my child's death."

"And Jorl believes it too, I suppose."

The Jamus sighed. "He is a mage of great experience and many circles, Madame. He is also the most gifted Healer I have ever met. If such a wise man believes, am I to mock him?"

"You are the Rivermaster."

"And a wiser one than the one who left here for Greenhope. I will not allow my Kingdom to drown in its ignorance. We teach our mages to reason here in the Keep. We should teach the rest of our subjects as well."

Joria leaned her chin in her hands, her elbows propped on her study tabe. "It's not been the tradition to educate more than those talented in the River, Sur. I'd never quite thought about whether others might derive benefit from formal education."

"Think of those who have one," The Jamus said, pretending to warm to the idea. "Some of the village families teach their children to read and cipher, it's true, but what about the rest? Shall this land I rule encourage ignorance or challenge it?"

"And you propose a solution?"

"I do. A school. In the village. But, I can't do it myself. I need a preceptor, someone to organize the place. I was thinking...."

"Thinking I might be interested in such an undertaking?" Joria asked, leaning back in her chair while she kept her eyes fixed on him. "A curious proposal, My Lord, and one I shall have to consider. You say this idea struck you since you've been back?"

He shrugged. "On the way back, actually. Salene was so silent, I had plenty of time to think. I kept trying to think of something to make amends for giving her that stone, you see. It was then the idea of a school, to train children came to me. It was something I could do to keep the Shadows at bay. I mean, if more people understand, then how much safer will we all be?"

Joria puzzled his enthusiasm as she considered a response. Little of what he said sounded like the Jamus she knew. First to believe in the curse, then to think the stone had caused his child's death, and now, to ask her to leave the Keep to open a school when there were dozens of lesser Mages far more qualified and even eager to take on such a task. Even the idea of a school coming from him now, when Salene needed his full attention, made little sense. Something was definitely wrong with him. "Give me a day or two, My Lord. It's not a decision I can make quickly."

"You'll consult with Sarena, I suppose?"

"She and I do often ask each others' opinions," Joria admitted.

"I'm going to be busy for a few days, but if you want to talk more about this, I'll find the time." He nodded to her and left. Joria sat, mulling over the conversation. The idea of a school was certainly sound, but Jamus' methods were even more disturbing than Salene's behavior. Sarena would be more than interested in these latest developments in what was proving to be a riddle worthy of the Way itself.

****

"You need to ward her, My Lord," Gira insisted as Jamus stood stock still in the room, simply staring at Salene. "She used the Whitefire again."

"She's mad," the first maid said. "And no matter what you think, your Magic is the only thing that will keep her under control."

"I tried to tell you before," Gira said, "but you just wouldn't listen. Well, look at this room and tell me now I was wrong."

Jamus ignored the two women, his concentration focused on Salene instead. Her gown was torn and rumpled, her hair tangled, and she seemed unaware of his presence. "Salene?" he said softly. "Can you hear me?"

When she didn't respond, he took a step closer. At first, she didn't move. Then, she glanced up for a split second and cringed closer to the wall. She took a lock of her hair into her mouth and began to chew on it. He knelt not far from her, his eyes seeking hers. "Salene? Why are you doing this? Please. Let me help you." He reached out his hand.

She screamed and leapt to her feet, her hand extended towards him. She snarled, her lips curling back to expose her teeth as she played her fingers readying a spell.

Instinctively, Jamus raised his own hand, and sent a ward against her before she could make another move. Her face blanked as the weave hit her and she rocked back on her heels into Gira's outstretched arms. Swallowing back his tears, Jamus finished the weave, tying its silver strands with finality. It would hold her Magic in check, and calm her for the time being. "I've warded her," he said hoarsely. "If only I could Touch her."

"She'd try to kill you if you did, like the last time," Gira replied, easing Salene onto the nearby couch. The maid beckoned to the other woman. "Resa, get me the laving bowl and some towels. Now that our Lady is peaceful again, I'd like to clean her up."

"I'll brush her hair," Resa said. "Perhaps we could braid it this time so it doesn't tangle so badly. My Lord, you could help a bit by cleaning the room for us. Magic does that part of our work more easily than we can."

Jamus nodded numbly and raised his hand to set the room back in order. Then, without thinking, he chanted a pitcher of calidew to the table to accompany a full meal for all three women. "Take good care of my wife," he said, his voice choking.

"Oh, we shall, My Lord," Gira replied. "As long as you keep paying us well."

Money, so that was it. Not loyalty, nor affection. He tossed a purse full of gold on the table beside the meal. "Don't disappoint me."

The image of Salene haunted him after he left, the experience completely unnerving him. He felt his hands shaking and he hid them in the folds of his tunic until he was out into the streets. Only then did he let the emotion take hold, when he was just another body in the crowds gathering in the Market.

Unlike his Magiskeep, no one seemed to know who he was here. Apparently, this lord spent little time with the common folk of

his kingdom. For once, anonymity was a blessing. With tears
streaking his cheeks, he would prefer not being recognized.

The crowd was busy and rushed, as if all the errands had to
be done in a matter of a wind instead of all day. When he heard some
of the bargaining going on, he began to understand why. Goods were
being traded at exorbitant rates and shop after shop ran out of
merchandise in a matter of minutes. The vegetable supply was
limited as were the fruits, with most of the produce of questionable
quality. Cloth at the fabric stalls appeared ill woven and nearly
everything else looked similarly inferior.

Confused by the lack of pride among the shopkeepers, Jamus
finally found a seat in the Tills Inn and ordered a mug of ale, some
bread and cheese. As he waited, a pretty girl in a loose, low blouse
glided over to his table. "Ye look lonely, Sur. If ye'd like, Melina
would be pleased to keep ye company."

Jamus laid a gold coin on the table, waiting to see if Melina
would pick it up herself, or leave it for the barmaid. She reached
down, pocketed the sovereign, and swung herself into the chair next
to him. "Then ye want company," she said, her fingers idly tracing
the contours of his hand.

"Conversation, actually," Jamus replied.

"For a gold ye can have more than that. Dost ye have a name
I can use?"

"Jess," Jamus answered.

"So, ye be of the Magic then?"

"Somewhat," he replied.

"I should wonder ye be here like this, sitting with the
common mortals, paying for thy food."

"As I said, I was looking for some conversation. It's not the
kind of information I can learn in the Keep palace. You see, I'm a bit
of a stranger here, from a Southern Hold."

"Oh, so ye don't know the Keepway, eh? No wonder ye pay
for what ye want." Melina leaned nearer her breasts almost spilling
out of the top of her blouse as she pressed against the edge of the
table. "Let me tell ye, Sur. Learn to use your Magic first and your
purse after. 'Tis the way here and no Mage who does else is
welcomed by his kind."

"Magic is the common way, then?"

"Aye, Sur. 'Tis a trial for the common folk who see no reason to sweat themselves if they can patron a Mage of their own." She slid her chair closer to be sure her thigh could touch his and rubbed against him. "I, for instance, might do well to share secrets with my own Mage in return for his favors."

"Tell me what I need to know and I'll favor you with no further expectation," Jamus replied.

"I keep my sheets clean."

"I have a wife and I keep my marriage vows, My Lady."

Melina sighed and sat back in her chair. "And ye have such a pretty face too. Pity it's taken. So, ask thy questions. I'll tell ye what I know."

"Lord Jamus, Master of the Keep. What do you know of him?"

"I've ne'er seen him, if ye so ask, but I hear he is a handsome man and most powerful, else he'd not be Keepmaster. I'm told he's arrogant and proud. Some even suggest he dabbles in the darker spells, but rumors have a way of riding on black wings when a man's not well liked. When he killed Sagari and took his place he let Magic fly as it had never done under the Golden Lord. Instead of holding it in the Keep itself, he let it roam into the village at will. At first it was good to have the right to use the Power at will, but soon the Mages grew tired of gifting every mortal who came their way. There are more of us then them, you see."

"So the Mages used to offer Magic to anyone who asked?"

"Aye, until they decided any Gift deserved favor in return. 'Tis now the way, you see. Mortals as I offer what we can in return for the Magic. A man with a warm house and a spare bed may patron a Mage who wishes covers away from the Keep. That's the most common exchange, as is mine."

"What of the craftsmen?"

"What hand can compete with the Magic's? The craftsmen have most long gone, with only the few who can produce goods quickly to earn their denerets still here. The rest, I hear, have crossed the Rim to seek fortune in Turan proper."

That would explain the market. "Is this Jamus beloved?"

"Only to those he pays. Like every Mage, he's only as loved as his purse. The Mages have taken more than they've given, I fear. Those of us who stay, offer no love without silver."

"I heard one of the Mistresses was teaching school in the village."

Melina laughed. "Poor old fool that she is. Joria, I think, is her name. Used to be a Master in the Palace. Now she thinks she can teach the mortal children enough of the Art to free them from the Mages' dominion. Everyone knows it's impossible, but she strives on. She's the laughingstock of the gentry in East Village and the Keep, or so I hear."

"Does Lord Jamus condone her actions?"

"Does he care one way or the other is more like it. I don't think the Mistress was his favorite when she was in the Keep, so maybe he's just as glad she's not there anymore. My friend, Licia, sends her son to the school and speaks well of the old woman e'en so."

Jamus took a bite of his cheese and washed it down with some ale. "I thank you, Madame. You've been a great help."

"Is that all?" Melina asked, her face wrinkling in disappointment. "Are ye sure ye don't want a roll for thy coin?"

"You are an alluring woman, Mistress Melina, and if I were a lord here, I'd hope to find you a gentler way to earn your keep. You deserve more than a different man in your bed every day."

"Would it were every day," she answered. "There's more'n enough like me to go 'round, I fear. Jamus slid three more coins over to her. "Sur?"

"Sleep alone for the next Sevenstin," Jamus told her. "For at least that long, I'll be your patron." He could see tears brimming in her eyes, but he shook his head. "I have reasons you'd never understand." He rose, nodded to her and left.
Melina clutched the coins in her fist and simply sat, staring at the door.

****

How many steps have you taken, Shadowspawn? Does their River yet bleed?

The Jamus closed the door of Jamus' study and locked it with a spell. "I have begun. I must be careful. This Joria is keen."

She is an old woman. Perhaps it is time for her circle to close.

"Not yet. Not until I have more masters in my hand. The harlot will be easy, for she harbors a lust for the Rivermaster. There are two more whose greed makes them easy prey. With three in my keeping the River will weep. I may trick one more, but after that, the path grows harder."

When the Rivermaster's Will breaks, the others will fall. Then their waters will be in my hand.

"The Dragon will sing your praises."

Do not speak of the Dragon, Lowling. This you do not in his name, but in my name. It is I who conceived this plan and the fruits will be mine to relish. I will be the Rivermaster to his wings.

"You'll challenge him?" The Jamus asked, barely hiding his excitement.

Who is to say which River runs stronger? I will not be minion to Blackwing forever.

"I will be honored to stand for you, My Lord."

Do this for me and the Thirteenth blood shall be thine. Now, go. I must revel in his pain.

The Jamus felt the presence leave and settled back to reading the scroll he'd found in the Great Library. The Arts of Comprehension and Elevation were still obstacles to his intent. Jired, Master of the First Art, was a simple man with few desires and a most basic grasp of the Magic's implications. Unlike Jorn and Senneth, who had ambitions of their own, there was little he could think of to persuade the Mage to bend his Power to any direction except the straight. Complex personalities were easier to control. Still, he had hope the old Master would recognize the futility of resistance once the others had been won. Savel, on the other hand, posed another kind of challenge. As Master of the Highest Art, his morality and principles were unyielding. Of all the Mages, he would be the most difficult to win. If anyone had to die, he'd be the most likely candidate.

But, that pleasure would have to wait. Patience scored more victories than haste.

He rolled the scroll back up and tucked it into the bookshelf behind him. It hadn't really helped anyway, but he was certain the Eldenlore had some clue he'd overlooked. When he had more time, he'd search again. For now, he would satisfy himself with handling those he understood.

Jorn and Senneth.

Of the two, Jorn had never quite accepted his secondary role in ruling the Keep, perceiving himself quite capable of full Mastery. Senneth, his closet associate, allowed himself his own delusions of talent, walking in his idol's footsteps of ambition. Neither one was really able to do much more than command his own niche in the River's currents, but The Jamus intended to let them think otherwise. With a little cajoling and an offering of promises, he could turn them easily.

He had forgotten about Sarn.

Left in charge of the Keep in the real Jamus' absence, the young Master posed an unexpected obstacle.

"You've been avoiding me," Sarn said when he finally found The Jamus in the dusty stacks in the upper level of the Great Library.

"Not at all," The Jamus replied. "I didn't know you wanted to see me."

"Sorem's Blood, man, you expect me to believe that? You left me in charge here while you were gone and when you came back you never even bothered to question me? Since when have I had to seek you out, eh? You're usually at my throat by now."

"I've been preoccupied with other matters, Sur. Surely you've heard."

"I've seen and heard more than enough to know something's far more wrong here than what I've seen and heard, My Lord. The Rivermaster's not a Novite naïve enough to be duped by a charlatan like Jorl."

"Who's to say the man's a fraud? He is wise in the River, Sarn."

"Bory, My Lord, the Shadows themselves are wise in the River. Would you trust their word? Think, if you can. Use your Master's reason. This is all chicanery."

"And what would you know of it, Sarn? Have you ever left the Keep to travel the world as I have? How many men beyond these walls have you ever spoken to? Do the deep waters answer your call? How are you such an expert in men's deceptions?"

"Because deception, trickery, and lies are the best of my arts, My Lord. It's the reason you set me to guard your precious Keep when you leave it. You know I'm an expert at cheating my way to what I want, and that makes me the scenthound you need to hunt out the lies while you're gone."

The admission delighted The Jamus, for it offered Sarn as an unexpected ally. "I've learned something from all this, Sarn. All this time, I've been tempering my Magic with Rule and Vow, no matter the consequences. Do you know where it's gotten me? Nowhere. Nowhere at all. And now it's cost me my child and…and my wife. I'm not going to play the buffoon anymore. I have Power and I intend to use it."

Sarn's mouth dropped in surprise. "Impossible."

"Grief can change a man, Sur. I've wept my principles dry."

Sarn checked his skepticism for his own sake. This was the chance he had been waiting for. "Then take away the wards you placed on me, and I'll join you in exercising this new revelation. Since you've been gone, I've seen many things I'd like to change around here."

"Can I trust you?"

"What difference does that make? You have a hundredfold more power than I can ever dream of. What threat can I be to you?"

The Jamus rubbed his chin thoughtfully. He started to raise his hand, but as he studied Sarn and began to scry the shield, he lost confidence. The weave surrounding the other mage was so far beyond his comprehension, he hadn't the slightest idea where to start. He thought he saw a pattern, but as soon as he sifted it, it shifted to another configuration, more complex and indecipherable with each alteration. This was the work of the Rivermaster at his best, and The Jamus couldn't measure up to an inch of it. "Threat or no, I will not free you until you prove your loyalty."

"By the Blood of Sorem, you have changed, Jamus. You're beginning to think like I do. Fair enough. What do you want me to do?"

"Turn your Master, Jorn, to my new concept of the Magic. Convince him to free himself of his honor and to use his Magic for his own purpose. I want the Gathering to support me in this. Rebellion here would be a dangerous thing. Turn Jorn and he'll turn Senneth."

"There are more than two Masters here."

"I'll take care of the others."

"How?"

"By appealing to their desires, Sur, as I've appealed to yours."

Now it was Sarn's turn to grin, even though, in the pit of his stomach, he knew it was wrong.

Chapter 11

In the world of the tapestry, the East Village Schoolhouse was located in what Jamus would have thought to be the West had he been home. But here, where all appeared to be a reflection of his own land, he had to trace at least half of every route opposite to expectation. North and South seemed to hold as far as he could tell from the sun, but elsewhere reality was reversed.

Thus, it took him an extra span of wandering to find Joria, and when he did, her classes were well into session. The building had about ten rooms, more than he had anticipated. Of these, five were delegated as classrooms and the rest as residences for her and her staff. At the door, he was greeted by a young lad, apparently a student assigned to some sort of hospitality duty, for he escorted the visitor to a small study and invited him to sit.

There, Jamus settled himself in a cushioned chair and began to leaf through a small book of poetry left on a little table. In a matter of minutes, an older woman appeared at the door. "Sur, you wish to see Mistress Joria?"

"Indeed I do," Jamus replied, rising. "Does she have the time to talk to me?"

"Her class is presently taking an examination, so, if your conversation will not be too intrusive, she will speak with you now. Come with me."

Jamus followed her to a back room where he found the grey robed Mistress of Illusion by the door, her keen eyes watching the bent heads of fourteen young scholars.

"Prentices to your Art, My Lady?" Jamus asked.

He heard her gasp as her head spun to him, her eyes locking on his face. "My Lord! What are you doing here?"

"I came to see how your teaching progresses, Madame. Your ideas fascinate me."

Joria's eyes froze on him and he could feel her sifting him. Her brow furrowed. "Class," she said, clapping her hands for attention. "Something of great importance has come up and I must cut short our lesson for the day. Please leave your work on your tabes and I will gather it myself. We will finish this test on another day."

Puzzled expressions and a few muffled sighs of relief answered her as the students filed out of the room, casting curious glances at Jamus as they passed. When they were gone, Joria closed the door and gestured for Jamus to sit.

Then, she pulled up a stool across from him and sat herself. "Who are you, Sur?"

Jamus shrugged, "The Lord of Magiskeep. Don't you recognize me?"

She shook her head. "I know Jamus as well as I'd know my own son, Sur, and you are not he. Your face can't fool me. You've come by the Way, haven't you."

"And what if I have? Does that pose a problem for you?" He felt her sifting him again and let his sphere slip just a little to see what effect it would have.

The results were dramatic. She stiffened, her eyes widening. "By the Blood, you are the True Rivermaster! What in Sorem's Name are you doing here?"

Jamus laughed. "Being right, for once. I had hoped you, of all, would be unchanged in this world, Joria. Everything else is all twisted and turned around, but you are the one solid force in a world spun 'round. Thank the Hand for that."

"The Lord of our Keep will not be pleased to find you here."

"He's away at Lord Sarkem's, from what I understand, so I have a little time to worry about it, I suppose. Perhaps I will have solved my riddle and been gone by the time he returns."

"So that's it. You're like the others, then, here to solve a riddle." She sighed. "It would have been nice if you'd come to rescue us instead."

"Maybe I have," Jamus answered. "That could be part of my riddle. I haven't figured it out yet."

"I'd take care, if I were you, My Lord. Rescuing us might well condemn your world."

His brow furrowed. "What do you mean?"

"Supposition. There've been a few who've come here before you, and each one of them has noticed much in this world quite opposed to what they left behind. Since they all came here through the Way, one does begin to wonder if one world is merely the reflection of another."

"I've met and altered reflections before. I've never seen a problem there."

"How many mirrors did you have to choose from when you came here?"

"None. Keldra sent me through some sort of tapestry." He thought a moment. "Although to get to her, there was only one choice."

"Have you ever faced a room in the Way like that before?"

Jamus had to admit he hadn't. Every other time, unless the room were a specific entrance or exit he had created himself, there had always been choices. Only one, of course, had been the reality he'd sought, but it was never alone. The passage to Keldra's forest had been a dead end. Now that Joria brought it to his attention, he realized how strange it actually was. "I hadn't really thought about it."

"Only one reflection to choose, Rivermaster, almost as if you had reached the end of the Way."

He shivered involuntarily, all too aware of the implications. "Your Jamus is not my true reflection, Madame. I have already met that. If you're suggesting otherwise, you are much mistaken."

"Don't be so narrow-sighted, Sur. One man does not make a world. Our Jamus, as you call him, has traveled the Way hundreds of times. I'm not so sure he has always come out." She shook her head knowingly. "Someone has always come out, but am I to say it is the man who went in? Once this Lord of the Keep was cruel and savage, beyond redemption in all things. He tempered some seasons ago into the Mage he is now. I asked myself then why he had changed like that and then, I had a chance to sift him as I have sifted you."

Jamus leaned forward, intent on her words. "What did you discover, Madam?"

"Reflections, that's all. I studied the Eldenlore a bit after that. Time and time again the legends hint of Masters who entered the Way and returned, to quote the bards, 'not as they were, but as they may have been if the world had turned the other way.' Many were ruled mad and so the tales began of the Way's dangers to a man's sanity. I believe men had gone in, and reflections had come out."

Jamus nodded. Her assessment had confirmed his own suspicions. Already, one of his more keen reflections had taken his place in Magiskeep with Naboth's help. Suppose this were not the first time such a thing had happened. "You recognized me easily, Mistress. How could a reflection escape detection?"

"Ah, but you forget. I am Mistress of Illusion. The very art the reflection practices is my specialty. Why do you think Lord Jamus sent me here to teach? Was it out of a love for the commoners? He wanted me out of his palace lest I expose him for what he was."

"Would you have?"

"What would be the point? He is far better than the one he replaced. Besides, if I were to reveal his true nature, what would happen in your Magiskeep as a result? If this world is your world's true reflection, then everything that's done here must somehow alter things there."

Jamus rubbed he brow. "And what's done there is reflected here."

"To some degree. You said you had passed through a tapestry to get here. That means this reflection has been crafted with at least some Art. I would say the weaver took some liberty with the pattern, offering some threads of his own. But who is to say which ones, eh?"

"Could that be my riddle?"

"It depends on what you're trying to do. As I asked before, what are you doing here?"

"Trying to get back home," Jamus answered. "A Shadowlord imprisoned me in a cave. He's cast a spell I cannot breach and the only way out was through the Way. But, as you've said, it was a dead end. I thought the riddle was meant to free me."

"Surely your people will go look for you."

"No. The Shadow sent another Reflection to take my place. He has some kind of plan to take Magiskeep for his Dragon. I can't quite fathom his methods, though."

Joria smiled. "Look to the mirror, my Lord."

"This world?"

"Aye. If ever a kingdom was ripe for Darkwing, this is it. Magic Unrestrained abounds and 'Mage' is a cursed title."

"My Keep would never fall to this."

"Do your Masters have ambition? Are they meek servants to morality, or do they battle their longings? If the Rivermaster leads them, will they not follow?"

"Joria won't."

"And Joria didn't here, either. But see where she is. An effective banishment, I should think."

"So what I see here might well be indicative of what may be happening in my Magiskeep, then," Jamus said quietly. "This is its opposition."

"In a manner of speaking," Joria replied. "I would take care what remedy you use here, for it may well be poison in its reflection."

He thought of the stables and shuddered. "But how can I leave this place in suffering? It goes against every instinct moving me."

"There lies your riddle, My Lord. Solve it, and perhaps the door will open."

He leaned on the study tabe, his head dropped in misery. Then another thought struck him. "You said others had come here before me. Are any of them still here?"

"If I were to judge, I would say at least one. There is a Healer here who is accused of the Waymadness. So much so, he lives as a hermit in the southern forest. His name is..."

"Jorl," Jamus finished for her.

"You know him?"

"I do, My Lady, and your perception is quite keen where he's concerned. I need to find him. Do you know exactly where he is?"

She shook her head. "Ask in South Village. Despite his madness, they trust his Art. Someone there can help you find him." Jamus pushed to his feet. "You are an amazing woman, Joria—in both worlds."

****

Jiala was such a simple matter The Jamus was almost disappointed. More used to hunting and stalking his prey, having it practically leap into his snare took much of the pleasure out of the chase. Then again, this prize had a certain pleasure all its own, and he intended to relish every taste of it.

She had called him to her chambers, with, she said, word about Salene. She'd insisted they keep it private, suggesting a meeting near Norwin's turn, when the palace was asleep and they'd not be overheard.

When he arrived she had a light meal waiting, with amberwine poured in two large goblets. "I hope you're hungry. Evenmeal was light this Weswin."

"Salads," The Jamus said, "because of the heat. The weather is out of sorts these last Sevenstins."

"Yes, the storms and now a drought. It is said in the Eldentimes there were mages who could control the weather. Have you ever tried? Would not the Rivermaster be the one the Hand might Gift with such Power?"

The Jamus took a sip of the wine as he decided how to answer. While hiding in the shadows, he had seen Jamus command the skies, not as a Weathermaster might, but enough. He had to be careful about what he said now, in case Jiala mentioned it to someone who might be more aware than she. "I have worked a spell or two, mostly to calm the rains. I've had a little success, when the River wished me to."

"Really?" she asked, her green eyes sparkling with excitement. She had chosen a low cut green gown this time, hoping the color would suggest modesty despite the neckline. "Skill in something like that would be a treasure to the Keep. How wonderful it would be to offer a beautiful climate all the seasons long."

"You'd soon grow tired of it, My Lady. It's the nature of man to grow weary of the same things day after day."

"Is it?"

"Change offers man a challenge to face, something to look forward to when the wind turns."

"Does that mean change in all things, My Lord?"

He sighed. "The sameness wears the winds long." He took a big gulp of the wine this time. "You had some news for me?"

Jiala idly cut a surlep and arranged the pieces on a plate. "Your wife, My Lord, she...she will not be consoled. I tried everything I could think of, but even with Sarena's Touch, she blocks every effort to free her of her grief. Until she decides it's ended, there is nothing we can do."

"So I'm left comfortless," The Jamus said hoarsely. He took another big swallow of wine. He let his eyes fill with tears and dropped his gaze.

"There is comfort here, if you want it, Jamus." She moved over to him and put her hand on his head, her slim fingers gently tousling his hair. He leaned into her touch, his head falling against her waist. "Come to the couch," she said. "You can rest a while."

The Jamus let her lead him to the cushioned couch where she pushed him down against the pillows. She knelt beside him, cradling his head against her breasts. "That feels good," he said softly.

"It's been here all the time," she said. "Waiting for you. Let me offer it to you now."

"My wife," he muttered.

"Is mad," Jiala said. "No one can keep a promise to a madwoman."

The Jamus smiled, his teeth white against the soft flesh of her bosom.

Such a simple matter.

****

Sarn had wasted spans considering his options.

He was torn between what he knew was right and Jamus' offer. Something was amiss with Magiskeep's Lord, but since it was to his benefit, should he bother to do anything about it? All his life he had wanted the freedom to use his Magic as he willed instead of being bound by Rule and Vow. Now, the Rivermaster himself had granted him the promise to do just that.

Why then, was he hesitating?

The offer stank of Shadows.

Setting him as some sort of surrogate to scheme against Jorn and Senneth was so far from Jamus' style it didn't even touch the River.

That left two possibilities. The first was that Jamus had gone mad, perhaps with one too many trips into the Way.

The second was that this Keepmaster was not Jamus at all.

That thought chilled him. He had a sense of Shadows, almost an uncanny ability to feel their work. Master Jorn told him it was because he really wasn't much different than they were, and a man always recognized his kin.

They'd laughed about it now and again. "If you hadn't been born to the River, you would have made a fine Darkmaster," Jorn had said. "I've never quite met anyone so bereft of morals."

"I have morals," Sarn replied. "They just don't quite match the Keep's expectations, that's all."

"Have you ever spent a span thinking of anyone besides yourself, Sarn?"

"Half a span, perhaps, and only if I thought I would benefit from it in the end. I do hate to waste time."

Now, here he was, spending far more than a span thinking about Jamus and what his intentions were for the Keep. Why did it matter so?

When he considered this, the answer came quickly. Jamus had woven a ward around him to prevent him from the very acts he now advocated. The promise to free him from his prison meant nothing from a madman and even less from Shadowspawn. Worse, if something had happened to the real Jamus, there would never be a way to escape. No other Master in the Keep had been able to sift even the first thread of the weave let alone the entire pattern.

Sarn needed Jamus alive and well. Nothing less would do.

In the meantime, he had to be careful. Whoever this Jamus was, he still held more Power than anyone in Magiskeep. Crossing him would be a fatal mistake.

He headed for Jorn's rooms, the decision made. He would do exactly as he had been instructed.

Besides, what harm could it do? There was always a way to turn back.

****

South Village was seedier and more rundown than Jamus expected. The houses had a forgotten look, as if their residents had neither the time nor the money to care for them any more than was absolutely necessary. He thought fleetingly of Becca and Jeamel, an as he did, a hundred other names raced through his head. Here, in this world, were the reflections of people he loved. So many it would take a full circle to look for them all.

Instead, he knocked on a random door.

A thin faced woman opened it. "Whatcha want, Sur? I ain't got naught ta hand out if'en yer beggin'."

"No begging, Madame. Just questions. I'm trying to find Jorl, the Healer."

"Ya don't look poorly."

"I'm not. I just need to talk to him. Can you tell me where I can find him?"

"When we needs 'im we calls. Jest go to the beckon tree an' knock."

"Knock?"

"Ya'll know when ya gits there. Take the levee trail an' foller it straight 'til the sun don't shine. The tree's there. Now git wid ya. I gots me work ta do."

Jamus thanked her and sent a quick spell to her larder, filling it with food before he left, but even as he did, he frowned. The waters seemed to hesitate in rising to his hand, as if reluctant or confused by his call.

More to worry about.

"The levee trail," he said under his breath, "and the Beckon Tree. I'm getting damn tired of having to solve riddles just to solve a riddle I haven't even started to look for yet."

The sun was high in the sky, signaling Sowin's turn. Though time had no meaning in the Way, it appeared to be passing here with reassuring regularity.

There was indeed a levee running along a wide stream near the village—a detail his own Magiskeep lacked. Good or bad, the occasional lapses from total reflection urged him on, offering hope that his world was not completely under this one's influence.

He walked for a full span as the path narrowed and began to descend into a small valley filled with pines and brellums. Then, ahead, he saw the tree.

Well shaded by a rocky overhang and its fellows, a broad trunked brellum stood in a wide depression. From it hung a wooden mallet. There were numerous indentations on the bark, as if it had been struck repeatedly. Jamus grasped the mallet and swung.

There was a resounding thump, bouncing back against the cliff and echoing down into the valley. The strange geography of the spot sent the thump scurrying off into the distance like a winged messagebird.

For insurance, Jamus hit the tree one more time and then sat down on a nearby log to wait.

When he got back home, he promised himself he would look for this spot in Magiskeep.

If he got back home. He looked up into the brellum leaves above, where the shifting wind had set the fronds to motion. How peaceful and absolutely normal it all looked. Up there, nothing was amiss. Nature traveled its course with no acknowledgement of his discomfort. Was it the same in his Magiskeep? The sound of hurrying hoofbeats broke his reverie.

He looked towards the valley and saw Jorl heeling his pony along at a jarring trot towards the Beckon Tree. When Jamus rose and headed for him, he reined hard. "You? I told you I was not your man. How dare you call me?"

"Does the wise Mage search only with his eyes, Master Jorl? Way travel doesn't encourage such limited vision."

Jorl pushed the pony back into a walk, nearing Jamus cautiously. "Why do you speak to me of the Way?"

"Because I think you are here because of it, Sur."

"And what if I am? Since when would that matter to you, My Lord? You've never cared before as long as I didn't cross your path. I thought we had a truce of sorts."

"You may have a truce with the Lord of Magiskeep here, but not with the true one. As a matter of fact, we've never met."

Jorl slid from the saddle. "Sogol's Sake, Sur, you don't mean to tell me you are the Rivermaster himself and not that pretender?"

"I'm here from Keldra's tapestry, if that means anything to you."

"Indeed it does. That old Seer pushed me through so long ago I find it hard to believe you even remember who I am."

"For all intents and purposes you are still in Sarkem's Keep in my world, Jorl. As a matter of fact, you're the one who led me to the cave where I found the entrance to the Way into this world."

"Impossible. I mean, I did take Jamus to the caves, but I never showed him the pool. I covered the hole with all kinds of debris just so he wouldn't find it. The last thing I wanted was for that creature to get to my Magiskeep, though to save my soul, I can't figure it out myself."

"You don't know how to get back either?"

Jorl stared hard at him, his hazel eyes searching Jamus'. "You mean to tell me you don't know how to get back there?"

Jamus slowly shook his head. "I'm imprisoned by a Shadowlord's trap and Keldra's damn tapestry. Supposedly, if I solve a riddle, I'll be able to escape."

"What's the riddle?"

"If I knew that, I'd be gone by now, I think. I haven't seen even the hint of a riddle since I've been here. The only thing I know is that this world is a reflection of mine and what happens here somehow influences what happens there."

"Or vice versa," Jorl said.

Jamus nodded bleakly. "What I don't know is just how perfect the reflections are. It worries me. Apparently, this Jamus is not my complete opposite, and Mistress Joria is hardly any different than the woman I know. On the other hand, my wife isn't."

"His wife," Jorl corrected, "is totally insane and has been ever since he gave her the Blessing Rock from the cave."

Jamus frowned. "Blessing rock? I thought the cave was cursed."

"Not here. The legend is that the Cave of Light blesses all who enter with life. The Lord of the Keep gave his wife a stone from the caves and almost at once, she conceived a child. She's convinced it's some sort of demon and has been trying to rid herself of it for Sevenstins. He's delighted with her pregnancy since she's proven barren for so long and will have none of it. He's demanded I assure the child is born." Jorl sniffed. "Now, how, I ask you, can any man be expected to reasonably force a sorceress of considerable power to carry a child she doesn't want to full term? I take my life in my hands every time she sees me. And let me tell you, she is a Master of Spellfire, that's for certain."

"Can't he ward her?"

"Pah! He's half a fool when it comes to wards—creating or removing them. He just manages to contain her in her rooms and soothes the worst of her rants. Why he'd want a son from her womb, I'll never know. One suckle and the babe'd be poisoned."

Jamus' heart lurched as Jorl's word's sank in. As much as that woman in the palace resembled her and as much as his heart ached to see her plight, she was not his Salene. None of these people were the ones he knew and loved. What appeared to be reality was as far from it as Crystal Lake from the Great Sea. Hard as it might be, he needed to divorce himself from his feelings for them, and use them to his own purposes to shape events in his own Magiskeep while he was away. Cruel? Perhaps, but the River demanded sacrifice. Already he had felt the banks eroding and the currents diverting to another course. His own grief had spoiled the waters and here, when he raised his hand, he'd already sensed just a hint of uncertainty. Could he cast aside his compassion and surrender this world for the sake of his own? "Can you take me to those caves, Jorl? This world is just skewed enough from my own that I'd probably get lost without a guide."

"Why would you want to go there? All you'll find is the other end of the circle. There's no way out there."

"I think, Sur, I've begun to see the first part of the riddle. Somehow, I think the rest is linked to those caves."

****

Jiala was his, her Art corrupted by the consummation of her desire. For The Jamus, the bedding had been one small pleasure in his short tenure as Lord of Magiskeep.

The problem was it had only increased his appetite.

Temperance was not his strong suit, and with a powerful Mistress like Jiala, he had to be cautious. Though her blood would have nearly been enough to satisfy his need for the thirteen sacrifices, there was no way he could use her to that purpose. Dead, she offered nothing to the Shadowlord, for it was only through her use of Magic that he would gain its benefit. Once he had twisted her to his paths, her part of the River was won. Though he might never be a Seven Arts Mage himself, control of the Seven was victory indeed.

But, Naboth's success was secondary to The Jamus. His own success was far more urgent. Two spans under Jiala's sheets had stimulated his lust.

And so, in the darkness of Norwin, The Jamus headed out into the village to quench his thirst.

He knew he needed to find remote prey—someone whose loss would not be quickly noticed. Better if it would not be noticed at all. Violent death was not commonplace in Magiskeep, but closer to the mountains, where tarks took sheep and cavil to their lairs, one lost herder might well go unnoticed.

He rode out to the Rim on a horse chosen at random from the barn. The little sorrel suited him well and took to lifted travel with casual indifference, making the journey quickly. He was delighted to find a flock of sheep grazing in a little valley cut off from the farmhouse and hold by a high ridge and a line of amberpines. Surely, where there were sheep, there was a shepherd.

To the west, at the edge of the mountains' shadows, he saw a faint flickering glow. He headed for the campfire, wasting no time in speculation. To his satisfaction, he saw only one figure huddled at the site.

The young shepherdess looked up and whistled at his approach. From the shadows, two sleek dogs appeared at her side, their teeth bared in warning snarls as the rider drew near. "I'll set them to ye, if ye move to harm me," she warned. "Best ye come in peace, though at such an hour, I'd mark ye for mischief."

The Jamus raised his hand, sending a feeble but effective ward. The dogs whimpered and shrank back as their mistress half rose, ready to run. He threw a dark coil at her feet, tripping her. She let out a little scream, quickly silenced by the binding.

The Jamus dismounted slowed, savoring her fear, forcing her to wait in growing terror.

He let the darkness fill him, expanding his body with its aura, coloring his features against the wavering firelight. He saw her cringe, her form contorting in a desperate effort to break free, limbs twisting, her breath coming in ragged pants, her mouth open in a silent scream.

He licked his lips, his tongue tracing his sharp teeth. She was young and vigorous, well fed on milk and mutton, her blood rich. Slowly, he descended on her, his lean fingers prying at the laces of her tunic, plucking away the coarse fabric. He scraped his nails into her tender flesh, smiling at her panicked whimpers, laughing as his hands stripped her naked, while her eyes darted wildly about.

He slaughtered her as slowly, a piece at a time, drinking his fill while her heart still pumped the precious blood through her limbs. Her terror spiced the kill, making it all the more sweet.

When at last she was dead, her shell white and empty, he used his Magic to score her flesh with tark's claw rakes, then tossed her remains down a rocky slope. His hand waved once to clean himself of any sign and then, he mounted his nervous horse and rode away.

The mournful howl of the dogs did not stir him. His belly full and he was content. Twelve yet to feed upon and immortality was his. It was a fine start.

Chapter 12

Sarena was disappointed to find the sorrel gelding missing from his stall at Easwin, and equally disappointed to find no Josep to suggest another mount for the trip to Greenhope. "I'm not much of a rider," she said to the new stableman, Donni. "The sorrel is a gentlemen and I've ridden him before."

"Lord Jamus took 'im hisself, Lady. They come back Easwin turn an' the hoss be all tuckered. I ain't sech a Master as ol' Josep, but I ain't sendin' a weary beast out fer no one, not e'en a pretty lady like yerself."

"Can you suggest another mount then? Something quiet?"

"Mistress Joria's already called fer Pebble, so's I cain't give ya her. How 'bout Topper? He's got some size ta 'im but he seems like a good sort."

"You don't know for sure?"

Donni shrugged. "I ain't bin here long enow ta be sure, Lady, but I can recognize a kind eye when I sees one. Word is Lord Jamus don't keep no bad animals in these stables anyhows. There's some what's a might spirited, but none what's mean."

"Then please, Sur, saddle Topper for me. I'll be back as soon as Earlenmeal is finished."

Donni nodded and went about his business as Sarena returned to the palace to change her clothes and pack a traveling bag for the journey.

Later, she met Joria in the stable and the two rode out together, headed for Lord Sarkem's Keep.

"I should think Jamus will not be pleased to know we've left without telling him," Joria said once they were out of earshot of the stables.

"I thought you told me he was trying to get rid of you."

"To the village, not to Greenhope. I doubt he wants me where he can't keep an eye on me."

"He's not the man who left the Keep. That Jamus would never even suggest such a thing," Sarena replied as she shifted uncomfortably in the saddle.

"Well, we'll have plenty of time to discuss the possibilities of what happened to him in those caves. At the rate we're going, the ride will take several days."

Sarena sighed heavily. "My bottom won't last that long. You've woven a lifting spell before, haven't you?"

Joria grimaced. "It's not one of my better skills. Let's ride for a while before I try. I have to consider the right chanting."

"That doesn't boost my confidence."

"Since when does your confidence matter to me?" Joria asked, laughing. "I'll tell you what. We'll ride until your bottom is too sore to go on and then I'll Touch it for you."

"Bory, woman, I'd rather risk your ineptitude with lifting to that!" Sarena laughed too, and patted Topper's bay neck. "What do you say, Topper? Are you ready to put yourself into Lady Joria's hands?" The gelding tossed his head.

"At least he trusts me," Joria said.

"More than you can say of the Lord of the Keep?"

"I'm telling you, Sarena, that is not Jamus. I've known that lad since he first set foot in Magiskeep."

Sarena nudged her horse closer to her friend, her voice dropping to a near whisper as if she were afraid to speak any louder. "He's not the Rivermaster, Joria, I'm sure of it. When he came to see me, he took my hand. Jamus would never do that. He knows full well how dangerous that would be, even with his Sphere."

"This man wears no Sphere," Joria replied.

"You sifted him?"

Joria nodded. "There was no Sphere. I pretended nothing was amiss as soon as I realized it, so I don't think he noticed."

"So, we do have a pretender in our midst."

"That leaves the question."

"Which is?"

"Where is Jamus?"

****

Jorl led the pony along the path, his long legs nearly matching Jamus' stride as they headed into the forest. They reached his little cabin well before Weswin's first breath, while the sun was still high enough in the sky to light the clearing. Jamus noted at once how this house differed from the one in his Magiskeep. Here, Jorl had built a small stone fence around a neatly manicured herb garden and inside all was neat and organized.

"Your counterpart has a more casual approach to life," Jamus said. "He had to sweep his pots away to find a place for us to sit."

Jorl shrugged. "Then he's one of my earlier reflections. I've not always been a tidy housekeeper, but since the villagers have learned to depend on me, I decided I'd better create a more professional appearance."

The Healer proved in informed Master, well schooled in both the traditional skills of Compassion as well as the secrets of native herblore. Like his reflection in Magiskeep, he had developed a number of creative concoctions he readily explained to Jamus.

"The other Jorl had an energizing potion blended from delf and sandel. Have you tried that too?"

"By the Hand, no, Sur. If any drug has aftereffects, it's that one. Surely it restores spirit at first, but once it wears off the patient often drops into an intense depression. I've had much safer results mixing the delf with putterweed."

Jamus was relieved to hear some of his suffering may have been driven by the drug Jorl had given him instead of his own weakness. While the loss of his child and Naboth's torment were certainly strong motivation, he still cursed himself for collapsing over it all. The River was at stake against the Shadowlord and he, as its guardian, had no right to forget his duty, no matter what. "I fell prey to one of Jorl's potions," he said. "Now I feel the fool."

"Why? If your Jorl is as charming as I am, why shouldn't you have accepted his care?" Jorl winked. Then he went on more seriously. "Few men would resist, My Lord. Delf in any form is almost charmed itself. Here." He handed Jamus several stalks of the blue flowered herb.

Jamus' hand jolted as the leaves touched him. It was as if they had grabbed him instead of the other way around. The herb's scent filled his nose and his mouth began to water. He dropped it quickly, forcing himself to let go with Master's Will. "By the Blood, that plant is potent."

"If you've used it once, you crave it again. The putterweed tempers its allure while it adds to its effect by relaxing the muscles. There's a market for delf in the villages around here and it's been said men have killed for it. Only the Healers are allowed to grow it and even they must keep strict records."

"We don't have the herb in the Keep proper."

"Not yet. It's native to these southern climes and needs the fullseason here. You'll need to guard against its import, My Lord. Sooner or later, someone will take it to your villages."

"It's not my nature to make laws controlling the lives of my subjects," Jamus replied. "I'd much rather teach people about the dangers and let them choose for themselves."

Jorl shook his head. "Delf doesn't always let people choose. It's like the Magic. Despite the force of Rule and Vow, the temptation if often too great for the weaker Will. Take care, My Lord. Promises and good intentions are not a guarantee of anything."

****

Jorn stared at Sarn for a long time, his hands clasped around his goblet, his wine untouched. "What proof do you have of this, Master Sarn? I'm not about to put my Mastery on the line purely on your word. You haven't the most silvrin reputation."

"Lord Jamus told me himself he no longer has need of Rule and Vow here in Magiskeep. Take a proposal to him for using your Art to better use and he'll confirm everything I've told you."

Senneth, called in as soon as Sarn told the first part of his story puffed in skepticism. "You have your own purpose in this, Young Sur, I'm sure of it. Do you mean to make us look the fools in front of the whole Keep to elevate yourself to our positions, eh? One taste of Magic Unrestrained from our hands and Lord Jamus would have our hides."

Sarn spread his hands, accenting his plea. "What else can I say, gentlemen? I cannot yet prove myself, for I still wear the ward the Lord of the Keep bestowed on me."

"If he's so changed his mind about using Magic for our own purposes, why then has he not freed you to do as you will?"

Sarn thought quickly. "He's jealous. He knows I will surpass him in indulgence."

"That doesn't sound much like Jamus. He clings to propriety like the ungalens to the stolen nest."

"You heard about his wife, of course, and the child?" Sarn asked. When the other two nodded, he went on. "There was nothing he could do to save the baby, even with the River in his hand. He's not forgiven the waters for that and he's vowed to make them pay. What better way than to set mages' hands free to play it at their whims? Think of it, gentlemen. What is it you want? Women to soothe your nights and serve your days? A palace of your own?"

Jorn rubbed his chin thoughtfully. "My own Keep, I think, with no one lording it over me would be quite satisfactory."

"No more wet-nosed Prentices," Senneth said. "I'd never again have to try to convince some ignorant brat that Transformation is a finer art than Illusion."

"So, you do have ambitions then," Sarn said. "The Rivermaster grants them to you."

"Let him tell us himself."

Sarn nodded. "I'll inform him of your interest."

The two Masters watched Sarn leave, their minds racing with possibilities. "Do you think it could be true?" Senneth asked.

"Strange things happen when a man wanders too long in the Way," Jorn replied. "If our good Lord is but a shadow of his former self, we would be remiss not to entertain his fancies."

"Ah yes," Senneth agreed, "It's the very least we can do."

****

Jamus had let himself get drunk on Jorl's home brew, relishing the freedom from his inhibitions for at least one night. He had talked freely of his feelings, letting the grief pour out in torrents of self-indulgence.

Jorl was a good listener, content to offer no recrimination or advice beyond one full glass of caliwine after another. Then, he put Jamus to bed on a little cot and staggered off to his own bed.

Easwin demanded payment. Jamus woke with a pounding headache. Jorl, as Healer, should have been able to ease it, but he was so sick and miserable himself, he hardly had the strength. Instead, Jamus groped his way to the herb cabinet and blended several remedies, downing the first himself and then stumbling to Jorl's room to offer him the second.

Jorl took a sip and grimaced. "Why is the cure for pleasure always such misery? This tastes awful."

"Better than mine did," Jamus replied. "I used the bitterroot."

"By the Hand, you are a glutton for punishment. Did it work?"

"Well, I'm not seeing double anymore and I can think past my nose, so it did something. I think I can Touch you if you wish."

Jorl started to nod and stopped quickly when the movement seared through his befuddled brain.

Jamus put his hands on Jorl's head, letting the waters wash away the pain. The River was even more sluggish and fading than it had been the day before. His brow furrowed as he found himself having to concentrate on the Healing. His usual ease eluded him. "Something is very wrong."

"I'm not dead, am I?" Jorl asked quickly. "It's hard to tell."

Jamus laughed then thought better of it. "Heal me first, Sur, and then I'll explain."

But when Jorl Touched Jamus to cure his hangover, there was no need to explain anything. He too felt the River's unresponsiveness, struggling to find Compassion amidst the churning currents. "It's as if the waters are so low the rocks are exposed, blocking the flow of my weaves. What's going on?"

"What I'm afraid of is that my imposter in Magiskeep is somehow taking control of some of the waters."

"But you're the Rivermaster, not him. How can he take Power from you?"

"If he can divert the streams to his riverbed, there's always a risk."

"I don't understand how."

"If the Seven Masters give themselves to his darkness, it's more than possible."

"Never, My Lord. Mistress Joria would never give in."

"If he drove her from the Keep and put another in her place she wouldn't have to. I've been here long enough to see the reflections of how my Kingdom yet may fall, Jorl. I know the Masters too well to trust their loyalty to Rule and Vow. Several of them have ambitions to higher seats."

"Mastery of the Keep? With the Rivermaster already named?"

"Being Master of Magiskeep is as much an elected title as any, Jorl. Usually, it's the most skilled Mage who earns the honor, but the Gathering makes the final choice. If the imposter fails too many times in his duty, or proves a poor guardian of the River's Will, he can be taken down and replaced."

"He'll never let that happen. He wants to take power, not lose it."

"Seven Masters against one can be a formidable foe."

"But would it be seven? You said yourself some of them could turn to his side."

Jamus nodded grimly. "We have to get back before he does any more damage. Too much more disruption in the waters and we may not even be able to get back."

Jorl shuddered. "A bane I'd do almost anything to avoid, My Lord. If it meant my life and being, I'd sacrifice them rather than be condemned to stay here knowing my world suffered under Blackwing's deceit."

"We need to get to that cave. It's the only place I can think of where we might find a clue."

Jorl nodded and led the way to his little stable. Soon the two men were mounted and heading South. This Jorl's cabin was many winds from Sarkem's Keep and the waterfall, but with lifted strides and a growing sense of urgency, they were within sight of Greenhope well before Weswin's darkening skies.

****

The Jamus arranged himself elegantly on the new couch in his chambers. He had dressed formally in one of Jamus' royal blue tunics, but had left the top unlaced, adding an air of rakish ease to his appearance. He'd invited Jiala and Siamel to a light evenmeal as part of the drama, then told his amazed servants to inform Masters Jorn and Senneth that he would be delighted to listen to their petition while he ate.

Then he settled back to wait for the rest of the cast to arrive.

The two Mistresses of Manipulation came soon after, dressed in similar gowns of fine green shaenis cut to fit every contour of their bodies and to reveal as much flesh as possible without insulting the servants beyond redemption. "What a pleasure to be asked to a private meal with you," Jiala crooned.

"Three does not make it so private," The Jamus replied.

"What can it inhibit between us?" she asked coyly. "My Apprentice is ready to learn all of my arts. She and I are of one mind, you know."

The Jamus stretched lazily. "I was hoping you'd say that. I've been so lonely without a wife to keep me warm. Two will ward off the chill much better than one."

Siamel's eyes sparkled with excitement. This was an opportunity she had only dreamed of. Though she had cruelly teased Jamus when they were young, once he had become Master of the Keep and the Rivermaster, hate had turned to longing. She craved the power, but more importantly, she lusted for the man. Jamus had grown from a skinny nervous boy into a handsome, vigorous, attractive man, the secret lure to half the women in the Keep. Being here, invited to share his bed stirred her more than she would have ever expected. "I know many ways to keep a man warm, My Lord. I'm honored you've decided I'm worthy of you."

The Jamus yawned. "You're the key to your Mistress' loyalty, little bird. I wouldn't want you if it didn't please her. However, finally taking you will prove interesting. After all these circles I'll be curious to see if you can live up to your reputation."

He'd won a point there, for Siamel's face reddened and Jiala had to put her hand on her Apprentice's arm to steady her. "Siamel has learned a great deal from me," Jiala said. "With or without me, she is more than your match, My Lord. Still, I am keen to you myself, so I won't step aside to let her prove herself. Let us just see how the evening progresses, shall we?"

The Jamus tossed a few grapes in his mouth. "It will progress according to my desires, not yours, Madame. You will remember who is Master here."

Jiala bowed, nodding her head quickly. "I cannot forget, My Lord. Your power surpasses me in all things."

He smirked, and sat forward, gesturing towards the table. "Then let's eat and consider the rest of the night."

A few minutes into the meal, there was the expected knock at the door. Although The Jamus pretended surprise, he was completely ready to put on a show for the visitors. "Master Jorn, Master Senneth, a pleasure indeed. I hope you don't mind witnesses to your plea."

Jorn snapped his mouth shut, his eyes darting from Jiala to The Jamus with obvious alarm. He managed to catch his breath. "I never mind the ladies, My Lord. Especially such beautiful ones."

"Then you had a petition? Speak as you will, Sur, but don't take the Wind. I have other plans."

Jorn coughed nervously. "Your surrogate, Sarn, brought us disturbing news, My Lord. He said you had decided to reject Rule and Vow in favor of Magic Unrestrained. Now we, Master Senneth and I, are not ready prey for his pranks."

"You didn't believe him?"

"My Lord," Senneth said, quickly. "Sarn is not noted for his honesty. You yourself have often chastised him. We'd never accept his word on such a grave matter without your confirmation."

"It is," Jorn added, "quite contrary to your nature, My Lord, though we do hear you have been under a great deal of strain lately. I do regret your pain, but for my own sake, I must ask you to be honest with us."

"Unlike Sarn?" The Jamus asked. "He has been my voice before. What hope could he have in lying to you about a thing like this?"

"My Mastery," Jorn replied. "If you set me down, he would be the logical successor."

"I could put you down at any time, Sur. I'd need no prompting from Sarn."

Jorn swallowed hard before answering. "It is your Will, My Lord. But, I would not like to be set down because I failed you."

"Do you relish the idea of Magic Unrestrained, Master Jorn?"

"What Mage of worth doesn't, Sur? To be free of Rule and Vow, to use Magic at Will and desire?"

"Then satisfy yourself, Masters. I have disavowed the lies beaten into us by the memories of Wizardchase. Why would the River grant us Power if we aren't supposed to use it? I'm sorry to say Sagari was right in his intent to return to Turan and teach the mortals there the worth of Magic. Though I'm not yet ready to follow his course, I certainly won't hesitate to change things here. After all, Magiskeep is my kingdom and I can do with it as I please."

Jorn frowned. No matter what anyone else thought, he found it hard to believe Jamus could change so. Still, the offer was too tempting to pass up. "You give me your blessing then? I can use my Magic as I please?"

"Who else should it please, Jorn? The River gave the Gift to you. Perhaps it's time you opened it."

Jorn raised his hand and in it appeared a golden goblet of amberwine. When Jamus nodded his approval, the Master of Recreation conjured goblets to everyone in the room. "A toast, then, to seal the pact. We are free of Rule and Vow."
The other revelers did not notice, but The Jamus did. The River lurched, as two more streams sheared off from the main course to carve new beds in Turan's heart.

****

"Damn," Jamus cursed. "Did you feel that, Jorl?"

Jorl grunted. "The River again. Another disruption. I wouldn't have noticed if you hadn't alerted me to the danger. Surely other Mages will feel it."

"Not unless they are working a weave. The River is alive, moving and driving with its own passions. I can temper it, but most Mages can't. If it shifts beneath their hands, they think little of it."

"So we've no allies but ourselves." Jorl looked up at the sky. "It's late. It will be dark soon. We shouldn't try to reach the caves now, as much as I want to. We can set up camp if you'd like."

Jamus shook his head. "I'd rather prefer a stopover in Lord Sarkem's Keep."

"But you said this world's Jamus was going there. Suppose we run into him there?"

"That's exactly what I was hoping," Jamus replied. "I'd like to meet this pretender to my name and see what he's made of. I can hardly believe I was sent here unless I was meant to meet him, and if that's true, then he may well hold part of the riddle."

Jorl sighed. "I can tell you I detest the man myself. The Hand only knows what you'll think of him, and worse, what he'll think of you."

Much to Jamus' relief, there was no Whim in Sarkem's stables. Instead, a tired Magwin stood in one of the stalls, suggesting he had been the Master's mount. While Jorl bedded his ponies in the stalls reserved for him during his Healing visits, Jamus inspected the black horse. Magwin was thinner than he would have liked and certainly not fit enough for the trip he'd just taken, but his eyes were bright and he seemed healthy. His coat shone and his hoofs were well trimmed and shod. Jamus fed him two surleps, stroked his neck and sent a cautious Healing to ease his fatigue.

By then, Jorl was waiting for him and together, they made their way to the main house.

The manservant at the door was too well trained to react with more than a raised eyebrow to Jamus' second arrival. He merely escorted the pair to Sarkem's dining room where evenmeal was already being served.

"My Lord," the servant said as he entered ahead of the new guests. "Master Jorl is here and," he pause, his eyes riveting on

Magiskeep's Lord already seated at the table. "Master Jorl and a friend," he finished.

Sarkem pushed his chair back and started to rise. "Master Jorl, an unexpected surprise and who…" He dropped back into his seat.

Across the table from the speechless lord, another Jamus wiped his hands on his napkin and sighed. "So, you bring more reflections to torment me, eh, Jorl? A new conscience to rouse me to your morality? Well, Sur, you've found a good specimen this time. He is quite impressive."

Jamus moved in front of Jorl, blocking the Healer with his own body in case Magic became an issue. "You are mistaken yourself, Sur, in judging reflection and reality. Were you a true Master of the Way, you would know your own face better than that."

"H-m-m-m-m," the other Jamus leaned forward, rubbing his chin thoughtfully. "You are confident for a shadow. Do you have a name?"

"Kiselor," Jamus replied quietly.

The other man stiffened. "How dare you claim that name?"

"Because it's mine."

"Liar. I am Master of Magiskeep and by right the Rivers Master as well. Who are you to come here and say otherwise? Take care or Spellfire will end your pitiful existence."

Jamus shook his head. "I'm not here to challenge you, Sur. I've merely come to see what you are."

"I am what you see."

"Is your kingdom your image as well? Can I truly see the Lord in his subjects and the way of his land?"

"Magiskeep of my making, and it is in my keeping."

"Then I must ask another question."

"Go on."

"Of all you have in this Keep, what is the most important thing to you?"

The other Jamus frowned. "A strange question, but I'll entertain it. I treasure myself above all. It's the precept upon which I've built my kingdom."

"A pity," Jamus replied. "The River has a greater purpose than the pleasure of one man. "

The other Jamus spat his disapproval. "Pah, what would you have me do, spend my life in study trying to find a way to benefit the commoners? Should I seek others' happiness above my own? A man's circle begins and ends with himself. If he wastes the time in between on anything besides his own needs and desires, why has he lived at all? It's an empty existence that does not satisfy itself first." He waved his hand in disgust. "But how would you ever understand that? You claim yourself the Rivermaster and that says it all. To you, life is sacrifice to the Dragon and you are the servant of humanity, destined to save it from the Darkness. If I were a pretender, I'd choose a more sensible claim than that."

"If I were a pretender," Jamus said, "I would choose better too."

"You're insane."

"Call it Waymadness if you will, My Lord. It might make it easier." He deliberately turned to Sarkem. "Sur, Jorl and I need shelter for the night."

"I...ah," Sarkem sputtered. Then he collected himself. "It's not for me to say, Sur. While he is here Lord Jamus commands my Keep."

Jamus nodded. "Then, Lord Jamus, I ask your indulgence."

The other Jamus laughed. "You're brazen for a madman, I'll give you that. There is a room in the servants' quarters you can share. I'm sure Master Jorl knows where it is. I insist you leave before first light. I would be loath to look at your face again."

Jamus turned and pushed Jorl out the door ahead of him. "Then, Sur, be quite sure you never look in the mirror."

Jorl heard cursing behind them as they hurried down the hall.

Chapter 13

"Sleep lightly, Jorl," Jamus warned as they settled down in the little room behind Sarkem's kitchens. "Unless I misread your 'lord', I have a feeling he will visit us in some form or another before Norwin's turn."

"To what end, My Lord?"

"I've piqued his curiosity. He'll want to know, one way or another if I really am who I claim to be."

"The Rivermaster? But he thinks he is."

"Not at all. If you listened, he never said that at all. This world may be a reflection of the reality of Magiskeep, but apparently there are some indisputable truths that defy the mirrors. For one thing, Whim isn't here."

"Your famous silver stallion I've heard so much about? What does he have to do with it?"

"Whim is part and parcel of my Magic, Jorl. Since he's missing, I can only conclude my Magic is somehow immune to the Way's control. Since I also believe Whim is the River's unique gift to me, as its Master, then I must also believe the Rivermaster has no reflection either."

"So this Jamus is a fraud."

"Only if he claims the River as his own, and I didn't hear him say that. But I'll tell you this; his ambition won't let him rest if he thinks I'm his rival. Frankly, I was a bit surprised he was a tempered as he was. I had set shields for us both, you know."

Jorl shook his head. "I had no idea. I never saw you weave a thing."

"I don't weave as you do, Jorl, though I must admit it wasn't as easy as it should have been. The waters kept slipping through my fingers as if the threads were too fine to hold the patterns I commanded."

"So you thought he was going to attack you."

Jamus nodded. "Spellfire's no idle threat." He blew out the lantern and lay down on the cot. "We're still warded, but that doesn't mean he couldn't use some other weapon against me."

"A dagger?" Jorl asked, shivering.

"More likely he'll try Magic first. It is, after all, his life."
Then he closed his eyes and drifted into a doze.

The door opened at Norwin's third span. Jamus didn't move
as the dark figure approached his bed. Only when the hand covered
his mouth did he react. He moved with supple strength, wrenching
his attackers' hand with a twist of his own, squirming out from under
the covers. His other arm snaked out to clamp around the man's neck
and an instant later, he had wrestled him to the ground. He felt the
sinuous coils of Magic licking at the surface of his sphere and then
heard a muttered curse.

Jamus sent Maglit to the lamps, lighting the room in a
silvery glow. Then, he looked down at the face of the pinned man. It
was his own. "Pitiful for a Lord to behave like a common thug. I
would have hoped for better."

"You knew I was coming," the other Jamus hissed. "You set
a trap."

"I only acted as you would. After all, we are kin."

"You are reflection then."

"It is a matter of perspective. If you promise not to attack me
again, I'll let you up and we can talk. I assure you, I mean no harm
here. In fact, all I really want to do is leave. Are you willing?"

"Anything, if you'll let me go. I can hardly breathe under
here."

Jamus suppressed his smile and pushed himself back up,
setting the other Jamus free.

The Sorcerer sat up, rubbing his neck and shoulder. "Quite a
trick. Where did you learn that?"

"Instinct, I think," Jamus replied. "I don't often have to
defend myself against physical attacks." He looked over at Jorl who
was still sleeping soundly. "Good thing it worked. I wasn't going to
be getting much help if it didn't."

"He's an old man and not very useful for anything."

"Jorl is a skilled Healer."

"To the commoners, not to my Keep. He's worthy to the
worthless."

"Have you always been so contemptible? A Master is responsible for the welfare and comfort of his subjects."

"More twisted doctrines espoused by the duskit hearts like your Jorl and that old hag Joria. You don't mean to tell me you believe in that garbage?"

"It's the way of my world—at least it was the way of my world when I left it."

The other Jamus frowned. "You're not of the Way?"

"As near as I can tell, your world and mine are true reflections of each other. Yours exists in my Way, and mine, I would guess, exists in yours. What I haven't yet reckoned is exactly how what happens in each influences the other."

"You've no right to change my world for the sake of yours. You don't belong here."

"I don't want to change your world, nor do I want your world to change mine. The problem is, I have a feeling I may not have the choice. Already I feel my River slipping from my hand. If I lose it altogether, the Hand only knows what will happen here."

The other Jamus sat quietly for a moment. Then, he nodded grimly. "I've felt it too and so have other Masters. The other day, Masters Jorn and Senneth came to me with a plea. They suggested I demand the Mages temper their use of Magic lest we use up the waters until there are none at all to draw on. They suggested I issue some sort of edict restricting Magic's use to absolute necessity. I told them they were fools. Now I'm wondering who the real fool is."

"I don't approve of your methods, nor the state of your kingdom, but its survival is as important to me as it is to you. Will you help me for both our sakes?"

"What do I need to do?"

"Jorn and I are going to the caves behind the waterfall not far from here. There I hope to find answers to a riddle I must solve. You must do all you can to discourage your Mages from changing things here."

"You want me to continue to behave like a common thug? You mean to tell me you're condoning it? What about all those subjects you say I'm responsible for? Suddenly they don't matter to you?"

"Sacrifice," Jamus said softly. "A word you used yourself, My Lord. This time I'm the one who has to refuse his nature and leave these people to their fate."

The other Jamus rubbed his hands together in satisfaction. "It delights me to have the upper hand over a man who claims to be the Rivermaster—to be sanctioned by his command."

Jamus gritted his teeth. Sacrifice. Surely he'd have to suffer no harder part to the riddle.

****

Joria and Sarena arrived at Greenhope shortly after Sowin's turn while the sun was still high in the sky. Though Sarkem was surprised, he had no trouble preparing rooms for them as well as a festive midmeal to celebrate the unexpected visit.

"We don't mean to impose, My Lord," Sarena said. "We really came to see Jorl."

"And would you expect he'd treat you as I do, Mistress? Master Jorl has but a small cottage and is a terrible cook. Accept my hospitality and rest here. I'll send for Jorl so you can meet him in comfort."

"You needn't bother, Sur," Joria said. "We can go to him."

"Nonsense, My Lady. Jorl comes here all the time. He is tending my wife. I'm sorry she wasn't well enough to greet you."

"Your wife is ill?" Sarena asked.

"Aye. Ever since Lady Salene lost her child, Delise has been…well, she simply hasn't been herself. Losing our child was devastating for her, and it took her a long time to recover. Then it happened again." He sighed. "She's taken to her rooms and hardly eats at all. She lets me visit during the day." Sarkem's voice trailed off.

"I am Mistress of Compassion, Lord Sarkem. I would be remiss if I didn't offer to tend your wife while I'm here."

"Jorl is a capable Healer."

"So he may be, but he is not Master of the River's tributary as I am. There are currents I may be able to turn for her sake."

Sarkem's gaze lifted hopefully. "Could you, My Lady? I'd be most grateful."

"I could visit her now," Sarena said. "Would she be willing?"

"Delise still loves me, despite everything. She'll do as I ask."

He led Sarena to an upstairs door, entered the room alone and came back out a minute or so later, nodding to her.

Salene entered the room, her eyes peering into the dim interior. The drapes were closed, and a few candles were the only light. Delise was in bed, wrapped in a pale pink comforter. "My husband says I am accede to your will, Mistress Sarena. For him, I do this. But don't hope for too much. Master Jorl says the curse has ruined me."

"I don't believe in curses, My Lady," Sarena said as she drew near. She held back her own distress to see how pale and thin the woman was. When Delise had visited Magiskeep, she had been vigorous and healthy, with a ready laugh and good sense. Now she was a hollow shell, empty of any will of her own. Sarena sat on the edge of the bed. "I can only imagine how dreadful all of this has been for you, Delise, but the Magic does not punish people."

"I am being punished. I dared to defy the Falls and the Cave of Secrets. I scoffed at the legends, and laughed at the power residing there. This is my sentence," she patted the bed. "My circle will close here in the shadows."

"Let me Touch you. My River loves life too much to let it slip away so easily."

Delise nodded and Sarena took the woman's hands in hers.

Coursing through the shallows, even these waters were muddied. What should have been simple demanded concentration and the full Will of its Mistress.

But the pain was unmistakable, sharp and keen to strike. It coursed through blood, muscle, bone, and spirit, infusing soul and mind with hopeless resignation.

Poison indeed. A thought planted as a seed grown to a noxious weed strangling the struggling life around it.

There was life—weak and submissive, fighting for air.

Sarena took hold of this, urging the River to nourish it.

But the poison flowed rich and dark, turning the waters again and again.

Compassion alone could only do so much.

She broke the contact.

"Mistress, you look pale. Are you all right?" Delise asked as the air lightened.

"It's common in a Healing for me to react like this," Sarena explained quickly. "I am going to need some herbs from my pack and a few from the forest to make you a medicine. You should feel a little better now, but I have more to do to cure you completely."

"I'm sure Jorl can assist you."

Sarena held up her hand in warning. "No. Master Jorl will have no part in this." When she saw the look of alarm on Delise's face, she tempered her remarks. "If I am to Heal you, no one else must be involved. My remedies are balanced to your needs and taking treatment from someone else could seriously compromise their effect. Please, don't take any of the potions Master Jorl has prepared for you until I tell you to. Will you promise me that?"

Delise nodded weakly. "As you are a Master of Magiskeep, I must abide by your command. Jorl has been so kind to me. I hate to reject him."

"He'll understand as soon as he finds out I've Touched you, My Lady. He'll be gracious enough to stand aside." Unless he is bold enough to stand against two Masters, she thought.

As she headed downstairs, she heard voices arguing. "I've always done right by you and your Lady, Sur. Why would you turn to the Keep now?"

"I cannot refuse a Mistress, Jorl."

"To the Sea with Mistresses, and all Keep Mages who presume superiority! I have as much Art as any of them!"

"Hush, Jorl, she may hear you."

"Let her ears burn! Let her hand burn for all that matters!"

"Sur, no matter what your provocation, I will not tolerate such threats," Joria interrupted angrily.

"I'm not your Prentice any more, Madam. So don't lecture to me."

"I have every right to call a fool for what he is."

Before it got any worse, Sarena glided into the sitting room. "So this is the fabled Jorl. Now why, I wonder, would such a man be so enraged with another Healer's efforts to soothe his patient?"

"Meddle is more like it, with all the high and mighty piety of the Keepbred." Jorl spat. "By the Blood, I've had more than I can stomach of your kind."

"Like Lord Jamus?" Sarena said quietly.

Jorl's mouth dropped.

"Lord Jamus is of the Keep, Master Jorl. As I understand it, you were most courteous and kind to him. Should one who honors him as I do deserve any less."

"You trod on my pride, Madam."

"It was not my intention, Sur."

"So have you healed our Lady?"

"I think you know the answer to that question better than I do. But, I do have herbal remedies to work where my Touch can do no good."

Jorl shifted nervously. "I gave her remedies already."

"Remedies? I told you I Touched her. Do you think I am a Novite? Was it wileroot or tammerseed you used? Either one would make her lose the will to live. I'd say you added some veldherb as well for appetite, and a few other flavors to steal her peace."

"What are you talking about, Sarena?" Joria asked.

"Poisons, my dear friend. The drugs Jorl has been giving Lady Delise are slowly killing her."

Sarkem shook his head. "No, My Lady, you must be mistaken. The strain, the strain has been too much for her, that's all. Surely Jorl would never hurt her."

"Master Jorl has harmed your wife, My Lord. I don't know why, but I do know how. Those precious herbs of his cure nothing but life itself."

"That is a dangerous accusation, Mistress. My Healer has been here for circles serving my Keep loyally and well. Why would he suddenly try to kill my wife?"

"I suggest you ask him, My Lord. I can tell you I am bound my Rule and Vow as well as the oath of my Art to protect Delise. I will not let this man near her again, My Lord."

"And what will you do to stop me?" Jorl sneered. "Touch me with your sweet Compassion and charm me into submission?"

"The Masters of the Keep are not limited by single-minded skill, Sur. It would not be wise to challenge my decision."

Joria stretched her arms lazily. "The Lady does not stand alone, Jorl, and I have circles more experience dealing with unruly young mages than she does."

Jorl tried to stare her down, but her sharp gaze drove him back as it had so many circles before when he was a Prentice in the Keep. He waited for the Darkness to rally to his cause, but the Dragon was silent, refusing him refuge. He had no choice. "I'll do as you say, Mistresses, but you have misjudged me."

"I think not," Sarena replied evenly. "But when my herbs cure the Lady, I'm certain Lord Sarkem will be curious about your cures."

"It's a lie," Jorl repeated, his eyes darting nervously from Joria's face to Sarkem's as he avoided Sarena's placid gaze. When neither of them made a move to support him, he straightened. "Well, I won't stay here to be insulted like this. I'm leaving." He spun on his heel and stalked out, his step quickening on the porch in case Sarkem had decided to send guards to apprehend him.

In the sitting room, Sarkem collapsed on a settee. "By the Blood, I put my faith in that man for over twenty circles. How could he do this to my poor wife?"

"He's changed," Joria said. "That's not the Jorl I tried to teach back in Magiskeep. I didn't have much of a chance to sift him, but the little I did looked suspiciously Illusive."

"A reflection?" Sarena asked.

"Dimly lit, suggesting Shadow," Joria replied. "He's keen, though, and clever in disguising it. I'd say he's had a bit of practice and has been here a long time."

Sarkem looked confused. "That can't possibly be. Lord Jamus is the Rivermaster. Surely he would have seen this reflection in my Healer. He never even hinted of it, and when he left, he'd willingly put his own wife's care into Jorl's hands as well as the care of that stallion of his."

"Whim is with Jorl?"

"So I was told. Lord Jamus said he was lame and needed tending. Then, he left for Magiskeep with his Lady and a pack of Jorl's remedies."

"That only adds to our suspicions," Joria said. "To begin with, there is nothing that could happen to Whim that Jamus couldn't cure. And then...," she hesitated, looking to Sarena for her assent. When the other Mistress nodded, she went on. "Neither Sarena nor I believe the Jamus who returned from your Keep is the one who left ours to come here."

"Another Shadow?"

"If so, we need to find out what happened to the real Jamus. That's why we came. If we're right, he's still here, somewhere in your kingdom."

Sarkem swallowed hard. "In Sorem's Name, I pray you're wrong, Madam, for if you're not, I may well have played a part in a horrible scheme to murder him." He shook his head sadly. "Before he left, Master Jamus convinced me to seal the caves beneath the waterfall because of the curse. Now I'm beginning to think he had another purpose in mind."

"The cave Lady Salene keeps telling us is cursed?"

Sarkem sighed heavily. "They are cursed, if, as I now fear, they are the Rivermaster's tomb."

Chapter 14

With Easwin, Jamus and Jorl rode out to the mountains and soon reached the caves beneath the waterfall. There had been a rockslide near the entrance, sealing it, but Jamus' Magic easily cleared a passage for the two Magicians.

With Maglits lighting the way, they cautiously made their way into the inner cave and knelt beside the runes.

"See?" Jorl said. "It's in the Eldentongue. All death ends in shadowed walls. Life flows rapid in the falls. Endings here shall never be.' It's really quite clear. These caves inspire life."

Jamus smiled. "What appear to be the same runes have quite a different interpretation in your eyes, Master Jorl. Your reflection offers far less hope than his translation."

"He'd have cause," Jorl replied. "These words 'life, death' could be easily interchanged. But it's the final two lines that define their meaning. Here." He brushed away the sand. "'Give thy life to waters' will, all ambition thou shalt fill. Give thy life for waters' sake, Light shall all thy circles take.' Do you see, My Lord? The word 'light" is the key here. These caves promise hope."

Jamus studied the runes himself, mulling the words over in his head, trying to put the pieces together. Once more he said the word he'd learned to understand here, "Sacrifice. Look at this, Jorl. 'Give thy life.' They're written twice. Somehow, I'm sure that's part of the key."

"But you have given your life to the River."

"No. I've always held back, keeping something for myself. My reflection here is the epitome of selfishness. If he is the true reflection of what I must be to again stand at the other side of his mirror, then I must give all of myself." He began to dig the debris away from the base of the runerock.

"This isn't the way out of here," Jorl said. "I came from somewhere closer to Magiskeep's stables."

"So did I," Jamus replied, "but that way in is all part of a dead end. We need to try another way back."

"So you propose going in there?" Jorl asked, pointing to the hole beneath the runes. "Isn't that how we got in trouble in the first place? Did you ever think it may just take us deeper into the mazes of reflections?"

"It doesn't matter," Jamus said. "Our lives aren't worth anything here as it is." Then he shrugged. "Besides, all life is a circle. Sooner or later, we'll meet the beginning again." With that, he lowered himself into the opening, and Jorl had no choice but to follow.

As Jorl dropped to the floor beside him, Jamus looked up. Above him, the pool in the cave shimmered a span above his head, offering a way back into the runecave. The only other way out was a single mirror, glowing with the unsteady light of another realm within the Way. He could clearly see there was no route to Turan's reality from here. Still, the misty image of trees beyond the reflection promised more than the caves he'd left.

It was exactly as it had been before. Not hesitating, Jamus beckoned to Jorl to follow, and then, he stepped into the mirror, and into the water.

A moment later, Jamus' head broached the surface of a fern edged pool in the middle of a forest glen.

Pale sunlight filtered in through the thick branches of elms, brellums, and oaks, rising like sentinels on all sides. Somewhere, not far off, a tarlet trilled, and a shy duskit darted to cover under a feathery brellybush.

Jorl bobbed up next to him, sputtering water from his mouth. "I've been here before," he groaned. "Too many damn trees in every direction."

Jamus waded to shore. As he dried himself, he looked around. "Do you remember where Keldra's cottage is?"

Jorl sat down on the moss and poured water from his boots. "East, west, what difference does it make? No matter which way we go, we'll get there sooner or later. You said yourself all life was a circle."

Jamus laughed. "So, my words bite back. Let's test your theory. I definitely didn't go that way the first time." He pointed straight off ahead. "We'll go that way until we're too exhausted to keep on."

"Sounds fine by me," Jorl said. "It shouldn't take too long. I'm tired already."

Jamus reached down, grabbed Jorl's hand and pulled the Healer to his feet. "We have to struggle on, My Friend. I think we both have to be ready to collapse before we find the end of the trail. I, unfortunately, still feel quite fit."

"I can fix that," Jorl replied. "Just a nice little potion of dallyweed."

Jamus started to reply, but the other man's grin checked him. "Dally not, Sur, or your tarrying will circle us a circle. I, for one, don't want to wander around."

This time Jorl laughed. Hopping on one foot he managed to put his boot back on and then he trailed along behind.

This time, though, Keldra's cottage appeared in its clearing after what seemed only a span of walking.

As they approached, Jorl grabbed Jamus' arm and yanked him to a stop, his audible gasp a clean warning. "Look!" He pointed.

There, sitting on its haunches near the door sat a great brindle tark.

Jamus shook off Jorl's hand and headed for the cottage. "Now we find out whether we've circled."

"How? By getting eaten? For Sogol's Sake, My Lord, we don't have to go on. That creature will kill us."

Jamus strode resolutely on. As he neared the cobbled walk, the tark rose, stretched and headed out to meet him. "Taba?" he said. "Is that you?" The great cat shoved her head into his chest and began to purr, as Jamus breathed a sigh of relief. "It's all right, Jorl," he called back. "She's a friend."

Keldra opened the door. "So ye have returned. 'Tis a wise man who finds the way back."

"I risked it," Jamus answered, "for the sake of the River."

"And the riddle?"

"I'd like to see the tapestry before I answer," he said.

"Then welcome. And welcome to ye too, Master Jorl. It seems ye have learned to follow the right man at last."

Jorl bowed slightly. "If that's what I was supposed to learn after you shoved me through that weave, then I can think of far easier ways to find out."

"Aye, but easy is not always as lasting a cure. Now ye've been dosed with pretender's poison perhaps ye'll realize the worth of the true Masters, eh?"

"I thought I was running away," Jorl said. "What I failed to understand is what I was running from. All this time I thought Magiskeep and its Masters were the enemy."

"So, now ye return to face thy fears."

"And to go on with my life, accepting what I am. The River didn't curse me, it Gifted me. It's my duty to use it to help people, whoever they may be."

They entered the house and Jamus walked over to the tapestry. He reached down and fingered the lower corner where the weave was at last complete. The whole picture had intensified in color and clarity, the walls of his Keep seemingly etched from real blustone instead of thread and dye. "The weave is complete."

"Aye, Rivermaster. The world of the tapestry is healed."

Jorl walked over to study the tapestry. "I don't understand what happened. If I'm not there anymore, then that world has no Jorl."

"Not yet," Jamus answered, "but once we restore you to your rightful place in my Magiskeep, you'll have a reflection again, though I don't envy the people who'll be taken care of by it. The better a Healer you are, the worse he'll be."

"Then I should strive to be mediocre for their sake."

"No. If you do that, then you truly don't understand the answer to the riddle."

"Sacrifice," Jorl said. "I have to be willing to sacrifice both myself and them for the sake of the River."

****

Joria, Sarena, and Sarkem clambered up the rocky slope to the waterfall. They'd been forced to leave the horses lower down since the rockslide had blocked the trail.

Joria muttered to herself and with a wave of her hand transformed her soft boots and riding skirt to a more practical outfit of breeches and solid leather boots for hiking. "If the Keep ever saw me dressed like this, I'd lose the advantage of my Mistress' image."

Sarena, already dressed as informally grinned between panting breaths. "I've been lazing about far too much, judging from the way my legs feel. How much farther, My Lord?"

Sarkem pointed. "Up there. We'll have to earn our prize, I'm afraid. The landslide I used to block the cave has ruined the trail." He gestured to call the Magic, but the feeble spell shifted only two medium boulders out of the way. "If I'm this pitiful clearing the trail, the Hand only knows how long it will take to open the caves."

"Three of us working together will help," Joria said, "but the River is sluggish to my call."

"To mine too," Sarena agreed, as she stopped on the hill, bent over with her hands on her knees to catch her breath. "The River's running askew and until we find its Master, there's nothing we can do to restore it."

"At least it's running," Joria replied, grateful for the rest. "That means there's a good chance Jamus is still alive."

"We'd know if he were dead, Joria. I'm sure of it." This time she gestured to clear a few boulders with hardly more success than Sarkem. "What bothers me is that we've no clue of where he may be."

Then, an instant later, there was a flash of silver on the slope above near the clearing beside the falls. Whim snorted, and began again to paw frantically at the rocks blocking the cave entrance. He'd made some headway in his long winds of vigil, the stones refusing to yield to his hooves, but a wide gap was open in the sand and dirt. He had been diligent in trying to rescue Jamus on his own, but now welcomed the newcomers with a tired nicker.

Sarkem rounded the trail first and called back to his companions. "He's here! He has to be. The stallion's at the cave entrance."

Sarena reached level ground a footfall ahead of Joria. "If Whim's here, Jamus can't be far away. But I can't understand why he hasn't used his Magic to clear the cave himself. If we can move the rocks as we have, he should be able to move the mountain itself."

"He could be hurt," Joria said.

"It would have to be serious to keep him from the River. We'd better get to work as fast as we can."

Joria nodded and raised her hand.

Whim, satisfied at last to have helped, nickered and began to paw again, sending up a shower of sand.

****

They had settled down by the meager fire to discuss the next move. Going back to the pool in the forest was, for the time being, the only option.

Jamus stared into his mug of soup. "The pool is the only entrance back into the Way. But where its mirror leads, I can only guess."

"Back to the caves of Magiskeep," Jorl replied. "If the tapestry's mended, it stands to reason we're making some kind of progress, doesn't it?"

"Since the tark welcomed me, I'm fairly sure this is the real Keldra and not her reflection, but the whole thing has become so convoluted I don't even know what to believe."

"The soup's good," Jorl said casually.

Jamus chuckled. "One bright spot in a maze of confusion."

"The woman is a Seer. Do you think she might help us decide the best course?"

Jamus shrugged. "All I can do is ask."

Keldra shuffled in from her back room, patted Taba on her head and lowered herself into a chair across from them. "So, what will ye do with thy riddle now, Rivermaster?"

"If I knew, I'd be doing it instead of sitting here, My Lady."

Keldra cackled, her mouth wide in a toothless grin. "Ye bear a sharp tongue to match thy wits, lad. Now use them both and think it through."

"If the River's Will be done," Jamus said, "I find it hard to accept I'd be thrown into the presence of a Seer if I weren't supposed to use her skill to my benefit. I believe proper etiquette requires me to ask you the favor of a Seeing before you will offer?"

"Aye, 'tis proper. And Keldra will grant thy favor." She reached out her hand and touched his forehead.

A shock jolted Jamus' body, cold as ice, chill as death. He cried out and tumbled to the floor at her feet, while she calmingly intoned a chant. Jorl leapt up ready to intervene, but Keldra's hard stare and a shake of her gray head warned him off.

Darkness. As impenetrable beyond as right in front of him. The muffled cry of terror and a thousand memories flooded his brain. The cave in the Rim and his mother's voice, echoing into the black abyss. Nightmare after nightmare tormenting his sleep.

And then, the ultimate horror of oblivion, the ever-present threat with its scraping tentacles engulfing reason.

He trembled, as if he could shake off the presence, but it was to no avail. Childhood's enemy enveloped him.

He could not escape. He had to face it.

"Get a blanket," Keldra ordered. "Warm him before he freezes near to death. He's faced the enemy before but ne'er conquered it. Give him time."

Jorl knelt at Jamus side and covered him with the blanket, rubbing his arms and legs to restore the circulation.

Through chattering teeth, Jamus managed to ask, "What did you see, Mistress?"

"I gave thee thy Vision, Rivermaster. Ye have always known the answer. Now ye must face it. Come, now. Get on thy feet. I'll scry thee a tale if thou wish it."

With Jorl's help, Jamus pulled himself back into his chair. "I do," he said.

Keldra nodded now and drew a small table covered with a towel over in front of them. With little ceremony, she took off the towel to reveal a beautiful ceramic bowl inlaid with ecrem and jade, and filled with a curious moving fluid shifting into a myriad of patterns.

The old Seer bent her face over the liquid, her blue-veined hands caressing the glazed rim of the scrying bowl, the bony fingers tattooing an impatient rhythm. She peered into the swirling waters, dim blue eyes searching, trying to sift a Vision from the magical liquid.

Why was it taking so long?

"I've not many circles of breath left in me, Algeeta," Keldra said aloud, as if the White Dragon of Fortune would actually hear the words of an outcast Seer. "Show me the Rivermaster's destiny. I need to know before it's too late."

Beside her hearth, Jamus pulled the blanket around his shoulders as if trying to ward off the chill of her words. "It's not the

Magician's way to listen to a Seer's prophecies, Madam. Perhaps your Agleeta will refuse me."

Keldra settled her gaze on him, her woman's passion, so long dormant, stirring as she studied the chiseled features of his face. "Ye are not an ordinary Sorcerer, My Lord. My Dragon sings for thee."

"Well, she's not singing now. Let her sleep." He shivered.

Shrugging ancient shoulders, Keldra rubbed her wrinkled cheek and shook her head. "She sings. I just can't hear her yet. See, the waters color now." And indeed, even as she spoke, the liquid in the wide ceramic bowl began to swirl with a rainbow of shimmering currents.

So bright were the hues, the old woman had to shield her eyes with the ragged sleeve of her amber robe. "Too many melodies," she gasped. "Too many Dragons singing. I cannot listen to her tune. How can so many sing at once for one man, eh?"

"By the Blood," Jamus cursed. He closed his eyes and leaned his head back against the warm stones. "I'm only here because the Shadows have trapped me. I don't know how to escape through that dark veil."

"Ye lie, Magician. Ye have solved the riddle and ye know full well the answer lies here, in my Vision." She tapped the rim of her bowl and the air thickened as a heavy presence descended into the little room.

Jamus took a deep breath, bracing himself against the weight of her Weaving, trying to defy the Truth. His own Magic rebelled and arced unbidden into a protective sphere around him, keeping hers at bay as she peered into the undulating liquid in her bowl.

"Ye shall escape, if ye so will it, Rivermaster."

He leaned forward now. "How? Every time I touch the darkness I can't bear the pain. It sears through me worse than Spellfire, burning my sinews so I can't even hold myself up. I can't escape unless I can get past that."

"Surrender thy fear. Use the riddle."

"I don't know how."

Keldra straightened and waved her hand over the scrying bowl, clearing the waters of their revelations. "Ye have always known the answer, Sur, and so have I. I was a fool not to have realized it before. But fear binds us with chains we refuse to see. I am an old woman, close to the closing of my circle. I, of all, should have realized the secret." She limped over to a stool beside him and gingerly sat, a grimace of pain tightening her lips.

Instinctively, he reached out, his compassion overcoming his revulsion for her Art. "I can Heal you."

She shook her head. "Why? To live another circle alone? Time has sealed my fate. Oblivion will be a blessing." Then she grinned a toothless smile and shrugged her shoulders. Then, like a silly schoolgirl, she began to giggle. "Ye wish to know what I saw in the waters?"

Taken aback, Jamus raked his hand through his dark hair and let out a puff of air. Was the woman mad? Her eyes glittered and her hands trembled as if it was all she could do to sit still. How could he trust a word she said? Yet, Magic and madness were too often kin. It might be wise to listen. "Tell me."

"Oblivion will be a blessing."

"You said that before."

"Aye, so I did. Ye'd be wise to heed me. It's why I can pass through the darkness and ye can't."

Oblivion. To accept that was to accept death. But accepting death meant being willing to surrender life. If the darkness imprisoned him because he feared it would kill him.

Then it made sense.

Sacrifice.

Chapter 15

Sarkem collapsed on a boulder and wiped the sweat from his brow with his sleeve. "At this rate, we'll never get the entrance cleared. Damn, what a fool I was when that imposter stood beside me and told me to raise my hand to send the avalanche to block it."

"Down is always easier than up," Joria said, rolling up her sleeves to hand-clear a tree branch from the pile.

Sarena pulled her dark hair back behind her neck and tied it with her scarf. "We should have brought more Mages. There'd be more people to take turns casting."

"More chaos," Joria replied. "We're making enough mess as it is. We need to organize our effort."

Sarkem rubbed his chin. "Or combine it. What if we all cast a lifting spell at the same time? Do you think the threads would join and be stronger?"

"A brilliant idea, My Lord," Sarena said, rubbing her hands together. "We should have thought of it sooner. Come, Joria, leave that twig of yours and join us in a trial spell."

Joria dropped the limb and moved over beside the other mages. Together, they raised their hand and together, they drew upon the waters, directing the weaves towards a boulder twice the size of any they'd moved before. In an instant, the silver threads coiled about the stone and threw it to the side.

Whim tossed his head and snorted as the boulder rolled past him and down the slope.

"Wonderful," Sarena said. "That was easy enough. Now maybe we can handle some of those stubborn rocks we couldn't budge."

Soon, the larger obstructions began to move out of the way, opening a larger and larger hole in the huge pile. Though one at a time seemed slower, the visible progress heartened the workers, and Whim's repeated approval cheered them on.

As Sowin drew near, hope brightened in the mounting sun.

****

This time, the forest pool was within sight of Keldra's door, as if space had narrowed once Jamus had resolved the secrets of the journey.

Taba rubbed up against his leg as he headed down the cobbled walk. He scratched behind the cat's ears, "I'll miss your purr, gentle Taba. Take good care of your Mistress for me." He turned back to the door where Keldra watched. "My Lady, I would like to think I will see you again."

"In a dream, Rivermaster, but not in flesh."

"Even if I return to this part of the Way?"

"When ye leave, this part of the Way will be no more. It has served its purpose in the River's Will."

"And what of you, Mistress?"

"Remember the riddle," Keldra answered. "May the Hand guide thee and bless thee on thy journey. Healer, honor thy Art and remember thy friends."

Jorl nodded. "I will, Madam. My thanks to you for the soup."

Keldra began to laugh and as the men made their way to the water's edge, the sound of it filled their ears.

It was a good way to remember her.

They plunged into the water.

Neither one noticed that the tark followed close behind.

"He comes."

"Hold, sister, mine is the hand he seeks."

"Over here, beloved. This way."

"Don't listen to her. She will lead you astray."

"Be silent. He will not listen to you."

"He will hear my song."

"Never."

The room opened before them, the mirrored image of the cave just above in the wall ahead.

"Give me a boost up, Jorl," Jamus said. "I'll pull you up behind when I'm sure it's safe."

Jorl clasped his hands beneath Jamus' foot and lifted as Jamus grabbed the ledge beneath the mirror. He slid easily through the reflection back into his prison cave.

It was darker than he remembered with the dark veil blotting out even the pale light from outside. Strange. Even if it were Norwin, the stars and moon would offer at least some glow. But there was none.

He lit several maglits, illuminating the chamber in silver light. When he still saw nothing amiss, he reached down into the opening below the runes and stretched out his hand, "Jorl, here, take hold. I'll bring you up."

The Healer grunted as he scrambled to his feet. "It's darker in here than I remember. Are you sure it's the right cave and not another reflection?"

Jamus pointed. "There's the black barrier I told you about."

Jorl frowned. "I don't see anything."

"No weave?"

"None, Sur. I'll go out into the other cave if you wish."

"No, don't. The barrier's there. I can see it."

Before Jamus could stop him, Jorl stepped forward. Nothing happened as he passed the black wall.

Jamus caught his breath. The Healer was on the other side of the darkness, completely untouched by the dark magic.

"Jorl?"

"Here, My Lord."

"I can hardly see you."

"You look fine to me. Is the darkness between us?"

"Yes. You didn't feel it?"

"Nothing. Evidently it's only your prison, not mine."

Jamus considered the idea. Suddenly, it all began to make sense. The riddle and Keldra's Seeing blending to a chilling realization. Naboth had woven the darkness out of Jamus' own dread, using a keen knowledge of the Rivermaster's mind against him.

Jamus peered at the threads of the weave with new understanding. The pattern was as intricate as the workings of his own thoughts, knotted with threads from nightmares he'd long forgotten. As long as he was Jamus, the barrier was solid and impassable to him.

As long as he was Jamus.

Sacrifice.

Oblivion.

What did his life matter if he were forever cut off from his Kingdom? It was no life at all. Here, he was nothing but fodder to Naboth's appetite and pawn to the dark Dragon's will. Better death than such a prison.

Better oblivion.

He closed his eyes, blotting out his senses as he extinguished the maglits. "Tell Salene I love her," he said, and he plunged forward.

Colder than cold. Darker than dark. More empty then empty.

Someone screamed.

His voice.

The night bellowed.

The Dragon.

He fell, into Jorl's waiting arms.

"My Lord, are you all right? I can't see anything in this darkness."

Jamus gasped for air and grabbed Jorl's arms with his fingers, groping up until he found his face. "It *is* you."

"Indeed, Sur. Who else would I be?"

"Thank the Hand. I'm out of there."

"Into another prison, I think. With this darkness the way out is still blocked."

Jamus regained his composure and raised his hand to float several maglits in the air surrounding them. Behind him, the black veil absorbed the light completely now, denying a view into the inner cave.

When the brindle tark leapt out of the hole, neither man saw her.

Instead Jamus was concentrating on the jumble of rocks blocking what was once the cave's entrance beneath the falls. "Stand off to the side, Jorl. With the River so erratic I may not be as accurate as I'd like."

With Jorl safely out of the way, Jamus raised his hand.

****

Joria had gone back to her log, determined to move it with her own strength rather than Magic. Meanwhile, Sarena and Sarkem were concentrating their efforts on a stubborn boulder lodged just at the water's edge.

Just as they cast their united spell, there was a powerful explosion from inside the cave, spewing rocks and debris in every direction.

Whim bolted and vanished in a wisp of silver mist.

Sarkem grabbed Sarena in his embrace and stumbled back with her into the stream as a large rock rolled past.

Joria, out of harm's way, dropped her burden and simply stared, her mouth open as the waterfall rushed into its newly carved channel.

Her eyes were the first to see Jamus emerge, brushing the dust from his worn tunic even as he squinted in the sunlight.

"Jamus! Thank the Hand!"

"Joria! What are you doing here?"

"Rescuing you." She laughed. "Though, as usual, you didn't need us. Sarena, Sarkem...." Her voice trailed off. "By the Blood, where are they?" She scrambled over the broken rocks towards the stream. There was no sign of the other mages.

Jamus hurried over to her. "Where were they when you last saw them?"

A voice answered from down the slope where the roiling waters of the falls steadied into a calmer current. "We were standing in the line of fire, apparently. Would you have aimed better, I'd be dry instead of sopping wet and half drowned." Sarena stumbled up the slope with Sarkem close behind ready to catch her if she fell. "My Lord, that was not your usual way of arriving. I do hope you have an excuse."

Jamus grinned at her and raised his hand to dry her clothes and set her bedraggled hair to right. "Didn't you teach me never to make excuses? The truth is I had no idea you were out here saving me."

"Ah, did you think we'd forgotten you?"

Jorl made his way down beside Jamus. "We thought you had fallen under the spell of the pretender who uses Jamus' name in his stead."

Sarena smiled. "And what of the pretender who uses your name, Master Jorl? According to Mistress Joria, he is a poor substitute for the Healer she once knew."

Jorl turned to Joria and nodded. "As ever, the Mistress of Illusion is sharp in her perception and wise in her ways. How did you know it wasn't me?"

"Illusions have no heart, Jorl, and the man I knew had more than most men."

"Thank you, My Lady. It's good to see you again."

Jamus was about say something when a snort interrupted. Whim had appeared again just a short way off, pawing the sand on the level ground just beyond the rubble. "So, the rest of the rescue party makes its appearance."

"Most dramatically," Jorl said, grinning. "This is the silver stallion of the tales, I take it."

"Whim," Jamus said, laughing. "Loyal to a fault until he decides to melt into the mist."

"Don't mock him," Sarena admonished. "He was here when we came, trying to dig you out of that cave. In all of Magiskeep, he's the only one who wasn't taken in by that monster who sits in your Palace."

"So, my pretender has managed to take my place, has he?"

"Too successfully, I'm afraid."

"Jiala, Jorn, and Senneth have joined in his side."

"Three Masters fallen," Jamus said. "The Dragon must be rejoicing. No wonder the River has slowed. Is there time to plan or do I need to go back at once?"

"Sarena and I are here. Jired is not likely to join without me and Savel is too removed from ordinary thinking to be an easy mark," Joria said.

"What about Salene?"

"There's nothing to do for her right now. She's refused to let him anywhere near her."

"She knows what he is?"

Sarena bit her lip, uncertain as to how to explain. "She's grieving, Jamus. She's not thinking clearly right now. She won't let anyone who loves her get close to her."

To her surprise, Jamus hardly reacted. "Good. As long as he doesn't touch her I won't rush in. I have another score to settle before I take care of him. Have you spoken to the Jorl who's here already?"

Still puzzled by Jamus' seeming lack of concern for Salene, Sarena answered quickly, "We've threatened him, if that's what you mean. It seems he was drugging Lady Delise and may well have been responsible for the death of her child."

"And mine too, if I'm not mistaken," Jamus added. "There never was a curse in the caves. The real Jorl has told me there are herbs a mage can use to cause all kinds of illnesses."

"Ending a pregnancy is actually a simple matter," Jorl said. "I'm afraid someone with the proper skill would have no trouble at all slipping something into the victim's food or drink."

"He's probably responsible for what happened to Salene too."

"So he's the target?" Sarkem asked.

Jamus shook his head. "I'll leave him to his own reflection. It's his Master I'm after—Naboth. He's the one who set all this in motion and imprisoned me in that cave."

"A Shadowlord?" Joria said. "How can you possibly find him?"

"I won't have to," Jamus answered. "Now that I'm out of his trap, he's going to come after me again. His plan's too far along to let me ruin it now. Only this time, I'm going to be ready for him."

"You won't be alone," Joria said. "You'll have us with you."

"No," Jamus said. "You'll only be in the way."

"But you can't face a Shadowlord by yourself. What hope of defense can you have against him?"

Jamus smiled. "Sacrifice."

****

The Jamus lay back in his bed, pleased to have accomplished so much in so short a span. Three masters were his and Jired, simple enough in his thinking, was finding Jorn's arguments in favor of yielding to Magic Unrestrained quite convincing. The two main complications in the matter, Sarena and Joria, had left the Keep without explanation, giving him free rein to act at will. He stretched and sighed with pleasure.

"Don't be so complacent, Face in the Mirror. You are not yet safe in the seat of power here."

The Jamus sat up. The room had darkened unnaturally and he recognized the voice. "Lord Naboth, I didn't expect you. Have you come to see how things progress? I've done a great deal since I arrived."

"A small beginning now," Naboth replied. "It means nothing."

"But, My Lord, I'm nearly halfway there. Three Masters ply the waters in your favor and another will soon join them."

"Three, four, it will not matter. The Rivermaster is free."

"What? You had him well imprisoned."

"He has mastered a dark secret in his soul and broken his bonds. We shall have to deal with him in his own element."

The Jamus grunted. "And will you lead the way, or set me up as sacrifice your ambition?"

"Don't be so presumptuous, minion. Best you remember who is the true lord here."

"In their eyes," The Jamus said, gesturing expansively towards the rest of the palace, "I am the true lord. If I call them to my side against you, will you be able to stand against them?"

"And if I kill you now, to whom will they rally?"

"You won't kill me, Naboth, because you still need me. "

"The Rivermaster has looked into his mirror many times, Pretender. You can be replaced."

"His true reflection does not exist, nor do any shadows with my ambition. I was born of a single moment in his life when the Master of Magiskeep forswore Rule and Vow for his own gain. Selfishness is not his robe and he will never so dress himself again. Where in the Way will you find another as suitable as I?"

Naboth snarled his frustration, unwilling to admit The Jamus had won his point. Not only would it be nearly impossible to find an equally worthy reflection to take on the task, but all his planning would go for naught as well. It had taken three full circles to prepare this imposter and even though time meant little to his immortal being, he was cursed with impatience. "Immortality is within your grasp."

"I have already taken nine since I've been here," The Jamus replied, licking his lips with the memory. He had traveled the outskirts of the kingdom in search of prey, finding more than enough flesh and blood to satisfy his growing appetite. Each kill demanded another, increasing lust instead of easing it. "All I need is a mage to quench my thirst."

Now, it was Naboth's turn to tremble. Though The Jamus might never be his equal in the Black River, once he was immortal, he would be a dangerous rival. Better to engender an ally now. "I will not rule alone, Shadow. This will only be a beginning of the Kingdom of darkness I will create. One alone cannot see to its care. I will need Lords to share its power."

"Share?" The Jamus asked. "Your word for 'serve,' My Lord?" He hissed the title as if the taste of it repelled him. "Why should I trust you?"

"I am the voice of the Dragon."

"And you deceive Blackwing even as you swear allegiance."

Naboth grinned. "Who better than to join in an alliance of deception than a master deceiver? For a true reflection like you, opposition is the ideal partner."

The Jamus smiled back. At least he knew exactly where he stood.

Chapter 16

Jamus rode off on Whim, heading back to Magiskeep, while Joria, Sarena, Sarkem, and Jorl rode to the little cottage in the woods.

Inside, Jorl's pretender downed the last of his homemade wine and began to work his way through a flask of amberwine he'd been keeping as a tonic. Drunk, he at least would not feel the cold creeping into his bones.

"Everendings ever be, dost thou fail the faith of me? "

"You weren't here when I needed you to help me defend myself against those hags from the Keep."

"Mistresses of River ne'er give the darkness need to fear. What is death but darker day to a spirit of the Way?"

"I was promised more than that if I served you loyally. I gave the Rivermaster's blood to your communion."

The voice hissed in anger. *"Blood served other shadow's will, for its taste I hunger still. You the pawn in Shadow game, falsehoods spoken in my name."*

"What? He told me it was all for you. I did it for you, Dread Lord, not for him."

"Truth's reflection ever turns when ambition's fire burns. With thy promise cast aside, in my River now abide."

Jorl the Imposter dropped on one knee, his head reeling with drink. "To thee I swear my fealty, Master of the Dark. Tell me what to do."

"Keep thy silence at thine end. I shall count thee as my friend."

The false Healer frowned. "I don't understand. I'll never betray you, if that's what you mean. Is it what you mean? Is it? I don't understand."

Silence was the only reply.

And then, he heard voices outside. He could barely keep his balance as he struggled to his feet.

524   Cave of Shadows

The door opened and he blinked his blurred eyes in confusion. Was he looking in a mirror? He was almost sure he was facing the door.

For his part, the real Jorl was just as astounded. His only advantage was that his travels with Jamus through the tapestry and the Way had faced him with other reflections. He was first to find his voice. "So, I've been impersonated by a common drunk, have I?"

"You," the other Jorl sputtered. "He told me he'd disposed of you."

"Whoever he is lied."

Joria appeared behind the true Healer. "I told you you would be disciplined if you misbehaved, Sur."

The wine was seeping into his brain more and more with each passing minute. "I'm not afraid of you."

"You are alone, Shadow," Jorl said. "How many lives have you taken in the name of this Lord who's deserted you? How much blood have you spilled for him?"

"I rarely spill my drink," the Shadow replied.

Jorl gagged, recovered, and raised his hand, "Filthy beast. There is only one end you deserve." The Spellfire burst from his fingers in a thin, white blaze.

The Shadow screamed once as the whitefire hit him square in his chest. He burst into flame, his form writhing in the agony of Magic's destructive violence. A high-pitched wail soared up with the smoke of his body until only a pile of ashes fell to the floor.

As the room settled back to silence, Joria took her hands from her ears and coughed. "We never asked him what he wanted as his epitaph."

Jorl turned to look at her, his mouth agape. When he saw the twinkle in her eye, he started breathing again. He didn't even realize he'd stopped.

****

Whim wanted to gallop, but Jamus checked him to a trot. "Slow down, my friend. I need some time to think."

The silver stallion snorted, skipped a few more strides, and then settled back down. His master's return had roused both his

spirits and his eagerness to get back home to the comfort of Josep's
stables.

But Jamus' desire to get home was tempered by caution and
another stranger attitude he'd not yet learned to reconcile. For the
first time in his life, all he loved was taking second place to a force
controlled by the Rivers.

And that was the puzzle he had to reckon. Whatever Naboth
and his imposter were doing, Jamus' River was being drained of its
vigor, its waters diverted to a new bed. But, were they flowing into
the dark waters of the Black Dragon's abode? If they had, he found it
hard to believe he'd had no contact with Shadows himself. The
Black minions tended to gloat and brag about even small victories.

So into whose hand were the waters going? It was here the
tapestry came into play. That world was reflection of his own, or, as
near as he could tell, the image of what his world would become if
left to his foes. There, Mages had fallen to the lure of Magic
Unrestrained, becoming easy marks for the Black Dragon's
temptation. But they had not yet denied the True River, lingering
somewhere in a dim existence between the light and the dark.

Naboth. The name bounded back into his thoughts. If
Magiskeep's Mages could pursue their own ambitions why couldn't
one of the Dragon's own? Were Shadowlords any more loyal than
those of the River?

Now he smiled to himself and nudged his eager stallion into
a canter before taking to the air in lifted strides. The puzzle pieces
were falling into place of their own accord.
He was looking forward to meeting the man wearing his name and
face in Magic's hold.

****

Salene—the one conquest The Jamus had yet to make.
Inroads with the Masters of the Seven Arts were worthy victories in
setting himself up as the political leader of Magiskeep, but he was
yet to establish himself as true Lord. As long as the Lady of the Keep
held him at arm's length, he was Master in name only.

He dressed in one of Jamus' finest tunics, royal blue with the
silver stallion crest on the right breast. Then he carefully brushed his

hair, setting it in place with a spell to keep the locks in place, slid a pair of soft dorrsett boots over his breeches and admired himself in the mirror. He was, he thought, lucky to wear the image of a man like Jamus. He could have been reflection to someone old and ugly, without the striking looks and bearing of the grey-eyed Magician. How handsome he was, and certainly more than attractive enough to appeal to a beautiful, discriminating woman like Salene. He added just a touch of cologne to finish his grooming and then headed out to establish his rightful place at the side of the Master's wife.

Salene was still in bed, despite its being well into Sowin. She hadn't been out of her room since their return to Magiskeep and had taken to spending more and more time sleeping as her depression deepened. Despite all the efforts of her maidservants, Resa and Gira, she often did not even bother to get dressed, preferring to stay in a loose dressing gown or night dress.

The Jamus' arrival barely roused her interest. But this time, instead of indulging her mood, he pushed in another direction. "Well, my darling, it's time you and I had a little talk, I think. This simply can't go on any longer."

"I don't want to talk right now, Jamus. Please. I'd just rather be alone."

"You've been alone long enough. At least three Sevenstins have passed, more than enough time for you to rid yourself of mourning and begin to live again. We have to get on with our lives."

"I have no life. It's all been taken from me."

"Nonsense. Your life…our life…is yet ahead of us."

"The curse, Jamus. It still plagues me."

"We're far from the caves and the stone's been disposed of. I have the River to bless our reconciliation. There's no reason not to share a bed again."

"No! Don't you understand? I've already killed one child. Why would I want to risk killing another?"

"For my sake," The Jamus answered. "I deserve your affection. I am your husband. You've no right to continue refusing me."

For the first time in days, her spirit sparked. "You've always given me the right, My Lord. How dare you demand now?"

"Time has changed me, Madam. I am, after all, a man, and men have desires. Why should I be deprived of my physical needs because you choose to wallow in self-pity? As my wife you have duties to serve me as I demand."

Salene's mouth dropped as she caught her breath, too startled by his attitude to answer at once. Then she managed to compose herself. "Changed indeed, Sur, if you insist on taking me to bed without my consent. You are not the man I married, that's for certain."

This time, it was The Jamus who faltered. Had she discovered his secret? But when she made no further accusation, he regained his composure and squared his shoulders. "After evenmeal and Weswin's turn, I will be back, wife. Then, I will take you as is my right, whether you consent or not. I am Master here and Master of the River. You can't deny me. Prepare yourself as you wish, but be warned, I will have you." He spun on his heel and left.

Salene pulled the coverlet up around her, hugging it close to her breast to help still her shaking. The curse had struck more than her heart, for like the heat of the forge, it had tempered Jamus' to stelin. Never in her wildest imaginings had she ever dreamed she would be afraid of him, but now, reality struck hard.

Weak and faint from too many spans of inactivity, she crawled out of bed and spelled on her traveling clothes. She hardly noticed the River's lethargy, thinking instead it was her own condition affecting its flow to her hand. She conjured a drink of rejuvenating herbs, swallowed it in one gulp, and took a deep breath, waiting for its effect to take hold.

She packed a light traveling bag, full of the necessities for several days on the road, and then, as the energy began to fill her limbs, she headed for a back hallway where she could slip down and out of the Keep unnoticed.

At the stables, she caught her breath again, as the smell of manure and urine assaulted her senses. Inside, she found the stalls half cleaned and spread with thin layers of bedding hardly worth notice. Without thinking, she gestured to set the worst of it aright, noting to herself to speak to Josep as soon as it was safe. She headed

for Flax's stall, found it empty, vaguely remembered leaving the
golden mare at Sarkem's, and then instead tacked up Magwin.
The black stallion seemed delighted with her attention, nuzzling her
pockets as she saddled him, then striding out energetically as they
headed out the narrow gate at the far south of the stableyard. He
needed no urging to canter off along the dirt path skirting the palace
walls, and not even a pat of reassurance before she lifted his stride to
cross out into the sparse trees of wilderness beyond. Only when
Magiskeep was out of sight did she rein him to a walk and let out a
sigh of relief. She had until Weswin before Jamus would realize she
was gone, and by then, she hoped to be in Greenhope. There was no
truly safe place to hide from the Rivermaster, but at least in Sarkem's
Keep she might find a clue to his inexplicable behavior. If not, she
would have the solace of Delise's gentle understanding when he
raped her.

****

        Jamus lead Whim uneasily down the aisle of Magiskeep's
stable, sensing Magic's taint in nearly every corner. While the stalls
were clean and the horses well fed and watered, it was evident little
of the work had been done by human hands rather than by the
River's Will. He had to worry now that what he had done in the
Magiskeep of the tapestry might well have affected this world as
well.
        His concern escalated when he came to the stable office and
found a scruffy man lounging in Josep's chair. "Donni," Jamus said
quietly, "have you finished all the chores yet? The brood mares need
alfalfa hay, you know."
        The man looked up lazily. "Aye, Me Lord. Wee Tatum took
the hay ta the mares afore he went back home ta his Maman. Took
'im near seven trips ta carry the three bales like I tole 'im, but it's
done."
        "Then I have another job for you, Sur." Jamus said,
producing a full bag of denerets and tossing it on the desk in front of
the laconic man. "Take this for your trouble and go to Josep's house.
Tell him Whim is here and needs his care at once. It's very important
that he come immediately."

His eyes fixed on the purse, Donni sat up, "Fer me, Me Lord? T'ain't much ta do ta earn so big a price."

"It's the rest of your wages for the Sevenstin and two more in thanks for your service here. I won't be needing you anymore, but I don't want you left without silver while you look for a new job."

Donni grunted. "I shoulda knowt better'an ta think me life was set. Still." He tossed the purse in his hand. "This kin hold a feller fer a good time iffen 'e has a care wid the coin, eh?" He rose and grinned. "I'll give yer message ta Josep, Me Lord. Then ya won't see no more o' me."

After Donni had gone, Jamus put Whim in his stall and set the rest of the stables to perfection, not holding back the sweet hay and fresh straw until every manger was full and every horse up to its knees in bedding. He noted with some concern that both Flax and Magwin were missing, and since the two horses were the most likely mounts for the Lord and Lady of the Keep, it was possible Salene and the Imposter might be out riding together. Though the thought worried him, he pushed it aside for the sake of the River.

Josep arrived within the span, out of breath from running most of the way. He rushed over to Whim's stall without even stopping to greet Jamus, and let out an exasperated puff of air as soon as he saw the stallion well and sound. "So, he weren't so hurt after all. I don't see no sign of no lameness 't'all. S'pose ya tells me the truth fer onct."

"Lame?" Jamus said, not hiding his confusion. "Who told you he was lame?"

"Ya did yerself when ya come back from Sarkem's widout him. Made up a fine story 'bout how's it were so bad ya couldn't do naught ta help 'im. So nows I come a'runnin' ta find 'im fitter an' finer than I e'er seen 'im afore. Ya gots a good reason fer lyin' ta me?"

"I never lied, Josep, but it's clear someone did. The man who came back from Sarkem's was an imposter, born of the Shadows to take my place. I'm afraid he's deceived more than just you. Have you seen Salene?"

Josep scratched his head. "Imposter, eh? What's ta say ya ain't one too? Ya call as ya might, but I ain't fooly enow ta fall twict fer the same prank."

"Whim wouldn't come back for just anyone, Josep, and you know as well as I do he has but one master."

"Aye," Josep agreed, squinting his eyes as he examined Jamus' face. "I cain't but see a difference, but I knows that horse can. So what are ya plannin' to do, Me Lord? The Keep's plumb upside downside ya knows."

"I know. I have to right it first, before I do anything else. But, Josep, Magwin's gone and so is Flax. I'm worried about Salene."

Josep shrugged. "The gold mare ne'er come back from Sarkem's neither. As for Mag, I cain't say I knows a thing. I ain't bin here since that lord," he jerked his finger towards the palace and then went on, "come back. He said I crost 'im, so 'e sent me packin'." He looked around the stable. "I see the beasts ain't bin sufferin' widout me."

"They have, Josep. I had to use the Magic to set things right."

Josep clucked his disapproval. "'Tis a poor man what lets the beasties pay fer his crimes. Ya send that imposter here when yer through wid 'im me lord, an' I'll give 'im a thrashin' fer what he done."
"When I'm done with him there won't be much left to thrash," Jamus replied. Then he headed up the gravel path to the palace.

****

Salene lifted Magwin's strides several times despite her increasing fatigue. Each effort seemed harder than the last, the River reluctant to answer her call. Still, she had managed to halve the distance to Greenhope and, after a rest, hoped to reach the Keep before darkness.

Now that she had reached the cover of the forest, she felt a bit safer, for there were plenty of places to hide should Jamus come riding after her.

She stroked Magwin's neck. "Running from Jamus. Who would ever believe such a thing? How has the world turned so quickly?"

The stallion snorted, then tossed his head, his hooves dancing a nervous tattoo in the dry leaves on the trail.

Salene snatched the reins and stroked him again. "What is it, fellow? Do you hear something?" She strained her own ears listening. There was a low growl somewhere off to the right in a thick cluster of brellybushes. She tensed, waiting to see which way to run.

Then, a huge brindle tark slunk out of cover and sat slowly down on its haunches a short way off, its golden eyes fixed on horse and rider. It made no further move in their direction, but simply lifted its great padded paw to its mouth and began to wash itself.

Salene held Magwin in check, trying to steady the pounding of her own heart. Then she nudged the horse into a slow walk away from the big cat. The tark yawned, stretched and walked slowly along with her, keeping itself a few paces behind the horse's gait while it still stayed several spans off to the side.

"Go away," Salene ordered. "Leave us alone. I'll use my Magic against you."

The tark seemed indifferent to her voice and merely yawned again. When she stopped to consider what to do next, it sat down and waited.

The mountain cat's interest unnerved Salene, but Magwin settled quickly to the tark's presence, as if sensing the creature intended no harm. She took some comfort from the stallion's behavior and again nudged him into a walk, hoping the tark would vanish. But the cat rose, and padded after, keeping the same distance between them.

Magwin balked when Salene tried to lift his stride, nearly bucking her off in protest. As used to Windstepping as the stallion was, his attitude caught her completely off guard. Once she was firmly back in the saddle, she patted his neck. "In the air, we can outrun the tark and my husband, my friend. This way it will take until Easwin next to get to Sarkem's even if we ride all night." When the horse nickered and bobbed his head, she sighed. "Then we'll do it your way for now." She pressed him into a slow, steady jog, with the tark still shadowing them, wondering how long she could keep up the pace before collapsing in exhaustion.

The answer came a span after Norwin's turn as the forest grew dark and thick around her and the wind threaded its way through the branches to chill her weary bones. She found a sheltered clearing, wove a simple camp, and used the last of her energy to cast a protective spell around her and her mount to keep the tark at bay before falling asleep on a bed of pine boughs.

****

Jamus shook his head in disgust once he reached the palace, recognizing too many details he'd already seen in the world of Keldra's tapestry. Magic's taint lay everywhere, suggesting Naboth's plans had progressed far more than he'd anticipated.

Were the Mages of his Magiskeep really so easy to buy? What had the Shadow promised them to make them turn to his cause so quickly?

He found a quick answer in his own rooms when Jiala greeted him at the door. "Back so soon, My Lord? I would have thought you'd take longer to recover your appetite."

Jamus glared at her, hardly noticing the flimsy wrap she wore as he brushed past her into the chamber. The rumpled furs and blankets on the floor attested to a relationship he was determined to end immediately. "You've been deceived, Madam, but that's no excuse for betraying the Rule of your Art. No matter what you were promised, you have no right to give the River to the Black Dragon."

Jiala's eyes widened in surprise. "What are you talking about, My Love? I've given the Dragon nothing of worth."

"In that you're right," Jamus returned, taking her by the arm and pulling her across the room to stand by the torches. "Look at your shadow, Mistress, and tell me again you've made no bargain and sold no part of your soul to the darkness."

Jiala looked down and gasped. Though the light streamed in full on her body, there was no shadow on the floor at her feet. "By the Blood! What's going on?"

"The man you bedded is Shadow, Jiala, my reflection bonded to a Dark Master. He's taken part of you already with his schemes. Your part of the River has twisted to his course and purpose."

"But you." She stared at him. "You slept with me."

"Do you really think I'd take you to bed? To what end would the Rivermaster seek satisfaction in your arms? Your paltry power is nothing to me and as for your…your feminine wiles, have I ever so much as given you a word of encouragement? Your wantonness disgusts me." He gestured once, replacing her revealing clothes with a modest gown. "By the Blood, indeed. If I could find a way to lock you away from man's lust I would, but now I need you to make amends for your crimes and restore the River's waters."

She stared at him. "Who are you to talk to me like that now? What kind of man are you?"

"At least one who casts a shadow instead of being one." He nodded down to remind her.

"I don't understand any of this."

"Use your reason, Madam. Have you chanted yourself so much with your own delusions that you can't sift me?" Jamus released her arm let his Sphere slip away. "Here, take my hand and tell me again you don't know who I am."

Cautiously, Jiala reached out. The contact was electric. Desire surged through her with incomprehensible intensity. Reason shattered as her mind reeled back to circles before when she had first felt Jamus' potent allure. Her pulse quickened as her heart thudded in her ear. She looked up into his eyes, her pupils dilated, her expression softening.

Jamus slammed the weave of his Sphere against her emotions, breaking the contact.

She fell back and he had to grab her as she nearly fainted.

Shaking in his strong grip, Jiala struggled to hold back her tears. "Jamus…My Lord, I am so sorry. What can I do?"

"Repair every tear you've made in the weave of Rule and Vow, and demand your Apprentice do the same, for I've no doubt she's part and parcel of this as well."

"And what of him?"

"You're lucky you're still alive, My Lady," Jamus answered, his voice softening as he let go of her arm. "He's a Flesheater with a thirst for Mage's blood. Sorem only knows how long it would have taken him to use you as his final feast."

Jiala shivered. "He's gone off with Siamel. He said something about showing her the beauty of Crystal Lake."

"Bory, woman! How could you let her go with him?"

"I thought he was you."

Jamus wasted no time, took the stairs two at a time and raced back out to the stables. He didn't even bother saddling Whim but simply leapt to the stallion's broad back and soared into the air in a lifted bound.

One stride was all it took to reach the misty waters.
One stride almost too late.

****

Siamel had blushed for the first time in circles when The Jamus had suggested he and she might enjoy themselves better alone. "You're far more tempting to me than your mistress, you know, my beauty. Jiala is an attractive woman, certainly, but a stale loaf appeals much less than a fresh one." He chucked her under her chin. "I'd be a fool not to indulge in a feast so tastefully arrayed." He kissed her, parting her lips with his tongue, hinting of far more to come."

"I am loyal to my Lady," Siamel murmured.

"I'll take care of her needs first," he replied, "and tell her I'm taking you on a picnic. She'll have no objections once I've finished with her. A woman's desire is easy to fill for a man like me."

"And will mine be too?"

"Yours especially, Siamel. I can't even begin to tell you how long I've wanted to return the favors you intimated when we were children."

"I was a silly fool then, Jamus, thinking myself superior to you. I teased you horribly, I'm afraid."

"It's time the tease was consummated, don't you think? Too many spans between an offer and its acceptance can't possibly be good for either party."

It was then she blushed. "I would be delighted, My Lord."

They'd ridden out well past Sowin's change, trying to reach Crystal Lake near enough to Weswin to catch the moonrise. The Jamus intended to finish his business there and still have time to deal with Salene.

The tall pines of the eastern forests filtered the fading sunlight into lacy patterns in the sofferns below. The two Mages rode along at an easy pace, lifting strides now and then to pass a twist in the path or a rocky outcropping, shortening the journey to the Lake nearly perfectly. They arrived as the sun was setting and the first silver drifts of moonlight began to caress the still surface of the water.

The Jamus dismounted first, set his horse free to graze, and then lifted Siamel from her saddle, his hands gripping her waist. She made no protest as he laid her down in the soffern bed by the lakeshore and slowly began to unlace the bodice of her riding gown.

"No need to hurry," she whispered. "We've waited a lifetime already. We should take the time to enjoy ourselves."

The Jamus smiled, his teeth white in the gathering moonlight. His hands moved subtly, weaving a bond to hold her once she realized what was happening. "I've reason to hurry, My Lady. I've waited longer than a lifetime."

"You flatter me, Sur," Siamel replied, arching her back to press herself closer to him. It was difficult to move under his weight.

His fingers dug into the soft flesh of her breast. "So long to fulfill a longing. How simple now."

She whimpered as his nails scratched her tender skin.

"Please, My Lord. Gently."

"Gently? Is that how you want to die?"

"Die?" She flinched at his hard grip, but she couldn't move now. Her limbs were fixed in place by more than his physical presence. She heard her own heart pounding in her ears. "Why are you doing this? I gave myself freely."

"Not for my purpose," he said, drawing a dagger from the air. "Even if I'd paid, you'd never lie still for this."

She tried to squirm away, panting hard as she strained against the lashes. "What are you doing, Jamus? My Lord?"

"Preparing my feast," he answered, tracing a bloody line across her breast with his blade. Then he lowered his mouth to drink.

The clearing exploded with a flash of silver light and a scream of rage as Jamus and the silver stallion burst upon the couple.

Jamus leapt to the ground, clutched the imposter's hair and yanked, pulling the Shadow to his knees an instant before his lips touched Siamel's blood.

The Jamus snarled, whipped himself from Jamus' hold and spun to face his attacker.

But Jamus had already raised his hand, with barbed threads of Whitefire snaking out from his fingertips, coiling and snapping about the Imposter like whips, slashing his clothes and wrapping him in bonds he dared not challenge. He froze, terrified to move lest the weave touch his form.

Jamus sidestepped his prisoner, and moved quickly to Siamel, pulling her away from the Shadow. She clung to his arms, falling back into his embrace as he sat down heavily, trying to catch his own breath.

"Thank the Hand, Sur," Siamel sobbed. "He was going to kill me."

"You're safe now, My Lady. Let me Touch your wound."

"I will, Sur, if you are a true Healer."

For the first time, Jamus realized she had no idea who he was. It had all happened so fast and now, he was behind her, so she had never seen his face. "Mistress, before you agree, I think it best you know who I am. Come now." He lifted her gently, turning her to face him.

She gasped, her gaze darting from his face to the prisoner's and back. Then, she reddened, awkwardly pulling the torn fabric of her bodice over her breasts as she bowed her head. "Master. I should have known he was a charlatan. By the Hand, I am blessed you came."

"May I?" Jamus asked again, his hand reaching towards the seeping wound. When she nodded, he gingerly placed his fingers on her chest. He felt her heart beating hard beneath his Touch and breathed a sigh of relief to sift the strong flow of blood in her veins. No harm there. The edges of the wound sealed at once, promising to leave little trace of a scar. Siamel would know it was there, lingering as a memory of how close to the brink of destruction her ambition had taken her. But to the eyes of her lovers, her skin would appear flawless. He wove another spell to fix her clothes, and then let her lean against him, finding solace in his strength.

"Who is he?" she asked at last.

"Shadow," Jamus replied.

"Jamus, Lord of Magiskeep," The Jamus hissed. "You are the imposter."

"Then tell me why the silver stallion rides for me, Sur."

The Jamus glared at Whim who stood not far off, his head low, his hoof now and then pawing at the sofferns as he eyed his master's prisoner.

"You've chanted him."

"And I suppose I've chanted Lady Siamel as well, Illusioning your attack on her to gain my own advantage?"

"You've said it, not I."

"And you're a liar," Siamel said quickly. "Do you think any true Mage could not recognize the Rivermaster?"

"You were in my arms, Lady. Wasn't I your precious Kiselor then?"

"I've never been in Jamus' arms before, but now that I am, I feel the fool for thinking yours were half as worthy. Even a perfect lie fails in the face of truth."

"Pah!" The Jamus spit. "What would you ever know of truth? Your entire life is based on deception—you and that whore you call a Mistress."

Jamus helped Siamel to her feet. "The only reason he can still talk is because I need him to rouse his Master's interest. Can you make it back to the Keep on your own, My Lady? I'd much rather have you safe at home while I deal with this creature."

"I can, My Lord," she said, brushing the pine needles from her skirt. She looked up at him, her green eyes wet with tears. "I fear I have amends to make."

"Your Mistress has already begun, Siamel. Follow her example and we may yet cast reflection aside and turn our world back." He lifted her into the saddle and sent her off with a lifted stride full enough to take her back to the edges of the east pasture. From there, she'd have a short ride to compose herself and consider the work ahead of her.

With Siamel gone, he wasted no time with the Shadow's comfort. Instead, he layered a silvrin sphere around him to protect him from the deadly touch of the Spellfire bonds still holding him captive. "Get on your feet."

"Why should I?"

"Because I'm giving you a chance to survive this. I lied to Siamel. I don't need you to lure Naboth to me. He'll find me no matter what I do with you."

"Then why spare me?"

"You are still my Reflection, as much as it offends me, and in the end, reconciling myself to what you represent in my image can only serve to benefit me."

"Reconcile? You mean to make a truce with me?"

"I need to know you first, Sur. You were born of the Mirrors in my name. I've already met and conquered my True Reflection, but that doesn't mean he was all the worst of me. A man is so much less the man if he refuses to face his faults."

The Jamus clambered to his feet and stared defiantly at Jamus. "Then face your desires, Lord of the River. Face the man you really want to be. Face your lust, your avarice, your rage at Rule and Vow. Face the cold bed of your wife's refusal and the hot blood of desire. Face me, Master of Magiskeep, and face what you long to be."

Chapter 17

Salene tossed restlessly in her sleep as the sounds of the forest rustled all around. Though her Magic protected her, being alone in the wilderness offered little peace. Baerwolves roamed the flatlands and already she had seen a tark stalking about. Had she not been exhausted, she would have simply stopped to eat and then pressed on, trusting Magwin's speed and her own weaves to keep them safe.

She'd built a small fire, but the chill air overcame its feeble flames halfway through Norwin's span. She stirred, shivered, and rolled over. The fur blanket seemed to have slipped off, so she reached to pull it back around her body.

The fur blanket snarled and then began to purr.

Salene froze with her face just inches away from the broad chest of the brindle tark.

Think. Don't panic. By the Blood, how could the creature pass through my protective shield? I wove it as Jamus had taught me, intended to keep out danger while admitting harmless advances. But a tark, a killer with a vile temper and no love for humankind? Cautiously, she reached out her hand and touched the cat behind its ear. It rubbed its great head into her touch and purred even louder. "You like that?" she asked softly. The tark let out a meow and snuggled closer to her. Somebody's pet? Was it possible? Well, it hasn't eaten me yet. Too tired to battle the questions, she dropped back into a weary doze, hoping perhaps it was all just another part of the dreams haunting her.

Jamus. Her love turned to a savage monster. His face loomed over her, his eyes cold ice, his lips leering into a twisted grin. He licked his lips, anticipating his conquest.

"Tasty, tasty morsel," he hissed, his tongue forking as it flicked her cheeks. "Thought you'd run, did you? I have wings, my love, and spies to mark your way."

His fingers were like tentacles, crawling down her neck, fondling her breasts, coiling on her belly as if readying to strike. She tried to squirm away, but he was relentless, holding her prisoner with his physical strength and a slow, insistent weave.

"I won't rush it, my darling, don't worry. There's no point in not taking the time to enjoy myself. After all, I've waited long enough."

"We've loved before," she said. "Why is it so different now?"

"Blood of the Blood, woman and the hunger I bear. You denied me. Now I take what I want. The Curse has freed me from my Vows. Now I live to please myself."

"I'm hurt, don't you understand?"

"It's not whether or not I understand, it's whether or not I care. Do you think you matter in this? I'm the only one who matters anymore."

"And what of your River and the duty you owe?"

"The River be damned. All she wants to do is take from me. Now it's my turn to take. My turn. My turn."

Salene woke up gasping for air. Easwin's first light was already sifting through the trees above. She sat up, wrapping her arms around her body in a vain attempt to keep from shaking.

The tark meowed again from its post a short way off. Not far from the fire lay a freshly killed duskit, an offering from the great cat.

Salene frowned. "I really didn't need that," she said. When the tark cocked its head and chirped more like a housecat than a dangerous predator, she laughed. "All right, then. I thank you for the meat to my table. I'll make a stew if you'd like some." She gestured carefully so as not to upset the cat, using the duskit with ingredients drawn from Magiskeep's kitchens to chant a fragrant stew for earlenmeal. She placed three quarters of it in a large wooden platter for the tark and the rest in a small bowl for herself.

The brindle tark lapped up its portion without hesitation, then it sat back on its haunches and began to wash itself.

Surprised to find an appetite, Salene finished her own bowl and spelled away the dishes, pleased to find her Magic coming more easily than it had the night before.

Soon, she was back in the saddle heading south, feeling no reason to lift strides. With the tark along for company, it didn't seem to matter how long the rest of the trip was going to be.

****

Jiala had stayed up all night righting the weaves she had conjured since Jamus' first return from Greenhope. As much as she had wanted that man to be the true Lord, as soon as the second Jamus had arrived, the hard reality of his identity had struck her like a falling brellum. There was no question in her mind that she had been deceived.

Jorn and Senneth were another matter.

"Don't be a fool, woman," Jorn told her when she warned him of the real Jamus' arrival. "You've been spurned and now you want us to suffer along with you. All my life I've wanted free rein with my Magic. Do you think I'll give it up now on your word?"

"He's ordered us to return to Rule and Vow. I'd not cross him if I were you."

"If you were me, you wouldn't have climbed into bed with him, Madam." He laughed at that, charming another flask of amberwine to his table and crooking his finger at the well-proportioned lass who'd brought him a tray of cheeses. He hooked his finger in the waist of her skirt and pulled her into his lap. "Go on your way, Jiala. Tell your tales to other ears more gullible than mine."

"You'll be sorry, Jorn," she said as she left. Frustrated, she sought out Sarn, hoping against hope to find at least one ally in her mission.

The young sorcerer was sitting alone in the conservatory, dressed more modestly than any Mage in the entire Keep and appearing happier than anyone Jiala had seen in days. Her news hardly even fazed him.

"So, he was an imposter. I wondered as much. He was far too eager to set Magic free to be the Jamus I thought I knew so well."

"Then why didn't you do something about it?"

He shrugged. "How could I? The Rivermaster has me pinioned in a sphere defying my Magic for anything but my own protection or the defense of the Keep. I tread a fine line with that false master. If I'd attacked him for the wrong reason, the spell would have come back at me."

"And now?"

"I'm not much better off, My Lady, but ready and willing to do whatever the real Jamus commands."

"Loyalty becomes you, Sarn."

He laughed bitterly. "It's not loyalty, Mistress, it's practicality. The Rivermaster himself is the only one who can free me from this weave of reflections he cast on me. The more I ingratiate myself to him the better off I'll be. He always said I'd rise to defend the River for my own sake. I suppose this qualifies."

"It's not fear, then?"

"Of what? Of him? By the Hand, no. Of all men in the world, Jamus is the last to fear. It pains me to admit it, but he is the most just and honorable person I've ever been tormented by. I'd wager if he could find a way to offer his Imposter mercy he'd do it."

"Never. The creature has nearly destroyed the River and must have had a part in the death of the child. Jamus will kill him." Sarn shook his head. "The creature will not die by Jamus' hands. Mark my words, Madam. It's not the Rivermaster's way."

****

"Where are we going?" The Jamus asked as Jamus' Magic prodded him along. Astride Dancer, one of the Keep's quieter geldings, the Shadow had ridden quietly for the first span of captivity, but now, he had begun to complain. The skin he wore was still tender and not used to long hours in the saddle. Naboth had gifted him with a body that looked like Jamus', but it had none of the true man's fitness.

"I want it to be easy for Naboth to find me," Jamus replied easily.

"To Magiskeep, then?"

"To the heart of his intent. I go where he thinks I'd look for him, back to the waterfall."

"The caves? They've been destroyed."

"The River carved them once. It can carve them again."

"So you turn the tables on him."

"I repay the debt, that's all."

"He won't be the last, you know. If you kill him, the Dragon will just send others. His store is limitless."

"And my waters run deep," Jamus answered.

"Your confidence will ruin you one day, Rivermaster. You think you know the secrets of the Way when you've only begun to travel its passages. Now you presume to match the Black Dragon. Pah! The day you learn his power will be one day too late for your world."

"How can you be so dedicated to him? Even in my greatest anguish, I never embraced his purpose. What reflection can you be?"

"Time has no meaning in the Way," The Jamus answered. "Who is to say whether I am what you have been or what you will be?"

The thought hit Jamus hard. He had always assumed reflections trapped in the Mirrors were simply those of moments in lives already lived. It had never occurred to him that the distortion of time had farther reaching consequences. But, if that were so, what could ever possibly twist him so as to inspire a being as dangerous as this figure on the horse ahead of him? He felt himself drawn to the Shadow, curious to know his mind. "What did you ever hope to gain by acting on Naboth's behalf?"

"Life," The Jamus answered. "I was close until you stopped me. Did you know I'd already tasted the blood of nine? She would have been the last. A Mage of consequence like her is worth four or five. Your blood would do for the full thirteen."

Jamus shook off the chill coursing through his veins at the Shadow's words. How could he have forgotten how these creatures sought life? He had loosed a demon on the world.

****

Greenhope lay in sight, just beyond the rise. Salene glanced back at her tark companion and urged Magwin into a trot. The great cat loped along keeping pace until they reached the first fence of the

Keep's pastures. Then the creature turned, paced off, and disappeared into the small grove of trees to the left.

To her surprise, Salene felt a pang of loneliness without her strange companion. But she pressed on, hoping for safe haven in the huge stone house ahead of her.

Guards signaled her arrival as soon as she crested the rise. By the time she reached the main house, both Delise and Sarkem were at the door with two others in the shadows behind them. A groom held her horse as Salene dismounted. "My Lord, My Lady, I've come to beg your protection."

"Thank the Hand," Delise said, hurrying out to meet her. "After all that's happened, I was so afraid for you."

"Afraid for me? You know, then?"

One of the figures stepped out of the house behind Sarkem. "The Jamus in the Keep is an imposter, Salene," Sarena said. "We found our True Lord here, trapped by a Shadowlord."

"It can't be. He's after me...," Salene began. Then she caught her breath. "What a fool I've been to be so blinded by my own misery not to see him for what he was! By the Blood, you'd think I'd be able to recognize my own husband."

As they met on the porch, Sarena took Salene's hand. "Not if you've been drugged, My Lady. You've not been allowed to see the truth."

As Joria moved in beside her, Salene shook her head. "Drugs. No wonder I've been feeling so strange. I didn't want to treat Jamus, or the man I thought was Jamus, the way I did. Losing our child was difficult enough, but losing him too," she stopped again. "The child?"

"Was killed, Salene," Sarena said, tightening her grip on the other woman's hand. "I'm sorry."

"There was no curse?"

Joria shook her head. "It's all been a lie from the beginning. Jorl murdered your child and Delise's as well. Who knows how many he'd killed for his Shadowlords."

Salene sat down heavily on the first bench she could find. "Shadows. Jamus? Where is he? Is he all right?"

"He's gone after them," Joria said. "He wouldn't let us go with him."

"Back to Magiskeep, then?" Salene asked. "I shouldn't have left."

"You're better off here, with us," Sarena said. "The Keep's no place of safety right now. As long as even one stream of the River is in the Shadow's keeping, its allies are better off together."

"You're welcome to stay as long as you like," Sarkem offered. "The Mistresses, my wife, and I were just about to sit down for midmeal. Please join us. Good food and companionship can make the time pass quickly."

"But Jamus?"

"There's nothing any of us can do for him," Joria said. "It's time we faced the truth about who and what he is. If there's any curse here, it's his to bear—the curse of being Rivermaster above all else."

"At the sacrifice of those he loves?"

"At the sacrifice of everything."

****

Jamus' spell cleared the cave entrance completely with just a little more effort than he would have liked. Facing a Shadowlord was chancy enough, but to face one without the full Power of the River at his call was not to his liking. Still, he had little choice in the matter. Going back to Magiskeep to sort things out first gave Naboth too much time to sort out his own strategy. Better to meet him on even ground and be done with it.

"What makes you think he'll come?" The Jamus asked as Jamus pushed him into the dim light of the cave.

"He wants me too much not to," Jamus replied. "Besides, he'll be curious as to how I escaped in the first place. He's not the kind to take a defeat easily."

"And what about me?"

"You're nothing to him."

"And to you? Am I still worth your interest?"

Jamus considered for a moment. He still hadn't quite puzzled out how this creature had ever come into existence. As many

times as the fleeting thought of Magic Unrestrained had passed
through his own thoughts, it had never reached the magnitude of evil
this reflection wore. To think such a being existed in any realm was
disturbing. He'd begun to think the Imposter was as much a part of
the riddle as the runes and the black veil had been. "I don't know,"
he answered with surprising honesty. "You're still a puzzle to me,
and like Naboth, I don't like unanswered questions."

The Jamus sat down on a boulder, wincing as he made
contact. "Time has no meaning in the Way."

Jamus grimaced. "I've heard that too often. So you're
suggesting perhaps you're a reflection of what I will feel one day?
I'll be damned if I ever sink that low, even in my imagination."

"Who's to say you're not damned already, eh? Those
Masters of your Keep spun quickly to my side and look at your
wife."

"Don't bother. I've already reconciled myself to my own
sacrifices."

The Jamus smiled. "So that's how you did it. Naboth will be
disappointed to find out how you passed that barrier. He was so sure
you were too noble to surrender everything you held dear for the
sake of your River."

"Only a temporary miscalculation," a voice said from the
back of the cave, just beyond the still shimmering black veil. Then
the darkness vanished, and Naboth stepped out of the shadows. "He
was willing to give up all he loved for the split seconds it took to
breach the darkness, but he won't abandon them for long."

Jamus smiled. "You've underestimated your opponent,
Naboth. Above all, I am the Rivermaster."

"Pah! You're a man. I've already tasted your blood and it's
no sweeter than any man's. I saw you weeping and wailing when I
drank. Do you expect be to believe that was just a show for my sake?
You'll be on your knees when I tear out the heart of that pretty wife
of yours."

Jamus shrugged, surprised at how little Naboth's threat
affected him. Then he looked at the Imposter and realized how much
the creature did resemble his thoughts at the moment. Right now, in
the face of the Shadowlord's threat, Salene and all he loved in the

Keep meant nothing compared to the River. "I'll do what I must for the River's sake," he said quietly.

Naboth took a step back, his eyes darting to Jamus' hands. When he saw no gesture, he steadied, keeping his own hands poised for a quick defense. "Do you see yourself now in your precious mirror, Flesher? You were so sure you could never be the corruption I sent to take over your Keep. But you've become him, haven't you? How far will you go into his world, eh?"

"As far as it takes to stop you and your kind, Shadow. If that means becoming him when I fly my Dragon, so be it. Ask your Master, if you need an answer beyond mine. Surely he holds Time's reins in his hand to see what is yet to be."

"Everendings ever be, Rivermaster calls to me"

"I evoke thy name, Blackwing, for the sake of Truth alone," Jamus replied.

"In defiance call to me, risk thy life and liberty. Darker darkness conquers all, waters to my hand will fall. Seek the truth and find a lie, on deceptions' wings I fly"

"And so do your servants, it seems. You've trained Master Naboth well."

"Hah," Naboth spat. "Do you expect him to take your word, Rivermaster?"

"Why shouldn't he? I've never worked behind his back for my own gain."

"What are you saying?"

"Look in your own mirror, Naboth. If you have any reflection at all, will it wear Blackwing's shadow or will it wear one of your making?"

Naboth shifted on his feet, his eyes darting back and forth from Jamus to the darkness behind him. "He won't listen to you, Flesher."

"Oh, he doesn't need my word," Jamus replied. "Do you really think he doesn't already know what you've been doing? Where have the waters gone, Shadowlord?"

"I've only been keeping them for him, he knows that. I'm the guardian, no more."

"Hot ambition rules thy heart. Yours was not the Keeper's part."

"But I was, My Lord! Of course, that's all I ever intended. It was all for you, I swear it."

"Swear not, tongue of twice deceit, ye the Everdark shall meet. Everendings ever be, end to all who challenge me."

Naboth screamed once as the inky coils snaked around him, but once the tendrils covered his mouth, all he could do was writhe in silent agony. Slim tentacles of black slid into his ears and he grimaced as they burrowed their way into his brain. His eyes widened and bulged as his forehead expanded. Dark worms augured into his chest and stomach, oozing dark blood already starting to coagulate as the ruinous poison worked into his heart, now pumping uselessly and desperately to keep him alive.

It would have been better if it had surrendered at once, for the torture was horrible, etching itself into his expression as tears streamed down his purple cheeks.

Then, almost mercifully, his skull exploded, and his body dropped to the sand, where it lay, twisting in its death throes before beginning to smolder.

Though he wanted to look away, Jamus didn't take his eyes off the sight, ever wary that the Dragon might try to catch him off guard.

He was wise, for one lone sliver of oily blackness snaked out in his direction. His hand was quick, shooting Spellfire out to slice it off a foot from his leg.

The Dragon screeched now as Naboth's body burst into black flame, consumed by hungry serpents until all that remained was a pile of ashes.

Then, there was silence for several minutes.

"Blood of the Masters," The Jamus gasped. "I don't want to die like that."

Jamus glanced over to see the Imposter on his knees, his hands clutching at the sand as he finished retching. "You won't. You're not immortal yet, and by the Hand, you never will be. For you, death will merely be the end of nothing."

The Jamus looked up, his eyes pleading. "I'm not just nothing. I'm a part of you. Kill me and you kill a part of yourself."

"I'm not going to kill you...yet," Jamus said, motioning for the Shadow to rise. "As long as you can be useful to me, I'll keep you as alive as you are now."

Rivermaster.

Jamus raised his hand as he stared into the deeper darkness of the cave. "I hear you."

We are not done.

"There, you're wrong. I'm finished with you."

The waters.

"The waters are mine. Already my Mages are returning to Rule and Vow."

Not all.

"They will. My word is law in the River's way. No matter what the cost, all the waters will answer to my hand. You've failed. Go back to your lair and think of another plan. Until you do, don't challenge me. I know the secrets of this one."

The Dragon hissed, and both Jamuses could hear it slither back into the depths of its realm.

Sunlight filtered in through the waterfall, filling the cave with pale, refreshing light.

"What now?" the Imposter asked.

"You will apologize to my wife."

****

"I need to go home," Salene insisted. "If my Jamus is back he won't look for me here. I need to be in Magiskeep."

"Not until you're well, My Lady," Jorl repeated as he'd told her several times before. "The drugs need to be purged from your blood before I can be sure you're safe."

"I feel fine. Let me go home."

Sarena moved over to the bed and added her support to Greenhope's Healer. "Listen to him, Salene. The herbs you were given were very powerful. You're going to yearn for them now that we've taken them from you. The Jorl who tried to ruin you was close to his goal and recovering will take some time."

"How long?"

"Two more days here before you're ready to travel. Then a full Warmmonth in the Keep until you're fully well again, at least."

"It's a hard journey," Delise said. "I've struggled myself for many winds already trying to escape. Jorl's reflection had me under his control since well before he took my child. Count yourself blessed it hasn't been that long for you."

"Blessed?" Salene asked, pushing up to her elbows despite Jorl's efforts to make her lie down. "Fine words now, My Lady. Cursed is more like it. First to have lost my own child, and now to have lost my husband."

"There are no curses in the River," Jorl said as he plumped up the pillows and motioned to Salene. "The whole thing was a lie."

"To what end? To kill my baby? Why? What use could an innocent child be to anyone?"

Jorl glanced at Sarena who shook her head. Better to be still about what Jamus had told him, than fuel Salene's emotions at this point. Perhaps later, when she was fully recovered, but not now. "That's something we may never know, My Lady. The Healer was a twisted creature, born of the Way. If we could explain his motives, we'd understand the Way itself, I suppose. Better to think it the work of a madman, without reason."

"Then I've even more reason to mourn. A senseless loss to live with the rest of my life."

Chapter 18

Still keeping his Reflection bound in silvrin and Spellfire, Jamus headed back to Magiskeep, growing well weary of the constant travel between worlds. Both horses welcomed the liftings, pushed to full power by the Master's hand.

They reached the Keep quickly, handed the horses over to Josep - who bit his tongue at the sight of two Jamuses - and headed for the palace.

The Jamus tried to drag his feet, but Jamus' Magic propelled him forward at a matching pace. The main hall fell to silence when they entered, dust rags poised over mantels, brooms frozen in midsweep, and more than one mouth dropped in open wonder.

Jamus directed his adversary to the center of the room. "See what you will with your eyes, but let your hearts perceive the truth. I am Jamus, Master of Magiskeep, and this...this man has been impersonating me in my absence. I see Magic freely used in these halls, for reason beyond need. It's not the River's way to deny Rule and Vow for the sake of personal gain."

"My Lord," Jeamel said, stepping forward from a side room. "We're doing as the Masters have ordered, much to our own distress."

"I've no reason to discipline anyone, Sur, much less those who obey the Masters of this Keep. They too have been deceived by the Shadow's lies."

Mercan, one of Jorn's favored menservants, fixed Jamus with a long, appraising glare. "How are we to know you're the true Lord? I can't say I can see a lick of difference between the pair of you. Some of us like the new way here. Why should we give it up on your word?"

The Jamus seized the opportunity. "He's the pretender, not I. He's bound with his evil weaves so I can't defend myself with anything more than words. Look at him, will you? Would the Lord of Magiskeep dress so shabbily? He wears road dust and a rustic's tunic. You'd think he'd dress to fit his station if he were the real lord."

"Lord Jamus never was much for ceremony," Jeamel said. "Though considering all that's happened here in the last Sevenstins I've seen some strange changes in his ways."

"That's because he was here instead of me," Jamus explained patiently. "Now that I'm back, the Keep will be restored."

"Not for me," Tulia said. "I like having a patronmage of my own."

"See?" The Jamus said quickly. "You can't just dance in and steal the mastery that easily. I think perhaps the Masters themselves have a right to judge us, don't you?" He smiled and nodded to Mercan. "It is the way of the Keep, is it not?"

"In matters of the Magic, it is," Mercan agreed readily and soon a chorus of voices joined him. "Call a Gathering and let the Seven decide who's telling the truth here."

It took only a matter of moments for Jamus to realize how far the Shadow's plan had progressed. He had a cadre of allies among the servants and lesser Mages and abundant confidence. There was little point in denying the Call. "So be it. Let the Call be made. I and my...my companion will be waiting in the Chamber for the Masters to assemble. The sooner this is over and done with the better.

As the two made their way to the Master's Chamber, the Shadow sidled up to Jamus. "So, you thought it would be easy to defeat the Dragon, did you? When minds are twisted to his way they don't turn easily. To all appearances, you and I look exactly alike, you know. Even your wife couldn't tell us apart when it mattered. Do you really believe tainted Mages will want to recognize the difference?"

"They aren't all in your pocket," Jamus replied. But, Sarena and Joria were still not back from Greenhope, and that left only five Masters to decide his fate, not the majority of support he needed to make his point.

Jorn had taken the seat of leadership, using his dominating personality and flamboyant style to take control of the situation. That

Sarn had been designated Jamus' surrogate seemed forgotten in the new order established by Magic Unrestrained.

Hastily called, the Gathering was far from formal, but each Master had spelled on the robes of his station to make a claim on each individual Art. Jorn's yellow gown was more elaborate than any others, reflecting his liberal use of Magic to embellish his life and when he rose, he made sure the elegant cut and shimmering jeweled trim was artistically displayed with each gesture. "So, two claimants to the Mastery. Indeed a puzzle worthy of our interest. The trouble is, which is which?"

Jiala, fully ready to speak up for Jamus, frowned as she studied both men. "I, of all should be able to tell the difference, but I see none."

"You won't see the difference, My Lady," Jamus said. "It's more a matter of intent than appearance."

The Jamus smiled slyly. "Golden words to charm you, Madam. All Shadows have liquid tongues when it really matters. Next he'll be telling you he's the one who believes in Rule and Vow and how disappointed he is to find how you've strayed."

"I've marked the error of my ways," Jiala replied.

Jamus was about to answer, but The Jamus interrupted. "Only once I'd confronted you about it, and, of course, after your Apprentice returned to tell how he attacked her."

Jiala's brow furrowed. "Private conversations between us. How could an Imposter know that?"

"By being clever," Jamus answered. "And through circles of experience watching me to see how I behave. I'm afraid I underestimated his abilities."

"I have sworn my loyalty to the Rivermaster," Jiala said, "crossing my way back to Rule and Vow as I so swore when I took my Mastery. But now, to tell which is which?" Her hand dropped loosely at her side as she shook her head.

Jired, completely intimidated by the whole situation, scrubbed his grey head with his hand, then nervously pulled at his green collar. "We could test them, I suppose. Surely the true Rivermaster is superior in the Seven Arts."

The Jamus puffed himself up despite the bonds. With the Black Dragon at his hand, he welcomed a duel of Magic. "I am bound by the Imposter's spells. Unless he frees me, I can't use my Art."

"Free him," Jorn commanded, waving his hand in an imperious gesture.

Jamus shook his head. "I will not loose a Shadow in this Keep."

Savel cleared his throat, the simple sound enough to quiet the others. When the Master of Elevation chose to speak, all ears listened to his wisdom. "If he is Shadow, then he's already been loose in the Keep, Sur, and so far, we have survived. With Magic Unrestrained so well entrenched in these halls, there are a number of Apprentices well armed with Spellfire. That is, I understand, the Shadow's bane. May I suggest we station our new warriors around the room to control matters? I, for one, need to be convinced we choose the right man of the two."

Jorn nodded, "Well thought, Master Savel. Let us prepare."

They stationed the Mages as Jorn directed and then Senneth turned to Jamus. "Take the bonds from your prisoner and allow him to use his Magic to prove his identity."

Jamus shook his head, "You're making a serious mistake, Sur."

"They have a right," The Jamus said. "Magiskeep law must be respected if this Keep is to be the rightful hold of my River. The Rivermaster would allow such a thing."

His hand forced by the Shadow's argument, Jamus nodded slowly. Carefully, he loosed the weave, but with each strand freed, he wove another, creating a much larger net around the edges of the room. If indeed the Imposter attacked once he was discovered, at least those outside would be protected. If The Jamus noticed, he made no sign, for he seemed quite focused on his own recovered freedom.

When the last tie was removed, the chamber itself was fully shielded. Only then did Jamus turn to the Masters. "I've done as you asked and freed him. Test us as you will, but I warn you, as my reflection, his Magic will match mine in all but Rivermaster's Art."

"Then what test can we demand?" Jiala asked. "Master Savel, this was your idea. Have you considered further?"

"None of the tests of Mastery will suit." Savel replied. "But it has been said Lord Jamus' stallion is of no ordinary ilk. Rumor comes to me the creature is chanted. I would think, if men cannot recognize the true Master of Magiskeep, a beast would."

"We've no beasttalker here," Jorn protested. "That lad who supposedly had some talent in that direction has gone across the Rim with Master Simen."

"Simen would know his brother," Jired said.

"Well, he's not here either," Jiala reminded him impatiently. "If he were, we wouldn't even have this dilemma."

"Asking a horse to decide is ridiculous," Senneth said unbuttoning the collar of his purple robe and tugging at the fabric pulling it away from his sweating neck. His hand fluttered back to his lap as he went on, "We can't depend on an animal to decide a matter of such importance."

"Nevertheless," Savel said, "the stallion is a capable judge, unfettered by the logic and prejudice we harbor."

"No one here is prejudiced," Jorn said.

"You're wrong, Master. You and Senneth have well benefited recently from the Lord's decisions here. Mistress Jiala seems quite ready to reform, but I do believe she too would wish one of these men over the other to be the victor. That leaves only two of us who can vote fairly."

"I take exception to your opinion, Master Savel," Jiala said. "One of these men attacked my apprentice and would have killed her if the other had not stopped him. Still, despite that, I cannot detect which is which. I would never choose a murderer as my Keepmaster, no matter what I might gain by it." She looked at the two Jamuses. "I am sorry, My Lord, but as the Keep is at stake, I dare not choose one of you over the other without being sure."

"You're forgiven, Madame," The Jamus replied before Jamus had a chance to answer. "I would not want a Master here to take such a chance. We must have the test."

Jamus hesitated at that. The Imposter had too much confidence. But there was no choice. To refuse the Gathering would make it look like he was the liar here. "I'm willing."

"Have Josep bring the horse to the courtyard," Jorn ordered.

"No," Jamus said quietly. "There's no need for that." Leaving the shielded room was not an option he cared to explore. "Bring Whim here, into the chamber."

"A horse in the palace?" Savel laughed. "That is indeed something the real Jamus would propose."

"The servants might object," Jired said.

"Then let them," Jorn replied. "They have Magic's aid to right whatever damage is done, and I, for one, would much rather stay here in the comfort of my chair than dirty my feet in the stables. Tell Josep."

But there was no need to inform the stablemaster, for a swirl of silver mist spun its way into the chamber almost at once. From its center, the great stallion materialized, tossing his head and snorting.

An instant later, another swirl of mist appeared and with it, another silver stallion, a match to the first.

Jamus sighed as the first horse nuzzled his arm, looking for surlep candies, while the second marched over to his reflection and nuzzled him as well. The only difference was the slight flinching of the second pair as they touched, something only the keen eye of a horseman would notice.

Savel grunted. "So much for that idea. Again we have two."

"Take them away," Jorn said. "It was obviously a worthless solution."

Whim moved away from Jamus and eyed the other horse. He lowered his head, his hoof pawing the floor. "No, Whim," Jamus commanded. "Not here. It's not worth it." The stallion squealed in defiance, his attention riveted on his rival. Quickly, Jamus stepped in front of him, breaking his glare. "No. Go back to the barn. This isn't the time." The horse snorted again and swirled away.

The Jamus patted his horse on the neck with little enthusiasm, making a show of pretended affection. "Go on, my friend. I've no more need of you here." The second stallion simply vanished, leaving no trace of mist behind.

Jamus spread his hands in a gesture of resignation. "We can continue this for winds," he said. "The Shadow will match me Magic for Magic."

"Then we need another test," Jorn said. "Perhaps someone here has a unique experience with the Lord of the Keep we can use?

"It won't matter," Jamus said. "He's been in my Shadow for circles, watching and learning my ways. He'll know my secrets."

"Then we've reached an impasse."

"Not necessarily," a voice replied from the back of the room. Sarn walked out of the audience to take his rightful place at the center of the platform where the Masters sat. He stared at Jorn for a moment and the Master of Recreation shrugged, rose from the Keepmaster's chair and moved to his own. Sarn turned and faced the assembly. "As you may remember, I am still under the penalty of Magic for my past deeds here in the Keep. Jamus, the true Master of Magiskeep, wove a web to inhibit my use of Magic."

Savel rubbed his hands in delight. "Ah, yes, the Rivermaster's weave, one even I could not fathom as I watched its chanting."

"And one no one but the Rivermaster can loose," Sarn said. He looked at the two Jamuses. "My Lord, whoever you may be, you put me in charge of the Keep to protect it from the Shadows. In your absence, I fear I have failed because of my own selfishness. I ask you to let me redeem myself. Give me my freedom so you may take your rightful seat in my place."

Jamus did not reply. Instead, he looked over to the Shadow. "Go on, Sur, prove yourself."

The Jamus paled. "Why should I free him from his prison? His sentence isn't finished. Besides, he's already admitted he failed in his duty."

Jamus shook his head. "He didn't fail." He raised his hand, gesturing slightly to untie the first knot of Sarn's weave. As complex as the pattern was, for him, it was a simple matter to undo.

"By the Blood!" Jorn sputtered as he sifted the chanting. "My Lord, Jamus, the Rivermaster indeed."

Sarn breathed a sigh of relief quickly cut off by the Shadow's retaliation. A blast of black fire burst forth, searing at the Masters.

Jamus cried out, throwing a shield at the platform too late to stop the fire, but soon enough to dissipate the worst of its power. Then he spun and faced his adversary.

The Jamus directed the next attack at Magiskeep's Lord, cursing as the Dragon's fury boiled in his blood.

But Jamus reacted calmly, accepting the dark Magic, his mind once more resigned to whatever fate befell. Oblivion.

The darkness enveloped him.

But it had no effect.

In one swift motion, he raised his own hand to the Imposter and once more wrapped him in Spellfire and stelin. "If I didn't need you one more time, I wouldn't bother," he said.
The Jamus screamed as the Dragon howled its frustration and then fell silent before the Rivermaster's superiority.

****

Salene opened her eyes to a new day and for the first time in Sevenstins, she truly smiled.

"Now that's a sight to warm my own heart," Jorl said from his chair by the bed where he'd spent the last winds watching over Salene. "The sun pales in comparison to you, My Lady."

"And who gave you such a silvrin tongue, Sur? If you think I'll fall for idle flattery, you're chasing a duskit's tail."

Jorl laughed heartily. "If your body's a well as your wit, then I'm delighted of the insult. How do you feel?"

"Stronger and somehow, lighter," Salene answered.

"Free from the worst of the drugs, then," Jorl told her. "I'll give you a restorative and then, if your mind is still set, I think, with care, you can begin the journey back to Magiskeep. Come now, get yourself out of bed and join your fellow mistresses in an earlenmeal downstairs. They'll be delighted of your company. I'll leave the potion and wait for you there."

As soon as the Healer left, Salene slipped out of bed. She was dizzy and had to hold the bedpost for support, but as soon as she downed the potion, she found her legs. She let the River bathe her, relishing the feel of Magic's cool waters on her skin and then let its flows weave a riding gown of soft blue as she hurried down the stairs.

Sarena, Joria, Delise, and Sarkem were already at the table when she entered the dining room. Jorl was filling his plate from a laden sideboard. "Fresh fruits, ham, eggs, and the most wonderful bread I've ever tasted, Mistress. Shall I make you a plate as well?"

Salene held up her hand. "I'll get my own, thank you. Like most men, you've no concept of a proper portion."

"Sparret's food, that's what you women like," Sarkem said as he swallowed a mouthful of ham from his heaping plate.

"Men are like a tark to the kill when the table's full." Delise laughed.

"Tarks…" Salene said, her voice drifting off. It was hard to remember why it mattered. Her mind raced through the last few Sevenstins in a blur of jumbled memories. "Something about tarks, I can't remember."

"That's natural," Jorl said, as he sat down. "The drugs will have affected your memory of the past, I'm afraid. You won't forget everything but remembering exact detail may be a problem for a while."

"But why a tark?"

"A dream?" Sarena asked. "Some people say our minds invent fantasies while we sleep to ease our pain while we're awake. The tark could be something you imagined."

"A fear, a danger," Jorl offered. "The cat could be the manifestation of something you were afraid to face."

She shook her head. "It's something more, but I just can't remember." She took some bread and fruit from the platters and sat across from Joria. "Master Jorl says we can leave for Magiskeep today. I'd like to go as soon as possible."

"No reason to wait any longer then," Joria agreed.

"Flax is in my barn," Sarkem told her. "I'll have her saddled if you feel up to riding. Otherwise, I can send a carriage."

"No carriages. We can travel faster by horseback."

Salene sighed. "I hope your Magic lifts more gently than Joria's, My Lady. My seat still aches to think of those landings."

"I told you I was no Master of travel," Joria replied. "Don't blame me for the River's caprices. I kept losing the weave just as we were descending."

"Jamus and I felt something wrong with the waters," Jorl said. "We think the Shadows were claiming the River bit by bit."

"By corrupting our fellow Masters in Magiskeep?" Joria asked. "I shouldn't wonder. I know of at least two who'd readily fall to temptation."

"Jorn and Jiala," Sarena said. "And where Jorn goes, Senneth is soon to follow."

"That's why Jamus went back to the Keep at once," Jorl said.

"Not to find me?" Salene asked, as she put down the bread and folded her hands over her plate, trying to steady them.

Jorl shook his head. "I won't lie to you, My Lady, nor will I tell you things you need to hear from Jamus' lips. He went back to the Keep to defend the River. That's all I can say to the matter."

"Then it's happened at last. She's finally won." Salene dropped her gaze to the plate of food and pushed it away, her appetite gone.

"The Rivermaster does as he must," Sarena said quietly, "but Jamus is still a man. He hasn't forgotten you."

Salene sighed. "I know. I've always known. I've fought it, denied it, and feared it for too long. Come, I'd rather be riding out to meet my fate than sitting here hearing things I'd rather pretend weren't true."

"I'd like to come with you," Jorl said. "Not only do I feel the need to keep my eye on you, My Lady, but I also have a debt to pay in Magiskeep. I left unfinished business behind me there and it's about time I went back."

"Good," Joria said. "Now I'll have the chance to treat you as you deserve instead of as I once did. You are a man of rare honor and talent. I'd be pleased to speak for you if there's need."

Jorl nodded and smiled. At last he was going home.

Chapter 19

Curiously, despite having set things right in the Keep, Jamus still found the River reluctant to his hand. Apparently the Black Dragon was hoarding the waters behind some sort of dam. There was no sense the Darkness had actually taken control of them for his own use, but at the same time, they were not his either.

Jorn and Senneth had resworn fealty to Rule and Vow as had every Mage in the Keep, but undoing all the consequences of Magic Unrestrained would still take time. Until then, Jamus remained on guard lest the Shadows sense the weakness and take advantage.

The Jamus was strangely compliant, making no effort to protest as they returned to the stables and again began the journey to Greenhope, this time in search of Salene. Once Jamus realized she was missing, he decided Sarkem's Keep was the most logical place to find her. If all else failed, at least he would have Joria and Sarena with him again and allies would be more than welcome.

The fact was that he was growing more and more tired as the winds passed, his energy sapped by the struggle with the Magic and the aches of his injuries returning. As Jorl had predicted, the false Healer's drugs had offered only temporary energy. As they wore off, Jamus had to pay the price of their effect.

When the second lifted stride fell short, The Jamus took note and broke his silence. "You seem tired, Rivermaster. Battle does not come easily to you."

"I've never claimed to be a warrior," Jamus answered. "The way of Magic seeks peace, not violence."

"Ah, yes, the benefit of mankind, the protection of mortals. Nothing for the sorcerer or his kind to enjoy. Did you ever ask yourself why the Magic even exists if it has no use?"

"It is the essence of Turan," Jamus answered. "A natural force holding the world in place. All the Mage does is call upon it to do his Will."

"Such a simple perception. Magic is because it is, and no more. You refuse to see the truth. Those who hold it are destined to seats of power dedicated to their own pleasure and joy."

"And the Black Dragon's way is joy? Death, destruction, and darkness offer pleasure?"

"They offer life to those who crave it and satisfaction to those who seek it. If we must kill to live, so what? It is our gain that matters, not their loss."

"So why is your life any more important than theirs? Why do they have to sacrifice so you can live?"

"Because I have the Magic and they don't," The Jamus answered, grinning. "It's all a circle, Flesher, and nothing more. One end meets another in endless repetition."

"And what do you find at the end? If it's only the darkness, you'll never be able to see to start again. You'll have nothing but the empty smoke of shadows to hold in your hand and no morning to wake to. How I pity you and your kind for the hollow hope your crusade seeks."

The Jamus laughed loud and long, his voice strengthening until it echoed with the rumble of the Black River's Master. *"Fool, ye dare to measure me with thine eyes too blind to see power's pleasure, power's gain in the blood of all the slain. Ye believe thy way is true, blessed by the deeds ye do. Yet for naught thy waters rise. Magic all thy hope denies. Empty is thy guiding hand, holding on to shifting sand."* His shadow grew with the words, a dark shape rising behind him as he sat taller in the saddle.

Whim reared and spun, held only by Jamus' certain hand and will.

One by one, the Spellfire bonds slipped away, leaving only the shield around the Imposter. "Now as Masters we shall vie, one to live and one to die."

Jamus reined Whim to a halt, facing his adversary. "Who challenges me then, the Dragon or his minion? Does the Great Lord himself face me? I don't fear your darkness any more, Blackwing, and if you mean to destroy me now, my Dragon will wake to fly against you. Is it time to end the Great Circle so soon? Where is your army?"

"Only blood from thee I seek, then thy Will be pale and weak so the River waters dry and thy Dragon cannot fly. In thy light my Will shall rule while the mortals play the fool."

"So, it's not yours to say when the Circle ends. Even you must yield to the Will of the Hand." Now it all began to make sense. The Black Dragon sought to only to control him, not to kill him. It was only the Shadow Lords who longed for his death. Like Naboth, they hoped to steal his power and use it for themselves. Blackwing tolerated them is if it were some kind of game. The victor would only be Rivermaster until fate decided an end to it all and the Black River's Master claimed the prize.

But this time, it was different. With Blackwing at his side the Imposter could win this battle--the deception would have no end. He would take the River and Jamus' identity as his own, shaping the

River to his Will and corrupting Magiskeep. The Dragon would have a victory and no one would be the wiser.

The battle line was drawn, Rivermaster against Shadow. They were evenly matched, Spellfire to Blackfire, with only one difference between them.

Jamus had learned not to fear death.

****

Salene and the two Mistresses of Magic had headed back to Magiskeep as soon as Firstmeal was over.

With Jorl along, the matter of taking Magwin back with them was resolved. Flax was delighted to have her Mistress back in the saddle and fairly danced as they rode away from Greenhope.

One tentative lifted stride brought them well into the forests, but then Flax balked and Magwin simply refused to accept the Magic's touch.

"What's wrong with them?" Joria asked, urging reluctant Pebble up beside Salene. "If we can't lift strides it will take eight winds to reach Magiskeep from here."

Salene shook her head and frowned, something nagging at her memory. Then, she heard a snarl off to the right and a great brindle tark stepped out from the bushes.

The riders stiffened, but the horses actually relaxed as if the huge cat was exactly what they'd been waiting for.

Salene rubbed her brow, trying to make sense of it. "She...she followed me before. When I came here, that tark was with me. By the Blood, if I wasn't just dreaming, I think that creature slept beside me."

"A tark as a fireside companion?" Sarena said.

But Jorl laughed. "Keldra's cat. She must have followed us through the Way."

"You know the tark?"

"Aye, My Lady. Her name is Taba and she belonged to a Seer your husband and I met in our travels. She was, as I recall, quite fond of Lord Jamus. I guess when we came be she decided to come with us."

"So that's why she followed me," Salene said, laughing. "She must have known who I was and hoped I'd lead her to Jamus."

"Fine thing," Joria grunted. "He goes off chasing Shadows and brings back a five hundred pound house pet. Does she like to sit on laps?"

"Offer her a lap big enough and I'm sure she would," Jorl replied. "She's really quite tame."

"The horses seem to like her," Sarena said, stroking Topper's neck.

"Maybe she makes them feel safe. I certainly can't imagine anything else attacking them with her around." Salene called out to the cat. "All right, Mistress Taba. If you're determined to come with us then welcome. We won't need your hunting, though, our packs are full of food."

Jorl was about to reply when they were interrupted by a tremendous crash up ahead on the trail as smoke and flame billowed out from the top of a huge pine tree.

"Magic," Joria said and she pushed Pebble into a trot, heading for the center of the trouble.

****

The Jamus struck first, sending a bolt of Blackfire searing at Jamus. Whim bolted sideways as Jamus threw up a silvrin shield to protect them both from the onslaught. The spell bounced off and shattered, spewing sparks into the upper branches of a pine tree, setting it afire.

Jamus threw a suffocating wind to smother the blaze before the entire forest caught.

The Shadow laughed. "Still you protect the world, even with your own life in jeopardy. Your virtue amazes me."

Jamus raised his hand to send a bolt of Spellfire in counter, but the Imposter's shield held as well as his, deflecting the white flame into the ground at his feet. He slid from Whim's back and sent the stallion off out of the range of danger, alert every second to the Shadow's moves.

The Jamus dismounted too, and circled around behind some boulders to taunt Jamus. "Blow for blow, we'll match each other until one of us wearies, Rivermaster. Who has the most to lose? I have no life, only hope. You, on the other hand, fight for a world. Will your arms grow tired holding up your responsibility?"

"Never," Jamus replied, sending a blast to split the boulders in two as the Shadow leapt aside and sent a returning barrage. The darkness exploded around Jamus, but this time, he dropped his shield, spread his arms wide and let the black force engulf him.

The Jamus roared in triumph.

"No!" Salene screamed, spurring Flax towards him.

"Salene!" Sarena cried, cutting Topper in front of her just as the Shadow attacked.

The chestnut horse reared, the dark bolt striking him in the chest. Sarena was thrown to the ground and the horse crumpled to lie thrashing in pain.

Joria cast a protective shield around them a fraction before The Jamus' next blast struck.

Beyond, a whirlwind of black flame spun where Jamus had stood, spewing leaves and pine needles in its vortex.

"Murderer," Salene cried as Jorl grabbed Flax's reins and held her back.

"Don't, My Lady. It's what he wants. Don't let him lure you into his trap. Stay within the shield."

But The Jamus would not be so easily thwarted. He began to stalk them, his keen eyes seeking the loose thread in Joria's weave to break her chanting.

As Joria's face registered her fear, he grinned. Finding the single flaw in her Magic, he raised his hand for the killing blow.

Suddenly, Taba, snarling and spitting, leapt out from cover and attacked the Shadow, tearing into his flesh with her claws, her fangs sinking into his throat.

The Jamus gasped and flailed, his body falling beneath her.

She shook the body until it was limp and lifeless.

But, it was not the shadow's end. From the shell he'd worn, a wisp of darkness swirled and in its true form, the Shadow that had been The Jamus emerged to avenge its body's defeat.

It billowed, huge and towering over the savaging cat and raised what might have been an arm to send the killing blow.

"No, Taba!" Salene cried--her reaction an instinctive urge to defend the cat. Unbeckoned, untempered by any sense of reason, Spellfire seared from her fingers.

The Whitefire rocketed at the looming Shadow and struck. An instant later another blast seared out from the dark whirlwind to meet it at the creature's back.

Caught in the crossfire, the Shadow bellowed, his screech ringing through the trees, rising to the highest branches, to echo across the hills and valleys with the Dragon's rage and agony.

Then, he exploded, sparks and flames torrenting like a flooding fountain of fire.

The trees bent with the force of the blast and the Sorcerers were thrown to the ground as their mounts plunged back in the horrendous wind.

Then, silence.

And from it a pathetic whimper when the Shadow swirled and drifted into a pile of ashes.

Topper grunted and lay trembling in pain.

Jamus stepped out of the darkness, turned to watch it melt behind him, and then rushed over to kneel at the horse's side. Gently, he placed his hands on the animal's wound and called the River.

The waters rose with eager obedience to his hand and the Rainbow Dragon trumpeted the victory.

Topper's breathing eased and a moment later, he rose to stand, completely Healed.

Salene scrambled to her feet and hurried over to Sarena, who lay pale and unconscious on the ground beside the horse. Without a word, she placed her hand on Sarena's brow and Touched the Mistress of Compassion. The warm, Healing waters flowed easily through them both, finishing the cure for both women.

Then, Salene looked up into her husband's face and smiled. "Welcome home, My Love. I've missed you."

Epilogue

"I still don't quite understand how you survived the Blackfire," Jorl repeated as they rode along back to Magiskeep. With Taba along, they'd stayed grounded, offering plenty of time for conversation.

"It's not something to understand," Jamus replied. "As a matter of fact, understanding it might actually prove fatal."

Jorl sighed, "Embracing oblivion wasn't exactly in the Magician's Book of Worthwhile Spells."

Jamus laughed. "Perhaps that's why it was my riddle to solve and hold then—Rivermaster's Art as old and arcane as the Dragons themselves."

"Then bless the Hand for it," Salene said, reining Flax close to Whim so she could lean over and kiss her husband. "I don't know what I would have done if I hadn't been able to tell you I was sorry."

Jamus smiled. "To hear you praise Rivermaster's Art is enough for me, Salene." Then he reached out to take her hand. "You've nothing to apologize for, My Love."

"We've lost so much."

"And we'll overcome it. We'll never be able to replace our daughter, but we will have more children and honor her memory by loving them even more. No matter what he's done, the Darkwing couldn't take that from us."

"He almost had the River," Joria said quietly.

"A part of it," Jamus replied, "but it seems to me at least two of its most potent tributaries simply would not yield to his temptations. For that, My Ladies, I am ever grateful."

"Nonsense," Sarena said, smiling sweetly. "How else should we have behaved once you'd climbed into Jiala's bed? After all, someone had to keep up appearances."

Jamus shuddered. "Did you really believe that was me?"

"I'm not even sure Jiala did."

"Well, whether or not she did, I certainly intend to have a word or two with her about it when we get home," Salene said.

Jorl laughed. "If I were you, My Lord, I'd make sure I was well away from the Keep when that conversation takes place. A man should never get in the middle of two women when he's the subject of discussion."

"Discussion is not exactly what I had in mind," Salene replied.

Jamus simply shook his head and urged Whim into a jog as the others followed.

****

Setting things right in Magiskeep required little more than affirmation of the Gathering's proclamations declaring Jamus as the true Lord. By the time the travelers returned, Jorn and Senneth had repaired the worst of the damage, and Sarn had taken charge of the rest.

Not a trace of Magic Unrestrained remained.

Jiala meekly accepted Salene's reprisals, gathering a collection of new students in penance and doing an excellent job of teaching them the merits of Rule and Vow.

For his part, Jamus made his way to the village, just to reassure himself the tapestry's weave was truly repaired. Once there, he made his way to the Tills Inn.

The tavern was cleaner than he'd remembered, with polished wooden tables and fresh rushes on the floor. The barmaids wore modest dresses of dark green cambric overlaid with spotless white aprons. When he found and empty table and sat down, a lovely young woman came over at once. "May I help you, Sur? We have fine ale and a fresh roasted mutton today. I'd be pleased to serve…" Her voice trailed off. Quickly she bowed, "My Lord, I am sorry. I didn't recognize you at first. Mistress Melina keeps the lights dim in here. She says it creates a better mood."

"Mistress Melina?" Jamus asked. "Is she in Innkeeper here?"

"Assuredly so, My Lord. She's been so for a season since Master Lucas sold her the place. She gave him a fine bag of silvrins I hear and though some say they were chanted coins, no one's begrudged her a deneret of them. She is as fine a lady as you'd ever want to know."

"I'd like some ale," Jamus said, "and a slice of that mutton too, along with a moment of your mistress' time."

The maid curtsied and hurried off as he sat back in his chair. Could his actions in the Way have actually benefited here?

He had his answer almost at once as the beautiful dark-haired Innkeeper moved over to his table. He rose, offered her a seat, then pulled up his own chair across from her. "Thank you, My Lady. Your maid spoke so highly of you, I wanted to meet you."

"Ye don't have to pretend, My Lord. You've come about the money, haven't you."

"Should I have reason?"

"Ye travel the Way, Master Jamus. I should think it would interest you."

"Everything about the Way interests me, Mistress."

"Aye, I thought as much. Well, I'll tell you, Sur, it was right strange. I was standing in front of my mirror, adjusting my dress when my reflection…" She shook her head as if wondering at her own tale. "It still amazes me, but my reflection reached out, a full purse in its hand and gave it to me. Then, and the story grows in madness here, it spoke."

"What did it say?"

"It, well, she said, 'I've been saving this for you, Melina of my Way. Now the Rivermaster's hand has filled it and it's time for you to have it. Make thy world worthy of thy life.' And then, the mirror went dark as if somewhere the torch had gone out. I haven't been able to see myself in it since. The money was real, though. I took it to Carvez the moneylender to have him look at it before I spent a deneret. Then, when Master Lucas decided to retire, I bought the Inn. If I've done wrong, I will make amends, My Lord. I've earned enough already to pay again with untainted coin if you so demand."

Jamus put his hand on hers and shook his head. "The money was yours, My Lady, and well earned by your generosity. The Hand be blessed you received it and used it well."

"But you are the Rivermaster. Did you have something to do with it?"

"In another world, I did," Jamus said. "A kindness repaid ten times over." His meal arrived then and he picked up the ale. "May I do the honor of offering a toast to one of the loveliest innkeepers in all of Magiskeep?"

Melina blushed most beautifully and then, with her Lord's approval, simply began to laugh.

****

Sarn had made himself scarce after Jamus' return, preferring solitude to the company of his fellow Masters. He was alone, reading a book in the garden when Siamel found him.

"I've missed your company, Sur," she said as she sat down on the bench near the grass where he lay.

"I thought you'd found a new companion," Sarn replied, not even looking up.

She shivered. "Don't remind me of that loathsome creature. I can still feel his slavering mouth on me. Blood, I don't know what would have happened if Lord Jamus hadn't come."

"Ever the hero, our Lord and Master. No wonder the whole kingdom worships him so."

"Don't begrudge him, Sarn. His virtues are real."

"Unlike mine."

She moved over and knelt beside him. "Who's to say a man needs virtue to be admired? Some men have other qualities to make them worthy."

Sarn slammed the book shut. "I don't. Not a one."

"That's not true, Master," Jamus said stepping into view. Then he held up his hand, gesturing to both of them. "Don't get up, please. Enjoy the day. I have to apologize for following you, My Lady, but I did think it would be the quickest way for me to find Master Sarn."

"Why, My Lord," Sarn asked, "to gloat, or to put a new spell on me so I can't foul up again?"

"You didn't foul up in the first place."

"I let the Shadow have his way."

"And what choice did you have? With the spell I set on you and the nature of his reflection, your Magic might well have killed you if you'd tried to use it against him. No, Sarn, when you said you had no worthy qualities, I told you you were wrong. You see, Sur, you are a survivor. Your life is too important to you for you to squander it in foolish endeavors. The Imposter counted on that when he solicited your help in turning the other Masters to his way. I counted on it when I left you in charge of the Keep."

"To what end, My Lord? So I'd be left alive to tell you how your hold had fallen?"

"No, so you wouldn't play the fool to Blackwing's plots and get yourself killed before you had a chance to determine how to defeat him. Had I not come back, you would have figured it out sooner or later."

"What makes you say that? I'd already failed miserably."

"You'd never let an imposter sit in my place," Jamus replied. "You see, that's your second quality, Sarn, ambition. As soon as you had the chance, you'd expose the imposter so you could take over yourself."

"My Lord."

"I counted on that, Sarn, and all in all, there's always been one thing I could depend on. You've never let yourself down."

****

Jamus insisted they erect a memorial stone to their daughter despite Salene's objections. While she wanted to find a way to forget